SARA

Glen "Rocky" Meyers

© 2023 Glen Meyers

<u>**Disclaimers.**</u>

All rights reserved. No part of this book may be reproduced or used in any manner without the prior written permission of the copyright owner, except for the use of brief quotations in a book review. <u>This is a work of fiction.</u> <u>Unless otherwise indicated, all the names, characters, businesses, places, events, and incidents in this book are either the product of the author's imagination or used in a fictitious manner.</u> Any resemblance to actual persons, living or dead, or actual events is purely coincidental. Let me emphasize that the stories in the NIA Series are Fiction based. All names, characters, and incidents portrayed in my novels are fictitious. All make-believe... No identification with actual persons (living or deceased), places, buildings, businesses, or religious institutions. In some of my writing, I may use names of entities, churches, or corporations. These manuscripts are totally fiction based and should be inferred as such. Surely I have fun with my characters, and some of them do too! ⚖. I appreciate your patience in reading this necessary legalese.

Library of Congress Control Number: 2020903428

Printed in the United States of America

**This novel is Dedicated to my mother,
Barbara Jean Hayes.
Thank you, mom!**

By Glen "Rocky" Meyers

Feral Eyes: Book One

Feral Eyes: Book Two

Sara

Kam: Book One

Kam: Book Two

Covid 57: Book One

<u>The 'NIA' Series.</u>

<u>'Sara' is the third of 13 books in the NIA series.</u>

<u>I printed some Incomplete Manuscripts a couple of years ago to test the market, called ACR's...</u> which stands for Advanced Reader Copies, and I had some Beta readers preview some of the storylines in the NIA Series. In a word, they were <u>'Awful'</u> and needed editing and punctuation, and many of the plots were discombobulated. I have been working on cleansing these books for publishing since 2019; yes, it's been a journey! Today the fruits of my labor are here to be read and hopefully enjoyed. I will publish Six books at the same time in May of 2023. ✀.

<u>The First Amendment.</u>

Freedom of expression is a fundamental human right and a central tenet of an author's work, livelihood, and American Society. The First Amendment protects freedom of speech, the press, and citizens' assembly to protest or march in groups. Freedom of expression is the freedom for us all to express ourselves. It is the right to speak, to be heard, and to participate in artistic, political, and social life. I am a firm and staunch believer in our First Amendment! Using someone's name. Image or life story as part of a novel, book, movie, or other 'expressive' work is protected by the First Amendment.

<u>The NIA Series… Book Three …'Sara.'</u>

<u>'A Preface.'</u>

<u>An introduction of how's and whys… with explanations.</u>

<u>'I'm a Felon… and enjoy using Disfluencies in my
manuscripts.'</u>

Within most of my manuscripts, I incorporate the use of disfluencies. There are many reasons why I do so. Many purists will find this form of writing unprofessional and of a lower standard… which is fine by me. Some authors have distinctive writing styles, <u>'prose.'</u> In writing, prose refers to any written work that follows a basic grammatical structure. Prose simply means language that follows the Natural Patterns found in everyday speech. It isn't well known that disfluencies pop up in everyday speech or conversations in most languages on our planet. In conversations, it has been approximated that about every 4.6 seconds, a disfluency is used. I try and combine disfluencies to emphasize points or for the reader to slow down and reflect on what was just read. I have fun using disfluencies, and I use them to directly communicate concepts, ideas, and stories to my readers. If you were to really concentrate on a person's speech or a friend's conversation… uhm, or listen to an interview, you might find yourself amazed at how many of these 'placeholder words, filler words you hear. Even some highly esteemed professionals use an abundance of disfluencies.

<u>Please reference this great piece of work regarding disfluencies ('Well, um, you know, you're saying more than</u>

<u>you think.) You can find this article in the November/ December 2022 'Psychology Today,' magazine.</u>

To paraphrase, some of the substance in this awesome article is that most of us use disfluencies; for example, have you ever been conversing with someone and lost track of where you were going? You pause momentarily and think of your next words... using Ah, Uh, Umh, then pick up where you left off. Disfluencies can be used to emphasize your topic of choice, aligned with appropriate expressions, and you see this at comedy clubs and in everyday conversations. We roll our eyes and pause and use 'Um'. Disfluencies are common in humorous or even serious discussions. Stop for a minute and truly listen to someone's interview, either on TV or the Internet, Social media sites; you will hear an abundance of Disfluencies. We as a society have become immune to the dozens of common disfluencies many speakers use them for repeating a phrase or revising the sentence structure in midstream. I use disfluencies in my writing for emphasis, and because they're fun for me, I hope they aren't annoying to readers, umh, especially the purists. If so, I apologize, ugh, right up-front. Um, I don't want any of you not to enjoy my books. I do believe that over usage of disfluencies can become a nuisance, Uh.

Okay, umh, so here's the rest of the info that I'll share with you regarding disfluencies. Now I'm not defending my overuse of these words, or maybe I am? In many of my 13-plus written manuscripts, you'll read and see or hear words such as... 'um, uh, ugh, ah, umh, huh, so, uhm, ughhhh, ahhhh, and other variations like... oh, yep, yup, yay, yum, ahoh, lol, lmao, huh, and the list goes on...

The argument can be made; according to some Professors of Psychological Science, disfluencies help listeners and readers concentrate better on the narrative, and the use of a disfluency sometimes tells the audience there is likely new information about to be disseminated. Disfluencies seem to occur at discourse points or are used to indicate a Major plot change of direction. These educated professionals have said that disfluencies 'focus listener's attention' and sometimes allow the listener to analyze what has been said, sort of like a pause for reflection. In testing theories regarding using Disfluencies... when appropriately placed in a narrative, they actually increase a person's attention and memory of what they have heard or read. 🌐

Disfluencies have been used to help emphasize the topic being discussed. They are proven to help the listener or reader to remember storylines or points of contention better than most other deliveries of verbiage.

To sum up, highly esteemed intellectuals use disfluencies, from our Presidents right down to street urchins. They have been proven to increase listeners' attention. Please try and catch disfluencies either by yourself or others. You might be surprised at how many of them are used in a single day. Like... Well, heck, that said a lot, lol... Umh, okay. Yup! 🌐

How I became an author after my arrest for growing and dispensing Marijuana.

I'm sure you've heard the term <u>'to make a long story short,'</u> which indicates that the story will likely not be short and concise. Lol. I've penciled over a thousand pages in a book named Sacramento County Jail, a harrowing non-fiction venture. Below is a short passage into what caused my life changes and thus led to my creative writing hobby.

In the year 2012, suddenly, health issues befell... my body and mind. I was beyond listless, with no energy or motivation to do anything felt like a Slug. I was a regular at the gym and in the past was active... this all stopped. I sought out professional help. First things first, I had to donate blood for a wide variety of tests. A sex hormone panel, 'SHBG' amongst other tests, was ordered since I was approaching the age of male menopause. The endocrinologist called me in and informed me that I had several anomalies. One was that I had extremely low… deficient testosterone levels, but what bothered her more was that I'd had the highest Estrogen levels she'd ever seen in a man. In fact, her words were with a smirk, 'Mr. Meyers, welcome to female menopause. Your levels are off the charts.' Thirty-five years of being an endocrinologist, she had never seen these numbers before. After checking with her colleagues, it was decided that I needed another hormone test because there must have been a mistake! My test numbers were impossible to comprehend. Well,… what would you know? Two weeks later, I was called back into her office. This time I didn't witness a smirk from her countenance, nope. She beckoned me to have a seat across from her magnificent mahogany desk. She folded her arms up elbows on the desk, clasped her fingers in a temple, and bent her head down. With her not saying a word, I'd automatically jumped to the conclusion, 'I WAS DEAD,' something terminal. I must be on my way out .

>>>>Please visit '**Gembooksrock.com**' and finish reading… Yep.

<u>Former Federal Inmate.</u>

I am a former prisoner and felon sequestered by the IRS… Federal Government on Marijuana charges… was imprisoned and locked up in Terminal Island Prison for about Seven years. A short synopsis of the events that led to my writing career can be found on my website 'Gembooksrock.com,' please check out my homepage. You will find some interesting tidbits… along with links to my arrest. .

We, humans, have many choices at our disposal in the short time of our existence cohabitating on this planet. We have many opportunities and alternatives. We can even change from the station we are born within, negatively or in a positive way, depending on our perceptions. Our genetic traits and heredity are not part of what we can choose for ourselves. No! Whom we resemble, our features, epidermis… ancestors are nonchoice. Of course, with the advent of plastic surgery, alterations exist; our external skin is our largest organ, not translucent No, but Opaque!

What we cannot see with the naked eye can be detrimental or advantageous. I'm writing about our internal biological systems. Our Skin is the largest organ; next comes our Liver, the second largest organ in human beings. However, the most vital Organ… that's in control of our human system and ranks solidly in third place is our 3-pound-plus Brain. This organ confounds scientists and neurologists. Even with all the technological advancements, we haven't a clue as to how brains truly function with memories and emotions, the limbic system, Amygdala, etc.

Many studies have been performed on individuals of their free will, and some experiments with humans being Guinea Pigs against what they wanted; many were prisoners. Throughout history, since the beginning of time, studies have been ongoing. Doctors endeavored to figure out what made a psychopath tick and why they were so different from other people, whether it was hereditary or instilled by learned life experiences. Psychopathic tendencies, why? How did these personality disorders manifest into extreme antisocial behaviors? Such as sociopaths that can lack a conscience and moral values. Many have discovered that these mentally challenged individuals can be highly intelligent and cunning.

They learn how to acclimate and pretend to be like any average person would, 'they are living amongst us and even could be your next-door neighbor!'

Schizophrenia is a word that can be stigmatizing, a label that none of us would generally want to be associated with but aren't we all just walking a thin line tightrope here? For indeed, we all are schizophrenic Umh, different people all in one. We wear masks, 'not Covid.' Our expressions can hide our true thoughts. We are actors primed for manipulations learned and manifested from infanthood. Think about how you react in different situations dealing with people... 'who are you?' In church, at school, on a date, in Court, dealing with police, authorities, children, your significant other, co-workers, or in a line at a store. Driving in traffic or with your friends, dancing and flirting at a Bar, during sexual conquest... acting with your parents, at a funeral or wedding, the list goes on infinitely based.

When we stare into a mirror, alone without outside noises, reflecting on whom that is looking back at us, who will it be in 11 years or 5, ask your inner voice Spirit, who are you inside? For none of us truly knows... we haven't a fricken clue at what we're capable of at any moment you might crack. It could be a natural catastrophe like an earthquake, a car accident, or any other form of a reckoned emergency. Instantly in a flash, you're now someone else pressure can make diamonds or spring leaks.

'<u>You and Sara' and I</u> have many common traits. '<u>Sara</u>' is your next-door neighbor, best friend, beautician, co-worker, sibling, or spouse. Just a warning that we cannot see what others think by looking into their eyes or gauging their expressions. Be careful out there, for inside, you and others could be demons just waiting to pounce. '<u>Sara types</u>' live everywhere on this planet; tread lightly... Keep the light on while reading or listening to her story. The disclaimer is done; yep!

<u>'Doctor Ame Amaya'… a 'Doctor of Forensic Psychology' in a counseling session at 'NIA,' a mental institution in Napa, California. Her patient is a Psychopath named 'Al.'</u>

<u>December 19, 1997, Friday 10:30 am Interview #11 'The Ventriloquist.'</u>

It was a positively glorious day, the sun a glow, a crisp and serene morning. The magnificence of this day was only magnified because it was the last day of high school at Terra Linda High before the Christmas break. I was a senior and was somewhat unpopular, but that mattered not. I had a girlfriend and the mandated cluster of wannabe friends, but they had no idea who I was, nor did I.

What was abundantly clear, transparent at least within my mind, was that I despised people, all people. What slithered under my skin and crawled upon my epidermis was the shameless, contemptible masses of loathsome humans. Who were sexually unfaithful, defrauding, and shredding hearts like wiping toilet paper from their asses, then flushing emotions down the drain ending in a sewer, and that's precisely where these deviates deserved to be.

Today I was on a personal mission to exact my form of justified retribution. The sinful teachers, Mr. Bayle, a History Professor, and Ms. Garcia, my Spanish educator, were pictures of infidelity, treacherous and adulterous. Both wore wedding rings and were married to other people. I accidentally caught them kissing when I didn't knock after school going to my homeroom. I just plowed through the door and opened it to see them in an embrace.

The expressions on their faces were etched in my skull busted; I turned around and tried to scamper away, not to be. Mr. Bayle shouted, 'Al come back in here,' 'I did!' "This isn't what it looked like; I merely thanked Ms. Garcia for making me some delicious enchiladas. Please understand that we don't want false rumors spreading all over campus… we're both happily married." I replied, "it must have been some tasty Enchiladas, no doubt. I'm sure I have '<u>A pluses</u>' in both your classes, so what I saw surely I didn't." Then I left with their teeth gleaming and mouths agape!

Since that afternoon over a month ago, I had followed the deeply incorrigible couple many times to hotel rooms in the low-rent district in San Rafael, the slums of the 'Canal Area,' 3 to 5 times a week, they met, lately in the same room 513 I followed them in my 1993 Dodge Ram truck.

(Al paused as if collecting his thoughts and memory, listening was an undervalued attribute, so a nod was all I gave Al, waiting patiently).

<u>'I'm brilliant'</u> as he swivels his head to one side, a quirky smirk slides from his cheeks, "I had my girlfriend rent room 513 for her best friend's birthday party. "Jenny's 18th a biggie, I guess, a week before… the party got rowdy, the cops were called in, and some arrests were made, but my girl and I had left hours before. The Key to all of this was pun intended, lol I took the Key to room 513! I had followed the teachers last week to the very same rendezvous. Unfortunately, room 513 was taken. Damnit, I was amped up, my Boy Scout Motto in force. Sadly, I drove back to my apartment with my disguise intact, changed back to being good ole Al, frustratingly locked my door, and drank myself to sleep; alcohol was a perfect escape."

(Al's inflection, he altered his timbres with different modulations of his voice, a deeper resonating tone exhibited,
an intrinsic implicit ghoulishness, his articulations and

pronunciations seemed to drip… with grinning drops of blood.)

Al continued with our interview, "I parked down the street at the 711 store and crept back towards the hotel. For me, this Friday, the 19th of December, was a perfect start to the holiday season. Watching above a hedge, the teachers entered room 513. I almost busted with excitement; yes! I gave them about 15 minutes, lurking closer to the door. Noticeably, room 513 was an optimal choice, for it was set back in the corner of the hotel with only one adjoining room. Placing an ear to the 'weathered peeling door' hearing the telltale signs of sex, slid the extra key out, hoping it would still work; it did. Now with my steel cutting snips in my hand, I cut the chain that I knew would be attached to the door, but it wasn't, 'no prob!'

So, I slowly opened the door and bent my head into the room. It was dimly lit, the slapping sound of flesh, 'oh yes, Yesss! Fk me harder' grunts, groans. 'Disgusting,' I slinked in without a problem and made my way directly to a small alcove um closet. Kneeling, I took off my backpack. After a few minutes, my eyes had finally adjusted to the light.

I saw balls bouncing and ass cheeks shaking with each thrust. He had her in doggy style with his long slender hands clutched to her shoulder blades, pulling, gaining leverage with each plunge. She was grasping the headboard, squealing in ecstasy, their naked bodies linked in mutual motion, moaning… *She > 'I Can't Feel Your Cock, You Cheating Bastard'* he ripped it in harder *'you fkn bitch, you're a slut and a whore fk ya!' Her 'Get off me, or I'm going to castrate your ass'* He *'what the fk is wrong with you?'* yet he didn't stop and continued hammering away. *'I'm not saying a word.* Who's talking? *What's going on?'* asks Ms. Garcia. <u>*It was Al, the ventriloquist speaking for the lovers.*</u>

I had already tiptoed inch by inch closer to their bodies with a red fire engine-colored hatchet, sharpened to cut paper, with all my weight and momentum. I hacked into the back of Mr. Bales, and blood sprayed. His head fell forward onto her back, his cock still attached like canines. She let go of the headboard and rolled onto her right shoulder, spinning her head to look back. Blood was leaking, pooling up. She looked right at me, and her eyes followed the swing of my handy Lil axe.

I hummed the lyrics 'the first cut was the deepest and severed her carotid artery, quickly chopping my little axe down three more times, uh or thrice. I was grinding my teeth, smiling so hard my dimples might crack. I took Ms. Garcia's head by her hair, swung it around, and did a tiny jig and twirl. Then I knew I was wasting time, for I'm smart. So I posed their heads together inches apart, gory art on display. The blood and body fluids were everywhere. Oh, how I wanted to taste and chew on them, but I was aware of the DNA factor. So, as efficiently as I could with haste, I took my Rose clippers out of my backpack, cut off Mr. Bale's ring finger, and put it in Ms. Garcia's mouth, bloodied side in, and did the same to her ring finger in his mouth. So their heads were facing each other, sucking on bloodied wedding ring fingers. Yes! Then I had to fix the pose. It was all messed up. His eyes were partially closed, so I took some duct tape and opened them permanently, making a mental note to bring super glue for the next fun time to cum!

I took out my Polaroid camera and took some scintillating shots. Then I needed to make my escape. I slipped off my plastic raincoat, dropped it next to the bodies, put a clean pair over them, packed up my hatchet, took a spray cleaner out cleaned the bottom of my shoes. Before my exit, I took a paintbrush out, dipped it into the coalesced blood, and wrote on Mr. Bale's back, 'Thou Shan't Cheat.'

Out the door I went; it was still oh so bright outside. I 'skipped to my Lou' away, my pants sticky from my body's orgasms cum and cum again, exhilaration. I hopped into my truck. The glued beard itched like mad, my wig irritated me, the look in the rearview mirror wasn't me, and even my colored eye contacts were a nuisance. "I pulled into a manual carwash, removed my disguise, and drove home, but 'Guess what'?" <u>"What? I asked."</u>

Doctor Ame Amaya… I sat across from Al, trying to act like his confession bothered me not; being his Psychologist, I'd heard some horrific revelations, but this killing event took me by surprise. Al's matter-of-fact detail of his double homicide and disgustingly crude description of the sexual act he'd engaged in unhinged me. . Raising my hands and palm up, miming 'What?' in response to Al's (guess what?) I noticed Al was sweating, yet the ambient temperature was 67 degrees in my borrowed office at NIA. I admitted I wasn't used to Al's expletives and his gruesome narrative detailing sexual nuances, it was low-class verbiage.

<u>Al continues to detail his crimes to Doctor Ame.</u>

This was the very first time in my life that I could be the avenging Angel in dual or separate locations. Check out my luck; are you paying attention, Doc? (I nod) Well, down the street from my apartment in San Anselmo was a home. Like five buildings away, the police were always there; in the last seven months I lived there, I counted 11 times, and remember I wasn't always home. You know I had a life too. This specific house had a fence around the back of the home with a dog, uh, St. Bernard, inside. I had been over the fence a few times, always bringing a doggy treat. We were nearly friends, um, the dog and me.

I had watched an Ambulance take away the woman and mother three times then the man in cuffs was led to the back of the police car. Their three children would be crying, screaming, and gesticulating all over the front porch. I watched a kind neighbor lady from across the street who would take the children into her home. She was called the nosy neighbor by many who lived in our neighborhood. One day she walked by with her bulldog on a leash and stopped and spoke with me. This was a couple of weeks before the incident; she'd said, 'one day, that man was going to kill his wife.' The lady told me how sorry she felt for the children who suffered. There was a 5-year-old girl, a 3-year-old boy, and a baby girl only 15 months old she was wobbling her head and said, 'domestic abuse at its worst.'

This was my Friday night, and I was on 'Double Duty' having disposed of my teachers, I jumped their fence and crept up to the kitchen window… staring over at the huge husband, uh, and dad who sat on his lazy boy chair drinking beer with a bottle of whiskey next to him on a table the dude had to have been 6'5" tall and well over 355 pounds a fat brute. His wife the mother of the children was petite perhaps 5'3" tall with an anorexic frame of 105 pounds.

I had fed my St. Bernard pal a Porterhouse Steak and some bones he was drooling away. Standing at the open curtain kitchen window, which was two-thirds open with the screen tickling my nose, I listened, "hey bitch where's my dinner? You're a useless piece of shit. I'm hungry; get your ass in here now!" She checks the oven and says, "honey, it will be another 5 minutes; please stop the name-calling. Our children can hear you" 'fk them, give me a snack now!'

(Al gleams an evil expression) say's this is why I love being a Ventriloquist, listen… Doc at how clever I am in the wife's voice, I said; She, me… says, *'one day I'm going to give you what you really deserve, you bastard!'* The mean, drunk man… knocks the whiskey bottle over, struggling to get out of his chair *"what did you Fkn say, woman?"* she, I mean, I said, pretending to be her, *"I should take this butcher knife out and stab your cold black heart, you prick"* <u>'Omg Ralph, I'm not saying a word, please its someone else Oh hell, what's goin on?'</u> In a rage of drunken aggression, Ralph grabs Linda, opens the oven, and shoves her head and upper body deep inside the 475°… coils. She is screaming, a blood-curdling howl as her hair lights on fire. He wedges her further inside the oven as the five and three-year-old children run into the kitchen. With one arm, he whirls on the kids. They flew into the air, landing on their backs, crying, barely breathing.

I sliced open the screen with my left hand. In my right hand were my throwing knives, sharp as a razor… tapered steel 5.5 inches long (Al's smirk accompanying a lick of his lips). My expertise proven out from barely 5 feet away, my first throw buries in Ralph's sternum; he lurches forward next toss into his groin in rapid succession. I throw the third dagger into his back as he falls over Linda's legs. The smell of fried skin and burnt hair sickens me with nausea gross. I spit onto the grass, drooling a little bit but remembered to crush the spot under my boot. 'From the corner of my eye,' I see the two children trying to pull their mother's head which was truly sad, from the oven. (Al then lets out an uproarious howl, "but their mother was toast.")

I left them… umh, the children with this. Being a supreme ventriloquist, I told them, pretending to be their mother… *('I Love You This Is Mommy Sweet Dreams… I Will Be Your Angel Forever I Love You.')* Then I bolted up and over the fence hidden by the large Oleander bushes. What luck I had. My girlfriend was pulling into my driveway; I snuck in the back door and check this out…

Suddenly the door of the 11 x 17 consultation room burst open three individuals in white clothing, garments covering their upper torsos with smocks on, crowded into their room. The men looked like blocks with their heads welded to their shoulders. Both were 6 feet tall, at least 200 pounds, meaty faces with popping pimples, steroids maybe; the woman nurse was thick and chubby with a triple chin. She said to the orderlies, 'take Al to his cell.' Al was up in a flash shrieking, wailing, 'leave me alone, get away from me. I'm only talking to my psychiatrist...' Al tried to kick the first man, but the guy only grinned, grabbing Al, who unleashed his wickedly long fingernails, clawing and ripping through the fleshy cheeks of the first guard. The other guy lifts Al up in a chokehold from behind.

As calmly as a Professional Doctor with authority could declare, I yelled, "stop; you could kill him. What are you doing here? We're in the middle of a Psychotherapy session." The rollie pollie nurse turns on me and says, 'we have a Red Alert Doctor; all inmates are to be returned to their cells immediately!' I see, for the first time, spray patterns like a mist of what was blood over the lower front of her smock and down her arm sleeves. Al is still in a combatant mood, squirming, spitting, and trying his best to bite anyone's skin that came close enough to his mouth. A camisole was handed to one of the brutes… Camisole is the politically correct term for a Strait-Jacket.

As they were wrestling with little Al, who was 5'5" tall and perhaps about 135 pounds soaking wet, just a guess, but I remember that from his BIO, intake paperwork into the _Napa Insane Asylum, NIA._

Then the nurse flicked out a hypodermic needle. Walla, Al's eyes rolled up like fluttering wings, his eyelids ceased to move, and one of them snatched up a gurney attached to a wall in the bright white painted room and strapped Al down. I was collecting my files, tape recorder, and stuff when the abrasive woman said, 'let's go, Doctor, time to leave here at once, immediately.' I walked over to Al, who was gasping for oxygen despite unconsciousness 'unless you want him to die, you should loosen the restraints now' as I left the room following nurse Judy's waddle. I finally noticed the screams and squeals the staff was scurrying all about, looking through the plate glass windows into an enormous day room in which the inmates were allowed to commingle. It was pure unadulterated chaos, naked inmates. Blood spewed like torrents of rain. Obviously, an artery was severed the projected stream of blood, like on a swivel, was everywhere.

A quick count of 13 inmates and twice that number of staff members, doctors with full body suits looked like a SWAT team in a movie, helmets masks in black, not a sliver of skin showing.

Judy spin's around 'please hurry up, heck.' I didn't know why she said that… I was on her hip "what happened, Judy?" "Aah, apparently, a female inmate attacked a male inmate with a sharpened piece of plastic and cut his carotid artery in one slice. I haven't had time to check the video, but I was told the male had stolen a crayon from her while she was coloring a picture." "Judy, aren't the inmates screened, strip-searched, or x-rayed? I have serious reservations about continuing Psychoanalyzing these patients; hell, I'm essentially locked into a room with each one during the counseling sessions!" "Doctor, the inmates normally have been scrutinized and gone over, even every cavity is prodded and scanned, and besides that, a staff member is at your door all the time, remember, everything is being monitored via real-time Video!"

I followed Judy down a wide hallway listening to her continue… and realized that my assessment of her was incorrect. Judy wasn't roly-poly. Nah, she was a big, strong woman, "if you want to waive the patient Doctor's confidentiality, we could have a guard sitting in the interview room with you." 'With my years of experience, this certainly encumbers any communication between Psychologists and Inmates.' "Listen, Doctor; it's a rarity that an attack like this occurs; somehow, X-Rays didn't pick up the razor-sharp plastic. The inmate could have hidden it under her armpit. We have to do a better job searching all of them." I replied, "Yeah, but in the meantime, a man was just murdered because of NIA's negligence!"

I was now at the counter after traversing three buzzed locked steel doors, going to my locker # 51, and retrieving my purse and phone. Then finally, I'm buzzed out into the spacious lobby. I'm in a cold sweat, and an odor excretes from my pores, a mixture of… "Hey Doc, ahh, 'Ame' I'm so sorry it's been a long while since anything like this has happened here," the assistant Warden stood before me, Mr. Larry Walden.

-2-

The perennial vines of grapes were as far as I could see.

The drive back from Napa was pleasant. Ame would have been tempted to stop at a winery for a taste or three if she was her sister… but Ame abhorred the taste of wine. The grape vines spread across the rolling hills as far as she could see. An hour and 35 minutes later, she sat at San Rafael Joe's Restaurant, enjoying some French Onion soup and a scrumptious Cobb salad.

Doctor Ame Amaya was only a few hundred feet from her medical office, Suite 155; her phone jangled a text from her secretary per preference, a male 'Donnie Feline.' 'You're 1:15 pm appointment is already here. Are you going to make it?' 'Yes, at

Joe's Seeya soon.' Ame strolls down the famous Fourth Street in downtown San Rafael staring up at her Gothic-like Victorian building businesses separated floor by floor. On the first floor were financial consultants, and the second floor had a law practice specializing in Civil law. Ame leased the top floor.

With a large sigh, she enters her building. Ame takes the stairs two at a time, wanting to believe she is immune to what happened to her incarcerated clients... after years of evaluating the Criminally Insane... she'd learned to compartmentalize all caustic interactions. Still, she shuddered with an intrusive feeling of terror. Ame had to reset herself; anxiousness flushed away from the corrosive exposure of the traumatic event only this morning. From the backside of her building, a private entrance, she went to the coffee machine, filled the cup with the words imprinted 'What's up Doc' sat back in her comfy ergonomic swivel deluxe $1500 chair.

With another sigh, she pushes the intercom, "send in Ms. Bender in 15 minutes, Don, thanks." Sipping her coffee leans back and glances at all the plaques attached to her wall. Not a large office, 13' x 17' suave and comfy; this was her office, almost like a home. Stanford, Business Administration, and a UC Berkeley Graduate Degree in Psychology. Her specialty and favorite part of her counseling practice was that she majored in Forensic Psychiatry for criminal and civil law and was hired to evaluate inmates to determine if they were legally insane. Ame's ability to access defendants added to her experience level during a 3-year internship years ago at NIA, which educated and hardened her. She rolled her head and saw her certificates in ECT or electroconvulsive therapy psychotherapy, rubbing her eyes. Lord knows, like 13 years of further education, was it all worth it?

She ruminated further, thinking she was home-spun, grown up locally, and had graduated from high school right there in the San Rafael area, less than 15 minutes from where her ass reclined. What a long ride it had been in hell. She wasn't even 40 years old yet; she grinned. Well, I guess it has been rewarding; after all, she indeed wouldn't be driving a 2017 Lexus LC with a 2016 'BMW 650 i convertible in her garage at her lovely home on the water in Marin County. I suppose it's been worth it. Her false preconceptions as a young adult student morphed. Ame had believed she was 'down-to-earth,' not about materialistic things, nor a capitalist… told herself she'd be happy driving a Volkswagen bus and living in a tent. But after signing her first lucrative contract, those ideas vanished… nope, Nada!' .

A knock at the door then enters Ms. Bender; Ame speaks into her recorder (1/3/17> 1:25 pm Lily… Wednesday.) Lily Bender wasn't in the door, and her face was blotched, dripping from her chin sweat "hi Doc," sniffling red eyes puffed out, "where do you want me, chair or couch?" "Wherever you're more comfortable, take the couch if you want to lay down with a pillow." Lily stops in front of Ame "they fired me after 19 years. They fired me… Omg, what the fk am I going to do now, howling?" Ame kicks her feet down, leans back, and thinks, 'this is going to be a rough session' "tell me about it, Lily, please." "As I told you last week, I don't think the new manager likes me" she reaches into her oversized purse for a box of Kleenex blowing her nose.

"I've been a server for 19 yrs., I opened that damn restaurant with the owners and was hired as the first waitress and server. I called in sick on Friday and Saturday, but I got a note from my doctor that I got the darn flu like a 48-hour bug," tears falling rapidly. "What am I going to do?" "Let's back up, Lily. Where were you on Thursday night?" "Okay yeah, I was drinking vodka at home, then I went out to listen to some music at the Tavern down the street. I don't remember much after that; I think I was drugged cuz when I woke up on Friday, my head was on fire naked next to a dude I didn't know. It was fricken loony. I roll over, head throbbing, and then choke on this skeleton of a man's back hair. Ain't kidding, Doctor. The dude had a rug coming out of his skin way gross. The hairiest guy I have ever seen. Geez, his toes could have been permed. Oh, shit, like aah, I peeked over to see his Dick. We were naked, the covers off, really; Wtf? The guy didn't have a cock, or it must have been lost in this mound of curly, kinky hair. I mean totally gross on the sheets around me… hair and more hair like he was freaking shedding." *I could only shake my head in acknowledgment that Lily was on a roll downwards, thinking, and this was only Thursday evening, surely she didn't make it to work. This most likely was why she was fired!'*

"Fk had to get out of that room. I threw my clothes on fast and saw a leftover bottle of vodka, crap. I gulped it down; yeah, no, this was traumatic. I stumbled to the window to see where I was… damn, in a Motel 6!" The dude was a serious locomotive train, like snoring insanely. The freaking walls shook. How the hell did I end up in this room? I had to take a pee, so I ventured into the bathroom. Lord, the mirror was like scary looking back at me. Ugh, mascara and lipstick are all over my face. I looked like a melted clown, and my tongue was bothering me, itching. I stuck my tongue out like a fricken hairball was clinging to my teeth… involuntarily I started dry heaving, which in no time became wet vomit. Wtf was his hair doing in my mouth? Uuhhh, are you freaking kidding me? This was a Dightmare ('daymare-nightmare combined') so I rinsed out my mouth, gargled with some rusty sink water, and was on the way out of the room."

Lily coughed and continued in animation mode… "then I heard, 'hey babe, where you off to? I'm starving. Can you get me something to eat?' Omg, the mound of hair was speaking to me, fk I thought to myself… 'Hair-Pie' just kidding, Doctor."

Ame had been counseling Lily for 5 yrs. The woman was once a knockout with gorgeous green eyes, mahogany hair, a pert nose, supple lips, and a contagious smile with a body to match implants for boobs, 5'7" tall and 139 pounds. Lily, now 55 years old, alcohol had deteriorated her teeth and added wrinkles and a red nose to boot. Alcohol has changed her looks, yet on a good night with the light down low still beautiful, her personality a major plus fun, always ready to laugh. Alcohol addiction, insecurity syndrome, paranoia, fear of being alone, and low self-esteem were the reasons for Psychotherapy counseling recommendations from her Probation officer and this was mandated by a Judge's order.

Lily has had three DUIs, is driving impaired, she drinks daily. Her husband left her five years back, tired of babysitting an alcoholic. Lily tried to commit suicide in November 2016 during the Thanksgiving Holiday in her closed garage. A bottle of Smirnov vodka opened on her seat, her car running, having passed out drunk. Lucky or unlucky for her, a next-door neighbor at her townhouse complex heard the car running and called the Police. Lily was saved from herself that day. Her excuse was that she was tired of being alone, no one loved her, her family had abandoned her, and she had no invite to her daughter's home on Thanksgiving.

I was sitting and sliding my ass back for more of a comfortable position. I mused and pondered how Lily would take the acidic results of her actions, not worried that I was missing any of her stories. My clients sign disclosure forms. All sessions are videotaped and audio archived.

Lily sucked down some of her bottled water and trudged on…"what a screwed-up weekend, right? Ahh, Friday, I don't remember much. I think I ate something in a park, and weird things started to happen. I had thoughts…." "Wait, Lily, what thoughts, weird things? Please tell me?" "Oh, Doc, just my past life when I was so happy, my husband and I would go on cruises, motorcycle rides with my friends, motorhome trips to Canada and Mexico. All the fun we had is over like toast because of my alcohol problem." Lily paused in reflection.

"My husband's last words were, 'I love you, Lily, but I am done being your live-in babysitter.' I only wanted to die sitting on that bench in the park, but then I reached into my purse and took another swig of a pint of vodka. Everything became better." "All right, Lily, I want to thank you for…." "No, wait, Doc, not finished, please listen. I rolled over late Friday night or Saturday morning, and there was a clock radio with a red digital display showing 3:55 am. I had no idea where I was. The room had several nightlights, I was freaked out naked again, and there was another fkn body next to me like a child's body." "Lily, did you black out? What are you describing, a three or four-day binge…." "Please, doc, lots of things are foggy. Let me get this out before I forget it; as I said, there was this small body, uhm. I realized my right arm was touching his skin. I leaned up on my left elbow; we were partially under a satin cream-colored sheet. I thought it was the hairy ape dude until my eyes focused. No, this guy didn't have any hair at all. Not a hair follicle on his back; his head was bald, and I was huge compared to him. He couldn't be 5 feet tall and maybe 115 pounds skinny. Wtf? I'm not making this shit up. It does sound bizarre. I woke up to find myself with a freakin midget. Where was I last night ughhhh… at a Circus? My mind bounced, then I couldn't hear this guy breathe. His bones didn't even move; geez, the dude was freakin dead. I lost it; my heart beating was the loudest sound in the room. Can you imagine this, Doc? I mean, like, really?"

I now nod, totally entrenched in Lily's story, perched at the end of my chair. Lily had my undivided attention, raising my hands with my well-manicured eyebrows beckoning her to continue.

"On the nightstand was a bottle of Absolute Vodka, expensive stuff. I sat up and gulped some of it down, then noticed pictures of family photos, the people smiling, an Asian family grandpas, grandma's children, a large gathering, and other images, and even a couple... of wedding photos. I reached over and finished the bottle of vodka, burning down my throat as I swallowed. The room's decor matched the chairs, everything in a light brown suede motif. I was lying in a four-poster bed, all matching. Damn, I was in someone's house; this isn't a hotel room. For a second, I felt embarrassed, like I was like a slut or something, but that thought didn't last long. I was a survivor, but where the fk was I?

I tried to sit up to itch my left leg and couldn't. It wasn't that I was so messed up; nope, my ankle had a suede leather cuff attached to the post on the bed. I flipped out, started kicking my legs, and realized that only my ankle was clamped down. Bam, the body next to me spun around, alive his deep black eyes I expected to see... NOT. Wide whitish blue albino eyes looked right back at me. A monster not 5 inches from me thought I would have a Heart Attack."

"Excuse me, Lily, our time is almost up. I will need the last 15 minutes of our 75-minute session, please. I know you haven't finished your weekend's tale recounting the events of a hectic, wild few days. Let's get to the point, Lily; at any time, did you call your restaurant for someone to cover your Friday and Saturday shifts?" Lily slouched down and hid her eyes from me "no, but I was too sick. I told the manager on Sunday night, got a doctor's excuse, ugh, note uhm, Doctor Ame Amaya."

"Lily, you are a lucky woman for you have outstanding medical insurance and the means to pay your bills out front. Your ex-husband left you not in the lurch but well provided for." "So, what are you saying, Doc?" "Lily, please listen, and I don't interrupt you; please let me continue; you're on Probation. If you violate the conditions of your Probation, they will lock you up in the County Jail for one year. You now have

16

lost your job on another alcoholic binge, and tell me, Lily, why the wrap on your left wrist… let me see?”

“Oh, I scraped myself, is all; I’d rather not unwrap the wound. It hurts when it hits the air.” “That’s fine, Lily; you will be checked out thoroughly soon. Will you please excuse me for a minute? Do you want a juice drink or bottle of water? I will be right back.” “Doc, I’d love to have some orange juice if you don’t mind… thanks.”

I exited the room and entered the reception area “hey, Donnie, could you call Lily’s Probation Officer and have her arrested here? She has violated and once again tried to end her life lost her job, and whatnot.” “I’m right on it, Doctor Amaya. Uh, Ame, sorry.” “Please get on this now, Don; my next appointment is in less than 25 minutes.” “Aah, Ame, Ms. Slim has canceled and rescheduled for next week.” I cock my head to the left, somewhat disgusted; Ms. Slim’s disorder can be terminal. I make a mental note to call her… Anorexia nervosa and bulimia are psychiatric illnesses that center on food and its consumption and is usually characterized by; excessive preoccupation with food and dissatisfaction with one’s body shape or weight. They can be severe disorders, and I needed to stay focused on Ms. Slim.

Grabbing two cans of OJ, I reenter my office, “Lily, what are you doing?” I catch her swiftly putting something back in her purse with a stare of Busted. “Umh, Doc, just taking a sip of a tiny airport bottle is all, umh, you know, before the OJ. I know, Doc, it’s like my first drink of the day!” I say, “here’s some orange juice. Listen to me carefully. I want you to comprehend what I must explain to you fully.” She blushed, bowing her chin. “I’m going to recommend that you be admitted to a rehabilitation center for 90 days.” “What? No, Fkn way… I don’t need any rehabilitation. I can handle myself, and I’m not going….” I place both hands up in the stop sign motion “let me finish, Lily; there is an awesome program at

NIA the treatment center is second to none. The place is like a 5-star resort 24/7 care...."

Lily is on her feet at once, scarily fast, pacing back and forth. "Wtf, that's a nut hospital for the criminally insane. I'm not nuts, crazy... umh, I'm leaving!" "Hold on, Lily, and please hear me out! The rehabilitation center is a complete complex, all separate and not even associated with the mental institution. I've sent other clients there, and I have to say with amazing results. Would you rather be housed there in a treatment program or rot in a cell in the County Jail, a rubber room locked in a cell going through Detox-Hell? You have so much to offer humanity; you can succeed and get this monkey off your back with help. I believe in you, Lily; you will be able to achieve anything you want to. You told me in our first session that your ex-husband would like to become friends with you again, even date you. He said he loved you still, right? He just couldn't watch alcohol destroy you anymore; remember his words, no more babysitting Lily. I have faith in you and will visit you at NIA."

My desk phone buzzes. I pick it up "yes, Don." "Lily's Probation Officer is here; she was in the area; convenient, right?" "Send her in, Don" the instant Lily saw her Probation Officer, the lights went dim, and an expression of dismay slapped her across her cheeks. "I thought everything I told you was in confidentiality. This is bullshit, Doc, straight BullShit a setup."

"Now you relax, Ms. Bender," as she looked at the leaking blood from Lily's left wrist bandage, "this is for your own good." Ms. Benders P.O. probation officer Ms. Vamp stated, frowning, "you tried to kill yourself again, lost your job, and appear to have lost 10 pounds since I last saw you. I smell alcohol from over here." She takes out a breathalyzer "blow in this, please, Ms. Bender, one of the terms of your probation was absolutely zero alcohol... zero tolerance." Lily blows into

the breathalyzer, "look at the reading B.A.C of 1.5 legally intoxicated anything over 0.8... your inebriated Lily!" "Ms. Vamp, that can't be right. I haven't drunk that much. I haven't been eating, is all." "Let me see your purse," she snatches it away and yanks out three empty bottles of the airport variety vodka, "not drinking, huh?"

"Stand up, Ms. Bender. I have to cuff you up." "Doctor Amaya, your secretary, said you have filled out the forms for her admittance to NIA's treatment center. Is that correct?" "In triplicate," as I rip off the bottom page, "Lily, this is for the best this is for your own good. I will stop in to see you in the next few weeks, is your car parked in our lot?" "No, I took the bus," a defeated Scowl of disdain and contempt upon her face.

-3-

Doctor Ame Amaya was plumb... worn out.

I walked them out and wished Lily good luck, then I collapsed on my couch with the door closed, been a rough day already! After about 15 minutes of peace, I hear tapping on my door, "come in" "sorry to bother you, Ame, you know your schedule is clear. Wednesday is an early day for us. If you don't mind me asking, what's happened at NIA?"

"Have a seat, Donnie," while I roll onto my side to face him, place a pillow under my head, then fill him in on my day's inner tumult, ugh. After a while, my secretary Donny... looking like he does toward me most the time a compassionate, soul... says, "So, Ame, they wouldn't allow you to see 'Sara,' and they took 'Al' away in a straitjacket. I don't know Ame, but from my perspective, taking on two more clients at the asylum is way too stressful and unnecessary with the drive to Napa and all the crap you got to go through to see 'Al and Sara' heck, you have a dozen referrals waiting. I could easily book you seven days a week, I realize…." "Don, of course, you make inarguable points. I respect your opinion and know you're only thinking of me. I'm concentrating on Forensic Psychology. I've grown somewhat attached to Al and Sara. I see a glimmer of hope, flashes of recognition; besides, I enjoy the drive through the vineyards." He frowned. "Donny, why don't you come with me next Wednesday on the trip, and we can catch lunch at a winery?"

He smiles "well, hell yeah, call that confirmed Ame," then with a subtle wisp and flick of his tongue, he falls forward on his knees, with a wink, "I've had lunch Ame but not dessert, mind if I indulge you, your due some relaxation!"

I kicked off my flats as he helped me peel back my pants 'yuh, no, I kinda understand why all those male professionals have cute secretaries. Turnabout is fair play. Yep!' As I grabbed his head and pulled him down to my already wet crevice one, two, three tongue lashes, he whispered, "Yummy, your clit is so hard; girl cum on, let's do this!" ❧.

Thursday evening: Ame is relaxing in her spacious 5,500 square-foot home in Bell Marin Keys, looking out her bay window and viewing her dock. Her neighbor pulls in with his charter fishing boat. She'd been on his Boston Whaler several times on fun fishing trips. That was years ago. Ame was an unrelenting workaholic glancing down at her iPad that sat on her desk. Her files on 'Al and Sara' inmates at NIA were within reach. She is enjoying a microbrew beer, her favorite alcoholic beverage; beer to Ame was the best, especially in an iced mug. She may enjoy the view of thousands of acres of grapes and vineyards, but she despised the taste of wine. It made her sick to her stomach, detesting white or red wine. It didn't matter;

she couldn't even stand champagne. She had determined that she was allergic to wine.

Her body shuddered, thinking of the last time she put her lips to a glass of wine at a wedding. She rushed to the restroom and vomited that was about 15 years ago.

Ame had been thinking about Al… gnawing in her craw, chewing on her mind. She was missing something, feeling odd but couldn't place a firm finger on it. Perplexed thinking, there must be a way to achieve a breakthrough with Al! 'How can I reach the boy inside?' This man, what made him tick? Can I help him to find himself? Ame decides to start from the beginning.

<u>INMATE #5155 NIA. Date 10/5/16.> First initial consultation, Al's words, who was Al?</u>

In a straitjacket sitting across from me, his eyes tracking my every movement, no fear in his countenance, only arrogance. After the introduction, I asked him to tell me about himself from childhood to where we were today… 'Doctor Amaya, I'm not going to communicate with you in this strait-jacket. It's uncomfortable. Please have the guards take it off me. I pose no threat to you nor anyone.' With permission from the Warden, 15 minutes later, Al was rubbing his hands, free of restraints, and he was given a bottle of water that was on the small table in front of us. A guard outside the door of the 11' x 13' room with video surveillance ongoing.

'I suppose I was three years old when my parents first realized I was odd; it's common for infants to mimic what they hear. It's the way they learn words through sound… a TV was on, and a show named 'Blue's Clues' was playing.' Dad turned it off and handed me a bottle.

I then repeated the sounds of the Blue Dog on the program. Dad smiled and said, 'Al, that's good.' I then replicated his exact words, 'Al, that's good,' but in his octave, his intonation tone, as if he'd said it himself. I took the bottle and sucked it, staring at his shocked face. My inherent talent, or as it was called a 'curse' several months later, caused me trouble. I was no longer amusing my dad or mom. I was being reprimanded by both my parents and severely spanked by my dad when I repeated the sentence 'shut the fk up bitch' in my dad's precise intonation; my parents were in an argument. I was trying to be funny.

I was only 3 ½ years old. This hurt me inside and out. I stopped talking much when mom or dad was around for a while. I only listened and then learned what was expected of me to be a normal kid. I was beaten bloody when I screwed up a little later using my mother's voice; my dad went berserk. I wasn't four years old, and I didn't understand why I was spanked severely… I only said, 'loving… to you is a two-minute hump and dump; I'm over it.' My dad was incensed, seething. My mom covered her mouth and giggled. He was in a rage, picked me up, and threw me down. My mother came to my aid to rescue me but was tossed aside.

I became more introverted; I could bark like our dog, purr like our kitty cat, and speak just like our Parrots. Shortly after that, my life changed permanently for my Grandpa; my mother's father had moved to Marin County from Las Vegas. He maintained a home in Vegas and bought a nice house in the Fairfax area. Grandpa Sloan was a world-renowned Ventriloquist, a showman celebrity, and a regular on the Vegas strip. Harrah's, Winn Resort, you name it, his name was the headliner. Grandpa did world tours and could throw his voice up to 25 feet. His lips nor throat moved as he spoke for each of his puppets, carrying on conversations and dialogues in various voices. His ventriloquist acts were second to none, Doctor Ame.

My parents both worked, and instead of being left at daycare at four years old, when grandpa was in town, he would watch me; my mother had told her dad about how I used to mimic everything I heard when I was younger. <u>'I stopped imitating and duplicating sounds months before.'</u> I was mortally afraid and didn't want to get into trouble again for being a 'copycat.' One day, I remember eating ice cream with 'PAPA,' and he told me not to worry about my mother having another baby. 'She was pregnant.' I was so insecure, crying. He picked me up and said Al, your special. I can tell you're hiding your secrets. Let me tell you one of my secrets.

Al… in your lineage in our ancestry that goes way back before the Roman Empire. Uh, we were Court Jesters in Medieval times, well-acclaimed Wizards, and had magical ancestors, both men, and women. 'Barnum and Bailey Circus' archives have pictures of your great grandpa, who was an amazing performer. I'll tell you some of the stories that have been recited to me over my lifetime that are nonetheless encouraging or, shall I say, inspiring. Al, as you get older, I will work with you and help you to refine your God-given talents; you are a blessed child. This will be our secret only. We must 'vow never to let anyone know for the time being.' You do understand how your parents feel about your mimicking. Your mother, my daughter, has made me swear not to encourage you in any way whatsoever. If you break our promise not to repeat what I tell you or what I'm going to teach you, then they will not allow us to be together, so, Al, do you promise?

I was sitting on Papa's lap. I flipped around with a dimpled grin, hugged him, and said, 'Yes, Papa, Yes, I Promise!' He put me down on the other side of the table to finish my ice cream bowl; the line at the ice cream shop was growing. Papa said in a whisper, but his lips didn't move; 'watch this, Al, and you try to do the same.' 'A customer said loudly to the ice cream guy, give me a scoop of sherbet and chocolate mint!'

"Give me a scoop of sherbet and chocolate mint," Papa said, those same words even louder. Then the ice cream guy spun around and said rudely. "I heard you the first time. There isn't any reason to yell." The customer looked around, befuddled… and perplexed. 'I didn't say a word shit; what's going on?'

Papa and I laughed hard; then, Papa said, "Your turn" the next customer in line was a hefty lady. She said, 'I will have a 3-scoop banana split with Caramel and hot fudge.' The ice cream guy grabbed the scooper and turned his back to go to work on the banana split, and I said, using the worker's voice, umh, I was able to throw the voice behind the counter, *"Uhm, Like You Need This Lady?"*

The lady became highly agitated: "what did you say to me, young man? I want the manager. You just insulted me." The ice cream guy held up both hands. "I said nothing at all" others in the line 'yes, you did; we heard you. That was rude,'… Papa and I busted up howling with high-fives, then Papa and I got up and left. He was serious all of a sudden. "Al, although that was funny, you must learn not to use your special gift to hurt people or get others in trouble, like you just did. We use our special abilities for positives and fun, okay?" I told Papa I was sorry, but I wasn't. From that day forward, Papa and I developed a unique bond. He was everything to me. We were so happy together. He worked with me whenever we were alone; the most challenging part for me was to be able to breathe and not move my lips or make facial expressions. Throwing my voice without contorting my face was an ultimate challenge and frustrating, but still, it was fun trying to learn.

Al was dealing with school bullies.

We worked on sounds like doorbells or a phone ringing, a choo choo train, a growling dog, Lion's roar, Omg. I was having so much fun; Papa was number one in my life. My parents left me even more often after my baby brother was born. I started kindergarten when I was five years old and missed Papa. When he was in town, he would pick me up after school.

During my first week at the school, a big bully pushed me down and took cuts on the slides; he continued to pick on me. I don't know why he did this. He would hit or push me whenever he was around me for no reason. One day in class, we were doing our ABCs. The teacher wrote on the blackboard and asked the bully what letter was next. Using <u>HIS</u> voice, I said, *'I don't give a shit bitch'* Omg, the classroom was silent, not a word. The girls next to me covered their faces with both hands, he was snatched up before he could say a word, and the bully was off to see the principal he was whining. *'I didn't say that!...' crying.'*

Back in those days' principals were allowed to use force or wooden paddles to swat your butt. The paddle had holes in it. I heard being hit by it hurt really bad; the bully got three whacks. Yep!

Ame let out a cackle, stood up thinking, Heck, the bully got what he deserved, reached in the freezer for another frosty mug, and selected some Hemp Ale, thinking to herself, where did Al lose it? Turned the page, amused at Al's antics.

Ame cherished living alone in her 5-bedroom flat. This afternoon she was listening to classical music playing on her surround sound, re-familiarizing herself with Al's earlier counseling sessions.

By my 3rd consult, Al's childhood tales were becoming increasingly foreboding. Even his changed voice turned unsavory, and his expressions morphed sinister-like. This was unscripted territory for Al. He had made the statement, *"I have never told a human what I'm telling you, Ms. Amaya… aah, Doctor Amaya, sorry."* I told him that he could trust me. Patient Doctor confidentiality, and so he did.

There I sat with my legs up, scanning the following interview I had with Al, taking a chug of my frosty beer and wiping my chin, watching the sunset on the water.

<u>8/5/16 Interviews with Al and Sara, # 5155 NIA.</u>

My mom had brought another baby home, a little sister. She was in the house; the sliding glass door was open a screen door kept the bugs and our pooch in the backyard with us. The baby girl was cute but annoying, crying all the time. She was 15 months old, and I was six years old… and was playing in a large dough boy pool; there was a deck connected all around the pool where we had a barbeque grill and lounge chairs. That was where my mom sat.

Mom was reading a 'Good Housekeeping Magazine' by her side, a plastic carafe of iced tea. My little brother was sitting in a baby tube with holes for his feet to dangle from into the water; he was like three years old. I had a raft; we were having a bunch of fun daddy was going to be home soon, and we were going to have a barbecue. Mom had caked us with sunscreen lotion. I was tossing some floating rings back and forth to my Lil bro. The pool had stairs at one end. It was about two feet deep by the stairs and almost four feet deep over by where I lay on my raft next to my mom on the deck.

I had a ton of fun jumping off the deck and doing cannonballs. That was my favorite dive. All of a sudden, my brother started crying, wanting me to play with him, but I was having my own fun with my imaginary friends, diving and playing tag. My mother yelled at me to pay attention to my Lil brother.

I spontaneously decided to alter the odds. I stood by the edge of the pool and mimicked my Lil sister's crying screams, throwing my voice through the screen door where my little sister sat in a stroller. My mom jumped up, shaking her head, saying not again, moving slowly off the deck. Once her back was turned, I gave the Evil eye to the pain-in-the-ass little brother, swam over, and turned his tube over. His head was stuck upside down in the water. His legs were dangling, kicking out of the water, and bubbles were coming up. He squirmed, but I held his legs in place tightly. After a few minutes, there were no longer bubbles coming up. His little fat feet stopped moving. I then started to scream for mommy. She came rushing out of the screen door.

I'm yelling, screaming, and gesticulating like a madman crying, you know, the total way someone should act if his little brother had accidentally drowned; I was holding him as my mom leaped into the pool. Sadly, my little brother... had accidentally drowned. It turned out to be a bad day for my family. Suffice it to say. We didn't have a BBQ. I did have a massive headache the rest of the day, all the shrieking and screaming; then the Sirens came; with the Police, it was like I was on a TV show. I wasn't as sad as mom and dad, but I acted like I was devastated; my parents sent me to Papa for the rest of the summer; it was a fun summertime, Yes! ✿.

Ame steps down onto her outside patio, decides to walk out onto her dock to view the sunset, grabs a light sweater off a bench, and meanders on, not really paying much attention to the gorgeous colors of the impending sunset, closing the sky off, for a darker pattern to take hold. She was lost in thinking about Al's words; how could she help her patient? Al's adolescence deviates from cultural expectations. It would be too simple to use generalized

An argument could be that Al suffers from various forms of psychosis... and has a manic-depressive disorder, sometimes referred to as Bi-Polar Disorder. Al was diagnosed as a sociopath. His decisions were made with little or no thought of consequences, and he was the only person who mattered in the world other than his grandfather Papa.

Ame closed her eyes. A breeze of the wind blew her hair back upon her shoulders, and a fantastic feeling brushed against her skin, matching the mug of beer she was clutching. She had an epiphany of sorts, a great idea. NIA's staff and leading psychologists have employed a belief of biological psychiatry, believing that mental illness was strictly biological, treatments always included Pharmacological modes using measurable biochemicals, pharmaceuticals parlaying some physical methods, and even employing biomarkers to calculate the severity of a person's mental disease.

Poor 'Al' had been treated with (ECT), Electroconvulsive therapy, called shock treatment, best illustrated in the horrendous film *'One Flew Over The Cuckoo's Nest.'* ... This archaic form of treatment is more akin to torture. This treatment is commonly used in patients with severe depression or bipolar disorder that has not responded to other treatments. The electrical stimulation of the brain is rarely successful. Ame's politically correct term, Al, was a sociopath with psychopathic undertones. Al, no doubt, is a clever, manipulative patient with characteristics diagnosable with a degree of narcissism, and there isn't a question that he knows right from wrong; it's just that he doesn't care. No feelings, none. He moved with machine-like discipline.

She walked back to her Rose garden and saw her greenhouse full of life with a whiff of a splendid aroma, leaving the garden to the bees and Hummingbirds, another brew in her paws. She settles down and scans her transcripts, stopping on a date that Al remembered clearly; Ame thinks to herself with her stomach growling. Psychotherapy with Al was useless years ago. The list of psychiatrists was overwhelming; researching the date of his brother's drowning, 8/5/86, the drowning is still categorized as accidental. Ame sat quietly, peering down at her hands, unfocused, squeezing her fingers abruptly in a gesture of futility, her eyes brimming with tears. 'How many murders can I digest?' An explosion of cerebral confusion and tension-filled emotions takes hold of me. A powerful sense of loathing regarding her occupation, confidentiality, and moral values be damned. 'Then laughs contagiously' loudly opens another beer. It's no wonder psychiatrists are in the upper echelon of Suicides... amongst professionals. Wiping her eyes, smirking, and glancing back at her iPad... Ame takes another swig of her beer and concentrates on her other patient at NIA... Her name was Sara Sloan. ◖.   But couldn't let loose of Al, flipping to the next counseling session in sequence.

8/27/89 Al... Interview 7 # 5155 NIA.

As society would say, I was an average 10-year-old, well, almost besides all the pranks and practical jokes using my art talent of Ventriloquism intonations, imitating voices... and sounds. Al's tooth-bearing grin was too much for me to overlook.

I make it a rule of thumb to refrain from interrupting a patient; my style was listening, analyzing, and assimilating the articulations from my diverse patient client pool. Recently I had taken on the 'Dark-Side' an overpowering desire to consult and debate with the Criminally Insane. I should have better judgment and more restraint, but his bragging swagger, that grin I attacked emotionally, Damn it, Al had succeeded in drawing me out. Professionalism be gone.

Al, do you think such pranks are harmless? I took a list of his acts… Purposely disrupting a football game, blowing phantom whistles when the other team had a breakaway run to the endzone, breaking friends up at school by saying awful things using their very same voices and causing fist fights in gym class. Appallingly during an award ceremony in the gymnasium, where the Principle spoke of an Honor student's well-deserved accolades, Al used the principles voice and said into the microphone to the audience and the Honor student, 'Your Ugly And a Loser!' Al started snickering, then ended up grabbing his stomach, cackling loud. I Stopped flabbergasted and asked, 'Al, you thoroughly thought that was funny?'

Al had caused an accident that hurt several children… *'Your abuse of the school bus driver resulted in an accident, Al. Sadly you were all about having fun at other's expense, using your ventriloquist skills to fulfill your pleasure. You sit there gleaming and smiling, describing your purposeful disruptions of every kind, including your referee whistles and stopping sporting events. There's no excuse for your torment of the teachers and your classmates. One of your escapades stands out when you stood at a bus stop listening to a Police Officer reprimanding a driver for running a red light. The young high school kid was terrified, but what did you do, Al? Uuhhh, you were able to say using the student's voice, 'Fk you, Pig,' then you laughed your ass off as the teenager was dragged from his car….' Al stops me and says, 'you wanna hear more with a wide-ass smirk.'*

Instantly Al swiftly moved and stiffened his hands grasp on the arms of the chair. His death-spiraling eyes bore into mine. I will never forget the evil and fright I was exposed to. In an instant, a snapping roar, a growl of horror, carnivorous teeth

clamping and nipping behind my left ear; the hairs prickled erect on the nape of my neck. I panicked, leaping from my chair… falling to the ground. In a split second, the door flew open, and a white-clothed guard stepped in. Al sat with his palms up as if he didn't understand my reaction or what was happening stoically, with no emotion, just the glow of his red eyes.

The guard helped me up and asked, 'What Happened?' I was shaken but said, aah, everything is fine. I remember snarling at Al. My panties were wet; my vagina let loose of urine, not just a drop or two. I was pissed 'Off or On' depending on your perspectives! Pulling down my blouse and re-adjusting my clothing, I was face to face with Al… 'Al, if you ever pull that stunt again, I will never see you again.' He only shrugged, non-committal. I turned away from the iPad screen.

Thinking back, it was like a salivating Saber-Tooth Tiger was on my neck. It was real, scary beyond any explanation. It's the adage, 'you had to have been there.' I could almost feel the Tiger's breath and smell the Feral odor. His ability to throw his words and sounds like within an inch of my ear lobes was uncannily insane, unbelievable, and way past Scary!

Al was a psychopath out of control, yet I was drawn to his self-confidence and his egotistical ways… 'Doctor Amaya' would you like to let me continue, for 9/27/89 was an important date in my life. Perhaps this part of my childhood or history could help you to understand my way of thinking, giving you the information to enable you to process and a simple formula to help me regain a foothold and once again be an asset to our society. Please help me, Doctor Amaya.

I nod affirmatively… Al drops back in his chair and into times past, to when he was but ten years old again; "I hadn't any friends, hanging alone, these boys would pick on me they were 6th graders, two years older than me. One afternoon I was standing in front of my locker, and there was a crowd of kids packing up to go home for the weekend. All of a sudden, my pants were down to my ankles along with my underwear; this older boy had 'Panced Me'… yanking them down.

I was naked… my butt and all were showing. I tried to cover up, but all the kids were laughing and teasing me. It was the worst feeling, so embarrassed. Omg, the boy's girlfriend was excitedly squealing, 'Look at his boney ass. He has no penis oohhh, gross!' I burst into tears and made it out of the hallway, kids laughing at me as I left. When I got on my bike with my backpack, I felt a sense of relief. I peddled away only to ride right by the girl and the boy. The boys' friend reached out and shoved me over. I fell off my bike on the concrete, bleeding.

The three of them, along with the rest of their audience, were literally crying and laughing so hard. No one helped me up; my books, all my stuff lay sprawled about on the sidewalk. I was bleeding from abrasions… hands, chin, and knees, and all I heard was addictive laughter, then I was alone. As I fixed my crooked handlebars, straightening them out, I decided that I never wanted to return to school again, Never! But what infuriated me much more was how hateful humans were. If it were the last thing I ever did, I vowed to get even, and as luck would find me, I did!

I had overheard them say as they laughingly passed by me, 'meet yah at the creek cave,' a place where the popular kids hung out, also referred to as the kissing cave. The water ran slowly and wasn't that deep. The sides of the embankments on each side of the creek were like 19 ft. high at least. Some older boys had dug out a cave in the 19-foot wall of dirt a few years back, and others kept digging, and it grew. They brought in plywood and 2X4s for reinforcement. It became a place to go and bring a 'Ghetto Blaster' and dance on the shore um beach by the running creek. I used to go there and throw, uh, skip rocks. Others brought bows and arrows and bee-bee guns, and pellet guns. I liked to kill the frogs and pollywogs while playing in the water.

Anyways Doc, there were homes adjacent to the creek. One was magnificent, like a Castle, with a giant swimming pool with slides and diving boards. I hid my bicycle by the crazy tall hedges and waited for the crowds to appear. I should have been home already. I knew I would get into trouble, but whatever. It took like forever, although probably not so long, about an hour, I suppose, and the boys showed up with the girl. They had bathing suits on, still laughing, and sang to the music box they carried. The three of them went right into the cave; I watched them for a while, trying to figure out how I would get my revenge, seething!

I only had a slingshot, and I was a rather good shot, though, with lots of practice and alone time, I could hit a bullseye from about 50 yards away. I spotted another boy and girl from my school jumping into a water hole, the one area with deep water sectioned off with rocks. On the other side of the water hole, a boy and girl laying on a towel were necking, uh, smooching and fondling each other, you know. A few moments later, the three bullies were in the water with the girl, all hooting and hollering, having fun. I wasn't… the music I heard was from 'Great White,' the band was on the radio, and the song I liked was playing loud. I still remember this day like this only happened this afternoon. The song's name was 'Once bitten twice shy.'

The three boys ran into the cave giggling with the girl, soaking wet howls of fun laughter. What they didn't know was that I had turned a valve on from a 3-inch hose that was used to empty the enormous swimming pool of the house above the cave. Taking the hose, I re-directed the hose from the creek. It must have been used to empty the pool for cleaning, I don't know, but where I placed it was above the entrance about five ft. back.

I had snuck back to the beginning of the hose and turned the valve on. Yup! Smiling all the way… Karma was on my side. Like an earthquake, in less than 15 minutes, the cave entrance, wet and soggy, collapsed. I ran to pull the hose out, but it was stuck… running fast to my bike; I rode home. Bad news I was in serious trouble mom was pissed off royally; I got grounded and belted by dad, but I smiled the whole time.

The news hit the TV… Damn! Three children buried alive Dead Oh… No. Yay!

-5-

1/11/17 Wednesday.

Don was enjoying his morning. It wasn't every day that he drove a $115,000 sports car Ame's 2017 Lexus L.C. taking the winding roads through Sonoma County on their way to NIA; abreast of him was Ame, concentrating on her last appointment with 'Al and Sara.' Last Wednesday, the 4th, she didn't even finish her consultation with Al when she was directed to leave the institution because of the stabbing death. Therefore it had been two weeks since she saw 'Sara' usually; she'd scheduled Sara first on her Wednesday. That was the case for today.

She closes her iPad down. *"Donny, I will try and get you past security. You're my assistant, all right? Worst case, you can hang out in the visitor's lounge till I'm done with the counseling sessions, okay?"*

Don mutters, "that's fine, Ame. I'm happy just being with you; I can see how your Wednesdays could break up the week, like a kind of escape for the day kind of cool, relaxing drive out of the city and humanity into the rolling hills of wine grapes. I wish I could accompany you weekly; heck, I could be your assistant and chauffeur. This is way cool, the wine country grapes for as far as you can see; look over there, Ame. Up in the air, look, there are like five air balloons so damn colorful what fun I'd like to do that, geez, what a life! Hey, Ame, can I ask you a question?" "Sure, Don; what's on your mind?" "Well, okay, here goes. Why does it seem you enjoy your work with Psycho Inmates? Is it that they are so dangerous, and you think you can save them, change them, or what?"

A chuckle, "you know I've asked myself the same question many times, but by far the most intriguing and challenging venue is the Prison Wards. NIA is renowned for the criminally insane and madness locked up of every conceivable form, shameless psychopathic killers, and remorseless child killers. Serial killers, every strain of evil, moms who murder their babies, on and on, even hyperverbal drug addicts who had lost their minds." "Man, Ame, it's got to rub off on you. I don't think I could handle it." "Don, all the insanity of this world locked into one place NIA kind of exciting to me, inmates from all over the world, Don, this is the most Notorious Prison in the whole damn world Psychopaths are shipped here from everywhere on the globe. I find it intriguing. Sure, it's ominous, but I'm learning a lot, okay!"

There was a pause as the wind blew a whiff of a pungent left-over Skunk into the open sunroof. "I only suppose I want to learn somehow what makes them tick… the dream of discovering an epiphany, a breakthrough, just bring one of them back from the brink of insanity."

Don slinks the Lexus to a stop by the guard hut; the grounds were covered in trees and grapes in neat, organized rows. It was an overcast day with Cumulus Clouds encircling the sky, a crisp winter day. NIA was a complex of 7 buildings, with the main one looking like an expansive castle retrofitted with a European architectural façade matching the other six buildings. The guarded compound was over 655 acres square, an enormous operation, paved paths going in different directions, and maps were handed out per request, although all visitors were monitored closely.

If not for the rows of chain-link fences stretching across the horizon, the sharp shine and gleam of razor wire coils of concertina wire, and a stainless-steel perimeter of razors, you'd think you were visiting a medieval castle. Matching the Castle façade was the round gun towers turrets at least 75 feet in the air, no doubt all of which underscored the asylums fortress like an impenetrable or inescapable image.

Don said, "Ame, I feel weird. Geez, hell, I don't like this place." Three gates later, he parked by the front entrance by the 7-foot sign in marble, 'NIA' <u>'The Napa Insane Asylum for the Criminally Insane.'</u> A sign by the triple sliding doors read, 'Anyone entering this facility is subject to full metal detectors X-Rays, Search. Have your Identifications out for processing... Thank you.' 'Warden Ursula Anders.'

Ame and Don slowly make their way out of the maze and are finally staring up at the magnificent cathedral ceiling five stories high. Inside the entrance of NIA were wrap-around moldings outset dormers, a checker-board design of brown and beige, a bank of elevators on the left with a mini escalator to the right lit signs directing all to the visitor's area for further processing. They walked along the marble tile with a terracotta color. The place was immaculate and modern, with rounded molding and 11-foot openings. The air was clinical. It almost smelled of cleansed ozone.

There were armed guards at each opening with wires and headgear; it looked like the secret service; instead of uniforms, they were in designer suits and jackets with ties. Don thought to himself, Wtf? He elbows Ame while they are waiting... seven deep in a line, "what's up with the guards, attire?" She smirks back at him, "it's policy. IMO it's a show for the visitors, inside the prison that all disappears, white coats and…." "Hello, Doctor Ame Amaya, room # 5, please," "Come on, Don, let's go!" A guard holds up the stop signal, "Please, Mr. Feline can you wait in the visitor's lounge momentarily? Thank you."

A scowl on Ame's countenance. "He's with me, my assistant." "I'm sorry, doctor; please follow me." They walked down an expansive hallway. The guy opened the door for her; Ame was stunned that the room looked like something out of a luxurious mansion. She stepped down onto the sunken floor… instead of chairs with tables, the typical office arrangement. There were leather couches. The high-back lounge chairs and the deep brown walls matched the Mahogany furniture. The size of the room also shocked Ame. It had to be at least 1,000 square feet. Who could have guessed? "Please be seated, Doctor Amaya," startling her, for no one was in this room… it was vacant except for her.

'Please, doctor, look over here on the screen' Ame then noticed a large TV monitor, perhaps 75 inches wide at least. She sat on the leather couch with her legs crossed. She recognizes Warden Ursula Anders at once. "Doctor Amaya, I wanted to speak with you in person, but I'm on another site here… at NIA. I hope this isn't too impersonal. I wanted to express my heartfelt sympathy to you for having to experience last week's horrific stabbing and fatality in one of our dayrooms. We are thankful that you didn't repeat to anyone what happened here in our dayroom. The management here at NIA knows that you kept this anomaly out of the mainstream news with much respect…." "Warden, I'd hardly call a murder an anomaly, but I didn't want to cause any trouble. I figured it was best for NIA to handle the corrosive issue." "Nonetheless, we thank you. As you well know, this is a public entity. Obviously, Doctor, there could have been massive losses for our shareholders and bondholders. You know what negative publicity would do to our stock price. Thank you, Doctor Amaya, for not allowing what happened to damage our present situation further and adhering to your contract of non-disclosure about whatever occurs behind our walls."

Ame stares back at the monitor where Warden Ursula Anders was posed and then looked up at the camera's inset in the ceiling and says, "NIA is like Las Vegas Warden Anders; anything that happens here stays here...." "Yes, so appropriate. Please stay diligent and be aware that everything remains 'In House' have a pleasant day, ughhhh... your patients are waiting in separate interview rooms. Sorry, but Mr. Donny Feline will have to remain in the visitor's lounge and garden area. Good day!"

Ame opens her mouth to express herself, but the screen goes dark. The double door opens, and the GQ guard 'please Doctor Amaya, could you accompany me?' 'She muses as one of her secret fantasies takes hold. 'I could think of something else I'd like to do with you, Mr. Guard!' Ame did enjoy a man in uniform, lol, even if it was a 3-piece suit.

Ame discards all her electronics, Bluetooth, Apple Watch, iPhone, and purse after pulling a pair of tennis shoes out of her haversack and trading out her high-heeled shoes. She locked all her belongings and stuff in a locked box, # 155. The steel doors are buzzed open she steps inside the room and sees Sara with arms folded just below her petite breasts, sitting erect impatiently. A Guard of lesser quality closes the door behind her, dressed in blue and white stripes.

<u>1/11/17… Wednesday, Sara # 4755… NIA Interview # 11.</u>

"Where were you last week, Doc? I waited and waited like forever." "I'm so sorry, Sara, I had to leave; it was out of my control," a sly squinted look, upturned lips. "That's right, the blood bath ole Henry bit the dust. That's what happened, huh?" I nod. Sara brusquely switched personalities with a jerky motion. She raises a make-up bag "look what I've added to my fun bag; I'm a real cosmetologist." She pulls out a set of combs, hairbrushes, safety razors, emery boards, nail polishes, a battery-powered shaver and mascara, cosmetics with blush, and eyeliners. "See, isn't this sweet Doctor Ame? Can I brush your hair and help accentuate your natural beauty, please… oh, Please!" "Where did you get all this stuff, Sara? You have twice the assortment of cosmetics you had the last time I saw you and even a safety shaver."

"Sshhh, Doctor Ame, I have contacts connections, and guess what? I have been here at this hospital for over five years, haven't had any trouble, and there is nothing in my Salon bag that could harm anyone. I fix other patients up, and a few staff members allow me to make them pretty, but for some of them, there's no hope, but I try." lol.

Not being able to restrain myself, I laugh, "maybe later, Sara. First, let's back up a bit; why don't we revisit our conversation from where we left off on our last visit?" I opened my 'Sara folder' "Doctor Ame, I've been having a hard time sleeping lately, been having 'dightmares' (day and nightmares) it's been horrible, the dreams are sort of surreal, lucid, and vivid it's like I'm actually there! I leave ah… I'm not here in Prison, kinda weird."

"Sara, why don't we venture into these dightmares and address them today? Where do they start? Why don't you tell me all from the beginning, okay." "Well, all right, Doctor Ame, but many of my dreams are not interrelated, like aberrations, yah know, disconnected, don't think there is any form of intervention, or how you could interpret or decipher any of it?" "Sara, enough; why will you not let me make those assertions? Please tell me what troubles you here, Sara. Please, you can always trust me. I'm on your side, Sara!"

She bows her head forward and fidgets in her chair. "Fine, it's weird, okay," she asks, "do you mind if I lay down on the examination bed, close my eyes, and relax?" "Great Idea Sara." Sara daintily postures up like a shy, unassuming small girl and mutters, "So it's strange the date is etched into my memory 7/25/10. I was overlooking the picturesque San Diego shoreline on a warm and brilliant summer afternoon. I walk into a 5-star hotel named the Palomar, with a swimming pool on the roof, bar, and lounge; I'm stepping into the 1st-floor kitchen area for employees. I duck into the swinging door. Then I am in another room, uh, the laundry room taking a maid's uniform and pushcart. I enter a bathroom, change into the maid outfit, and check myself in the mirror; who am I?"

I lean into her prone body, listening intently; she continues, "the reflection in the mirror back at me isn't me… my long Raven black wig, thick bushy black eyebrows, blush, hair in a tie with a scarf, my eyes are a dark brown, contacts, not hazel and they itch already. I am a different person. I'd brought with me a medium-sized backpack. I placed it on the third shelf on the pushcart after attaching a plastic name tag with a clip of my new look on the card. My name that day was Maria Santo!"

"Were set, sir, in place, all three rooms secure; how do we know she's going to show up?" Brock listening on his earbud, dressed to kill in his Armani Suit, speaks into his microphone to his team of FBI Agents… "don't worry, she will be here. Remember to be diligent, suspicious, and aware of any person. She is like a chameleon, a camouflage expert. Listen, under no circumstances do we arrest her until she enters our 'Johns' hotel room. She will not be able to resist this trap. We have been working on the online dating site for nine months. Terry, as I said during our briefing. I'm almost certain that she is going to show up. She has 27 murders associated with her modus operandi, yet she has left zero evidence or clues at the scenes. This time will be different!"

Brock swivels around in the white Crown Vic. "Lucie, whatcha thinking? From a female Agents perspective, am I, or are we missing anything here?" Agent Lucie Link leans forward, pressing the air-conditioning vents upwards into her upper body, dressed in a pants suit with lite brown flats, cherubically angelic features, pouty lips, dainty nose, and ocean teal eyes, a stunning beauty at 5' 7" tall and 145 Lbs. a body that screamed fk me. Brock was enamored and transfixed with her assets, which included her long strawberry blonde hair, a natural. She made her Swedish descendants proud. What made this woman stand out, though, was her intelligence and intuition. These, by far, were her most outstanding attributes, at least within Brock's mind.

"Brock, you're the man. Top field Agent supervisor, the hero, Mr. Brock Dame, the one and only, huh? Why bother to ask me for advice? You're a macho egotistical chauvinist?"

"Lucie, stop it already. It's not as if I wasn't tempted; you're a knockout girl. Sorry, shit, if I had crossed the line and become romantically involved with you, girl, I couldn't be objective, unbiased, but…." "Shut up, Brock. Don't fricken patronize me, and I don't need your condescending high and mighty moral justifications. You're the first and last man to rebuff my advances. My package will remain wrapped up. I will not tolerate your misogynistic points of view; you're an asshole!"

"Oh, great, Lucie, now I'm a misogynist; you're unreal. Next thing I know, you will accuse me of sexual harassment." Lucie elbows him… "Sshhh, Brock, look at the front entrance by the Valet." Brock raises his binoculars "it's her; I think Lucie, your right!" Lucie was already on the radio… 'Valet lobby woman in black and red dress with a black suitcase,' the reply. 'I got her, ma'am.'

Lucie smirks and states, "Agent Dame, sir, we have her, video surveillance in all directions. There isn't any place she can go but the restroom; we have her every step; she will not evade us this time, sir!" He drops the field glasses open-mouthed and stares across the seat. "Oh, now I'm Agent Dame, Sir! Stop the high school stuff, Lucie. Our relationship doesn't or hasn't changed. Call me Brock, all right." She grins, and a dimple leaves her cheeks. He will regret it, she thinks… Over the radio… 'Agent Link, the suspect is in the lounge sipping a Bloody Mary.' 'Okay, we're on our way inside… stealth mode; give her room to breathe.' Brock and Lucie exit the Crown Vic slowly and purposefully with new conviction that this time will be different. They would capture this murderess.

Brock watches her seductive strut go right past him… he drifts back and muses to himself within his testosterone-induced fervor, 'Damn, Agent Lucie Link is a hot bitch. If she only knew how gratifying my stroking of BJ, ole Brock Jr. was in the hot shower earlier this morning. A definite double explosion, shit, the bitch turns me on as his crotch tightens up; damn BJ, relax, we have real work to do!'

Lucie's mind was in likewise mode as the car doors swung open, Lucie a smidgen damp 'that rabbit vibrator isn't getting it lately, this bastard and the fantasy of him deep inside me clamped, rabidly a furious, frenzied love session, oh screw him.' She blinks and discards the fantasia, for now at least. "Jeez, woman, what the hell is that look for, Lucie?" "Let's do this, Brock," as she rubs her Glock… holstered. "Yes, I feel she will not escape our trap this time!"

Sara… on the prowl at the hotel.

Sara pushes # 5 into the service elevator and checks the watch on her left wrist. It was 5:55 pm. She keeps her head bowed away from the camera's vantage points.

Why must I? Do I have to meet the challenges for real is it because I am so egotistical, arrogant, a self-professed mastermind, self-indulgent, and mentally superior lol Yep! Good ole Agent Brock has been tracking me for over five years, futilely since like 2005. I fell off the radar in 2007, and then I re-emerged the classic 'coup de grace' I didn't think ole Brockie would recover from the Magnum Opus. Yes, my intricate scheme was pure genius. Aah, but that's another story; What do I know for sure here at Hotel Palomar? 'Think Sara!' no mistakes!

By this time, my female date should be sipping a cocktail drink on the bottom floor in the Lounge, dressed to detail in a black and red dress. At precisely 6:05 pm, she should enter the elevator and push the number 5 button to rendezvous with me! The cheating bi-sexual lover matches her own obsessions. She will knock on room # 555. Oh, surprise, Yay! .

Tech-savvy Sara had her Bitcoin accounts since the inception of electronic monies, Cyber Currencies, and she also had several Websites on the 'Dark web browser Tor' and the other Internet, lol. In her backpack was a handheld electronic blocking device that effectively disabled all powered electronics. A simple tap on a button and 300ft. in all directions were mute. She had also purchased a 'Nicotine based nerve poison chemical solution from a North Korean contact, a light mist or spray that would kill humans in less than 55 seconds. It was nearly instantaneous if sprayed in the eyes, nose, mouth, or face area. Once the poison hit's the skin, it systemically enters the bloodstream, the main assault on the lungs freezing them; the person suffocates, gagging for oxygen, clenching their throat, hacking, convulsing to death, literally asphyxiated. Oh, so much Fun!

Gloves were a must. Sara had tested this new formula on dogs and cats she took from 'Haven Humane Societies' animal adoption centers. I'm a fricken genius, surely unstoppable, a force to be reckoned with, no doubts, she mutters over her breath. The service elevator opens on floor #5; Sara looks both ways, then pushes her cart out and scurries down the hall, flicking the blocking device on as she exits. Now, no video, Yep!

('Sara stops lifting her head from the pillow, glancing over at the entranced Doctor Ame at full attention in front of a small table… 'please continue, Sara!')

Okay, in my dreams, I've been forewarned, uhm, I know FBI Agents are in adjoining rooms, or on each side of the room, you know, the 'man doors' ready to pounce on me from rooms #554 and # 556. No questions remained that the enemy, the Feds occupied those rooms, how many I had no way of knowing, yet I was overly confident. The Feds sting operation worked the sites I browsed, such as 'MarriedHotHorney.com.' 'And Cheatersanonymous.com,' so many websites for the philanderers, lascivious betraying, deceitful masses to click on and arrange their adulterous rendezvous.

These websites fed me an ever-ending supply of the deviant miscreants that I would devour; of course, the Fed's and the public referred to them as Victims; lol, not! 'Thou Shan't Cheat' is my motto. If you are a cheater, you don't want to be meeting with me. True that!

"Silence, no radio contact unless an emergency exists states Agent Brock Dame; the time was 5:57 pm. The perp was sucking down the last of her Bloody Mary. Brock and Lucie grabbed a table closest to the exit lobby. He had two Agents each in both stairwells on Floor # 5 and in rooms #554 and #556. Brock's best friend, Agent Travis Yuck, waited, in charge of the agents in both adjoining rooms that the murderess, they assumed would soon meet her client in, prospective 'John.'

The perp 'SARA' had already reserved room # 555. Lucie asks, "Brock explain to me once again why we must wait till Sara goes to room # 555 before we take her down. We catch her with the deadly spray. The case is 'Open and Closed' immediately hell… she has given us her description on the cheater's Web Site, black, red dress with black nylons, that's her sitting right over there!" Brock scowls, thinking over his plan, and says nothing.

"Brock, what are we waiting for?" "Lucie, two trains of thought have engulfed my mind. I'm in tumult; first, as you well know, I have been on Sara's trail for over five years now my name has been left out of the investigation. But it has appeared in many newspapers, syndicated news services, and local news channels, so Sara must know what I look like. That's why we're hidden here in this booth. I can hide my face with this menu when she gets up to walk by. My question to you, Lucie, is what if I show my face to the lady in the Red and Black dress and she doesn't react? I guess what I'm trying to say…." "I get it, Brock; if she reacts, we take her down immediately before she can reach a spray bottle, or if she doesn't react, we let her go about her way, watching her. But how do we know if she paid attention to any of our planted publicity? Nothing is for certain, right?" "Correct Lucie, my second concern is what if we, the 'FBI,' are being played and it's a reverse like a sting and the alluring lady over there is part of Sara's scheme?" "Wait, Brock, how could she know? Please, just last night on the Cheater's Website in the San Diego area, there was a minimum of 1,300 hits, thirteen hundred fricken hits, and Cheaters galore. I know we set certain parameters, looks, sexual orientations, fantasies, body types, and all that, but please, Brock, there's no way she could know this is a setup. No Way!" "Okay, Lucie, the plan stays the same. I will conceal my identity as best as I can..." "Oh, shit, she is on the move; Lucie, it's Game Time!"

Sara rolls her cart down the plush carpeted hallway, pretending to be a maid while Brock and Lucie were occupied watching her diversion on the first floor, Maria/Sara was humming in Spanish a song… <u>'The girl from Ipanema'</u> by the <u>'Tijuana Brass Band'</u>… Sara pulls up directly across from room #554.

"Can you believe this shit? Agent Ruiz says out loud, peering through the peephole. The Serial Killer is on her way up here, and I got this Fkn Mexican maid rummaging around." Bang Wtf, as the door rattles. Agent Julio Ruiz opens the door and leans out, "Hey, get out of here; come back in an hour or so, all right!" He's flabbergasted that his fellow Agents allowed somebody to break containment; the FBI had the stairs and elevator covered. All the other Hotel rooms in this wing of the Hotel were empty because of the sting operation.

Time 5:59 pm, "I'm so sorry, sir." As Sara holds a clipboard in her left hand, a poison water squirt gun is just below. Her hands are gloved with see-through plastic. She methodically lifts the clipboard, trying to see within the room. Her trusty 38 caliber pistol was in her apron. She pulls the trigger, and a direct spray hits Julio's face; Sara moves lightning quick as

Agent Ruiz falls backward, gasping for oxygen. Sara catches him partially beyond the threshold, lowering him without a large thud.

The room was empty. Yes, she scampers over to the pass-through man door and knocks loudly. Agent Travis Yuck was waiting for a knock on the other door, umh, front door, nervously pacing and peeking out the peephole. He was excited and would be a hero! The second Sara arrived at the front door. He would open it fully masked, protecting all his skin which would be covered. Then he would take the Fricken killer down, throw an elbow at her face, bust her up properly, and knock some teeth out her nose pulverized Fk the murderous bitch he had lobbied his good buddy Brock for this assignment, and God knows he was going to enjoy it.

His full-face mask was in his left hand just in case Sara had her spray bottle or squirt gun with her. This was her M.O. the female poison spray killer was the most wanted female on the planet, top of the FBI's list; the Vipress was his! He would be a National Hero Celebrity and maybe even do TV interviews. Why not? He hears his name and a pounding on the inner man door of the hotel room, checks his radio, and says into it in a whisper, 'Julio, what's up? Damn, he quickly walks over and opens the inside man door. He sees a red pump pistol, a damn water gun. It was the last thing he'd ever see… done, bye-bye now. His face shield mask slips from his hand as he grabs at his throat, no air, no breath left, in excruciating agony clutching his throat.

Sara re-bags the squirt gun, zips it shut, then reconsiders whether it is better to keep it available calmly, pushes the cart out of # 554, closes the door, and moves back to the service elevator. As the door slides open, the customer and public elevator doors open, and the woman in the black and red dress walks out. Sara checks the time at 6:03 pm. She's a little early and pushes 'B' for the Basement in the service elevator that the Fed's paid no attention to as the slow clucking elevator descends, then it stops. Wtf? No panic in Sara's demeanor.

A sizeable Hispanic gentleman walks into the service elevator; a handsome man of full girth stares down at her "who are you? I've never seen you around, and I know all the maids." Sara sees his badge Head of Security West wing. Sara holds up her blouse, grasping her name tag… he bends down to take a better look. His eyes become misty, unable to focus with one direct spray. He was dead in seconds, grasping his throat, gagging for breath, oxygen that would never come. Sara giggles 'good thing I didn't bag that squirt gun. Yup!'

She is out the door, walking past and under an employee lounge parking lot sign. She takes a right out the exit door, the maid uniform she left on top of the dead head of security's distorted face; in the apron was a friendly note to her favorite FBI Agent! Her blocking device… she lets do its magic till she parks at the beach. What a breathtaking Sunset, life is grand, and a stroll on the beach is in order… Sara kinda felt awkward and disheveled, for her plan wasn't to kill anyone except the lady in red and black who was supposed to meet her on the 5th floor, unfortunately, Brock Dame had run interference, and the FBI Agents became collateral damage. Damnit!

-7-

Sara's 'Ground Hog' days…

Sara picks her head up from a pillow cocks her head towards her Psychologist, Doctor Ame Amaya saying, "that's it, the dightmare. It's like the movie 'Ground Hog Day' for the last week. It keeps replaying in a loop when I close my eyes.

Weird, huh? can you help me get it out of my mind, Doctor? Ame shook her head… Sara said, "wait, I'm not finished yet!"

The suspected perp under surveillance in the lounge got off the elevator on the 5th floor of the 5-star Hotel Palomar. She ambled confidently in her cute attire to room #555, anxious for her sexual interlude. A break from her heterosexual lifestyle curiosity to quench and satiate a thirst she had developed since she'd been in high school. She was bored and tired of watching her favorite type of porn, lesbian loving is what she desired, and now she wanted to taste the real thing. She grins in anticipation, with her tongue peeking from her plump lips. Her lips below slid without hindrance. The proof was found with the subtle probing of a sliding finger over her slickness… indulging the flavors of her juicy and ripe chasm, which was wet and inviting, ughhhh, if she could only go down on herself! Knock, knock, Knock…

Brock and Lucie are on their way up to floor # 5 in the elevator right behind the salacious perp. "Sir, Travis isn't answering the door." The elevator opens to the lady in black and red impatiently banging on the door of #555. Brock yells in his hidden mic, 'take her!' both stairways open, FBI Agents careen out, door #556 slams open the woman is ordered face-down. She was trembling and quivering; a soulless noise reverberated as her air was squeezed from her chest as a 205-pound Agent's knee bounced on the small of her back. Her being secure, Lucie, with gloves and full body cover, starts going through her oversized purse and working her body for weapons. At the same time, Brock was pounding on room # 554. Frustration was mounting. No answer on any of the three doors, and he didn't have master keys. The Agents started the assault on the door, which gave in on the third attempt.

Brock was the first past the threshold, waved his arms violently… shouted, "stay back!" Face up the bug-eyed reddish-blue face of Agent Julio Ruiz. He'd bitten his tongue off; pieces were stuck and coagulated on his bristled chin. The look in his glassy eyes was of terror; he… An Agent burst past him to try and give resuscitation; Brock hit him with a powerful right cross punch and a left-legged kick… "Stay Away, get back. That's an order! He's been sprayed with a toxic poison. If you touch his skin, you will also die." This was learned when we lost two agents trying to give mouth-to-mouth, in lifesaving efforts, at an earlier murder scene. Suddenly masks were the theme of all who heard Brock's words.

He already knew but couldn't accept the reality as Lucie called in the Forensic Teams and helped tape it off. With the toe of his Brooks Brothers shoes, Brock wedges the adjoining door open a ghastly, pallid vision, foam from his nose and mouth. His friend no longer lived. Travis is dead; ugh. OmLord, he screams out loud. How could he face the wife of his friend and their five children who would be left in the horrific wake? Brock knew that the responsibility was his to bear, the burden almost too much to comprehend. The weight stifled his own breath as he made a beeline out into the hall and down five flights of stairs. He had to escape this as he dry heaved, sucking in oxygen, sick to his stomach and spirit.

Nine days later, 2/3/10 Wednesday afternoon, Agent Brock Dame was sitting at a coffee shop on the beach strip watching the traffic pass… humans of every dimension, race, and ethnicity, most barely clothed, the Pacific Ocean swirling and pounding the surf. San Diego at its best, he sat in his shorts and t-shirt. "Hey buddy, you looking for some company, or are you saving that chair there?" Agent Lucie Link had arrived. "I was saving it, but since you're an upgrade, have a seat!"

"Upgrade huh well, mister, I ain't in no competition for nothin!" They both grin. "But upgrade. I like the sound of that!" "Ahh, I meant an upgrade cuz the seat was empty, was all" "You're an asshole, Brock." "That be me." They smiled and laughed.

A server appeared at their side. Lucie ordered a Latte, Brock a refill, an adjusted somberness consumed the ambiance, three funerals as Brock lowered his head, like, Omg, life certainly isn't fair. I feel guilty for allowing Travis to coerce and manipulate me into assigning him to be in room # 554, the supposed first initial contact with 'Sara.' "Really, we don't know if Julio was the first she killed." "I guess you're right, Luce. With the blocking device, we haven't any video proof." "We must also feel sorry for the security officer. Who she also liquidated the poor guy had three children and had lost his wife to Ovarian Cancer only five months previously," utters Lucie.

"Brock, it was fair. As I recall, they drew straws. All of the Agents wanted to be the ones to take her out." "True, Lucie, but Travis had five children and was my best friend. It's gut-wrenching to watch his children and wife shattered." She reaches her hand onto the top of his with a gentle caress. "I know. I'm so very sorry… you said it earlier life isn't fair, Brock."

"This is no longer another investigation, no way, now at least 30 murders can be attributed to this 'Sara' it's personal now. Seriously she's fkn with me. I can't sleep or think of anything else, even during my self-imposed escape into that alcohol binge of like 25 hours straight!" "I know I picked you up that night, downtown saloon, after you had been kicked out of 'Old San Diego Bar and Grill,' man, you were a mess, dude Brock, you got a bit Handsy. My left boob is still bruised." "Oh crap, woman, I'm sorry." "No worries, but I must say that SARA has a set of humongous balls or lips, that is, yes, just the audacity of that psycho, her cocky attitude that fkn note to you!"

He sucks down the rest of his cooling coffee. "I need a real drink; you down for that, Lucie?" "Sure, let's do it." The note that Lucie referred to was something he couldn't get out of his mind. *'Brocky, I missed you this time, but 'In The End' you will be mine; I Promise you that you're my boy, and I'm your girl… yum, 'Sara forever, Luv ya.'* Damn, I can't get those words out of my skull. To hell with her! Brock turns to Lucie and says, " you know Sara's note ughhhh, those news-clipped letters, the paper will have zero DNA… hell. We have yet to be able to filter a slither of evidence; if she didn't leave her calling card a few months back, heck, we'd have nothing. What was her original message, huh? Oh yeah, *Sara avenges the brokenhearted-betrayed, death to adulterousness, take the cock out of cuckoldry, unfaithful, duplicity. Stop me if you can… Sara!"*

Brock finished reading the laminated card, Sara's first correspondence! Lucie shook her head and displayed a grimace, and said, "whoa dude, geez, Brock, you took her words and laminated them on a plastic card. Whew! Gotta say that's sick." He didn't bother with a reply.

He slaps some cash on the table, waves to the server, and off they go. "How many times have I asked you this, Brock, 'what does take the cock out of cuckoldry mean?' The words are not gender-based; she's an equal-opportunity killer. Shit, out of the known 30 kills, 11 are or were women." "I know, but none of it matters here in Southern California; there's like over 23 million people at a minimum, a million cheaters, just a guess, shit the online hook-up sites are still multiplying, Lucie!" "Right, Brock… speaking of that while you were on your binge, I was the one who served the Search Warrant to ole black and red dress 'Trudy' talk about awkward. Her husband of 17 years was in the process of moving out Trudy's belongings, she was balling her eyes out, and unfortunately for him, we stopped and ceased all the items he was moving out of hers. He argued for a moment, then turned on Trudy and said, 'I'm going to my beach house. Why did you marry me if you are into women? I know it was always about my money ughhhh, stay away, Trudy.'

Then the disgruntled husband handed me his business card and said, 'please call me when you're finished here.' "I mean Brock, this guy was nothing but money; the mansion on Coronado Island was like 25 million dollars. He was handsome and fit, maybe 15 to 20 years older than her, a Dream catch if there was one. His last words as he stomped away were, 'You will not be able to break the Pre-nuptial. You will get what you deserve. You're a tramp!' Trudy was another casualty hoping to hook up with Sara. Ugh, well, at least she's not dead.

"Lucie, that's a man after my own heart," as they slip into the beach bar. "I have never said a word of my private or personal life, but I don't trust your gender. I will not commit to ever entrusting my tattered heart to another woman… sex is what I'm after; I don't need to love them emotionally, just physically, orgasms galore, and then leave them panting for more. The bullshit line *'I love you'*… is strait superficial hogwash."

"Geez, Brock, whew, panting huh hum, just say it like it is, why Dontcha, I mean, are you a misogynistic womanizing hater or what? Don't answer that I get it," giggling and slapping his shoulder.

Three weeks later, Brock had lost weight from 227 pounds; he was now touching 213 pounds. He had missed regular visits to the gym, and last week's events weighed heavily on his mind remembering a letter addressed to him, his name below the letterhead. 'Agent Brock Dame from the 'Consumer Protection Agency.' Fortunately, any mail or correspondence sent to his office was thoroughly vetted and X-Rayed this particular letter didn't have any prints on the envelope or papers inside. It was opened in a lab with all precautions in effect; the three neat blank pages were <u>soaked in a non-oil-based poison. If a human</u>

<u>**hand or finger touched the paper inside the letter, it would equal a human life Voided!**</u>

Sara had raised the bar; she was now on the attack. This had now progressed from being merely personal to life-sustaining for Brock. He was paranoid; from the Pursuer to now the Prey… the Hunter to the Hunted, the definitive 'Final Straw' happened on a pleasant Wednesday. Brock's morning started like any other 'hump day' bowl of cereal and coffee. He had nine years left on his mortgage on a modest single-story home in Santee, California, just east of San Diego. Brock activates his alarm and hops down his three steps. The company car in the driveway, his actual garage, had a few of his toys, a dune buggy, a Harley and two quads, and his other personal driver, a 2007 Ford Explorer.

Startling him to a quick Stop, a pink envelope wedged between the front windshield and the hood of the Crown Vic. He slips his briefcase on the hood, pulls out some gloves, and thinks, jeez. I'm paranoid it could be from one of the neighbors, and I carefully slide the envelope out by a corner. He then saw the tell-tale magazine letters glued to the envelope, left it there, and lifted his cell phone in one hand; Glock had already been leveraged in his other as he scanned his surrounding area.

Forensics would be at his home in less than 45 minutes. His reaction to this trespass stunned him, shaking, grinding his molars yet defiant with unnatural calmness, pissed, angry, uh, violated, but his resolve, determination, and discipline took auto-drive. This foray into his private life strangely had an opposite effect empowering and pumping him up… like a gunslinger in a stare-down; he wouldn't blink!

He drove his Explorer to the San Diego Federal Building, thinking, 'so Sara wants to play hardball, huh? Who the fk is Sara?' Is that her real name? There is no use in checking all the cameras on his street or his security system. Sara always used

a blocking device; he would check with Cal-Trans for pics of
the East 8 Hwy, but already conceded this would be futile.

He picks up his ringing cell phone, "good morning Lucie"
listening, then saying, "Oh, news surely moves fast." "Okay,
see you in 25 minutes; I'm fine, thanks. A Serial Killer had only
stopped by to say hi!" "Brock, no reason for sarcasm. I'm your
partner." "I know, sorry, Lucie; I'll be in my office in a few.
Thanks for the call."

*<u>Ame flips through a condensed set of files, catching Sara trying
to resist a flashing smile, "Sara, as I recall, I read something in
your files about the Palomar Hotel; you were the leading suspect in
those three murders, in fact, you were the only suspect right?"</u>* ✍.
*"True, Doctor Ame, the Feds tried their darndest to pin me on
those murders and too many more to count; by the way, that wasn't
a confession on my behalf, but for some odd reason, well, who
cares? Perhaps if it were something I would have endeavored to do,
um, that's how I'd see it play out. You know I'm Innocent, just
making up shit, Doctor." "Now, what about a makeover for you,
my favorite Doctor? Come on, Ame?"*

*"Sara, why don't you slide your chair over here? While you give
me a manicure and style my hair, we can try once again to get to
the root, pardon the pun of the question I've asked you to answer
several times, and you promised me five visits back. Remember, I
wanted you to do some self-analyzation about your past. If so, what
conclusions or realizations have you come up with thus far, Sara?
How do your life experiences relate to this new hair Phobia? I
mean, where did it come from? You love to work on other people's
heads of hair, yet you're shaved bald?*

"Doctor Ame, you're talking about the hair thing again.
Why is it such a big deal, huh? You tell me you're the fkn
shrink." "Sara, hey, stop, remember our rules on bad language;
think not to be redundant when you were arrested in 2011, you
had long blonde hair in the pictures of you from the San

Francisco County Jail mug shots. You have had a ponytail, eyelashes, and lush eyebrows since your incarceration here at NIA. You have resorted to pulling out your eyelashes, shaving your head and eyebrows like you have a hair phobia hell, you shave your vagina bald, no hair on your body." Sara giggles again "you wanna see again" "no Sara, this isn't a game, I want to…" "stop jerking your hands around doctor I only started shaving my body hair last year!"

Ame sits back calmly and rationally says, "Sara, within our therapy sessions, we need to accomplish small strides, mini breakthroughs, or this is a waste of my time and yours." Sara cackled, then stared at Ame with a wry smirk. "Doc, things change, people change!" Ame barked back, "damnit, Sara help me, okay? Since your hair-phobia change occurred in the near term, I want to know what happened. Sara, you are obviously not repulsed by the feel of hair. You have the tools of the trade, a hairstylist, and work on the staff's hairdos. Didn't you say you worked on your sister's hair for hours just the other day?"

"Doc, I not only give my sister a pedicure and manicure but also wax her peach fuzz, brush her thick raven's colored hair, style and use a curling iron… look! I even have a new hair dryer. What's so cool is that I am allowed to practice on other inmates in the dayroom or out on the terrace or picnic areas; it's a bunch of fun, Doctor Ame." I smiled.

"I like to help others look pretty or handsome." "Sara, why do you pluck out your eyelashes, causing such pain? Another question where do you get all your cosmetics? Is there a beauty?..." "Doc, I see where you're going with this. Let me only say I give out some favors and receive some back; likewise, um, this isn't contraband… all safety stuff approved."

"My sister visits every Thursday most of the time unless her piece of shit fiancé takes her away from me." Ame snaps, "please, can we stay on point, Sara?" "Doc, how about Fuchsia Orange for your nails this time? It's such a bright color, so perfect for you!" "Oh, thanks for the compliment. There you go again, not only changing subjects but avoiding any of my Inquiries. Can't we try and accomplish one thing, one question, such as your eyelashes? What happened to change your feelings about body hair, uh, Your Body Hair?"

"Doc, we are most definitely accomplishing something. Take a look at your gorgeous fingernails!"

<u>**-8-**</u>

<u>Jan 10, 2017 'Al' #5155… NIA Interview #12.</u>

"I was afraid you wouldn't return to visit me, Doctor Amaya, after the frightening stabbing last week." "Yah, no, I'm a celebrity here. All the fellows are jealous that I have such a 'Smokin Hot' Psychotherapist, blonde and petite."

"That will be enough, Al… I appreciate the compliments… but let us continue down the path we decided on together. I want you to bring me to the present date in your life, any life experiences that linger in your subconscious, so we were last at!" "Doctor Amaya, I was only this morning dwelling on a lost opportunity with 'Papa' he wanted me to join him once school was let out for the summertime for shows on the Vegas strip. He said we would bring the house down unique, never before a Grand-Pa and grandchild on stage, with puppets, speaking without moving our lips or throat, throwing our voices both Ventriloquists. Gosh, we even sat together and worked on skits and scripts. It was fun, although not really at times, cuz I wasn't like Papa. He viewed the world through kind eyes."

"I saw the world's inhabitants for what they were transparency shown through and through, true human traits of greed, self-serving evil selfish and jealous, self-absorbed, egotists,

narcissistically, shallow…." "Enough, Al. I believe you made your point long ago. No need to expand your vocabulary with negative words, so you detest all other humans besides yourself… why?"

"Doctor Amaya, that's plainly wrong; I like you. I thought I was doing a pretty good job explaining why I detest other people, aren't you… ugh!" Al waves his right hand before his face. "Whoa, are you not paying attention to me?" Ame couldn't stop herself from rolling her shoulders, and yes, with a wobble of her head, "Go on, Al." "Okay, but you're not going to interrupt me all the time when I start this true story of my past because I will lose my place, Doctor." "No, Al, go ahead. I am all ears, as has been said many times from my chair."

"K, The date was 4/10/95, a Monday. I was fifteen years old. I was doing my best to contain my inner turmoil and hadn't used my talents for pranks or practical jokes for over a week. Well, since I got this bully back, we were getting ready for the gym and had to dress out. I was able to replicate 'Tim's,' the kid's voice next to the bully 'Sam.' I was sitting on his left side like five boys were stripping off clothes to put on our gym shorts and shirts. This was so damn funny that I still laugh at it now. So, I said, using Tim's voice, that's what one of those inverted cocks looks like! Where's your dick, Sam?

The laughter in the dressing room was off the charts; I was howling… Sam wasn't. He reached over and grabbed Tim by the back of his neck and slammed him headlong into the metal lockers not once but three times blood squirted all over the place; oh, such Fun. Sadly, it didn't end there because later that afternoon, I watched Sam, the bully, being escorted from the school's grounds, and he was suspended for two weeks. After poor Timmy was taken to the emergency room, I think Sam got into even more trouble. Timmy had broken teeth and a flattened nose. Timmy never looked the same after that day; he had a brutally horror-stricken Chain-Saw Massacre, uhm, type of face through High School hell. I wonder what he looks like now?"

"If you're going to ask me, Doc Amaya, if I felt bad for Timmy, the answer would be a resounding no! My Golden rule was no deferential treatment to anyone. It was Timmy's bad luck to be in the wrong place at the right time!" Lol.

Al snickers, "anyways, I had my first massive crush on this girl named Shannie. She was rocking Hot, both of us 15 years old. I had a hard time(pun) keeping my boners down, popping up when least expected. Horrible times actually. I know girls go through periods and such but try being a teenage boy with a body part that grows when least expecting it. Please, a mind

of its own… sort of scary. That's why men name their appendages, for they have lives of their own. Shannie and I had been together in my bedroom, and then Pop goes the Weasel.

Like so many times in my shower, she never let me down; all my imagination uncountable times of sex, but all of this was fiction, false. Although it was suitable for solid masturbation ejaculations galore, she was a dream boat that I had to make a reality, so on this day, my virgin life changed. Yep, that morning, as I passed Shannie's house, she yelled from the porch, 'Hey Al, hold up' I stopped on the sidewalk as she trotted out with her backpack on. She said, "you want to walk with me to the bus stop?" I thought this was a silly question cuz we walked all the time together. I said, "sure, Shan, but we walk to the bus stop almost every day" then she slipped her hand into mine. "OMLord, we were holding hands shit boner-time damn each step to the bus stop was Fricken painful, our hands sweating. We were so happy… at least I was. After school, we rode the bus next to each other I knew then that Shannie would be my first-ever girlfriend and lover. ❦.

I was on fire all day and got picked on by two of my teachers for not paying attention in class. I didn't know what Love was, but I was sure I felt it. Weird, I was so nervous but calm at the same time. After school… I held her precious hand all the way to her house, it was terrific, and she said, "after I finish my homework, you want to meet me at the Kramer's to talk." I said, "well, hell yes, that would be great." The Kramer's house had burned down months before. It was now a condemned, dilapidated place and was fenced off, but we kids used it as a fort or clubhouse. We would sneak in from broken slats in the backyard fence. We sometimes would be caught by nosey neighbors then our parents would read us the Riot Act.

**Some older teenagers played games like 'spin the bottle' and 'truth or dare.' I thought maybe I could talk Shannie into playing with me. At the Kramer house, I'd bring a blanket, a cooler of drinks, and some snacks.**

"Doctor Amaya, this is way, kinda cool telling you this story, um, it is like being back there, like it's really happening again. I can see all, like reliving it all. I feel alive in person seeing everything as it was occurring!" "Al, I appreciate your willingness to share your life experiences."

"Wow, anyways, I was pacing by the landline phone, waiting for her call like a predator stalking its prey; well, the phone, that is. I could barely remain still. Being so horny, I went into the bathroom, locked the door, and pulled out a bottle of 'Jürgen's lotion' talk about premature ejaculation. Whoa!"

I cleaned up and felt way less tension. I even was able to sit down by the non-ringing phone. Then it rang, so trying not to act impatient, I let it ring five times, not wanting Shannie to think I was so preoccupied with our first date. I answered the phone with my sexiest voice ever. 'Is that you, Al?' 'Papa, no, well yes, I gotta go.' 'I hung up on Papa; we didn't have call waiting damn, don't you know the ole fart called right back. I got rid of him quickly, but then I was worried that Shannie might have tried to call and got a busy signal, so I was forced to call her. She didn't answer, but her mom did.

"Al, Shannie is in her room doing her homework. I will let her know you called goodbye." Before hanging up the phone, I started to imitate her mother's voice, saying… **umh, like Shannie is in**

<u>her room, then said bitch…</u> *Oh no, I'm a fool; Shannie's mom hadn't hung up yet. Oh, crap, started swearing, "who is this, Al? Is that you?" 'whew, I hung up and slammed the phone down!'*

I tried to remain stoic like a good doctor ah, but busted up giggling… "Not funny, Doctor Amaya" "oh, sorry, Al, just your facial expressions were hilarious. Please continue," I said to him, "so what did you do next, Al?"

I remembered it was only after 5 pm, so I decided to try and sneak over to Shannie's house. She lived only seven houses down the street; her bedroom window was in the backyard, but they had this annoying 'Beagle' who would bark at the wind and had a damn super nose on that dog.

I was lucky the dog must have been in the house, so I zipped over the fence, jumped down quietly, and slinked, sliding my back down the wall to her bedroom. I knew her dad got home from work after 6:30 pm. He was a mean man, and everyone was afraid of him. Anyways I tapped on her window after peeping in. I'd been there several times before to talk with her. Shannie opened her window. Her screen had been torn up months before when she climbed out with me to sneak over to the park, which was fun. She looked down and said, "sshhh, Al, what did you say to my mom on the phone? Did you call her a bitch?"

I shrank down "no, Shannie, no way," she cackled, then said, "shit, she is a bitch," and we both laughed slightly. "Let me finish my math assignment; my mom wants to check it out, and I will meet you at Kramer's in 45 minutes. Dinner is at 6:30 when my dad gets home. I will see if I can escape after dinner." She leaned out her window, and suddenly I stood on my tippy-toes and kissed her right on her lips; she opened them like surprise, and I felt her braces with my tongue. She kissed me back OmLord I was in heaven. We stared at each other, and then the door opened simultaneously when we heard a knock.

Her mother with the yapping dog, shit. I shot out of the backyard fast as I could… hearing her mom screaming at her and yelling my name at the top of her lungs, cussing, not good. I almost leaped the 5 ft fence; I heard, 'your father will beat your ass, Shannie'… Damn!

All I could think about was that Kiss. I was in 7th Heaven, my very first kiss, 1st kiss of a real girl… not a make-believe fantasy felt her lips and braces and tasted her spit. I sprinted home in ecstasy, made another visit to Jerkens, and was happy and worried at the same time. The phone was jangling within minutes. Whom could it be as I dried off my right hand? I figured it couldn't be Shannie. I was right!

"Hello, Al… when your dad gets home, have him call my husband. What were you doing in our backyard trespassing? Shannie is grounded. Wait till her father hears about this. You stay away from her, you hear." "Yes, ma'am, I'm very sorry. I was only trying to help Shannie with her math. I have straight A's in math. I am the T.A. teacher's assistant in Geometry. I tutor some other students, and again I'm so sorry."

"Ahh, Al… Ummah, what? Hold up for a sec. So you are good at math?" "As I said, ma'am, straight A's" in the background, my slick ass new GF, I heard spout out. "Yeah, mother, he was only helping me on problem # 5. You don't understand it, so I needed some help, that was all. Sorry does daddy really have to know mom?" Paused silence… "your father can help you with the Geometry Shan." "Daddy just drinks when he gets home; he never helps," dial tone, and she hung up.

I was in sweat mode for hours, but Shannie's dad never called. I could replicate Papa's voice and be him if her dad did call. The problem was that Papa was home that whole nite. I couldn't sleep the following day. I was up about an hour early, wanting to see Shannie. I went outside, sat on the porch, and saw her dad drive off to work… on a date I will never forget as long as I breathe. It was 4/14/1995, a Friday.

I hear the house phone ringing. I opened the screen door and shouted to Papa. I got it and ran over, picking it up. My intuition was dead on, "Hi Al, I know it is, uh, 55 minutes early. Are you up?" "yes, Shannie, dressed and ready to go." "Okay, you know I have a major final exam today. It's like one-third of my total grade. Can you come over to my house now, Al?" "What about your mom?"

"Oh, she knows that you have been teaching me some of the formulas and equations in Geometry and that I wouldn't have even passed last semester if it weren't for your help. It's the truth, Al. Heck, you've helped me tons this semester already!" "Be over in a sec!"

Knocking on the door, Shannie answers. Her cute 5' 1" frame in tight jeans and a cowgirl shirt, plaid with her hair in ponytails. Fricken adorable, I could love this girl, did I already? Yep… Smokin' hot.

Her mother was on the couch, a Cosmo Magazine on her lap "hey Al, thanks for coming over… from now on, just come to the front door, no more windows, alright? Her father and I appreciate you helping out with this useless Geometry. When the hell would she use it anyways? Required courses, please!" Shannie said, "let's go out on the back deck." "What the hell got into you, Al… I've been thinking about that kiss all night." I grinned "me too, I have been thinking the school dance is next weekend. I want you to be my date, Shannie, please?" Shannie opened her math book, hesitated a little, and then said, " Can you help me? With # 5, 7, and 11, I don't get 17 through 29. Isn't there any way to cheat? I mean, you are the teacher's assistant; don't you already know all the answers, Al?"

I felt a little frustrated because she like ignored my plea for her to go to the dance with me. It was my very first time asking a girl to a prom dance, and I was like terror-stricken and now kinda hurt, and I said to her. "Shannie, yes, I can get you the answers, but it would be better for you to know how to do the work, but you didn't answer me. Will you go to the dance with me?" I then even surprised myself and followed that question up before she could answer with this; "will you go 'Steady' with me? Be my girlfriend. I'm going to get you a ring. I got like $35.00 saved up?"

Then I surprised her. I unzipped my backpack and opened my Geometry book "here is the actual test you're taking today. I took mine last week and didn't miss a single problem look as I proudly pointed to the 'A+' 55 questions zero wrong!" I smiled, large dimples exploding, proud of myself. She winked at me, looked back at the Livingroom to her mom, then swiftly kissed me again. 'Wild' right there, like yes. "Yes, Al, I will be your girlfriend and go to the dance with you for sure!" I felt warm all over my first girlfriend ever. I could jump to the moon. Oh, I was so high with excitement I could barely keep from shouting out, like Right on!.

She was so fricken pretty. Oh geez, I was a lucky boy. Shannie gave me a quizzical expression… "ahh, what if the teacher changes the test or mixes up the 55 questions, Al cuz why would she give the same test if others have already received back their graded ones?" "You're so silly, my girlfriend. I want to kiss you for hours. French kiss like forever, listen since I'm the T.A., the teacher made an exception she was hyped up and happy that I ACED the exam. I'm the only student to get the test back; she trusts me!" She squeezed my hand, "Shannie, if she changes it, I will get you all the answers, so don't worry, sweetheart."

I watched her copy my answers down then I knew I Loved her; another boner emerged. I wished I could put her hands around it as I slyly rearranged my tightened crotch. Soon she would be the first girl to touch me there! She then said I guess I should know how to do some of this math, pointing to several questions. I then switched my attention and started trying to help her with different equations.

Soon we were off hand in hand to the bus stop; I felt like 'Skipping to my Lou,' but she stopped me. No worries… she didn't want to be embarrassed. My heart was beating so hard… I wanted to kiss her all over, hug her, my first girlfriend, Shannie!... Yes!

We had decided that since she had a D+ in the class, it wouldn't look good to have her pull off an A; smartly, her test score was going to be like a B+, which was perfect. It was a fantastic Friday, with the weekend looming with all kinds of possibilities. I didn't sit next to her on the way home. She sat with her other girlfriends, but I held her hand all the way to her front door. We made plans to get together at Kramer's after dinner.

My papa had a meeting that evening, so it would be easy for me to escape and sneak out of the house. At the same time, the plan was for Shannie to ask her parents if she could spend the night at one of her many girlfriends' houses and spend the night in my tree fort! Perfect plan. I was so anxious. I couldn't stop thinking of her and about her. I went into the backyard, climbed up into the tree fort, and swung from the rope swing. I couldn't eat anything, for my nervous tummy was filled already with anticipation. I set up my sleeping bag and got the Coleman lantern and some playing cards. This was going to be the night of my life!

I sat on our porch swing for a while, kicking back and forth saw Steve walking up the street with a few of his friends bouncing a basketball. He stopped on the sidewalk and shouted, "Hey loser, you wanna play some three-on-three ball? I shook my head negatively, for I had more important things on my mind. He was a Sophomore a year older than me, 16. I was a Freshman like Shannie in the 9th grade. Steve was an Asshole towards me, always picking on me. Even the sight of his putrid self-couldn't harm my optimism about what the night held in store for me kissing and holding my girlfriend!

I was checking my wristwatch-like every five minutes… at almost 7:15 pm; oh, so excited, our rendezvous time. Yep. I jumped up and went to do a final cleaning. I washed my face, brushed my teeth again, gargled, then put on some of my Papa's cologne. I was primed… Yes.

The Kramer's burnt-down house was just down the street, and Papa was leaving for his meeting in 15 minutes. He asked me to help maneuver the Satellite system, for he was going to record a TV program on the VCR for later. I then told him I was going to my room to play Atari games and listen to music 'okay, Papa, have a good night, seeya in the morning.' He seemed not to pay any attention to me channel surfing trying to find his program lying back in a Lazy Boy chair with a cold beer next to him.

'All right, Al, I'm going to be leaving in a few minutes; there is leftover pizza in the fridge for you to have for supper.' I told him thanks and exited in a hurry to my room. Seconds later, I was out the window. Heart beating fast, I went out our gate, darted across the street, down the block, and through the broken slates in the fence at the Kramer's house. I first noticed a flickering light in the back bedroom, maybe a candle, or it could be a Coleman Lantern. It was the only room in the burnt home that didn't have significant fire damage.

Damnit, someone else was invading Shannie and our meeting place. Then I heard the unmistakable patented giggle and rushed over to the smoked and stained window, cracked… and smeared with soot. "Oh, Stevie, yes ok, I love you slow-down let me take… here, help me with my bra!"

I instantly melted, tears runneth crocodile droplets, my body shook and shivered, sick feeling OMLord. I slid my back down against the exterior stucco wall, hearing these words, which broke what was left of my heart. 'Can you believe the nerve of that

Nerd Al to think I'd go to the dance with him and be his girlfriend? He's such a loser!' They laughed in unison-howling uncontrollably, "yep, Shan, it worked out fantastic you will not be grounded for failing Geometry for the summer. I wish I could have helped you, but I'm no good at math." "Sshhh, Stevie, I know what you're good at. Enough talking; climb up on me, boy!"

"Here, let me turn on the cassette player; I watched through a splotch of soot I had cleaned from the window. He undressed to his underwear. She was already naked in her panties. Oh, she had fabulous tits, so sweet pink and pert, and taut her sexy body, whoa! Delicious, um, her body was mine to hold, not his, my pain, hurt, betrayal, I wanted to die. .

The following vision warped my already distraught heart, watching him hop on top of her… uhm, of my Shannie. "My first Wallop collided with the back of his skull; the three protruding nails buried deep inside his cranium. Ugh, head, I had to step onto his back to pry and pull the partially burnt 2 X4 out. Shannie shockingly stared up at me. My next swing hit her in her used-to-be beautiful face. I pulled the wood stud up. A nail had caught her left eyeball, dragging that out as I pummeled… both of them a blood bath all over their sleeping bag.

Her nipples were still hard… tasting like Iron; after I was done, I snuck back to my room. I'd only been gone about 25 minutes. But I had blood spray on my clothes and face, uh, skin. I stripped and jumped into the shower; lucky I wasn't that messy, but my shoes were soiled with blood. I re-dressed, grabbed some Orange Juice from the Fridge, and devoured the leftover pizza. Yum!

Later that night, Papa came home, and we watched his favorite show, Columbo. We barely spoke or acknowledged each other, both, I suppose, content. I was numb, not confused, but oddly relaxed. Then we stayed up even later that Friday night, just Papa and I, and watched the best movie ever, "The Good, Bad & the Ugly with Clint Eastwood.

Late that evening into Saturday morning, I was moving lightning quick, carefully taking my shoes and clothes, putting them into a paper bag, and racing to the creek, putting rocks in the bag and throwing it as far as I could. I was gone only 17 minutes.

I watched my patient Al fall into a silent stupor, not moving, his head rolled back, leaving his eyes wide open, non-blinking, staring directly at me. It was as if he was elsewhere, "Al, what are you thinking right now?" The first sign of life as he tilts his head sideways, "aah, Doctor Amaya remembering how chewy and tasty her nipples were, yummy!"

I stopped, mouth agog, then recovered, trying to keep my composure for if I acted disgustingly shocked, Al might clam up! "Al, let's discuss…." "I know what you're thinking, Doctor Amaya; what if I didn't burn down the Kramer's house in the first place?"

<u>'If I didn't burn down the Kramer's house in the first place?'</u> These words he kept on repeating. Ame listened to Al repeating this mantra over and over repetitively, Ame pushed the beeper in her left hand, and a guard in a white uniform opened the door. Al was obviously somewhere else in his warped, distorted mind.

Ame went through security and finally out to the lobby searching for Donny, wanting to get back to Marin County; this wasn't a good session with Al. She had to re-analyze her approach and diversify the nuances and strategies she was instituting. Al was going to be a challenge, but Ame never shied or backed away from a Challenge.

Still lost in her thoughts, a process of culling past histories of 'Sara' and 'Al,' then she would strategize all the optimal formulas to Psychoanalyze all facts and then try a paradigm shift, a new form of therapy. Possibly a breakthrough for Psychologists, Worldwide who knows, she could write a book with her discoveries of how to maneuver a delusional mind into a rational asset and heal a human being; maybe she could bring Sara and Al back to living within our society.

One thing was sure Ame had found her destiny. She'd be a famous Psychiatrist writing best sellers about how she brought Al and Sara back from their lost fugues. Ame was buzzed out of the Lobby, standing outside looking at the glorious sky. Where was Donny? She turns around and sighs at the entrance of where her long day had evolved from, uhm. It seemed like so long ago.

With an urge to use the bathroom, she retraced her steps spinning around and looking everywhere. Where was Don? She entered the visitor's lounge and restroom, washed her hands, and mused in the mirror. I'm worn out. The consultations with Sara and Al are killing me… another suppressed yawn, super exhausted.

As she pushes the door open at NIA, she thinks the Napa Insane Asylum is a suitable moniker indeed. No, Donny… she walks to the visitor's counter "please page Donny Feline and tell him his ride is leaving; thank you." Don hops off a golf cart and trots over with his hands… palms up without speaking. They walk to the car; she takes the wheel and cruises out of the Institution. NIA gates close behind them. After a long necessary silence, Don had his mouth running as fast as Ame was driving-motor mouth. He had been on a tour of NIA and was overwhelmed with the amenities offered at the facility.

"The damn place has more to do than a 5-star hotel. That place is amazing Olympic swimming pools, a Jacuzzi for therapy with a steam room… saunas, please. The crazy, demented patients depending on their custody levels, could be out playing handball and freakin tennis, really!" "Don please," as Ame switched on the stereo, "I want to relax, no communication. I've listened to enough this day already. Sorry, only one question what's my afternoon schedule look like?"

"I'll be quiet, and you only have one client at 2:25 pm." He reclined his seat and started surfing his phone. Ame contemplated how or if she would positively affect Sara or Al, realizing how preoccupied she was with her two patients glancing down upon her Orange Fusion nails glowing. The girl has talent and could make a fortune as a beautician, hair stylist, and manicurist; Sara was gifted, no question!

-9-

Present Time 1/12/17.

Thursday morning, Kamryn passed through the final obstacle; the buzzer rang, and the door opened. She always looks forward to visiting her sister Sara, a tradition of sorts. Kam visits every Thursday. This was sister time, and she felt sad with contemplation and walked while glancing in the rear-view mirror back at her life thus far, a woman from the era of the 70s. A fiercely independent soul, a woman liberation stalwart staunch in her beliefs that equal work should equal the pay that all humans receive.

All races and genders should be held as having the same rights, not corresponding with anything other than being human; we should be paid for our production and worth. Not stereotyped into a category because of the color of our skin or sex; true, this is a man's world, but she was going to make it her oyster. Kamryn controlled her destiny.

Kam was a gym rat who worked out like a maniac. She was a champion gymnast with flexibility and taut muscles to match her interior and exterior beauty. The fearsome alarming number, ugh, 40 years old, was just around the corner! The closer that ominous number came, the harder her resolve became to get in the best shape of her life. She idolized her

Coach, Apollo, who was 21 years older, had relentless energy and looked barely 31 years old. Oh, how she adored him. They worked out three times a week together.

Kam was considered unquestionably a 'Catch' beauty, mind-body with quintessentially a symmetrically based personality that could assimilate all of life's difficulties with unbiased integrity; time was ticking like a leach had gripped her by her Loins a time bomb, emotionally biologically the chronological clock wouldn't cease to be the past.

Womanhood, umh, motherhood was obliterated long ago. She quickly dropped that subject off the radar. Not a possibility, fortunately, was always on hold. Several reasons for this way of thinking, secondarily being a mother, would have restricted her advancements in her field of expertise. Ah, that was her opinion. She smiled and then frowned, lingering ineptly into a peculiar scowl. Sure, she had her flings or sexual encounters, even several one-night stands, yet never a long-term relationship that just wasn't in the cards!

Kam pinches her nose and thinks, 'what the heck am I saying now? Wow, it's so easy to lie to yourself. Truth be told, anytime she felt love, pangs of nervousness with angst overwhelmed her. A fear of commitment existed. It was an anomaly, uh, a false belief that she could commit herself with undeterred determination and discipline to anything that resembled a long-lasting intimate commitment. If I decided something was worthy of accomplishing, then I could be dogmatic and relentless. But this didn't include personal relationships with the opposite sex. She had a tainted soul, and as far as Kamryn was concerned, this wouldn't change. She recalled that once she'd fallen head over heels in Love, accompanied by her fluttering heartstrings and unbearable addiction to being with him, she would bail, run away. Her inner soul and mind took precedence, and fear and the paranoia of having her heart annihilated again caused her to listen to logic and purposeful arguments to self-destruct, eventually imploding the relationship.

Kamryn knew the truth of why she ran from serious intimacy hell. She lived the trauma of being abandoned on her Wedding day, standing at the Alter her husband was caught infidelity to the maximum, ugh… No!

I was called onto the carpet by one handsome hunk in New York City. He was also a successful Commodity trader on the Stock Exchange floor. I nearly didn't get away! The career woman, me, Kamryn, passed the exam… Series 7 license, stockbroker financial advisor consultant, Vice President at the Schwab Corporation, her office on Market Street, downtown San Francisco. Kam had another trip scheduled for next week to NYC. She just was so enamored by Wall Street, the mecca for capitalism. Oh, how she enjoyed her life of trading in the markets. Thus far, her life has been full of achievements, accolades, and money. Kam wasn't lacking… umh, for anything materialistic that she desired, comfortably wealthy, yet she felt empty at times. Kamryn was alone and realized she wasn't a loner type of individual.

Alas, she conceded that inner strife or emotion kept zinging along, some opaque apprehensive feeling, like was all of this worth it? What she would have done to have a baby of her own and wasn't averse to adopting. Kamryn stopped staring into the elevator at NIA, ready to visit her special sister Sara. Hindsight 20/20 vision, foresight up ahead around the next corner, or bend. This was it. 'Live for today and the future; can't change the past … Geez, Kam, shake it off!'

Kamryn had finally met her Prince Charming, the one and only man of her dreams. All the pain in her heart was now part of her history. Well, she had met him like five years ago but had only started dating barely three years now they had fallen In Love. He was everything that every man she'd ever been with was, in total, accumulation.

Yes, add them up, he was the sum of all, yes, always an equation, rational, love though wasn't about equating math oh how he turned me on we were so natural together it was easy like we were the dreaded moniker Soulmates. Yep, lol, but alas, he was so similar to me. We were so. Self-Driven! Integrity-based, I know enough. He was career-oriented, had one failed marriage, and no more commitments always wondered if it was worth trying to reel this one in. He doesn't even want children. It's all about his time, like my time; wow, she no longer had to worry about reeling him in. She was hooked and being pulled into the boat, a net waiting… All In!

Kam hears her name and flinches. A guard… The correctional Officer she met almost weekly said, "this way, Kamryn, I hooked up your sister. She now has her own room. She calls it 'Sara's Salon.' It's normally used for patient attorney visits, but there were seven rooms, and never are they all occupied at the same time. Come here; let's peek in." Walking alongside him… then she sees her beautiful sister Sara grinning from cheek to cheek. So happy, Kamryn's heart rose with thrills. Kam felt energized with love; oh, she loved her younger sister Sara. Who suddenly spied her, stood up, jumped, clapped her hands together, and waved her into the room. Sister Sara leaps into her arms for their traditional hug. Her customer sitting in her only beautician seat was a homely nurse. 'Could have been an anteater in a previous life, not nice Kam… 'Stop it, my bad!'

"Kam, let me finish with her blush. I'm almost finished!" "Sara, you go right ahead. This is so cool, girl, your own salon room." "Yeah, guard 'Carl' said he would help decorate it for me. Look, only one camera on us, no audio. This was a place of private, confidential meetings, like attorney visits." "Yes, sis Carl already filled me in; listen, I'm going to the cafeteria. Get us some beverages and a couple of fruit slices, BRB." "I will be here," Nurse Renae added "my break is almost up; Sara, please can you hurry? I'm going to a party tonight. I wanna look the best I can."

Kam stepping out of the room, thinks, 'then save your money for a nose job' she sarcastically whipped that through her mind. Other than that, nose, she'd maybe be a five on a rating scale of 10. Her final glimpse of her sister from 9 ft. away, yes, she was a Hottie, would be an '11' if she had any hair. Sara used to be drop-dead-gorgeous with her curly locks that bounced on her shoulders. A fantastic head of hair that was naturally a strawberry-blonde fluffiness. She couldn't get around Sara's hair phobia, a new thing, but she was encouraged by the leaps and bounds this new therapy had on Sara.

Why am I so critical of the staff? Ahh, because the nursing staff had abused my Lil sister in the past, although I couldn't complain recently, even the Correctional officers were a bit more pleasant remembering her first month of visiting Sara. All she received was dirty, nasty looks. Now it was like business as usual. Yes, her younger sister was an Insane murderess, but she was a person that could be saved. Sara could return to society, and I will be damned if I don't stand by her side and help guide her along her journey. Hopefully, it will be one step and a day at a time leading to her release. They'd be together in the outside world, spontaneous dimples shown. ❦.

Sara escapes… working her magic in her Prison salon.

I was on the finishing touches of nurse Renae as my sister returned, taking a deep breath -Kam was glowing, gorgeous, and vitality oozed. She had the oomph, and the pizzazz sexiness dripped from pores, 125 pounds of taut skin muscles and a 5'3" frame, a hot petite body, luscious butt… that was enhanced by her high-heeled pumps, form-fitting blouse with matching leggings.

Then add in… her Raven brunette hair, naturally flowing with those insane curls matching eyebrows, high cheekbones, and unblemished skin, and toss in the three dimples and a tiny chin cleft. Did I also mention her round angelic face and her greenish blasting hazel eyes with golden flecks that changed with her moods, bright, glorious teeth, her cute ears a match for her almost too small nose, thin waist with her pert, perky breasts, even her thighs were exquisite what dude could turn that package down? She was a throbbing hard-on strutting by.

Sara wasn't jealous, not in the least, only being objective, facts keeping it close to herself; personally, she had to admit it. She idolized her older sister Kamryn! She would strive to emulate Kam in every way. She patted Nurse Renae on the back, "have fun at the party tonight and knock them dead." "Thanks, Sara. With your makeover, I might get lucky. It's been a while. I don't mind telling you. Now, if I don't get into too much trouble for extending my break!" Sara thought, what a wild statement. Renae might get lucky, hell. I thought she was married. Sara follows her out the door and grabs her sister's hand… "come on, it's your turn, Kam!" "Let's go for a stroll first around the lake. How about a paddle boat ride like we did last summer?" "Kam, it's not summertime; there is a chill in the air," as she tightens her sweater. "Oh, I guess you're right. It would be colder on the water. Let's go to the park and sit on the swing together. I need to talk with you, sis, about a few things!"

Sara stops in her tracks, "why, what's going on? Is it bad news? What's wrong, tell me?" "Nothing bad; please relax. Come on and walk with me." They were swinging, watching Mallard Ducks, Peacocks, Geese, and Swans cruising on the water. Across from them was the spacious screened-in aviary with rare Macaws and Parrots. This seemed like a paradise, well, at least for the birds. A scenic, peaceful spot to break the news, thought Kam.

"Sara, I want you to listen to me. Please, try not to interrupt me till I am finished. There is something I want you to understand, okay." "I'm scared, Kam, your acting weird." "Stop and listen, sister… I will not be able to visit you next Thursday, 1/19/17, because I will be in New York City… because of my job. So please remember that you have my cell number we talk all the time, so call me next Thursday. We can spend time together that way. I can let you know how crazy the City is. So we will mark this down on your calendar. No visit on…." Sara's head was down. Kam felt terrible at once, but she had started this and now had to finish dropping the additional bomb. "Sara, you know I've been seeing a guy. We've been getting a bit more serious. I'm happy, no sister, I'm thrilled; he wants me to join him up in Shasta County for a four-day weekend. His parents have a vacation home up in the Whisky Town area. It will be the first time I will meet his parents. I'm nervous."

"I'm going to help him winterize his parent's 75 ft houseboat, which is docked at Lake Shasta. It's goin to be my first vacation, sister Sara since you have been locked up here. So, I will also miss 1/26/17, okay? I promise I will make this up to you, sis, by visiting you all day on 2/2/17."

Suddenly an ear-popping shriek, Sara leaps up and runs headlong towards the small lake and across a short ramp, crying, her arms flailing and gesticulating the whole time. Face first… she hits the cold water with a splash. Shocked, Kam was 50 ft. behind her; from three paths came an onslaught of Golf carts with guards, some on foot merging at the ramp's entrance.

Kam dived in and was able to snag Sara. Then both are pulled up on the boat ramp from the Icey water. They were freezing cold, shivering. Sara convulsed, crying hysterically, sobbing without control. Kam felt horrible that maybe her sister wasn't improving. She misjudged the effect that this news would have had on her… depression guilt took hold. Kamryn held her screaming, sobbing sister to her breast rubbing her head. They loaded her in a cart, Kam by her side. They parked at a curb by the entrance of the hospital. A gurney, standing by nurse Renae with three guards, one being Carl. He yelled 'Sara was having a tizzy, a temper tantrum' into his radio. Nah, suffice it to say this was better described as an episode of a seizure, arms wailing, feet kicking, a rambunctious tantrum of proportional dimensions needle in her shoulder injected by Renae. In seconds she stopped flopping around like a floundering fish and stopped moving. Sara slinks, sinks, and is strapped down on the gurney, rolling away with Kam by her side.

"Kamryn, it has been many months since Sara has had an episode like this, maybe over a year. You will have to check in with the front desk, speak with the Psychologist on call and make a full report. You can't go where I'm taking your sister. She will be lodged in an observation room, and when she recovers from the sedative, she will be confined to her cell until she meets with the staff and her doctors," sadly explains Nurse Renae.

Kam screams, 'wait for a second' the gurney slows, and Kam kisses her sister's forehead, "I'm so sorry, sweetie. I love you, darling little sister sweet dreams." Kam slowly ambles away with cloudy eyes and damp cheeks. As she stops at the Psych counter, told to please have a seat, she falls onto a couch landing awkwardly in a daze. Felt odd stress; she didn't feel well.

She ruminates about other visits with her sister; they always had a great time, and fun was the theme on every occasion. Always laughing together, makeovers playing Ping-Pong, games, Scrabble, video games dancing even. We'd go for walks along the mini lake and ponds and take the paddle boats out when the weather was nice. The 75-minute drive was pleasant, with the rolling hills and grapes forever. The only drawback or negative that Kamryn would experience was during some of her visits, Sara would nod out, pass out, and her eyes would roll back, showing white, mouth gaping. Kam thought her prescription regimen caused this. This always would scare the shit out of her. Besides those untimely events, her sis was as normal… as she was when they lived in the same bedroom as small children. Kam steeples her fingers with a short, concise prayer for her lovely insecure confused little sister, 'I love you, Sara.'

-10-

Past times, Oceanside, California. Agents Brock Dame and Lucie Link before Sara was captured.

The Jazz music playing on a low hum soothed the ambiance and matched the view of the tavern's large bay windows facing the Pacific Ocean. The relaxing tune and sounds of 'Toddi Reed' on his Saxophone were amazingly sensual, alluringly romantic, almost too much for Brock.

Lucie had picked the meeting place and location. Brock and she had been there since 5:45. By 7:45 pm… the party-goers were packed in thick. The tables were filled to the brim, and the clients were primarily upper-class. But there was a proper mix of customers right down to the wanna bee 'hippies and a smattering of surfers,' all engaged in conversation or lost in the sounds of the Saxophone. "Well, it's been nice to have a reprieve. Nothing from Sara in almost a month. Could she have dropped off the face of this earth?" "I doubt that Lucie; she has been ingenious, cunning, and shrewd in her last acts, only recently… of sending a letter to our office and a note on my vehicle. Her disguises are as diverse as the crowd in this place. Hell, we can assume her height and weight is between 5' 1" and 5'7" tall. What 115 to 175 pounds, approximately 30 to 45 years old, her eyes are ever changing from brown to blue, heck, she must have a container of colored contact lenses."

"Don't forget Lucie. She also adds moles to her face and even wears padding around her abdomen and upper body to appear much heavier than she is…." "Brock, hold up here if I didn't know it, you seem to be raving, extolling your admiration for this Serial Killer like you're in some sort of Awe. Must I remind you that she is responsible for at least 31 murders, 31 killings! She is lethal, and dude, she is stalking you!"

"No, that's not necessary; just stating facts, Lucie. I want to figure somehow what makes that woman tick, get into her subconscious mind, think as she does, you know," as he empties the bottle of Cabernet into her glass. "That's easy. The profilers all agree she comes from a dysfunctional, broken family with possible molestations, incest, and physical and mental abuse… obvious and probable infidelities."

Lucie takes a long draw-sip and continues, "Sara has scorn and utter hatred towards Cheaters with apparent contempt in her many missives and letters. She routinely expresses a ridiculed and derisive narrative. With despicable undertones, check the reports out; the profilers have reported or indicated she could have had her heart and life shattered before, and she is lashing out. This is her life-long plight to enact retribution on the philanderers. Hey Brock, the experts are all on the same page with this assumption!"

Brock raises his right hand, waving towards a server for the bill, as Lucie continues her rant. At least his mindset aligned with hers, 'she was speaking to the choir.' "She is rational, not psychotic her schemes and attacks are intricate, conceived with brilliance, and her arrogance will be her undoing. Mark my words, Brock. Listen; her skill set includes fluently speaking Spanish, French, and German. She's tech-savvy, aligning herself with the latest and greatest gadgets bought over the dark web. Every time we seem to have her trapped, she escapes ughhhh, it's not luck, umh, bordering on an uncanny and intuitive sense of survival." He interrupts. "Yes, she surfs the net on whatever establishment she is in via Wi-Fi services and uses those throw-away burner phones. We know she accesses the Dark Web heck, she purposely leaves a record of doing so. The poison she uses is purchased off the dark web. Our labs have not been able to discover all the various compounds, yet we know it is Nicotine based." Lucie sips her totty.

"Think about this, Lucie. Look around. How many people do you see?" "Aah, the plaque by the door says a maximum capacity of 55, but I'm sure that isn't including the patio and decks. Let me wager a guess, like 75." "All right, let's just suppose Sara is sipping a drink in this establishment; look above your head. What do you see?"

"Brock, please get to the point. I don't appreciate your patronizing tone, but I will play along for now. I see vents with ductwork, and there weaved throughout the ceiling." "What else do you see?" Then it smacked her, what he was getting at. "Oh fk, excuse the language, Jesus, she could as simple as pie pore her liquid poison into the ductwork or the A.C. unit, poisoning everyone here!" "That's right; this air conditioning system is described as a closed re-circulation system that constantly re-cools the air in this room. She could eliminate masses of people in one act, like a gas chamber." "Brock, I never gave that a single thought. I…"

"Excuse me says the server. Would you like another bottle of wine?" 'Yes,' says Lucie, staring at Brock, "come on, the night is young, will catch a late dinner, my place is only 7 miles away live a little dude, relax!" The server winks as 'Herbie Mann,' jams out the song 'Comin home baby.' 'okay, I will be right back with your bottle.'

<u>Sara is spying on her next victims.</u>

Sara tells the bartender, "yes, thanks, I shall have another Martini, 'Perfect' just like the last one." She closes her eyes and stretched her neck back and forth; this was the 5th restaurant or bar she'd followed the insidious couple to in about a month.

Cozy and lubricated… the Vipress, a venomous female, is closing in on her prey; he may be unsuspecting, yet he's far from naïve. His armored loin belt shows a tinge of rust, and the seduction is in full bloom. Sara watches Lucie's gestures, her provocative swooning, bobbing her head, licking her chops, drooling. Sara smirks under her breath 'bet she's nearly stuck to the seat,' laughs at her rhyme Seat in Heat, will she finally have him succumb, full-on consummation?

It seemed clear to her that they hadn't crossed the panties line, but lust was furiously steaming at their table; Sara saw Brock adjust his shorts 'little snug there, buddy, huh?' 'From the corner of her eye' warily prudent, cognizant of her surroundings specifically, keeping track of another handsome gentleman who had been making his turns on the dance floor… slow dancing chatting up the ladies, now he had settled on one gal. Cleverly he had separated her from a girlfriend. The hookup was in action; she was a full-breasted lady, maybe 27 years old, with a tiny waist and a tan line around her missing ring finger.

She was no doubt 'hot to trot,' she constantly glanced at her girlfriend, even going back to her table several times for consults or small talk, trying to ensure that she was okay. Comfortable since she had abandoned her for him. But wasn't this the strategy from the beginning? Chasing Dick is usually a single endeavor unless 'Ménage a Trois' is in play. Yep!

Sara's perception of the ongoing courtship went like this the girl's friend was egging her on, go for it, big boobs was apprehensive, even circumspect shy on guard, not all in, boobs was in an uncomfortable quandary. In a two-on-one scenario, Nah, her GF wanted her to experience this dude. The guy wanted to screw her like mad, and there was no doubt as he purposely brushed his hand over her left nipple with a gleam and a wisp flick of his tongue. Sara reaches for her Martini, takes a sip, and then looks back at the Agents. Oouhh, Lucie's hand covers his flat on the table, and their eyes are locked on each other gosh, what I would give to be a Luvbug on the wall.

"I know you've been unlucky in Love Brock, burned left and right, trashed in a junk pile, but it's been over three years since that bitch shredded your heart!" "No, Lucie 'snickering,' I'm not celibate, that's for sure, but…" "don't you like me? We have been partners for 15 months. Am I not desirable to you, Brock?" He takes his hand back, rotating his eyes and raising brows with a matching roll of his shoulders, "Lucie, honestly, you scare me; if I cross the line with you, it might be too…." Lucie, now grinning with a tooth display, retakes his hand "look, if we're being honest about this topic, I haven't been with a man since we became partners." "Aah cum on Lucie. I saw you hanging all over that guy last month; what was his name, umh, Gary." "Purely plutonic we used to roll around in the hay… sheets a few years back, so you were a bit jealous, Brock?" Huh, as she squeezes his hand.

"Nope, not really. Only happy for you was all." "Stop the Saint crap; what do you do with all your pent-up testosterone Brock?" A pause with a sly grimace and another readjustment, "oh, I think I will leave that unsaid woman." "Ahh, woman shit, we're both adults here. Man, we already have an integrity-based relationship; we can talk about anything you said yourself, dude!" "Dude, umh, okay, as far as my pent-up unsatisfactory sex life, as you aptly said, pent-up testosterone, we'll deal with that as they click glasses with smirks, having fun for sure!

"You ready for the truth, girl? Yeah, wanna hear it, every minute detail?" "Well, duh, Brock." He sits back, takes a mouth full, and swirls the red wine around. "Okay, don't say I didn't warn you; Lucie, here goes! I release my pent-up juices, usually squirting my cum into the shower drain or laying my iPad on my chest, and slowly tease myself to climax by watching assorted porn. Then I rub my cream over my face, a natural mask with the smell like an aphrodisiac, dip my finger erotically in a droplet, and place it on the tip of my tongue after squeezing every taste I can from my cock… Yum!" He started howling, laughing loud, banging the table hysterically… 'I Gotcha, girl. How'd you like 'that?'

Lucie periscoping around at the crowd, now staring unblinkingly, shushed him with indignation, 'Brock almost knocked the bottle of wine over.' Lucie's eyebrows furrowed, a peculiar sideways 'Scowlishsmirk.' "That's 'freaky shit.' I wasn't ready for that. Whew, you're pulling my leg!" Brock cackled largely, "no, I was pulling my um…" then they both erupted with laughter. "All right, you got me, Brock!" "Lucy, what if what I just told you was the actual truth?" He smirked and thoughtfully stared into her eyes with a long-lasting gleam.

"Uuhhh, well then my reply would be and is Brock. I have three orifices that would welcome you inside, and at least two of which are hot moist, and will mold around your cock and milk it dry of love juices devouring all, not dripping a drop." Serious issues resulted in his tightening shorts. She then returned a Raucous, raspy howl as Brock stood up to shift the throbbing bulge to the left. Three tables of patrons turned around to hear 'you bitch' tears of joy fled from her grinning eyes as she grabbed the table, trying to catch her breath. "Yuh, see, I can play your game too."

Then Lucie says, dabbing her cheeks and eyes, nodding her head at his crotch, "since your public display is on 'BLAST' being your gender, I will admit that my panties are soaking wet and the seat I'm squirming all over, clenching my thighs tightly has an odoriferous wet spot that I'm gliding upon." "Lucie, stop enough, I can't take any more of this sex dialogue, or I'm going to disappear in a bathroom stall. I'm done; you win, Lucie!"

"Not true, Brock. We can both be winners here. Please cum to my place for the night. I Promise we can do this and remain friends with no commitments. Instead of making love, we'll call it making sex, yay… let's make sex." "Brock, why waste your nectar? Share with me, cum on, let's have some enjoyment discovering new horizons, exploration of intimacy, taste me, and I'll swallow you." He had dethawed melted; he had to have this damn woman. Her words were sexy and lustfully intimated, articulated, and just what he needed to hear and understand. She had broken his resolve to hell with full-on promises of celibacy. He said, "all right, just this one night, how far is it to your house again?" They both giggled as tongues flicked out simultaneously. Her lips formed a circle as if sucking on a Lollipop with those plush lips; he almost lost it.

My place is only, like, just nine minutes at the most away; they were more than slightly buzzed, the wine now liquidated. He grins, "we're acting like teenagers… look at us, girl," smiling. She retorts, "so what? We feel it, and why not keep each other company, face it! We're both lonely, Brock, and hey, what's wrong with acting like teens? Hum, why not?"

Sara was in high gear. She was hot and bothered just imagining and observing the flirting going on between Brock and Lucie from afar.

She turns her attention two the ongoing saga of boobs and the suitor; why didn't she call her GF over to join them. Heck, boobs was Butterflying back and forth while the guy had ordered a second bottle of wine and was engaged in pouring boobs a full glass of vino. NO, Ugh, NO in an instant, a Cold Blooded Scowlish-Sneer, no way he didn't do that, please, why?

Sara had witnessed Romeo take something from his wallet and drop it into boobs drink as both the girls were in the bathroom. Now he was stirring her drink, eyes darting guiltily about looking to see if anyone had noticed. Most likely a date rape pill. Why would this guy need that? He was a good-looking man with a decent body, heck, better than the majority in here. Hell, he had plenty of willing bait on the dance floor. Sara stared him down; boobs was already goin to roll with him, probably!

Sadly, she had only brought two doses of the special poison, both designated for the FBI lovers. Well, they would get a reprieve. She placed both minuscule pills in her dainty gloved hand, meanders over to the scandalous creep, and dropped her small purse in his view next to his table reaction as she expected, he reached down to pick it up for her to be the gentleman he wasn't.

A drop, little fizz-water soluble, she took her purse from him, then shielded herself from all and did the same to boobs drink. Just as the girls were returning from the restroom. Sara ducks inside the bathroom to pee with a perplexed demeanor, thinking, whew, she was losing it. That was way too spontaneous and dangerous. Not thought out and analyzed… fk I'm losing it; not planned… like was her rule of thumb always, how criminals got arrested is precisely like this Ad-

Libbed, not good. She washes her hands as the bathroom door swings open. Screams are heard over the music.

Sara calmly exits out the doors, past the valet, and out, not bothering to look around at the chaos and panic-confusion 'death was satiating.' Good!

<u>Lucie and Brock were primed and ready to roll around in the hay or… whatever!</u>

Lucie was paying the tab; it was her choice, her date heck; he drove up to see her for the primary purpose of discussing 'Sara' the Serial Killer investigation. Smirking because her plan worked smooth as Exlax soon she'd seduce his ass not only mentally but physically, I waylaid him, got him… Yum!

Brock was gathering his briefcase when he saw a man across the room collapse backward… grabbing at his throat, gasping for breath, eyes bugging out of his face. He was hacking. A woman yells I'm a nurse and rushes over to aid him. Brock instantly assimilated all like a Shark. He leaped over a table and threw up his hands. 'Stop, FBI.' Badge flung out in one hand, his gun in the other.

Lucie from the cash register area shouts that 'No one leaves. Lock the doors'… as she hurries to the exit. Brock had seen this before; he knew the look as <u>Foam Formed</u> at once from the man's mouth and nose. He held back the nurse, who kept screaming, 'the guy is choking on something.' 'No,' he states unequivocally, "he wasn't eating anything. He was poisoned!"

The manager rushes forward; barbacks, bouncers, servers. The entire staff was in a frenzied panic, and the manager yelled, "Police are on their way. It was controlled chaos as everyone spoke simultaneously; boobs ran over to her GF's table Omg Wtf, nervously said, 'shit, the guy had a heart attack. He's freaking dead!'

Most everyone was standing in shock, and… boobs sucked down the rest of her wine in milliseconds. She dropped like a rock, coughing, spitting, choking, then started punching at her throat, the whites of her eyes shining, no sounds but gurgles, gasping, no oxygen. Her throat seemed to close instantly. Brock bellows an ear-shrieking scream, "no one touches their drinks, no one drinks anything, nothing! Everyone stand back against the closest wall. There is a lethal poison inside this room. Don't move. Don't panic!" The partygoers were silent as if they were at a Wake ugh funeral. Two patrons now lay dead on the floor, asphyxiated lungs collapsed.

-11-

<u>Three Hours Later.</u>

Lucie and Brock were scrunched shoulder to shoulder with Oceanside detectives, a team of Forensic technicians were working the scene, and the owners of the Tavern Beach Bar and Grill and several of his employees were still present. The patrons deserted the place hours ago after they were interviewed.

A voice on the surround sound speaker system 'Brock, can you come back to the main office?' Lucie followed as a squat, hunched-over woman said, "the closed-circuit video is top of the line here; it was coincidently upgraded only three months ago. The video and dot-pixels look almost as sharp as an HD broadcast."

No questions would remain of what occurred. It was plain and simple. 'SARA' sat at a single table, and the technician was able to zoom in on her portrait… profile. She moved deliberately, observing both of them, "her focus was on us,"

Lucie says. "Yes, that's the God-awful truth," replies Brock. Then they watched via camera's view at what Sara had witnessed, the guy slipping the date-rape pill into the ladies' drink. The culprit had another three in his wallet.

<u>The scribbled letters in Red lipstick at the bottom of a lady's bathroom stall summed it all up; 'Brock and Slutty Lucie till next time… 'UR lucky nite .'</u>

For the 9th time, they ran the entire video. All eyes were focused catatonically on Sara walking calmly as a cucumber right out the exit, not a care in this world. Other cameras pick her up, peeling off her stilettos and black nylons. Then she was barefooted; she strolled away onto the beach's white sand, the Pacific Ocean in the foreground gone. She was just a dim silhouette lost somewhere on Oceanside beach.

The lasting reflection and what stood out from the videos was Sara rolling her shoulder-length auburn hair, glistening from the streetlight's luminescence. Her only gesture under a passing lamp post was a middle finger in a firm ridged shake on both hands. 'Look at that hateful bitch!' declares Lucie… Five hours later, at 1:45 am, they decided to take her car, landing at her house, barely able to keep their legs moving.

She poured matching shot glasses of Patron Anejo Sherry Tequila they quickly swallowed them down… moments later, he crawled over to the couch and undressed to his T-shirt and boxers. She doesn't argue or debate his decision; she stripped naked, her moist, lubricated labia's lips from before were glued shut, dry as the Sahara, and both fall asleep in mere seconds, done… yep!

Brock wakes at 3:55 am, bladder pulsating cold, and doesn't even have a cover or sheet; in a daze, he finds her bedroom, slips in beside her, and they unconsciously cuddle, like this was the way it had always been, both out-dead tired exhausted. <u>*Sara was only 45 yards from them like a Panther in the blackness, sipping coffee, gnarly teeth glistening! Ugh!*</u>

<u>Forensic Psychologist Doctor Ame Amaya.</u>

Ame, chugs the rest of the contents of her mug and stumbles back over, opening the freezer and yanks out another frosty mug, her 5th brew. She smiles at her reflection in the stainless-steel fridge, pops the top off, and watches froth foam to the top.

Pats her tummy. 'It's a wonder I don't have a beer-belly' chuckles, yet she couldn't grab an inch on her taut midsection. I'm one hottie, for sure. Ame checked the calendar for Monday, 1/16/17. She had to be at NIA in the morning of 1/17/17 for another consultation with Al and Sara, having received an email and text from Doctor Liz Honcho regarding a mental collapse and breakdown by Sara when her sister Kamryn had visited her last Thursday.

Damn, she was anxious to visit with Sara. In her assessment, she was gaining a lot of ground. Lately, each visit showed improvements. Sara finally seemed to open up, speaking of her past, and they had a comfortable bond; confidence was being gained with the needed trust, almost a mutual give and take. At times, laughter could be achieved, albeit a Doctor and patient form of interaction.

Ame took her beer and walked out onto her dock, reflecting on why she was pounding the brews. It would be a faster process to just down some hard liquor, and stopping at one of her patio tables, she sits down and buries her head into the palms of her hand. <u>'What a total failure... I am!'</u> She contemplated how she had tried in vain a few hours ago and couldn't prevent a patient from jumping from the Golden Gate Bridge. She had been in a meeting in Sausalito when Donny had called her from her office in San Rafael with an emergency. "Ame, oh crap, we got problems 'Mr. Flight' is perched on a ledge beyond the nets that extend out from the bridge. He is asking for you. Bridge security and the S.F. Police are on the scene; he is threatening to jump!"

She sucks down and swallows more suds, staring out at the white caps rolling across the water, wanting to forget the earlier trauma. Mr. Flight's demons had returned false beliefs that bugs were eating his body from the inside out. His skin was crawling. The symptoms resulted from a severe Meth addiction that had him in and out of mental hospitals and rehabilitation centers. He was a Desert Storm Veteran who was a pilot and flew Blackhawk and Apache helicopters.

He lay sprawling and fidgeting around the edges of the net that was in place to save the suicide jumpers that came from all over the world to die at the 'Infamous Golden Gate Bridge'... below was the ocean, incoherently shouting words of a language that he only understood naked and bleeding from his ripped skin in his left hand a wire brush.

Fred's high-pitched shrieking unhinged all who spectated... screaming, 'Worms, Bugs, uh, worms are eating me alive,' he would take the steel bristles and scrape his skin off peeling layers from his epidermis. He was raw with deep etched red grooves. His arms, legs, umh, chest, and stomach, any place he could reach with the steel prongs of the brush, were damaged. He had scrapped off most of his beard in splotches, and pieces of his lips were missing. I was lost and had no... Zero answers, like helplessly futile attempts to talk, communicate or get his attention. It was a hopeless situation, only getting worse. Damn!

He seemed not to hear me in oblivion... heck, now I couldn't even recall what I had said to him. Whatever it was, it obviously wasn't what he wanted to hear, that's for sure. A San Francisco Cop leaning over me said, "I should shoot him and take him out of his misery, Lord. I've seen it all now." Next, Mr. Fred Flight took the wire brush and attacked his genitals. The police and onlookers around me started shouting, screeching, shrieking, freaking out in visible pain themselves, turning their vision elsewhere. A woman bystander heaved vomit, and the scene morphed into a horrific hell fest. 😵‍💫.

I heard a traumatic, piercing, shrilling sound. It was me. I then yelled loudly, words I still can't believe I yelped. "Please leap fricken do it... Jump Fred, do it, do it now, Fred... Jump!" I'm sure the San Francisco Chronicle will have my astounding staggering statement to my patient on the front fricken page. Most likely, it was all over social media by now, like 'Viral!'

I could see it and read it now... 'Psychologist Doctor Ame Amaya pleaded with her patient, war veteran Hero Sergeant Fred 'Flight to take a leap' to Jump from the Golden Gate Bridge. Do it, Fred, jump." Fk, fk...fk who's the nut, am I going crazy, Wtf, I'm sure that I....'

I need something more substantial than beer... whiskey. Damn, Fred did as I ordered him to do. How could I ever forget his last statement or expression? No way, he said, 'yes, ma'am Doctor Ame.' He twisted his face-distorted. 'I'm jumping!' Off he went wailing, tumbling downward, nearly landing on a rescue vessel below... dead on impact! I can't inhale any more alcohol and be functional tomorrow. I decided it was time for a long shower. Better skip the local news. I can't handle hearing anymore about Fred's suicide.

Instead of a shower, it was the hot tub her eyes closed afterward, and she'd indulge in her own patented form of therapy. Ame needed some self-medication which has always been drawing and sketching with a paintbrush in her hand. Drawing and painting calmed her. Ame was a touted Artist, literally selling many of her pictures! Since she was a small child, her talent just exploded from her fingers. She would draw acrylic, pastel chalk, pencils, and magic markers on the walls of her room. Now on the walls of her office were her favorite paintings.

-12-

<u>Doctor Ame Amaya was a professional artist.</u>

She was lost in reminiscence, lulling her head back after a quick dunk under the hot tubs water jets… once when she was at U.C. Berkeley. A friend's dad, who was a renowned contemporary artist, had seen some of her paintings, and he'd made an indelible impression on her. He was going into the hospital for minor surgery. Her friend asked if she wanted to take her dad's place at a park overlooking the beautiful San Francisco Bay. With the scenic, panoramic views unmatched anywhere in the world… from Sausalito in Marin County, across the bay, seeing San Francisco and Alcatraz… tourists by the droves would walk by the vendors on the sidewalk. He had a booth that he rented alongside the other vendors and wanted her to set up there, enjoy herself and see what the public thought of her talents. Ame couldn't wait. She couldn't sleep the night before!

Thinking back, oh, how much fun that day was. She would draw comical caricatures like cartoon figures of couples and family portraits, like a parody with exaggerated facial features and characteristic traits. Ame was a natural. From start to finish, she could draw a family of 5 in just over 90 seconds and accurately amazingly made a ton of tax-free dollars.

Peering out from her hot tub seeing several stacks of 11 X14 inch sheets of thick paper with depictions of her life's experiences resting on easels, she could churn them out quickly and naturally. Ame had several closets stacked high with colorful canvasses and decided that she would take the time to draw the day's events right down to Fred dropping into the Pacific Ocean, kinda like her form of therapy. Unscrewing the 7th beer, it was still early, 7:25 pm uhm... got to get something to eat as well. She whips her wet hair back, and the hot-tubs jets massage her body with steam rising, a deserved relaxation.

The urge for a sexual release took her focus. She slinked over to her favorite water jet body in the middle, straddling, controlling the pressure. Her clit was tingling. The throbbing sensation was enhanced and regulated by her distance from the jet. She flashed closer to her third close encounter; she enjoyed teasing herself almost to orgasm, then she'd sink down in the water until she couldn't resist spreading her legs wide and lulled her blonde head back... bracing her hands clinging to the edge of the hot-tub, knees planted a climax of triple strength desired, aah the jets never got tongue cramps she bit her lip 'cum on.' Nope!

Suddenly her answering machine from 7 ft away blasts off. It was Don, her secretary. 'Oh, darn no, Doc, OmLord, you didn't ... oh shit, they got you on the news. You're all over the Internet, Ame. You screwed up royally this time!' Her clit goes numb and shrinks as she drops to the bottom of the hot tub; after a few moments, she raises her head out of the water. So freaking frustrating Donny was still chattering and babbling, reading a news bulletin 'Celebrity and renowned Forensic Psychologist Doctor Ame Amaya told her patient, ordered him to commit suicide to jump to his death from the Golden Gate Bridge, 'Just do it!' We are so Screwed, Ame. I'm sure his family will sue us for everything you have; shit, how could...?' The machine finally had run out as the air left her lungs, sighing regrettably.

Ame tossed and churned for part of the night, then finally, with unrelenting hyped brainwaves, wired-like, shook her head, and said aloud, 'to hell with it.' She decided to take a lukewarm shower while her coffee maker was jamming out a super strong jolt of expresso coffee, glancing over at her 11 X14 drawings of her life on paper, walking over to her three easels, the awaiting canvas's paint brushes soaking in liquid, but then realized she hadn't any motivation.

Instead, she wandered over to her laptop, feet up on an ottoman steaming coffee, not surprised to see gobs of new emails, some from people she hadn't heard from in eons of years. She thought they had lost her email address, grimaced, visited an old AOL email site verbalized, 'you've got mail' she thought that was a gone era. Every one of her email sites was lit up with new messages and hordes way more plentiful than on a typical day. Ame didn't dare open her Facebook account and had put her phone in a drawer. At last count, she'd had 117 texts.

It didn't take long to see what all the chatter was over. Yeah, the suicide-assisted verbiage that was accredited to her, and now the exaggerations were beyond bizarre 'Ame, despite her morose disposition, chuckled.' Remembering the oldest of strategies, you start with a simple sentence in a classroom of 25 students, like, 'The woman died in bed' by the time this sentence reaches the back of the classroom to the 25th person. This sentence had evolved -expanded with embellishments and sensationalism. 'The woman was raped and murdered in bed. Her body mutilated, her head decapitated, a bloody mess indeed!'

According to a few Web pages, Ame had said, 'Jump Fred, just do it before the bugs eat you alive jump now; I command you do it, let go of the nets railing. You can do it, Fred. You can fly. Fred, flap your wings, Freddy… fly like an Eagle.'

Ame, in reality, knew there wasn't a recording of her saying these words, just again second-hand information, hyperbole with exaggerations. Funny though, of all the onlookers, the majority would have said the exact words to Fred. In fact, Ame was tempted to snitch out the cop who said he should shoot Fred. But she wasn't a Rat!... Nope!

<u>Aah, she had to grow a thick skin in the coming weeks. She picks up a file with the name and date 'Of Sara 8/13/16 Interview #5 Historical events of 12/5/92 Friday.'</u>

-13-

Some of Sara's childhood of trauma.

My mom was away. No way to talk with her; she died. I needed her so badly, Loved her, and missed her. Exhausted from crying constantly, I bit my lip and locked myself in my bedroom. I would lose myself playing games on Nintendo and couldn't sleep nor concentrate on top of mom dying; an older boy I liked had leaned over my locker, grabbed my tits, and kissed me. Omg. My first ever kiss in my life. It was so neat that I wanted more kisses. I was in love, sad that school was going to be out for the Christmas Holiday Season. So I wouldn't see him for a long time.

I wrote in my diary about my new boyfriend, well maybe, wrote a poem for my mother and read it out loud to her… strange noises unhinged me. I heard giggling voices and my dad's deep resonating tone and looked at my clock radio. It was 2:57 am. What the heck was dad doing?

My room was on the second floor, so I grabbed my favorite Cabbage Patch Doll and carefully sneaked to my parent's room. The door was cracked open. I got on my knees, crawled over, and stared into the master room… sheet's covers were strewn about, but my dad wasn't in the room. So, I snuck down the stairs, not making a sound. It was good that even the steps were carpeted. I neared the bottom banister, hearing more laughter and now music playing on low what was going on?

I was afraid because the house had morphed into creepy darkness. No one was in the living room-den, family room, or kitchen. I squeezed my doll and followed the music. Then it stopped, ugh… louder than the music… I listened to human moans of pain, I heard 'no, no, stop-oh yes-yes, yes,' and then the music started playing again.

That's when I noticed the sounds were coming from outside the house. On our Redwood deck was a Gondola covering our Jacuzzi tub, enclosed on three sides with the ceiling all glass. So, you could see the stars at night and the moon. I looked up, and the clear cloudless stars lit the night, blazing bright with a full moon. It was so damn cold that my bare feet were stinging numb, goosebumps were popping up, my nipples were rock hard, and my teeth were chattering as I neared the Jacuzzi. I recognized the music; it was a song that mom and dad used to sing together, smiling 'Slow Ride' by 'Foghat.'

I was crawling; my knees hurt badly and were bleeding; I felt splinters in my skin. I pulled myself up to the lattice siding and looked through a square opening, and almost shrieked out a scream. I saw my best friend's mom from next door, her red hair flopping back and forth and up and down, facing my daddy on his lap, shocked. Then it all became crystal clear that she was screwing my dad. Oh crap, the sluts husband had been in an automobile accident only the day before and was in the hospital in ICU. I'd heard he might not make it. He had awful head trauma.

There was a large bottle of Vodka almost all gone, and my dad was trying to cover her mouth because she was making these weird high-pitched squeals. I bent on my knees, transfixed, shocked into a stupor, and couldn't move, watching. Then I had this emotion, and a feeling came over me like I was someone else. I could see myself, but it wasn't me. I was no longer cold no but was sweating something terrible. I profusely had to wipe my eyes for sweat… they were stinging badly.

I was floating in the air, looking down upon the translucent me; I could still see the moon and stars. I was also glowing, felt dizzy and uncertain, then watched from above, seeing me standing onto my bare feet and walking through the fog-steam behind my dad and the slut doing the slow ride. All of a sudden, '4 eyes found mine, my dad's head hung back over the fiberglass side of the tub, her eyes locked into mine too.'

Yet she didn't stop hopping up and down on daddy. My father shoved at her to get off the mount; she smirked. I took the Ghetto Blaster and tossed it into the 'Fk-Tub,' causing a smell of static electricity, um, crisp popping noise. I will never forget their naked bodies twisting and convulsing-faces twitching eyes, veins popping out, like being electrocuted. The Jacuzzi jets stopped, then a wall socket exploded. My body had been re-joined in a trance. I did breathe. I don't know; it felt like an illusion. I went over and picked up my Cabbage Patch doll. There was a flesh-stinking stench in the air like burnt skin and hair and a smell like an electrical short, oh, well. 🐢.

I went back to my room in a daze and fell soundly… asleep. Dad and the slut died that night, apparently from accidental deaths… yup!

Doctor Ame Amaya leans away from the computer screen, swivels up, tilts her head, and muses. An already confused adolescent who had endured trauma as an infant and as a pre-adolescent had Snapped. 'This was the proverbial 'Ahh moment' this was the very first time that Sara had struck out at infidelity-based Cheaters.' She murdered the neighbor and her father only five days after her mother had succumbed to breast cancer. Not a week… had passed until her dad was having sex with the neighbor woman.

Ame paced back and forth, scanning her notes. The double death remains accidental in nature even to this day. Sara got away with murder... with a double dose. The wheels were starting to revolve her destiny in place at a young age. Her life's calling... her demented, psychotic mind had found a release and purpose, using her disjointed Schizophrenic visions of watching her commit this crime from outside her body.

-14-

Present Time 1/21/17 Saturday.

Kamryn was having fun driving over the rolling hills on highway I-5 North her first glimpse of Majestic Mt. Shasta, the snow-covered peak like a mirage growing right out of the two-lane highway, and yet the mountain was over 105 miles ahead.

California's drought was over, water spilling over all the Dams, Trinity Lake, Orville Lake, Whiskey Town, and Shasta Dam filled to the brim. Even as far south as Folsom dam, which was topped, the snow melt would be the most productive in almost a century. Kam was trying to adjust to the open terrain, landing in Sacramento, California, which was a far cry from her business trip to New York City, Wallstreet was fun. She took a sip of her iced tea; it was a strange comparison... open hills and roads.

The topography couldn't be more incongruent, or in contrast, Kamryn grins with the vision of last week fresh in her brain. NYC wall-to-wall humans stacked on each other the blitz, rush chaos, the city every evolving alive like 25 hours a day, nite like a gigantic hive of ants in motion on paths of design, for purposes of the unknown. Self-serving most often, eyes cold, weary, always on alert mode, predators at every seam in the sidewalk.

People wore masks, it's a dog-eat-dog environment, and mentality beware or get chewed up and spit out like gristle from a well-done steak. Strong survived. Gosh, how she adored that city! Wallstreet was a pump of adrenaline, invigorating competition in the free market, which was entirely manipulated by the powers that be. Of course, now, nearly 87% of all market trades are done electronically. The paradigm, like the mantra, remained true (it wasn't what you knew but whom you knew). True That!

Kamryn blinked out of her thought, inspiring a reflective mood, and checked the digital display. The time was 4:51 pm. The sun was still in full bloom, and the air outside was at 57 degrees. Definitely not a time to have her top down on her special edition Z 08 3LZ convertible 4WD wearing dark purple shades that enhanced the colors of her tri-colored glossed purplish rocket ship 'I freaking Luv this car!' To her left, she passes a casino outside the town of Corning, 'Rolling Hills Casino,' besides truckers; she hadn't passed many vehicles.

She enjoyed the open spaces and miles of sereneness, a natural peace... sighing, and this was going to be a fun weekend, anticipation squelched in a flat jack second. Her blood pressure shoots skyward 'oh fk.' She saw lights on her ass, uuhhh a freaking CHP damn, she yanks to the soft shoulder, feeling the pellets like bee-bees bounce up from the loose gravel 'uh, my paint.'

Kamryn hits her window down quickly, unfastens three buttons of her blouse, and pulls her bra down snugly. Valuable cleavage slides her skirt up to show a flash of her inner thighs, watching him saunter over, not a big man, relatively short with the proto-typical CHP sunglasses. Shit, not a good sign he was carrying the ticket book. I would have to put on the provocative, sexy available fk me... display, a natural default all desirable women had learned early in life, flirt, smile, and act like she was approachable. Pretend like he was delicious, be engaging, eye contact a must… play the alluring Damsel in distress act, a strategy that men fall for at the females beckoning call, more often than not. Lol, dumb!

Kam checks her look in the mirror. Her sexy provocative cum and get-me look should win over and warm up that testosterone. Kam had no wedding ring. She'd flash that ringless finger at once when the show began. Tags from Marin County could either be a positive or the opposite. He might think she was one of those rich snobby yuppies. She would put him to ease, heck. She had beat the last three tickets with this same sexually enticing production act, given warning citations. No Prob! ❋.

"Can I see your license, registration, and Insurance card, please, ma'am?" Kam looked up at him, and it was a Her… who gave her a knowing smirk like, nope, it isn't going to work, girl. "Why did you pull me over, officer?" The reply wasn't the norm "it should be apparent to you, ma'am, you were exceeding the speed limit."

Kam hands over all three of her requirements and peers up at the officer's left breast area to see her name tag, 'Officer Citation,' so apropos; she thinks sex play will work with this lesbian too. Smiling, turning on her charm, she stretched her arms up and out flauntingly, "this is God's country up here, Officer Citation. I'll be moving up to the Redding area; you're lucky to be…" the bitch ignored her and just walked back to her police car. This isn't going well; moments later, her identification and paperwork are handed back to her through the window, "do you have any idea how fast you were going?"

"Umh, I had my cruise control set at 81 mph open freeway, right? I'm sorry. Can you give me a warning, please?" 'Ms.' "call me Kamryn" "Kamryn, okay, I would suggest you get your speedometer calibrated. The airplane that tracked you had you fluctuating between 89 mph and 95 mph, which, at least in my own mind and certainly any other rational mind like at the Tehama Courthouse, the Judge will know your Vette wasn't in cruise mode, Kamryn!"

"Kamryn, I also watched you from my patrol car via your mirrored visor getting all sexy for me," a cackle "hell might have worked out if Rory had pulled you over… nice try. Here's your ticket. Can you sign the back for me?" "Crap, Officer Citation? You're writing me up for 91 mph. That's going to blow up my insurance. Can't you give me a break here? Come on?"

"Sorry, hey, you might want to button back up. It's going to get colder," a shit-eating fkn grin displayed as the bitch struts back to her piece of shit CHP car 'I hate her.' There goes a beautiful blissful afternoon! Kam pulls back onto I-5 and, this time really sets her cruise control at 77 mph, then drops back into her subconscious mind what was chewing at her. Oh yeah, Sara, her sister.

The replay of what happened at NIA was fresh in her mind, and she felt so helpless and guilty that somehow she had to make it up to her, hey maybe visit her twice a week. Her thoughts bounced to another precarious ledge, the situation shifting from Sara to meeting Edward's parents. Her stomach was upset. Her nerves were on edge; she would roll with the punches. How bad could it be? This is a giant leap, uh, step in our relationship, the ominous meeting mom and dad trip syndrome, serious development with ramifications across the board. Her phone sings a tune she clicks on her blue tooth "hiya sweetness, what's your 20?" "Ahh, just getting the hell out of Tehama County; thank goodness I'm in Cottonwood, like the tree, if I recall correctly, just over the next bridge is Shasta County." "Babe, I need a stiff drink; I just got a speeding ticket for going 91 mph and am nervous about meeting your parents. I just…"

"I feel you, baby; I'm off Cypress Ave; you will see the Hilton Garden Hotel on your left. It's on the west side. I'll meet you there in 11 minutes." "Sounds great seeya there."

<u>Sara.</u>

<u>1/16/17 Monday 3:19 pm at NIA.</u>

"I can walk Carl now. I'm much better. Stop with the baby trip, will yah?" "Sara, it's only been four days since you freaked out… besides, we're on camera. Let me push you at least back into the dayroom." Sara obliges and mulls over guard Carl's motivations "if yah check out your client calendar, you missed like 11 appointments, seven inmates, and 4 of our staff members. You're getting quite the reputation around here. The word is spreading fast about your God-given talents, Sara!"

"Heck, that makeover you did on Nurse Renae was freaking unreal, like amazing. That proves that you can make a pig look appealing!" "Carl, shut up; that wasn't nice." "Oh well, I'm sorry, but you didn't hear she got laid the night you made her up. Oh, shit, don't look no; here she comes!" Nurse Renae skips over like a teenager. "Sara, geez, I was worried you were still out of it. I was hoping you could make me look exactly like you did last week. I can't get my hair even close to how you did it. I don't know how you do the stuff you do, but I got a date with the same guy that I met at the party. My break is at 5:15 pm, and my date is at 7:35 pm at a bowling alley in Novato, so pretty please, will you?"

Sara rolls her eyes. A bowling alley, wow. "Nurse Renae, let me clear my head, take a walk, and I will meet you in my salon aah attorney visiting room at 5:15 pm, okay?" "You're a darling. Oh, I almost forgot I bought you the stuff you asked me for blush, makeup, and hair dyes." She scurries away. Carl says, "see what I'm telling you? You're getting really popular around here, girl. Wait till you see what I've done to your salon, even added wallpaper the Warden has given the green light. You can now use that room permanently, Sara. The only time you will lose it is when all the other attorney rooms are filled, and missy, let me tell you, in the 15 years I've been here, not once has all the rooms been occupied at the same time." "Carl, I thought NIA wasn't that old, and wait, isn't Nurse Renae married… hell? I thought when she said she might get lucky, it meant like to revitalize her sex life with her husband!"

"Oh, Sara, the Napa Insane Asylum has been around even before the grapes at the turn of the century, I believe. The brand-new ownership came in 2007, and this place has been renovated into a Country Club in the last nine years. There's always construction going on, never-ending. Heck, they're working on a humongous greenhouse called a Solarium, the garden area where we're even going to grow orchids, I mean super expensive strains." Carl stops and stares up at the cameras, nodding.

"Nurse Renae is married, Sara, and I'm sure it is her husband that's role-playing with her at the bowling alley. Who else could it be? Don't worry, your pretty head over her." "I'm going for a walk Carl to the cafeteria and get something to drink. Don't you worry about what the other guards and staff think when you're always like clinging to me? Really like smothering, man." "Wow, that's the gratification that you show me. How rude of you. I've gone to bat for you constantly, fk. I've smuggled in loads of contraband for you and helped you out on the streets. Do I have to remind you of that…?"

"Shut the fk up, Carl. I'm the hottest commodity at this freaking nut house ward; you're sloppy and obese and, at best, avg looking. Worst of all, your married and cheating on your fat-ass homely wife, you know I'm accused of killing philandering cheaters, but I'm innocent. If that were true, I mean, if I were a murderess, you'd be at the top of one of my lists! Besides, you never had your dick, ugh, cock sucked like I do deep throat with the velvet squeeze. So call the kettle black and get out of my way; give me some fkn space, dude. By the way, I need a new Curling Iron tomorrow Carl; aah, thanks!"

She pushes by Carl's tonsil wagging open-mouth and hairy nostrils, who instantly morphed into red-faced angry, even pissed off. He whispers, 'you slut' she stops and spins around, "no more 'head' for you." "I'm sorry, Sara, I didn't mean it shit. Please forgive me, and I will get you a hair straightener, too, okay?" She scowls at him with a vicious sneering wink... "that's my boy Carl... good boy, now get out of my sight!"

-15-

FBI Agents Brock Dame and Lucie Link.

"It doesn't really matter in the scheme of things. Every lead has to be vetted, no matter how small, right?" "Easy for you to say, Brock, you're not sitting on the 405 freeway parked. I've literally moved like... 55 feet in the last 35 minutes. The radio reports of another motorcyclist dead. I mean, if you want a death wish, all you have to do is drive a bike in LA!"

"Lucie, I'm walking into a conference with the facial recognition team. Let me tell you something you already know Sara is the master of disguises. She is so adept at altering her appearance were even checking with Hollywood. I met a Lionsgate studio producer who told me they'd hire her in a flat-jack second. In one picture, her cheeks are swollen and baggy. In the next, her eyebrows are thick as a mustache. It's a skill that is hard to come by even for a supreme makeup artist, heck the producer said he wouldn't be shocked if Sara used Botox to swell her face up to change the angles of her features."

"She can't change her bone structure or height unless she wears high-heeled shoes. I am not so impressed by her, Brock." "Gotta go, girl; good luck with the parking lot freeway; want to do dinner later?" "Yes!"

Later at dinner, "this is scrumptious as she swirls her fork through the Caesar Chicken Salad," he smiles at her with peace in his heart; she has passed the barrier. No longer a conquest, no urges to dominate her body, power deep into her thrust all of his manhood make sex-not love, 'funny what happened weeks ago they almost crossed the panties line' he sat back and watched her swallow some more wine, just a friend no pressure, albeit a cute friend.

Brock was glad they hadn't consummated their physical desires; his pants remained slack. Oh, he felt relaxed and comfortable with this lady. Across the table from him, a noticeable transformation took place. Lucie's eyes narrowed like a Hawks measuring her swoop down to capture the Rodent, swiftly turning the report on the table over with emphasis. Brock kept silent, only observing his friend. She seethed with contempt as if, in her past, she had some severe psychological scars that were constrained behind a mask of cruelty, shown imposed on and in her. "So, the lab came back with the date rape drug called Rohypnol," her words bordered on agony. An exquisite, odd sense of pain and sadness prevailed. The presence of which, like a Killer Whale, unhesitatingly... swallowed their corner in the restaurant whole.

Lucie broke down, tears shaking forth "that piece of shit rapist that Sara murdered. His picture was in the LA Times, and the San Diego Union 27 women have so far come forward, reaching out to our hotline at the Police station. Some of which are still in counseling; he brutally sodomized them with foreign objects and an assortment of dildoes.”

Brock drops his fork and pushes his plate to the center of the round table… swigs the rest of his wine, gets up, maneuvers over behind Lucie, and wraps his arms around her, “hey babe, let’s take the rest of this to go okay!” He kissed the top of her head and squeezed her shoulders. “I concur or agree with your opinion and feelings. The rapist got what he deserved.”

She shook her head negatively… unfurling his grasp, “let’s finish our dinner; this salad will get soggy. It’s too delicious to waste, Brock. Still, my last words on that subject, I disagree that the vicious rapist got what he deserved. No, he got it easy, dying quickly from Sara’s poison. *He deserved to suffer castration without anesthesia and to be tormented like his victims. The women he raped will live a lifetime of uncertainty… violated, and never to be the same. He dropped those pills in their drinks and then carried them to purgatory!”* He nodded as she finished drying her cheeks; inside his heart, he knew there was a story of pain that Lucie endured at the hands of a predator, ughhhh better to leave it alone for now… as a large breath of carbon dioxide exited his lungs.

Lucie said aloud the letters… C.O.S. (change of subject) is an acronym my father was fond of, which meant enough. Switching the topic, “so obviously Sara has us both on her radar sitting not 27 feet from us in that lounge in Oceanside, it must be assumed that wasn’t the only time she tracked us. Sara had already been to my residence, and now I bet she knows where you live. The assumption could be made that she intended to poison us three weeks ago. No, it’s a fact. We would’ve been on the menu if she hadn’t seen the Rapist drop the pill in his intended victim’s drink.” “Yeah, Brock, remember what she wrote in lipstick on the bathroom stall” he nodded.

"That's it, Brock; the confusion runs rampant; her victims are the lecherous, lewd, adulterous, unfaithful, and scandalous betrayers wrought with infidelities. Neither one of us fit that mold; M.O., we don't meet her requirements for the death sentence doesn't fit in her puzzle. So why is she so hellbent on attacking you, Brock?" She paused and said, "Now, I must be included in that same equation. Why cuz we're her adversaries, we want to end her reign of terror?" "Lucie, that makes sense to me; we are like bait in a sophisticated trap; look around us, what 19 to 25 customers?"

"Sara might be right here under our noses again, Brock. Who knows, the next bite of salad could contain her devilish poison." They both stop chewing "geez, I've had worst conversations while eating. I just can't remember when… suddenly I'm not so hungry." Her eyes wobble back and forth, surveying the room they dined in. He pours the rest of the Red Zin into their glasses and leans back on two chair legs "let's get out of here, Lucie."

She nod's her head affirmatively "heck, we haven't heard from Sara in over three weeks. Maybe she dropped dead from her own poison" lol. "Girl, we couldn't be so lucky; still haven't figured out how she knew the woman she murdered with the rapist was a cheater?" "Could have been the obvious ring finger tan mark line shown?"

He waves down the waiter and does the mime gesture cutting the throat with a karate chop; done a bill, please. They're from a blind spot. A dish is slid in front of them, and the manager says, "our very special Blueberry cheesecake. Enjoy," Lucie grinned, "well, I think I can find room for some of that" as she lifted her fork, they froze. 'Excuse me, ma'am,' as Brock gets the manager's attention, "why the cheesecake is it on the house?" "Oh, it seems you have an admirer. It was 'called into our servers' station. No worry, it's been paid for! Enjoy!"

Lucie pulls out her badge "we need to speak with the person who received this order, all information credit card used, a trace on your phone line, we will need a box for this cake, let's move." Brock adds. "I need access to all your surveillance cameras; also, let's go!"

<u>Sara watches Lucie and Brock via a tiny camera.</u>

Sara had struck again! Sara hilariously claps her hands, a mirthful sidesplitting laugh, then a second howl uncontained oh damn, a drop or three of urine is felt, which starts the joyous state of hilarity going back to a full roar. I guess I need to invest in some Depends.

Sara had followed Lucie, who'd met up with Brock at the restaurant. Sara had walked in and sat at the counter looking over the menu. After they were sat by the host… Sara had placed the tiny wireless camera in a picture frame facing the FBI Agents. The camera was on and shone real-time video on her iPad screen. She had another bout of humor when she again checked herself in the rearview mirror. 'She was African American, her hair in braids, and she was having the time of her life.' On the passenger seat was her itinerary. She had to get on the road to LAX or miss her flight back home to San Francisco. She had a return flight back to San Diego in 13 days. Her rule of thumb is never shit in your own backyard.

Southern California was her hunting grounds, and if she could multiply herself by the 5th power, she would never meet her life's work and the demand for vindication for the faithful minority. The supply of polygamists, insatiable sluts, and cheaters would take her many lifetimes to avenge… aah, enough. As she slides the transmission into gear, her rental car juts out into traffic.

Sara was always super careful in almost everything she endeavored to do and accomplish; she picked her way past vehicles, obeying all traffic laws, and muses how much she loved Brock; what a fkn stud she had thus far been toying with him like a cat, and mouse. She could tell by their body language and chemistry that they hadn't done the wild thing yet, even though it was a fact that Ms. Lucie had burned many holes in her panties thinking of just that with him.

Lucie was forever… slip-sliding away on the seats facing the 'Brockster.' Sara was taking the overpass to LAX. Sara had learned all about Brock's past relationships and read every single one of his social media posts. A decision was formulated by Brock that he would remain celibate… abstinence from sexual relationships ever since his adulterous slut of an ex-wife shattered his life over three years ago. Sara had hijacked Brock's personal Facebook accounts showing the formerly happy couple the wedding in Maui, Hawaii. Another heart ripped out of the chest cavity. 'I need to comfort that man, make love to him, have him feel emotionally, spiritually, and soulfully connected, that I'm a woman who can be monogamous, trusted true love one cock one man at a time, forever do us part 'I Love Brock!'

Her inner self felt a warm glow naturally, but how would I get him alone to prove to him that I could and would be his protagonist, his heroine! What would it feel like to be really heart to heart-mind to mind melding into only one human being bound by the flesh of his body-skin, his tongue deep down my throat, our bodies interlocked in bliss! <u>Just one truth sex comes and goes, not Love. Uh, Love can be forever… eternity based!</u> .

Sara stares at her manifesto, a truism that she had on all her computers and phones; she would read it verbatim before entering the fray of morphing into being the Equalizer. Her moniker in many publications and online was 'The Vipress.'

<u>**'The Vipress Manifesto.'**</u>

Loving sex is by far the most rewarding of human experiences. Being In Love enhances all our erotic senses morphing and multiplying us into euphoric blissfulness. Aah, a sexual encounter or one-night stand is exuberating strange body conquest sex screaming orgasms. Even bad sex is good, and then it's over. You roll over and visit an alien. Yes, Sex, again and again. Why not? But then, besides the sex, there is no connection. Love can have sex last forever, good as the first time as the last time. Never let loving become routine or on demand or reflect life's struggles of monotony and tedium. This can bring lackadaisical boredom to the once cherished joy, drop the inhibitions of the soporific humdrum, change the style, experiment, even role-play a lifetime of fulfillment within your grasp, and reach out to the one you love. Love them in all the strange ways that you can.

<u>Never let them go or thusly live a lifetime of regret, an evil nasty, vile systemic stench that will be in your skin excreting from your every pour. Don't allow complacency into the bedroom, for when it rears its ugly head, the erotic senses dull and wither like a Rose pedal, DEAD! Bye-Bye Now! 🙃.</u>

<u>Don't cheat on the one you vowed to commit yourself to 'till death do you part' for I'm waiting in the lurch for you. I will avenge the shredded hearts that you shall trample upon, me Sara, trust that!</u>

<u>If you wanna stray, then divorce, break up, separate, move out, have an open relationship, and Communicate with your previous precious partner. Have the Balls or Lips to set the fkn record straight, or so Devil helps you. I will one day look back at you in the mirror, a reflection that will Kill you! Sara has spoken done-toast. Yay!</u>

<u>**-16-**</u>

<u>**Ame… 1/17/17 Tuesday visit to NIA.**</u>

<u>**Interview with Al & Sara #12.**</u>

I did get three hours of sleep. The coffee helped clear the cobwebs from the seven beers the night before climbed out of the shower at 6:45 am, and my phone was already making noises. I'd missed seven calls in the last 15 minutes or less.

At 7:05, she was ready to walk out her doors at her Bel-Marin Keys home with yet another jingle "yes, Don, I've seen you have already called" "good morning, Ame. Aah, doctor or, maybe it's not, I'm parked outside our office, and there are already five people with placards and posters walking back and forth right here on 4th street. Let me read one 'Doctor Death says, just do it jump!' and another 'Doctor Ame Amaya is a murderer." "Okay, Don, enough. We will have to weather the storm, don't speak to the press or anyone. Only say that you have no comment if you are pressured. Is that understood?"

"Yes, Doc, check it out. The San Rafael Police are also parked across the street with a few News vans that look like reporters pacing back and forth with camera crews. I have been here since 6:35 am, and the five protesters were already set up here. What's it goin to be like by noon? Oh hell, here comes more poster carrying?..." "No worries, Don, relax, damnit, take one of the muscle relaxers in my medicine cabinet. 'Chill, dude' I will see you at around 2:15 pm for my first appointment."

"Doc, you sure I can't accompany you to NIA? I can drive while you gear up for the interviews." "Not this time, Don, but I am looking forward to some of your tension-releasing technics, which will be much needed by the time I make it back from Napa!" "You got it, Ame, willing and ready bye."

Ame rubs her crevice and then pauses by her security monitor. Well, I will be darned, a news van parked in her driveway; they are on her like the proverbial stink on shit. She climbs into her Lexus-LC, pushes the garage door opener, and backs out; in an instant, a reporter with a mic hops out of the sliding door of the van camera woman rollin. If Ame continued her backward momentum, she'd run them over.

Pushing the button on her door, the window slides open, "listen to me, I have no comment other than to say that my words were misinterpreted, totally misconstrued, all out of context, pure unadulterated hogwash, full-on exaggeration off the record. This is all fkn Bull Shit; now move out of my way. Your trespassing." 'Honking her horn and wheels on by the newsies.'

She makes her way through the labyrinth maze from her home to Hwy 101 North. She lightly taps the accelerator down and zips into the fast lane, her two-thirds full triple shot latte in its place on the console. Mulling over her actions from yesterday, 'if she had used other words, could she have saved Fred's life?' One way or the other, he intended to jump, and when he ripped the most tender skin on a man and exposed the inside of his scrotum, it was just too much to absorb. He was better off at peace, a mercy kill; he had mangled himself, oblivious to pain or reality. No, I would have handled it the same way, as a lame horse put him out of his misery! I wonder, besides the gawking onlookers hearing what I'd verbalized, were there any recordings? Maybe with the wind blowing like it never ceases to do on the Golden Gate Bridge, perhaps no one could hear her precise statements. For sure, the cops wouldn't collaborate with the reporters, or was this wishful thinking? Duh!

Ame passed through the gates at NIA with 25 minutes to spare, having the pedal to the metal lost in space and time; her first appointment was with Sara, who was traumatized just days earlier by her sister's visit. Kamryn meant well and visited Sara nearly every Thursday.

Ame can feel the vibes as she traipses into the lobby and stands in a short line to be processed. "Doctor Amaya, can you please come over here?" A man she recognized as Assistant Warden Larry Walden meanders towards her. She felt his daggers and glowering stare 15 feet away, his Werewolf brows furrowed and forehead like a Chinese Shar-Pei.

Doctor Amaya, I need to have a discussion with you about the catastrophe that you were involved with yesterday afternoon. With conventional and professional wisdom, proper etiquette mandates us at NIA." Ame tosses up her left paw. "Hold up. Mr. Walden, before you read me the riot act here, let me clarify that I'm innocent of all the malignant embellishments. This character assassination will be dealt with by my legal team, which I've already contacted."

"The maliciousness will be brought to heel, and now, I hope that NIA will honor our contract that expires in 2025. Do we have a problem, sir?" She smiles inside as she imagines his balls shrinking. "Aah umh, well the Warden is in Washington D.C., and aah just let me say if the news reports were and are accurate, and all the Psychotherapists told their patients just to Jump and commit suicide and kill themselves, then this hospital would be empty."

Ame disregarded his comments, "Please inform the staff that I haven't anything to say about the slanderous, disparaging, false statements. I'll be filing several defamation Lawsuits. It's plainly a smear campaign. No comments, please!" "That I will do, Doctor; let me expedite your check-in and move you through the entrance obstacles at the front desk and get your patients ready in separate offices. BRB, be right back."

Ame sighs and drops her cold coffee into a garbage can fk. I don't need any caffeine now. She is ushered through the steel doors and signs in at the front desk, "Sara is on her way over from the gym," says guard Carl, "would you like something to drink, Doctor Amaya?" "Wow, that was some horrific shit on the Golden Gate, huh, crazy crap like what the hell was he thinking?"

"Carl, let's just say that Fred was not thinking and wasn't rational; he was out of control, delusional, and didn't have one-third of your commonsense." Carl grins and taps his head "your damn right, Doctor." Ame almost chokes, thinking, what a 'Dumbass, her eyes roll.' Anyone can work here at NIA… K-Mart or Walmart security guards should all apply. Oh darn, I think I just insulted them. As she sees Sara jog through the double doors breathing sporadically, "hey there, doc!" "hey there, Sara, why don't you cool down, and I'll meet you in room three in a few, okay?"

Ame sat down; directly in her view was a courtyard fountain, plush green grass benches, tables, and four inmates playing shuffleboard; from where she was, they appeared as usual as anyone, including herself laughing childishly and pushing one another after a good or bad shot.

In a pamphlet she had read, now recalling all the classification levels of the individual inmates, five was the less restrictive level, with far more freedom only locked down in their single cells from 11:45 pm till 5:55 am. However, if you were classified as a level 1, you were in solitary confinement, never to breathe fresh air or have a glimpse of the sky.

Lucky level 5's had breakfast between 6:05 and 7:05 am. afterward, you could roam around and about be free to enjoy all the amenities 5's could sign up for college classes online or could attend classes where outside educators came in to teach courses, drama classes, plays in the new Amphitheater or essentially you could hang in the finest library this side of the downtown Napa's Central Library. Arguments had been made by the public which held water, or credence, around Napa.

The citizens said that NIA's facility was akin to an enclosed country club, newer than many available to the public. 'On the chance that you only wanted to play in the pool, jacuzzi, or swing on swings. Take your visiting children to the sand and slide down intricate spins in the park, or heck, go row boating in the large ponds. Play Tennis or Handball workout in the huge gym; go for it. It was the inmate's time; everything was supplied for you only if you were level 5's, though.'

These notable inmates could have their own wardrobe, although they must always carry a chipped card, ID, and G.P.S. ankle monitors on each so the staff would always know precisely where to find each inmate. Like snails across a monitor color-coded, of course, the 655 + acres had many areas that were 'Out of Bounds' with bright red paint drawn on the ground and pavement. The inmate didn't cross those lines without repercussions. Once you had achieved level 5 status, you didn't want to drop back to 4 or have your level reduced.

Of course, razor wire fencing kept everyone in check. If your level declined, there were far fewer privileges. This was the leverage on the level 5 inmates to maintain their status after being free to roam. Can you imagine being an inmate that was a level five, then for some reason had their level drop and were relegated to their cells and locked down? That can lead to depression and become caustic for these prisoners. Many times inmates were fully restrained in strait jackets or shackles, without windows in their cells. The majority of those cells were 7ft X 11ft with a 9 ft ceiling height, concrete and steel walls insulated soundproof, and inset camera systems with built-in speakers. Level 1 wasn't deemed the worst inmate status or label for the Criminally Insane. You could move down to 1 minus status. A padded cell restrained naked in the dark 24/7 with only a tiny hole in the floor for a toilet, a pushdown knob that sprays or shoots a stream of water when pressed on with a timed shut-off valve for drinking water. You lived entirely in the dark.

The cell door remains shut until a moving module unit on tracks like a trolly car that would automatically stop and attach itself to the cell door, which then opens this small additional space would have a shower inside, completely self-contained. The inmate never saw other humans. A robotic system would deliver their food. Slots through the steel door. Mentally this would break many because you saw no one, not a single human being, no mirrors, the hard floor rubber, no clothes, sometimes or once a month, a Psychologist Doctor would speak to you over the speaker system or give the inmate a video checkup, or assessment right from inside their cells.

The inmate had no utensils to eat with, only could use his or her fingers, no TV or radio, and many times nothing to read or to keep their mind entertained, only solitary white walls to stare at, no time clock. No Christmas or New Year's holidays if you caused trouble, disobeyed, or a guard didn't like you. The subsequent torture was that you would find yourself in complete and total darkness, not a speck of light for days or weeks. Then there were the chambers of Torture.

This state of art Modus-Operandi had one controversial arrangement, a method of disabling the inmate prisoners that would never make it to the Supreme Court. This form of control was kept in-house at NIA. A habitual offender, dangerous, even deadly, could be anesthetized and knocked unconscious by a formulated tasteless, odorless gas that entered the cell via a wall connection within five minutes. The inmate was made lifeless. Except for a shallow heartbeat, inmates that were treated with this measure of punishment were in the minority.

These prisoners would continue to regress with hallucinations and psychotic delusions, only exacerbated by the torment of their incarceration. So, therefore, once you were

116

categorized as a level '<u>One</u>,' you might as well kiss your life goodbye. The ascension to level 2 was beyond assailable very few had climbed that ladder. Only winnable strategy came from the outside world, attorneys, members of Congress, and family pressures, without anyone that cared for the inmate he or she Rotted. Some evil-intentioned individuals that worked in the facility kept track of this modicum. Who would know or care if you lived or died? No contact from the outside meant precisely that the incarcerated had zero recourses.

There was another way. In actuality, it always boiled down to money and not what you knew but whom you could buy or parlay into your corner money notoriety helped the climb out of the abyss.

Amazingly 'Sara' had bolted out and up from a Level 1 Classification in just under five years, an ascension unheard of a record by NIA standards. 'Al' took much longer. Still, it was a rarity for anyone to climb from the gutter up to where both now resided. Ame had read in Sara's NIA files that she had been offered 5+ status, which was an advancement, depending on your perspective. You could work as a trustee, wear a uniform while working, bring books and mail, and run errands for the higher security inmates, such as dispensing clothing and commissary from the inmate store. Sara refused to work as a trustee for 35 cents an hour. It wasn't as much the money but her negative feelings about why she should help the jailers and the system that leveraged her downward. Sara had her sister Kamryn who supported her while she battled the IRS for her own monies.

Doctor Ame Amaya had filed the necessary paperwork and had recommended that NIA raise Sara's level to a seven, then she could work on the outside of the Razor wire... those fortunate inmates were called the 'Work Cadre.' Inmates who were allowed to work outside and live at NIA. The fire crews were invaluable for the California fire season. Also available to the notable inmates was a fully functional winery of about 555 acres outside the Prison. NIA cultivated many different wine strains. Needed were grape pickers and processors, all manned by inmates. Every phase of the production had NIA inmates working like slave labor, from barrel manufacturing right down to loading the Semi Trucks with forklifts with the finished product barrels and barrels of wine strapped down. The warehouse on the grounds employed 17 inmates working 53 hours per week. Of course, you were always behind the razor wire towers, guards, and machine guns. The illusion of being free was obtainable to some.

What had held back Sara was that she allegedly killed 39 people. Some of the investigators had the numbers much higher, well, as high as 53, with many of the victims being Law enforcement officers. With that being said, Sara was named the most notorious, infamous female Serial killer in the history of the United States. Bad! She made an impression across the globe because of her stunningly sensual looks, she was a beauty, even called gorgeous. Sara was model material and fodder for publications from Newsweek to Playboy. One such headline was, 'would you kick this beauty out of your bed?'

Although this disgraceful, shameful reputation stuck like superglue, what was more bothersome was that she never repented nor admitted to a single murder, denied it proudly, claimed her innocence alive without remorse, always staunchly repeating she was innocent and one day she would be vindicated. She had contacted 'The Innocent Project,' who never replied to her letters.

Ame blinks, tilting her head, saying to herself, on top of all that I've learned, that she has a boatload of other victims. Who knows how many people she extinguished from existence, only her. Recalling that Sara had even killed her own father and a neighbor woman in the Jacuzzi, those murders were labeled accidents in the Police investigations and Coroner's reports.

**She hears the voice of Sara, joining her in the consultation room. 'I'm ready, Doctor Ame Amaya.' Who simultaneously pushed in the recorder 1/17/17 Sara NIA # 4755... Interview # 12, the time was 9:35 am.**

They both relax in facing chairs. The door is closed there alone, as always. A guard is near... 'Carl' and a camera blinking red with the audio or recording function enabled; it was up inlaid in the ceiling tile.

"Sara, can we discuss what happened last Thursday when your sister Kamryn visited with you?" "Doctor, I'd rather not; that would cause me extreme pain. I'm trying to put that behind me. It was awful like I completely lost it, was dizzy, couldn't think, and suddenly wanted to hurt myself. I ran and jumped into the freezing pond. My sister isn't going to visit me for three weeks, or until Feb 2nd. Therefore, I wasn't going to see her face for like 21 days. I just freaked out. I didn't know what I was going to do, frustrated, because I look forward to hugging, touching, and talking with my older sister; it's like everything to me!"

I fix her hair, and you know, makeover her already beautiful features; I don't know Doctor Ame what I'd do without my sister. I love her so much and always miss her, and now I'm worried, umh, scared, even petrified that she'll abandon me here. Kam has this boyfriend who's beginning to get in our way. She is up in Shasta County this week to meet his parents, which is not good, and you know, Doctor, the ole meet the parents trip is Super-duper relevant. This could become a serious thing. We need to stop it, end this relationship, uh, stamp the seed out, squash it, and prevent it from being fertilized, uhm, from growing. I need to figure a way to end this toxic relationship for my sister's sake!"

**"Sara, my rule is never to interrupt my patients, but I must do so now. First, there is no 'We.' Second, your sister deserves to be happy. She has been here for you week in and week out for over**

"I have communicated with Kamryn, heck, many times, if there is a more compassionate and benevolent ah selfless soul I haven't met them… she hired me. We signed a contract… your sister is funding your entire treatment/therapy program. Sara, your sister Kamryn is your Angel; beyond that, I can tell you she is a loving and sympathetic person. Who adores you and love's you unconditionally? Kamryn has always been your advocate and supportive number 1 fan behind you. Sara, you should be thrilled for her. I'm disappointed in you, your selfishness, and…" "Excuse me, Doc, geez, I was only joking. Christ's sake, the way you're acting, you'd think I'd led you to my poison stash and ordered a damn hit on her boyfriend, who has evolved to be her fiancé. It's just I'm afraid that this could be a trend, yah know, a negative change instead of Kam coming to see me every week, then or now twice a month-next thing it will be one time a month, then Never!"

Sara cracked an evil grimace which manifested into a snarl, then a teeth-gritting smirk "yeah, no, Doc, I dreamed last night that you said to her fiancé, "just to do it, Jump off the Shasta Dam… like the Golden Gate dude!" Lmao!

"Sara hold up!" as Ame choked on her own saliva, "how'd you hear about that, I?" "Doc, please, it's made its rounds through this hospital; I think what you said was freaking awesome. I can't lose my sister, and her heart will be destroyed. You know all men are untrustworthy like women, all cheaters. We should save my sister Kam…." "Sara, for the last time, there isn't any 'We' this is the wrong way to approach this…." "I have to save my sister from inevitable heartbreak. I…" "Stop this now; your being completely irrational and self-centered, egocentric, and downright mean and rude to your only ally!" "Wait, you're not my ally Doctor Ame?" "Sara, don't think I'm going to put up with you trying to twist this around.

120

You know exactly what I'm saying, so this is how I want you to approach this subject from a different perspective. Okay, think about this; next time Kamryn visits on Feb 2nd, show her how happy you are for her. Tell her that you want to hear everything that happened at her meeting with his parents. Be happy… show her you love and care about her?" Sara frowned largely.

"Then Sara, you're going to ask her to bring him to visit you so you will be able to get to know him. Wouldn't that be way cool if the three of you could have a wonderful time? You let down that force field of distrust, and you might even surprise yourself and grow to like him. Also, not all humans cheat. I realize how you have been hurt in the past, Sara, but remember our Mantra and the new and improved Sara. Well, what do you think about what I just said?"

"Doctor Ame, okay, yes, I like your idea of getting Kam's fiancé to join her and visit me. My quandary is a simple one where do I get some poison?" Ame slaps her palms violently on the table. Sara busts out in raucous laughter, "just kidding, geez, Doctor. You're the one that is going nuts," more hilarious giggles. In between gasps, "just playing around with you; you know I'm not serious!"

"Actually, that is my concern. I believe you are deadly serious speaking of poisons. I read in an old file that you purchased the Nicotine Poison from North Korea. Umh, coincidentally, I saw a news report last week that North Korean Dictator "Kim Jong Un's regime was behind a Hit on his brother Kim Jong Nam' two women assassinated him by smearing a toxic 'VX' nerve agent on his face 'VX' an oily liquid which kills a human in less than 9 seconds. The chemical component is always lethal. He was murdered right at the Kuala Lumpur International Airport. He wasn't sprayed, just wiped with a rag of 'VX' I thought you would find that interesting, Sara."

"Doc, there are plenty of liquid poisons produced in sophisticated laboratories all over, um, throughout this world. This will always be a fact; look at the Nazi's gas chamber's poisons and experiments on humans for producing lethal killer sprays and poisons."

Ame decided to end this counseling session, leaving her some time to add some content to her ever-expanding manuscripts. She needed to spend some additional time reading her manual on how to change a mentally challenged person's ways of thinking. Ame had been writing for the last nine years. Soon she would publish her thesis and educational lessons on locating and exorcising the Psychopathic Brain's inner demons. She handed Sara a worksheet to complete regarding the lesson she'd hoped she'd learned from her counseling session. The title of this chapter was 'Letting go of past mistakes.' A moan expelled from Sara... "what, Sara, you don't want to participate in your own therapy? If you can fill out this worksheet, it can help me... "No, Doctor, that's not why I groaned... it's because I haven't used the bathroom in over a week, and my abdomen is tender and hurts."

Bang like a lighting bolt hits Ame... that's right, Sara, I read in your files that you were diagnosed as having 'Coprophobia' at a young age, I understand that it's an extremely rare phobia. It's the irrational fear of feces or the act of defecation. Sara, do you experience a high amount of anxiety from merely thinking about feces? In fact, when I researched Coprophobia, a person with this affliction can endure a full-blown panic attack aligned with an increased heart rate, an increased rate of breathing, higher blood pressure, muscle tension, trembling, and excessive sweating... can, in extreme cases, cause a heart attack. Sara, do you avoid public restrooms, how uhm... tell me about how Coprophobia affects you, my dear." Doctor Ame stood from her chair and reached over to embrace Sara, who was bent forward in obvious pain.

Sara muttered in a low monotone… "Doctor, I can get sick to my stomach just thinking about poop, uh shit, or feces, like facing a loaded gun in my face. I have to eat laxatives to be able to poop. I was first diagnosed at about five years old I was in kindergarten and went to the bathroom. I stepped into a stall, not looking at the toilet, for toilets always had given me the heebie-jeebies, I locked the door and glanced back…Ughhhh, there was a huge pile of shit on the back of the toilet seat. It was smeared everywhere. I started uncontrollably shaking and convulsing and got dizzy, like having a seizure. I awoke in the Nurses office, with a hematoma on my small head, bruised and bleeding. It's awful, Doctor Amaya, ugh."

Ame rubbed her bald head and held her close, all along… Carl weirdly leaned into the window, looking at them through the door with a worried look, Ame didn't see it, but Sara winked and rolled her shoulders, letting Carl relax… she couldn't have him all worked up thinking that she was divulging… "so Sara how can I help you?" asks Ame. "Doctor, there is nothing that you can do, I take laxatives, and have a routine, when using the restroom, I have Baby Wipes and only use my peripheral vision to spy the toilet seat, I've learned I have to watch what I eat, don't want to experience diarrhea, and most often don't sit on the toilet seat. But hey, I have it down… umh, having a bowel movement about eight or nine times a month. I need to go and try to have one now, please excuse me, Doctor Ame Amaya."

Ame shook her head sadly and pushed her beeper, Carl immediately opened the interview room door. "Please take care of yourself, Sara, and complete that worksheet. I will see you next week." Sara walked past her, not replying. Ame was a bit drained as she made her way to the cafeteria, leaving Sara to return to her living quarters with Carl. Coffee is needed before her next appointment with 'Al.'

-17-

1/17/17 Tuesday Interview #12 # 5155 time 11:37 am… Al.

"Doctor Amaya, I sure look forward to seeing you. I feel that with your guidance, I'm being able to see myself and my previous actions from afar, umh, from a different and unique perspective," said Al. "You have helped with this. Thank you for the first time in my life. I can almost comprehend what society must think of me in the way that I lived my life. There wasn't anyone more important than Papa. I'm not ready to discuss with you the events that led up to Papa's death." Ame nodded her approval.

"But if you will, I'd like to release or vent some pent-up anxiety of a repressed time that I hadn't recalled till last night in a wicked dream, and it's like your therapy and counseling have brought out hidden compartmentalized feelings and emotions. That I wasn't prepared to assimilate into my conscious state of being… Doctor, I am no longer scared or afraid, a tad bit leery though I don't want to break the dam all at once; thank you for caring for me, Doctor Amaya." I nodded with an inquisitive expression.

"I was never a suspect in this horrific re-enactment of my past indiscretions. Since we speak in total confidentiality, I'm compelled to open my suppressed mind and explore this topic that may seem oppressive. The lists of my brutal misdeeds are uncalculatable."

"Al, I am thrilled to hear your words. Yes, please tell me all that you dreamt of last night. Let's analyze this dream together, your growing by leaps and bounds. There is hope for your future, Al! Before you continue, I want to express my gratitude and feelings for some of what you've expounded on. Suffice it to say that you have amazed me from my first consult till now; you've moved mountains. I am proud of you, Al!"

"Thank you, Doctor Amaya."

"The date etched in my psyche was 5/16/98 Saturday that was the end date, the day and night that all my planning and violence culminated in a successful reap of benefits, but let me bring you, as they say, up to speed about three months prior.

"Okay, now let's go into the time warp back in history mine; so, I was like 20 years old, taking classes at U.C. Berkeley, lived in a 5-story apartment building lucky to be on the first floor, even had a tiny garage. Directly across from my place was the biggest dealer on campus. Well, that is an exaggeration, but let me say he had all the toys: a super nice sailboat, speed boat, sweet-ass new red Corvette, Harleys, and a tricked-out Trike. He owned a home in Piedmont Hills, an affluent area." Al's face contorted, constantly morphing from frowns to smiles.

Al continues perched at the end of his metal chair… "No doubt he dealt his drugs out of our apartment building. The guy was only 25 years old. His name was George. He was originally from Boston, Massachusetts, and still had this wicked accent, but his whole family was from Peru, South America."

His looks were sub-par, IMO, 5'7' tall and perhaps 155 pounds with angled sharp features-beady black eyes, yet he had to beat the girls off him daily. His parties were always the Bomb like Rad. Anyone who was anybody showed up, at least for a cameo.

On one side of my Apartment were five residences or rentals; he rented four of them. I was on a corner next to his first apartment rental, or call it like it was his drug dealing business office, um, headquarters, he liked to call it. I would sit and stare out my front window as one woman would leave and another arrived a little later. George was Mr. Popular; he used the other rentals for party space and sometimes storage. He allowed other students to crash in them at times. The cops showed up about once a month; one second, he was driving a brand new Trans-Am, the next a Porsche. Doctor Amaya, my only car was a beater, Ford Pinto. Yep, I was major league jealous who wouldn't be? Please, like, be real. Damn, he had everything I wanted… the chicks and money, car prestige, and respect. George was held in awe, like a Hollywood Porn Star.

I learned sometime later that the reason he had so many rental apartments was that he used them cleverly. He'd put the buyers of kilos of Cocaine in #2 and his supplier in #4, and he used apartment #3 for his 'Cut' lab. This was where he Re-Packaged the Cocaine after putting filler, uhm, cut into the kilos… smooth as Ex-Lax, right?

George was smart and had zero cash outlay. He was the ultimate middleman. I had to figure out a way to get some of that cash to infiltrate his business organization somehow. One afternoon, I took a chance; I'd seen this Caddy 'Cadillac' low rider before… it'd drop by once a week. In the car were three black boys who always showed up together. They were buyers from Oakland, easy assumption! With all the Oakland sports teams stickers on the Caddy.

They'd constantly be pacing back and forth in the parking lot, like they were nervous, waiting on George. One afternoon, the Police had been patrolling the area and stopped to ask them what the three of them were doing. Like they were out of their environment, you see back then, the blacks stayed in the ghetto's didn't hang out around U.C. Berkeley, especially these gang banger types.

After the cops had driven off, I went out and whistled to get their attention one thing led to another, and I told them they could wait for George in my apartment. It would be a safe haven away from the cop's eyes. They offered me some pot and a pipe full of 'Crack' I pretended to indulge. I didn't do drugs. More of a nerd, I guess, than anything else, not to say nerds didn't use drugs, like Duh!

The leader was pissed off. He had his pager in his hand, tapping away, then asked to borrow my landline. Back then, in 1998, flip phones were around, but the dealers still used bulky large telephones. I learned that dealers were creatures of habit. They still used beepers and pagers and preferred landline phones. I sat and observed their gestures, slang, and voices. I could imitate them in less than 25 minutes. My Ventriloquist skills were enhanced with this new form of language, words, and Ebonics. I continued to listen, learning all I could about how they spoke. They were supposed to be buying their largest purchase ever, 3 kilos of raw Cocaine. I practiced using their accents and slang. It was more difficult than I had thought it would be in the beginning, but I mastered it. I'd call the Pizza places and speak with them in my new black voice. It was way cool; I was treated differently being black… not quite sure why, but hey, it works.

The total cost was $75,000 for the purchase of the cocaine they wanted, so I assumed that they had to have 75 grand cash on them. I fed the brothers beer, and they used my obsolete stereo to place their cassettes into. I was the host. We listened to Oakland Rapper 'Mac Dre' while watching out the windows. Next thing you know, a van shows up, I knew it was the supplier, yet George was nowhere to be seen.

A month later, this had become a weekly program the three black men had regularly stopped by when I was home, sort of like a comfort zone, away from the scrutiny of neighbors and the police. I even helped them to hide their Cadillac in my garage.

One afternoon I took the ball and initiative and decided to do it on my own why not? I told my three guests I'd be back and walked out to a flowerpot where George hid the <u>'keys'</u> underneath to apartment #4, took it, and opened the door. I know what you're thinking, Doctor Ame… kinda brazen, ugh, ballsy or stupid, uhm, perhaps all of the above. It was a warm afternoon in the lower 90s hot, actually having spent all my extra time scrutinizing George's operation. I suppose I was obsessed after my college work was accomplished; that is, I knew what the game plan was!

I then went to the van, where there were three Hispanics. Spanish was only spoken. I learned they were from Peru and Bolivia. Of course, an added feature to my repertoire came into being super handy. I could speak fluent Spanish, Yah!

I told them to set up in Apartment #4. George should be here soon. They were relieved to get out of the van and parking lot. One of them grabbed a duffle bag and followed me, entering Apartment #4. Both groups, the buyers and the sellers, were upset at George. He didn't understand what the word Punctual meant. He was nowhere, Doctor Ame. I did wait for about 35 minutes till I took control of the situation, putting the buyers and sellers in the apartments they'd be in, typically using the hidden keys that George kept stashed!

Doctor Ame was, as always, mesmerized by Al. His delivery and articulations were second to none. He definitely was a character; anytime Al told a story from his past, he became animated like he was in the present tense. Here he had the gestures of the black man who was the leader and primary buyer. His name was Tyrone… his tone, slang, and voice… imitated him. I could close my eyes and imagine a black gangster sitting several feet away; it was terrific. He would become the leader of the sellers or the suppliers from South America, mimicking them, gesturing with natural ease, again speaking fluent Spanish; the guy was unreal. Ame smiled within herself, musing I couldn't remember what happened last month sometimes, and here Al was playing back an incident from nearly two decades ago as if it only happened yesterday!'

"R U with me, Doctor Amaya? You seem to be drifting?" "oh yes, Al, please continue" *"let me shorten it; cut right to the meat already."*

'So, like another 25 minutes had passed by, and the buyers were about to drive back to Oakland super angry, cussing, and upset, same for the Cocaine distributors... With a ton of trepidation still wavering. I decided this was my chance to Adlib, so this is what I said; now, mind you, I hadn't even sold an Ounce of pot before, never ever sold any drugs, but I was a quick study-learner. Saying to the brothers, go get all your stuff to do this deal, I left and then crossed the sidewalk down the path to the sellers who were like, per usual, set up in #4. In Spanish, I told them we were ready and that I would handle the transaction for George!

They gave me only 1 kilo at a time. I took it to the buyers, and it was tested and weighed on a triple-beam scale. Then I was given $25,000.00, which was run through a money counting machine. Off I went to the sellers with the cash; the Peruvian leader took the cash and flipped it in another money counter... and wrapped the bills in bundles. All checked out three trips done, and they all left satisfied. I didn't make a penny myself. They gave me $3,000.00 to give George... a thousand dollars per kilo as profit for the middling of the transaction. Well, night came and went, George wasn't around, and I worried; Wtf happened? But I did have three grand, a lot of money for me for sure!

Come to find out, George was arrested and in jail for a DUI; after he sobered up, he was released. He had set up the 3-kilo deal before being pulled over driving his Corvette, tilting a beer right in the open. A CHP officer saw him and yanked him over.

When George finally showed up, he looked like leftover shit. I explained to him that I took care of the deal for him and handed him the three grand. He said, 'thanks, what was your name again?' and gave me a whopping three hundred dollars, cheap asshole. For all my trouble, he kept $2,700.00 really righteous, Huh!

That is how I started infiltrating George's drug business; what he didn't know would definitely hurt him. Within a month, I had the contact information for the 'Oakland buyers,'… group, and the South American sellers. I could easily replicate George's voice right down to a tee. His raspy-throated cuss words were no problem for me.

'So, this is what I did,' a sinister, sneering, teeth-baring look exploded upon Al's countenance. Then I watched Al's face move from a grimace to a ghoulish grin; he was enjoying reliving this experience, literally getting off on his description of his ingenuity and brilliance, an egotist, no doubt. *"R U following me, Doc?"* I nodded yes, "okay, being clever and creative as I am, I completed another five transactions. George was so busy he turned this trivial deal over to me but still only gave me a measly three hundred dollars. He took the 2,700 dollars, and it became clear he was abusing me and using me. I decided it was time to get even. Yep!

Once a week, this deal was done like clockwork. The 3-kilo deal was routine and easy. The timing of my Mission Impossible Operation was everything. The Oakland protagonist Tyrone had beeped me on my pager Friday morning. I was in Physics class. It was 5/15/98, a Friday. Uhm, I never forget a date. I stepped out of class and sent him a coded message about when we could get together."

I followed protocol likewise and phoned George on his giant phone. He was in San Francisco with a girl and not due back until late Wednesday night. I explained that I was leaving for a family emergency and wouldn't be available for a week or so. I didn't know when I would be back. George said, "too bad for Tyrone; he would have to wait till I get back." "Al, I'm going to turn off my phone and pager. This little honey could be the one I'd been looking for all these years; she's a real keeper!" I chided him with a disdainful cackle, "oh yeah, sure, George, I've heard that before" click, he was gone.

The time had come. Did I have the balls to pull this off '<u>not really,</u>' but I would do my very best. I slinked over to George's business, Apartments #1-4 (I had the keys copied by then to all the apartments # 1 through 4 easy peasy enough.) The place was vacant the last Friday night party left his Apt. in tatters. I went into his bedroom in the closet. I took out George's showpiece, umh, his favorite weapon. A 45 caliber 1945 Tommy Gun, a fully functional sub-machine gun with a 25-round clip… one shell was chambered.

I put it in a laundry bag and entered Apartment #2, hiding the gun behind the couch. Then back at Georges, I paged Tyrone from the landline; of course, I wore gloves. Tyrone called back in less than 5 minutes. *I swapped my voice out for George and played him to a tee…* 'Hey George, what's up, man?' 'Hey, Tyrone… Al has to leave town for a family emergency. I'm out of town but will be back for your 3-pack, so we will revert to our business model before Al took over. I will be at Apartment # 2 at 6:45 pm. You know where the key is.' "Okay, George, thanks, my bro, uuhhh, I appreciate it. I will be there at 6:45. Try to get me the same stuff as last time. It blasted everyone's mind; business couldn't be better.' 'Will do TY… later.'

Al's brows drop with an amusing trickle and evil glimmer exposed as he looks at me. "Doctor Amaya, for all intents and purposes, I was 'George' my voice, mannerisms, and intonations exactly so," he chuckled anyways. Next, I paged the Peruvian group, Mario, in less than nine minutes. George's house phone rang again. Lol. Now answering using George's Spanish tongue, 'Mario Apartment #4 at 7:25 pm same as per usual three pack.' 'Si Jorge seeya then my amigo.'

I returned to my apartment and packed all my essential things, umh, well. I didn't have much. I would leave almost everything except my college books, assignments, and the one picture of my childhood. A family photo before we as a family had imploded… Papa was holding me on his lap. I was but five years old.

Weeks before, I bought a face mask and handcuffs, all I would need, along with 'high-heeled boots.' I was once again in George's place. I changed into George's favorite Raiders jersey, 'Ken Stabler' quarterback in his clothes with the additional inches I was almost his height, and then I slipped into Apt. 2 at 5:55 pm. I peeked through the curtains, and I saw the black Caddy park. Then Tyrone and his brother headed to where I lay in wait.

I slid down against a wall, and they entered, talking about some girls from last night's party; they were at ease and relaxed as they put down their duffle bag with the scale, testers, and money counter. The briefcase with the 75 thousand dollars was next to Tyrone's leg. As per usual, they flipped on the TV and started watching Soul Train.

I waited anxiously, almost backing out; apprehension with fear had taken hold, and I pinched myself so hard, almost causing blood, building my nerve and resolve to follow through and do it. I put on my ski mask, became 'George,' and stepped out with the machine gun, waving it back and forth at the sitting brothers.

Their brown eyes went white with fright and shock. Tyrone screams, 'What the Fk, George? What's this?' I said I mean, George said, 'Shut the fk up on your stomachs now!' Ty was moving his right hand as his brother did the same with his left hand… guns, pistols in their pants, and waistlines.

I hit Ty with the butt of the Tommy Gun 'put your hands in front of you or your both Swiss Cheese.' I had them cuffed, hogtied gagged in less than 95 seconds. I took off my mask. <u>They never saw my face and assumed exactly what I wanted them to perceive: I was George. The first thing I did was grab the briefcase. Yes, $$$!</u> .

Silly, uhm, they didn't even lock the briefcase, lol put my mask inside and hid the 45-caliber machine gun behind the shower curtain in the bathroom, and strutted out the front door drowning out the slurred moans and expletives of the brothers… was Soul Train; yep, I turned the volume up for their listening pleasure!

Phase 2; at precisely 7:11 pm, Mario showed up with his typical entourage, took the hidden key from under the rock, as per usual, and ducked into #4. I had discarded George's Raider jersey and my George costume. I looked like myself, um, little passive Al again… Lol.

I stopped at a gas station to fuel my Ford Pinto up for the last time, put a dime in a pay phone, called the Berkeley Police to report a Major drug deal of kilos of Cocaine, gave the address to apartment #4, then drove off with a 'Pink Floyd' song playing on repeat, 'MONEY!' Yep!

Next to my torn and shredded passenger seat was $75,000.00. I would find a lovely three-bedroom flat in the best of neighborhoods, no longer 'broke Al' poor, barely surviving waiting on probate from Papa's estate. No more macaroni cheese, peanut butter sandwiches, and Hamburger Helper, pot pies, Swanson TV dinners, or worse, powdered milk. I was rich!

In the following week, the aftermath, I called it the 'Event' 5/15/98, hit the newspapers, and television news channels Internet, of course, sensationalized to the max. The Cocaine bust arrests of the South Americans and the brother's front page, then in less than five days, a drive-by shooting claimed the life of George dead as a doornail, 'Poor boy George!'

"That's the end of that saga, Doctor Amaya, umh, I did graduate from U.C. Berkeley and…" "Al, we will address this entire subject matter next Tuesday, 1/24/17. Thank you for sharing. We are out of time today, unfortunately."

Ame stood up and pushed the button, and Carl appeared. Carl walked her to the steel door exit and buzzed her out and into the maze of NIA; her mind back in 1998, she would do an internet search of the timeline of how many people Al was responsible for killing. No one knew but her. Al had killed many more people than what was known. His murders were in addition mode, no question, as he felt comfortable divulging confessing the stories of his past life, his evil became more transparent, and Ame felt she was close to a breakthrough with Al. He seemed to trust her unequivocally.

-18-

Ame is driving back to her San Rafael office from Napa.

She wondered if her profession was driving her mad between 'Sara and Al' the insanity of irrationality melted in her subconscious, then thawed front and center in her conscious state. Did that even make sense?

SARA, in the past… 4/17/10.

Saturday afternoon sitting back on an outside terrace sipping an Iced tea, Sara had now been at the downtown San Diego Mall for going on three hours the bitches she was tracking were carefree sluts as far as she could surmise, from shop to shop, both going into the dressing rooms together like high schoolers… giggles and show and tell models bouncing around like honeybees dancing in the mirrors. Sara spies them, um, at this instant, they were in Victoria's Secret doing the lingerie strip show.

Sara said to herself, plain and simple. The difference between the genders was face-front men and women acted so differently; heterosexual men, that is, when in the hell would two men enter a dressing room together trying on undies? Yep, in the same fkn dressing room. How gross? But for women, it was nearly normal, like, let me help you latch that sexy bra girlfriend, uh, such a stark difference hum.

She had followed Lucie from her home in Oceanside down the coast, then watched her meet with this long-legged redhead they'd been shopping ever since. Sara had on one of her all-time favorite outfits. She was covered from the top of her head to her toes her dark blackish contact lenses finished the ensemble. She liked it that the crowds were cautious and weary of her. Most gave her insulting stares. She wasn't well received by nearly all except other Muslims.

Her black full Hijab Niqab veiled Burka was of traditional attire for women in Arab countries and the Muslim faith. The only negative thus far is that the Burka was too snug-tight. In her shoulder bag was a high-powered squirt gun, watertight, the kind that you could pump up for a more substantial, tighter stream of fluid. Her shoe flats were black, matching her gloves.

The mission was to eliminate Lucie; she was competition for her Brock; Lucie was hot to trot and heavy on the pursuit mode, no doubt buying some salacious thongs that barely covered her pussy-lips, with one of those narrow strings wiping her ass as she strutted her stuff.

Also, in her bag of tricks was a 38 caliber Snub nose pistol and stun gun that she retrieved from a storage that she had rented years ago, well, ever since she'd been traveling south when her cover business or actual business expanded from Marin County. She and her partners decided to open up an office in L.A., and now the third one in San Diego, lucrative and highly profitable, the Real Estate business was booming. Although she would never permanently leave Marin, the area was second to none, her safe and secure home base. Nest!

Should she walk right into Victoria's Secret and to the dressing room to spray Lucie dead? Right now, although her escape was not certain, dressed in full-length clothes was a disadvantage for quick movement couldn't full-on sprint or run too fast, but she was prepared with a complete outfit underneath. Where to change, was the question?

The original plan was to catch Lucie in the elevator, but of course, as life has so many choices, good ole Lucie took the escalator, and she couldn't get close enough to her. Sara made a staunch commitment to her modus operandi. She wasn't going to do what she'd done at the bar in Oceanside again, no change of plan, no Adlib, nothing spontaneous unless it was life or death.

I just needed an open area, not even just a clear shot with my squirt gun, then done sealed deal. It would be nice to find an alcove or follow the bitch into the restrooms; um, a smattering of privacy was needed. The mall was fricken packed. She checked the time. It was already 15 minutes to 5 pm. Maybe I'll get next to her car in the parking garage; that will work!

Oh crap, look who the hell just appeared, damnit; bad luck walked right past her, no way. Brock was dressed casually in shorts, sandals, and a Polo shirt, and by his side was a tall string bean of a man with black curly hair. They went directly into Victoria's Secret fk now what?

Geezus, was it now time to abandon today's attempt? She watched as the string bean kissed and hugged the redhead, then took her drove of bags in his hand as a gentleman would do or a pussy whipped guy would… you make the choice.

Which one? She didn't give a crap, her eyes Hawkish at the back of Brock; no kiss, no taking her cumbersome baggage, communication only, it seemed. Uh, damnit, then he reached out to help her with a load of bags… they were smiling like four cockroaches. I felt like spewing vomit as they walked out together; Brock glanced over and caught my eyes for a sec. He squinted with a menacing glare until one of the group must have said some words, and he turned away.

But suddenly, like a magnet, he swiveled his head back around to look at me again. By then, I was on the move in the opposite direction. Lol, he must have been attracted to my Pheromones. Yes, she takes the steps down the escalator by 2's. Brock had stopped cold, and the others were staring in my direction like Wtf? I know, weird, I shouldn't have but couldn't resist, ah, really childish. I waved to them rather than flip them off.

Being mindful, aware of not wanting to leave my DNA, the iced tea was still in my left gloved hand. "Did you see that, Lucie?" "Of course," "I'm going after her" "For what, Brock, because she was waving at us, since when is that a crime? Come on, dude, we're here with our friends; let's give it a break. I mean, Sara, that is, please! She could have been waving at anyone around us. Stop with the paranoia, please; we're going out to dinner. It's a double date, right?"

Dan turns to his friend, "what's up, Brock?" "I don't know, Danny. I just had a bad feeling in my gut about that woman who just waved at us. Do you mind if we stop at mall security on our way outta here for a few minutes?" 'Sure,' was the unanimous reply. *They watched the replays of the security cameras as tempers flared. After 13 minutes of watching, the lady in black follow Lucie and Jean to five shops from the food court.*

Only one conclusion was absolute. It was Sara, and dinner was postponed.

Sara looked all about in the parking garage, wondering why she'd forgotten her blocking device in the very storage that she had visited only this morning. She needed more rest or nutrients and vitamins. She was losing her focus and then shaking her head; uhm, no biggie! She drove out and was gone safely. Besides, what use would the blocking device be at a mall with over 155 cameras spread out?

Security would have noticed the malfunction, and the range was like only good for approximately 300 ft. So, as she walked with the device turned on, all systems within range would have been frozen. As she continued, the same cameras would unfreeze a major bust ultimately, justifying her rationale as she headed to her San Diego office. She would have to retire this outfit for a while; oh well. Tomorrow was another day; she'd get Lucie. Only a matter of time. Yes, time was on her side. She grinned, then her face twitched to a Frowl (growl frown) that prick Brock. He's trouble, indeed.

Meanwhile, as Brock and Lucie bid Adieu to their friends, raincheck, a promised dinner at Dan's house in three weeks was agreed upon, their friends depart their back staring at the small screens in the mall security office, the supervisor and a couple of security guards sitting in chairs trying to line up the camera's to be able to follow Sara's movements.

"Brock, there was a family of Muslims and several others dressed alike; what in the world made you suspicious of that one woman?" "Lucie, I can't put my finger on it. It was like I was drawn to her, a 7th sense, uh, premonition, a hunch, call it a weird feeling. I saw her zoning into Victoria's Secret. Her attention was on the front door as Dan and I entered; no biggie."

"Then, as we all left 'from the corner of my eye,' I saw clearly her head following us out as we turned away, then an urge shot to my brain, so I strained my head back to take a final assessment of her." "She hadn't a single shopping bag at a mall, not shopping, had a drink. I thought I saw a distinctive black shoulder bag that we had seen at the Palomar Hotel. It was like I had X-Ray vision." Lucie rolled her eyes as the security guards listened to him.

"I could see her evil scowl right through the burka. I wish I would have reacted proactively, but even now, all we have is a Muslim woman waving goodbye or hello as she goes down the escalator. There's no law against 'people watching' at malls. In fact, it's like a lazy sport nowadays, right?"

"Let's back up. How, if that was Sara would she know on my day off that I'd drive down here from my Oceanside home, then meet up with Jean? Sara would have had to be following me; I met Jean at the mall before lunch. We ate at the food court; what yah think she has a GPS chip on my car? Although that would be rather difficult, it's always locked in my garage." "Okay, let's get down to it, Lucie. Let's review the video from when you pulled into the parking garage; we'll watch your every step."

"Agent Brock Dame, on your right, the three monitors are only of the parking garage. These others will pick up Agent Link as she starts through the mall. We only have video of the escalator walkways outside the stores and the food court. We'd have to access individual shop security cameras for other views once Agent Link and her friend exited out of our main camera's views," exclaimed the mall supervisor, Ms. Shield. "No problem, Ms. Shield. Thank you for all your assistance," says Brock.

They watched Lucie enter the 3rd floor of the parking garage and pull up to Jean's vehicle, which was waiting; then, seven cars later, a brownish Honda Accord, a 2010 model new, passed by and parked. The woman in black exited quickly with the same shoulder bag only five rows away, perhaps 25 yards off, from where Jean and Lucie were seen hugging and walking off to a bank of elevators.

This was when the woman in black increased her pace, reaching her left hand into the bag-she closed the gap, "shit, look at her. She's nearly right behind us, OmLord." A crowd of seven surrounds the elevator, the door opens, and 'wow, look at her, try to shove her way past the waiting people… holy Crap.' A rotund guy with a quadruple chin knocks her out of position out of the elevator.

They paused the video; Ms. Shield stated, "look at her hand; she's got something grasped. She wanted on that elevator badly. The large man might have saved lives." "Nothing for certain, Brock, yet the woman in black takes off running up the stairs, now ain't that super strange… Lucie?" silence.

Jean and Lucie exit the elevator on the 5th floor of the food court "uhm, let's call her Sara. So Sara knew the arrow was pointed up. You could only be going to floor #4 or #5, so check her out." They watched the stairway door bolt open on floor four… out she peeks, omg, Sara. Then the stairway door opens on floor 5 "damnit,' she's behind you girls. Look, she is merely like 11 ft from Jean. She's definitely on your tail Lucie!" "Yes, I see her; fk what's wrong with me? Why wasn't I on alert less than a month ago? She attempted to murder us…."

Brock answers his phone 'yes, okay, thanks, shit, it's what we thought. No, we're still at mall security. Aah yeah, I will check in with you when we leave, all right, but a BOLO (be on the lookout) for a brand-new Honda Accord brown. Yeah, that's the best we got, okay, thanks.'

"The license plate was stolen, Lucie. This confirms it was Sara" as Ms. Shield is tapping away, following the three women from shop to shop. *Lucie and Jean were chatting it up, laughing, having a grand time, oblivious of the danger that lurked in the shadows.*

Brock jumps out of his chair, nearly spilling his coffee 'wait, he shouts!' And lunges towards the monitors that were still displaying the earlier time period when the three cars had parked on floor #3 'right there, he yells, look!' A San Diego Police Officer was parked behind Sara's Honda, leaning over the windshield. They Zoomed in and noticed the uniform. It was a Cadet, a young kid. They took another look at the patrol car, a sign in the window, 'Not in Service' in large black fonts on a white placard. Car 557… *Lucie was already on the horn to S.D. Police Dept.*

Fast forwarding now through the security video of Jean, Lucie, and Sara with more vigor was, Ms. Shield, Brock, and Lucie, certain the Vipress Serial Killer was on the prowl 'her prey was Lil Lucie.' They see Sara rush out of the stairway to her Honda Accord and, wasting no time, drive out the exit paying her toll. By this time, Lucie was not only sweating and lite headed, but she was also totally embarrassed and feeling guilty. What a fool, she thought. Not only was she in mortal danger, but so was her best friend in this whole wide world, Jean. She vowed never to let her guard down again.

The call came back as Brock and Lucie were leaving the mall in his car; Lucie's car was left in the mall compound to be checked for a GPS chip and a thorough screening. The next challenge was accessing other cameras by Lucie's home in Oceanside and Cal-Trans pictures on the freeways. These were relatively simple requests, but all took time.

Lucie's cell rang. "Agent Link, the Cadet's name is 'Cassie Binge' she is in her 1st year. She is on a task force that is on the lookout, searching for stolen cars. Like another 11 Cadets, Cassie searches public parking places for stolen cars. They travel to all the malls, stadiums, and beaches…." "Excuse me, please, is Cadet Binge available to speak with me right now? If not, I can leave her my contact information. Please make sure she contacts me; thanks." "No, she is off until next

Monday. I checked already. Hold on, Agent Link." Lucie had the call on speaker phone as Brock maneuvered through San Diego's Saturday evening traffic.

"Umh, you still their Agent Link?" 'Yes' "K, I'm now texting her contact info to your cell. Cassie failed to file the report on the Brown Honda and probably has it in her onboard computer system. Sorry, not protocol. If there is anything else I can do for you, let me know?" "Well, yes, Lieutenant, can you run a log on what Cassie called in from the downtown mall for me today and check back in, please?" "Yes, sure will"… click.

Brock decides to stop by the College pub next to Junior Seau's restaurant off Hwy 8 East. "While we wait for the log to come in on Ms. Binge from the Lieutenant, let's get a drink, girl. What do you think?" "I'm down for that Man, ahh, boy." Lucie smiles and paws him on his shoulder. "All right!" "Lucie sends a text to Cassie's phone after the third voicemail call. They settle in a corner, their backs against the wall. Once they swallowed their second Cape Cod cocktail, a measure of relaxation was exhibited; sighs, shoulders… drooped slightly.

Although anytime the doors swung open, so did their B.P. pop up… as their heads were on a swivel. They ordered red hot Chicken wings, fries, and chili. All were scrumptious. Lucie's phone vibrates as Brock dips the last fry into the remaining chili. On her screen is Ms. Binge's number, "hello, this is Agent Lucie Link from the FBI; hi, Ms. Binge." Loud noises could be heard in the background, and lots of laughter and giggling… fun stuff going on.

"I'm sorry, let me slip out on the patio deck. I'm at a birthday party. What can I do for you, Agent Link? Oh, please call me Cassie." "I'm Lucie; sorry for bothering you on your time off, Cassie, but this is urgent. You were at the downtown mall this afternoon. We have a video of you checking out a brown Honda Accord. Do you remember that?"

"I think so; there were other Hondas in that parking garage. Did you know Lucie, it was the number one stolen car nationwide just last month, 11 Honda Accords were ripped off, in San Diego County, there are many auto theft rings that are…" "Cassie, not to cut you off, but we need to address the brown Honda on level #3 in the parking garage." "Let me call you back. I have all the written reports next door at my Apartment; ugh, that's right, I didn't upload them to the department yet. My bad; I hope I don't get into trouble. Damn!" "Could you hurry, okay? Thanks, Cassie." Click!

'Well Luce,' "oh, now I'm a single syllable, Luce, not 'loose' right with the double Oh's?" Brock grins with a shiny tooth display "you know I like you a lot Lucie." She giggled "wow, commitment, huh dude… So, what is it? Do I get one of those Mood Friendship rings or what? Umh, I like you more, Brock!" They cheer, touching glasses.

"Oh, Cassie is getting her reports and is calling me back." "You do know, Lucie, that Cassie had to have made a near fatal error, blunder, because Sara's Honda had stolen plates. If Cassie had called them in, the car would have been towed, and a Police Officer would have been posted close by… to approach the driver of the Honda when she arrived back to the car…." Vibration Lucie's phone, "Hi, Cassie, thanks for getting right back to me," "No problem Agent Link umh Lucie." "So, here's what I have brown and tan Honda Accord 2010 model license plate YZL5177 VINs." Lucie interrupts with an adamant, admonishing tone. "Cassie, why didn't you call that plate in?"

"I did; hold on, wait a sec. oh geez, I screwed up, but the vehicle's VIN number was registered to Enterprise Rentals here in San Diego and…" "Cassie, isn't the proper protocol when working on auto theft patrol to check the tags first and then the VIN?" "Well, yes, so what are you trying to say, ma'am?" "Simply that the license plate on that Honda belonged to a Chevy Blazer, and the plate was called in stolen last Thursday if you had done your job? We'd already had the...." "Wait, I'm sure, oh no, you're right, I didn't check that box. This is so terrible. Omg, am I in trouble? I'm so sorry, and it was my last car of the day. I did call all the rest of them in Agent Link... are you going to report me?" Lucie shrugged her shoulder, staring into Brock's frowning face.

"I can't believe I screwed up." Lucie leaned back in the booth deciding whether to tell her that the car had been rented by the infamous 'Vipress Killer,' the woman that was murdering humans right here in San Diego. <u>'Sara was all over the News.'</u>

"Cassie, which Enterprise office was the car rented from?" "The San Diego Airport, the contact is Dick Peterson. He works the night shift. A nice guy, I deal...." "Cassie go ahead and text me over his phone number with the Vin number of the rental. Now get back to the birthday party." "Actually, It's my 23rd birthday party my best friend put it together for me as a surprise; I'm so sorry, Lucie!"

"Happy Birthday, Cassie please remember the details. The smallest of them can save lives. A lesson for you is to always triple-check your report and write your initials at the top afterward." "Yes, from now on, I promise Ms. Agent Lucie Link, I'm texting the info now. Good night."

Brock caught the drift "birthday jitters, not thinking, trying to speed up the day and get off work, huh shit." 'Manager Dick Peterson, please,' Lucie explained the situation to the manager, knowing full well that 'Dick didn't have to provide her an inch of customer information without a search warrant. Privacy policies, Lucky for Brock and Lucie, ' Dick' was easily massaged and pliable with the right stroke of words.'

"The car is to be returned Monday at 5:45 am, and the customer's name is April Bane. She flies out to San Francisco on United Airlines flight number 535." "Thanks, let me have her driver's license number… great have a good night, Dick." Lucie finishes typing the info into her phone, "what, why the look Brock? You look worried. What's with the peculiar expression? What's wrong?" Lucie takes a head spin checking the other patrons, "it's worth a try, Lucie. I thought that the new Hondas had an onboard computer system. Try, and call Dick back to see if that is the case? Lucie, if you can Pump him up again, maybe there's a GPS or tracking system in the onboard computer." Lucie nods. "I should have thought of that damn," she pushes redial. Better give ole Dick a second shot to help her out… Really!

Within 15 minutes, Brock drove back into San Diego, the business district financial hub, office buildings banks, and Safeco Park. The Padres were hosting the Dodgers tonight, and traffic was horrendous.

Sara was sipping her 3rd Martini with her legs kicked up inside her 5-story office building that was nearly vacant. Her suite #725, she could look out at the Baseball field from her perch. She had a long client list the day before, worked past 6:45 pm, then spent the night in Oceanside following the Slut Lucie. Now fk another failed attempt to seek revenge upon Lucie? I have had no luck.

Lucie kept on trying to seduce her future husband, her delegated soulmate. He didn't know her yet, but he would once their skin became interwoven, eyes met, true love was Undeniable. Brockster would melt within her touch. Oh Yeah!

-19-

Sara was incensed with building animosity toward Lucy.

Sara relaxed, knowing tomorrow was Sunday; she had nothing planned and would fly back to Marin County on Monday heck, she was a bit tired and could crash in the back room on a comfy pull-out couch. But first, like an addiction, she zoomed into some of her bookmarked Porn sites. She opened her deluxe specially configured laptop, so let me search out a few more future victims. 'Marriedboredsameole.com' Sara logs on. On one of her other favorite cheater's websites, there were over 71 hits. AshleyMadison.com grinning, thinking… in her fun extracurricular hobby, there was an unlimited number of choices.

Little did Sara know Brock and Lucie on foot were now focused on the Brown Honda, walking around it parked in a lot that charged by the day. The 2010 model had an onboard computer system that showed everywhere the vehicle had been driven. The first thing that Lucie saw was that the correct license plate was back on the car. A little coercion led to them checking out the cameras in the lot office, and there she was, Sara in Black, walking away. Yes!

So, as they grilled the dopey watchdog guy for information not helpful, he said, "the Muslim paid cash, no never saw her before, the first time was on Thursday night, left on Friday late, and now she's back parking her car that's it. Look, man, I don't like no Feds cops or the Law; that's all I got… get a fkn search warrant. You ain't touching that car, aah it's on private property now I'm busy tootalou!"

"Wow, what a fricken punk caveman. He's got a hair up his ass. We'll have 24-hour surveillance on this place from here on out," declares an agitated Lucie. "Listen, first things first, Luce, we're lucky the new Honda's have an onboard GPS. Now we can back check it and see where the car has been since she rented it. This could be a huge Coup!"

Sara has a unique situation going as she bites her bottom lip; she stands up from the cheater's site and goes to make another Martini, stretches her body out, then her BP blood pressure is highjacked and blows up.

She runs to her desk and clutches her binoculars in the lot three buildings over where she parked. Nope, her eyes didn't deceive her Brock and the Slut. Damn, oh crap! How the hell? What did I miss? Musing in warp speed accessing aah, even at this hour, dozens of office personnel were working in these buildings. No way she would be found, but now what? If they knew more, they would be at my door. I left no prints. I guess April Bane is history. It was an excellent I.D. Sara thinks, well, it's time to get out of town! Fast!

Well, she'd be busted if it weren't for the one-hundred-dollar bill she gave to the slug working the parking lot. The text from him that someone was looking for her came in on a burner phone. Within 17 minutes, she had three sites up and checking times and availability of flights out of San Diego and settled on another ticket to fly back to Marin in the morning. She had other IDs in her storage. Unfortunately, it was too far away. Damnit, she'd have to use her real name and felt cramps in her tummy… nerves exploding, sending acid up her esophagus. The Feds were closer than she thought; I needed to lay low for a while… No Shit!

Nice that she only uses rental cars when she was working on cleansing society of vile deviates. With her additional IDs, this incident would not hamper her. Her regular driver was down in her parking slot, a sweet green Jaguar XKR Convertible. She'd drop by her storage in El Cajon to pick out a proper disguise and to drop off the peripheral stuff of Sara's enjoyable other life… Vipress paraphernalia!

Sara repeated herself, now hopping in the shower for a hot rinse; since childhood, she'd jump into the hot streaming water when stress encapsulated her. When not planning on working her enjoyable second life as the Vipress killer, she'd always used her actual real identification. She was totally legal, and her company leased three offices in California. Heck, she even paid the IRS their extorted monies. Okay, I'll drop off my outfits and the poison spray gun, pick up another ID for security reasons and then drive to LAX instead of S.D. Airport to fly out. Park her car in long-term

One week later, Lucie was sitting facing Brock in his corner office at the Fed building in San Diego. So "let's recap in the past month, Sara using April Bane as her alias, took two separate flights out of San Francisco, one to LAX and the other here in San Diego. All photos show her in the same outfit with the black-covered burka. She rented cars at both airports. The address on her fake identifications led to a San Francisco homeless shelter. Forensics found no fingerprints or DNA. Her latest rental, another Honda, sits at our lab for further Forensics. We can assume it will be clean also."

"Lucie, we're missing something here; look at what we know. Sara's last two trips revolved around us. The Oceanside murder of two that we sat and watched last month; we know she trailed you. Since then, there have been no other killings because I believe she's dialed in on us. Sara has both our addresses. We have photos of her Honda in Oceanside by your home, Cal Trans Hwy pictures, not seven cars behind you. So, I'm saying we should be able to use us as bait. Am I off-base, um, target?" "No, it's a fact that we're being hunted, or at least I am. I was in both places; you were not yet at the mall. She'd followed me. I now am 'numeral uno' sure months back she dropped a note on your car windshield and sent several threatening letters to the local news…."

Raising his hand as a stop sign, "hold up, Luce, we've been over this a dozen times already. Think out of the box. What can we surmise from all we know first; Sara is the Serial Killer in Southern California. Yet she flies to San Francisco and the Bay Area and disappears for over three weeks, then back no killings up north, so she doesn't murder where she lives. How else can we look at this?" "Brock, that's true; how else can we look at that? It's a good assumption, and so is the fact that her alias April Bane wasn't used on her return flight on United Airlines back to S.F., and she left her Honda at the pay lot. Somehow she knew we had surveillance on the Honda."

"Yes; as he pounds his fist on the desk, we checked all Taxis, Uber, and Lyft services and buses. She walked away, and the last video of her was ducking into another parking garage. She knows how to avoid the cameras in the business district. It's not a residential area. Let's assume she works in the area; she had to have a visual of the Honda, or how else would she have known it was being watched? Her slinking into the parking garage area could warrant another check of any videos that we're missing. Let us conclude that she has another vehicle. How else did she get to LAX? She certainly didn't Hitchhike." They let some stress release with laughs. True! "What's bothering me? Is this Brock? How does she support herself? Is she independently rich? We know she's tech-savvy. No, I believe she has an occupation that allows her to travel, and she lives in the S.F. Bay Area, and she's not Insane, no chance. Nope, she's a cunning adversary with a very calculating brain, a Psychopathic Killer?" "Lucie, maybe she was hurt or abused, as our profilers have stated, was born into a dysfunctional family. Perhaps her parents were involved in adultery. We should canvas any cases of murders relating to infidelity going back 15 years."

"Could have been a witness in a terrible assault," silence, a long pause, they both nearly busted out laughing like really… there was no way to research all the murders relating to cheating. The stacks of cases would be at least three stories high, Lol!

Present Time; 2/2/17 Thursday.

Sara is just finishing a manicure at her third-floor prison Salon, a Supervisor's nails painted hair and makeup besides a pedicure the whole 9 yards. What was on her mind wasn't the woman… she was beautifying, but it was her sister Kamryn who was visiting her today. She'd talked to her on the phone last night, but where was Kam at? It was already 9:49 am.

Kam liked to watch her perform her makeovers, and she was near complete with this homely bitch. Damn Kam, where are you? Then like an instant wish come true, Kamryn's gorgeous face walks through the door with guard Carl on her heels. Sara pops up like a Jack in a Box, and the sisters hug with happy tears. They hold each other, bouncing joyfully.

It was pouring dogs and cats, so Sara took Kam around the inside track course on the 5th floor. As they walked along, her sister spoke with enthusiasm, excitedly animated. At the same time, Sara listened discontented, spewing in vileness how dare she goes off on how much fun she'd had on vacation and spewing how wonderful her piece of crap fiancé and family were. 'R U Kidding me like I wanted to hear this… how about me, huh?

"Sara, I had an awesome time with his parents. The only negative…" she stops. "I got a damn speeding ticket going, uhm, like 91 miles per hour on highway 5. Other than that, I had a ton of fun; you're going to love him and his family." No comment by Sara. She would have preferred Kam to have had an awful time.

"Omg, Sis, wait till I print out all the pictures. Edward's parents own a 3-story log cabin just like the ones we built as kids, with wrap-around decks overlooking a serene landscape and a dazzling view of Whisky Town Lake and Mt. Shasta. It's truly God's country up there; we drove quads down to the lake, enjoyed barbeques, and went sailing. The parents have this

freaking houseboat with more square feet than many of our apartments had while we were in college." Sara hid her facial expressions, asking herself why her sister would be bragging about how much fun she had, with me being locked in this mental hospital, saying nothing.

"Sara, it was frigid cold on Lake Shasta, but most of the houseboat is enclosed. The super-duper deluxe master bedroom has a full jacuzzi bath shower and a sauna, and on the top deck is a huge hot tub, and there are two slides you can take down splashing into the water." By this time, Sara was near nausea, seething with anger, but doing her best to do as Doctor Ame Amaya had suggested. That she was to listen to what her sister said and think of peaceful, tranquil times in life. Don't get too anxious or let tension and stress control your mind and body. Be mellow, be happy, adjust and meld, become one with my environment, and show my good side, the Lying side. Ugh!

"Oh, Sis, they have all the toys connected to winches to drop them into the water and to retrieve their toys. I mean, it's an awesome setup with Sea-Doos, Wakeboard, and a ski Boat; I mean you...." "Kam, I am sorry, but I can tell how exhilarated you are about this damn houseboat. It's kind of depressing for me to listen to, for I will never get to see it in person or go for a ride with you on it. I'm thrilled for you and happy that your relationship with 'Edmund' continues to grow and gets better every day. When can you bring him to visit me? I wanna meet Prince Charming already."

"Sara, his name is 'Edward, not Edmund,' Please stop with this nonsense defeatist attitude. You always drop mentally off into this mucky murky quagmire. It's simply not true; the odds are that once you're deemed rehabilitated and certifiably sane, you will be released, sister. I'm positive of this, and all our attorneys are on the same page heck, sister, look how far you've gotten in barely over five years. NIA has given you your own Salon Room, and

you're like free to come and go for the most part unless it is count time or the facility is locked down. It's amazing. I am so proud of you, Sara!" She gives Kamryn her obligatory smile, fuming under her skin.

"For Christ's sake, you have gone from being locked up 24/7 now your freedom of movement is stunning heck, it's like we're at a Country Club. Now let's get some delicious lunch. Come on now." Kam reaches over and hugs her little sister again. "And I will talk with my boyfriend BF and get him on the visitor's list. We will visit you, no worries; I love you." Sara almost flinches, then shuts her mouth and adds, "I love you too, sister." But in the front of her mind, she knew full well that Kam's BF would not visit her at this Insane Asylum. It would be a cold day in hell. The guy isn't stepping a foot onto this prison ughhhh, that's a no-brainer. Duh!

Kam's words had already left her mouth when she regretted making promises, that she wasn't sure she could keep cognizant of how Sara had a mini breakdown when she told her that she would miss some visits. She had yet to really broach the subject with Edward. He was averse to entering the gates to NIA.

But wedding bells were in the works, and she could feel it in her head and loins, at least in her fantasies; maybe she was delusionally hopeful. True, as of yet, her fiancé hadn't popped the question, but hell, this was 2017. What rules are there that the woman can't ask as she pops off a huge grin? "What are you smiling about, Kam?" Blushing, she says, "oh, nothing really, sis." After a buffet lunch, Sara says, "come on, sista, let me do your hair and wax that hair lip!" Kam shoves her playfully "okay, let's do it."

"How are the prettiest sisters on the planet doing?" Sara rolls her eyes. Kam squints with a partially restrained frown. 'How inappropriate of a guard to be openly flirting weird.' "Got some

news for you, Sara. Guess what?" as he holds the door open for them to enter the Salon 'what, Carl?' "The top hospital administrator of Psychology has heard how everyone is raving about your talents. You're becoming quite the celebrity around here, famous like anyways. <u>Ms. Liz Honcho</u> wants to schedule a full makeover tomorrow morning!" 🦋

"It's her 35th Anniversary, goin to be a big party. Doctor Liz Honcho saw what you were able to do with Renae and was simply astounded. She is like biting at the bit to have you work your magic on her! She doesn't want the staff gawking at her or being nosey and wants to keep her appointment private. I was privy because I'm the one that will bring you here to your Salon during the lockdown of the other inmates after hours. Isn't that like, umh, Fricken crazy, Huh?" Carl is fidgeting and openly excited like, mesmerizingly even emitting a spray of spit as he goes on. "Oh man, Sara, I betcha you'll get the Warden herself down here. I'm bringing in two Lazy Boy full-on recliners and am supposed to ask you if you need any supplies. You should be Pumped, Girl!" "Wow, how fun, that's great news. I will make a list for you, Carl, after I finish with my lovely sister; now, please leave us be."

<u>Ame and Donny Present Time.</u>

"I will tell you; I'm sure glad the stalkers and protesters, uhm, posters and sign-carrying bleeding hearts have finally disappeared. That was like crazy, Ame; please don't tell any more of your patients to Just do it, Jump!" They both laugh heartily. Ahh, that felt good, Donny. We still have the medical board and Fred's family Lawyer to deal with. It's a relief that we're old news now, for sure. "Hey, since we haven't a patient this afternoon, yuh wanna catch an early bird dinner with me?" "Damn right, Ame, thanks. Let's roll."

It was 4/28/17, a gorgeous afternoon. A pitcher of Ice-cold beer was sitting on their table, the second such fill-up. They were seated in the corner booth at their favorite restaurant San Rafael Joe's. The place was jumping, already buzzing the Friday crowd building, with music in the foreground, 'Billy Joel' 'The Piano Man' played over the speakers.

Don watched his boss, lover, and friend intently, mesmerized almost in a vapor lock of Awe, what a talent, a fantastic human being Ame is. With all that, a knockout body and looks that still turned college boys' heads, brains, and <u>beauty equals 'Ame.'</u> Don't forget talent with a quirky personality and sense of humor. He didn't care that she was over 15 years his senior. He was in love.

Ame had all the crayons rolled out in front of her, usually reserved for children, to keep them busy in the restaurant. She had even asked for a few extras of the colors that were missing, and Sara was on her third paper drawing, requesting the server for several more. He looked over the table. No, she wasn't doing crosswords, Tic-Tac-Toe, number games, or the frustrating finding of Waldo. She flipped over another page in less than three minutes, her crayons moving like possessed.

He picked one up, and 'R U kidding me?' The depictions were mind-blowing caricatures of a couple at the bar and the server at a table full of customers. They were like a moving scene in a silent movie in sequences, a pause in time, our server with a tray at our table pitcher and two mugs and a munchy bowl of nuts and pretzels all in the drawing! Don started to laugh, then he saw himself with a blown-out humongous nose and floppy ears. But it was undoubtedly an imitation of him as a cartoon figure straight-up amazing, yet he didn't care for his distorted look. In the last scene, he and Ame held up beer mugs in a salute, tapping and grinning, showing exaggerated teeth… smiling. "Ame, if you ever got tired of Psychiatry, I'm damn sure that Walt Disney would hire you in a flat jack-second." "Your hand is like a blur using various colors of those crayons. In less than 9 minutes, you churned out like 13 pictures!"

Ame smiles with a glimpse of her hidden dimples and holds up her glass as Don refills it. At about that time, their food was delivered. Oh, it looked delicious roast beef, gravy, red potatoes in garlic butter, asparagus, and hot fresh garlic bread; they dug in immediately. Conversation waned; beer warmed good stuff. Don spun out some 'shop talk' during breaks in chewing with an extended swallow. He wipes his dripping chin "jeez, if you could only get Ms. Slimson to eat a meal like this one, Ame, I can't help it, but every time she shows up for her appointments, she seems to have lost more weight, her clothes are loose and baggy already like a skeleton, bones breaking through her skin, she's what 25 years old but looks to be, umh, 45 with all those greenish veins, thin skin I...."

"Donny, can we enjoy our meal? Please keep those thoughts to yourself, okay? I certainly wouldn't invite you to dinner if you were going to bring up negative crap. This is exactly what I am trying to escape from this evening!" Don sort of missed chewing and accidentally swallows... a hack, coughs, choked, and nods with a swig of brew. The damage is done. Ame shakes her head. "We need to have her mother check on her, Don. She didn't show up this afternoon; please remember to call her. The combination of disorders that Abby Slimson has... can be terminal as Ame cuts another slither of succulent roast beef with her fork, with no need to use a knife. Yum!

She continues, "Anorexia and Bulimia, her obsessive desire to lose weight OCD obsessive-compulsive disorders with the deadliest post-traumatic stress disorder the ladder the loss of her son and daughter and husband in that fiery crash on Hwy 101 like 15 months ago." Ame takes a warm chug of beer "wouldn't you know it the drunk driver walked away from that wreck I'd be surprised if Abby makes it to 27 years old." With that being said, Ame retorts with her arms flailing in the air. "Why don't you leave your car in our lot and drive me home? Donny, no more drinks for you until we get to my place. I don't need you driving drunk. I need some of your warm, comforting touches with love this evening," as the server finally noticed her flailing arm.

'I'll have a Grey Goose Martini. Please Dry' as the server skips away; Don has his own warm feelings inside "that sounds like a request, or was that an order? Ame, either way, I can't refuse you. I will call Ms. Slimson's mother once we leave and text them. How about some dessert?" He says to a passing server, 'dessert menu, please' the evening will be blissfully fulfilling, he thinks. He will make the night a Remembrall experience for his lover Ame.' They left the restaurant just after 6:15 pm, driving to Bel-Marin-Keys homeward bound. Not a phrase was voiced… both lost in their own minds. The music wasn't heard, yet it was a welcome break in the silence that permeated the car. The texts and calls resulted in nothing, no returns of the voice-mails. Ms. Slimson and her daughter Abby were out there somewhere. Oh well.

Finally, the gorgeous drive out by the water to Ame's sprawling home, they were on the deck, overlooking the Bay… Don took the role of the bartender as Ame started the bubbles blowing, and the jets were pumping a pre-action to what was to become. She undresses naked and steps into the Hot Tub as he brings a tray of drinks, Absolute Vodka with a splash of Cranberry juice, 'Tracy Chapmans' album played on the surround sound system 'New Beginnings' the song 'Give me one Reason.'

<u>*** WARNING SEXUALLY EXPLICIT WORDING… PLEASE Skip underlined words and go to Chapter 21… don't read if your easily shocked by descriptive salaciousness.</u> ✸.

***

<u>Ame and Donny in the her Hot Tub… love tub.</u>

<u>Ame floats over to Don and climbs onto his lap, CowGirl-style sensual lips kissing him all over his neck, taking Lil nibbles, finds his ear lobes, bites down ever so tantalizingly, then engulfs his entire ear in her mouth while pinching his nipples hard. He moans in ecstasy, ohhahhyes, then her tongue whips around in his mouth, hearts now matching synchronous beatings screaming in lust.</u>

<u>He takes her breasts in his hands, with a gentle twist of her left erect nipple. Has her squealing in delight; she couldn't resist and mounted his rigid cock facing him. Her hands clenched his shoulders, kissing deeply lost in the scintillating moment, insatiable, slowly matching each other's motion, grooving hips swaying to the music in unison. They were veterans who knew each other's bodies and moved in sync.</u>

<u>They move ever sensually in no hurry, gyrations, her feeling him inside filling her up, him moving and rotating her luscious pussy to rub the ridges of his cock, oh gloriously making love the world could implode, who cares?</u>

<u>The tempo speeds up. Ame is gliding, clenching the back of the hot tub, sliding up and down and side to side, hastening then a faster pace, hearts pounding. Their tongues danced, matching their body's motion, synchronized movements. She purposely slowed, pulling his cock side to side and high then low, squeezing him with spontaneity forcing his cock to rub her pulsating clit, letting the erotic rapture take her to heaven. His hands find her supple ass, and he ups the RPM's lifting her and pulling her body down in a furious fervor in a heated fever. She earnestly passion laced had to climax, soon teasing herself until she would blow up, explode intensely, peaking close oh no, yes, Orgasm cometh! No!</u>

He disrupted her intent with his insatiable appetite selfishly. Now in a Rage, he grasped her by her hips, jamming her down on him ughhhh, he had to have her Fkn, now, Cum on. He buries his cock in her depths while their mouths breathe the same air, tongues moving, nipping nibbles, sexually enticing all nerve endings on Fire. Omg, blissful moments lingered, hands finding all the crevices and erogenous zones, bodies intertwined as One. Water is flailing in waves over the sides of the tub. Her fingernails dig into his back, and then suddenly, she raises up like a Jackhammer in a frenzy. She squeezes his manhood, the last frictions against her swollen clit, and her body falls quivering, convulsing backward. He's not finished. He rams her like a bucking bull and pulls her up in a vice grip; she shrieks ahhohhnoNOOO! Orgasms multiple climaxes: she twitches like roadkill!

Gasps for control of her lungs. Donny picks her up, spins her around, still engorged puts her ass on the top step. Her hands clutch the side of the tub as he grabs her hips aggressively and slams it home… doggy style as she whimpers with each stroke raising her butt, backing into his cocks pressured pounding. He lifts her vagina up to take him to the hilt. He's Rocking her, Panting. She lets out a guttural, visceral Feral growl, then FK Me, Fk Me Oh, Fk me harder, Harder, HARDER! Oh yes, Oh, no, Oh Yeah, they CUM in unison Climaxes like earthquakes, Volcanic, she loses grip of the tub. He Bites the Nape of her neck as his last contraction explodes and spews sperm, his cock pulsating so sensitive he jumps as nerves tickle the head of his swollen penis, nearly painful, the good kind. He rolls her back over. She is well-done toast spent her hair looks like a mop that had gone through the garbage disposal eyes dilated, her breathing still hyped out as her breasts heave, lifting with every intake, exhale he re-positions her again on her back on the top step of the tub one-third of the tub's water was on the outside now.

He winks at her foggy eyes and wobbles his tongue, flicking it like a voluptuous Luv Viper insatiable. She wiggles her nose… head back and forth, and manages a single word, 'No,' versus his word… was, 'YES!' As he drops his tongue between her swollen crevice, her clit immediately welcomes his flicking tender smooches, circling her now engorged clit ever so tenderly now swelling to full potential; AME'S hands have his head in a Vice Grip he wasn't getting away, as her hips grinded his face, animalistically. Her moans started silently increasing in duration and speed, accompanied by louder and louder inhuman words. She Screamed as his fingers gently pulled her labia's apart, fully engulfing his mouth in her pussy. Her love tunnel was flexing with fingers, a dual action. He then naturally went full TILT to triple action, his tongue slipping across her rock-hard clit in a circular swirl, two fingers with the palm of his hand manipulating her mound, pulling her clit too and fro, in sync with his tongues flicks, fingers actually gyrating in sequence with his tongue. Clit about to explode up and back side to side, he slips only her clit into his mouth, deep throat like and teases, so evil like in total control of her gyrating body. He again slows and sucks, nibbling on her labia's completely ignoring her clitoris, driving her beyond Insane. She tries to fight him off, Screams, 'Please stop Teasing me,' kicking her legs, but he has his own Locked down Grip. She's unable to move. 'Stop U Fker,' he purposely allowed her to squirm under his pressure. His and her intensity builds as he plays teasingly. His head was buried between her spread legs, which were flopping and kicking over his shoulders. This was the main course he wasn't going to waste a drop.

He engages her body with both his hands and all his fingers in motion with his swirling tongue. Sucking and flicking her clit in circular taps, then dived in for the finish! She Shouts stop, STOP Now, stop it, You Fker she becomes enraged like a maniacal demon. Her body Juts up, and she screams In a RAGE outside of her body with pleasure she had never felt before. OMG, up and down, squeezing his face head, convulsing, Vibrating his passion, strength, and force controlled her... sensations so enhanced it almost hurt. She slapped him across the face, then again viciously right left right combinations, his face stung of blood, she Yells out I'M GOIN TO KILL YOU FKN STOP." His triple swirl continued on, swiveling her mound in unison. His tongue rotated around her genitals, her clitoris erect... throbbing her back arches again, then a final Shriek as she pulled her own hair. Her eruption was VOLCANIC, shattering the neighborhood... shouts and screams of either Ecstasy or Murdering moans could have been heard on the sailboats in the Bay.

Her body emptied, and she could no longer move, paralyzed, flaccid, with no tension in her. She goes entirely limp with deep heaves and sighs, eyes closed. He then ran his tongue over her loved gap one more time. With the last flick of her Hiding Clit, she barely flinched, numb with climaxes spent burnt toast. His grin couldn't be seen as he had his way with her subtle hips and re-mounts her in Missionary position, not minding the dead lay. Her hips body stayed limp, but his hard-on, Erection was RAGING. Smirking now is perfect timing. Aah, Yes, he'd wake her up to a raucous giddy-up. He slipped his cock a little lower, right past her taint, reached over for a squirt of lubrication, and slowly worked his raging manhood in the tightest orifice on her voluptuous body. Yep, FKED her tight ass. She couldn't fight him, for she had no strength left, spent. Sara tried but gave up, no energy left as he kept slowly adding a half inch at a time, working 'RJ' in snugly his way in tighter than a virgin. Her Virgin Ass was his finally; with each stroke, he hit Pay dirt Ohyeah! Fully submerged, he could no longer hold on zero control and felt dizzy in heat. It was impossible. Oh, his Cock, Rocking back and forth, Spying on

AME's glassy eyes, giving him the evilest STARE. His eyes rolled back; Blast off… Earth Shattering Missile Exploding like never before in his life. He fell forward, flipping her and biting her left nipple. The orgasm was never-ending best ever. He flopped about like a fish on a dock, still remaining in the tightest orifice he'd journeyed into, slowly shrinking inside of her.

Ame gave him the last 'Stink Eye' as if to say, 'oh boy, I'm going to get even with you and get you back for this. It will be your ASS next, boy!' The jets had been hissing, spurting not enough water. He finally acknowledges this as he regains his consciousness. She was sprawled over on the steps in recovery mode. He lays back and checks out Ame's swollen crotch and thinks, bet she's goin to be pissed. She'd always said or drawn the line at her Ass, never no way. Still, I got it now. I have to have it again, whew, he says out loud. I got to stop thinking of sex and lay his bruised head and still stinging face on a stair. Wow, she beat the shit out of my head. I might have black eyes; heck, If I had hair, she'd have yanked it out by the root; AME is an Animal.

I love the Bitch. Man, she can be physical, but hell, it's all worth it. His dimples cramped as he slipped off in a daze.

-21-

Donny and Ame after the lovefest.

Don's eyes opened one at a time. No music, strobe lights still on, and no Ame. He climbed out of the tub, his skin wrinkled, puffed up like he was 101 years old, looking for Ame, and found her legs splayed wide open in the master bed naked, uncovered…

asleep Donny knew that he better cover her still swollen genitals before another urge filled his manhood.

He put a sheet and cover over her, dimmed the lights, and wandered out to the kitchen with a cold beer in his hand. Time to catch up on some of Ame's patients. She allowed him to listen to her interviews with the patients and to read her reports and diagnoses. Donny attended classes at night and dreamed of being more than a male secretary but a Psychologist himself on equal standing well, never with Ame. Perhaps he would one day ask Ame to marry him, and she'd say, well, HellYeah! This was his ongoing fantasy. Why not?

Don went into the archives and pulled up an 'Al' file, he kicked his feet up, and instead of reading the file online, he checked the bookcases for the hardcopy that was printed out, took it opened it up in a slot, found in the interview folder a memory card the audio of the Interview between Al and Ame.

He inserted the memory card into his laptop, paused it, and made a quick bathroom run to take a leak, ouch kind of sore, fondly smirking, tucked <u>Rock Junior</u> RJ back in his pants. And grabbed one more beer and checked to see how his lover was doing. Wow, she was down for the count.

Don reflects, 'I screwed the shit out of her laughs hysterically umh the shit out of her… get it! I bet she wakes up in the morning with a major attitude. He smirks; yep, I deserve it, I suppose, but if yah ain't ready to hang with me, get off the porch. Whew, that didn't sound right. What was it? Oh yeah, 'If you can't hang with the big dogs, stay on the porch!'… Pooch!

He kicks back again, scans Ame's initials, inserts her passcode starts the interview. <u>*"Al seats himself directly in front of me despite having chairs on both sides of me. He is dressed in cargo shorts and a green T-shirt, with an Oakland A's hat turned backward matching his shirt.*</u> *His pencil-thin mustache is trimmed, and he seems relaxed, even smug. Then I say, 'let's talk about your mother's cancer. Al, his demeanor shifted like the wind "Doctor Ame, can't we talk about something other than my mommy, uhm mom, I mean Mother?"*

"No, Al, this was discussed last week. In fact, it was your idea even." "Okay, I'm going to make it short; this hurts my stomach's insides and gives me a headache too." Mom had excellent health insurance and regularly saw the doctors since the cancer was prevalent in our family, especially on the female side. She took precautions, and preventive measures, constantly testing and screenings, and was prudent about having regular mammograms.

But not surprisingly, errors were made, and one day mom came home from work with her makeup smeared, crying. Dad had already started staying away from home. He had ulterior motives and had to jangle his sorted sick affairs. I was in 9th grade. She rushes past me into her bedroom. I listened to her cry so hard it was scary. I cried along with her knocking on her door. She said for me to come in… raising her arms up for me to hug and cuddle her. Al, I have breast cancer Stage 4, a hidden tumor deep in my left breast; we sobbed all night.

Later, after Chemo sessions that nearly killed her, she looked like a scarecrow. Her skin had turned yellow; instead of looking 41 years old, she appeared 97 years old. Her eyes were sunken in and black. She resembled a scary movie about the living dead, a zombie. She stopped Chemo… her double mastectomy was horrific.

I watched my mother die daily; her cancer had metastasized, and the malignancy had spread to her lymph nodes. My mother was terminally in pain all the time, tears dried up, and I couldn't keep my head straight; mom was a skeleton with grey skin. Her eyes were now hollow. They had her on this drip Heroin-Morphine I.V. all she had to do was push a button. We had Hospice at our house. Mother was reading the Bible one night and asked me to sit next to her. We both again started balling crocodile tears.

You're going to move in with Papa, she told me; even with the Morphine, she hurt all the way in her bones. She wanted to die. Her doctors had said she could live maybe for a month or two, possibly, worst case, a week or two longer. She asked me to give her the bottle of Crown Royal in her dresser; she needed a drink. I did. I got her a glass of ice.

I left after a great big hug and kiss on the cheeks to do some of my homework. After a while, I heard her wildly loud praying, shouting, begging God for peace and death, no more Pain. "Please kill me now. I want to die, God; please have mercy on me. Heaven, peace, please. I couldn't take it any longer using my Ventriloquism skills, using a deep Holy Voice I was able to throw into her room.

<u>"I am waiting on you, Sharon. 'Heaven' is yours. I am God. You have nothing to fear; God is Love. Join me in Heaven now, Sharon, take your entire bottle of sleeping pills, finish your whisky leave your physical body, and let your Spirit free... be with me in Heaven!"</u>

Mother died that night, an overdose of sleeping pills mixed with booze. Before momma pushed her intercom for me, I was hidden by her door. *My Godly voice imitated Charles Heston in the Ten Commandments movie.* At least, that's the voice I used.

I waited a few moments, then entered her dreary room. There were a few cards from well-wishers from mom's work; mom was the black sheep in her family, with no love. I pulled one of the drapes open, and mom wheezed, her lungs eaten alive with voracious cancer. My vivacious mom was no more; she could always swivel heads when she cruised into an area now at death's door, on her last legs, one and a half feet in the grave, and couldn't catch her breath. Her mouth opened in exhaustion; she was straining for an ounce of oxygen, gulped, and heaved up some bile. I wiped her chin, kissed her sunken cheek, and told her I loved her with all my heart and soul; panting, she said. 'Al, I love you with all of my Spirit. We will be together again in Heaven, with short puffs, catching her air. "God has spoken to me, Son; please get my bottle of sleeping pills in the drawer,' I did.

I helped her open the child safety cap, her cancer-stricken fingers now like claws raising her head, her left-hand shaking, holding the Crown Royal. She nodded. 'I'm leaving you now, but I will always be your Angel Al watching over you!'

She opened her mouth with no expression, no tears, and total resolve. I poured the three-quarters full bottle of super strong sleeping pills, even dropping a few, which I grabbed quickly, all of which went on her white filmy tongue. I helped her gulp and choke… them all down, with the Crown swallowing and gagging, then gently laid her down on a fluffy pillow, kissing her forehead. She smiled as best as possible, then gave me an air kiss, her chapped lips pursing.

With her right index finger, she pushed for another dose of the liquid Morphine, holding her bony hands. She shuttered and remained still. A little later, she squeezed my hand with amazing strength, a partial grin still upon her countenance. Dead, my mom was Dead! Sad!

I then let torrents of water flow over her blankets. My eyes were stinging then the ear-piercing siren of the heart monitor broke me from my outright torment. I yanked the plug, dumped the pill bottle down the garbage disposal, then, to my surprise. I finished off my mom's Crown Royal in three fierce gulps, pulled back her sheets, climbed into mommy's bed, and cuddled her dead body all night!'

<u>Donny and Ame.</u>

A noise tore Donny from the interview he was listening to between Ame and Al in NIA's counseling room. He had been wholly enthralled and then torn away by a broken-sounding raspy yell. As he got closer to her bedroom, it was, umh, an only could be Ame. "Get your ass in here, you Prick, get me some Ice water. I can't move my tongue like Freakin sandpaper; my Ass is raw. You're a dead man!"

Oops, I believe Ame is mad at me, lol he peeks his head into the room like a mole popping his head out of a hole in the ground. "Hi babe, umh, Ame, I'll be right back with a pitcher of ice water." She had her knees up, laying on her back, feeling herself. "You bastard, ouch oh, you're going to pay ole Donny" he hand's her a tall glass with a straw and then puts the pitcher on the nightstand.

"Hey, Ame, wasn't that the best ever?" He rubbed the knots on his head and bruises around his forehead and cheeks where she had pummeled and battered him. "You got me drunk… took advantage of me, raped my butt hole. You Raped me!" "OmLord Ame, no, you were down with it; you were totally receptive, I promise." "I told you to stop, Don! No, Don!" "That's true, Ame, but you say NO, no, No… Stop, stop, Stop, even when we're making love… how was I to know that this one time no meant No?"

"Women gotta understand how confusing this all is like no, no… no Noah Nah-nah, Yah. Oh yeah-oh oh oh, stop, oh Yes, yes… yes Fk yes oh fk yesss don't stop Yes!"

"Oh, you fricken prick, fine, now your making fun of me, huh, Don asshole? I'm taking the cuffs out, chaining you spread Eagle to these bed posts on your freaking belly. We will see how much you squeal with a dry 9-inch dildo is rammed up your poop chute, you prick." "Gosh, Ame, you're not joking. You're really angry with me. Butt, don't threaten me with a good time, lol." He lets out a roaring howl. At the same time as he is laughing, Ame takes the pitcher of ice water and pours it directly on his naked crotch. Don shockingly screams out, squealing in frenzied pain, trying to breathe, spasming in a fetal position. Now she's the one Howling. "Oh, this is only the start of payback, buster!"

166

<u>Sara at Napa.</u>

Carefully with fantastic skill, Sara is working the curling iron, her hands moving in a manner only professional beauticians could. She thinks to herself how far she had come, mirrors now all-around privacy in Prison full vanity with five drawers of the tools of the trade, Scissors… R U kidding me; they allow me Scissors. R They Insane?

'I'm supposedly a lunatic Psychopath.' Surely hordes of loony insane criminals walk the yards of this prison or are confined in their cells, not I. Of course, a metal detector is embedded in the threshold of each door to catch anyone trying to hide shanks or knives. She was a bit proud that she moved from the Dungeon to the Salon in only a little over five years. Doctor Liz Honcho was a good customer. She followed my orders, staying still as a Possum. I finished her mascara. The base perfectly matched her skin color and full-on blended into her old acne pockets of long-ago pimples disappearing. Sara was smirking, musing like she was a Body and fender man, some Bondo fill, sandpaper, some paint Walla, almost as good as new!

Sara was beyond an expert; Sara could be an instructor and a top-of-the-line cosmetology university. Sara could no doubt work in Hollywood using shadow techniques. She blushed a stroke on the cheeks, giving the appearance of a daintier nose to the most famous doctor at this establishment, the top Psychologist here at NIA, Doctor Liz Honcho. She finishes with her top-of-the-line glued eyelashes from Hollywood itself. Sara couldn't wait to start applying permanent eyebrows, hoping Carl would get her the Microblading device… she'd ordered.

Liz was attending a fancy Gala, a dancing celebration, uhm, retirement party for an affluent woman, the former Mayor of Napa. Doctor Liz Honcho was attending this occasion with her husband of 35 years, coincidently their

anniversary too. Nurse Renae knocks on the Salon door. 'Come on in,' Doctor Honcho says.

Renae stops in her tracks, her feet glued to the floor, stupefied with utter astonishment. "Doctor Honcho, you look ravishing, I mean brilliantly sensational." Liz starts to grin. Sara says, 'stay still.' "I'm not allowed to see myself, Renae; this Sara is a tyrant…" 'sshhh, please, I'm nearly done!'

Several moments later, a medium-sized mirror was handed over to Liz, who just stared. All she could do was gasp in delight. Her eyes didn't leave the mirror, yet she swiveled all about for at least 75 seconds like she didn't know the face that bounced back from the reflection.

Then Liz looks up at Sara. "Oh my, I'm gorgeous. I've never looked more beautiful. My hair… my everything, you're a miracle worker! She stands up and takes little Sara in her clutches for a warm hug. 'How can I ever thank you, your amazing Sara,' then she checks her watch "wow, it has almost been 5 hours since I came into this room. It's the very best perm style and makeover I have ever had, Sara. Thank you." "Doctor Honcho, please, all I want is to hear what others and your friends think of your new look. That's it."

"Sara, I think I can sum that up with just one word, Jealous." "Sara, you need to get over this hair phobia. Your lush blonde hair would be fun to play with, girl, this Bald is beautiful and is fine, but you don't have hair that's allowed to grow on your body. I'm scheduling appointments for you next week with me. We must get to the bottom of this phobia. That's the way that I will be thanking you!" declares Liz.

Sara smirked sideways, 'yeah Bitch, if you only had an inkling at the shit that was about to go down.' She quickly erased the thought, "I look forward to meeting with you. Thanks, now get out of here. It's almost 5 o'clock."

Renae and Liz skipped out the door; the ladder thrilled with feelings of oh how sexy I am, strutted away like she was going as 'Queen at the Highschool Prom.'

-22-

Sara, long before apprehended.

<u>Sara drifts off in her warped mind. It was 5/21/10 Friday in El Cajon, California, at 11:17 pm, almost seven years ago.</u>

Patti pulls into her garage; her door closes behind her; she lives in an upper-level subdivision just east of San Diego. In her 3rd marriage, a Veterinarian by occupation still got the looks, only 37 years old. Her new husband Rick, of barely two years, was a Dentist from a super wealthy family.

They were opposites in so many ways, which was discovered after they were married; while both single, they went on dates dancing and cavorting at all the parties that were notoriously valued by the Who's Who. It was non-stop go mode. What fun they had. He was a party animal. Yes! It Was! Uhm was like fricken Past-tense… Patti evilly cackles. The woman usually lets herself go after she captures her man-husband. No need to super priss and workout like a feign nope. Yuh pulled one into the boat. Now you could get comfortable and let it all hang out, roll with false security… intimacy goes from daily to weekly, then once a month, so Passe relationships. Not for me. I keep the fires brewing with new meat, lust, and desires!

Her husband Rick had morphed into who he always was, a homebody, a stay-at-home slug 51 years old chronologically but much more senior in attitude, stuck in neutral, now he avoids the lights, crowds simply happy to sit back, reads a book, and visits with his daughter and three grandchildren. Since marriage, he stopped working out entirely and allowed himself to slip into awful cardio shape, his BMI off the charts, at 6' 1"… he weighed 311 pounds, his sports model trophy wife maintained her body type was 5'7" and weighed about 145 pounds intimacy had already waned.

The last time he engaged in the standard missionary position, he started wheezing a loud whistling noise coming from his nostrils and throat. Patti thought he would have a heart attack and croak right there. She asked him to lay down, hopped on his sweaty body, and cowgirl up, not cuming close to orgasm herself.

In the last three months, his demand was always for cowgirl action. She turned him on… his trophy wife, and the admiration of all his colleagues, many swooned over her at the Country Club. He had put on 55 pounds since the wedding, so by GOD. He wasn't in glorious shape before; Patti knew what she was getting into.

You see, Patti had her own agenda with tunnel vision. She didn't waver from her destiny. Her obsessions, in order, were Money, Men, and she was a sexual creature who couldn't get enough of strange dick and bedfellows. Labeled a Nymph during her college years, that moniker still applied. Patti had only left one of her BF's 77 minutes before, after disappearing in his bachelor pad for over an hour. She didn't drink much alcohol and made up for the difference in Sperm.

Sara giggled as she watched the lights turn on in room after room; she got out of her rental with a miniature Chihuahua on a leash that she picked up from an animal shelter just days before. Walking leash in hand, she moseyed over next to Rick and Patti's luxury villa. Yep, the fireworks were cracking!

The pictures Sara had sent to all five of his Dental practices and partners did the '<u>TRICK</u>' well; poor choice of words, lol.

The videos and photographs of Patti as she performed her tricks were beyond graphic. The interesting bit was that all Sara did was copy them off her advertisements online and on her 'OnlyFans' site. Simple one and done!

Her secret life of online prostitution was coming to a halt; unfortunately for Patti, she'd never inherit the 35 million dollars which was allocated her way. Her cash cow dentist was the gravy train off the tracks!

Oh, Sara was having real fun, but the climatic Zenith was only milliseconds away! Suddenly the garage door bolts open. Patti is crying, screaming, 'It Wasn't Me,' a song that was appropriate for this occasion sung by 'Shaggy.' Rick is throwing her wardrobe onto the garage floor. Patti peeled her tires rubber frying, nearly running over the loose Chihuahua who had served its purpose throughout the three days of surveillance. The pup was free as Sara tried to stay on the bumper of the speeding Patti in her Mercedes, not an easy task, but Sara was up to it.

Patti wasn't bothering with a Bluetooth. Her phone was glued to her right ear in apparent panic, almost sideswiped a truck; she blew through a Red-light, Sara being pinned behind a Volvo, slamming on her brakes not to worry though Patti was soon on the side of the road, Yup. El Cajon Police. Aah, not a good night thus far for Patti; Sara planned to add to her demise as she yanked over into a 7/11 store parking lot, watching Patti try to talk herself out of the Red-light ticket; that wasn't going to happen.

Sara, in another of her favorite costumes, was a grandma-type attire, matching her wrinkled face with a congruous mop of grey hair. She carries a cane in her left hand and picks up a cold 12-pack of beer, chips, and bean dip with her other. Why not? Granny was thirsty and had no dinner and worked up an appetite walking a Chihuahua up and down Patti and Ricks street.

The young man from India didn't 'bat an eyelash' bagged her stuff up; then ole granny said, 'give me a pack of those extra ribbed condoms, the pink ones, please' snickers are heard behind Sara in the customer line-up of three. Sara turned her attention to the snickerers 'never can be too careful even at my age, remember safe sex, a wink, then she wobbled out, carrying her cane.

Sipping on a cold one waiting for Patti's signature on her ticket to be completed, finally, Patti is on the move again. Heading north to Hwy 8, maybe, Sara is on her bumper when she flips on a blinker for a right turn into a Vonn's grocery store parking lot. She stops abruptly. It's now 1:15 am, not the grocery store but the bar and grill lounge named 'hook-up' that was Patti's stop. With intent, she strutted past the bouncers under the red enter sign blinking.

Sara had energized her electronic blocking device eliminating any video camera. Nope, she hadn't forgotten it this time. A pleasantly cool breeze wafts in the air. She could hear a tension-based conversation, Patti standing outside the lounge, "Rick, please, it's all a mistake, honest, that's not me. I know the resemblance is uncanny, but you know they say everyone has a twin, babe. You know I only LOVE you. Let me come home and show you, prove it, let me in the saddle. Your Cowgirl is waiting, babe cum on. How about some Reverse Cow-girl action tonight."

That didn't go well as apparently good ole Rick hung up on her; Patti now slumped over in the driver's seat. Sara carefully scanned the parking lot while approaching the Mercedes, leaned on Patti's car, her window down, listening to sobbing; she took out her purple squirt gun and then roared. 'Hey, Patti' Patti twists her head towards the sound and is shot between the eyes. She drops her phone and starts gagging. Sara cackles 'aah, Patti, I thought you were a Pro Yuh got past the gagging Reflex, Lol… Not!

By 6:49 am, the El Cajon detectives had roped off the Mercedes Sedan. There was a 11X14 sheet of thick paper, a message to 'Agent Brock Dame,' which lay on the passenger seat. The FBI was alerted and was on site. They were principally the same team that was under Brock's command.

Agent Brock Dame and Lucie Link were doing their own things on their day off, and Brock was kidnapped by his good friend Dan on a surprise offshore deep-sea fishing trip. They had departed on a charter fishing vessel at 4:25 am, out of reach 27 miles off the coast of Mexico. They were enjoying themselves with cold beer and fishing poles.

Agent Lucie Link was in recovery mode, having been the hostess of the mostess and entertainer extraordinaire with the male stripper from out of the cake, traditional Bachelorette party for BF. Jean was so sweet and shy, and it was nice that Dan had taken Brock out. Jean, with Dan, had set a date and were going to tie the knot. Ironically, Brock and Lucie shared opposite positions meaning there weren't any wedding plans. Ugh, they had none, uuhhh.

Jean and their friends had a wild party, and they got so loud they thought the cops would be called lol. The 13 girls had finally wound down by 3:57 am; Lucie found herself one-third of the way on a sofa with a G-string on and a slinky black lace bra attached. Wild, Wtf happened? They were at the Marriot on the beach. It was 7:37 am. Lucie's phone was on Torch. She staggered up by rolling over someone's shoes to her knees, felt like her mouth was glued close, and her temples. Omg, the headache was rattling her ears. The song by 'Foreigner' 'Double Vision' took on an entirely new reality. Felt like death warmed over. Trying not to giggle, the song should have been called 'Triple Vision' she was only able to crawl to a bathroom, over several more body parts, to pee, screw the toilet paper she'd drip-dry, nods back out, blocking the entrance.

By 8:21 am, the Feds had their CSI team of Forensic Scientists on site, and Patti's vehicle was towed to the lab. Patti was taken to a specialized quarantined autopsy facility controlled by the CDC. The chemical sniffers confirmed that the Serial Killer had struck again.

After the second pot of coffee and three trips to the porcelain Goddess, Agent Lucie Link was on the slow-mo road to recovery. Bloated from a gallon of water, lucky for her, a patrol officer was driving her to a meeting at the lab. Agent Dunbar was the lead investigator until Brock, or she took the reins from him; she was in no hurry and felt years older. There was nothing to do besides hydration, food, and time that would soothe her massive migraine and hangover. She flashes her ID, inserts her computer-chipped card, stares into the facial recognition lenses, and then continues to enter the building.

Lucie went straight to the bathroom… another running biological function, burning hot putrid juice sprays from her anus shit warmed over, now she's got to deal with the arrogant wanna-bee Dunbar. The ultimate male chauvinist with a raw and burnt butt; damn. She checks her reflection in the mirror geez one night, and she looks five years older. Wow, muses, 'alcohol definitely ages you.' She opens the door to conference room three.

To her surprise, only Agent Dunbar was sitting in front of a laptop. He wagged his salutation with an audible grunt. Lucie finds a seat directly across from him, ready and on the defense from the always sarcastic, demeaning verbiage that spewed from Peter Dunbar's thin lips. He reminded her of one of her grandfather's favorite comedians Groucho Marx right down to his Werewolf eyebrows.

"Well, what do we have, Dunbar?" "Just a moment, please." Lucie takes the time to log in to her FBI account via her iPad. Opening J-Peg pictures of the murder scene, when he looked up and said, 'this isn't good, even personal.' His words were unnatural, almost empathetic... somber-like. 'When will Agent Dame be here?' She frowns behind her mask, and there he goes with his preference to deal with a man. Women second-class citizens belonged in the kitchen raising children. It's a man's world. "Brock is out on the ocean on a charter fishing trip and not due back till much later, so you must deal with me!"

He holds both of his palms outward. "I know we've never met in the middle nor seen eye to eye-that is my fault, so I will be brief and hand the ball off to you once I get you up to speed." "Thank you. Why do you have this ominous look of a forebearer of bad news?" "Good perception... The woman whom our Serial Killer murdered is none other than Patti Rockefeller. That was her married name; previously, it was changed from Dame. Brock Dame was her ex-husband. Her birth certificate shows Patti Lynn Sutton."

It took Lucie longer than expected. Still, in the cloud of substance abuse, and alcohol melting, "Dame, Brock's ex-wife... No-no way are you fkn with me?" "No," He lowers his eyes, "no, I mean yes, the one and only Patti Dame. I had met her at several functions years past. It gets worse, though; you remember when you were a kid and at some birthday parties. Or at the circus, a clown would make you puppy dogs or kitty cats out of various colored balloons, twisting them together well; check this out!" as he flicks on the flat screen.

The wall monitor lights up. He clicks the mouse and says a picture is a better way to describe it. A pink condom was blown up to form a penis with testicles; the head was jammed down Patti's throat the balls rested on her chin. Looking at the other pictures and video Patti's skirt was ripped and shoved up with the same-colored type of condom design between her legs. Lucie felt another surge of diarrhea loosely teasing her sphincter. Was that a drip-shit, 'please excuse me, Agent Dunbar.'

Lucie washes up and re-enters. Dunbar looks upon her with unrecognized sympathy shit if he only knew I was torn back from a late-night party, alcohol-based, but she played her part, as she again sits down even more gingerly. "Okay, here is a picture of the message or letter left for your partner on the passenger seat of Patti's vehicle. <u>"Hey there, Agent Brock Dame, a smile for you, darlin; now you owe me BIG! I did what you wanted. I killed your cheating wife; she was up to her old tricks. Get it tricks, lol; watch your back Darlin for you got another 'Man Eater' sniffing your crotch, ole Agent Loosey Link!"</u>

Heat went right to her cheeks, wildly induced blush of proportional measurements, instant sweat perforated her epidermis… like a steam room engulfed, yells 'What?' she exclaims "what; OmLord how delusional is this Psychopath?" He stares over at her, aah 'did you see the last line?' Lucie leans forward, blurred, her head tingling… rushing shivers down and up the spine. In tiny fonts, it read, "<u>Agent Loosey Links will not have you. She's dead already, just doesn't know it, your all mine!</u>"

"Umh, let's interpret that as you're on a short leash or list of being her next victim, Agent Link. I'm sorry. She carefully cut all the letters from the San Diego Union Newspaper. We haven't done anything thus far. We know she used her typical blocking device to alter all security systems; I'm afraid we don't have a lead yet. Forensics hopefully will turn up something positive."

He sighs and kicks his chair back. "I'm sorry, that's the whole ball of wax. Patti's husband hasn't been notified as of yet. Patti is in the back on ice with our M.E. all files will be forwarded to your account, and Agent Dames, there's a conference called for the both of you from our central office and Wash. D.C. on Monday at 3:45 pm. Oh, if I can be of assistance in any way, please get in touch with me." Then Agent Dunbar pleads with her, "this forgery ring, counterfeiters case is slow and methodical, like watching molasses roll uphill. I've been on this case for seven fkn months just between us. I'm bored to smithereens. If you can use my aid on anything, I would gladly help."

"Thanks for all you have done; I will let you know once I fill in Agent Dame. Thanks again," as Lucie makes her way out of the room, about to vomit again. Sweet girly shooters, never, Never, never again, those sugared alcohol shots, Yuck!"

-23-

Hungover Bachelorette party victims… Brock's ex-wife Patti Dame & Fishing buddy.

Sitting at the dock of the Bay, watching the charter boat coast effortlessly to its mooring spot, was Lucie; Brock quizzically mulls why his partner would be greeting him. She should be enjoying herself, and then he recognizes Jean from the corner of his eye. Dan's fiancé, Brocks, paranoia bounces off the waves. He puts two thumbs up, and Dan whistles. They reach a distance so that they can shout to each other Dan yells, "we killed em" the men are widely grinning with pride… "Black Tuna, Mahi-mahi, even landed a Sailfish and did some bottom fishing for Cod and Red Snapper. We're going to have Yellow Tail filets for days…" shouts Brock.

The 47 ft Boston Whaler pushes up against the bumpers. The first Mate leaps out to start securing the vessel, and that's when the men notice the slacked, washed-out faces of the women. They showed no emotions to match their own "Hey babydoll, how was the Bachelorette party?"

Jean, with a lopsided smile that vanished as soon as it broke the surface, "we had a blast; some of the girls are still at the hotel in recovery mode. I love you, Danny." "I love you too, babydoll; why the glum faces?" He steps onto the dock to embrace his lover and best friend "why are you here?" Jean nodded towards Brock, then rolled her shoulder in Lucie's direction.

Lucie takes Brock by the hand. Hey, "I got some terrible news. Obviously, you don't have your phone?" 'Yeah,' adds Jean, "neither do you, honey." "Oh, we both decided to leave them in our vehicles. Have a boy's day without the always intruding phones, and most of the time, we were too far out in the ocean to pick up a signal or service anyways!" declares Dan. "What's the bad news, Lucie?" asks Brock. He flicks her hand away from his arm and faces her with his hands now clenched to her shoulder blades, staring into her eyes.

The Captain interrupts, 'excuse me, guys' the first and second mates are busily fileting the Catch. "We will bag em all up and label them. We'll need those Igloo's Coolers you said you brought out of your truck." Brock says, "I'll grab them." Then, Jean flashes a glance at Dan. "Nah, bro, give me your keys; why don't you and Lucie talk? Go for a walk, okay!" Jean strolls hand in hand with Dan giving him the updates, while at a slower gait, Lucie had re-acquired Brock's hand-intertwined fingers and followed a step behind her colleague.

"Girl, what's up? Why are you acting as if your dog has died? Spit it out already; why drive two hours to meet us here? What couldn't wait? You could have just called me later, sweetheart?" "Sara struck late last night again, sometime after 1 am!" 'Ugh!' Brock stops 'well, shit, where at? Who? Do we have any leads?' Lucie then does an about-face, spinning into his path face to face, "Luce, you're beginning to scare me. What's up with this act like we've lost our firstborn?" "Sara murdered Patti, your Ex-wife!"

3/21/17… Tuesday, 8:35 am, Doctor Liz Honcho meets with Doctor Ame Amaya.

Ame entered the main lobby at NIA and was ushered into a room, the supervisor said, 'please have a seat; what would you like to drink?' Ame shook her head in the negative. 'I'm fine….' A few moments later, Doctor Liz Honcho appears. This alarms Ame, who stands up, 'what's wrong?' "Thought it was time for us to have a chat, Doctor Amaya. We have the same goals regarding Al and Sara."

Ame sat back down once again. "I am spread thin here even with a full staff of 15 Psychologists, and I've taken a special interest in some of our inmates. In the past, I realize we butted heads when the Warden, due to outside pressures, started allowing privately hired Psychologists, such as yourself, on-site. I felt like I was being undermined, losing some control of our patients. In hindsight, I was wrong! Doctor Amaya, it's been a Godsend in actuality having families, and loved ones take a concerted effort at…." "Excuse me, Doctor Honcho. I certainly respect your position here. Without your guidance and help, Al nor Sara wouldn't have shown so much improvement. You and your staff have done an exemplary job."

"Thanks, Doctor Amaya. Let me get right to the thick of things; we have concerns with Sara. She seems to be regressing in the last three months plus; we've had to restrain her five times and had her in Lockdown seven times." While speaking, Liz is busy on her laptop. She looks up "strangely, these episodes are linked to visits from her sister Kamryn." Ame scowled at Liz... squinting her eyes but only listening, not interrupting like she wanted to do.

"Sara has extraordinary skills. She is so very talented, way beyond what she believes. Her work at the salon has the staff literally fighting for appointments. I've never had as many compliments as I received after only one visit with her, amazing like she's magical."

"Doctor Honcho, you realize I have my regular practice in San Rafael, and I contract out for patients Al and Sara. That being said, I have to be back in Marin by 1:30 pm, which doesn't leave me much time; pardon me, but I am here to see my patients. I...." "I'm sorry, but today you will be unable to see either patient. An assistant was supposed to have notified your office of that yesterday, shouldn't have had you drive all this way out here."

Ame blasts to her feet "what, why would you...." A hand swiftly was pushed out like Stop! Liz barks "please Doctor Amaya... Sara is sedated. She had been having paranoid delusions since her sister's visit last Thursday. We thought she would be fine by Sunday, but she had another bout with her Schizophrenia, causing deluded misconceptions of who she is... uh, Sara claims there has been an Escape here at NIA, and she is not Sara and..." "Doctor, none of this adds up for me. Sara's sister is her Lifeline look. Kamryn has been through thick and thin. She is Sara's number One fan... uhm, and advocate. Doctor Honcho, all you have to do is look at the excitement on Sara's face when she speaks about her sister and their visits. It's no doubt the highlight of each week for Sara!"

Doctor Honcho frowns, peering into Ame's face, but says nothing.

"Listen, please, Doctor Honcho… it is because of Kamryn, her money and influence, and the connections of renowned politicians and legal advocates that Sara is even here at NIA. She also fits the bill for my services; heck, she loves Sara. That's solid and apparent, and I'm distraught that you and your staff allowed me to drive all the way here just to inform me that I wasn't allowed to visit with my patients. What's your excuse for not allowing me my consultation with Al? I will be billing for my time, Doctor Honcho!" "Fine, Doctor Amaya, I will not dispute your billing, but can we stay focused on what is relevant? Apparently, we want the same results regarding Al and Sara."

Liz bows her head, "let me continue. I agree wholeheartedly with you, and that's why I wanted to have this one-on-one conversation with you. Something is amiss. Can you please get to the bottom of it and speak with Kamryn about this change in her sister? Next Tuesday, maybe you can analyze what's also happening in Sara's head!"

Ame shakes her head in disbelief "the only anomaly, or shall I say stressful change between the sisters, is Kam is engaged now. Maybe Sara is afraid that she may be replaced or she could lose her sister to him. I will keep you posted, Doctor."

"Yes, we need her back in her salon room, that's no joke. Speaking for myself, I have a company party to attend in three days… or this Friday." (<u>Ame can't believe the selfishness of this woman, sure she wants Sara back in her Salon for her own selfish reasoning</u>). Liz switches subjects. "Okay, that leaves us with Al; my staff here at NIA have exhibited admirable tolerance despite his pranks on my staff and his other obscene antics, his practical jokes are way out of control, and he needs to stop all his immature behavior immediately. He imitates my

damn voice better than I can myself. Ame, I could spend hours reviewing written complaints and reports along with watching videos of him. It's not a pretty picture Al's negativity is off the charts. He isn't just a pest. Nope, he's dangerous. There isn't any arguing. Al needs to be reined in, and hell, I'm not even touching base on a fraction of his foolish behavior. He will be brought up for a classification enhancement, and his level will be reduced from a '5' to a '4', which will strictly alter his movement here at NIA." Ame crosses her legs, pondering her response… listening to Liz.

"Last Wednesday, one of our Janitors was emptying a large 55-gallon drum filled with toxic medical supplies, blood, and body fluids, as the poor man had it up to the brim of an industrial garbage dumpster to pour it out. Al using his ventriloquist skills… threw his voice and yelled. Don't freakin move! In the man's ear, he dropped the entire load all over himself. It might seem funny, but that was hazardous waste. The Janitor is in quarantine as we speak, with burns over one-third of his body. Since then, Al has stopped messing with the staff, but that didn't stop him from picking on the inmates. He should be on stage doing Vegas shows for his Ventriloquistic skills. Here are a few stunts he's pulled lately after the janitor.

In the Chow Hall, the dessert for the inmates was a special Blackberry Cheesecake. Well, guess who had a table full of it? Yes! Al. He waited as select inmates received the dessert. Good ole Al would throw his voice and imitate the guard on duty, 'give your pie to Al' some of them did." Liz was on a roll; Ame could only listen to her rant about Al.

"He caused trouble awhile back between two employees making derisive and lude comments using the voice of a Supervisor, the list goes on, causing fist fights with patients playing games like Chess and Checkers used the Warden's voice replicated the alarm and said 'Lockdown, Lockdown all inmates to their cells,' even our guards bought that one. He is just like an angry, spoiled brat child. He wants to punish everyone; at least we've been able to contain his derogatory and prejudiced sexism against some of our female staff members." Liz paused for a second.

"Doctor Amaya, his last stunt two days ago was just too much. It was the proverbial straw that broke the Camel's back. In one of our Olympic pools, specifically the pool we use for special inmate patients who have benefited from water therapies, Al decided he'd become our pool attendant Guard. Using our employee's voice, Al said to one of our patients, "Jump into the deep end of the pool... go ahead, you can do it, you can swim, you have to believe God says dive in!"

Ame nearly laughed, then said, "well, Doctor Honcho, besides getting wet, why was this particular practical joke so..." "The patient he picked on was in a wheelchair, paralyzed from the waist down. She drove her chair right into the deep end of the pool."

"Here's the video,"... as Liz turns the laptop around. Look! Ame watches in horror as the paralyzed woman topples into the water, strapped in the chair with a hand covering her face... holding her nose. She could be heard saying, 'Oh fk' in the background on the monitor. Al was rolling all over the tile by the pool, laughing so hard he was holding his stomach. A correction officer dived in with the Lifeguard on duty, who was able to save the woman from drowning after a long-concerted effort of mouth-to-mouth resuscitation.

"The woman survived," Doctor Honcho says as she flicks off the screen. "She suffers from Dementia, and when Al put the words, GOD says to ride her chair into the pool, she did it." Liz kicked her feet up, "In the scheme of things here, we have enough chaos to have a fool inmate cause us any more trouble. What if she had drowned? Then what? Al will be on Lockdown in his cell for three weeks, but I will not prevent you, Doctor Amaya, from counseling him. Next Tuesday, the

28th of March, you can visit him. Still, I suggest you somehow get his attention and have him stop the pranks. No more games, no more chances, or we will be forced to drop his custody level and classification here at NIA. Even now, I don't know if I care to stop the process. He won't like being reduced to a level '4' that I guarantee you!"

"I understand, Doctor Honcho. I will have some appropriate words for him, thanks." Ame gets up, shakes the doctor's hand, and leaves.

-24-

<u>Brock Dame and Lucie Link.</u>

He sat alongside Lucie, two-thirds of a bottle of 15-year-old Chivas Scotch gone. He had this forlorn stare lost in thought from years back; memories danced before his irises, the fun, exhilarating good times with his ex-wife Patti. Sex was the best because he genuinely loved her. This enhanced all the stimulating touches between their bodies. They were in tune and enjoying loving sex... knowing it would be just sex without love. Loving sex was the epitome, the ultimate show of Oneness... soulmates.

She had shredded his heart, mind, body, and soul, which was integrity-based, and still, that was a constant. He remained forthright and fully disclosed, um, admitted his emotional upheavals, not hiding as some people would from the truth that resided within. What Brock projected to others was precisely how he felt. He tried to be transparent. In the beginning, this was also Patti Dame. They were quite a match. She was vivacious, full of positive energy, gorgeous, even mesmerizing and scintillating in the sex department, but hey, their relationship wasn't only physical but mentally and emotionally matched. They, indeed, were in sync!

Then her demons took her away, her addiction to other's flesh, essentially a Jones for strange cock, promiscuousness for sexual partners she had never had. She would never keep her Vows Oaths of Matrimony. Brock poured another straight shot of Chivas and gulped it down; why, Oh, why his eyes wet with unshed tears locked into the abyss.

Lucie held him on her bed as they looked out on the Pacific Ocean; she had no answers, her feelings instincts of nurturing… estrogen peaking as odd as it seemed she was wet for him, even now knowing he was elsewhere only physically being comforted in her arms, but mentally with Patti. He staggered to his toes, wobbly his equilibrium out of whack, and mumbled as he almost fell. She helped him to the bathroom and even undid his belt buckle and jeans as she held him steady instead of standing. He sat when he urinated. She was there not trying to see or feel like a nurse, but in her heart, a girlfriend one day or night she wished, hoped!

He sat later while she helped him take off his boots, leaving only his briefs and T-shirt on. She pulled back the sheets and put him to bed. No words were spoken or had been in over 55 minutes, and none were needed. His body lit up her senses, umh, endorphins, pheromones secreted, causing a dichotomy of sorts. Her instinctual urge… mothering maternal feeling of protection shielding holding Brock, mixed convolutedly with the pull of desire to have him inside of her, making love as one kissing and touching… Lucie needed his masculinity, his maleness, animalistic tastes… then she dreamed of cuddling afterward with post-coital bliss, oh when, 'oh if ever?'

Lucie drifts off, listening to his light snore, finally relaxing, leaving this conscious state of being off to the other world of subconsciousness. In her mind, it had always been this way. They held each other loosely tonight and forever, a puzzle of body parts under the sheets, hearts beating together only to be apart. This was their destiny.

She wakes up to emptiness, alone. Her dreams were fiction; was he even there? Spying his boots, then her nose an aroma of coffee. The blurry clock digital display flashed at 4:55 am, only three hours ago. They had gone to bed; how could he be up? Wearily focuses on the last remnants of Scotch, the Chivas coagulating at the bottom of the bottle. She slides out of her bed, and then a shocking revelation is exposed, uh, that she is wearing her Sexy Sheer Red and Black Negligee. Whew, when did she put that on? Blushingly quickly slipping on a robe, she slowly meandered to where the light shone along with a low jazz sound looking through the cracks of her bedroom door.

Perched on a swivel chair with a white towel over his head, like a turban, was Brock. She snuck up from behind and saw that he had been busy… the printer was beeping pictures in an order displayed on the table in front of him, stacks of hard copy files. Sara's latest 'VIC' Patti's picture was front and center. "Oh, hi there, Luce. Did I wake you? I'm sorry." "Nah, I had to do a potty run, and the smell of fresh coffee had me curious how you could be up and able to concentrate on anything after all that Scotch?"

Brock tapped his wrapped head… Ice in a plastic bag enclosed by a towel. He turned his bloodshot eyes into hers. 'I need a break Luce' he barely stands. She takes him by his arm back to bed, and he falls back into a silhouette that was him, then surprises her. 'Please hold me.' She disrobes, pulling him in for snuggles to her breast. He was asleep in no time, and she wasn't.

Brock's subconscious led him down a pleasant path. He dreamt of all the beautiful times with Patti of what he thought their relationship was evolving into… children, travel, retirement, and lifelong commitments. On their last romantic vacation before the implosion, _Sara intercepted his blissfulness like a Lightning bolt. 'Your mine. I will have you. I will kill the_

<u>*slut holding you now,' he fights back. 'You have to make a mistake; I've missed something. I will find you, Sara; the hunted will become the hunter bitch, Sara I will Kill you personally!'*</u>

Brock crept back into his netherworld, trying to find a better world in an attempt to escape the painful reality that had become his present life. He felt the external stimulation of the warm, inviting woman who could be a refuge for his pent-up frustrations, physically, mentally, emotionally, and sexually.

Hours later, between the 'wake state' and 'dream state,' a lineup of assumptions was being analyzed, his mind playing detective in slow-mo. Everything he had read and seen unraveled, from diverse angles, flipped upside down a vagueness, an intensity, alternative outlooks, incompetent concepts, paradigm misrepresentations, quintessential and prototypical patterns. His mind was boggled with theories, hypothesis goals, and objectives, a motion picture in 3-D, then a replay. The supposition postulated a bitter, angry taste hit his glands-wait, stop… conclude, focus, help me remember what's inherently irrational!

Sara, at the mall stalking Lucie in her Burka, flashes by, then he is off in a moment, thinks she used the blocking device in the parking lot of the 'Hook-up' Lounge, but Patti's Mercedes was thoroughly screened for tracking devices, none! How did Sara know where to find her? She had to either have contact via phone, unlikely that they were talking… not the Vixens M.O. she had to have physically followed Patti from her home or shortly after she left, wait a sec, the El Cajon Police had ticketed Patti for speeding and running a Red Light.

This occurred on El Cajon Blvd. this ticketing process took 17 minutes for Patti's identification and the typical checks. The officer noted that she had been crying and disheveled and asked her what the problem was. The question is, where was Sara during this time frame? She was sitting somewhere observing. Did she engage the blocking device?

'I need to consult with the police officer and check out his onboard camera system and body cam. Perhaps Sara got a bit lackadaisical. It's a possibility. Brock rolls over and kisses Lucie's arm, which held him tight. 'I do want to make love to this beautiful woman.'

Slipping back into the 'Twilight Zone,' he awakes to the distinct smell of delicious bacon. Yum, her side of the bed is empty. He went to the bathroom to clear the Chivas Cobwebs. He dropped his drawers and T-shirt and entered the shower stall. He sat under the flamingly hot water on a convenient tile seat, the spray blasting… invigorating him. He hadn't time to mourn Patti. No, it was time to nab the perpetrator to be proactive and nail Sara to the Wall.

Suddenly the steam evaporated as the shower door sucked fresh cool air into the enclosure, a female naked succulent Venus model, her ample firm tits like a ski slope bobbing, her one-half-an-inch rigid nipples met his upturned head in need of a suckling. He felt surrender. The luscious, mouthwatering tasty body displayed open like a book to drown himself in 'you scrub my back, and I'll do yours.' She whispers and spins her sway-back Ass in his face, not before she takes in the view of his ripped abs and his thick hanging package. Oh yum, she silently moans.

He stands and suds down the contours of her spine leans forward, and nibbles on the nape of her neck, sending nervous tension across the expansions of her epidermis goose bumps that need to be popped arose. He takes her shoulders. The hot spraying water is welcoming. With an aggressive twist, he forces her around. His tongue invades her lips, and they breathe in each other… oh, for so long. He freezes momentarily and drifts apart, his back now at her front 'your turn' as he bends down so she can reach his shoulder blades. She soothingly rubbed the sponge over his skin with gentle force, and then, just as quickly as she had appeared, the steam left with her. 🌀.

"Breakfast will be ready in about 15 minutes. How's a bacon and cheese omelet with Avocado sound, sourdough toast, blackberry jam, and grits?" "Lucie, you're such a tease, your just an Angel. Thank you so much!" "Yeah, but I could be your naughty Lil Angel later," giggles…. 'Oh, fk, what the hell is wrong with me, his ex-wife was just murdered, and here I'm trying to seduce the poor guy… scandalous indeed.'

"Lucie, my body, wants to devour your naughty side up and down, lick, suck, bite, taste every centimeter of your erotic skin, it's my mental being that needs to catch up, and I'm getting close to the finish line Babe, I adore you, Lucie!" "I kinda like you too, Brock, more than I should; seeya in the kitchen" Whoa!

Lucie dry's herself off. Sheesh, I'm so Horney for him, 'I wish I had the time to 'rub one out' better get with the breakfast.' With two-thirds of a hard-on, he knows a few well-positioned strokes, and the current visual of Lucie's bodies orifice's her swollen crevice the landing strip like a guidance beacon oouhh turns the faucet to cold woe oh owwhho for sure throw some cold water on it, done. Thinking tonight, he will love her. Who in his right mind couldn't indulge in her sweet package?

"This is so scrumptious baby, aah Luce umh" "baby works, babe," smiles creased their cheeks; Sunday morning was going to be a workday. They have a meeting with the patrol officer who gave Patti the ticket at 11:15 am.

She was driving. Brock sat next to her on the bench seat in front of them. Driving a marked police car was the El Cajon cop, who pointed to where his patrol car was parked; Lucie pulled over and parked behind him. They get out after introductions. He says, "this is the exact spot that I pulled her over at, and here are the copies of my body Cam and the onboard systems surveillance camera." Lucie asks, "was there anything peculiar or different about this pullover?" "Well, other than her being emotional, obviously been crying and seemed highly upset, nervous, and angry all at the same time, you can see this in the video!"

Brock thanked him graciously for taking time out of his off day and for meeting them at the scene of the ticket. They stood with the 21-inch monitor on the trunk of the Crown Vic, watching the onboard video nothing popped out at them after the third time, zero out of the ordinary other than the obvious point that Patti had makeup running down her tear-stricken face, upset of course.

They could see the oncoming traffic and other vehicles parked nada, but no sign of Sara. The body cam showed similar results. Still, they were striking out; one thing was for sure if Sara was in the vicinity, she didn't use her blocking device. Lucie's puzzled expression on the fifth looped projection increased, 'what do you see, Luce?' She yelped, "wait, back it up, slow it down. Can we enlarge that shot right there?" Directly across the 5-lane thoroughfare was a 7/11 store blurry picture of a lady staring into the camera unwavering, she could be just another gawker or another nosey citizen, but she was out of focus.

They made their way over to the 7/11 store 'can I speak with the manager, please?' asks Brock. "I'll do you one better good help is hard to find, ugh, even or especially when you hire your own family. I'm the owner!" A dark-bearded Indian puts forth his hand, "now your obviously Law enforcement; how can I help you?"

Lucie goes through the narrative with additional verbiage thrown in by Brock. It was as if they had melded into one being, all copacetic thinking in unison, goals aligned. Brock looked on, watching her, thinking, why haven't I noticed? I mean, where had I been? She is... "Brock, what are you doing?" He blinks back to the conversation. "Yes, I was just thinking."

The owner was kind enough between customers to locate the tape that coincided with the precise ticket time, the premise being well it was worth a chance to see if the blurred-out woman in the Police Cam was Sara. Sitting in a small alcove, they watched the line of customers… again, nothing out of the ordinary at the gas pumps. The cameras showed the same, all normal, then Brock pounced. Lucie almost drops her iced Chai tea. What the hell a 'Granny type buys a box of pink condoms!'

"That's her; that's Sara all wrinkled up. I wish there was audio… also, look, she doesn't even need her cane after paying cash. She strolls out carrying the cane, a case of beer, and condoms; damnit!"

'What an incredible disguise, like a show from Mission Impossible.' After another 35 minutes, they had a cash receipt, copies of Sara's store video, pictures of her automobile, and photos of her leaving, following Patti driving off in the distance. The plates were again congruent with her M.O. stolen, and the car looked to be another rental like the one she used when her I.D. was April Bane.

"I think this is the closest we've been. This is a major breakthrough," exclaims Brock. By 3:45 pm, stacks of photos were wired to all car rental agencies at LAX and SD. And SF airports, knowing that April Bane had flown in and out of the SF Airport, all direct flights to SF or connected flights were on the lookout for 'Granny Sara.' Too bad facial recognition wasn't further advanced! Brock and Lucie had sent a dozen plus agents out and also utilized the local police to canvass all the rental car agencies, and also had the LAX security agency on alert, cameras, and video of every person who entered the airport were being gleaned everyone's eyes were peeled looking for Granny Sara!

They decided to alleviate some tension by bringing some comfy workout clothing along. Both disappeared in restrooms and changed into jogging outfits, moments later on Mission Beach, San Diego, smiling into a run, running off some frustration of unmeasurable increments. Three miles into this exercise, an alert came over her phone, 'Get to the Airport tickets waiting to San Francisco' memo from Wash. D.C. Director of FBI.

-25-

Brock and Luci are on the hunt… for ole sneaky Sara.

They landed in San Francisco at 8:25 pm. They were immediately whisked off to the Southwest Airlines security department; also joining them was an Agent with Homeland Security. Sara had only passed through the turnbuckles a mere five hours before. How close yet so far? The next step was to follow Sara to her vehicle, knowing full well the Serial Killer couldn't have boarded the airplane with the cloaking-blocking device. Optimism wasn't diminished nor misguided. In actuality, they were only five hours behind her, and Brock was anxiously hopeful, trying to squelch and compartmentalize all the emotional upheaval; the energy levels were on a high!

Sara lays back on her comfy futon with a gaze through her round portal windows, the low ceiling fan circulating slowly. In her quaint loft full of nick-knacks, she was always enamored with her majestic views overlooking Mill Valley, her favorite county in this world, 'Marin.' She reflects on her excursion south with a grin; yeah, a successful trip, yet she was tired. Umh, almost famished, starving mixed with exhaustion shrugging at a couple of empty beer bottles, alcohol, uh, an added factor to why lethargy was setting in. Even so, she closed her eyes! Not her mind!

She awoke in a dreamworld; then an out loud uproarious howl, memories of the weekend events, a firm decision she'd made... no more Granny. The disguise, the masquerade, was perfect in appearance but hampered her and slowed her down. When she had to move quickly, she was out of character almost to the point of bringing unwanted attention to herself, like when she was running late and torpedoed through bystanders to board the trolly and escalator. No, there would be times for Granny for now, though, she sighed. Granny is retired. Lol

She had already bought tickets for a return flight to Southern Calif. On 5/30/10, she had a full day to deal with clients and business matters and to readjust her investment portfolio. She'd called her sister Kamryn, who worked for Schwab in New York City, and she advocated moving some of her assets into higher growth investments since she was young enough to weather any market downturn. Higher-risk investments bring on more risk. Therefore, hypothetically reaped higher gains, umh, typically... got to be in the game to win!

So with the elimination of Patti... Slut Dame, the only obstacle that remained was Agent Lucie Link. How strange life is as she mull's over her infatuation with Agent Brock Dame in the infancy of this 'cat and mouse game,' a war ensued between him and me. It was settled... I decided I would murder the asshole, but after further analysis, um, due diligence... research, and observing him. I had an epiphany and, no doubt, realized that he was such a perfect man.

A man with integrity, not a man to ever cheat, be unfaithful in any of the ways humans are, a total gentleman and a Stud on top of it, handsome as they cum, and that fkn body. His life was about the pain caused by women hurting him. She could count the last three women in his life-after hijacking his

Facebook account; I'm surprised the man could even get it up for a bitch after the tumultuous whores that ate his heart bite after bite!

Sara said aloud, 'I will prove to Brock I'm worthy of being with him, Brock, and I forever and ever. God has brought us together; he would not tear us apart! I love him more today than yesterday, more than anything or anyone... I love him unconditionally.'

Now I must eradicate my last nemesis, be conscious of my surroundings, and be alert. They have my April Bane identity, the S.F. connection, and downtown San Diego. She will fly down using her real identification heck, she was legit. Unless she had ulterior motives, she regularly flew down to her offices in southern California, using her real name. Sara was the CEO of her Incorporated Real Estate Business, which was wildly successful. She was a top-notch female entrepreneur. I will be Sara then I can set up from my storage in El Cajon. Lucie, I'm coming for you, girl 'ain't nowhere to hide, nowhere to run!' Sara will get her man. She had to stay focused and not let superficial nonsense cause her to waver!

Agent Homer Lan, Brock, and Lucie.

'Okay, we have her flying south on 5/17/10, Monday, and out to S.F. on 5/21. In every video, 'Granny Sara' wore gloves, and pictures of her drinking beer, eating a sandwich on 5/17 and walking through the terminals. We are in the process of interviewing the passengers who sat next to her on both flights Agent Dame.'

Lucie pipes in, 'we appreciate all that you have already done, Agent Lan' "He seemed to ignore her with a bout of tunnel vision and a steadfast focus. "Excuse me, Agent Link, our primary goal is to see how she left the airport, and San Francisco is one of the world's most innovative and technologically advanced cities. We're hopeful; look, we have her on the air transporter bus, then she got off in the Fisherman's Warf area down by Pier 19. We lost her in the crowd," explained the Nerdy, paper-thin Homeland Security Agent Homer Lan.

"I have our resources scouring the businesses down near the Wharf. There is a multitude of long-term parking lots. We can't discount the fact that this Sara doesn't reside within walking distance of Fisherman's Warf! Let me also add that we have the support of the SFPD currently... There are 11 field Agents on this case, seven from SFPD. We don't want this Serial Killer in our city; we need to hem her in so..." "Agent Lan, could you take us to a car rental? We want to participate in the reconnaissance," asks Brock. "I can do you one better. I will drive you into San Francisco to the Federal Building, and you can have a loaner company car. I already set you up in adjoining rooms at the Holiday Inn in Fisherman's Wharf;

how's that sound?" asks Homer. "Thanks, that's highly thoughtful of you," espoused Lucie, "hey, call me Homer" "okay, I'm Brock; this is Lucie" "tell the powers to be much appreciated for the hospitality if you ever make it south give us a call ahead of time and we will certainly reciprocate Homer."

'Sweet,' he states, his explicit, deliberate manner aligned with an apparent preference for maleness; homosexuality ensconced his aura. This was a refreshing change for Lucie, who now realized she'd grown tired of the macho, flirtatious Agents. Homer was wildly attractive, a bit on the thin side. He again interrupts her speculation, "so let's catch this, Sara, killer," as the three of them take the elevator down to the garage.

5/23/10... Past time 9:15 am Sunday... Sara relaxing, until!

Sara had a long day scheduled for Sunday. She dried off and put on a sleek robe, spent 7 minutes blow drying her thick blonde hair, seeing her greenish-emerald, speckled ever,-changing eyes beaming back at her. Smiling!

At times she had a difficult time versus inertia pulling herself from the mirror, sometimes spending hours before her reflection. As per her ritual, she was propped up on a body pillow and took one of her five portable computers. This one, in particular, was loaded with apps from The Dark Web and the other internet.

First checking on her Bitcoin investments, the fluctuations in the last five days had brought gains of over $5,000.00, and she was pleased. Next, she accessed the wireless camera that was attached to a tree limb just across from Lucie's home in the town of Oceanside at 9:35 pm, and it didn't seem Lucie was home. Backing up in time via the memory chip that was installed in the miniature camera, she replays the day, skipping and fast-forwarding to 5:57 pm. There were no changes scanning forward in time.

Oh yes, as she sees her honey Brock, his Crown Vic parked by the curb then, her sleepy heart gyrates and twitches to attention. In his hand was a suitcase put in the backseat they seemed in a hurry, the car sped off, the Vixen Lucie with him.

Where the hell were they going together on a Sunday night? Both had to be on the job in the morning. At least, that had been their schedules and her assumption. Sara pulled out her 'Ace in the Hole' in her thorough vetting of Brock. Not only did she access all his online accounts, but she also had his cell number, the same one he had used since 1995.

Sara went to one of her favorite sites, 'illegal tracking website via Dark Web,' punched in her entry code, a monthly charge billed to a 'PayPal Mastercard' Visa. Swiftly her Blood Pressure went to Boiling abruptly. Jumping skyward up and rolling over, holding onto the laptop. A map filled the 19-inch screen, a blinking Red light depicting a GPS coordinate of where Brock's phone was at this precise second… Ohfk.

Mesmerized in a state of disbelief, her brain wasn't registering, her mind like a strobe light flickering then refocused, entering warp drive. She pounces across the floor. A ferociously, savage, FERAL Wail flaps from her distorted lips, teeth bare veins popping a barbaric, cannibalistic merciless metamorphized Alien. In the mirror was no longer Sara, blood dripping from her chin savagely, teeth mashing into her tongue and inner mouth.

Brock was less than 33 miles away in Fisherman's Wharf Wtf. Sara was dressed and in her car in less than 13 minutes, heading for the Golden Gate. She parks across from Chrissy Field and then fidgets about watching Brock's movement not minutes away. Parking at the Safeway Marina store even on a Sunday evening, the park beach was overflowing with tourists, lucky her inner mouth had stopped bleeding as she wiped her chin for the last time.

Sara hadn't a plan. Her storage building was in the Tenderloin District here in S.F. with her weapons of choice. She had lost perspective, sprinting in her tennis shoes and jeans through the manicured grass; breathing heaving, she continued to run. She had to clear her head finally another 330 yards later, sprinting the last 100 yards, finally spent. She sat on a bench overlooking the water. Cold sweat poured over her skin; she needed to get her sense of direction... bearings.

Her head was dizzy; she felt flushed, rushing waves of spent stamina, having emotions of awkwardness felt disjointed, disoriented, and confusion was spazzing her out. She entered other dimensions in her Vast collection of personalities, trying to maintain equilibrium, control of whom she portrayed she was at the moment, and who the fk was that she mused. 'Sara, stay strong and relentless. Where's your composure?' I'm calling on you, 'Sara the Almighty,' says a familiar voice reverberating, bouncing in her skull. She Listened!

Calmness took hold with a form of tranquility before the storm. She regained a tempered disposition, inhaled… exhaled, and clarity with fervor compelled a translucent composure. Sara would steadfastly analyze the caustic situation with a calculating resolve. She drove back to Marin County to her 3 ½ stories Victorian home in Mill Valley, black sharp… rod Iron gates closed behind her… the garage opened. Inside, she lurked.

So, the Feds have traced her to Northern Cal. how, why… what mistakes did she make? How close was she to being apprehended? They'd already been here if they had a real clue… as to who she was. Sleep wasn't in the cards for Sara. Only one positive could she grasp upon; with Brock and Lucie miles away, her prey was now in her backyard, a trap, a kill… but how?

-26-

Al in his cell at NIA, 4/3/17 Monday… Present time.

Al had been up for 37 hours straight-wired on the mixtures of pharmaceuticals along with his own messed-up biological system. He'd accomplished hours of calisthenics and burpees. His cardio exercises had finally exhausted and shut him down. He was going to crash hard. As of late, a fear existed when he entered his subconscious, the dream world that he journeyed in, like a locked morgue sometimes mocking him, didn't want to release him, a phobia of always being in the Nether World.

The lucid, vivid reality was overwhelming at times. He couldn't tell the difference between this world and the next many times he'd awaken, being covered in blood, with scratches, and sometimes naked and bruised. What had happened? Al was taught that most humans found solace, peace, and comfort in their sleep cycles, some even inducing so by sleeping pills. Al never desired sleep, but it was but a necessity.

If it would help him, he'd use some glue to keep his eyes open. He was fearful and anxious whenever sleep reared its ugly head. Where would his dream expeditions take him too? Why not a friendly, fun dream? Just once, please; as his eyes close, he slaps his face hard, takes water from the sink, and splashes it all over him. Al yelps internally. Please… don't give in. He starts pacing back and forth in his Solitary Confinement cell. He was locked up because of his antics… shit, having fun with the wheelchair lady who took a roll into the pool's deep end. Really no one saw the fun in that practical joke. Well, a few other inmates did; I saw them hide their faces with constrained smiles. Yep!

His reoccurring 'Ground Hog Day' dream, the haunting remembrance that was always below the epidermis like yellow-greenish pus about to squeeze out from his pores, music was loud 'Polka' the entire VFW dance floor filled to the brim 'Papa' sat at the end of a long table. Only just leaving the dance floor, the atmosphere was upbeat, must have been 55 partygoers at least. I was one of the youngest seniors at Terra Linda Highschool in San Rafael, Ca.

The gathering and celebration were for my Papa's best friend's 50th Anniversary, a full-on banquet band, and a 'roast' of the unsuspecting couple; Papa was my Legal Guardian.

Earlier in the day, Papa and I had the most terrible argument of our entire relationship. It wasn't very pleasant. The only time he and I would have disagreements was when he would try to convince me or manipulate me into performing on stage with him, like in Las Vegas. He wanted us to be a team of ventriloquists, a Grandfather-Grandson puppet show for the ages, the whole 9 yards. And we would pick people out of the crowd, bring them on stage, imitate their voices, and tell jokes, a one-of-a-kind, professional Ventriloquist show for sure!

This was Papa's goal and fantasy. I wasn't into entertainment, nor had any aspirations to make a career out of performing on the Strip of Vegas. I had other plans.

Okay, back to that day of the party, the worse day of my life, it started like any other Saturday Papa had breakfast already, as I sat at the table, Steak and Eggs with crisp bacon and a few slices of Banana nut French toast with Blueberry syrup the best yup! After breakfast, I left to visit with my only friend, who was like a hermit. She had been caught plucking her eyelids out, pulling the eyelashes out by the root. 'Our sex was about pain and degradation, mortifications Yum, oh, such a Blast!'

Lisa's father was a frenetic, manic-depressant with an OCD disorder magnified with Narcissistic undertones. 'I know, sounds like a fancy dinner plate, lol. Anyways my friend Lisa had major stress that resonated from her… kind of fun to be around.' She had torn clumps of hair out of her head, and her mother had died like three months back from a Heroin overdose. This had exacerbated the 'trauma domicile,' not a fun house. Her father had seen the scabs on Lisa's stomach and upper arms. He had made a call to her therapist. I was afraid that she would be committed to a Psycho Ward. Lisa was a 'cutter' like deep wounds, with rows of scars on her skin… way before her mom had dropped dead!

Lisa's father was happy that I showed up that Saturday morning, and so was I. Yeah, see, I had a terrible crush on Lisa. Still, nothing in this world got me more excited, tightened undies pulsing than running that straight razor over Lisa's skin. Oh, it's the best, then I sometimes, if she let me, I would lick and suck the blood from the cuts. Other times she would be selfish and take the honors. Lately, I had moved the razor to Lisa's back, lol, so the blood was all mine! Yum! 'Lisa couldn't cum or Orgasm without a Cut!' Cool!

While Lisa and I were having our fun, what I didn't know was going to destroy Papa and me. Because Papa surprised me and bought a load of new furniture for our house, I received a four-poster Oak bed like King-sized… yes! He was getting a whole contemporary bedroom set. So, before I left for Lisa's, I took apart my Queen-sized bed for the furniture delivery service that was going to take our used furniture and donate it to the Salvation Army.

'Damn, I awakened for a second, and I rolled over, fk realizing I was locked in a tiny Jail Cell in Solitary Confinement inside of NIA Insane Asylum. Obviously, my dreams went awry, so surreal that I was alive two decades after the traumatic memories of what the hell went wrong. Why relive this?... no way to alter the past, make different decisions, 'stop please… leave me alone, no dreams, memories.' 😵.

While I was 5 miles away, 'carving up Lisa yum,' Papa had run into a problem the solid Oak dresser he had ordered didn't fit in his master room cuz of the angles, so he told the movers that my room had the space. It could easily be moved down the hall. This is where things got a bit sticky and hectic was it Fate or just bad luck? This changed our lives instantaneously. Papa went from overjoyed to overwrought with despair. A cyclone of devastation engulfed him. His vitality and spirit were plundered because as he emptied the contents of my dresser onto my new bed, taking each drawer out carefully, he stumbled onto my Secret! Stash… Damn!

Crap, I can see it now; OmLord, the bottom drawer concealed a stack of old newspaper clippings and my Journals in bright colors. The pictures of the two boys and girl that were buried alive in the cave were right on the top of the bundled newspaper articles, an excerpt I'd highlighted with smiley faces 'others around the accident swore they heard other voices!'

It only got worse from there. The teachers I had murdered, Mr. Bales and Ms. Garcia, fk! For closures, the worst of all was the damn little 5-year-old kid telling the Police that she'd heard a voice and seen a boy standing at the screened window of the kitchen where I had thrown my knives into their dad Ralph after he had barbequed Linda his wife and Mother in the Oven, leaving the three children orphaned no this wasn't good!

My journal was the last straw, no deniability. I hadn't any defense for all my crimes. If that's what you want to call them, I was guilty as sin, and Papa went berserk. I was going to prison. He waited for me to come home, all of this on his best friend's 50th Anniversary, which he helped host.

I was running late from my visit with Lisa… still, with the taste of the iron from her blood, the movers were gone as I opened Papa's front door. I'd lived with him since my mother's death from breast cancer. I saw a sight that nearly dropped me to my knees at the kitchen table. Papa had tears flowing; in his left hand was my Journal and all the newspaper clippings I'd cut out on the table.

His red glowing eyes saw right through me. He was stoic yet shaking in emotional distress, "you killed my daughter, your mother, and three children? You murdered four other adults using your 'God Given' talents that I not only encouraged you to realize and utilize, ugh, and master. I taught you Al… voice modulations and how to throw your voice." Papa stops shaking and blows his nose on a worn-out handkerchief.

"How could you, Al, murder your little brother in the swimming pool using your talents of throwing your voice pretending your baby sister was screaming from the screened door? Your mother, my daughter, ran to see what was wrong with the baby. When she was out of view, you flipped your little brother upside down in his rubber raft, pinning his head upside down in the pool. You are the 'Devil Incarnate.' You should be tortured to death. How many people have you Murdered? It's mindboggling that you'd kill your brother, my grandson… you're lucky that I don't have the Police here right now to arrest your slimy heartless soul."

No longer was tears falling. He was resolute; steadfast a firmness had evolved throughout his countenance like he had made a decision. You see, when Papa decided on something, he never wavered. Stubborn was an understatement, and I guess I'd inherited that trait from dear old Papa!

"I nurtured you, Al, and we had an uncompromising and unconditional bond, unbiased in my love for you… you are my blood. Al, I was there for you, always enhancing your Ventriloquism prowess. I helped you harness and develop your skills that are unmatched 'tonal inflections,' perfect pitch, accentuation, your ability to emulate and duplicate anyone's voice accent, to reproduce and impersonate after hearing barely a sentence spoken by any person. You're much more talented than I have ever been. What do you do with these unique talents, Al? You go out and proliferate Evil; you're a Monster, a Counterfeit Human being. I weighed the decision to call the police and have them here to arrest you when you showed up."

In this Dream, and even back then, I tried to speak. No, he wouldn't listen; he became impassive, impenetrable. Papa only said I must attend my friend's Anniversary tonight.

"This Anniversary I planned for the last five months. Your options Al, are to turn yourself in to the Police, or I shall report all that I know as he waves his thick-aged, spotted hands over the contents before him. Think about it, either way; you're going away to Prison for the rest of your life. Now I have to get ready to go," as he climbs out of his chair.

I can view this in my mind as clearly as if it was just two minutes ago, not two decades past; from above, I analyze how I can manipulate a change in venue, umh, to mitigate the inevitable conclusion. I can see my head in my hands at the very seat Papa had been perched in. He had taken all the damning evidence to his office, surely stashed it in his safe.

I watch him wind his way down the staircase, and, walking towards the front door, Papa only says, "Al, your killing of your mother, my precious daughter, could be rationalized. She had maybe a week to live and was in excruciating pain, a mercy kill. I might have done what you did if she had begged for death as she did per your Journal."

"But the rest of your Murders proves your inherently Evil and a demon in flesh and blood like an Anti-Christ. I will be back this evening; I suggest you turn yourself in or run away to hide. I'll give you that, Al. Get out of my sight, you are no longer my family," as he slams the front door.

By the time I hitchhiked 'my car's carburetor was messed up' to the VFW, the dance floor was filled. It was after 7 pm. He saw me immediately. Papa's face was acidulous, a corrosive glower framed in a full-on sneering scowl. The seat adjacent to him was my reserved seat. It was empty, so I slumbered over with some of Papa's friends patting me on the back, all smiles, the band's accordions in unison, the 'Polka' music contagiously upbeat, no one had a frown displayed no one except my 'PAPA!'

At 7:45, the feast was served food of every color and taste, a banquet style all in formations hot bar, salad bars, and even a dessert station. I waited my turn. The lines grew shorter, the music Bohemian and lively; Papa had slid his chair as far as he could from mine; I remember being so sad and lost, feeling sorry for myself.

Not remorseful, not guilty, or mad, I couldn't understand what the big deal was? am I a Sociopath? No, anyway, I guess

I was just angry to have been caught by Papa. I had no one left in this world but him. He was not only my legal guardian but my Idol, and I loved him! Papa didn't say a single word to me, he kept making trips to the soup bar, and once he had his full meal before him, all but dessert, he took a silver spoon and started ringing his champagne glass for everyone's attention. He made a toast for his beloved friends, warm words spoken of the couples decades together, and others joined in. All the partygoers got serious with their silverware.

Papa wouldn't even acknowledge that I was there or even alive. I felt so small and unwanted; he was the kind of man that nothing stopped him when he finalized something or made up his mind. He was relentless, unbending, undeterred. He remained as cold as an Iceberg towards me, but I understood. I knew Papa much better than he knew me. Sad!

I floated up above this huge spacious room. My view was in full 5 D Color, but the only person that my vision was locked on was my Papa. He was speaking to a lady on his right, enthralled in her description of some waterfalls she and her deceased husband had played and splashed in about ten years ago on a cruise to Jamaica.

I sat on Papa's left and felt awkward and out of place; he coughed then choked, and a shrilling wheezing whistle came from his throat! Oh no… He tried to catch his breath… his face was ashen pale, snorted, with his mouth wide open like his eyes, straining for oxygen. Something was terribly wrong. People from the party were at once at Papa's side. A doctor was behind Papa, and we were helping him from his chair. The doctor yelled, 'hold him up! We need to ensure that there isn't any food lodged in his throat.' The doctor was one of Papa's friends who performed the Heimlich Maneuver. A crowd surrounded us. Papa had a bracelet on his left wrist with a compartment that held a small pill, an antidote, a remedy that counteracted his deadly allergic reaction to 'Peanuts' his body's adverse effects would close his esophagus. His face became flustered and discolored.

I accidentally must have dropped his Lifeline; you know that small yellow pill, or did I? Then a Stare that I will never be able to overcome emblazoned, etched on my mind forever, weird Papa locked eyes upon mine. Papa's glare wasn't misconstrued, and I wasn't the only person who saw it. He looked through me with an evil scowl. Right past my Spirit into my soul, he knew that I had poisoned him, the glassy wide-eyed expression unwavering; I shouted, "he's got a serious allergic reaction to peanuts." The doctor friend pulled back his shirt sleeve further, knowing Papa had that damn bracelet. Shaking the bracelet, where did the antidote go where the hell was the pill? Yeah… Where?

I was torn out of the way by a swift shove as they laid him on his side, and 911 was called. An ambulance quickly transported me to Marin General Hospital. I, of course, rode in the back of the Ambulance with his best friend's umh, the Anniversary couple, and the doctor. I even held Papa's hand. I loved Papa… ugh, past tense, lol. He was in a coma for five days, and then he died, never regained consciousness, which I made damn sure of. I didn't want him lingering in pain! Nope, Mercy!

Earlier that day, before the 50th Anniversary party, I had dropped by a Safeway store and bought a pound of peanuts… took a blender, and ground them into a fine powder. I wore a long-sleeved shirt, took a baggie, put tiny pin holes in it, and walked from the salad bar to the soup bar, distributing the added ingredient. I even made a pass over the delicious Lasagna; I was having fun but remained focused and paid particular attention to Papa's plates. Sorry, Papa, Naw, you shouldn't have fked around with me. I am the true king of ventriloquists.

Just in case, before leaving the house and stopping for peanuts, I had retrieved all the incriminating paperwork from Papa's safe. He didn't know it, but I had his combination since I was 13 years old; it was my mom's birthdate!

I had tossed the blender in an Industrial garbage container behind a restaurant and skipped to my Lou away, singing with glee. In retrospect, all foods were tested, and the Detectives were all over the place. There weren't any peanut derivatives in any of the food that was prepared, None, so where did the peanuts come from? They had classified Papa's death as a Homicide. The cameras were so old at the VFW that they were not of any usefulness. I was the primary suspect. No one could figure out where all the nut powder had come from, and the tests proved the powder was on all foods. After a while, it became a Cold case like 'Dry Ice Cold!'

'Al hey, Al, wake up, take your fkn lunch tray' oh, thank God the guard on the intercom had woke me up. A food tray was stuck through my steel door slot. Now, if I could only stay awake. I don't want to have any more days and nightmares, 'dightmares,' Please! No!

-27-

4/27/17 Thursday, Present time… sisters Kamryn and Sara.

"Oh, you're awesome, Sara, thanks so much," as Sara covers her older sister's face and sprays the finishing touch of hair spray to hold a brand-new Gorgeous look, with a modification of the typical French braid, teasing her bangs in a reverse curl. "Let's go for a walk in the water park, sister. We need to talk." "Okay, Kam, let me first put all my stuff up. It's super nice that the staff here has given me like my own Salon."

"Sara, my sweet Lil sister, you deserve it. You're the best. 'Carl' peeks his head in after a fluttering knock on the door.

"Kamryn, geez, you are even more beautiful; I love what Sara has done to your hair. Wow!" "Thanks, Carl. My sister is an artist for sure; when she gets out of here one day, she will be famous and maybe work in Hollywood." "Oh, stop it, Kam… I'm not that good?" Carl leans, closely touching Sara, and says, "Sara, your way too modest everyone here at NIA raves about your skills and transformations. I should know; I have my ears open. Look at your appointment log. You're in demand, girl!" "Thanks, Carl. I appreciate all you have done to help make all of this possible," says Sara.

Sisters 15 minutes later, walking hand in hand past splashing fountains, Ducks, Swans even a couple of pink Flamingo's floating by. The sky was cloudless, bright blue, the temperature in the upper 70s, and the wind was blowing calmly, just enough to pass the scents from the flower gardens.

"Sara, Doctor Honcho contacted me a couple of weeks ago. She is concerned that my visits with you have become disruptive. You seem to change your personality and become distraught after my weekly visits; you have had to be sedated, even placed into a straitjacket, and locked down. I don't want that to happen anymore, Sara; please tell me what is happening. How can I help you, sweetie?"

"I've been visiting you here for over five years, and what you have achieved is beyond spectacular; my gosh, your so trusted here. They adore you. The strides you've achieved in your recovery are stupendous, and each report I read from Doctor Ame Amaya has me grinning from ear to ear. You're on a fast track out of here, IMO."

"I don't know, Kam. I guess I miss you so much and love you with all my heart. When you leave, I suddenly am lost alone, and I want to be with you to leave with you; depression engulfs me." "Sara, you're not being honest with yourself or me. We both know when this alternative behavior started, the time you ran and jumped into the pond, it was because of my not being able to visit you for two weeks!"

"Come on; it's because of my relationship with Edward. Isn't it the truth that your insecure and worried that he will take me away from you? I know this, Sara, but think. You just said how much you love me; don't you want me to be happy too? I was so lonely; I hadn't been in a serious relationship for years. "I do Love Edward, and I Love you." Sara twisted her hands around and bent her head down, kowtowing.

"I will never abandon you. I will be here to visit you like always," as she reaches out for a great big hug, but Sara… steps away. "Kam, a part of my mind tells me that I'm being so selfish. Yes, I'm jealous of him and am petrified that he will change our relationship. I'm sorry." Kamryn grabs Sara's shoulder. "Time will prove that you have nothing to fear. I will remain faithful to our sister; love, you're the only family I have, and that should be the same way you should feel about me, Sara. Which means we should be on the same page; we're all that's left of our family, right? Think, Sara haven't I been there for you from the very beginning?" "Yes, Kam, I couldn't have ever asked for a better sister; you're the greatest!"

"Doctor Honcho and I have discussed this fluctuation and shift in your moods and personality. Since I told you that he asked me to Marry him and we were engaged, your episodes have progressively worsened. Would you rather me not be forthright, honest, and not keep you abreast of what was going on in my life? Sara, I never want to regret not being candid and honest with you. I will never deceive you, for <u>deceptions are lies of omission</u>."

A long pause of silence, only the trickling of the stream over the rounded boulders. It's as if Sara was deciphering, formulating an appropriate response. "I asked you to bring him here so I could meet him over a month ago. Is he afraid to meet me, for I'm Insane, right, a nut? What because I'm a supposed lunatic crazy as a loon," as Sara's face contorts-then morphs into a sneer. Her lips flex upwards, a snarl of evil intent; she looks away, ensuring her sister doesn't see the Real Sara.

"I'm Psychotic, demented, right, Kam?" 'Stop enough, Sara!' "No, Kam, why don't you say it? He thinks I'm a murderess, Criminally Insane, but sista, I was never convicted of anything. The Fed's piled like 39 murders on me, a bunch of copycats. Who is to say I killed anyone?"

"Sara, let's not regress back into the abyss of the corrupt judicial system. This argument is in the past move forward, okay? I will have a talk with him and pick up some visiting forms when I leave today and see you next Thursday with a firm answer and game plan. Is that good enough for you, sis?" This time Sara relents; the sisters hug, and with a hidden snarling scowl, she exclaims, "Kam, yes, it would mean the world to me to get to know your future husband and soulmate."… Right!

Kam snatches up both of her hands and gets her full attention "we have set a date, and I want you to know before anyone else that our Wedding will be on 9/9/17, a Saturday morning!" Sara squeezed and dug her nails into Kam's wrist… Kam held steady, trying to meet her sister's eyes, and whispered, "sshhh, relax, please" for a split-second, Kam felt she saw a 'vicious hatred FERAL sneer of wickedness in Sara's eyes, which she'd never witnessed before, like a flash of Red Toxic fury then it left as fast as it appeared.'

Kam manages to help her shocked little sister… to sit back down on the bench. They stare out at the waterfall while other inmates are walking or being pushed in wheelchairs, a nice day for visiting families to have a picnic. The food was provided in the cafeteria to whoever asked, with picnic baskets filled with treats.

NIA was there to accommodate all the visitors. It was a first-class presentation… what the visitors didn't know wouldn't hurt them for now, thought Sara; this place is fake. If people really knew what was happening here! lol.

Sara finally shook it off, not really, but emphatically played it off; shocking as it was, she tilted her head sideways "why so fast? That's less than five months away; what's the hurry?" She follows that up, not waiting for the answer. "Where are you going to tie the knot." Kam's smile should have been contagious to anyone else except her sister, but nevertheless, her voice grinned from ear to ear; she was in love, really 'In Love.'

"Why wait? We'd been dating for almost four years and were not getting any younger. I've never felt like this, Sara. It's like, at times, my feet don't touch the ground. We're getting Married on Lake Shasta, you will be able to see all the pictures, and I will get permission from the Warden to bring the videos!"

"Edward's parents have a 70-plus foot Houseboat. Their friends will tie a total of five houseboats together in the Lake by Shasta Dam. It will be like a massive party barge; we're also renting an entire campground with cabins on the Shasta arm of the lake for all our wedding party friends and his family. We are driving tomorrow to Redding to take out the Houseboat and make other arrangements, Sara. You will be there in my heart; know this. I promise you will be able to watch the entire wedding!"

Sara bit her lip, had a significant pout on its way, then bounced back like a super ball, jumping up clapped her hands together "yes, sista, it will be a perfect wedding"… Nope!

5/24/10, seven years in the Past… Sara.

Sara landed at LAX. She flew south undisguised and had canceled her appointments till Wednesday morning so she could escape the Bay Area for a few days. She was on another mission. It was only supposed to be a quick turnaround. She also had changed up her routine this trip and flew with a private airline that had a service from SF to SD and then Las Vegas. Sara stepped down the stairs into a waiting taxi off to Hertz to pick up her driver. If her timing was good, she could be back in SF the next night while Brock and Lucie scoured San Francisco for her perfect ass, sweet!

"She didn't just vanish, Agent Link." "No, Homer, that's a definite for sure, although it's a distinct possibility she lives right here by the Wharf," mutters Lucie. Brock was busy working with other Agents trying to track Sara, the Granny, then the radio cackled with static… "we got her was heard over the radio ahhhh, video at the Rainforest Café."

Within minutes the three of them converged on the restaurant. Brock sprinted five blocks, breathing heavily as Lucie and Homer hopped into a vehicle. On the Rainforest Café's security system, they watched the video for the 3rd time, 'Granny ducks into the 2nd floor bathroom then in nine minutes slipped out the door the only resemblance of the old lady was this person was female also.

Sara transformed into a new vibrant Red head with deep blue eyes and a cute mole on her left cheek. A scarf covered much of her forehead and ears; the suitcase was identical, a new Sara on the prowl. One hundred fifty-five pictures were printed and passed to all local SFPD officers on duty. All Agents were given a super high gloss, high pixeled shot of Sara, now on all electronic devices and online. On Tuesday morning, the San Francisco Chronicle would run a Sara photospread "Have you seen this woman?" The reward had reached 175,000 dollars.

On Monday night, all local news stations would be broadcasting the pictures and no doubt sensationalizing her alleged crimes of evil and mayhem, as they always do. The reward would then blow up the phone lines and tip sites online.

Sara was South of the Agents at the time, about 357 miles.

Sara had only landed less than 24 hours ago. The pressure was on; the grill was on a low simmer with heat rising to a Broil.

Sara's new disguise look was exceptional. She had worked hours with products, materials, and makeup from her Storage building in San Diego, adding 55 pounds to her petite frame having solid pieces of foam lodged in her mouth to blow out her fat cheeks contact lenses of deep brown eyes with thick eyebrows a brunette with many wiggles and Curves call her Curvy she had a room at the Hyatt Hotel close to the L.A. Courthouse, where she was on the steps with a wave of reporters, her timing was impeccable. The astonishing trial results ended on Friday, another travesty of justice. Most of the naïve public expected the jury to quickly render a 'Guilty Verdict' in one of the highest-profile cases in the last seven years.

'Timmy 'Big Time' Grope,' the leading 'scorer' on the Lakers, was going to walk on another rape charge. It was his third high-profile case, and he'd walked free on the other two. His attorneys had ripped the intestines out of the witnesses. Some failed to even show up to court for the well-publicized trial. Suddenly noise erupted like a winning basket in overtime at the world championships, cheers then jeers. It was a mixed gathering indeed.

Rumors spread that monies were paid… lots of cash doled out because the number one eyewitness for the prosecution had waffled, had gone against her deposition, and faced Perjury charges. Cash was in charge; therefore, Timmy Grope was the King his entourage came strutting out of the Courthouse doors.

Broad white teeth shining now, the press surrounded him, the circus was in vogue, and he was hell-bent on altering the public perception of him being misogynistic and chauvinistic and a person who held contempt for all women. Timmy was aglow and barely could contain himself… his egotistical, self-centered, narcissistic 'Hero am I' persona had to take a backseat, and he realized he had to display some humility for the 'Double XXers' ugh females. The publicity he garnered had to be positive,… said his sports agents, for he had another huge contract to sign after the season. With cameras in his fan's hands, he was in righteous form and would answer all questions with a gold tooth display.

"Look, I was found Not Guilty; I'm Innocent. These women were after me for my millions of dollars to be with a celebrity and the honor to hang off of my arm." The TV cameras rolled, ESPN, FOX, MSNBC, and TMZ, too many cameras to count; everywhere you turned, there was a microphone.

In the middle of this mass of humanity was pudgy Sara. In her black-gloved hand was a microphone, patiently waiting her turn. Upon her head was a hat that she had sewed the acronym 'BBC;' this was congruent with her accent British all the way. "Timmy was kept in the center of the mass of newsies by five large bodyguards. He enjoyed himself immensely, shouting like a Rock Star to his fans and the people who came out to support him.

<u>*Yet there was another faction that carried signs and placards for women's rights… for human rights, that had megaphones and were ranting about the injustice of allowing Timmy to go free…*</u>

"He took the opportunity to point at the lesser group and said, "I love those women, for them to say that I'm a misogynist, a hater of ladies. They need only to interview my mama. It's easy to get on the bandwagon against a superstar. It's merely a hate smear campaign for money. This is why I believe that in the USA, you are innocent until proven guilty, and as you all can see, I'm innocent of all charges once again. The Witch Hunt proves false! 'Proof I'm Innocent!'

He let out an uproarious Howl, and his followers were laughing along with him high fives and pats on the back; fist bumps and grins were congruent. Timmy Grope was a happy narcissist; his entourage and everyone around him were paid to uphold his ego. 'To hell with moralities turning blind eyes and wickedly squinting… it was always about the money.' Ugh, despite many of their inner feelings or beliefs, money talked and walked, Timmy… was speaking into microphones and grinning at the cameras from all angles.

Sara tried to get closer to him. He was now answering questions from selected reporters. In her quaint British Voice, "Mr. Grope, your overseas fans, your world base of fans, would like to hear from you!" This immediately got Timmy's attention. He beckoned his hand out and pointed to one of his bodyguards who went to retrieve Sara and make a path for her to interview their boss. Sara stepped forward with her satchel on her left shoulder and microphone in her gloved right hand attached to a retractable line. "I just heard you say that you donated $300,000 to Orange County's women's shelters. Could you please tell the world full of your loyal fans who idolize you why you're doing this?" asked chubby Sara. 'Timmy 'Big Time' Grope' looks down upon her and then asks, 'where are your cameras?'

Sara points to a throng of assembled cameras. He grinned large, reaching out as she handed him the microphone, "to my world fan base, I want to say <u>I…</u> his last word spoken was so Appropriate <u>'I' I, I</u> he fell backward, grasping his throat an odd expression of the cat that swallowed the Canary whole suddenly chaos reigned the crowd acted as if a gunman was in the area and had fired a smattering of bullets.

Sara calmly pulled back her oily, jelled, soaked microphone, making sure no one else could accidentally be touched by it, swiftly put it in her bag, and nearly fell people shoving and pushing… screams are heard over the shouts for a doctor, Sara knew no doctor could 'save the already dead bastard.'

Timmy Grope 'Little Time,' the poison systemically entered his blood system through the pours in his skin right past the epidermis of his left hand. Yep! Sara carefully maneuvered away from the scene. In 25 minutes, she had changed into her hotel room and vacated. Her first stop would be a payphone, and she mused how difficult that would be in the year 2010, but her 'throw-down phones' were in her storage in SD, so she decided a payphone would work this time.

Sara was lucky, parking across the street from a convenience store, a pay phone unused with a load of coins, she dialed or pushed the numbers. Brock's cell phone... he didn't pick up her call, but on the 5th ring, his Voice-mail did. "Hey, there, Brockster, it's your number One... uhm, numeral uno fan, Timmy Grope, was found innocent by his paid peers, I found him guilty when the mice are away. Kittie will play Seeya."

She returned to her rental car that had stolen license plates and drove south to San Diego. It was 5:31 pm on a typically pleasant day in Southern Cal.

-28-

Brock, Lucie in San Francisco.

Brock and Lucie were positioned at a table in a hotel room on a video conference call with their superior Director, Tanya Firm, who was in Washington DC. Who was reading them the riot act? Not in the least bit happy with their performance in their investigation of the Serial Vipress 'Sara.' Things weren't going well. They didn't need telepathic vibes. They only had to see the countenance of the US Attorney General and the rest of the uppity powers to be.

A special Agent investigator from Washington D.C. was going to take over the Serial Killer Sara case. Brock's task force would be eliminated and shifted to other investigations and divisions. Part of his team would be reassigned to the new Special Agent that was going to be in charge of the Vipress case. She would pick and choose her own task force; a debriefing was scheduled for the following Monday.

Brock stood with Lucie, who clicked off the real-time video conference call, leaning and bowing their heads... together they dropped into despair. He speaks first, "how could they do this to us?" then he raises his hand, "no, don't answer that!" they were both aware of the politics. Justifiably Sara had been on a rampage for years, still going strong. But Brock was given the lead investigation status only three years prior, and they were closer now than ever to catching Sara... Lucie exclaims, "well, that gives us a full seven days to nail that bitch!"

"Let's see what kind of tips turn up from our Blitz of the media. The reward is substantial; we know Sara is somewhere near you and me, Brock!" Lucie turns the flat 55-inch screen on the wall towards them and switches on the channel to the local 6 pm news. They were lost reading messages and updates on their phones when instantly their mood changed. A bold flashing headline blasts across the screen 'Timmy Grope' is dead at 25 years old, an apparent heart attack right on the L.A. courthouse steps. Brock sucks in a large breath. "Heart attack shit, the guy was in phenomenal Basketball shape cardio-wise! How the hell, geez, I guess you never know, huh? When it's your time, it's your time, but Timmy just was getting ready to sign that Whopping contract with the Lakers, who would have gone over him medically with a fine-tooth comb... wow!"

Lucie sounded off with a disdainful growl, "yep, God works in amazing ways, that's for sure!" "What not a fan, woman?" "Nah, man, I was a fan of his moves on the basketball court, not his moves off the court hell, rumor had it he had his Juvenile records expunged. The guy, even as a teenager, attacked several girls that were younger than him, even allegedly drugged some of them, and was accused of the rape of a 13-year-old, of course, all 'Off the Record." "You're right, Luce; he was a monster off the court." Then the news segment they had wanted to see was on the screen.

Sara's picture was plastered over the entire screen. "Well, if that doesn't draw some attention to our cause, nothing will. Let's get back out there, Luce!" They packed up and rolled down the elevator into the Crown Vic. Brock was listening to a few VMs on the second recording. He slams the brakes down they spin sideways into the curb, stopping on a dime!

Luce is shockingly caught lunging forward by her seatbelt "fk Brock, what the hell was that? Was there an invisible dog in the freakin road? I mean, seriously, dude, what…."He activated his speakerphone, listening once again to Sara's recorded message. They both exited the car. Luce was on the line with the home office, and Brock was with the Forensic team. Sara had struck again; while they were in S.F.… she was in L.A.

"Brock, where did Sara get your cell number from?" In between calls, he didn't reply; instead was busy arranging a private flight back to L.A. He'd already sent in a request to trace the number that Sara had called from… his stomach was whirling upset, sick.

"Brock, how did Sara know 'we Mice' were out of town? Referring to the message they had listened to on a loop her, the… Kitty Cat, she'd referred to them, uhm, as ahh rodents or mice. We know she has my address, your home's whereabouts hell. Sara was in your driveway now, your personal cell number, eerie, almost paranoid, is my feeling." "You're right, Luce… Sara even did her due diligence research like a bloodhound located my ex-wife Patti and killed her!"

"With that being said, perhaps we could set up a trap; let's get to the airport. We can leave Agent Homer Lan in charge up here in Northern California."

<u>5/2/17 Tuesday present time, Ame and Donny.</u>

Don knocks on Ame's office door 'come in' "Hey doc, umh Ame, wow, you're doing something right; Ms. Slimson looks like she's put on some weight. I couldn't see her cheekbones when she came in; they were not as sunken in her face. She even had some color. Ame doesn't comment as her phone thrips, 'hello, Doctor Amaya.' "Hi Doctor, this is Doctor Honcho. I just had some time to not only go over your report but spend time with Sara and Al umh, what a magnificent job you've done, Ame. It was nice to see Sara back to being herself and working in her salon again." Ame blinks and says, "your welcome, Liz."

"This after her sister Kamryn gave her the news of her wedding date and plans; Sara seemed to take it with a grain of salt. I'm impressed, and Al is back in population acting the fool but watching his 'P s and Q s' just called to thank you for your expertise in handling a few of our difficult patients!"

While Ame spoke and listened on the phone call, she sketched on 11 X14 inch drawing paper… and churned out three caricatures. Don was amazed at the quality of one of them. Dr. Honcho was on her phone at her desk, details down to folders, a lamp and a curtain blowing in the air, a window open, and even a tree in the background.

Ame hangs up. "I don't care too much for ole Liz Honcho, can't place my finger on it, aah perhaps it's her weekly makeover by Sara that seems to be of most value to her remember Donny all Sara's expertise and work is free to everyone, in my mind she's being used. But hey, she enjoys what she's doing, actually loves doing it, but Honcho is really working her weekly." Don laughs "yeah, I've met Honcho; she could double for the wicked witch of the South in the Wizard of Oz, I'd like a before, and after picture of her taken by Sara still I'd say she would have to create a miracle to make her a 5 out of 10!" "Stop it, Don, looks aren't everything!"

Ame swivels her desktop monitor around "here are the latest updated pictures of NIA staff members 'look at Doctor Honcho!" "No way, shit, she got plastic surgery," Ame giggles, covering her mouth. "Donny, stop that man… that isn't nice, geez." Donny reaches past her and clicks on NIA's board of directors. "Now, see what Honcho really looks like" they lean in on the monitor. Ame says, "you've made your point, Donny; let's get some dinner." Don looks over at his boss-lover friend, "sounds like another night of fun… Yum."

Ame winks at him, "I still haven't got you back for your violation of my body." "Aah cum on Ame, you dug it. You only don't want to admit it, lol!" "PBMF,' says Ame, 'payback is a mother fker' boy. I'm going to getcha." "Oh Ame, I'm like shaking in my boots or tennis shoes, so scared, big bad Ame is going to get me, should I run and hide? Naw, I don't think so. LMAO…."

They both chuckle, Ame a smidgen longer than Don. "I will shut down the office, be ready in seven minutes," he says as he turns to go out the door. Slash, snap as Ame reaches down and picks up her just purchased Black leather whip. With a perfect crack, she popped Don on the left ass cheek. He fell forward, squirming. She snaps it, again and again, Don's chirping like a castrated puppy dog. Now Ame rolls over on the floor, Howling Yep! "Who's laughing now?" She hysterically holds her belly. Don kicks the door close, "you bitch, ouch, that still stings, damnit, Ame!"

<u>**4/29/17 Shasta Lake Saturday 5:05 pm.**</u>

"Whatcha think, my lady?" "Umh, I'm exhausted, is for sure, Edward. I'd say we've had an eventful and successful trip up here. What do you think, honey?" "I love the area; your parents are fortunate to have retired here. As your dad says, it's God's country!" "Kam, your so cool, girl… to think that we found each other through all the adversities. Our story would be one to write about. I adore you." Kam shifts her weight forward and clutches his left hand. "Yuh, I know I hated your sight, literally despised your every breath. All I can say is that it's our destiny and that love can overcome all obstacles. We're living proof, babe." "no argument here. I felt the same way towards you, that's for sure, sweetheart. Who woulda thought us In Love" he steps out onto the deck "wow, it's still hot out here."

Edward takes another pull on his iced mug of beer. She raises her white <u>wine glass</u> and cheers on their excellent fortune, their love, and commitment, 'check it out,' she points up into the air, an Osprey with a fish in its mouth flying to its nest. Flying way up to the top of a pine tree, 'it's so beautiful here, I could sit out here forever' he choked down a gulp and snickered, 'I agree.' "Kam, we're at the dock and haven't even gone anywhere. Wait till we take this houseboat for a cruise!" they were anchored-tethered off at the mooring spot for his parent's houseboat on the top deck, relaxing after doing a complete cleaning and dusting preparation for the upcoming wedding and party. They were going to have dinner on the water at the Bridge Bay Resort, a fantastic restaurant named 'Tails Whale.'

"So, Kam, as I've told you, it gets hot as Hades up here. A few years back, my dad sent me a front page from the Redding Searchlight, the local newspaper; the headlines were, 'The Hottest Place on Earth' was Redding, California. One hundred nineteen degrees, it's not a rarity to have like nine days in a row of plus 110-degree temperatures. That's when an ice-cold brew tastes the best how can you drink wine when it's so damn hot?"

"Edward, as I've told you, I am allergic to hops, uhm, beer. Besides, I can't stand the taste. I enjoy the taste of wine well, only white wine when it's hot. But my favorite is Red Zinfandel …" "I have never met someone allergic to beer another first. I enjoy red wine and will be indulging with you." "Okay, Edward, there are so many flavors and varieties. I've ordered a special bottle for dinner, a 'Staggs Leap' Cabernet…." He nodded, then shared, "I want you to at least try this special beer. It's a 'Doppelbock' from Germany before you stave off beer forever, Kam. Oh, so tasty shall we get changed?" Kamryn thinks, didn't he listen to what I have been telling him I abhor? Beer, oh well, no reason to rock the boat!

"Kam, we have plenty of time dinner isn't until 6:45 pm, and it's in walking distance, but we will take the Golf cart over to Bridge Bay." He takes her by the elbow "we have enough time to make love, then shower," she skips to her feet, 'well, Hellyeah!' The best kind of appetizer-yummy my 'stud muffin'… off they go. Yep!

They had finalized all their wedding arrangements earlier. The rest of the evening was about rest, hugging, cuddling, and loving tomorrow… a brunch with his parents, then back to the city, the Bay Area, another world indeed. Kam and Edward forever, she mused after her horrendous breakup five years before. She couldn't believe she had 'fallen in love' and trusted another man, but she did! Aww!

29

Sara was in the Past in 2010, the same day she eliminated Timmy Grope! Sara wasn't much fond of her moniker... 'The Vipress Serial Killer.'

Sara sits back on her stool with a pitcher of beer, grasping her cool ice-melting mug and sipping away with a picturesque view of the town of La Jolla east of San Diego. The patrons were abuzz with the chitter chatter of the death of Super Star Stud Timmy Grope, but what had bothered her wasn't that topic, which only brought internal satisfaction. Nope, she had other major league issues to deal with. Looking at her iPad, a picture of herself, she punched the headlines, and multiple websites popped up OMGod with a reward of $175,000. A few sites even had her Granny disguise; the Muslim and Maid outfits, her disposition drops into the toilet. Many internet sites had her descriptions from other sightings and many different pictures with aliases, height, and weight variations. The nape of her neck tingled; tiny hairs were prickling, and a nervous tension took hold as she filled her glass a 3rd time.

Sara wasn't a stress-laden gal, always 'cucumber calm' even putting up with the typical macho show-off amongst the bar's crowds. About that time, she watched from her peripheral vision the same annoying Romeo that was with a group of men who sat nearby at a table, get back up. The guy wouldn't take 'No' and strutted back to her. "Why don't you join us? It has to be better than sitting here alone?" "I doubt it. Can't a lady be left alone, or is it your duty to invade my personal space? Please leave me alone for the 3rd time!" He tilts his head back to the table of guys after being rebuffed, deflected, and shunned once again. A hoot and holler erupted from the drunkest of em.

Romeo then bends over to within inches of Sara's nose… angrily declared, "you ain't all of that, lady, last night I had a better lookin woman than you by far. You're a lesbian, probably a bitch for sure!" Sara then taps her purse; his whisky breath lingers on her skin, the spit from his loose mouth she wipes from her cheek. She, in a flash, whips her open hand forward to slap the shit out of his face, which remained near hers.

He must have anticipated this retaliatory action and easily blocked her swing, laughing heartily. The bartender was upon the table in an instant "madam, is there a problem here?" "No, I was just leaving, only talking with the lady Ralph!" Ralph waited with a gesture towards her "aah, everything is all right, only boys being boys," she said, "could you bring me a shot of Dewers?"

Romeo wipes his forehead; damn, thinks I don't want to be 86-d from here again like last year "your kinda cool, lady," he says as he returns to his table. Sara, angered, 'I don't have time for this crap. Why can't a single woman go out and get something to drink and be by herself like a dude? Double standard 'man's world, it's bullshit!' muses, maybe I should start a T-shirt business for women that just want to go out and enjoy themselves without the obligatory sexual pick-up lines, 'not interested' or 'please leave me alone.' <u>Ughhhh, 'I need alone time' she stares around the pub, counting at a minimum nine guys drinking, watching sports on the tubes, and relaxing by themselves, because she has a freakin Vagina. She's like open Meat, so Sad!</u>

She was not in disguise… just being herself, blonde long curly hair, greenish speckled eyes, her petite self all of 135 pounds, 5' 3" tall in heels, all muscle and lean taut skin, every feature aligned pert nose matching luscious ears, her neck a sensual paradise she knew she was a beauty. She could have opted for breast augmentation enhancements. Nope, her B-cup boobs were a solid attribute. With her sway back and upturned tight little ass, she felt confident, desirable, sexy, and erotic in all the right spots as she reflected on her gorgeous body. Too bad she masturbated so much and didn't share her flesh with other lovers, but her body was her domain, owned and manipulated by yours truly. Oh well? The last lover was a hot ebony-skinned lady. She rarely went with her own gender, but the black woman eked out sexual energy I couldn't resist... into men 85% of the time, but hey, I was an equal provider 'secure in my skin!'

She glances back at the five guys. Romeo was sweating and seemed to be gawking in her direction, maybe whispering. Then she spied three other candidates in slinky attire, females on the floor in heat... who were there to meet the males on the prowl, and she wished she had time to watch and observe the pickup scene, the meat market in full bloom.

But the reason Sara was still in the San Diego area was that while surfing on 'Tor' the 'dark web,' she'd found another illegitimate advertisement and followed up on it. The purchase of children from Mexico... she had an appointment with a pimp who bought poor little children, girls, and boys from across the border to Prostitute, a smuggler of human flesh. For the deviates that paid for sex with children, she had posed as a high-dollar buyer online. The Coyote was to meet her at a Casino, which would be texted over on her Trac burner phone, a convenient throwaway.

Sara had stopped by her storage and selected a delectable, proper disguise with a few of her toys and weapons. She would stop at a gas station and change into the costume for this task. Sara patiently waited for the text to let her know which Casino she would meet the Coyote and the children. What she couldn't hear over the jukebox music were these words, 'no, I'm not wasted, not drunk. I'm telling you what I saw. Ain't no question that the resemblance is indisputable. It's got to be her right there. When I leaned over her, I saw her iPad screen... I'm not bullshitting, dude. No, it said a $175,000 reward. I couldn't read it all, only parts… Man, it's like she's the fkn Serial Killer that's been all over the news and social media!'

The table fell about itself. The other guys were mocking him, laughing at him in total ridicule, calling him drunk and a fool. One said oh, I'm so scared of that tiny woman; please don't sic her on me. Lmao, have another one, dude! Sara's 7th sense was on alert. She downed the Scotch. It did nothing to numb the intuition, a strange transference of odd ambiance… that took ahold of her like a thick fog. They were all eyes peering at her, not interested in the five felines now sitting at a nearby table, who were doing their 'best or worst' at getting the guy's attention.

Something was way wrong, but what? Then she looked 'from the corner of her eye,' her iPad screen went to screensaver. Pushing her finger over the pad, Omg, and there she was Vibrant full color. Oh fk, no, even with the many disguises, the resemblance was beyond uncanny Romeo could have seen the screenshot. Wtf. That is why I'm getting the Evil glares. Then she hears, 'I'm going to call the police' Romeo's mouth flapping.

"This is for real, dudes that bitch is worth a Buck 75 thousand dollars, and I plan on collecting it!" Sara had a bagged squirt gun of deadly poison in her purse, plenty to kill everyone at that table. She also had a 45 Caliber pistol in her car, now with shivers up and down her spine. How could she have been so stupid 'this is how most of the brilliant Serial Killers were caught, plain bad luck, by accident. If she paid the bill and strolled out, would they follow her?

The plates on her automobile were not hers. Could she make her way out of this pub? Closing down the iPad, she waves to the bartender, mimes her hand as if writing for the final tally, gets up, and walks past the men to go to the ladies' room.

Suddenly Romeo snaps her picture with his phone, not once but machine-gun style, maybe even with video. She stops, grabs her water pistol holds it tight, pulling on it inside her purse. "What the hell are you doing?" she angrily shouts; once again, the bartender was 'Johnny on the spot.' "Why are you harassing me? Let me have your phone… delete my pictures. You're an asshole; what the Hell?" Sara was Livid, furiously ripping at Romeo's phone.

Romeo blurts out, "be careful; she's a Serial Killer, a murderess fk there is a 175,000 reward for her." Ralph, the bartender standing over the table, says, "Your cutoff; you're out of here, Marvin. Get going!" Sara throws her arms up in utter disbelief, "OMGod, R U kidding me? I'm a Serial Killer?" "Yeah, see, she just admitted it. She said she's a serial killer," growls Marvin.

Behind Ralph, the manager appeared. "Ms., you owe nothing. I will comp your bill. Sara takes out a twenty-dollar bill, stuffs it into Ralph's top pocket, and instead of going to the restroom, spins abruptly towards the door but has to hear the last words ominously prophetically, "Marvin, where the hell did you escape from? Was it Napa Insane Asylum?" NIA. Ironic? Huh!

As the door closed behind her, she heard another voice coming from someone she'd seen roaming, um, surfing the internet on a laptop. He yelped out, 'Marvin isn't lying!' He screams, 'don't let her go!' Not running, but with one hand on her unwrapped squirt gun, gloveless, hoping it doesn't leak, her pace quickens. The door blasts open 55 feet from her, and a couple of guys burst out. She's already close to where she'd parked, always using 'forethought' finding an advantageous position, always backing her vehicle into an easy access spot. She opens her car door as the first guy, Marvin, is running only 25 feet from her, yelling, 'stop you fkn bitch!'

Others are now crowding out of the pub; she spins the gravel at Marvin and takes off-lucky she knows the area well. La-Jolla had been a City she had lived in for a short time. From the vantage point of the rearview mirror, a truck sped after her, followed by several other fools. Oh great, now she was in a race. She had a good head start and took the chance running a Red light... she knew that if a cop saw her, she would be arrested, busted, and jailed. She needed this Bullshit like a hole in the head. This was freakin Brock Dame and Lucie Links doing. They would suffer slow deaths! Plastering her pictures all over the fkn Internet, oh, they're So Dead!

She could face the death penalty. No, they had Zero evidence; she was sweating with the Chevy Camaro's AC on Freeze mode. No one was in the rearview mirror. She took the downtown exit nine minutes later. She parked down the block from her San Diego office; her options were to park the rental car at the Hertz office at the San Diego Airport and pay the difference because she rented it at LAX.

Her vehicle was parked in her space at the office building. Flustered, she wasn't thinking. Slow down, analyze, stop freaking out; you escaped Marvin 'Sara, get a grip!' Relax, breathe. Should she fly out tonight, go home, and forget the Coyote... pimp? Her mind flashed and jumped from subject to subject. She couldn't concentrate like she had drank a pitcher of espresso coffee. The alcohol had left her body with the adrenal glands rush, feeling anxious and jittery, like wired out. Mistakes had already been made. How did they track her to the Rainforest Restaurant Bar?

She was Granny Sara. Where was the fkn camera that took my picture? I wasn't careless; I added a mole and colored contacts to my eyes, changed my hair color, and altered my body's proportions; this is beyond perplexing. Marvin was right. I didn't change my appearance enough at that Café in Fisherman's Wharf, but that was because I never thought the

Feds could trace and track me to the S.F. Airport... shit becoming complacent.

Surely letting my guard down got lax crap. I'd done the same exact trip 35 times, no less it was always secure, damnit! No way they could find her real name; if she could have flown with her blocking device on and a 45 Caliber gun... with more toxic juice spray, she would have. She had dozens of disguises. She peered over at the floorboard, knowing her stun gun and handcuffs were tucked away; oh, what the hell? She had a suitcase packed full of accessories, but she was limited. The Airport couldn't function with a blocking device on full tilt. She was forced to play by the rules; therefore, she was forced to play their game here. Vulnerable and weary, she soldiered on.

Onto the next subject, she used her real name on the flight to LAX, so what? Another voice said so what? Her mind was like an echo chamber in normal and in abnormal times. She could maintain Sara until stress slammed her. Now she was broken in all directions; should she return home to Mill Valley and forget the Coyote, umh, the pimp?

What if someone looked beyond the color of my hair and eyes and the mole and picked me out? The only reason Marvin put 2 and 3 together and found five was that she was sitting in front of the freakin pictures on the iPad screen at the bar, and he nosed in and saw the reward. She had a carry bag with the new disguise, a simple change, blasting back well, the Feds now would know she was down here in So-Cal hell. She called Brock and left her calling card regarding Timmy Grope now Marvin at the pub had her actual pictures on his phone... not good.

Geez, I'm genuinely screwed. They now have my white Chevy Camaro rental. How long will it take them to locate the airport rental agency? Answer duh uh, not long... decision fly home and drop off all incriminating equipment at combo locker and storage in San Francisco. I needed to beeline back to my storage building and then get home. Grab the laptop that I work with on the Dark Web. Check Brocks Dame's phone… search to see what he and the FBI are doing. Then research all my clandestine accounts and Bitcoin transactions, take everything to the S.F. storage must be prepared for a Federal onslaught of Search Warrants. Even though I hitchhike on other people's Wi-Fi systems, the Feds could trace my actions, If they get any of my computers.

You can't catch me there, Brock. Am I being a bit too paranoid… shit? Damnit, I have Real Estate offices in San Francisco, Los Angeles, and San Diego, uhm, they haven't any proof. Paranoia is methodically attacking my internal self… stop! Nothing in any office, zero phones with harmful material, and no DNA, but wait, ugh, now they have some actual pictures of me at the pub. I could be in trouble… if not for bad luck, I'd have no luck at all. My co-conspirators within my skull are itching, spoiling for a fight, and are upset with me. Yep, I should have jumped back on the airplane after disposing of Timmy Grope… Indeed if they broadcast the pictures that Marvin had taken, '<u>clients of mine will be calling the Hot Lines.</u>' <u>The FBI could link the pub pictures to her actual identity!</u> .

Sara then compartmentalizes all with resolve, 'let's go to storage, then LAX next to the warehouse in S.F., then home and lay in wait for Brock and Lucie to knock or bash down my door, convinced clearly, they will surely be coming for me. She was nodding at her reflection in the rearview mirror. Let's do it with discipline and determination. I will persevere; I will never be caught, never apprehended. Lol, well, maybe arrested and charged with all that bullshit, but how could they convict me? This Sucks!

<u>**Lucie and Brock are on a flight to LAX… to investigate the Timmy Grope fiasco.**</u>

Lucie taps on Brock's shoulder "hey, hon, get ready. We're on approach to LAX," he rubs his eyes "well, heck, how long was I out, Luce?" "not long enough, I'm sure, but you did have a baby snore raging," she grins. "Looks like we have about a week to solve this case, or D.C. Agents will kick us to the curb. We will be relegated to clean up," Lucie declares. "Naw, I will fight them all tooth and nail, Luce; let us nail Sara. We're so close I can smell the bitch!"

They powered up the electronic devices getting ready to exit the private jet and follow up on the Timmy Grope death. Their phones were Blowing up; by the time they'd taxied to a halt. Brock and Lucie had another destination, supposedly, someone had taken pictures of the serial killer Vipress 'Sara' down in a drinking establishment in San Diego. Brock asked the flight attendant if they could remain on the plane to its final destination, San Diego Executive Airport. He was told, 'sorry; you both could be knocked off the plane. All the seats were booked for the entire flight to San Diego… This was their original destination, so you must depart here at LAX. I'm sorry; thank you for understanding.'

Lucie and Brock watched as the private jet filled with executives and the Who's Who knowing it was just a matter of time until they were booted from their seats… 'whatever, I'm FBI, I'll pull a power play,' mutters Brock. Luce was on the phone to Wash. D.C. strings were pulled; egos massaged 15 minutes delayed. Lucie and Brock continued south to an arranged meeting with Marvin, his friends, and Ralph, the bartender at a La Jolla Pub called the 'Brigg.'

"I wonder how sober any of them will be? Luce… this has the likelihood to be the major break in this case, although all that Marvin spoke about was the rewards, the reward he wasn't given up nothing without that." Lucie shakes her head affirmatively "yeah, Homer's FBI team in San Francisco splattered social media and arranged all the publicity on the internet, we live in interesting times, where you can put out on the airwaves pictures of a wanted person within 35 minutes the information is worldwide Twitter, Facebook, Instagram… Google and on and on, how somebody sitting in a bar almost 1,000 miles away looks at a woman and then picks her out of a crowd… Karma equals our destiny, Brock!"

"Luce, it didn't quite happen like that. Supposedly Sara was surfing the Web and had found her pictures and reward under female fatal Serial Killer or something like that." "Still without the Internet, we'd be in L.A. dealing with the Grope murder!" "You're correct… I have a positive vibe, babe, about this trip." 'Babe huh' a slip of the tongue, oops, another slip as he gently elbows her with a pig-eating grin.' Lucie smirks "you're outta control, dude; I've now learned that P.T. can stand for two other words instead of 'Prick Tease, Pussy Tease,' they grin as they touch down in San Diego.

"The P.T. is not intended, Luce, my best and hottest female friend. I truly adore you. Can we talk about us later, please?" "Absolutely, I will hold you to it; Brock, let's do it!" The drive was smooth, parking at the Brigg Pub 39 minutes later; they'd preplanned the meeting with Marvin on the short drive. Standing in the middle of his friends was Marvin. The time was 11:25 pm. Only three of the group remained a workday the next day, a Tuesday. They no longer were drinking alcohol well, not much. The group settled for Irish Coffee, lite on the booze, and across the top of their table were remnants of chicken wings. Ralph worked till closing and served the three of them with whirling confusion. Musing, 'I had her at my bar. She was so calm. She always seemed to have a hand in that purse of hers. Could she have had that 'VX' type of poison spray inside? Well, perhaps, although I shall never know,' then his manager said, "Hey, Ralph, you have customers over here." Duh, Ralph thinks, what an asshole. Why didn't he serve them himself? The pub was brimming with people. It was a full house for a Monday night!

The buzz in the Pub called the Brigg was about their infamous visitor this afternoon, 'check this out. This is the best pic of her white Camaro.' As Marvin shows a video clip, then he flips back over to the still pictures. "Does it get better than this close-up? Look at those Emerald eyes." "Yeah, but Marvin, the woman's picture shows her with dark black eyes, brunette with a mole the size of a fkn dime!" Doug, the nerd of the 3-some, slapped the table and yelped, 'I got it.' Doug was in his 3rd year of a 4-year degree at the Art Institute, a touted learning Academy in downtown San Diego.

He slides over the small screen of his laptop. On the left side partitioned was the S.F. Sara on the right, the La Jolla Sara 'Photo Shopped' with another type of morphed software Doug had used. See, identical, and it's fricken her… that's $175,000

sitting there, blurts out Marvin. "I'm not giving up the pictures, nothing Dougy. Don't show anyone that comparison till we got a deal, or they will steal the reward money." 'Yuh got it, bro' as he closes down the computer at about that time, Brock and Lucie show up at the entrance.

'The suits are here,' says Doug "keep it cool, let me do the talking, shouts Marvin, don't act overanxious they need us. Heck, that's a fine piece of ass on that cop bitch, like the way her skirt rides up on those muscled thighs… I bet she's a mouthful in the sack and probably likes it rough, lol. You know, cuffs, chains, cop women, you wanna let them play dominant!" Doug chirps in, "I'll play subservient to that hot ass cop, but I bet she likes the young studs. She looks to be in her mid-thirties. You know that's when they're dripping."

The manager has Brock and Lucie in a secluded corner of the pub. All of them stare down at Ralph, and the bartender then sets their sights on Marvin's table. "Hey, Brock, why don't you handle the guy behind the bar I will take on the table with the threesome? A few of them are giving me a drooling look, yah no 'lady in uniform' with a discreet elbow to Brock's ribs.

Louder than he intended or wanted, the music had lulled, 'No, we do this together.' "Oh, Brock, do I sense a tinge of jealousy?" "I guess you do if you have an overactive imagination," he elbows her right back.

They enjoyed the flirtatious play on words, a form of foreplay at that very instant as their eyes melded. Lucie knew he'd be inside her as one, if not tonight, real soon, 'he conceded the testosterone urge he wanted to taste her explode deep inside her boiling loins. Stop concentrate. You're on the job; was I jealous? He asked himself, nada Yeh!'

Marvin and his pals wait, sipping their drinks as the detectives interview Ralph and the Manager with grainy blurred images in their grasp from the outdated bars security system. Doug says, "I can see from here, Marv, the pictures the manager gave the Agents could be almost any of the 25 women in this pub." "I know, bro; let's hold our water. We give them nothin without a signed contract agreement, okay?"

He warns again, 'we need not be acting too eager' as Brock and Lucie approach the table, Ralph on their tail "hey, why don't we take this little get-together into our banquet room" the manager said, 'that would be cool, follow me.' Ralph waves and points and unlocks the door… and hits the lights. 'I gotta get back to the bar, folks,' he turns to the Agents "if you have any follow-up questions, you know where to find me!" 'Thanks,' said Brock as Ralph exited.

30

Marvin Payco snitches out Sara…

Marvin takes the lead vocals in the introductions, "I believe with all that's me I deserve the reward for if not for me, neither of you Agents would be sitting here now," holding his phone up. "I have close-ups, uh, digital images of this Sara, pictures of her vehicle license plate; I tried to follow her, but she lost me at the entrance to Hwy #1, so before I turn anything over to you guys, I want this in writing!" "It's you 'Marvin, who originally called in the tip,' is that correct?" "Yes, Marvin Payco is my name."

Lucie continues, "we cannot promise you anything; we're the lead investigators. I can tell you that if the evidence you believe you have is used in an active apprehension of this Sara, you will receive the full reward. Better yet, if your information leads us to her identity, which you seem confident of… then you're in the driver's seat!"

"Let me interject some additional info," says Brock, "a further incentive. The reward is now $350.000, double after her murder of Timmy Grope earlier today in L.A." Marvin shifts eagerly on his stool. "Hellyeah, I want it in writing. I don't trust anyone. No way, really, she killed Grope?" Lucie pulls out her digital recorder "shall we proceed with this interview?" "No, I want a signed…." Brock slams his fist into the table "what's wrong with you, Marvin? This woman has killed over 39 people that we know of. You will get the damn reward if your information leads to her arrest. This is a fkn verbal agreement, a statement with your two buddies here to validate…."

"Stop, Brock, calm down; here, give me a second." Lucie reaches into her briefcase. Staring at the obstinate Marvin, "I will give you a written agreement of what we've informed you of, Marvin… my partner Brock and I will sign it. Will that suffice?" The three guys were leaning back away from Brock, Marvin's face flush, "umh, yes, that works for me and us, right." As his friends affirmatively nodded paperwork handled, he added, "I don't need the intimidation theme or the good cop bad cop semantics, so skip it!" said Marvin. "Hey, Dougy, can you start out by showing how you worked your magic with my reward shot of the killer on your photoshop? That software is awesome?"

Doug explains the nuances, his expertise glowingly shown on the laptop's screen. They watch Doug's transformation of the pictures of Sara in disguise into the images Marvin had taken mere hours ago; omg! Brock and Lucie had differing reactions and opinions. Brock was wide-eyed, choked, and leaped up from his stool 'yes, he screamed' Lucie's face went pale, features quivering, then her complexion morphed to beet red 'no fkn way, please' no, removing her hand from her mouth.

Lucie, like now in a state of Shock, "I've had several conversations with that woman; only weeks ago at a Whole Foods Store in Oceanside and a gas station down the block from my home, she told me that she had bought a home in the area just small talk, chit-chat. Something like her husband was killed in Iraq, uuhhh, and she was a widow. I thought nothing of it. Oceanside is like a mecca for women who have lost their husbands or significant others. It's a military town, Camp Pendleton, down the road. The last thing this Sara said was I guess I will be seeing more of you around town; then she drove off." "Hell, she could have killed me at any of those times dead in a split second. Why? Explain why she didn't pull the trigger of her poisonous squirt gun?"

No one offered a reply or answered, not even the bewildered Brock, but his warm hand found her's then Marvin's pictures were scanned over to the Agent's computers.

The statements by the three witnesses were recorded and videotaped, and the articulations of the evening's events played out right down to the chase in Marvin's truck. It was already 1:31 am. Brock and Lucie head for the exit after saying their goodbyes and exchanging contact info. Last words "Marvin, you're a betting man, I guess?" 'yes, I am.' "Well, I think you have a mortal lock on that reward" he shakes his hand and thanks again.

"How can I be so tired and wired simultaneously," Lucie asks, "were like two peas in a pod, girl. Let's go to my place and get some rest. We have a huge Tuesday coming. We should try and get like 3 to 5 hours rest; believe me, we will need it." "Let the wheels of justice work while we sleep. Every car rental agency with a white 2010 Camaro on their lots will have Sara's pictures from LAX to S.D. airports. Let our Agents do the work we have finally…." "No, Brock, let's not get overconfident. Okay, let's grab a hotel close and not drive all the way to my place in Oceanside or your home in Santee. Hell, it's almost 2 am. There are plenty of hotels here in La Jolla!" "All right, let's do it." He slips his arm over her shoulder and then opens her car door to show that chivalry still lives.

In retrospect, it was an excellent decision to bed down at a nearby hotel. They no more than hit the door and were in the sack. The only notable change was that they slept in the same bed with underclothing. They had developed a bond of friendship, trusted their relationship explored their sexualities verbally, and uncannily laid that to the side. This had the initial start of an overused term, 'SoulMate's best friends evolution, next stop, Lovers.'

'They already frightfully finished each other's sentences, intuitively moved cohesively like a hand in a glove, sock on foot. Would they be sexually adaptable?' She lay next to his warm body with these musings, whirl-winding chasms, um, emotions bouncing off her Amygdala. On the other side of her, he had the testosterone bursting early morning Wood… erection. Unlike most mornings, this morning, he had a place to stash it temporarily, albeit inside a warm and inviting body. What to do? Nope!

Finally, by 7:11 am on that Tuesday, they drove on Hwy 5 on a direct line to the Hertz Rental at LAX with a tentative match. You could cut the excitement and anticipation in the interior of the Crown Vic with a spoon. With the earth-shattering breakthrough, they were lost in their minds. You would have thought that their mouths would be churning like motor mouths, but instead, lost in contemplations analytics, evaluating the competition against them, it was fierce.

Federal Agents from Sacramento, San Francisco, Los Angeles, and San Diego, and as far as Washington D.C., were on the move, blood in the water. Sara, the Vipress Serial Killer, was a Prize catch anyone, and everyone wanted to put their name on it. Authors were coming out of retirement; Newbie journalists and novelists were chomping gums at the bit 'A Sara biography would make millions. Movie producers had agents in the air from Europe to China… Sara was on VIRAL.

No one was Naïve. This arrest and bust would make headlines Worldwide. The So-Cal Director of the FBI stood steadfast. This was Agent Brock Dame and Agent Lucie Link's investigation. He was adamant, nervously Brock said, "I don't know, maybe I should get my prostate checked. I gotta pee again, Luce." She "maybe we should start bringing one of those hospital urinals?" "Hehe, you're a wise ass," she giggled. His amused feelings sort of broke the mysterious fog that had hovered engulfing them, torn apart then reattached due to the pressures mounting "better a wise-ass than a dumbass, right?" She retorted.

Just as quickly as her words drifted by, the meeting room emptied, and they were alone again. Next, a high-level conference call meeting at the L.A. Federal Building loomed… the Who's Who would be linked to D.C. The USA Attorney General, face to face, every move would be calculated and scrutinized, a master plan would be enacted, mistakes wouldn't be tolerated, this case was a 'Game Changer' could make or break a career! 'politicians were lining up!'

The others involved in the 'SARA' case… didn't realize, couldn't relate with, or calculate how Insanely possessed the partners had become. Lucie and Brock lived, and breathed this investigation over the last three years of chasing this Vipress…This was Fkn Personal for both Brock and Lucie, the vile subtle attacks on them by Sara, her notes, letters to the FBI, her snide verbiage gloatingly with Nefarious undertones bragging about her murder of Brock's ex-wife Patti. The Narcissistically brutal mind games and threats the Psychopath, Sara, had intimated toward both of them, had systemically been rooted beneath their epidermises. Like a colossal wart or pimple about to burst or the spread of shingles… a film of slime, oil-based water… a shower could never wipe away Sara's grime.

They briefly caught each other's eyes as she turned into the Hertz main office. Their doors clashed close robotically without a thought in auto drive, human emotion devoid. They went about all movements, heads on a swivel. With confirmation affirmed 45 minutes later, they entered the Fed Building. She broke the silence "that brazen hussy knows we're coming for her; she is lying in wait mode." "Yep! a shameless inhuman being with the audacity to use her real first name Sara unabashed why would you use your name, Luce?"

"I don't have a clue. Maybe perhaps it's like the dozen of profilers that have analyzed this case 'Sara,' somewhere inside her convoluted insanity, wants to be stopped, caught her time in the limelight, you know, the fifteen minutes of fame thing, umh. Still, truly that doesn't add up either, Brock. Maybe when we interview her, she will shed some light on this very question, quandary?"

"Luce, let's listen to the powers to be you play off of my words; I'll follow your sentiments like always. You and I are a formidable force together!" Brock squeezes her upper arm as they pass a few suits entering the expansive conference hall, a 55ft long table with only two chairs remaining, a dormant video camera on a 75-inch screen that showed an empty chair behind a glorious desk, an American Flag unfurled a real time hookup with D.C.

They take their seats with extra oxygen, filled lungs with resolve and certainty. They unloaded their briefcases from their designated areas others drank beverages. Lucie's instant feeling was, "this must be what it feels like being in a Zoo on display. The screen fills with the USA Attorney General, who sits down. Salutations automatically begin, and greetings are completed with serious tones; time is now!

Afterward, the meeting is a blur as Brock and Lucie depart on a plane Agent Homer Lan the head of Homeland security, awaits them in Nor-Cal, waving at them moments later. The three leave the Executive Airport North on Hwy 101 to S.F. "We already have her residence and business in San Rafael under 24/7 reconnaissance. Believe me when I say a leaf doesn't blow across her lawn in Mill Valley without us documenting it!" "Thanks, Homer," exclaims Brock. He drops them off in front of the exact vehicle loaned to them only days ago "all right, Homer... Lucie and I will get settled in Marin County at the Sheridan. Let's call for a team meeting at 7 pm." "Sounds good, Brock. I'll await your call?"

"The speed that all of this has worked out is phenomenal. How many of Sara's clients had seen her pictures posted on the net and on TV? They called our hotlines. We did it, babe. I mean, YESS! He kisses her romantically inside the closed elevator. She gives as good as she gets... yum! Hearts beating rapidly, the door opens and back to plutonic partners where their eyes sparkled with a gleam, exchanging winks. Aah, a bit more bothered. However, they'd both felt there would be closure soon enough!... Yay! 🐟.

Proper etiquette with conventional wisdom, they booked separate rooms with a pass-through door to uphold the decorum of professional conduct, but they both knew they'd sleep side by side. Finally, alone he reached over as she sat in front of the coffee table of their fully furnished rooms and rubbed her shoulders. She moaned ever so slightly, "Uhm, that feels so damn good." He applied more pressure. "I think a jacuzzi soak in one of our tubs is in order tonight!" "Wish we could jump in now-but in less than 75 minutes. We have a scheduled gathering of select Law enforcement Agents on the first floor in the Seminar Room."

He climbs over the couch and sits beside her, so let's prepare ourselves. Bam... spontaneously, he grips her neck tenderly, pulling her head and lips toward his, and kisses Lucie profoundly so damn enticingly slow molasses-like no hurries romance-filled passion bringing a sensation like nothing either of them had ever felt. Hearts beating sporadically, she holds the back of his head, not wanting his darting tongue ever to depart; he gently tugs on her ear lobes; 25 seconds later. He rubbed his nose upon hers, "I just had to do that..." she, not finished, yanked him down to indulge once more. He gently disengages and raises his forefinger across his moist scintillating lips "no, we must maintain our composure until later." 'Both grin synonymously, knowing precisely how exhilaration felt, euphoria, was this love?' Is this Luv?

Now leaning and touching the computer, she displays on her laptop screen Ms. Sara Sloan from childhood to the present times, her life as an open book on the computer. "So, she's a trust fund, baby, huh!" "Yes, she will never have to worry about money. That's for sure monthly allocations are deposited on the 5th of every month. Last month's amount was $115,000. It fluctuates with the stock market gyrations."

"Her Real Estate business is jamming, uhm, growing vigorously, actually thriving in this economy her offices in L.A., S.D. and here in Marin County." "I can't wrap myself around it, Luce. Wow, aah, she's a multi-millionaire. What the hell makes Sara tick? Why?" "Yes, we have to cross our every 'T and dot each i' because Sara has the money to clam up and hire the best lawyers in this State, uhm, World." "Even worse Lucie… attorneys will be throwing themselves at her… The gauntlet will be thrown down tomorrow morning. Our Search Warrant will be in place for her vehicles, offices, homes, and anything she owns, including all financial records, transactions, and credit cards. We cannot make a mistake, or it's our heads that will roll. Lucie, we know she flew back home last night. Still bizarre that she used her real Identification!" "Yeah, Brock, Sara is plainly unafraid resolute, waiting for us. She is an analytical mastermind with zero scruples and a super high I.Q. intellect off the chart. Some of her Professors ranted and raved about the way her mind formulated her many 'A+ conceptualizations.' Surely she has a plan in force."

"Geez, babe, the way you said that seems to put us on the defensive side. Remember, we're the good guys. She's the one who should be sweating bricks; we caught her ass, Luce. We got her ain't no place or anywhere for her to hide or run to. The killing stops now… she will most likely get a Life Sentence, right?" "Don't know, we could be in for a hell of a battle on many fronts, but in the end, we will win the war!" "Well, Hellyeah, we will. We got her by the lips, girl!"

He leans over to give her a peck on the cheek. But, she is too quick, tilting her head and finds his mouth, their lips locked, her tongue this time slips through yum yummy moans taste of mint. He clutches her head in his hands. He matches her tongues rotations, dueling tongues as they exude pent-up lust. He thinks a quickie might be in order, then hears knocking on the door. 'No, she sighs. No, just plain wrong No!'

Sara had decided that Lucie Link had to die…

The doorbell rings, then aah shit, he leaps up and must fidget a bit with his snug slacks. She wiped her face with the back of her hand and readjusted her blouse, flipping her hair. Then, as he headed to the door, she slyly took her index finger, slid it up her moist crevice, then brought it discreetly to her nose, inhaling once, twice, three times. She was cool in her skin and enjoyed her smells. Yum!

He opened the door in a huff. After eyeballing through the peephole, the courier held out a clipboard for him to sign afterward and handed him a sealed envelope. He cruises back towards Lucie and stops. She stands perplexed 'who is it from? 'It's from Fed-X,' he places it on the counter "whom the hell knows that we checked in here?"

In Brock's hand was a hard rigid envelope with a menacing structure and no name or return address. He went to his suitcase takes out a pair of gloves, "stand back, Luce," she looked at him, didn't speak, then said, "be careful." He peeled the opener with two fingers, then widened it to look inside and saw 8X10 inch pictures. At least 25 of them that were taken when Sara had flown South on her last trip. Both sigh with relief that it's from the L.A. office forwarded by Homer. They shuffle through them, then freeze!

Pictures of a rather rotund-heavy, maybe obese woman reporter with BBC credentials identification and a microphone that she put forth to Timmy Grope… it was Sara uuhhh had to have been. Still, there is no way that anyone would come to that conclusion. Her disguise was impenetrably perfect. The following picture was of the 2010 white Camaro with no tags and no inscriptions on the back. The next one was of the plump reporter driving away again with no plates, no defining marks on the car, a post sticky note 'we couldn't locate a clear picture of the license plate on the Camaro Cal-Trans all businesses in the area we struck out sorry.'

He spins around "wow, we're like paranoid? Shit, if you would have seen your face, Luce, you would have sworn that the Fed-X was from Sara herself." Lol… she flips up her hand "no, dude, it was you who freaked out. You were barely holding it with two fingers like it was boiling hot. Lol, then you ran to your briefcase to get gloves." "Shut-up bitch. I didn't run!" They both collapsed laughing and rolled over for a hug, 'yeah, that Sara has us creeped out, honey' "Honey kinda like that, Luce, well let's get prepared for our 7:11 pm get-together."

Sara was on her 3rd brew, relaxed in her extraordinarily complex 153 IQ Mensa intellect. The inevitability, bound to happen scrutiny by the FBI, it was only a matter of time. Teflon, since childhood untouchable like the mastermind she was. Her Preparation for the inevitable was already in place, just another hurdle… phase for her to tread past if they thought her killing spree was over. Lord knows they were clueless, not even fkn close! Across from her Victorian home was a community park. The Feds had been parked there for hours. Welcome, boys and girls. Hello!

I guess I became a tad-bit lackadaisical, even indifferent toward the FBI's ongoing witch hunt against me. She was a necessary force, vowed early in life to extract, uuhhh, exact revenge and eliminate the evildoers, spouse beaters, rapists, heartbreaking cheaters, the ruthless scandalous humans who lived by their own rules. She would uphold all moral values!

Sara had many opportunities to take Lucie out, vanquish, expunge, and purge her from the equation, yet she didn't pull the trigger. Why did she stall, hesitate? Was it going to be a pure kill or self-serving jealousy for her infatuation with the man she or both of them loved? Unfortunately, with all due respect, Brock Dame was the perfect match for Lucie as she admired her reflection in a wall-sized glass mirror.

I couldn't find that woman Lucie to be an immoral person. She wasn't flirtatious or superficial, or she'd already been exterminated and executed months ago if she were a philandering, frivolously amorous whore, actress, or seductress. Sadly, she maintained vigilance in her wanted dalliance with Brock; Lucie just wanted him just like Sara did; what was the crime of that, and furthermore, how could she justify wasting the competition?

Although now she will die. Time has come, push to shove, her claws are clenched upon Brock pulling him in, and he would one day cave in and be all hers, no way. She'd made this promise to him and her Soul & Heart. Enough… Sara moves into the computer room, checking out the five active monitors' especially studying the video of the park directly South, two Agents on the outside of her 11-foot black sharpened rod Iron spiked gate fence wrapped around her property, a Fed car down the street, and one at the bottom of the hill.

A live shot from her backyard camera positioned two-thirds of the way up an old Oak Tree trunk. At the back of her 3-acre parcel was a drop-off cliff. You were not attacking from behind her house unless someone was an experienced mountain climber with the appropriate climbing gear. She had a team of lawyers on speed dial as of yet and hadn't sought any counsel. I don't want to go into this premature merely a defensive maneuver; Sara was best as a counterpuncher. Let the Feds fire the first rounds. It wasn't like she wasn't prepared with her own arsenal, Armory, and plenty of ammunition; ugh, soon, the fun was going to start.

Best of all, she would meet her destiny, her Soulmate, up close and personal. I would be able to reach out and touch him. Would he feel the attraction of our Pheromones, no doubt fused magnetism heat from her body and his? The reaction indubitably would alter the outcome of this whole situation.

How could he fight what her body already knew? He was hers. She was his… only needed our eyes to connect our skin to sizzle. He would wilt, melt with my touch, Delish!

Sara switches to her cameras in remote positions, views of her offices in three different cities… live action, her wireless surveillance systems second to none even at this late hour the Feds were posted, her night vision lenses didn't disappoint. Tomorrow will be Blast off; better get some rest.

At 5:27 am, Sara's alarms blasted so did the task force Forensic vans, the vanguard led by Brock and Lucie at the substantially impervious opening to Sara's fortress. The bells were ringing. There was no way to bust down the doors, although various alternatives were nixed, like blowing up the front gate… but that was only the first of three gates. So, they would secure Sara's perimeter and place a chopper in the air trying to make this an easy takedown. Sara had way… too much money and financial wherewithal to be Swat Teamed… by rappelling Agents from helicopters.

Sara rolled up nude from her satin sheets, seeing the security screen at the front gate smiling, then heard the sounds outside her home, a megaphone, a voice she had longed to meet in person to verbalize with, "This is the FBI we have a Search Warrant, and your place is completely surrounded open up, or we will force our way in you have five minutes."

She reached out with her thumbs and index fingers and twisted her nipples, ripping at them. Oh, so hard 'ooh, that hurts so good I'm awake now Lol' better than coffee sometimes; simultaneously, she unplugs her cell phone and pushes her intercom button that's connected to the front gate, 'I will be right down!' she says this, not waiting for a reply. No Worries!

She throws a Flounce Kimono Silk Satin robe over her shoulders and puts on her most comfy slippers, Burberry Vintage while dropping down her spiral staircase. As she did so, she pushed speed dial the emergency number and direct line to the Terrance Hallinan Law offices based out of S.F. an answering service picked up her call and switched to the suddenly alert Attorney. She was already filling him in as she reached her 13 ft front door.

Within milliseconds, another attorney affiliated with the Hallinan group, who was local right down the street in Mill Valley, was already on his way up the hill to her home as she swung open the second steel security gate. A spectacle before her lights flashing cars filled her driveway, even a damn News van in the background. Taking her 'sweet-sour' time, she meanders through her Iron gates before she gets within 7 ft. Brock says, "we have a Search Warrant in place for your home... automobiles, all three of your offices, and everything associated with you." Smug was his expression.

"Now open the gate, Ms. Sara Sloan!" Sara calmly holds up her phone and takes several pictures. "Umh, here, whoever you are, someone wants to communicate with you, one of my many Attorneys." "You know damn well who I am, Sara, don't fk with me." He takes her phone through the rod iron and pins his back against the black iron gate. After a few moments, he passes the phone back, wanting to keep it for... justice's sake!

He and Lucie walk aside "her Attorney will be here in less than five minutes to validate the Warrants, then we will do our blitz on Ms. Sloan." She wiggles her head into his eyes "it's always a different playing field when we deal with the wealthy affluent if Sara were a no-name non-rich, we would have raided her home blown up the doors, and rammed down the gates, kicked in her door. She'd already been in handcuffs so fast that her pretty little head wouldn't have had time to blink three times. Sadly, it's not only whom you know. It's how much money you have, and Lil Ms. Sloan is Loaded in just one account... Sara has net cash of 15 million dollars. Crime and justice aren't fair, not synonymous look at her with her coy, unassuming demeanor like not a worry in this World, albeit even Cocky on her phone. She's a Serial Killer standing in front of us, rubbing our faces in her shit like the control freak she is. I…." "Lucie, Lucie, please, you're preaching to the choir. We were admonished, plain and simple… to move cautiously with no mistakes and give her no loopholes to escape the Hangman's Noose. Remember, my sweet cheeks, what we have thus far is, at best Circumstantial Evidence we were lucky to get these Warrants signed."

The Nuclear Reactor on the Pacific Coast was lighting up, dawn was breaking, the Sun was warming up, and her Attorney had already stepped out of his Lexus dressed to kill impeccably, even at 5:49 am. "I'm here to see and scrutinize the Search Warrants. I represent this fine human being. This is an atrocity that you're trying to insinuate or to impose all this unsubstantiated nonsense on Ms. Sloan. She is a fine citizen, a philanthropist who only gives of herself for the betterment of society," Sara finally buzzes open the gates.

A large crowd moves forward with Brock and Lucie at the forefront; Sara says, "what is going on? Why the circus, all these people for lil ole me you'd think I was like Osama Bin Laden or something I can't …" "Please, Ms. Sloan, don't say another word, not one word remain silent, please Terrance himself is flying over from the city in his chopper let me thoroughly vet, scrutinize these Search Warrants Please, just relax I realize this is traumatic."

Brock and Lucie are now speaking into their phones, updating their superiors. 'The one and only Mr. Terrance Hallinan, the Celebrity Attorney of the Stars World renown, was handling Sara's case personally. "Yuh, gotta be kidding me? Says the Fed Director, who the hell is this Sara Sloan anyways?" "I don't know, sir, but we're at a standstill on her sidewalk entryway as we speak!"

"Relax, Agent Dame… she's going nowhere!" Lucie receives the exact verbiage, 'Okay, sir,' she mutters, then turning to her partner, "that didn't sound so uplifting on our other fronts. All three offices of hers are also on hold. She has high-end partners who will fight us 'tooth and nail' we are positioned for action once the Warrants are validated." Even though the morning lite was still subdued, Sara wore an expensive pair of sunglasses, super dark. She was only 15 feet from her man Brock and a few more feet from the bitch who was her interference. Brock never even looked her way, but the witch did. She sat down with her arms crossed, talking with her business partners in S.D. and L.A., explaining to them what to expect.

Sara was on a conference call already explaining how utterly preposterous aah ridiculous this all was a literal joke, a witch hunt… stand up for your rights! 'I told all my associates exactly how to handle this bullshit and don't waver to the Fed's manipulations. I am going to be exonerated. I am innocent. This is ridiculous and beyond bizarre! We will be countersuing.'

"Luce, remember we're here for all her victims," points over at the smug murderer. "Hey, she attacked us too, babe, she would have killed me, Brock, at the mall in San Diego if she'd got the chance!" "I'm well aware of that," "ugh, and she was stalking me in Oceanside. I'm bummed out my adrenalin was pumped up honey, yet now it's like shut-down were at her doorstep, yet she seems far away from being arrested and in our custody," whispers Lucie.

In the air, a chopper is heard dropping out of the sky. Sara's attorney says, 'the cavalry has arrived for you, Ms. Sloan, Mr. Hallinan himself, the Man!' Terrance walks up with a mini entourage on his cell phone, a conference call with a Federal Judge and AUSA Prosecutor… 'That's not the point here, 'Judge Willingly' with the circumstantial evidence, there isn't even a case, in my opinion, how can you justify signing all those Search Warrants.'

<u>**Nine hours later.**</u>

Attorney Terrance Hallinan was calmly trying to manipulate his prey…. "Umh come on, Judge, the FBI was still tearing apart Sara's residence and pummeling her offices, and not a single incriminating item was located, not a piece of paper, nothing," "Mr. Hallinan, I will discuss this no further with you." "That's fine. I will be lodging my numerous complaints you will be hearing from me shortly," he hangs up. He mulls over what he'd learned from the Search Warrants and his multitude of connections throughout the FBI and all associated agencies all the way to the White House.

He taps his cigar into an ashtray in his Limousine, looks up through the moon roof, and swigs a shot of Glenmorangie Scotch… Terrance muses, so could Sara be the Serial Killer for real? The evidence is beyond weak umh they have over a hundred pictures of a woman in disguise, not one picture that was definitively depicting my client. He watched the monitor, squeezed his nose then rubbed his eyes until the video at the Rainforest Café started.

Terrance replays the video… 'Ms. Rachel Graybar, the Granny, disappears in the lavatory, the same Granny seen in Southern California, who allegedly murdered the ex-wife of Brock, what was her name, uh Patti, that's right. The Granny with the cane, his eyes flinch, no cane hum granny was in the bathroom for nine minutes while inside, three other ladies had shuffled in then out. Next came the stunning redheaded beauty with bright blue eyes, with a large mole, and without a cane. She strutted out and walked down the stairs and out onto the street. The Fed's Software Program had deleted and morphed the woman's hair and subtracted the lady's eye color, then added Ms. Sloan's characteristics Photo-shopped… busted, they got zilch, uh, all wrong!

Irate was Terrance 'Shit. If the Feds wanted, they could take a picture or video of him and morph it into him being Ronald Reagan, please.' Although the perplexing conundrum was where did Granny Graybar go? She never left the restroom, never seen exiting, and we know she didn't climb out the second-floor window with her cane. The cane was never found, but what does this prove?

Terrance sits back in his limousine, mulling over what evidence they had on Sara … why would a Serial Killer use her real first name in all her correspondences with the FBI? Sara wouldn't be so stupid, please! It doesn't add up… the killer is a master of disguises with intellect and savviness, a talent to blend in like a chameleon, and a Hollywoodish makeup artist. The Feds haven't found one outfit, not a stitch of evidence thus far. They have her renting a white 2010 Camaro as the most damaging evidence. Ms. Sara Sloan did drive away from the Brigg Pub with tags that didn't belong to the car. Uh, 'stolen' license plates are in evidence in digital pictures. But when she dropped it back off at LAX, it had the correct license plates that belonged to that Camaro.

How do we explain this to a Grand Jury, prosecutorial team, or Judge? This was the Red Herring, the unexplained quandary of the murder of the basketball player by the heavy-set reporter. However, it was reported that she also drove a white Camaro with no tags seen. The Search Warrant was based on freakin license plates. That's it in a nutshell-all the killings were in Southern California. Ms. Sloan has offices in LA and SD, but her alibis were solid. She was here in Marin during many of the murders.

The Fed's arguments were that she used phony names… aliases, and disguises. This will be an interesting case for the ages. Fun thought, Terrance… 'they haven't enough to arrest Sara well unless something harmful or substantial is discovered.' He looked forward to sitting down with Lil Ms. Sloan in the morning at his main building downtown San Francisco office. He pours another drink and blows a puff of his $300.00 Cuban cigar out through the open sunroof.

Life was good; this high-profile case was going to be Sweet… at this stage of the Sara Sloan case. He wanted her to shun the limelight, no news cameras interviews until the time was ripe, 'Ripe for his audience!'

<u>Sara relaxed… Cool as the cucumber.</u>

Sara has her feet up on an ottoman, sipping a beer. The Feds were finally finished with her Den and library. She was looking out on her swimming pool and deck. Her exercise obstacle course had dogs roaming around and through. Her backyard looked like it was part of a freakin dog show. With their FBI handlers, canines in different areas on her 3 acres, metal detectors, and wands of various sizes… X-Rayed her walls and floors. What did the fools think? Ugh, that she had bodies buried in the basement or attic like fkn fleas. They were all over the place.

All of this happened because of the Romeo Marvin asshole at the pub in La Jolla. The Feds had warrants to seize all her personal computers and phones and the computers in her Real Estate offices. Sara relaxed and let her excellent legal team intervene and counter the Feds at every impasse. They provided all the answers the Feds were asking for. At this very second, she had three attorneys on her property, watching and videotaping all that the cops were doing, ransacking… and tearing apart her home. Brock and Lucie were in charge but invisible to her, not even saying a word in her direction… weird?

Another team of Attorneys directed by Terrance Hallinan was in charge at her other offices; she just needed to kick back and get a fine-ass Beer buzz! One thing was certain if she didn't have the legal team at her disposal enforcing the Feds to be respectful following due diligence, she'd be in an interrogation room shackled and cuffed by now. Sara catches the TV blurting out vileness on the screen, a loose-lipped braggart boasting that he would collect like three hundred and fifty grand. *Marvin was in the same bar as when he'd spotted Sara grinning largely, damnit. He couldn't buy a drink… everyone patted him on the back. Marvin smiled, and then an idea sparked… smirking. While the news reporter had the video camera rolling… Marvin changed his phone screen to the picture of Sara being served a search warrant. Smirking wildly, slipping his tongue out, and held his phone screen up with a thumbs up! Messages constantly crossed the screen's lower part: "Sara, the female umh femme fatale serial killer, was allegedly arrested in Marin County." Sara would have to carefully do some research on ole Marvin* .

Sara found the snitch's Facebook Account… Twitter and Instagram pages; he even had several YouTube videos on display. 'Marvin Payco' was the culprit as she downloaded the videos to her phone, the same one the Feds earlier had in their grubby paws, she had to be careful they had access to her cell phone service, which bothered her, but via the Dark Web, she could cleanse all Lol!

After analyzing the culpable parties, she had to place a sliver of the blame on herself for leaving up the reward picture on her iPad when Marvin approached. This caused a domino effect with the stolen tags on the fkn Camaro. For sure, she had a percentage of the blame, her being there to rid society of another predator of children and others, Coyotes, Pimps, and human traffickers of adolescents. She was going to leave La Jolla with all accomplished, but for the assholes, the freak Marvin taking pictures with his darn phone. He violated her space, and soon she'd return the favor!

Marvin will pay, the fool… hasn't any idea whom he screwed with. Suddenly he catapulted to Numeral Uno jumped right up to the most wanted dead on her enemy list. Marvin was the reason her life was upside down. He would never see one silver dime from the reward, lol. Bad-boy Marvin leaped past Lucie Link on the soon-to-be Dead list.

One lingering, apprehensive issue caused significant anxiety and concern. No matter how she evaluated the situation, there wasn't anything she could have done differently. She rented both storages, one in S.F. and the other in S.D., under aliases that matched her description. She wasn't in disguise because if she had rented in disguise, she would always have to have that around, which today would be a bust. The Feds were searching precisely for that... disguises and aliases. There was nothing Nada anywhere but inside her two storages. The scary part that hovered over and in her Cerebral Cortex was whether the managers of those storages would remember her face... in her favor was heck, it had been years since she'd rented them; they were on Autopay!

Again Sara sighed... good Omen was that those storages were rented over seven years ago. She tapped confirmation on an airline ticket to San Diego in three weeks for her to meet with her Real Estate partners at the LA. and S.D. offices. Sara had to visit with her loyal client base, wondering if she would have any travel restrictions from the Feds. Why she nearly laughs? Did they not wait before playing their cards, catch her in the act, or something like that?

She sucks down another frosty beer. My Gawd, that man in person close up is so much hotter, a definite Hunk. He smells of masculinity, and Brock is a man's man. I can see his muscles popping from his clothes, his ass tight. I want him, those dimples, the way he walks with confidence, yum, so sexy is Brock. One day, he will be all mine. That's a <u>'VOW' till death do us part!...</u> Yup.

Forensic Psychologist Doctor Ame Amaya, 5/23/17

Tuesday… Almost seven years later, in the present time.

Ame is on her way back from NIA. She felt a sense of satisfaction on her winding route out of Napa and the thousands of acres of wine stock. The drive went by without a negative thought, pure bliss. Her nine years of education and training were paying dividends. The interviews with Al and Sara were the best of all time, the progress wasn't Ame's imagination, nope, evident to all the staff, and Doctor Honcho had reaffirmed the positive steps her patients were making.

Al had nearly stopped all his practical jokes; he had taken up reading and was now taking College courses from an offsite accredited institution associated with the College of Marin and, thus far, was carrying a 4.1 GPA. Al was very bright. You could see in each of her participant's eyes that they were growing stronger and understanding their past events, coming to grips with the insight of why they were not only locked up in the mental facility but how to grow and find peace within their souls. Ame hoped they could reach reconciliation in their hearts.

Ame smiled into her rearview mirror; Sara was her prize patient. She was 'happy as a lark' and had a full schedule of clients, other Inmates, and the staff of NIA. As absurd as it sounded last week, Ursula Anders, the Warden herself, sat in Sara's Salon for a total makeover for the first time ever. The entire staff was raving about the skills of the makeup magician; I had to face it. She was remarkable indeed.

Sara seemed to adjust easily after our last counseling session regarding her sister Kamryn's impending wedding. She'd been able to compartmentalize the marriage. It was put on the 'back burner.' Doctor Liz Honcho had sent me a text earlier and stated that Sara had finally accepted her sister's engagement. She was only upset that Kamryn's Fiancé hadn't been approved yet to visit her at NIA.

Ame hears the ringing interrupting the cool jazz that played from her car's speakers and clicks on her dashboard screen, answering her San Rafael office phone… "yes, Donny," "your 2:30 has been confirmed, Ame. This will be your first new patient in like five years." "I know, Don, that we discussed not bringing in any new patients, but a professor friend of mine had personally asked me to take this one on. He is a Kleptomaniac," Ame snickers. "Better put away all your 'knick-knacks' on your desk. This guy will steal your teeth if there loose. He is a harmless individual but will pocket anything."

"Wow, Doc, this will be a new experience for me; you want me to have lunch ready for yah?" "Nah, Don, I'm going to stop to eat something. Thanks though, seeya soon!" 'Bye, Ame.'

<u>About seven years previous … 5/27/10… The Taskforce vs. Sara Sloan!</u>

The entire task force, all the Agents in the three cities canvassing Sara's properties and offices, were utterly exhausted. Nothing to show of significance, and no evidence was found or located anywhere; Sara's vehicles had been towed to Forensic Labs and were clean. There wasn't a speck of incriminating evidence. It had been going on four days since the Warrants were served.

"Lucie, our Forensic teams haven't found a single clue on any of Sara's computers, phones all legit every single transaction from her Real Estate business and all her financial expenditures, transactions are being vetted by the IRS, who are still breaking the spreadsheets down, thus far all above board an IRS Agent off the record said that Sara maybe was owed monies back where the hell

do we go from here?" Together they take the last steps down from the S.F. Fed building… heading toward the Crown Vic. A few minutes later, they were driving back over the Golden Gate into Marin County, the Sheridan Hotel destination, sitting on a bench not relaxing now, both with sugar-free Red Bulls in their palms, overlooking the Courtyard the tourists mull about unaware that mere miles away was a 'ruthless killer.'

"Brock, if she weren't a Millionaire, she would already be in custody!" "I know, Luce, but honey, in my heart, it wasn't a mistake to push for the Search Warrants." Their downtrodden moods couldn't be elevated by caffeine. It increased their anxiousness and worsened their despair. Maybe a few beers might be a better choice. She thought, "look," as she slung the pictures of Sara in the Camaro with the stolen tags. "These were taken at the pub. What more proof do we need? Damn." She then tosses Sara's following picture at Hertz's return gate with the actual license plate that belonged to the Camaro, which proves that unless a person was an idiot… Sara had changed out the license plates…fk. How do you explain this? How can she be free to come and go? Why not an arrest?"

"Lucie, we've been over this dozens of times. The license plates being changed and stolen doesn't prove that she altered them. It's not enough proof, total circumstantial evidence." "Bullshit, Brock bullshit. If we were in any other country but the USA, that Bitch would be behind bars instead of going about her life without a concern!" "She's laughing at us, rubbing our noses in the blood of her victims. She murdered your Ex-wife Patti. She has stalked both of us, sent messages to my office, and dropped a note on your car right in your driveway in front of your house Brock. This is as personal as it gets. I want to put a bullet between her eyes. I'm not…." "Stop, stop, babe, we've at least reigned her in. She's under 24/7 surveillance right out in the open; she can barely take a piss without us not knowing it. Hell, we have a van parked right outside her gate." "Her pictures have gone Viral on the Internet, on television, and all-over Social Media sites. Sara couldn't go to a gas station without being recognized. Believe me, news or something will break, and somebody out there will come forward. We know she must have a secret place where she keeps her clothes, disguises, weapons, and poisons, inside a storage building, maybe a house she owns under one of her aliases fk. Lucie, where are all of her props, like the cane? Remember, Sara owns a darn Real-estate company, uh could have a hidden property or three!"

"Yes, Brock, the assumptions from all the genius profilers and Investigators say the same thing: Sara has a storage building or another residence where she has her hidden trove of illegal paraphernalia. We know she is a master of disguises and identity changes. Her picture is out there; in my mind, it's only an eventuality that we will apprehend her soon!"

Sara slammed down her phone these fkn Feds; she hadn't considered the blowback from all the negative press. 'The allegations had not only curtailed her Real Estate business but alienated her business associates.' Her partners were trying to distance themselves. Two of her three partners have resigned, wanting to break away from the dark cloud that has become Sara.

Sara was beyond irate, pissed off to the max. Everyone assumed she was guilty before any evidence. It was pure speculation hell. There wasn't a shred of proof. So un-American. In less than two weeks, she had lost 35 percent of her client base, and another 17 letters sat unopened on the coffee table of most likely ex-clients that had fired her company. Her Real Estate business had slowed to a Turtles crawl. Her company email was like reading the obituaries. Her name was filth... terminal.

It was as if she was the return of the Black Plague; in front of her on Van Ness Ave in S.F. was a couple of FBI Agents, and behind her were a few more followers. The same as if she were a Mafioso… Sara glanced out her window, passing a sign for Pac-Bell Park alas, no helicopters with a cackle. Sara was on her way to the airport to try and circumvent her Real Estate business imploding, her partners wanted to Oust her. Suddenly the FBI vehicle on her tail almost slammed into her bumper. Sara had to brake instantly… Those pricks are ruining my life. It's time to ratchet up the pressure, a vice on their testicles, some super glue to close the vile lips of the females too!

She takes the turn-off to South 101 Hwy and the S.F. Airport, knowing fair well that the FBI had her itinerary. The millisecond she tapped the confirmation into her iPad… later today, she'd be in San Diego… and so would they? An impromptu meeting with the Board of Directors of which she was the Chairwoman President, her professional life on falter mode, aah, she didn't care. Nah, untrue; she was adamant about payback for all of them, fair-weather friends. Now she got the cold shoulder, colleagues… partners, her social life in shambles, calls and emails from people she had forgotten were alive, uh, so-called friends not calling her back, it was a complete 360 degrees… Flip from her being in popular demand en vogue. Her speaking engagements were canceled. Even the charity events that she sponsored had backed out. Sara enjoyed being a philanthropist for many children's charities; she no longer had clout, and now with the negative publicity, she would only harm what she wanted to support!

The only demand that Sara had an interest in following through on regarding interviews was if Brock Dame wanted to speak with her! There were wishes for interviews lining up. Just the numbers requested were mind-blowing by themselves, an upcoming exposé on 60 Minutes… and a 3-hour segment on Dateline, the Producers, who had contacted her publicist.

You name it, even TMZ was harkening for her attention, but as per her legal counsel, 'mums' was the word she remained mute. Her major regret was losing the connection with Brock. Soon, the dust would clear, and Brock would be back in Focus! Her attorneys had flatly refused her to have any interviews…including her wannabe paramour Brock.

She hadn't seen him for 11 days and counting; Sara was in for the long haul. The scrutiny would wane. They'd let their guard down then she would pounce! Sara would play dead, boring the Feds to death. It was only a matter of time which was on her side. Yup!

'Yes, sir, we have her entering her office on the 5th floor. We're positioned in the hallway. No way for Ms. Sloan to escape us unless she grew wings and flew out a fixed window. Nope, Sir'… Brock pushed end, thinking about his partner and wanna-be paramour. Weary Lucie had the flu and was sick as the proverbial dog. He wondered where that saying came from… dogs were not sickly creatures typically. They could lick their genitals and other doggy assholes and then chase balls or sticks, no, not a sickly bunch.

Oh well, what the hell was he dwelling on? Dogs, for Christ's sake, he was losing his mind. He texted Lucie to see if he could pick up lunch… soup, or anything for her, only 33 miles from Oceanside. Every waking second, he went through the stacks of reports on all of Sara's killings. There had to be a mistake. A clue had to be somewhere. Right there in front of us, we're overlooking something as he lets himself into Lucie's home with his extra set of keys in his hand… up the stairs, he spies the woman he'd fallen for. Luv!.

"Hi, there, Lucie," she was sitting up in bed with pajamas on… pale as a ghost, aah, her laptop on her lap, reading glasses on her face, and a stack of papers on her nightstand. Lucie was sound asleep! He didn't wake her; he only silenced his phone, sat in a cozy chair, and started working on the Sara case. He would heat up her chicken noodle soup when she awakened.

Sara's trying to circumvent with obstinate avoidance of what she'd cost the Corporation with her name attached to it, namely lucrative contracts many mega developers demanded her ouster. Needless to say, Sara's well-meant strategy went awry, not as planned. The unanimous vote proved her removal was imminent. She rationalized that she hadn't any recourse and that her ouster would be the ultimate or foregone conclusion, uhm, outcome. Unfortunately, the board that she'd put in place was correct, and a buyout clause was in order. She would have to walk away from her L.A. and San Diego offices. Her business was done essentially; she was fired, terminated 'seeya wouldn't want to be yah,' at least she would have a massive windfall of cash, not bad. Still, it hurt her pride and ego horribly. Sara, it seemed, would be able to hold onto her initial Real Estate business in Marin County. It wasn't the money; she had plenty of that. It was her innovative entrepreneurial concepts that she had initiated, building an empire from nothing but an idea.

Brock listened to the latest news from his posted agents about Sara's demise and grinned hugely, and now she would be terminated, ousted by a mutiny by the hierarchy she had put in place. The same humans she had hired and placed on her Board of Directors. Omg no. Sara had an ego the size of Texas, which was eviscerated, Lol. Brock knew that Revenge was what motivated her, so they better keep a close tether on the killer bitch.

<u>Sara was losing it!</u>

Sara was biting her tongue while others were speaking to her. Within her head, her diverse entities were getting louder. The voices were screaming at her now, between her ears. Her diverse mindsets were angry with inner conflicts and in-fighting. Sara was a mess. She had to take control and shut up her demons!

Sara sometimes spun around, thinking others could hear the same voices she did, or strained her eyes to see if someone was yelling at her, but always it was the same outcome, the chatter within her mind lingered, creeping on the fringes, jockeying for a voice. Could she maintain her Vigilance, Eagle-eyed, sustain? Could she remain to be Sara? Or was she going to morph once again into another of her personalities? She emphasized control, struggling to shut down the voices… that were reverberating in her skull, knowing precisely how to shut them up. Violence was the only cure to squelch their voyeuristic appetites. She knew now she had to Attack, Kill again. Yep!

-33-

Poor Lucie is sick as the proverbial doggy…

Brock had taken and muted Lucie's phone, sat back, and listened to her congested mini snore. It was soothing to his ears to hear her sleep. Sleep had become a commodity for them, Lucie moaned; he rubbed her congested head, 'sshhh.' Then unwittingly fell to the wayside… sound asleep in less than 11 minutes at 1:43 pm. He'd submerged… plunged into the same genre haunting style of a nightmarish dream state. Sara had infiltrated his Psyche and was part of his subconscious world no way to turn her off; she roamed freely, always there when he closed his eyes, wishing he could close his mind off and truly recharge his internal batteries rest. Nope!

This afternoon was nothing out of the ordinary, her devious countenance prevailing, ughhhh, blood dripping from her canines always the same, dightmares consistently impossible to reconcile, the pressures on Lucie and him... were taking tolls!

Sara stood looking out on Petco Park, the Padres playing a doubleheader against the S.F. Giants. The so-called meeting had convened only minutes before; she glanced at the parking garage. On her monitor, the Feds parked next to her rental, her vehicle sitting as always in her space, was returned from the Forensic laboratory with not a shred of negative evidence... she was innocent. Lol.

Another Agent was right outside her office door; they had her pinned in, probably G.P.S. devices on her rental and her Jaguar. How to escape? She had to get to her storage. There was a will and a way, but how? Pacing back and forth in her main office, there were five employees, Realtor's secretaries, and...! Wait, what if she exchanged car keys? No, these brazen pricks would get on the elevator with her. They were like bodyguards and never out of sight... heck, in public, she couldn't sneeze without them saying 'Bless you' out of contempt.

The FBI was harassing her, yet this was legal. Even if she wanted to, she couldn't assault them, umh, only this morning, she was in line at Starbucks, not 15 inches behind her, was a stinking slob of a woman Agent, or was she imagining them? They had unlimited resources, but contrary to what they believed, she had her resources to unveil soon enough, like today. 2-Day!

Isolating her thought process, thinking her synapses were firing on all cylinders, her multifaceted brain discarded her Amygdala underpinnings. It morphed into her emotionless Sociopathic slash Psychopathic self with reinforcement, and it was 'Time.' On the first floor of this commercial building, there was a restaurant and a separate Café gift shop with miscellaneous items, tampons, newspapers, etc. Sara decided to visit this establishment and called ahead to order some food. Having a craving for a French Dip with crispy fries and extra Au Jus for dipping, the time was 3:25 pm. She stepped out into the hall, and a large shadow joined her at once. The Agents were like gigantic ogres. One brute with no neck, maybe 6 ft and 275 pounds, followed two feet behind her.

She clicks the elevator button #1 he accompanies her. No words are ever spoken as most of them were wearing sunglasses like clones, wires connected to a radio, and one ear, a tiny mic attached to the top of his suit collar. Sara wore her sunglasses, a small-sized purse absolutely no makeup.

She had adopted the plain Jane look 'au natural' strolling into the restaurant to the hostess counter. They all knew her. She walked into the dining area like a Movie Star. Ugh, not quite uuhhh, the opposite actually, the whispers began, talking, chit-chatting about her spreading hateful rumors. She was a celebrity in the negative tense. Their viral words dripped like water off a duck's feathers, calmly stepping from a pond. I guess the restaurant could have refused to serve me. I'm the Vipress Serial Killer. Lol. As her meal was served on a hot plate, Sara even wondered if she should risk even eating it. What did the cooks do to it? Hey, they didn't know she ordered it using an alternative name.

A stiff double shot Bloody Mary was on the way as she dipped the fries in a mayo-mustard ketchup blend. 'From the corner of her eye,' she saw the Agent drinking perhaps iced tea and perusing a menu. She dipped her sandwich into the Au Jus and relished each bite of succulent roast beef, melted cheese, onion, and bacon. Delish! It should supply some needed energy in a few minutes! A long pull on her straw resulted in a shiver as the taste of the Absolute Vodka found her throat. The big man at the bar watched her. His Club sandwich arrived about the same time as her second drink; checking the Agent's attire out, what struck her as an advantage was his hard shoes and his bulk, which could and would be his downfall.

That certainly was a miscalculation by the FBI because it was a male, uhm, was a He! If Sara were in charge, a Female would be assigned to her 24/7, like in most of the last 19 days since the Search Warrant. A woman shadowed her as well. The oversight today was a 'Fatal Error.' The FBI would come to suffer major humiliation for making this shameful mistake. Heck, it is on them, lol. What the brute had missed was that she'd changed out her shoes in her office; instead of wearing 'Pumps,' now Sara was wearing running shoes!

Her hair was pulled back into a Ponytail, also most likely missed by the brute, a change from when she entered her office. She was known to run for fun 5 miles on a whim all the way around Petco Stadium and back. Sara was in prime shape, all 135 pounds tight tempered steel. Leaving one-third of her drink on the table and 35 dollars, she moved across the dining hall to the women's restroom, which immediately elicited action from the Agent. As Sara reached the bathroom door, a couple of ladies laughing stepped out. She knew this bathroom well, knowing the windows and screens were on hinges that swung downward… Then locked into place, a simple exit for Sara. The Agent stops, almost knocking two ladies into the wall that were entering the restroom.

Sara is cloaked behind the door; she was quick and made it out the window in less than 15 seconds, kicking the screen out. Her tiny, petite, small frame easily maneuvers out behind a bunch of large shrubs, off and running… 'Gone Girl' Yep!

The humongous Agent's apprehension held him for too long. He then knocks on the door and cracks it open 'FBI' 'I'm coming in, please excuse me!' The bathroom was vacant. He saw the window. Ain't no way he was going to fit through that opening; fk, he cussed yells into his mic and ran out with a beastly growl, not paying his tab… out the lobby, the hunt was on, and the dogs were let out of the canine unit, in less than 5 minutes the alert hit the streets.

It was 91 seconds too late; Sara melded perfectly in the cross-traffic. The timing was flawless, impeccable obviously, Sara had done her due diligence. The first San Diego game was letting out. The second group was rushing to the gates for the doubleheader; under her light sweater was a dainty San Diego Padre frilly blouse with the name Tony Gwynn on the back.

Sara was now free to make it to her storage, next to the downtown mall, where she kept some IDs, costumes, disguises, cash, and, best of all, her purchased Poison. Oh, how sweet freedom felt, breathing again now that she was back in control. She had no phone and left it in her office. But lol had plenty of throw-away burner phones where she was headed; the time was <u>'420</u> pm.' 'A toke would have been sweet, no… she would indulge later.' Yep! 🔲.

Back in Oceanside, Ca. Brock would release carbon dioxide Lucie would take in Oxygen in unison. They were in a state of oblivion, and the first to blink was Lucie at 5:11 pm. Her neck was cramped up. She saw her man well, almost her man.

<u>Present time 6/15/17 NIA Thursday… Kamryn visited her sister Sara.</u>

Even though she had watched her sister for years learn to add to her repertoire, uhm, prowess and innate abilities, God-given talents a natural she could have worked in any movie production studio, her makeovers were like historic second to none. Kamryn wished she had half of Sara's inherited gifts. Sara enjoyed the challenges of transforming blemishes, scars, or flaws to bring the best life to her client's faces.

Finally, Sara finished up and took pictures with her client's phones. The ecstatic staff members could only smile. Her clients, amazed with many dazed in 'Awe at their new selves' overwhelming appreciation and thanks, were bestowed on Sara with an occasional hug; what a portfolio she was building of before and after photos. Kamryn couldn't help herself. She sat in the magician's chair as her baby sister curled her long, raven-black hair. Kam loved to have her hair brushed. Who didn't, as long as it wasn't pulled on? Aah, there were times for that too. Lol, the final cut of the dead ends and last curls a spray to Set her hair, and Walla Kam grins in the hand-held mirror. Purrfect!

Later after lunch, the sisters walked along winding paths past ponds, other inmates, and visiting family members. If not for the Razor wire in the far-distance towers and the occasional guard riding by in marked Golf carts, one wouldn't even guess they were inside a Maximum-Security Mental Institution "hey, sis, what's up with Carl? He seems to be obsessed, even like infatuated with you?"

"Sister, he's followed us on each trail and stays far back there. He's back by that large Cottonwood Tree, watching us with binoculars. Weird, really creepy does he ever bother you, sis?" "Kam, he is like overprotective of me like I'm his personal duty harmless, but now that you mentioned it, when Carl's working here, he is never far away from me. It's been an advantage having a guard like Carl on my side, sister. He's helped me tremendously with the Salon." "Lately, though, it's like he's possessive of my time, even jealous when I cut other males' hair or trim up their facial hair… haven't given it much thought, Kam, but perhaps I should?" "Sara, you want me to report his actions to the staff and Warden?" "Gosh, no, I will handle it. He could cause me a lot of trouble guards here stick together and could set me up easily."

"What, how, sis, what are you talking about?" "Kam, this may appear like a hospital, but don't be fooled, don't forget, Kam, this is a Prison. Depending on the inmate's classification, Level One's can find themselves chained to a gurney naked in a rubber room... soundproof-torture. All a guard has to do is claim that they found contraband on me, plant drugs on me or a shank, um, weapon, and even though I'd be set up, I wouldn't have any defense. It would be the guard's word against mine like I have zero rights; I Lose!" "Wow, sister, that is so unfair" Sara waved her hand and continued.

"I would be locked down in solitary confinement. Kam, one thing I've learned in the five-plus years that I've been locked inside NIA is that the guards are in collusion on any matters that affect one of their own. So to answer your question of why you cannot report any of Carl's weirdness, uhm, no, please don't report our peeping Carl because all you'd be doing, sister, is hurting me in the end. I will handle him unless he becomes uncontrollable, then most certainly I would ask you for help... thanks, Kam!" Hugs tightly, the sister's bond is solid; what a moment but a sly wink was missed by one of them? "Now, let's talk about your wedding Kamryn. It is less than three months away. How excited are you, um, getting anxious, huh?" "I feel like I'm in a live real Fairy tale. The only thing that would make this experience better is that you could be there for me, Sara. You know we have only each other our dysfunctional family was decimated a generation ago."

"One day, you will be released from this Hellhole, and we will be together again, free; you must believe this. If it's meant to be, then it will be so, sister! Oh, that's right, I brought a selection of wedding dress colors and designs. There are so many shoes for you to choose from, Sara; it's mindboggling just trying to decide on what theme to go with for my wedding; you'd definitely be the best wedding consultant. The stack of catalogs are in your Salon in my carry bag. You must help me pick out everything because you're always with me in my heart!" Hugs again, "Kam, I love you. Thanks for being here for me; I'm so grateful and Blessed that you're my sister. I'm so happy for you, sister. If anyone deserves happiness, you do after that awful, hurtful relationship with that scoundrel and cheater, your former piece of crap… Fiancé Rocky."

Kamryn froze, and her palm covered her heart. She kneels slightly, the pain culpable; Sara huddles around her. "I'm so sorry, Kam. I forgot! I shouldn't have let that slip out. How could I have brought him up, Rocky, who left you on your wedding day nine years ago? He was having an affair with your best friend, Bridesmaid, sick disgusting facts. I'm so Sorry, Kam!"

After a few moments, Kam recovered her composure, and with both hands, she pulled Sara's head within inches of her face. "Listen to me, Sara… Edward isn't Rocky, nothing like him. Why would you ever say, umh, bring that up again? Sis, damn, don't hurt me, I thought I'd recovered from the wounds, the scars of that wasted, rotten relationship, but nope, I haven't. My Heart would burst if something happened like that again. I'm still hurting, please Sara, don't ever…."

"Okay, Kam, I apologize, relax, stop crying. I was wrong; please forgive me. Let's not look back at the past. Your future is brightly awaiting you. I promise I will never say that piece of shit Rocky's name again!" The shaking, trembling Kam hugs her sister once more. Walking hand in hand, the sisters make their way back to Sara's private Salon. Strangely, only one camera was turned on in Sara's Salon… typically at the high-tech mental institution, there were at least three cameras filming every nook and cranny. The only rooms that were not 24/7 under surveillance were the bathrooms and some of the select Attorney visiting rooms, Officers' suites, and the Warden's deluxe suites, being exempt from the eye on the wall.

Sara fondly remembered getting even for her sister Kamryn's betrayal… ending that cheating bridesmaids reign on this earth,

smirking 'that was fun. I never got that bastard Rocky, though…
he was still on her list to deal with.'

"Everything all right, sisters. I saw you both holding each other. Why are you crying, Kamryn?" "Carl, please leave us alone. What are you doing stalking us? Give us some space, please." 'Geez, Sara, oh, all right, wow, I meant nothing by…' Sara shuts the door of her Salon in his face with a biting sneer. Kam was still anxious and said, "that guy is out of control, sis." "He means no harm. Don't you feel at peace now, even a bit more tranquil inside my salon? Here sit, Kam; let me fix your mascara. It's bleeding. It's my fault I caused your tears. That won't happen again; I'm sorry."

Suddenly the door pops open 'you sisters want something to drink?' "Yes, that would be so sweet of you, Carl; iced tea for both of us, thanks…." "No problem, Sara, be right back."

Kam wobbles her head and then tilts her chin up "sister, really, what's up with that guy? He is now your waiter. He's a Jailer… a damn correction officer, and he's like glue on ur ass, Sara. I don't like that dude; he's got ulterior motives. Uh, something smells wrong… to me." "I know, but hey, iced tea sounds good to me right about now and delivered on top of it!" With an unnatural gleam in her eyes, "Kam, please, I hope I will be able to meet your honey fiancé Edward before you get married. What's the hold-up with the visiting forms? He isn't a Felon, is he?" She nervously releases a loose chortle "nope, far from a Felon or Criminal. He should be approved next week, I think."

"Speaking of Edward, I want to forewarn you, Sara and don't want you to get upset, but in July … hold on, let me check the calendar. From July 7th to the 15th, Edward and I are going to do a houseboat vacation with all the toys, Sea-Doo's, a Ski boat, and some fishing on Lake Shasta." Kamryn pauses with a hand on her sister's knee. "I'm going to learn how to drive a quad motorcycle in the mountains. We're going to do a picnic up in the Shasta Forest because of that. I will miss you on 7/13/17, our typical Thursday visit. Still, I will be bringing bunches of pictures. His parents will be on a world tour in Europe, so it will be just Edward and me for over a week out on the water barbeques… water sports. Oh, Sara, I wish you could be there like I said one day, sis!"

"No worries, Kam, as Sara takes out her calendar so you will visit me the week before on 7/6/17. Is that correct?" "Yes, that's a Thursday. I'm only going to miss the July 13th visit, sweetie."

-34-

6/13/10… Past Life, Sara is finally free of scrutiny. .

The Pacific ocean breeze blew her long, flowing strawberry-blonde hair. She had accentuated her sharp Scandinavian nose and pale dusted blue azure eyes. Her accent was Swedish, umh; Sara was again fully equipped and had her latest and greatest laptop; her electronic spree at Best Buy was rewarding. She was wired for sound, ready to be the predator that would sequester her comingling inner minds, now leaving her storage. She had plenty of spending cash and identifications she had purchased on the Dark Web and the other Internet.

Tunnel vision enhanced with vigilance zoned in with special attention from this time forward, no more errors or misjudgments again. She had logged into her home pages and accounts and was currently in the process of locating Brock via his cell phone. Then she would go to priority mode. 'Marvin Payco' was her objective first in line, biting her inner lip, Yum blood. It had been three days since she had made her escape.

Funny though, after a thorough check, there were no Warrants out for her arrest, but the Feds put out a BOLO (be on the lookout) and were actively hunting her. She was their 'numeral uno,' wanted prey. Brock and Lucie were undoubtedly at the San Diego Fed Building in a freakin tizzy, or at least his phone was probably going bonkers. I wonder why he still used that phone. Didn't he figure it out yet? as she saw its location in his office on her interactive map. Sara knew thus far she was out of this world lucky... she wasn't arrested and therefore didn't have to bond out of jail, the FBI and other Law Enforcement Agencies had zilch except for the change-up on the Camaro's license plate. Truly she didn't have to report in, nor in reality, could have gone anywhere. She'd even retained her Passport. But it was legal for the FBI to be her shadows, and harass her by following her everywhere, the American system had its flaws, but Hey, I was a free woman! Lol.

What Sara would have paid to see his face when Brock was told she had escaped... and vanished? Her Attorneys were livid. Terrance jumped down her throat; her Attorney had a valid point. Why run? But my argument was that I was tired of the FBI being my shadow and told Mr. Hallinan to give me a week to lay on the beach, and I would resurface. I would see him personally at his S.F. Law Office. He laughed and told me that was a slick move going out the window. The lead Agent, Brock Dame, was furious there was a 'woman hunt' in the process... Lol.

The last three days and nights had been total chaos, emergency meetings, and an entire task force hunting Ms. Sara Sloan, San Diego Police North to L.A., the Bolo had turned absolutely nothing, up Zero even Lucie's home in Oceanside was under surveillance. The afternoon that they had woken up and powered up their phones, you would have thought that Brock had been jolted by one of those Heart shocking defibrillators. Lucie's adrenalin was pumped up, then her fever from the flu beat her down again, leaving her in bed for nearly another three days; now, they were together and setting up computers running, searches for any signs of Sara.

Lucie says, "this is bizarre, Brock. It's like we're back at square one, as if we don't know who Sara is again. She is on the loose we have zero leads. It's like all we can do is sit and wait for her to make the next move, shit, still waiting on that Bitch. Doesn't that sound familiar?"

"Damnit, Luce, she should have already been behind bars with no bail amount. Her being a danger to society, her slick escape was legal in her Attorney's eyes. Hell, we hadn't any hold on her in their minds. The circumstantial evidence was enough, but over 25 days of thoroughly searching her properties and anything with her name on it, not a thread of damning evidence as if she's a fkn Nun… nothing we cannot even freeze her accounts."

"Well, all we can do is monitor her accounts. Darn it, our hands are tied." "Don't worry… she will turn up; Sara will need money sooner than later. She wouldn't be stupid enough to commit another murder, for it would obviously point directly at her. What did the Asshole lawyer say to you yesterday?" "Aah, Luce, he said that Sara felt claustrophobic. We were like her shadows, harassment personified… she couldn't breathe and needed a break, some peace, and solitude. We, the FBI, had ruined her life and her businesses… had alienated all her friends; we were the Evil ones!"

"Okay, so where would she go for solitude and peace? We have the trains, busses, and airports under surveillance, canvassing the Mexico border, her pictures plastered at rental car agencies. She couldn't have gone far, right?" "I don't know, Luce." As he rubs his hands through his hair, "we're lost. Where would she strike? You know she's threatened both of us; we best be on high alert!" "Umh, like we're not, babe?"

<u>**Sara dresses to kill…**</u>

It's time to move as she lays down a valise, unzips it, and pulls out five separate outfits, all stylish in their own ways. I popped open another suitcase that had an assortment of shoes. Sara looks down at her flip-flops with little roses on them. Looking up at her, Sara revises her hairdo into a French braid, then stands nude admiring her curves, her reflection no time for any self-manipulations. As she rubs her mound and leans in, staring back into her face close up meticulously works the applications of makeup, still astonished at how effective age reduction can be accomplished with cosmetics easily 5 to 15 years could be lifted from facial features.

Back at her bed, another look at the wardrobe she'd brought from her storage, her choice a favorite slinky chartreuse silk sheath dress so feminine and sexy, but which shoes? A pair of classy pumps or shiny flats, or a pair of high-heeled strappy sandals, maybe stilettos, the choice was the pumps, clearly the winner. The heels were not too cumbersome, and she could still stride confidently.

Checking her look once again, sexy, sophisticated professional, only in a way a woman could look too bad, you men, as she winks at herself, air kisses. With her briefcase, she struts from the Tropicana Hotel's 5th floor, the Grand Suite, with Mission Beach in the foreground, tourists and regulars congesting the strip. She drove her rental Ford Focus east on Hwy 8, her destination an older sub-division in the city of La Jolla her G.P.S. chirped as she made her way along the hilly drive. She remembers her assortment of pictures and flyers at the Dollar Car Rental office. Be aware that ole Sara was on the hot list, albeit not this Sara.

Wherever she drove, she had a stealth forcefield surrounding her for approximately three hundred feet. Her electronic blocking cloaking device was initiated, and a plastic 34-ounce container of water sat in her cup holder. On the passenger seat, buckled in by the seatbelt, she had her special jug of poison in what you would see a runner or jogger carry on a strap. The contents sloshed back and forth, sealed tight. The home she would be visiting was on the next block. She squirmed with excitement. Sara had an appointment with the 'Big Mouth' eyewitness who had brought her World down to her ankles. She giggled. The Feds would never guess that her next victim would be Mr. Marvin Payco. This guy was an extreme egotist. Besides referring to himself in the 3rd person, Romeo believed he was a lady killer. He had made three YouTube videos of his exploits, right down to his address and phone numbers. A self-promoting fool, he had been interviewed by Channel 7, 2, and 3; all local channels bragged that next week he would be on a show called 'Good Morning L.A.' His claim to fame was his sharp mind. And how his intuition led to him recognizing her. He would constantly take his index and middle finger in his videos, point to his eyes, and pat his head. Yelping out, 'I knew it was Sara the second I saw her at the bar sitting there all alone! I catch all my Vibes… and I'm almost Never wrong. I see more than other humans. I'm a paranormal seer and have a 7th sense.'

Sara cackled. Soon enough, she'd be testing that theory a 'paranormal seer with vibes.' What a fool to believe any of his bullshit on social media. Well, an idiot was hatched every second on this putrid planet.

Sara had called him on a burner phone to set up an interview with him at his home, a private meeting playing up on his ego told the idiot she was a reporter from the S.F. Chronicle. Sara borrowed a name from the newspaper, her appointment at 5:15 pm, which was only minutes away. Parks, below his property, looked up the 75 or more steps to a large bay window and wrap-around deck. The driveway was roped off; apparently, it was being re-sealed. A glossy black glistened from it with the odor of tar. She turned her wheels inward at the curb in her passenger seat. She snatched up her satchel over the shoulder bag and had a briefcase in her left hand. In Sara's right hand was the jug of poison.

Sara starts to step up and out of the Ford… a howl, hoot, and holler from above. Marvin and the two girls are jumping, laughing, dancing, and cavorting about the smoke of a barbeque in the air. Once the sliding glass door was opened, music entered the mix. A furious scowl took hold. She had called for a private interview, not a damn party. This wasn't going to work; her entire attitude and demeanor sank. Without even taking another glance, she was behind the wheel and gone. Fifteen minutes later, I parked in front of a 'Traders Joe' calling Marvin.

"Hello, Marvin, this is Ms. Lane of the San Francisco…" "Hi, are you having trouble finding my place Ms. Lane? You can't miss it. I have the driveway…." "Sorry, Marvin, something came up not going to make it this afternoon, but what are you doing later on this beautiful Southern California evening? I'd wear a sweater if I were back in San Francisco." Marvin laughed… Sara forged on, "I have to fly back tomorrow… Sunday morning, so I would like to meet with you before then. If possible, umh, my boss will kill me if I don't get this interview. It is supposed to be included in an Exposé about your magnificent awareness and catching this Sara, the alleged Serial Killer, for a Sunday spread in my newspaper. Oh, I'm sure your aware that she's on the lamb, being sought by every Law-enforcement entity in the state of California!"

"Yeah, I heard that; it's all over the Net and news. I can't believe she wasn't arrested. I have been in a battle, having to hire an attorney trying to get the $350,000 reward that I deserve."

"Marvin, I hope you don't have a problem with me uploading images of you when we get together. I need vivid color pictures for the paper…." "Aah, Ms. Lane, I will make myself available… the only thing I have scheduled is a quick appearance at a pub here in La Jolla for a friend's B-Day party; I will be there from 7:30 till maybe 8:30 tonight, sort of a cameo… then I can meet you back at my house or at a coffee place wherever?"

Sara could hear squeals and noise in the earpiece "sounds like you're having a party over there?" "No, my Lil sister and girlfriend and I are having a BBQ wish you could have made it. My famous Tri-Tip is sizzling on the grill!" "Marvin, save me a slice or three. How about I meet you at your place at 9 pm? That should give me plenty of time to interview…" "Or you could meet me at the 'Brigg,' I'll be around. Just text me gotta go. The Tri Tip's ready, and the potatoes are Smokin' seeya! Ms. Lane," click. Gone that obnoxious prick, seeya huh yeah that's right seeya Marvin DEAD! 👎.

At 7:45 pm, she watches him pull into the parking lot of the pub in La Jolla named The Brigg, his oversized tires on a dark green Dodge 4-wheel drive with the woman she saw on the deck of his house clamoring out the passenger side. With a pair of mini binoculars, Sara watched as best as she could. The sun was down over the ocean almost. The floodlights of the parking lot had already been initiated.

Damn, she mused that the place was packed. What a business, yes, a Saturday night, but at another time, this could be the place she would have entertained an investment broker or a client for her passé Real Estate Business.

Live music swirled out of the Brigg each time the double doors of the entrance were opened by the bouncers, who looked at all entries like vultures. The steady mix of genders was consistently pretty, handsome, evenly matched, and most looking for sex. Some were discreetly looking to cheat to get laid, while others wanted to move up the food chain to find a wealthy mate. Others were hunters waiting to pounce, or the subtle games played by the wanna-be Prey, players of the most alluring kind, the flirtatious, the raunchy, they all found a place at the Brigg!

Sara waited, anxiously digging deep for her renowned fortitude, one of her best virtues. It was time she texted his phone. 'I will be at the Brigg soon. Can we meet?' She leans up against her car and mulls over her plan for the umpteenth time. Was she missing anything?

Marvin's phone would have her texts and calls; she deleted the text before pushing send. Ugh, it would be better to call him but wait, what if the freak had an App to record his calls? Sara, couldn't and wouldn't leave a speck of any evidence? The last three calls went to his VM. She left it blank and said nothing. The time now was 8:11 pm patience was wearing thin; what could she do? Well, she could enter the 'restaurant bar, uhm, the Brigg.' After all, she was 'dressed to Kill,' a smug smirk gone as fast as it was revealed. On the 5th call, he answered, "Marv here!" "Hey, it's the reporter from San Francisco, Marvin." "Ugh, hold on, I can't hear you!" as she listened to the music exploding… out of the bar, there was Marvin holding one finger in his ear hole, the phone to his other ear, standing at the entrance of the Brigg!

He was stepping down the steps "okay, I can hear you now. What's up?" "Can I meet you by your truck in like five minutes, Marvin?" 'Ohahh oops…whoa' hesitation "Aah, umh, howya know I drive a truck, Ms. Lane?" Silence 'hello?' 'ummah,' she pauses. "I read it online where you gave chase and tried to catch that Sara Vipress!" "Oh yeah, that's right, I drive a green Dodge with a lift kit. Yuh, can't miss it; this place is way too rowdy. Maybe we can do the interview in my truck?" "Sounds like a plan, Marv seeya soon!" She clicked end pulls into the lot, nowhere to park by his monster truck. So she parallel parked her Ford Focus, backing it in directly behind the truck, and the motor remained functional, running for a quick exit. Yes, this will be her mode, a quick getaway.

278

Marvin stepped up a little buzzed. She got his attention instantly, exactly like… was her plan. With his libidinous tilt and eye-popping stare, lust filled his pants. He was typically the macho dude who would be in reaction mode. Oh, she was so fkn desirable thinking how luscious she appeared <u>'men are so crudely obvious, simple easy as pie to play'</u> read them like a graphic cartoon. "Hi, Marv…" "Well, umh, wow uh hello there Ms. Lane Dontcha look ravishing heck you look much better than you sounded on the phone, aah I mean umh I didn't mean that I was…."

Sara once again grinned, allowing her dimples to flash giddiness, raised her eyebrows with a noticeable wink, then dropped her chin and smiled. "Once we're done here, Marvin, perhaps, aah, maybe I can get you to buy me a drink," as her skirt blew up in the breeze. "But let's get this interview started so we can get in the Brigg and have some real fun, Marv! Do you like to dance… close dance?" "I'm the best dirty dancer you'll ever dance with, Ms. Lane. Lol, she reaches into her passenger seat for her shoulder bag. "Why don't you turn your car off, Ms. Lane?"

She ignored him as she pulled out her laptop and opened it "see this…" as she put it on the roof of her car, he took another step towards her and started to bend over. That is when her right hand came forward. Holding the liquid poison, the lid already off, she tossed it upwards into his leaned-forward face moving away, retreating from any blowback spray or splash.

Marv's first reaction was a gut-wrenching Scream, and then he started to roll over on the asphalt. At the same time, she tried to pour the rest of the solution on the back of his head, tossed the container onto the ground, put her laptop back in the Ford Focus, and drove away calm as a cucumber when she was far enough down the road she took a long, satisfying breath… Yes!

Later that same Saturday evening, past tense at Mercy Hospital in San Diego, in the crowded waiting room filled with family and friends, Marvin's little Sister said, "if it were me, I wouldn't want to live. His face was eaten away, part of his tongue melted off, his eyes boiled blind, and he was still being kept alive. Where is the fkn Mercy here at Mercy Hospital?"

The dynamic duo was listening from a row of chairs on the other side of Marvin's family. "I agree with her, Brock. They need to pull the plug; why didn't we have surveillance on Marvin? Damnit, what the hell? He will never see them again. Most of his scalp has been burned off. It was Sara what the hell… we should have considered protecting him!" "Lucie, hindsight is twenty-twenty. There was never a threat of retaliation. Remember, we brought this up at the task force meeting. We both spoke of our concerns for Marvin, and they thought it was a low priority."

"But when she gave us the slip, we should have put someone on him. I know it didn't make sense, not her M.O., but do I need to remind you she killed your best friend and others at the Palomar Hotel who hadn't done anything wrong either? In her missives, she called it unfortunate collateral damage. We can't second guess this now, Brock; it is obvious that she wanted him to suffer excruciating and humiliating pain, not a kill like her normal M.O. this was a purposeful example of the evil Sara can exploit from within. We haven't a shred of evidence that it was Sara Sloan… Marv was, Omg, I mean is, a womanizer. There could have been someone else who attacked him. He was a known misogynist?" "Jeez, Luce Sshhh, please keep it down!"

He pulls her down the hall. "Yes, Lucie, but who else would disable the security system at the Brigg using a blocking device to freeze the cameras at the pub? The report states that the entire system was disabled for just seven minutes. Coincidently, we see him walking through the parking lot towards his truck and talking on his phone. Once he got near his truck, then that was it. The video paused, and a few patrons leaving the bar heard the ear-splitting curdling shrieks from Marvin." "Your correct Brock, and to add to that detail... the phone calling him was a burner!"

One of the surgeons Lucie and Brock had spoken with previously... pushed open the door-his countenance shown of horror, "Agents, I've been a surgeon for 23 years, burn patients, mutilation victims. I was a medic in the Desert Storm campaign on and on, but let me tell you, that's the worst of all time. It's as if he wasn't a human ahh but resembles a lizard or alien. Whoever did this to him wanted him to suffer unimaginable pains and didn't want him to die immediately. This was about vengeance, absolute hatred I.M.O. Oh, Btw he just expired."

Lucie stares over at the Chaplain and other nurses and staff, cajoling and empathizing with Marvin's family and friends, thinking there is Mercy here after all. The doctor glances at Brock as both arose... from the uncomfortable chairs. "Thanks, Doctor. I guess we will have to wait for the analysis of the container found at the scene in the parking lot, most likely some Industrial Acid."

The Doctor stopped and spun around "you know, I read a few weeks back that England was having a spate of attacks at nightclubs, and in London, gangs are using Acid that can be purchased at local hardware stores. The populace over there doesn't have the access that we do here for guns, so the alternative was spraying or throwing industrial acids on enemies, might check that avenue out!"

'Thanks, Doc,' as they hit floor number 1 on the elevator. "Wow, Luce, I've peaked and am exhausted; uh, don't feel like driving out to Santee." "I feel yah, babe. Let's use our allowances, get another downtown hotel room, and start fresh in the morning." "All right, let's do it, Lucie."

By 10:35 am on 6/13/10 Sunday.

The Forensic analysis was complete. The mixture of the killing brew, umh, the solution that Marvin had succumbed to, was Muriatic Acid (pool cleaner), and Drano blended with Clorox and topped off with Chlorine. The percentages are nearly exact, around 25% of each, approximately that is. A deadly concoction umh combination that any Ace Hardware or corner hardware store would have... all the contents are shelved at Home Depot and Lowes.

They sit in the breakroom at their office, discussing their latest orders from Wash. D.C. and the fatal mistake that the Special Agent who oversaw the Sara case had made. Her catastrophic blunder of not having a female Agent with Sara and surveilling her everywhere she would go was a devastating miscalculation that only a novice would make. An atrocious egregious error neither Brock nor Lucie would have made.

Lucie sighs "so our orders now are to spend the next week going through Mr. Marvin Payco's online activity, all of his friends, umh, girlfriends. Was there anyone else that would seek revenge upon him?" "Duh, Luce, we both know it was Sara." "Please, Brock, this is our assignment, so we better get to it." "It's a total waste of time; she didn't use her Nicotine or VX Poison sprays. It was a personal Kill her mindset was to change up her M.O. so we couldn't pin this killing on her butt...." "I'm as frustrated as you are, dude. I mean, babe looking at the list his sister has compiled, he did make his rounds and did have enemy's hell take a look at his ex-girlfriend's. He was a busy guy. She shows him a list of names, "whew, what a player in the last three years. Is it possible 27 women? Shit, lucky he didn't get Aids or a bunch of STDs!" declares Brock. "Sooner we get on this... the better off will be.

Let's start with the current GF and go back from there, all right," he concedes with a nod.

They were returning from a quick lunch, passing on the elevator and taking the stairs; Brock's secretary "Hey, sir, here are some of the preliminary results from the forensics on Mr. Payco's iPad. I sent you an electronic file, but here is a set of hard copies." "Thank you very much." He looks at the top page, 'let's go' as he hands them over to Lucie. They take the steps two at a time down towards the Crown Vic. On a roll, she says, "Oh no, listen to this" as she reads from one of Marv's emails; 'you piece of shit castration would be too good for you' or 'you small dick mother fker I'm going to pay you back if it's the last thing I do in my life!' "Ugh, listen to this one," 'three months of my life wasted on you, you're a pathetic piece of shit', or 'I hate you, Marv, you're the scum of the earth, hope you die in a car crash!' Umh, or 'you ripped me off… you're going to get what's coming to you. You promised to pay for half of our trip to Hawaii. I'm in collections. You owe me $7,000. I'm going to kill you, Marvin!'

She exhales, "geez, that's just the beginning or start of the Hate that ole Marvin brought on himself. He had made some women angry enough to harm him. The Playboy was getting some valid threats on his life."

"Unfortunately, we have our work cut out for us, Lucie, sweetheart. Do you really think that Sara isn't the culprit? Please, it's Sara, right?" She slams the folder down. "I uh am not 101% sure anymore. Look, he's got multiple threats on his life right here on my lap, and why wouldn't Sara spray him and be done with it." "Luce, remember the cloaking device the security system froze up? Was that a coincidence? I think not!" "I realize that, but don't forget what the owner said. The system froze up from time to time!"

She yanks out another page "shoot, he's had three different restraining orders by women, his truck was vandalized, oh fk sorry, excuse me, someone poured an Acid solution all over his hood… insurance claim, police reports, this leads me to think it might not be Sara." An exasperated yawn "all right you have my attention woman this could very likely turn out to be one of his jilted lovers, just weird coincidence maybe. Still, Sara is my #1 suspect."

<u>6/18/10 Friday 12:55 pm.</u>

What a fun five days and nights, yes, major relaxation; Hwy 101 up the coast stopping in Monterey for the night was a highlight, three bed and breakfasts all on the beach. She left San Jose this morning. "Sara had one more stop in San Francisco, which was at her storage building; then, she'd return the rental car… rented under the name of Ms. Sweden and take Uber over to her Attorney's building. Sara had an appointment with Terrance Hallinan for 2:45 pm. She was running late. ⇜.

Sara stepped off the fancy spacious elevator and directly into a reception area… suits and skirts like guppies flushed out by a Shark were fluttering in and out of cubicles. These were the 'minnows, minions' offices duplicated as far as she could see. Then she saw a gold plate plaque. It read Mr. Terrance Hallinan, Attorney of Law. She followed an arrow down the corridor of exquisite tile, a blue-grey feldspar of the Spanish granite Azul Aran directly from the quarry in the 'Pyrenees' in northern Spain.' Uh, and she should recognize it. Having gone in on the deal with Terrance for her Mill Valley home, the path ended. She opened the door.

A gorgeous model material woman, secretary yummy, a female of deliciousness, hello Sara 'I'm Ms. Jewel,' 'with diamonds to match, I noticed.' "I'm Mr. Hallinan's office manager. I'm afraid he is not here. He went up to his penthouse at a little after 3 pm. He told me to have you join him.

Ms. Jewel slides a card over to Sara, "take this card, put it in the slot, then push P-1. The elevator will then take you to Terrance. I will let him know you're on the way up, and oh, use the elevator on the far left. The other ones don't go all the way up to his penthouse." "Thank you so much, Ms. Jewel." Sara cruised out the door into the elevator on the left and pushed P 1. Moments later, the door slid open to a magnificently huge foyer, plants in pots, and sunlight through the clouds lit the entire area up. A Solarium, she thought, how beautiful!

Over a speaker system, 'Sara, please take your 3rd door on the left,' she wonders as she passes artifacts, alcoves with lit portraits… paintings statues like a museum, what the costs of these artifacts might be. "Sara, please take a seat. Would you like something to drink?" He gestures to a maxi fridge and open bar… juices, coffee, and alcohol. Go ahead and help yourself." "Thanks, Mr. Hallinan" "call me Terrance, as I've told you too many times to count, Uncle Terrance. No need to be so formal! Get over here and give me a hug, doll. We're family, right?"

Sara grabs him with a big, furious hug. "I thought you were going to be mad at me… Uncle?" their embrace cools. She reaches for a cold energy drink. Rockstar added a dash of top-of-the-line Vodka to the top, snatched up a straw, and wandered back over to her amused Attorney. Eyes wide, looking amazed at the humongous Mahogany desk, at least three times the size of any she'd ever seen. Music lightly played, dropping from the ceiling, which had to be 11ft high… artist 'Toddie Reed's' song 'Anglo Sax' was playing. "Sara, let me get right to the point here. I've known you and your entire family for as long as my life has spanned."

"I am here to support you with legal advice and counseling on how to maneuver through, and past the legal hurdles that seek to restrain you it doesn't much matter to me if you are culpable of any of which the FBI alleges, with that being said

I will put up with no more stunts such as you pulled off down South, yah got that little lady?"

"I need to be kept in your thought-processed loops. Can you comprehend the pressure the Attorney General, the Director of the FBI, and several Federal Judges applied once you vanished?" "Remember, who your Advocates are, it's my Law practice and our expertise that will either save your ass or allow you to sink into the abyss. We are your voices of truth, a necessary buffer… if you will."

"We handle all inquiries, publicities, all negatives in hopes we can reverse perceptions by the public and the Federal Prosecutorial team meant on your destruction arrest, and conviction for life not excluding the Death Penalty doesn't put us at a disadvantage again Sara, the only reason you're not dressed in Orange and sitting bare-assed naked on a cold stainless-steel toilet is because of me!"

Sara leaned further back, sitting uncomfortably in an ergonomic cushy chair, and felt like she was a child being reprimanded by her daddy. She takes a long pull on her straw and sways her head back into the silence. She felt compelled to break this long uncomfortable pause. "Aah, they were stifling me, smothering me. I had a bout of claustrophobia and bolted Uncle Terrance. I betcha you would have done the same thing that I did… when the female Agents were glued to my ass. They'd follow me and wait inside the restrooms harassing me derisively, but when the idiot in charge of the surveillance team failed to put a female on me, I took advantage of their stupidity, Uncle!"

"Sara, my Niece… save the semantics and bullshit for some buffoon with a moronic mental capacity… that is entirely untrue! I'm warning you now for the last time no more dishonesty; remember when you were in Highschool and were busted in the Principles office, and I presented the lesson to you that truth and integrity are all that your Uncle will deal with and that 'Lies of Omission' are plainly Lies do you get that Yet Sara?"

"Your absconding was orchestrated and premeditated, planned to the 8th of an inch calculated to the minuteness of details. I saw the pictures and the video from the entrance to your board meeting; the alteration, come on, dear, you changed your outfit and running shoes, even put your hair in a wrap and pre-ordered your French Dip lunch, all precisely enacted a search of your phone that you had to leave showed you researched when the San Diego Padres double header would likely start, etc."

"I would have asked you to call us. After all, we did supply you with a secure phone, did we not?" "Yes, sir, you did. I feel embarrassed. I truly apologize. I will be forthright with you from here on out, sir!" "Stop the Sir crap. You're now on notice, Sara… anymore screw up's, and you will be locked up, where I will know where your fkn ass is, yah got it?" Sara kowtows only with a respectful nod.

"Now I have the compulsion to enact a fail-safe strategy to alleviate much of the upcoming stress leveraged on you and us, and we can meet our adversaries on an even playing field. We must, with forethought, make the first move, which will be this. I am going to provide you with a couple of bodyguards. This should help keep the FBI at Bay."

"Sara, here is a credit card and a new iPhone. All you need to do is click on the app on your screen, and a female professional bodyguard will accompany you wherever you want to go; conveniently, they have an office right in your hometown of Mill Valley… okay?" "That's great, Terrance. Thank you, bunches. What have you learned of the ongoing witch-hunt investigation; do I have anything to be concerned about?"

"My dear Sara, your portrayal of naivete is such pretense and a waste of your energy and mine, no need to posture. You come from a long line of intellectuals, your very much aware that a special task force has your identities plural and have attributed your handy work to about 39 to 45 murders. Whom the hell knows at this very instant in time? Most likely, teams of Forensic Scientists are retracing their steps taking each victim under the proverbial microscope. Searching for a speck, a sliver of DNA, a loose hair from your scalp, make no mistake; they plan to incarcerate you until you're so old you will not be able to wipe your 'cobwebbed' own ass! The plan from their side of the room is to be there in person when the Lethal Injection is jammed into your veins. The Death Penalty is what they plan for you, Sara, so again, with that being disseminated, please work with us, not against us. Let's try and keep your pretty neck from the gallows noose!"

Sara was by then sweating, and it wasn't from the energy Vodka drink, nope! "But Uncle didn't California vote down the death penalty…." True, Sara, but Texas hasn't, and you are suspected in three killings in the Dallas area!" A jangle emits from his desk phone, "that's my next client, so I will have to bid you adieu, my dear Sara." Sara stands, bows courteously, her head ever so slightly, puts her glass on the stainless-steel sink, then says, "Uncle Terrance, I want to thank you again. I have a firm understanding of what is expected of me and the danger to my freedom. I will not let you or us down again!"

"I will keep you abreast of any personal decisions that could affect our relationship or the upcoming litigation. I trust that the funds that I have provided are sufficient and accessible to your firm, and if they are not adequate, let me know again. Thanks for the phone and your guidance Terrance." Sara reaches the elevator doors, about to cross the threshold. "Lastly, My dear, I will inform the Feds your back with the living, so expect there to be a shadow or three to re-emerge, don't speak to anyone about anything, not even the bodyguards. Oh, BTW, what an unfortunate occurrence seemed like a violent act of revenge and retaliation on Marvin Payco. He had many enemies; lucky for us that it was Acid that took his philandering life and not some form of poison spray!" he chortles, morphing into a gruesome cackle.

She spun her head around quickly just in time to see his upside-down Smirk, even from a distance between them 'four eyes Zoomed in and met all four eyes, understood eyebrows flinched in unison. Did he fkn wink at me? She turned the corner… Yes!

<u>**-36-**</u>

<u>**Present Time 5/31/17 NIA Thursday, Sara scheming!**</u>

Sara didn't schedule any makeovers, haircuts… nor styles, Pedicures, or manicures. Her salon was closed, and her sister Kamryn would visit later this morning. A sort of quandary she'd been mulling over as of late, what to do about correction officer Carl? His usefulness had run its course. Sara was tired of the janitor's closet and walk-in freezer and the sneaking around to satisfy his cravings and every whim, his smelly groin shoved up into her face.

Yes, Carl had been a great coup and major asset, but his value had been diminished to a non-necessity, and daily he'd become more of a nuisance. Carl had been maximized and used up. She could visualize the pot at the end of the Rainbow. She'd accomplished as much as she could using the idiot. It was a waste of effort to keep him hanging on, pun intended. The blowjobs were beyond boring. She suffered humiliation each time she kneeled before the fat smelly slob having to take a box of 'clean wipes' and a spray of Cologne to make the deed palpable.

He was now once again pushing hard for penetration. He wanted more than just Oral sex. His demands and overt threats were taking a toll on her mind. Was it time to have him busted for sexual harassment of an Inmate? He would be fired at best, at worse, moved to another floor or area of NIA with mixed emotions, none of which were desirable. She wasn't in the least bit fond of the adulterer cheating Carl. He was merely a helpful cog Hell, and his moral turpitude stood for every reason she was incarcerated at NIA.

But what of retaliation by the staff? This could be the end of her master plan, her 'Mission Impossible'... convoluted irritation about what to do, what of self-preservation, hell if she needed him on the outside again? Then shit, he knew many of her secrets, but who would believe him? What proof was there? But being a sex slave to his smelly genitals was too much trauma, ugh, maybe nose plugs and cologne. One thing was certain Carl was loyal and would go down with the proverbial ship, that Sara was confident of... that being mulled over, Sara would have him busted somehow anonymously!

Again Sara mused... one thing for sure is that she could trust him, and for now, for over three years, she had him hire Private Investigators; the reports were made monthly and then destroyed. Carl was her outside source, eyes her oxygen. Damn, if he would stop the pressure of sex... he was a loose link but had been her everything since her imprisonment!

Hey, gulping and slurping down some semen 3 or 5 times a month is a small price to pay physically. However, she did sometimes help him, allocating money from her secret accounts to purchase cryptocurrency that couldn't be traced into his account. It wasn't just a sexual arrangement. Nope, he sucked from her financial benefits. I could have his ass in a sling simply by saying to the Head nurse, 'Carl is sexually harassing me. Please watch him.'

Carl tried to force me into one of the Janitor storage rooms, only earlier this morning, knowing where all the cameras were, an added advantage for the man. I could even get him busted with his pants down. He was so dumb he'd haven't a clue, wouldn't know the difference. I'd be A-Okay if he didn't suspect I set him up. Whatcha think, Sara? I mused and let these thoughts bounce off, uhm, of my skull of hidden entities, which remained sequestered for now. He was done, she decided, like burnt toast, but the question remained... ugh, How?

Maybe I could use Sista dear to say a few sentences about ole Carl to the staff, and she's already creeped out by him. No, the best result was to eliminate Carl from this dimension. Kill Carl... Dead men tell no Lies, but how?

Hellyeah, the pros outweighed the cons time to take him out of this equation. There were plenty of cleaning chemicals in those closets. Her mental adjudicator, umh, arbitrator's voice bounced off of her Cerebrum, her always logical thinking and reasoning, problem-solving purifier, stepped up to the plate and put a stop to that meandering thought... No, I couldn't murder Carl yet! If I did something like that, killing ole Carl, the authorities would link the Marvin acid trip down in San Diego to me, Naw. I'm so close to fruition that I can't make any stupid, dumb mistakes or miscalculations. Everything I was to do had to be vetted at least 13 times. Then again, once more, just before initiation, one thing is positive Carl was the only liability she had. His benefits were pallid and feeble, and they'd peaked weakened and now inconsequential... his usefulness was history. How to put the slob in the morgue?

How? Aah, Kamryn waves at her with that gracious warmhearted gleam in her gorgeous eyes umh, my big sister had arrived just in time, huh? I gotta hear, listen attentively, pretend to be all excited, be fake, and give her the expressions that match her wonderful fkn life and pending marriage… she's so happy it's fkn pathetic. Ugh, I feel like vomiting.

Sara hops up with the patented fake spring in her step. "Oh sister, I love you so and missed you. Yah want me to style your hair? Do your nails; you wanna get lunch? I'm so happy you're here," she says, but she barfed under her epidermis. She hurled vomit metaphorically…

<u>Doctor Ame Amaya… present time, perplexed and annoyed.</u>

Ame's secretary Don peeks into her office after a series of taps on her door. Ame was preoccupied drawing away on her 11 X 14 art and craft sheets. She looked up "hey Doc, it's after 5 pm. I'm going to be heading out 15 minutes from now. Is there anything I can do for you before I leave?"

"No thanks, Donny" "What's wrong, Ame? Since you returned from NIA, you have been in a funk. Even your last client said you were not yourself today!" She puts down her Art "yeah, know one of your quick back rubs could help with the tension in my neck and shoulders."

Ame moves over to a comfy sofa and explains to Donny, "last week, on June 6th, there was a subtle change in both Al and Sara, like a different dynamic was in play that day. I had tapped on my watch, trying to bring Al back to our conversations, but it wasn't to be… Al was agitated. He was lost in his mind. He was involved in a Shakespearean Play, and his mannerisms and voices were being replayed. He kept reciting 'Macbeth' like he was on a stage." "Well, was his medication changed?" asked Don. "No, Don, that was my first question; he came out of it by the end of my interview and was cognizant again and fluent. I don't know if I or we were making major strides, leaps, and bounds, then it's like taking a big step backward. It just has me in a rut! That's all, Donny, just in a blasé mood, sorry."

"Ohh, that feels so good right there," "geez, Ame, your neck is in Knots" "umh, wow, I needed this, thanks." "Then take Sara was lost in her mind, confused and muttering nonsense, and she had this far-out stare going... eyes were glossy, only giving me lip service. It was a struggle for me to communicate with her. It was like I was a bothersome nuisance to her; Donny, you ought to have witnessed the relief on her face when I got up to leave. Usually, she begs me to stay longer. It was as if she was oblivious to my presence, engrossed in some form of mental distraction. She clammed up when I reached out to her for an explanation!"

"Ame, there must have been something in the air... next Tuesday will be a better day. I'm sure of it. Relax, please!" "I appreciate all you do for me, and Don, thank you" "No prob, Ame close your eyes. Let me help you out of your slacks. I know just what your doctor would prescribe you... relax, babydoll!" Tasty!

Past... 6/21/10 Monday, in San Diego.

"It's straight, unadulterated hogwash, Luce. Did you read the statement from her damn attorney uhm, yeah, sure, she just needed some alone time, huh? That's why she escaped out of the window; she wanted to hang on the freakin beach B.S." "I know, but what could we have done if we had enough to arrest her? We would have Brock... at least Sara is back at her house now!"

"It doesn't make any sense for us to work on the Homicide of Marvin. We should be up in Mill Valley on the job. After all, we were the ones who broke the case wide open." "It is what it is, Brock," they were knee-deep, cringing over Marvin's spiteful, hateful girlfriends. Lucie parks the car "all right, this one's name is Evonne."

They ring the doorbell crying, and screaming children are heard when a chubby middle-aged woman with curlers in her hair answers. She stares up at them both, "what the fk has she done now? Don't Freakin tell me she escaped the rehab center?" "Excuse me, ma'am, we're with the FBI and are here to speak with Evonne Furtal," says Brock. "This is Agent Lucie Link, and I'm Agent Brock Dame." Lucie hands the agitated woman their inscribed cards. A child grabbed her thigh from behind, and another peeked through her Mumu dress at them.

Lucie steps in front of Brock, "who escaped the rehab center, ma'am." "Aah, never mind, what are you doing on my doorstep? I have nothing to say to cops?" "Can we speak to Evonne Furtal, please?" "Don't you listen to what I say? She is in rehab?" "How long has she been in rehab, ma'am?" "First, you tell me what this is all about, and then I might answer your questions!" Lucie says, "we're here to interview Evonne about the Homicide of Marvin Payco." The woman's face morphed, then a twinkle lit her eyes, and she started hysterically laughing, pushing the children off and away from her. They just stood there watching this woman, laughing uncontrollably, then, after a while, she caught her breath. "Yes, it couldn't have happened to a better Pig than Marv. Two of these kids are his, he is a no-good, cheating, lying piece of shit, and he drove Evonne to drugs. Prostitution, my daughter has five kids now. She's been locked up for three months." Brock and Lucie back away from the porch "umh, so you knew Marvin?" "Yeah, I knew the dick; he started dating my daughter before she graduated High School. He's a child molester as far as I'm concerned."

"Could you be so kind as to give us the name of the rehab center your daughter is at, please?" "I can do better than that" the children were breaking stuff, and fighting in the background 'here is one of their brochures,' the door shuts.

Brock and Lucie had left their daily morning meeting at the Fed Building. In collusion with their beliefs that their boss was only a figurehead, they were uncomfortably watching and taking orders from the man who oversaw the San Diego FBI. Lucie sat close enough in the packed conference room to nudge her foot into Brock's leg. They played Footsies like children while listening to the reports about the Vipress case filed by the FBI team that had taken over. Feeling chided and disrespected, they were called in later that afternoon for another impromptu lecture after interviewing another of Marvin's ex-girlfriends. The boss used to be an ally, but lately, Washington, DC, had superseded him.

They were beckoned back to the office when, following up on another tip about the Marvin murder, they finally found the leading suspect, who was supposedly in Las Vegas when the attack occurred. A few months prior, the woman was arrested for pouring Acid on Marvin's truck! The tickets were stamped, and they didn't mind the two-night quick flight to Vegas!

On their way back to the Fed building, they wondered why what else was there to say... the boss was a kiss-ass. Brock yelped out loud to Lucie that he guessed the reason was because of their constant meddling in the Sara investigation. Lucie concurred, for she had sent a scolding email only the day before regarding their complaints of being taken off the case! Now relegated to the sidelines chasing their tails and the dozens plus of countless suspects who had motives to splash Acid on Marvin. They were on the sidelines and were treated unfairly, and their boss didn't have the balls to stand up for them... atleast. That was Brock's assumption, and the guy always wanted to hear himself speak, verbalizing useless chatter.

Now sitting across from one another, listening to their used-to-be ally and boss, he had a peculiar expression and then spoke, "Brock, Lucie, try and empathize with my position here. You're my best agents combined. At least your arrest records could attest to that. Angrily my authority was subverted. I was superseded by the powers to be in D.C. It wasn't my call when they sent a special Agent to take charge of the task force that you oversaw. Listen, I understand your resentment and frustrations; I have read unrelenting grumbling emails and get your standoffish attitudes." he stands up from the cluttered table. You both should put this in your 'pipes and smoke it.' Lucie nudges Brock's foot. Like, here we go again. Ugh...

"I fought tooth and nail to have Ms. Sloan arrested and indicted all the way to the Grand Jury. We all know this whole pig and pony show is a farce. The Grand Jury is a constant across America. Uh, over 97% of the time, they earmark any charges we put before them, but in the case of Sara, she had unyielding opposition, a defense team right inside our hierarchy."

Brock spins Lucie a perplexed, confused squint. She again nudges his leg. Both had heard these similar words before, redundantly. Where was this conversation leading? "This is the crux; yes, we had photos of, aah, Sara in the white 2010 Camaro with the altered license plate that was stolen. This assumption was futilely flawed. Yes, Marvin was able to take a slew of pictures on his phone of her leaving the bar, the 'Brigg,' but not one shot was to be had with her face and the license plate together, not one."

"Come on, boss, don't we have enough circumstantial evidence?" asked Brock. He shook his head no... "her legal team pointed out that in Southern California, including both SAN and LAX airports car rental services, a total of 19 white Chevy Camaros rented on the same day, same models. Sadly, since we didn't have a clear picture of Sara inside the same white Camaro with the stolen tags at the L.A. Courthouse murder of Mr. Grope, the basketball player, all we have are solid pictures and video of Sara dropping off the Camaro with legal tags IMO, we need only one tiny break! No question, what we needed for an indictment was just one photo of her next to the stolen tag of that car. In our extensive searches, we could not substantiate a Link, no pun Lucie, or even a thread of evidence. We vetted all her electronic devices and did Forensics for DNA. Sorry, we have been chasing our tails."

He paused and sucked down the rest of his bottled water, "the tips called in have overwhelmingly added to nothing, Agents... Nada!" The straightforward narrative was refreshing, so Brock felt compelled during this small break to throw in his 11 cents, "but boss Agent Link and I were the lead Detectives investigating Sara. We were the ones that broke the...." "That's why I called you this afternoon. The Special Agent in charge of the Sara investigation has been called back to D.C. along with her team on some terrorist activity. An insurgent group from Iran is trying to intimidate a few Government officials." He waved a memorandum in front of them.

"So, despite the Wash D.C. opposition, I'm re-assigning the both of you to the Vipress Serial Killer Investigation. You're now back in charge. You fly out on Monday morning, July 15th, to S.F. this will be where you will be based out of the San Francisco Federal Building. All the files and data gleaned thus far will be uploaded to your accounts. We are currently taking a case-by-case re-analyzation of each murder, working around the clock. I guess that's all unless either of you has something to add?" Brock and Lucie didn't let on how excited they were, acting like business per usual. But they failed and were overwhelmed that they were back on the case. 💲.

"Get packed up and enjoy the weekend." Popping up like 'Jack in the Boxes,' the pleasure couldn't be misconstrued "thanks, sir, thank you, we won't let you down," says Lucie...

He sounds off just before they exit with fresh air in their lungs, "both of you, be careful. She has already thrown down the Gauntlet. Your lives have been threatened. Watch your backs. I trust you will finally bring this case to a close thank you, agents!" 'Yes, sirs.'

The door shuts. They both grin. She jumps in for a quick hug… 'Yes!' Not a word was spoken down the stairs. 'Marin County, here we come,' says Lucie! Brock kisses her fast and directly shouts, 'this is Awesome!' Like anything newsworthy, the stories in the paper, on television, and the social media sites were wearing thin. The sensationalism of a possible Serial Killer living in Mill Valley stimulated the masses especially being a woman and one of such beauty. Like any story overemphasized, it went cold and old without any closure based on pure speculation. The Masses fell back into the belief that if this were true that she was a Killer, then why wouldn't she have been arrested, please, okay?

-37-

<u>Sara was frustrated… sequestered, and locked down like an animal in a Zoo!</u>.

Sara looks out her loft window at a glorious day, not a news van for the first time in sight. She had turned down every interview paid attention to her attorneys, didn't put gasoline on the fire, and showed the other cheek. Now or soon, it was time to flip the tables on the accusers and hold them accountable their purposeful deliberate personal attack has to be reconciled.

The police and the Feds leaked all types of information and never came right out and said that Ms. Sara Sloan was a Serial Killer. Still, it was insinuated and galvanized dramatically, and who suffered me, Sara? Significant losses in her client lists, which had evaporated entirely. A trip to the grocery store was caustic and could become traumatic. The hecklers were everywhere; her snobby neighborhood had revolted against her like she was the return of the Black Plague. She couldn't go anywhere anonymously, even shunned at gas stations. Just yesterday, in line at Dutch Bro's for coffee, her bodyguard by her side, a man came up and said, "you got some nerve coming in here prancing all about... your evil and going to hell!"

She was the epitome of malignant cancer metastasizing across her favorite County of Marin. The press and social networks had propagated this evil disdain for her. Even the Vice-President of the HOA homeowners association asked her for her resignation. Now, the neighbors walked around her sidewalk, sometimes even crossing the street with their dogs and poop bags... Aww Gross.

Gawkers, to hell with all of them; I wish I could put a bullet into their viewfinders and shove the camera's phones up their asses. But on the positive, the number of gawkers and tourists had been reduced... been there and seen that. Like showings for Christmas Lights in the middle of January. It was getting old sitting outside her fortress and taking pictures and videos for weeks. People would park across the street aah as she stretched in her Yoga outfit; time for a shower! Screw em all.

She contagiously started to grin, and a sudden smirk evolved had glistened on her dimples 'the worm has turned' now retribution vindication. Her legal team was now prepared to avenge her malicious... cruel, uh, venomous treatment. It's time to go on the offensive! Growling!

A day of reckoning, Yep! Lawsuits to be enacted defamation of character, slander, false allegations, false and vindictive injurious statements written and spoken liable parties too many to name she meditates in silence. The list goes on and on, the New York Times, L.A. Times, San Diego Union, and S.F. Chronicle. Not only were her attorneys seeking monetary repayments for slander, but they also wanted the media to acknowledge in writing corrections and apologize for demonizing her.

Sara suffered negatively in all arenas; wrongly dispersed rancorous propaganda could cost Sara her Real Estate Business. She checks her look in the mirrors, downs her beer, and does a little twirl, for just yesterday, she had seen Lucie and Brock at the park across the street from her home. Yep, party time! It was time for her to strike back. Ahh, fk so glad the cardboard box of a Special Agent was gone; back to the dynamic duo, lol. She sought to eliminate an adversary, uhm, time to go, Lucie Link, the smug cute ass Lucie, gosh, I hate that bitch!

7/23/10 Wednesday. Mill Valley, California.

They sat at the quaint coffee shop just a few blocks from Sara's home; introspection was their theme or narrative, disjointed conversation, unnatural pauses, reading memos, and rules. Both were fully aware of the onerous regulations that the 'Bureau' mandated that the FBI Agents had to adhere to.

They were in the process of disintegrating one such rule. In fact, only hours before the threshold was almost crossed... The Bureau demanded loyalty, especially within partnerships, trust, allegiance, fierce devotion, a brother & sisterhood, an alliance, and a sorority, not intimate relationships. This wasn't condoned.

The fastest way to dissolve a partnership was to exhibit emotional bonds between Agents signs of this physical and mental bonding were not tolerated; lessons learned through history. Each of them signed pacts like all other Agents intimacy between working partners was shunned. If validated, they would be separated and placed with other partners, sometimes in outlying districts in the USA.

Lucie mulls this mandate once again, sure this was even part of the curriculum back in Cadet training, but now years later, it meant they had to navigate a quandary of sorts. How do you not have an emotional connection with your partner? It was unavoidable no matter what, even without sex. Hell, you spend more time with them than your significant others, like 40 or 55 hours together side by side. Sometimes days on end… continuously on lookouts in a week's time, a team or partnership could spend more time breathing each other's body odor than several months with their significant others.

Yet once you crossed the line to love and the physical attributes of the same, it was the end of the team. The 'writing was on the proverbial walls.' After reading the same literature, Brock looked across the small table and smiled "well, I guess we're rule breakers, huh?" "Yeah, sometimes people must make their own rules. Remember, babe, rules were made up from someone's life experience pre… us." "He laughs, well-said woman!"

They had met Homer previously and were driving the borrowed Crown Vic and were allocated hotel rooms in San Rafael, down the road from Sara's residence. Purposely leaving a few miles of distance between them, a partition otherwise like an addiction, both knew they would be shadows on the street she lived on. "Come on, let's venture over to the vixen's neighborhood," mutters Brock. They park in the community lots directly adjacent to Sara's Victorian home.

The Agents on duty acknowledged them and had a short, concise conversation which consisted of "Ms. Sloan had left her house only once at 9:37 am a female bodyguard showed up. I followed her to Whole Foods Grocery Store then shadowed her back here after another stop at an Apple Store, she…" as he looked down at his monitor "she bought an iPad and Apple ear pods also picked up an Apple Watch then arrived back here at 11:59 am that's it real quiet around here, its calmed down around here too, only a few tourists rubberneckers taking pictures of her place, that's about all to report Sir and Ma'am."

'Thank you,' states Lucie as they walk down a wooded path by an artificial pond, children on swings, and a merry-go-round on a very pleasant afternoon in July. After they were in a secluded area, Lucie reached out and clutched his hand. He twirls her around and dips his tongue, swirling in unison deep in her mouth, her arms pulling him in close, clenched now under his muscular arm which held her head tight, breathing and tasting… a snap of a branch nearly an accidental bite as they release like High School kids busted by a teacher!

Three skateboarders laugh and roll past them, the flash of heat between them subsides, and they stroll along an unspoken bond of Love that has undeniably engulfed their hearts and spirits.

Sara caught just enough of this intimate exchange from her loft to fall into a tirade of cuss words. Expletives that sailors would shun… livid was an understatement. Her rant lasted a mere 15 seconds, but it was enough to blow off some steam. Firm decisions were made, and the debate within her multiple diverse mindsets that they hadn't been intimate yet… the operative word was Yet… although this holds no water. Nope! There wasn't any way of denying it. Sara seethed, admitting jealousy, envy hatred with no way to control these weaknesses except one with Termination! The decision was now a foregone conclusion. They'd done the wild thing; the big nasty the Slut Lucie Link finally weakened his resolve. He broke weak; well shit, what did she expect, the constant pressure from the 'cop' bitch.

Now a respectable distance apart, the agents made it back out of the cluster of Eucalyptus Trees, definitely not holding hands. Never in public, they approached Agent Tom, who sat on a bench with binoculars by his side. They stop by to say seeya later on. Tom grins, "hey, the lady sometimes puts on a Hella of a show, almost like a strip tease show in the Tenderloin in San Francisco. It gets kinda wild up in that bay window." Tom points to the third-floor loft "a full-length mirror reflects right down here. It's as if she enjoys being an exhibitionist!"

Brock shakes his noggin. 'What?' replies, "well, that's all fine and good; at least we know where she is, right? Okay, text or call us if she goes out on the prowl and stay on her ass." "Lately, she only leaves with her so-called bodyguards. My shift is up at midnight. I guess I'll see you tomorrow. Agents Dame and Link."

Lucie turns, "we have a team meeting at the Hilton Gardens at 9:30 am on Thursday. I will be texting and emailing the rest of our team since Agent Dame and I are back in charge. We want to get caught up to speed with all your thoughts and feelings. We want to enact a change of venue umh strategy shortly!" "All right, that sounds good. I'm happy that you are back in charge. Our team is looking forward to working with both of you. Good afternoon!"

She reaches over as he drives back to the Hilton Gardens for some dinner and drinks and squeezes his right thigh. As per usual, they had adjoining rooms 315 and 313. The façade was a necessary evil. They even went to the extent of messing each room up to show they lived in each.

Brock parked... Lucie busts out laughing a contagious cackle, causing him to chuckle, then giggle, "what's up girl, what's so damn funny?" She's trying to catch her breath and mumbles. "I just got it. Agent Tom's trusty binoculars are watching Sara's soft porn show like a peeping Toms umh, get it 'Agent peeping Tom perfect' Yes!" It had been a long day already. They'd left So-Cal late the night before, a night not to remember… it was historical and had major credence for their attempted intimacy. The ice had been broken, a 'forgettable moment.' But a hint to cum… 💲.

He snaps her from her reverie "hey, let's shower and get dressed into something relaxing and revisit last night's effort at loving." She elbows him "it wasn't just me, dude." "Lucie, you're a real playgirl." She smirks and morphs into a lopsided grin "what you weren't down with…" "okay, it's 6:45 pm. I will knock on your door at precisely 7:15 for our date!" Lucie wiggles her nose and winks subtly, "make it 7:25. A girl needs more time." She laughs, and they kiss; he pinches her nose slightly… into their rooms they go.

While in her shower, Lucie replays the evening before nervously twitching her shoulders. What the heck happened? Brock and she closed the bar downstairs. How many bottles of wine, at least three after dinner? The conversation got silly, then profound, and the following emotions exploded. The topic naturally morphed to sex, their lack of it, their feelings of pent-up anxieties, and past relationships of pain, both of them devoured and eaten with shredded hearts and souls.

They were afraid and terrified of commitments… celibate for oh so long. Some of the conversations, like a dream, played in her mind as she washed her long hair hot shower feeling great. She remembers playing back what he'd said to her. 'Babe, we've kissed romantically, showered together, and slept naked many times. Don't you want me or desire me?' Lucie lets out a hoot and howl. Wow, the alcohol took hold. 'I said fk yes, sweetheart, I lust for you. We have been so close to making love, and you know that, Brock.'

Brock then said, 'I'm afraid of this affection for you. We're beyond best friends, together all the time, and I love being in your company. I don't want sex and intimacy to change us, who we are, and what we are together. It's not worth that! We have never even argued once, I'm worried that once we become lovers, that will complicate us being us?' Lol, I wasn't going to let him off the hook that easily as I pressed onward, so I said, 'us being totally frustrated sexually is not A-OK. Making love is the most natural evolution to bring us to fruition. It is meant to be, babe!'.

'I'm tired of self-stimulation of fantasizing about you making love to me and me loving you. Masturbation takes me just so far, and now I want the real thing tonight, Brock!' Yep, I had grown some big lips. I said that! His mouth opened… even with the glow of Red wine, his complexion grew redder a blush, and he smirked wildly. He said nothing. Instead, he reached for his glass, his eyes never leaving mine, but they were smiling at me, not his face, his eyes!

He placed the wine down 'wow, a lady who says what she wants, how provocative?' 'Since we're being so forthright regarding sexual desires, I've nearly rubbed poor BJ raw, Brock Junior. Yeah, raw in the shower because of your ass; at least my arms get a good pump. It's a workout, but it's your body that I stroke too. Down the drain goes all my Love Juice!'

It was her turn to be shocked 'really, babe, you stroke your cock lusting for me and only me?' <u>'No, sweetie, I stroke my cock for me, lol'…</u> they fall backward in their booth, giggling, her covering her mouth. OmGod, so funny! The bottle fell over on the table; lucky it was empty. 'So enough of this, our relationship needs to take the plunge, the next step, geez, what a fricken tease we've been to each other, 'shit Luce, it's after 1:37 am were the only ones here, look they're staring at us keeping the bar open for us let's get out of here get busy, drink!'

Lucie reached over the table 'what do you say?' he raised her hand, kiss's it tenderly, then gave a suck and a nibble on the top of her hand 'let's do it.' She was walking on air upstairs, with no time for the elevator, nope! Even though they were heavily inebriated and exhausted, they were on a mission to consummate their Love… last night!

Impatiently, at 1:53 am, he failed and couldn't even get the keycard in the door. After the third try, she says here, let me do it. On her second try, the green light showed on the door. They frolicked about, dancing into the room. 'I gotta go pee, be right back,' she says. He retorts, 'I'd better empty my bladder too!' After months of foreplay, none was needed. They drunkenly tore each other's clothes off, pulled back the bedspread and sheets he tossed her in, and leaped onto her like a caveman, both tittering and giggling like teenagers. They were breathing in gasps like locomotives with intense lust. The anticipation had him with gobs of pre-cum. Her lips were dripping, no kisses, no fondling. He aggressively grabbed her legs, pinning them in a vise grip onto his shoulders. She willingly lifted her ass up prime for entry. He dangled and hovered, taking Aim at the hot pink velvety opening beckoning him inside. She yells, 'Fk me damnit.' He plunges in a deep stroke to the bone mashing her runway strip with a powerful clench. She applied grinding pressure on him inside her, pressing on her clit. She let loose with a Porno Scream, earth-ear-shattering. Feral wild tremors scrapping his back with her embedded nails climaxing in orgasmic convulsions gasping with spasmatic twitches, barely audible words 'fk I I I Luv you' she had locked him down and in like dogs in heat. He trembled, quivering, vibrating in volcanic eruptions. Semen flowed and pulsated in frozen ecstasy of euphoric bliss, a piece slice of yummy Heaven.

Not one gyration or stroke, not a pump buried to the bone exploded, yet they were both puffing and huffing as if they had just finished a marathon. His grunts and deep moans slowly faded away as he shrank inside of her warm tunnel. Their embrace unwound like they had been together for a decade. She said, 'OmLord, I needed that!' He only said, 'HellYeah' she then rolled over her back to him, he pulled his chest and hips towards her, and their fetal puzzle was in place. He held her tight, smelling her skin; in less than 75 seconds, both were visiting their subconscious, oblivious to the world.

If she had taken out a stopwatch, their First love-making action 'started at 1:57 am and 25 seconds later or 1:57:25 caput, drained Yep! Precisely 25 seconds, uuhhh later and done, history. But that was all right. She thought as she grabbed her large beach towel and dried off. Just thinking of those 25 seconds had her lubricated, all ready to go, giggled sporadically, nothing to write home about or to brag to her girlfriends. They spontaneously prematurely ejaculated in under 30 seconds. Whew, it was something indeed!

Brock's way of thinking was along the lines that he was glad that tonight he wasn't going to be drunk, and he planned to take his sweet time and love Lucie because he could no longer deny that fact. After all, she had told him during her orgasm that she Loved him! Did she or was that exhilaration of the typical jabber that left one's mouth, during umh, caused by the intense sexual orgasmic thunder? Love, what a weird conundrum! Not so strange, however. There weren't any post-coital conversations, just their faces smashed into pillows.

Tonight would be different. He felt this inner peace now, worried… he'd never believed he could ever overcome the infidelities and shredded heart syndrome that his deceased ex Patti caused him. His ego and pride were lost with it… along with his macho sexual confidence. He didn't want to venture backward into a painful disaster. He didn't want to again indulge in a physical relationship with a woman, but Lucie was what the doctors had ordered. She was fate, his Fate. He Loved

Her and was sure she Loved Him too. They would soon be married! No Doubts lingered!

-38-

6/29/17 Real Time… NIA.

"I can't, not now, Carl. Stop bugging me. Relax, damnit, you're getting out of control, dude. I told you I would give you a damn blow job after my sister left." "Sara, it will take less than 5 minutes" "when the guard on our favorite corridor is on break, the closet is waiting on us, babe!"

"Carl, it isn't my favorite corridor. Did you shower this morning?" "No, I got up late; I will wash up cum on. I need your magic throat; why don't you bend over and let me do you doggy style? I don't have to keep telling you, Sara, I've done everything for you. I'm getting somewhat frustrated, like you have been using me all this time. You know I get zero sex from my fat cow of a wife. She gives the term Frigid a picture in the Dictionary, Antarctica hers!"

"Sara, honey, I could be imprisoned, fired, prosecuted for all that I… "All right, damnit, Carl. After my sister leaves, I will take care of you. I promise we'll find another closet, okay?" "I don't get it; your salon is offline. Umh, I mean, there's a blind spot in the back corner. I've checked it out in the security room, and all but one camera has been disabled. Why don't we do it in there?" "Because it's my salon, and all it would take is for someone to flip a switch in the control room panel upstairs. And turn back on the cameras. You wanna risk that, Carl?"

<u>"I suppose you're right, but don't stand me up as you have; it's getting way old, Sara. This whole week you have been</u>

<u>saying hold on, I'm warning you this time I'm serious; you'll regret it!"</u>

She scowls at his back as he walks away 'that's it, Carl, time to take you out of this equation; eventually, it had to happen; why not sooner than later? Screw you, Carl,' she bites her upper lip! Carl's unveiled threats would be his undoing! Yup.

Kamryn enters the cafeteria wearing an adorable Sun Dress, looking for her sister. Over the intercom, Sara is alerted to go to the cafeteria. *Kam spots her Lil sis and meets her part way... a hug, "hey, let's get some breakfast, Kam!" "Okay, I brought all kinds of magazines for us to pick out my wedding dress and themes. I'm so excited, sis. I want you to be as much a part of my wedding day as is heavenly possible!"*

"We haven't decided where to go on our Honeymoon. There are so many destinations. Wow, like a ton of options, sister. Next week before our mini vacation on Lake Shasta, I'll bring all the hordes of brochures I've compiled. That way, you can help me pick out where to go?" "I love you so much, Sara!" Sara looks at her older sister with utter disdain, hardly being able to restrain, ugh, not show a negative expressive Sneer. She bends down to scratch her ankle, and a loud flatulence shakes the Cafeteria. Oops, 'OmLord, that's so embarrassing.'

Kam looks around. A few of the incarcerated pretend not to notice, and some clap and he-haw. Kamryn thought, hell, we're at a mental institution. Then the seated inmates started a... 'fartfest'... inmates trying to outduel one another with louder flatulating sounds. It was pathetically sick and disgusting. Sara plugged her ears with her forefingers... regaining her composure and playfully holding her petite nose. Sara barked, "oh, Kam, I can't even come close to being able to express my Love for you. Thank you for always being here for me. I wouldn't know what to do if I didn't have your love and adoration."... scowling deviously below her skin... sincerely pulled it off, ugh!

Sara spins her head like a Demon and mouths 'fk you, Kam' away from her sister's eyes, then turns back and smiles, "let's go for a walk. There is a pair of mating Pink Flamingos at the nearest pond!"

Sitting at a picnic table underneath a Weeping Willow Tree, they went through catalogs of colorful wedding dresses. Sara was doing her best not to barf and be somewhat helpful, trying to show high-spirited happiness and enthusiasm to exude and display what a Real loving sister would act like... it was difficult indeed. Her exuberance was ill-felt, full of apathy; her stomach was upset and nauseous, and a loathsome, foul taste met her lips. Her blood pressure was rising by the minute, and she was anxious with anxiety churning. She said, "excuse me, sista, I have serious gas! After all this time, I still haven't gotten used to prison food. I think it was the Frijoles de la Olla... uhm, Pinto beans. I apologize, sorry my stomach is upset."

Kam bent away from her, not watching Sara step away, mesmerized by all the various pages of beautiful dresses she had to choose from. Sara sits back down and quickly points out her favorite outfit, a pink and black floral-patterned theme. Gosh, this silk-laced white and cream wedding dress was absolutely to 'Die for!' So True! 💐.

Sara, sick of this hyper bliss, decided it was time to disintegrate any positive vibes. She twists her left nipple, fingernails digging in, and bites her tongue till the warm taste of blood fills satiates her... blood drips down her throat, which she gladly swallows.

A warning sign blasting a siren... for her to only hear from within... was she schizophrenic or plain evil um 'both? No doubt she didn't care. Another mood swing, change of personality, and tears flowed instantly. She gasped for her breath with squinted eyes watching for Kam's reaction, waiting to feed on her sister's emotions.

Covered her face with her hands, peeking through her fingers, Kam caught a partial glimpse and moved spontaneously from across the picnic table, hovering over her Lil sister, rocking her head between her bosom. She totally misinterpreted the reason why Sara was so distraught. "Sara, baby, I know how much you want to be at my wedding, sweetie. I'm so, so, so sorry. I wish I could do something to have you there, baby girl. You are going to be part of it. I promise you I will have all the pictures and the video, sweetie. I will even…." "Stop, Kam, stop it now, no, no, please help me, my big sister, it's not that. I understand I can't be at your Wedding. I love you and want you to be the happiest bride alive, but I need your help!" Sara goes into full anguish mode with an audible whimpering balling, sighing now harder, crying with heart-wrenching sounds of emotions, her expressions in sync. An Academy award performance was breaking down, metaphorically displaying hopelessness. "OmLord, what am I going to do?"

This show of emotions didn't go unnoticed and had the staff's attention. A couple of guards driving carts started converging, and Carl called them off. As the yard supervisor, 'I'll handle it' Carl takes charge. Sara looks up, mascara running down her face resembling the 70's Rock band 'Kiss' she was a mess, snot boogers flam Kam takes a Kleenex out of her purse "that's him! Oh no, here he comes, Kam!"

"What, who, what's going on, Sara?" "Please excuse me, Kamryn. Hey Sara, is everything all right here? Do you need any assistance? What's wrong? You need a doctor?" Sara only glares up at him; Kam says, 'everything is fine, thanks Carl, for your concern. We're fine,' he looks down at all the wedding pictures and guesses, 'girls will be girls' "yes, ma'am, just was concerned."

"She just got upset because she will not be able to be at my wedding, is all!" He still doesn't drive off. "Sara, hey, you all right?" lifting her head up, she nods affirmatively, blowing him a hidden kiss. He winks back and then waddles off, shaking his head, muttering, 'females, how can a man understand their infantile emotions!'

Once out of earshot, Kam follows up on the last words, "Sara, what do you mean that's him? I'm lost. What's wrong? Has he hurt you? I don't get it?" In between sobs, "it's Carl. He's sexually abusing me, sister!" "What the hell, that bastard? What? Tell me what's going on Now!" "I'm so scared they will lock me back up in that rubber room?" "Why, what's Carl doing?" "Why haven't you said anything until now? Have you mentioned this to Doctor Amaya?"

I spoke with Ame aah Doctor Amaya just this morning. She told me you were achieving incredible leaps and bounds you... Ame said if you keep progressing at this pace, she wouldn't be surprised that you may one day apply for and receive gate passes with supervision, Sara. I will try and get to Doctor Amaya's office in San Rafael next week. I want to meet her and personally thank her for all you two have accomplished. You know I adore you, Sara, right?"

Sara disregards this spin following her planned dissertation. "He has threatened me he would set me up with a shank or a weapon, and I would lose my Salon and go to the SHU Solitary Confinement locked down. I'd lose my top classification, and if I said a word, I'm afraid he is purely sinister, a disguised devil. He might hurt me, even kill me, Kam!" "Calm down, please I'm here. Tell me, from the beginning. I knew the dude was a weirdo. How long has this been going on? What's he done?"

"He has forced me to give him oral sex uuhhh gross," she spits "sickening makes me swallow his sperm, so no mess." Kam stiffens, grabs her throat with one hand and her forehead with the other, and gags, "that fkn prick, bastard, that piece of shit." She walks away adamantly, directly nonwavering, stomping with a purpose towards Carl, who is in his golf cart about 35 yards away. "OmLord sister" she yells. "Stop! no, Kamryn," Sara jumps from the picnic bench and pulls her back from behind 'stop.' "Sara… I've read about stuff like this. When and how long? This is insane, Omg. I have feared this because you are so beautiful, Sara, this had been a worry for so long, and now it's come to fruition! Okay, fill me in. We are now in attack mode, Sara!"

"Sista, it's not been going on that long, um, ever since I've been out of my lockdown cell, ah free to roam about since my level change to trustee status uhm, #5 classification. That's when he started, and he nearly raped me one time. I'm so terrified" as she shakes and shudders, Kam is back on top of her holding her. "I've lost how many times he's forced me to suck him, but today he's demanded intercourse. Oh, I'm so afraid this is disgusting, so wrong. Please help me, big sister!"

"Your damn right. I will put a stop to this. I'm going directly to the Warden right now. You stay here!" Kam stares down the predator Carl and says, "No, come with me, let's go. I can't leave you here. We need to make a report out now, Sara. Let me help you up. Oh my, you poor, poor darling girl, damn,

isn't it enough your locked up in this hell hole mental institution, but you have to deal with a predator guard. He should be castrated, the prick!" Regaining her control, "no, Kam, we don't want to make a public display of this abuse. No reports, no, we need to keep this on the 'Downlow,' meaning we have to think this out cuz my life depends on it, sister, please!" "What do you mean 'low-down we deal with this head-on. We attack sis like we always have. We get him fired and prosecuted we…."

"You're not even listening to me; please pay attention, Kam. It isn't like we're on the outside at a legal business or something like that… Look, I'm in Prison here; if I or we snitch out Carl, then my life is worthless. You might as well nail the coffin shut yourself cuz...." "We go to the top of the food chain, Sara. How else do we deal with this? I need to call Doctor Ame Amaya. She will know what to do. We need to get you out of NIA!"

"Please, Kam, don't interrupt me. Let me finish. I realize you mean well, but you are totally naïve about the dynamics in prisons such as this one. The guards stick together like fkn glue here, and if we snitch or rat Carl out, then one of them will get me, either kill me or set me up. That's just how it works, really."

"Check this out just this year... there have been seven pregnancies here. How do you think that happened, like Duh sex being forced 'Rape' or mutually agreed upon, no one ever hears about this on the outside, abortions tell me Kam have you heard anything about this huh?" "Well, hell no, I haven't otherwise. I'd..." "Exactly my point, sista. Yes!"

"You gotta be kidding me, Sara, without any repercussions, no way?" "Oh yeah, the guards are fired DNA tests, but it's never publicized non-disclosure forms contracts, you will never read about it it's slowly slipped, squirmed under the carpet! This is a hell-hole here, and like Vegas, what happens inside of NIA's Razor wires stays right here!"

"Sara, what are you trying to say that NIA is corrupt...?" "Kam, I know you explained to me over five years ago that you had placed a substantial amount of money into investing in NIA stocks and bonds...." "Yes, I did. I also brought other investors in. It has been one of my best-performing stocks in my portfolio and has paid handsome dividends."

Kamryn takes up Sara's hand and says FYI, it has helped you by investing some of my largest clients at Schwab into NIA. I have met the board of directors; ah, it doesn't hurt to have our Uncle being the CEO here." "Sister, I am grateful for what you have done to raise my classifications, but I have a predator guard to deal with; I...." "Sara, are you not listening?

I have met the top echelon and have a great relationship with the lead Psychologist, Doctor Liz Honcho. Let's not forget that with all my pull uuhhh. Accordingly, it's no secret how fast your resurrection from the basement and level #1 classification had happened. Inmates are generally stigmatized and pigeonholed once placed in the worst category, um, classifications. I have been spending all access monies to help you. Doctor Amaya is being subcontracted by me, and you know what? Sara, I have never met this wonderful Doctor Amaya. Our communication has been only on the phone, I will drive to her office later this week. Doctor Amaya is like me, a steadfast advocate for you, Sara… and look how far you have evolved; we're only starting. I'm getting you out of here eventually. Look at you now with your own Salon. There was a 'method to my madness,' which revolved around you, my Lil sister!"

"All right, big sister Kamryn, you get all the investor newsletters and correspondences Online. You're kept abreast of all the news about how NIA is expanding all the grandiose facts and proper propaganda… figures with outrageous expectations." Sara points… "Look across the way the stadium-sized training facilities NIA is now being accredited as a learning institution… but did you read anywhere that there were five suspicious deaths here since May first? Ugh BTWay, when an inmate is murdered, tortured to death, and dies, do you think the outside world finds out lololol? No, it's all kept in-house. The M.E. Medical Examiner works here, and no one ever sees the body, but NIA professionals, then it's buried in the back '40' uhm… most are Cremated… quickly poof gone!" "Geez, Sara, I don't understand your logic. I…"

"What, Kamryn, you think you're going to run to the Warden and say Guard Carl is Sexually assaulting me, with forced copulation and rape…." "Okay, fk Sara, I get it, then what the hell do we do? It's unbelievable, unfathomable, what you're saying. Come on, aah, no way. Are you kidding me? Are you sure? Why wouldn't there be newspaper articles? You can't hide that type of information. I mean, five people dying here, the families would have been up in arms, lawsuits, etc."

"Am I sure, sis? Am I sure, really, you ask me that? How freakin silly… please, I live here 24/7! Look around how peaceful, even serene a mirage façade, two of the five died from over medications one by an accidental fall, a suicide another inmate murdered the other so…" "Sara, why not a peep of this in any newspaper or Online how could they cover up such atrocities like I said those inmates had a family it doesn't sound right?" "Do you remember the theme song at NIA when I was first brought here? It was on their homepage before or until there was so much negative flack!"

"Oh yeah, wasn't it 'Hotel California,' a song by the Eagles, uhm." "Yes, the verses that stand out for me living inside this devious hellhole, the words are ringing in my head, sometimes I awake hearing the tune. It reverberates and bounces in my skull, probably like some of the other sane inmates incarcerated within these musty rotting walls. Sure, this could be heaven or hell; yep, welcome to Hotel California… (NIA.) 'My mind is twisted.' Voices are calling from far away; yes, my ancestor's evil spirits are most likely chanting in an aligned dimension right here with me in my prison cell. Every night the raving lunatics start howling and screaming up and down my hallway. Even stuffing my ears with toilet paper can't stop the incessant hollering of pain.

"NIA is programmed to receive, but Kam, this is the line in the song that vibrates on High '<u>you can check out anytime you like, but you can NEVER leave!</u>" "geez, Sara, you got that song memorized, girl. That was good… but come on; it's a song." "This place isn't what it is perceived to be. Please, listen to me; there is Mega money behind this operation. You see those warehouse buildings over there the size of like three football fields. What do you think is inside of them?"

Kamryn now thinks her sister is delusional with paranoia and doused with conspiratorial theories and fabricated narratives. She indeed needed more counseling but decided to play along, not wanting to upset the full Apple cart. She humored her. "I don't know what is inside those buildings. Why don't you tell me, sister?" "Don't patronize me, Kam. Listen, believe me or not 'it's a training site meticulously designed for terrorist acts. This 655-acre property ever expanding is over a mile square it's owned and controlled by the Russians, the Mafia!"

Kam tries to maintain her optimism, concentrate, and find lost composure. She was encouraged and led to believe by Doc Amaya that her sister Sara was regaining her sanity. This matched her own feelings that she was getting better. Nope!

Kam honestly thought she was coming out of her psychotic delusions, evidently not so ughhhh how sad. Better to let her expound and complain. She wonders if the 'Carl thing' is also a figment of her lucid imaginary psychopathic mindset. Kam listens non-attentively to Sara's meanderings, only partially giving credence to her ludicrous ridiculous narrative 'she was definitely sick... Lost her heart fell!'

"Kam, the special inmates here are mercenaries, uh, geniuses, Masterminds, some of the most gifted Killers this world has ever seen, notorious. Kam, this prison hospital rehabilitation center is the Who's Who for the Criminally Insane from all over the USA. The most notorious of them all in one place skills unmatched by snipers, Navy Seals, and Army Rangers who were deemed insane surely they committed crimes on USA soil. But they were lost in their minds in the Middle East, or truthfully were they? Lol, it was the old 'P.T.S.D.' game. Now I'm sure some of them were legitimately diagnosed and had the serious and debilitating disorder, but most, in my opinion, were working the system to get off for their brutal crimes playing the PTSD card because of their caustic military services! This is all a positive for NIA's militia; it is loaded with military intellectuals. Incendiary expert bombs technology wizards. There are some Scary IQs off the charts. NIA imports criminals with unique abilities from all over the Globe. Remember that sensational case involving Wendi Feral about the children being kidnapped by some out-of-the-country faction? The dude that's an Army Ranger is in charge of this NIA militia. Tell me you haven't heard the name Jax Foul.

"Sara, please, do you hear yourself? Yes, I read about that case… do you really believe this nonsense; this conspiracy theory stuff is for …" "Lastly, I will only say you remember that old show on TV with 'Mr. T' it was called the 'A-Team' well compared to the stealth clandestine squads of mercenaries that resides here right now. That 'A-Team' would be nothing but children who couldn't hold up the Jockstraps of the special operatives that reside here. Uhm, ah, experts in every field of mankind, mad scientists. Look at me, Kamryn. I'm actually being actively recruited. I'm the master of disguises. There are missions, the Russians!" Kam jumps up from the bench. "Stop this, Sara. At once, I've heard enough!"… Not!

-39-

Mill Valley Past History 7/18/10… Brock, Lucie at Hotel.

Lucie was looking through the closet. She'd hung up her clothes of choice inside from her suitcases and selected a sexy alluring mini skirt, and then she drifted back to their 25-second

318

love-fest session. Lucie gritted her teeth, slipped out her tongue, and smirked. Oh yeah, well, this night, um-yum, tonight. Their bout of loving would be considered a love feast! Grinning apprehensively, nearly blushing, ruminating on the facts, she oddly started cussing during our sex and told him I loved him; she blushed for absolutely it was the truth and consistent with every beat of her heart.

Her phone rang in room 313. "Hi baby, I ordered a bottle of wine to be delivered. Is that all right, sweet stuff?" "Yes, babe, that's great. I will be over in 15 minutes or so… tonight; let's not overdo…." "No worries, Luce, it's triple shots of expresso for our after-dinner drinks, lol," they laugh. "I hear yah babe tonight. I want to taste you, smell your body feel every centimeter I…." "Luce, yah better stop, or you're going to be on my appetizer plate. I'm already horny enough for you, so how about a quickie before?..." "Quickie, Brock, there's never been a faster quickie in the annals of time than last night's mini love sex session not complaining; I was fully satisfied completely, but hey, what was it? A long 25 seconds, lol!" They howl appropriately in the phone's speakers.

"Let's try to hold off until after dinner; however, uhm, if we start up, I'm not going to want to leave the room. Which means no dinner, just you, my dear, dessert!" "Okay, Luce… oh, that's the wine at the door gotta go!"

<u>Sara and Kamryn Present Time at NIA.</u>

Kamryn was worried that her sister Sara was once again living in her own make-believe world as she'd done when they were small children… could it be true that Carl was sexually abusing her? Kam moaned, "please enough, Sara, please, sister." As Kam stands up and grasps her sister, "I love you' you have to stop thinking this way, or you will never get well and never be able to leave here. Your imagination is unreal like this place is a mercenary training facility. You should write a book of fiction!"

No smiles from Sara "like I can check out but never leave… right Kam? Do you know how many military leaders are locked up, uh, incarcerated here with PTSD and other diagnosed maladies, ugh, abnormalities? Law enforcement officers who are supposedly crazy playing the only cards they have in Court. Oh, I'm insane, hoping to be sentenced to a lesser amount of time, you know, kept inside a medical facility until deemed sane!"

"Stop; how did you get on this tangent? Anyhow, we were discussing Carl. Remember now, are you sure what you told me about Carl is absolutely the truth, sister? I'm beginning to think you are not thinking rationally. Your…" Sara stood up, pushed her sister away, and started down the path alone "get away from me! So you don't believe me, you" as tears fell again from her… sullen fake face, "come on back to the shade and sit back down, please, Sara. I'm sorry, so how do we proceed to stop Carl's abuse? If you're going to be retaliated against, what's our method for stopping it? Uhm, what's the plan? Do you have a strategy?"

"Yes," sputtering, "let me run this by you?" Kam hands her another tissue as Lil sis is sniveling. You usually leave on Thursday at around 3:30 pm. Today you must leave closer to 4:35. I know the traffic back to San Francisco…" "For God's sake, Sara, I don't care about the traffic. You're the one I care about. Please go on; I'm listening, all ears!"

"All right, sista, Carl works 9 to 5 pm today. He is anxious for you to take off, so he will have me do this sultry sickening act. If we time this perfectly, we can bust him without anyone suspecting that it was a 'set-up' your acting has to be passable!" "I can do it for you, sister. I would do almost anything for you!" Aah!

"Okay, at the main desk that you have to check out at, there's always like 2 to 3 staff members, and maybe if we're lucky, Doctor Honcho will be doing her daily reports on a desktop computer. You should be able to see her from the counter. By 4:15, Dr. Honcho will have already left her upstairs office. Her last task before she leaves is the daily reports where you check out at. It would be nice if she follows her regular routine, for the guards will not notice any modifications; they relax after the Boss leaves."

"Now, how do I communicate with Liz, umh, Dr. Honcho? Without bringing suspicion on this scheme, I'm not allowed a phone until I am on the way out of NIA. At the desk, I could use one of the office phones, and oh yeah, there are several phones on the wall for emergencies or whatever, but how…?" Sara shakes her head, realizing how naïve her sister was, and takes the reins.

"Let's go. We have time right now. Doctor Honcho will be having some hot tea in the cafeteria," handing Kam a note. "I already wrote out a detailed plan for you to give to Liz Honcho. Just go over to her table and slickly hand her this note. Remember the cameras. Let's pick out a magazine for you to take to Liz, with the note inside, carefully open it up, showing Doctor Honcho the note. She is pretty savvy, and she will catch on. You can do it, Kam!"

Sara picks up the stack of magazines shuffles through them "this one, yep,… so after you drop the note off and, we will hopefully have Doctor Honcho onboard, who will be alert and waiting for when you catch Carl pushing me in a janitor's closet. Kam, this is how it should play out. You'll be checking out, placing all your stuff on the countertop, stop suddenly and say to the Officer, 'oh crap.' I wanted to give this magazine to my sister. It's all about hairstyles. Then I want you to, at a fast pace, go to the corridor on your left. About one-third of the way down is a broom closet. That's when you'll see me being guided by Carl… Perfect!" 'Even Kam smiled at her sister's dramatic flair…' thinks this is all a figment of Sara's bizarre imagination… but acts like she's all down with this premeditated show.

"The closet is in a blind spot from the cameras. Carl will have ushered me inside. You then rush back and loudly scream, catching all the nurse's and Correction officers 'guards' attention. Hopefully, Honcho will be raring to go. You yell and shout, "hey, that guard down the hall just forcefully pushed my sister into a room… grabbed her aggressively by her arm!"

Kam stands and stares at her sis "R U Sure of this?" "Absolutely… Carl will be in a frenzy because he's wanted sex all week, and it will be almost 5 pm. He will have to clock out. This will work like most of my elaborate schemes did when we were little children!" Kam grins "okay, I'm down for it. Let's get this scoundrel." "We need to head to the cafeteria where you can slide this note to Honcho," 'from the corner of her eye,' coincidently, Carl cruises back up on his Golf cart with a smirk. "Everything is better, I hope, here?" "Yes, Carl, excellent now, thank you," a grinning Sara said.

He then looks at his wristwatch "jeesh, it's getting late, Kamryn. I know you like to get out of here before you get caught up in traffic?" "How did you know that… Carl? I've never said a word of that?" He turns red as a beet displaying a major blush "aah, Sara told me, well gotta go seeya later!" "What a creep and is as homely as a mud fence. His sweat stains under those cellulite arms are so gross the man must stink!" Sara puts on a show plugging her nose, and laughs, 'Yep! Gross!' "Well, I totally believe you. No doubt he is beyond frantic, so obvious…wants me the hell outta here like now!" "Yes, disgusting for sure it's been stressful, sista. After I get him off my back, umh, off my knees, I will finally sleep sound, and his torment will end."

At 4:27 pm, holding hands, Sara and Kam walk up to the checkout counter. Sara follows everyday routines, with traditional hugs and kisses on the cheeks, saying their heartful goodbyes. Like clockwork, at the counter were three staff members and Honcho, obviously on alert, after nonchalantly receiving the Sara note, acting per regular routine, and finishing her last tasks.

Carl is anxiously checking his watch, leaning against a wall squeezing his penis indiscreetly with anticipation. He was set up closest to the hallway. He knows exactly where the blind spots are. Sara eyeballs him. He subtly nods his head like a horse's up and down, beckoning her to follow him like, 'cum on!'

She does exactly as per usual and starts down the long expansive hallway. About 95 feet later, he is up against her pressing her inside the open door "move, Sara." Quick and expeditiously, he closes the door rather aggressively, takes her by the shoulders, and spins her around with both of his hands, shoving me to my knees 'now, you little cock tease, you're killing me with anticipation as he has his pants down past his knees in a split second, grabs the back of my head and directs me to his rigid penis.

Kamryn, on cue, "Oh, crap, I forgot to give this magazine to Sara." Holding it up 'it's all about various hairstyles. The latest and most sexy' Dr. Honcho, peaks up. Kam hurries over to the hallway entrance, then she stops and sees Carl guiding her sister into the room, grasping her arm aggressively. 'Whoa,' shocked, 'it's really fricken happening. Omg, she wasn't lying,' Kam spins around and says rather demonstratively emotions in each vowel and consonant 'why did that guard just manhandle my sister into the room down the hall' at once, Honcho springs into action, "what are you talking about?"

Kamryn didn't wait for anyone to catch up to her, on triple pace down to that door. A nurse, a guard, and Honcho were only steps behind in the rears. Kam yanks the door open to see her cute sister's head in Carl's hands, pulling her towards his groin area. Carl almost couldn't stop. He was so damn close, fk it, but when Kam screamed and leaped into the room and literally socked Carl right on the nose! He bent his head down. Kam had her claws out, trying to gouge out his eyes. Sara had fallen back over and was getting back up to her knees to stand, tears now violently cascading down her cheeks. She had purposely scratched her face, and her knees were now bleeding. Sara's BALD head was also leaking!

The nurse frantically screamed, hollering; Honcho and the guard were right behind her. They saw everything; Kam pulled back with a well-placed kick to the already swollen scrotum sack. Down went Carl, his flabby ass widely cracked and displaying a lost square of used toilet paper. Gross! Honcho helped the now full-on hysterical Sara, with the nurse's aide, out of the closet and into the nearest female's bathroom. Honcho yells orders, "cuff him up. Get the Warden and the assistant Warden down here. I want a report filled out now!"

Kamryn was in disbelief and couldn't reconcile what she'd just witnessed "what the hell kind of place is this, OmLord I've brought over 15 million dollars from investors here to NIA," wailing, running into the restroom. She sees her sister and loses it. Her bald head was bleeding from the bastard's fingernails. Her face was marked and clotting.

In a nervous tizzy, Kam, distraught and shaking, screams and moans… putting her head into her hands and slides her back down the wall crying uncontrollably and frenzied as the nurse hovers over Sara, cleaning up her wounds. Honcho enters again, trying to console both sisters, "believe me, this doesn't happen here. This is an isolated anomaly, uuhhh, situation?" Then the door busts open, and another nurse clamors in.

Dr. Liz Honcho directed her verbiage at Kam, who paid her zero attention. Her head tingled no; 'if her sister were correct and honest about this sexual predator, how could I discount all her wild conspiracies? What if the story about mercenaries and all that bizarre stuff, umh, all her accusations?... 'Could Sara have been telling the truth about NIA? Is it possible?'

Lucie and Brock indulged in a delicious dinner that included Steak and Lobster, red wine 'one bottle' after dinner expresso. The night of the 18th of July was the one to forever reminisce about, unlike their loving first quickie encounter quite... um-yum, the opposite for hours and hours. They explored each other's bodies, smells of lust, body fluids, tastes of insatiable love, a twosome orgy... orgasms climaxes in the double digits. They were hopping, bouncing um, rolling, sweet sweat, slamming, and slapping bodies, blind fury, gritting teeth in insatiable thirst, twitching in quivering ecstasy. DNA on the couch, floor, counter, kitchen table, and walls, water out of the jacuzzi, and even the beds in both rooms, were Hit. They were spent, raw & sore it was the infamous all-nighter, endurance, depleted energy gone in each other's arms, asleep exhausted, and the alarm goes off. He punches snooze 11 minutes later she hits it... again.

His eyes were barely focusing. Saw the clock alarm. Oh, shit, 8:45 am. It's the 19th. They have a team meeting in the conference room downstairs at 9:30, yet he can't move. He is sore in spots he didn't know had muscles, felt like he'd ridden a bronco bull, and was thrown and stomped on by hoofs. Ugh, damn, his throbbing quads calf's cramping. His stomach felt like he had done over a thousand inverted sit-ups.

She was in even worse shape her entire body throbbed in... not a good way, and her muscles twitched like Roadkill. She had a feeling she'd pulled a few muscles. Her body was contorted into positions a Gymnast or Yoga instructor would have been proud of. Besides being raw in appropriate spots, her body screamed at her for a huge helping of hot swirling water. Hot Tub help!

Three Weeks Later, 8/11/10 Wednesday… surveillance of Sara Sloan.

Calling Lucie for a wake-up… salutation, she was always on his mind, his cell phone in his hand, wanting to hear his lover's voice, "Hi, sweetheart, it's like we're slowly being bled to death with small knife wounds" "whoa, a bit too graphic this morning, Brock. Let me finish my first java k." He paid her no mind having been up with the early birds "we have lost five Agents. They have been reassigned, despite Sara sitting within our grasp. Why? Because she hasn't struck again since shit, she has been under scrutiny since her last escapade. Unfortunately, Luce, not a speck of DNA zero evidence links her to the murders." "How do you wake up so damn hyper? Please let me warm up. Men like you are toasters; women like me are into a slow pressure cooker, okay?" they chuckle!

"Honey, she is only laying low." "Laying low, my ass… we're under fire, haven't you been following the news, Lawsuits, all the negative press public sentiment is gaining for her on the positive side, websites are calling us hyperbole bullshit. I read a post on Twitter that gained momentum stating that Law enforcement is a freakin joke either arrest her or shut the fk up. Sara just leveled another Harassment charge against us, naming you and me Lucie and…" "Of course, Brock, let's not let our frustrations disrupt our focus or who we are. The last thing we want or need to do is bicker; we are 'In Love,' are we not?" He wanted to reach out through the phone and put his hands on her muscled thighs 'yes, I love you.' I'm just bored sitting in the Crown Vic directly across the street from Sara's home. At least there is some laughter in the park. It's already packed with children and families, a typical Marin County

weather day gorgeous. When are you going to be bringing breakfast, babydoll?" "Soon, babe…"

A few hours later, Lucie… had joined her honey Brock across from Sara's Victorian structure… the gate starts to open, and then the 3-car garage door flips up slowly. A Porsche Cayenne pulls out. Sara is dressed in a dark blouse with even darker sunglasses and a stylish hat; she takes a left and waves at them. 'On the move,' Lucie barks into her radio. This was way out of character. This is her first trip from home without bodyguards accompanying her. Uh, perhaps she would meet up with them. Brock pulled directly behind her and hit the radio again, giving play-by-play street to street. They exit the security guard gates of the patrolled subdivision of the upper-class neighborhood. Another Fed car joins in the pursuit… or call it like it was a meandering slow grind of tailing a suspect who could care less.

Sara looks at her rearview mirror and thinks, damn feels like she's the Big Dog driving down the road with the Fleas chasing my tail; it's almost 10 am, so a shift change is in order. She could make out Agent Lucie Link on the radio and Brock Dame driving, it's like another monotonous day in and day out. Tonight the pervert Agent Tom should be watching my body in my set-up mirrors from his demented park bench. The dude was magnetized to my ass… wearing his binoculars on his eyes later tonight! Yup, all part of her plan… Oh, how she enjoyed the voyeur's concentrated stares, purposely provocative the shows must go on!

I feel so unsatisfied inside, so pedestrian, like normal humans, so dull. My life's aspirations were squelched. It's always disconcerting to have eyes on your private life. Locked and free of eyeballs only behind the walls of her domicile, feelings of anxiety building to a peak, umh, non-climatic. I have to do something not going to be subdued and restrained much longer; I'm going to explode! I will humiliate and squash all of them like fkn roaches. In the last month, she had left her house several times by the cover of night, with the only light of the moon. Now that her escape route was clearly planned... from years ago, it was time to react.

Her legal team was on the offensive. They were firing on all cylinders. The press had reversed much sentiment, even correcting the many false accusations, insinuations, Libel, slanderous, and defamation suits that were filed. She even considered bringing back some of her previous so-called friends and clients. Even the precious Homeowners Association was calling again. Her sister, Kamryn, who lived over 3,000 miles away in New York City and worked for a financial firm, was in constant contact. Their bond continued strong, the only person who loved her truly for who she was and is maybe, uh... that might change if Kam knew who I really am.

Although the damage was done, it's impossible to cleanse oneself from the aspersions, slander in most people's minds never clean again scarred nothing could wash away the slimy blight film oil-based, she was and would always be guilty in the moral majorities attitudes and beliefs. The primary arguments in her favor on the AM talk Radio shows and channels held water, for as per usual, the ultimate conclusion was the same "If Sara were guilty, she'd be in fricken Jail." Duh!

The learned pundits questioned why all the murders were enacted in So-Cal when she lived in Nor-Cal. Not one of the stigmatized groups of deceased cheaters was North of L.A. Mr. Terrance Hallinan had been excellent, like a Savior and Father figure. His legal team had enormous clout and aligned precision. After she returned home from the 'Marvin Acid Trip.' Her legal team had private investigators who took a device and scanned her Victorian Home and property... and found seven hidden cameras with audio. The FBI played by their own rules, ruthless and evil, and illegal the difference with them was that they wrote the rules. Supposedly the good guys, but they resembled what they indeed were Wolfs wearing citizens' clothing. FBI's more Criminal than criminals; she said this out loud! Sara now had permanent scanners running 24/7. She could never be too security minded.

No doubt it was time to level the playing field a little anyways. She felt ornery and smiled with a devious smirk as she parked at the Sheraton Gardens Hotel, the same hotel where Agents Dame and Link stayed. A cackle erupts, thinking, why not have a drink at the lounge and a snack? I wondered how the Dynamic duo, ugh, love Vultures, would feel as she trounced on their turf, lol.

"Luce fk, she's pulling in at our Hotel Wtf." "How does she know where we are staying, Brock?" He only stares in disbelief "that bitch that cocky bitch is playing with us, toying with us." "All right, babe, as the boss told us last week, don't fall into any traps. She is a clever conniving woman with a powerful advocacy group behind and in front of her. They have leveraged strings being pulled in and out and all the way to Washington DC." "Yes, Luce, the question still remains how did she know we stayed here?" She says, "are you thinking like I am that her bodyguards informed her of where we're staying?" "Yeah, Lucie, either them or one of her lawyers, we know where she has been 24/7. Ugh, well, what do you want to do? You wanna go in?"

"Yes, that's exactly what we should do. Let's get some iced tea or coffee alert Agent Toms that he needs to get over here and take up her watch, Luce." The other Fed car parks next to Sara's Porsche with orders to stay put. Sitting on a barstool at the far end of the lounge was Sara watching the door and the morning news on the TV above the bar. A crock of onion soup was in front of her. "Her audacity, man, I don't like her. What a shameless impudent hussy" yelped Lucie. "Wow, woman, tell it like it is. How about we have a stiff Martini, at least one? Didn't we plan to go to the city tonight for dinner and a show?"

"We still are. It's a spectacular day to enjoy San Francisco's nightlife." At 1:15 pm, Agent Tom finally staggers in with an awkward wobble, the result of an apparent vicious hangover. 'Tom looked like a leftover with crooked sunglasses on his face… looking around the lounge. Ironically, at the time Tom arrived, a butch-type biker-like woman bodyguard joins Sara at the bar.

<u>Later that afternoon, Brock and Lucie were enjoying themselves in San Francisco.</u>

Love runneth over… walking hand in hand, dinner was scrumptious, some red wine they'd booked a Hornblower voyage on the tourist boat around Alcatraz. With his arm over her shoulder, she is holding a bag of caramel popcorn "you know, I've always known that sex is always better with someone you're In Love with. Sure, 'strange' or one-night stands are kinda fun like they say. Even bad sex is good." A pause ensued as Lucie couldn't believe what Brock blurted out without any forewarning. They'd just laughed and clicked a couple of pictures overlooking the San Francisco Bay!

Lucie stops cold and tilts her head up "what the hell are you trying to say?" as she shrugs under his arm about-face. "Ugh, oh shit, I'm not good at this… I was only trying to say because of our relationship, um, friendship first, yeah, uh, shoot. So I guess what I'm trying to say is we should get married, I suppose…." She jumps up. "Oh crap, that's the way you're proposing to me. R U kidding me?" Lucie busts up, spitting popcorn, howling hysterically with tiny squeals, laughing, and doing a jig in a circle crying tears. 'A marriage proposal,' she hacks, choking on a kernel in between spurts of breath. "Umh, you guess we should just get married, huh, you suppose, is that it?"

He puts his index finger over his closed lips sshhh and pulls her back down to the bench as tourists act like they're not being nosey. She spills part of the popcorn, and he says, "fk, I didn't want to do it this way. Why can't you make it easy on me." "Sit down here now…." He drops to his left knee rather forcefully. In his right hand was a jewelry box. "Will you marry me, Ms. Lucie Link, and be my wife for life?" 'OmLord from laughs to a stream of crocodile tears "Oh um, Yes, yes, uhm Yes, get up over here, you big Lug, and hug, kiss me OmGod, I Love You, Brock!"

Noise erupts and explodes as whistles and clapping, hoots and hollers, and pictures are taken on phones. A crowd had stopped to gawk at the lovers. The Warf was packed with people on this glorious evening, one to remember 8/11/10 she slips her finger up into the air he slides on his Grandmothers 3 Karat Diamond ring he had it already sized to match her dainty finger being In Love, best feelings in this world Yep!

NIA Ame 6/29/17 Thursday 5:35 pm. Present times.

'Hello, Doctor Ame Amaya. This is Doctor Honcho; damnit, I was hoping to catch you at your office. I know it's after 5 pm… please call me as soon as you receive this message. It's imperative, thanks. I need to bring you up to speed on the last couple of hours. Things have imploded at the Napa facility for your patient Sara Sloan.' Ame stood there with her briefcase and satchel, preparing to step out of her office, suddenly bolted to her answering machine and picked up her phone. "Hello, this is Doctor Amaya?" "Oh, I'm so glad that I caught you this late. Please disregard the message I just left on your cell phone. This is Doctor Honcho." "Liz, what's wrong? You seem out of breath or panicky; please tell me what's up. Is everything okay with Al and Sara?" "No, Ame, that's why

I'm calling you. I wonder if you could somehow work in your schedule to come here to NIA first thing in the morning. I'd rather not discuss this sensitive subject on the public airwaves if you know what I mean. It's an issue with regards to Sara!" "What, what happened to Sara?" "Ame, we need to keep this in-house, no outside publicity. You know we are a publicly traded company. The negative press could harm our shareholders!" "For God's sake, screw the stockholders. What about the patients? Tell me now what is going on. Do I need to drive out there now this evening… cuz I will!"

"Calm down, calm down. It would be a waste of your time to drive up here tonight. Sara has been heavily sedated. No worries, she's not in a life-or-death struggle. Just make time to meet with me tomorrow, okay?" "Liz, why the mystery Sara is my patient? I'm under contract. Does Kamryn, her sister, know what's going on? Should I contact her to come with me tomorrow?" "Ame, I will not go into details on this phone, and Kamryn has been here through all the chaos; she's here right now; she is leaving in a few moments!"

"I don't get it, Liz; what are you so afraid of? You're acting like someone is eavesdropping or something like we're playing a bit part in a spy movie. Why the secrecy what the hell?" "Sara was only attacked, umh aah she's fine all right very traumatic that's all I can and will say?" "All you will say, Liz, well, I'm her psychiatrist, uh therapist, and I need to know what happened right the hell now. It's total bullshit to keep this from me. I will be filing reports with the board at NIA. Now let me speak with Kamryn?"

"I have to go seeya in the morning, Ame," click. She looks up with a scowl… and says into Don's face, "that bitch just hung up on me, imagine the blatant gall." "Well, what I overheard is that Sara is in trouble! Liz said that she was sedated and that she had been attacked, but she was all right. How incongruous does that sound?" "Attacked, given narcotics to drop her off into a dream state, yet she's A-Okay… fine." "Oh, then why even call and inform you of this, Ame? What I can only think of… boss, is that Liz wants to make sure you clear off your work schedule for tomorrow?"

"No, Donny, this is a classic! Liz doesn't want any negative publicity. What happens at good ole NIA is a private business, wonder what kind of institution NIA really is, how much is hidden under the musty carpets inside that prison?" On her 5th attempt, Ame left a VM on Kam's phone 'Please call me the second you get this message!' "Donny, cancel all my appointments for tomorrow. Right now, try to catch them, email them, and text them to ensure we have a track record of proof that we tried to cancel. We will not be in the office tomorrow." Sure thing, boss-woman, um, maybe I should spend the night with you. That way, we can wake up and roll towards Napa?"

Ame scowled then loosened up, thinking what a character she had for a secretary. "Sure, I will need your company in the morning, so with that being said, you can spend the night at my place. We're going to make it an early one. I want to be at NIA no later than 5:45 am?" "No problem, Ame. I will have to go to my place first and feed my cats. Then, I will be on my way to your house; let me address our patients and reschedule. I should be there by 7 pm. Aah, I need to get a change of clothes. I should use one of the dressers at your place, Ame, to keep some extra clothes!" "Thanks, Don. We can talk about that later. I will have dinner on and ready. Why don't you stop and buy some beer? I'm on the low side." He smiles and remembers, "Oh, that's right, you're allergic to wine; I almost forgot?" "No, not allergic to all wine. I can tolerate White wine. I wouldn't say I like the taste, in any case. But Red wine causes major Hives. I can't stand the tannins of the red grapes. It tears my stomach up and cramps me up. Next thing you know, I'm bending over the toilet… with the runs… why does White wine not bother me. Don't have a clue?" She patted him on the back, "Seeya a little later, Donny," as Ame was out the door.

-41-

9/3/10 Past Time Mill Valley Sara.

Brock rubs her shoulders. It is Friday afternoon; he whispers in his lover's ear, "Agent Tom has a fever and is hacking up and coughing…sadly, Lucie, I'm going to have to work tonight. Damn, I don't have a choice since our team has been reduced further. Heck, cutie pie, it's either you or me? So it looks like I'm forced to pick up his shift, and babydoll, you're a bit stuffy, blowing your cute Lil nose." "Oh, I think it's just my allergies, but you're right. We should give Tom the night off, although I will miss your warm and inviting body next to mine, Brock!" They kiss gently, hugging. I'm just a text or call away. He packs up a cooler… it's 6:15 pm. "Tom's 12-hour shift ends at 5 am. I will be crawling into bed with you then. 'I love you, my wife, to be." She smiles largely. "I love and adore you, my husband-to-be!"… Aah! 🚂.

Brock parks his Crown Victoria… across the street from Sara's home.

Brock sees Agent Tom's slumped over on his mainstay, a Redwood bench. "Hey, Tom, go get some rest. I'm relieving you tonight." "Oh, shit, thanks, boss. I'd argue with you, but I feel like 'death warmed over' a freight train running through my head. Hey, boss, here are my special binoculars. If you click this switch, this enables you to have a Night Vision view kind of epic cool military, the latest and greatest, and ole Sara might put on one of her patented titillating strip-teases for you tonight. It's Friday night. She normally does a routine in the mirrors up in her loft, don't mind me saying this, that serial killer woman is off the charts, Hot!" Tom grabs his shoulder bag and laptop and wobbles to his feet.

"Enough, Tom; let's not forget that woman most likely is responsible for over 39 gruesome murders, and if you counted others, we suspect she would be at 43. She'd love to spray us with her special poison potion… now, get going!" "Yes, sir, thanks again. Oh, here's the key to the new restroom. The park close's down at 11 pm. I borrowed it from a security guy at the entrance gates!"

"Hey, can I just ask you something that's been bugging me, Agent Dame?" "Sure shoot, but you better get going, or I might change my mind." "Oh, I feel like shit, sir; I'm going. It's just that this is a gated community. There are only three ways out of here for Sara to take, and that's through the gates that are being manned; why don't we let them do our work for us? I'm not complaining. It's…" "Tom, that's true and good, but do you propose we ask the shacks guards to retain or hold Ms. Sloan till we get there to follow her? Or do you think the shack guards will tailgate Sara for us?" "K, boss, good point. I'm outta here. Thanks again."

<u>**Sara watches Brock and Tom in the park across the street from her loft.**</u>

Sara watches the interaction between the Perve and her man-to-be with her special binoculars. 'Oh, I must put on a stimulating show for him tonight, she thinks. <u>He will never forget this night… Yep, that's a promise, and I never break a promise!</u>'

Gotta get busy as she struts away. What a night this is going to be! The Sun was setting over the ocean as Brock did a set of 25 pushups off the bench. Then with both palms and his body in the forward position sitting off the bottom bench did the same amount of tricep repetitions, lowering his body slowly with controlled motion.

Then he takes a Red Bull sugar-free big boy 24 oz. from his cooler and gulps down about one-third of it. At the same time, a couple of teenagers stroll by in teen love holding hands, yammering, and stammering in a daze of adolescent innocence. He smiles as the kid leans in, gives his Lil G.F. a peck, and then nervously looks around. A sneak date, Brock thinks.

He texts, 'hey, sweet stuff, have a relaxed evening, babydoll, it's 7:11 pm, and all is well, Luce.'… 'I already miss you. Are you sure you don't want me to catch a ride up there and keep you company, babe?' 'Nah, you get some rest. I hope it's a 24-hour bug that Tom has… did you grab a sandwich or enough snacks?' 'Yes, I'm good to go!' 'Okay, I'm going to hop into the tub and kick it for a while, then call room service for a club sandwich with Avocado, then tumble into bed. My phone will be glued to me, so don't hesitate to ring me. I love you!' 'I love you too, honey!'

Not much time passed as Brock settled on the picnic bench before the lights at Sara's second-floor window loft flipped on, then the drapes were pulled wide open; he quickly raised the glasses then dropped them in his lap, nearly blushing busted but wait, this was part of his job. To watch the suspect, Sara waves at him and blows him an air kiss, dressed in a sexy Spandex workout leotard, and her hair pulled back in a bun. He raised the glasses once more and saw her running on a treadmill at a decent pace. He stood up and did another set of push-ups guessing the exercise was a bit contagious.

The Red Bull was pinging his bladder, so he went off to the bathroom. His phone buzzed a text came across his screen; 'I love you, babe. I wish you were in the bubbles with me right now.' A selfie popped up on his phone. Whoa, he shook his head in a glimmering grin, staring longingly at a sexy full-frontal breast shot with suds on her nipples and nose, the top of her head suds with a sexy expression. He nodded his head. Gosh, I love that woman! He shook himself off… a mini scrub in the sink, and texted her back. I wish I were there, sweet 💋 my sexy darlin'. He returned a selfie with him smirking, and his tongue lapped out.

Brock takes his seat on the bench… once again and picks up his laptop to do some follow-up work on a report. He was typing away and heard another chirping sound, another text with a picture grinning as he opened it. Geez, more boobs, he thinks to himself. How the hell am I going to make it tonight? He should have hit Luce for a quickie. She was driving me crazy now, and he was becoming extremely horny.

He leans into the phone and enlarges the boob shot. Wtf. Those aren't Lucie's boobs, a set of pert sweaty tits he enlarges more, a cloverleaf tattoo over the left nipple… the boobs were glistening, the caption underneath 'nice, huh?' 'Look up, Brockster!' He looks up directly across the street into the second-floor window. A figure not in focus too far away, he picks up the glasses, bouncing tits touching the windowpane glass, and drops the binoculars. The laptop goes sprawling on the grass, as does his phone.

Winces and lurches up, springing to his feet, 'How the hell does she have my private unlisted phone number? He had switched phones only a month back,' pissed and irate with anger… making his face distort, twitching, rolling his shoulders, and spitting, picking up his phone from the grass.

Brock decides to confront her, but first, he forwards the text to Lucie's phone and his Cloud Account, then calls Lucie. "Who's tits are those?" 'her voice is definitely enraged.' "Where did you get that picture? What's goin on, Brock? What… I'm not enough for you, dude, huh, I don't get it.

338

You're watching porn on your phone, ugh, why the hell did you send me that?" "Calm down, Luce; check the time stamp. Our blonde Serial Killer just sent me that pic. Yes, notice the tattoo. It's been documented in her files." "That fkn slut, I'm getting dressed. I'm on my way; how did she know your number?" "Stop please, babe… relax, sweetheart. That's exactly what she wants. We're not going to play her games!" "What the fk? I'm going to relax; she's sending nude pictures to my man. I feel like putting a bullet between those fricken tits. I am…." "Please, Luce, let's not overreact. That's precisely what she wants, and she's not going to control us. I'm not replying." "That's too bad, Brock, because I just clicked on the link and sent her a message right back to her with the caption, 'soon bitch someone is goin to be smashing those ugly boob's into prison bars 🔫.'

"What, no, don't antagonize the bitch no, don't send her another text, damnit Lucie, your out of control. Stop!" "Too late, babe. I just forwarded you the next text," he looks back at his screen. *'Sara, what ugly tits, what didya borrowed them from a pregnant 93-year-old cow… sorry for you 'leave my man alone,' you pathetic witch!'*

Brock shouts into the phone, "no, Lucie, look, now you have put our relationship on blast, ugh… on front street. The Director might learn about this and break us up. Think rationally; stop Luce, please!" Damnit, thinking to himself, I shouldn't have forwarded her picture with her number. My bad! "Like everyone doesn't already know about us, Brock, look at us. Our chemistry is on 'Front Street' haven't you seen our team's eyes and reactions to us."

Sara returns a text to both of them…. *'Your man, huh, lol once he has a taste of this sweet meat, your down for the count down a garbage disposal. Your nothing but a Whore!'* They read the text from Sara. He yells into the phone, pacing back and forth, "Agent Lucie Link, think please, babydoll, cease this retaliatory stuff! Please, stop this. It's so high schoolish, sweetheart. Take a deep inhale!" "Why did you call me Agent Link? Oh, now we're back in the formal mode well...."

He slams his palm into his forehead, temperature rising "no, Luce, get a grip. You're acting like a pawn. She's under your skin. She's got you!" "Not true I'm going to kill her!" "No, sweetie, what you're going to do is open a bottle of wine and hop into bed. Please take the Kindle out or a book, no more texts." "What I'm going to do is catch an Uber ride to be with you" "I know you are feelin' a little under the weather, babe" "aah, not any longer. My adrenalin has blown whatever bug or virus out, kicked its ass; my heart is racing!"

Sara decides to up the Ante; *'Cat gotcha tongue Lucie Lou?'* texting them both. He sees it and quickly says, "she's baiting you, Luce" "Lucie Lou, I hate her" "I know, don't fall for her sarcasm; I love you. Now relax." "It's going to be a long night, hell. It's not even 8 pm. This is personal, Brock, but I'll try to settle down as long as she stops this crap!" He has a friendly ploy to administer as clever as he can say, "Hey, babe, where do you think we should spend our Honeymoon, Sweet-stuff? You know we're taking three weeks off, maybe we can go on a cruise. What do you think?" "Umh, nice try, boy. Changing the subject ain't going to work, but let me think about that talk to you later. Love you too."

Sara tries again. *'Brock will be mine, all mine that I promise you both I never break a promise. I will have you, Brockster. One day the touch of my body will sizzle, caress your cock, you'll be mine forever, or nobody's...* 💋*.'*

"That's fkn it, I'm done screams, shrieks oh, I hate that woman" he takes the phone from his ear, picks up the binoculars, and sees Sara's wide ass smirk and both hands up with single fingers pointed at him... middle fingers. He abruptly runs across the street up next to the rod iron gate and shakes it as if it were Sara's throat! *"Hi. My big hunk, you wanna piece of me, Dontcha? Yeah, want me to buzz you up, handsome?"* Brock regains a smidgen of his composure and speaks directly to the gate speaker that had just spoken Sara's words. "Sara, I'm warning you seriously, stop this dialogue. I'm going to make sure you're on… Death Row. I wouldn't touch your Skanky, scrawny body if you were the last female on this earth. You make me want to vomit."

He waits impatiently, nothing, no reply, steps away, thinks I shut that bitch up, stepping off the curb, faintly hears, *'you hurt my feelings, Brock, you should never have done that… now you sealed her fate!'* He rushed back to the intercom system. The screen went blank pushed the button. "Sealed fate, what is this a threat, Sara? It's only a matter of time before I will arrest you, and you will die in Prison, and that's a promise that I will keep… all right now. Go fk yourself!"

That was the end of the verbal attacks and communication. He called back his Fiancé's phone it just went to VM. He texted her to please pick up the phone, and then she rang him back, "sorry honey, I was in the bathroom. I had my shoes on and the Uber app ready to access, but after calming down, yeah, you are correct on all accounts, babe. I will stay put as you have requested."

Timings everything in life at that precise time, Sara sends her last dual text of the night accompanied by her picture while the lovers were talking, Sara's blonde hair in a French Braid, green eyes with a twinkle, and bright ruby lips with a black outliner, neither could Lucie or Brock deny that the psychopath was a beautiful woman… Sara's texts a link; 'Here's your 'SWAN Song…' Lucie and Brock I dedicate 'Halestorm' song 'Love Bites (So Do I)… *Brockbaby you hurt my feelings,* 🦢 *… but I forgive you, we will be lovers one day real soon* 🐝*.'*

"What is she talking about now? Did you speak with her 'Brockbaby?' Huh, here you tell me not to fall for her antics and traps, and you do the opposite of what you asked of me, kinda hypocritical if you ask me…” “Lucie, I lost my temper and did go to her gate, your right, sorry!” “well, what did you say to her?” “Umh, in a nutshell, I was going to arrest her and put her on Death Row. She would die in prison!” 🕸

“Man, she’s obsessed with you, has so many disorders, neurosis’s a raving lunatic psychopath….” He had been thinking about this off and on for a long while, but in the last several days, it had become all-consuming. Just this afternoon, multiple times mulling over it again now, he verbalized, “you know Luce, what I’m thinking, maybe the both of us should walk away from this investigation. It’s becoming obsessive, very personal, and truly if I had the smallest justification, I’d unload my 9-millimeter into her skull! This is getting dangerous for us, babe.” “Me too, honey. I concur with your thought process, and in fact, I’ve been replaying the same thoughts. Let’s get back to So-Cal as fast as we can, okay?”

“I want you to Remember this girl. This is a one-in-a-lifetime high-profile, uh, Octane case. Whoever cracks it wide open can write their own ticket….” “True, boy, but thus far, no DNA traces, nothing nada.” “Boy, ugh, Luce, well, we have one major positive, and that’s not disputable. Sara hasn’t murdered again. At least human remains haven’t turned up with her M.O. since we’ve had her under surveillance.” “I don’t care anymore about the limelight, and all the accolades let someone else get all the credit, Luce I….” “We’re on the same page as per usual let’s get outta here!” “He glances at her house. The third-floor loft lights bright like floodlights, and he sees her reflection in a humongous mirror. In fact, recalling when he and Lucie searched, the Victorian loft had mirrors on all the walls, the ceiling, and even some mirrors on the floor.

“Sara is up in the loft right now; I will not correspond with her again. I love you.” “Okay, babe, I love you too. When we get together in the morning, we will figure out how to exit this case and which direction we should go in. Like always, we are the best team. My phone will be by my side, Brockbaby!" giggles. "Stop it, Luce," they bust up laughing. After a pause for breaths, "Yes, I agree, Brock. Let's get off this case… Time to spread our horizons and return to Southern California!"

"Okay, that makes me happy, Ms. Lucie Dame. Kinda like the way that sounds hum." He chortles. She says, "in today's World… perhaps you can change your name instead of me; how's Mr. Brock Link sound?" More laughter explodes from the speakers, "funny girl, all right, seeya in the morning 'I love you, sweet dreams, Lucie." "Sweet dreams, Brock." Still feeling antsy, he was walking in large circles and figure eights. He couldn't get those words out of his craw <u>'you have sealed her fate'</u> in his mind. There was only one conclusion this was a blatant threat… on Lucie's life.

Finally, after 25 minutes, he again perches himself on the edge of the bench, lights still blazing in the loft; must be some halides super bright. Brock sees a silhouette, then a dark shadow in the background of the loft. All of a sudden, Sara appears in a slinky negligee, one hand on a golden pole Bing-bam he didn't remember a pole up in the loft, a strippers pole. She swung around, touching herself slowly 'this must be the show' Tom was referring to that he had enjoyed.

She let a breast fall out subtly seductively, pinched the nipple erect… miming pleasure, then tucked it away with a smirk, her left hand pulling on her crotch. That's when he realized the binoculars were glued to his eyeballs. He takes them away, covering his eyes with his palms, mesmerized, then shakes it… ah, them off. Sara was provocatively playing around. Her alluring and seductiveness could even be described as scintillating to most males and some ladies. Not to Brock. It was disgusting and sickening. It was as if she was Mocking him, poking fun, teasing, taunting him. She made a nasty bitter taste creep and crawl up from the back of his tongue secreted by his saliva glands. 'Sara was a chronic disease!' &.

Twenty-three minutes later, an evoking soulful, ardent subtle invasion flashing sharp pain squeezing his abdominals, a recognition a cognizance grasping and clenching at his heart, the emotions hit him like 3 tons of bricks! Jeez, was he having a heart attack? He surged up, tingles of intuition of impending trauma startling him to totally erect. Standing shivers ran up his spine, instantly… hair on the nape of his neck spiked, sizzling on fire. Cold sweat dripped… following a 7th sense, but what? Nervous anxieties stress spilling over an eminent emotional loss, his subconscious reacting way before knowledge of a foreboding yet ambiguous and uncompromising upheaval of danger… Omg panic-stricken. Without a second to spare, a definite known fact surfaced unwittingly. He tossed everything into his car and sped away!' A magnetic draw, all he could do was rush back to Lucie… Feelings of calamitous ruinous endings screamed from his aura.

He was at the guard shack when the visions of lucidity played across his irises. His brain was instantly in wired mode, analytically canvassing the firing synapses. His brain was informing him of vibes of eminent catastrophe, cataclysmic torment. For the 5th time, he pushed Lucie's phone number down… nada! He drives like a bat out of hell, all the while glancing at his screen. A picture of Sara with her bright red Ruby lips outlined in black moments before her strip tease shows Sara had the same lips and makeup, but the color had changed. Her lipstick was pink, black outlined, instead of minutes before being Ruby colored. He had been watching a recording of a time earlier, and she was no longer in her house. He knew this as sure as he was breathing! His intuition was heartfelt and reality-based. He nearly drove right through the gates of the communities' guard shacks.

Sara On the Prowl.

Dressed in black, her blonde hair now covered by a Cold Raven dark wig, her eyes matched. She had slithered out of her backyard on the other side of a Popular Tree. A section of her rod iron fence was designed just for this, a small opening but large enough for Sara. Her motion sensors on this side of the yard were in disabled mode. Knowing the only spot she had vulnerability was crossing the street into the park, the timing was everything!

Her sexy video should keep the testosterone-filled Brock busy, entrenched in hot sexuality and desires for her sensual skin. Grinning profusely, knowing what man could resist her 73-minute projection of Sex on fire, the dildoes would bring him to a wet climax. What a performance, all synced with her laptop displayed in the large mirrors. Lol, if good ole Brockbaby knew this was a video from seven nights ago. She was checking her Apple watch… Yep! I will have enough time to do what is necessary. Her alibi was irrefutable, the lead FBI Agent Omg, this was fking fun! Good ole Brock is watching her slink around her golden pole in the mirrors. He would be her alibi. The slut Lucie was but 21 minutes away at the hotel she'd scouted out and visited just days before.

Thinking as she hurried once again, going through the broken area in the fence at the perimeter of the closed gated subdivision the neighborhood children had used as a shortcut to the Circle K store at the bottom of the hill. She was relieved to spot her Saturn four-door sedan parked as she had left it days ago in the mini shopping center parking lot. Throwing in her props, empty suitcase, satchel, and backpack, she was off and driving to her fateful rendezvous. This was her 3rd trip out this week, the idiot, ugh, incompetent Agent Tom with his hand on his pecker watching taped porn shows of her all the time, and women were the weaker sex… lol.

Having acquired a 38 special with an attached sound suppressor from her S.F. storage building, she wouldn't be held to her M.O. as the poison Vipress Serial Killer. Yes, the Worlds media had finally relented and settled on this moniker, 'The Poisonous Vipress Serial Killer.' Duh, she never left her home... he watched her in the loft, her alibi FBI Agent Brock Dame to attest to precisely that. Uh, I'm too smart for these mere mortals. Just a fact. Yup!... Lmao!

<u>Brock, in a panic, drove as fast as he could to their hotel... he had to save his Lucie.</u>

How long of a head start did she have? This could 'seal her fate?' Yes, it was only a robust and vibrant vision; uh, hunch, why wasn't Lucie answering his calls? Again the VM picked up, and the calls to the Hotels front desk had been in vain also thus far. He ordered the manager to send someone to her door; now! He thought this all could be an overreaction. Maybe his bride-to-be was sound asleep, dreaming of their lives together!'

The time was 9:45 pm. Was she sleeping? She didn't feel well, probably passed out. He drove like a maniac and waited to hear from the Hilton Gardens Manager. He flipped the Crown Vic's lights on, and the siren blew through the Red lights. He would be there in under 13 minutes.

Sara's pre-registration worked like a charm, and she was already in room #321, only a few doors from Lucie... before she got her empty suitcase into the room. Sara had rang the front desk for housekeeping 'the shower stall is filthy, there's hair in the drain... gross' 'I'm so sorry, Ms. Rancor, I will move you to another room' 'no, send someone from housekeeping on the double I wanna take a shower now, please... I'm already unpacked!'

'*Ugh,* right away, ma'am'... in World Record time, a maid appeared breathing hard, knocking on her door, hypodermic needle in gloved hands; Sara aggressively plunged it into the woman's shoulder to the hilt. Sara quickly redressed and opened her room door, a small blood dot on the maid's outfit. No prob, the uniform was much too large with strait pens; she managed to make it presentable in less than five minutes.

Taking the Mastercard Key for all the rooms at the Sheraton Gardens Inn out of the maid's apron, a ghoulish gleam as blood shaded her white teeth, another bite of her tongue with the key in her clutches left her props except the satchel that held the gun-silencer and tools of her trade lol in room #321. She stepped out into the hall, turned left then noticed a manager knocking on Lucie's room. Then walk away. She waited until he cleared the hallway and approached Lucie's room #313, knowing the scandalous duo had the adjoining room rented #315 also. .

The Lovebird's rooms had a man door or pass-through door, which meant they could play in one bed and sleep in the other room. This wasn't Sara's first trip to floor #3. She had left Agent Tom one of her other titillating videos while she'd visited the hotel. He was such a pervert sucker... pun intended. *Now the only uncertainty was could she get into Brock and Lucie's room? Undoubtedly, the chain and deadbolt were locked tighter than a drum. Her maid outfit should do the job. How fast could she shoot the bitch 'Cold Dead?' Time was of the essence. Checking her watch, 37 minutes remained on her video that Sara knew... Brock was salivating over with tunnel vision... her tunnel, Yep... he wished. .*

'Timing is everything in life,' Sara's mantra; first, she tried sliding the maids' card into one of the doors blocking the camera's view not opening fk Dead bolted, then she moved to the other door in stealth mode she pushed the door open. Yes, then the steel chain lock stops her dead in her tracks. Stepping away with only a few alternatives, one to knock on the door lol or patting her satchel with the only way to proceed... obvious that room #315 was mainly

dark inside, so Lucie was either asleep or in room #313, the deadbolted door.

Looking back slyly towards the ceiling cameras conveniently placed at the ceiling height on each side of the hallway, she wondered if anyone was manning screens, for she looked nothing like the robust maid she had replaced. Sara anxiously knew she needed to expedite this fk and couldn't knock on the door. Lucie was no fool, slicker than most, and a good cop better to catch her off guard. She puts the card back into #315, opens it, and the door again stops at the steel chain. Sara, admiring the 'Girl Scouts Motto, Be Prepared,' pulled a pair of steel snips made for cutting steel studs from her satchel. One snip and she eased the door open. The room was vacant with a lamp on by the bed, the drapes closed, and she took each step with anticipation as quietly as a mouse.

Sara nearly tripped as the hotel room's phone started ringing. Sara ducked behind the bed and waited as blood rushed to her head. She could faintly hear someone knocking on the door. The 38 Caliber pistol was in Kill mode. She was swinging it cautiously. Finally, the noise ceased. Obviously, Lucie was inside the next room, with both doors being locked from the inside. Crotched down almost at a crawl heading for the inside bypass door, which was wide open, Sara was cognizant of one mistake, and Lucie would shoot her dead… now on her knees, moving inches at a slide.

Peering her head past the threshold, eyes becoming acclimated and adjusted to the lack of light, on the bed, not 29 feet away… was a form of a body under the covers. Her heart was pounding, trying to lessen the rapping against her ribcage ssshh adrenalin squirted like a fire hose. She closed in and slowly slithered, crawling like the Vipress she was. The sound of a hampered little snore became evident, uh, stuffed up nose. 'Aah, poor baby is sick' tic, tic, tic oohhh, better put her out of her misery, lol. Ssshh.' Sara thought this was too easy, a bullet in the chamber, then her knee crunched down on an empty potato chip bag. Lucie sat up instantly, surprisingly, and quickly, her right hand reaching under another pillow for her Glock.

Sara yelped out, "don't move you, Fkn Slut" as Sara's gun was leveled, not three ft from Lucie's head. Under the sheet, Lucie could see her flashing cell phone with her pinky finger moving snail slowly. She pushed send to return Brock's phone calls > speed dial number One.

Brock, meanwhile, was frantically swerving past all vehicles, then his dashboard computer screen clicked on; "Sara, you're not going to get away with it… put down the gun." "Shit bitch keep your hands where I can see them, or I will shoot you dead right there!" Brock's flashing lights siren now breaking Nascar speed limits, the sounds of squealing tires brakes, and the ear-piercing siren stunned Sara. Lucie rolled off the bed at high-velocity speed. Sara fired three bullets. One hit the bed, and two others the wall behind the bed. Lucie swiftly made it to the open sliding glass door to the outside balcony patio, busting right through the screen, falling, then tumbling up her head down as another bullet shattered the entire glass door.

Lucie had no time to grab her Glock from under her pillow, and another shot was fired in her direction… glass shattering all around her, the sound of Sara's shoes crunching the glass coming for her laughing like a Mad Woman 'Your Dead Luce… Slut!' Lucie looked down three stories to the asphalt.

The Crown Vic was sliding and swerving. Brock slammed down the brakes, careening to a stop. Climbing out of the vehicle as fast as his human body could… it was Lucie's Fiancé, um lover… and best friend Brock Dame, who caught Lucie's eyes somehow through the incandescent streetlights, his gun out. Just as Sara walked onto the outside deck with a gun held in both her hands. "Your dead bitch… ✣" as Sara squeezed off three more shots, but Lucie wasn't there. Lucie had leaped over the balcony railing and was tumbling down to the dark asphalt parking lot. Her terrified eyes locked onto him, begging him to catch her to save her as she screamed downward, tumbling towards him. No more screams, but her mouth moved. He saw 'I LOVE YOU' as she smashed into the unforgiving blacktop.

The sickening sound of her body when it impacted the asphalt... a gut-wrenching nauseating thud-like squish and snapping cracks as she bounced and rolled. Landing a mere 7 ft from where he ran trying to catch her, he stopped and stood shocked, her blood splatter smeared across his shirt and forehead. He rushed over to her fallen body blood was everywhere, flowing from her mouth; her body was contorted. Her legs were bent in an unnatural position underneath her and pointed toward her pale face. He lifted her head, and part of her scalp fell into his hand's brain tissue. It was surreal. Not real, instantly in shock, he couldn't focus. His heart was going to implode, rocking her in his arms, tears falling, sobbing, and crying like a baby; he mutters, <u>'I Love You, Lucie, I Love You... forever. Your, my only soulmate, please, you can live, fight, babydoll.'</u> .

Just then, or was it his desired imagination, her lips parted, and she whispered words heard, <u>"I will always Love you, Brock..."</u> already the sounds of ambulances; someone had punched 911. He bends his head, blood soaking them. He kisses her lips ever so slightly. She couldn't respond suddenly 'from the corner of his eye.' He sees a brunette stare over at him from across the parking lot viciously, scowling into a smirk. She jumped into a car, starting to back up. Brock had broken records sprinting and was already at the Crown Vic. He hit the ignition and shoved it in gear as Sara pulled out of the lot. Brock hit Sara's Saturn... at 45 mph on the back quarter panel spinning the car like a top or a hat ride at a Carnival! The airbags exploded in both vehicles, and neither occupant moved for a while. Then Brock...with superhuman strength and willpower, popped out of the driver's side and crawled to his feet, taking his holstered 9-millimeter out. He would empty the chamber into Sara's head till only brain matter was left splattered.

Staggering over to the instantly wrecked accordion-looking Saturn, Brock saw the back of Sara's head. The wig had been torn away; her blonde hair filled with a rust color of blood. <u>'Put the gun down and get on the ground now!'</u> Marin County's finest Police Force. Sheriffs and Mill Valley cops' guns drawn and pointed in his direction, Brock drops down to the ground in a daze, exhausted, running on pure adrenalin with a major concussion and broken bones, nose smashed from the airbag deployment. .

Later that morning, he was unconscious; with tubes, wires, and beeping machines, he was a mess with a fractured nose, busted and torn clavicle, and his left forearm endured a compound fracture. Brock was left with a significant concussion. His eyes opened, barely cracked. He lurched up and fell back; three of his Agents were immediately by his side. Agents Tom, Lola, and Kayla, the mascara makeup smeared down both the female's bloodshot eyes, puffed up and red-faced. Tom had also been emotional as he held onto Brock's leg. He shouts, 'where is Lucie? Please tell me I love her, Lucie.' he screams with a pitiable wail... Brock evaporates energy gone!

Agent Lola bends down, water dripping from her cheeks "she's in surgery, Agent Dame Sir. They're doing everything they can to save her life, but it doesn't seem like it will be enough. I'm sorry; omg, we're all sick," more tears fell. "Lucie has so many bones broken, too many to count, and massive Hematomas... her skull is fractured in a few places. Bleeding on her brain is the focus of the Neurosurgeons, sir!" "A Neurologist specialist just arrived, flown in from Redwood City. She's a professor at Stanford University. She is in the operating room with Agent Link right now, sir. I'm so sorry, sir!"

He was upset and dizzy, spinning in a quagmire of depression... spews vomit from his mouth, choking. As a nurse enters the room, she says, 'please leave the room,' pushing the emergency call button, 'can you all go to the waiting room now?' They rush out, staring back at Brock. 'I will let you know when you can return,' then a Doctor walks in. A time warp of 7 nights and days later, Brock was released from the hospital, yet he went nowhere but lodged his broken body beside his fractured lady. She was the image of a Mummy with tubes and wires casts with harnesses and pulleys. It was a scary sight. Brock was allowed into ICU and slept on a gurney within a few feet of her. He wasn't a Pious man or God-fearing person, but he Prayed. He spoke to her constantly, holding onto who they were, the future and the past. He would not give up on her... loved her so much at times that it was hard for him to take a breath, a chore!

It was way... too early to know how much brain damage she had sustained in the fall. The list of broken bones was all-encompassing. Her entire body was in a twisted puzzle when she entered the operating room. If there was a blessing, only five vertebrae were snapped, no longer connected to her spine; she wasn't paralyzed.

Her entire family had all been to see her. Lucie's mother and father were beyond distraught and torn down. They rented a home in Tiburon, being retired, they lived at the hospital, literally all the love they could bestow on poor Lil Lucie, their precious daughter they gave of themselves and more with unrelenting optimism support, with posthaste he was accepted a meteoric ascension, he was their son-in-law. He had taken a leave of absence, but the DOJ kept his salary ongoing. After all, Brock, along with Lucie, were heroes. They had finally ensured that Sara was locked away and arrested for the attempted murder of Agent Lucie Link. She'd not see freedoms daylight for a very long time, if ever!

Brock eventually gave up on his career. His life was Lucie Link. The medical staff at the Neurological Hospital allowed him to move in. He was not the mourning type of man. He always had tried to exude optimism; Lucie's parents embraced him Son-like after a while. This was where you would find him. For the rest of the time, Lucie showed no signs of recovery. Unfortunately, without machines, she would expire. Faithfully, he read fun stories to his fiancé Lucie… stacks of books. He talked to her, praying that she heard him, and Brock slept beside her. She was and is his Soulmate for life! Super Sad! .

<u>Sara survived… shackled.</u>

Ms. Sara Sloan was in another Hospital in Sacramento, U.C. Davis, under chains and shackles with three Federal Marshals. She was lucky not to have a single broken bone but had internal bleeding, concussion some bleeding in her cranial cavity, thus her admittance to the U.C. Davis hospital. Once she was released, Sara's destination from there would be a Federal Holding cell and isolation; Sara hadn't spoken to any investigators, and her Attorney, Terrance Hallinan, was already politicking for her. One of his many contentions was that Ms. Sloan was driven Mad by the stifling scrutiny of the FBI and Social media. All the negative notoriety drove Sara Insane!

Sara had gone crazy and become claustrophobic. She's not a Serial Killer, AKA the Poisonous Vipress. The proof was as clear as the nose on your face. She sedated the maid and wielded a gun, no poison whatsoever. She murdered no one. Agent Lucie Link jumped from the third story of her own volition. Attorney Hallinan stated to the press, "who of you would jump from a third-floor balcony? We believe it was a possible suicide attempt maybe, but we can't rule anything out at this time. This case will prove that Ms. Sloan is innocent of the charges of "attempted murder of an FBI Agent. Sara was driven insane by the constant prodding and unusual tactics deployed by the FBI. Thank you!"

Those were the last words from her legal advocates. Sara lay on the gurney with hands cuffed, legs shackled, a stern expression under her epidermis, blinking with a hidden grinning, ghoulish scowl. Solemn vow oath… she was determined to exact revenge she would get even with Agent Brock Dame. If it were the last thing she ever did in this lifetime, she would take control of him mentally and physically. How? When? Where? in the Abyss, yep!

__Suddenly a brief smile flashed, then was gone, grinning, restraining an inner giggle reminiscing, 'I did take out Ms. Slutty Lucie Link… Brockbaby would be a lifelong project, though!'__

-43-

__Current time about seven years after Lucie's horrific crash to the asphalt… 7/6/17 Thursday Morning… Kamryn was freakin amazed at how Sara had bounced back!__

It's only been one week since her attack. Amazingly look how fast she has recovered. Her resiliency is admirable. Three days after the unfortunate incident, her Salon was re-opened, and she returned to work. Doctor Liz Honcho whirls her head about, raising her hands to her face, "I had 2 hours with her yesterday afternoon." Kamryn takes in her sister's work. The remarkable transformation not only was Liz's hairstyle beneficial to her overall look facial features, but the makeover did amazing things to her appearance staring at the before and after pictures.

The disparity of a picture from apparently years ago was astounding; framed on her desk and sitting before her now in the here and now, the improved Liz Honcho appeared much younger. Wow, 'my sister was and is a magician,' mused Kam. Kamryn's epiphany rang true not only did her sister Sara take years off of her client's faces… enhancing their natural beauty and best attributes, she unwittingly massaged her subject's ego, mentally engorging, stuffing them with self-confidence. They always felt a Cloud 9 feeling of self-worth value. She brought out the inner beauty to match the client's perceived outer beauty!

Doctor Liz Honcho smiled knowingly at Kam, watching her look at all the pictures on her desk, saying, "Sara had healed completely from all her wounds. Most were superficial, at least on the physical side. She refused to discuss the Carl Assault, so this is why I wanted to speak with you before your visit today." "That's fine and dandy, Liz, but what is going to happen with the Carl investigation, 'you can't just sweep this under the carpet!' this was not a fricken isolated attack, nope, no way, Liz. This was an ongoing terror for my lovely sister… tell me, how long was my sister abused, living in fear of being assaulted at any dang second?"

Liz bows her head calmly and rotates her hands downward, "Kamryn, this is a sensitive situation. Ah, matter, uhm, please let your compassion for your sister be your guide on how we proceed from here. We know your sister has been traumatized enough, so my feelings are for you to tread lightly. I believe we are doing the right thing here regarding your sister Sara. She is strong-willed and will be okay. Let me assure you that we are following company policies and proper protocol Carl has been placed on administrative suspension. We will get to the bottom of it!" Kamryn blurts out, standing… Aggressively "bottom of it. Bottom of it, that's BullShit. You saw with your own eyes as I did that Bastard had my sister by her Bald little head, tugging on her trying to bury his cock down her throat. She was forced down on her knees as he had her ears in his hands, pulling on them. Luckily, he didn't yank Sara's ears from her scalp. Wtf do you need as proof? I'm going to post all of this on social media and across the world… I won't let you keep this under wraps, Liz. NIA will pay. I think this attack warrants an investigation into…." *Bang Kam has a flash of enlightenment, dang her sister could be harmed and retaliated against if she forged onward. It would be better to try and have Sara sent to another institution before filing grievous lawsuits. Umh Kam stopped barking angrily… trying to regain her composure, took a huge breath, and paced in front of Liz's desk.* Liz sat stupefied at how Kam had just gone quiet but waited until she was done venting.

"Please, Kamryn, I realize that what your saying is factual. Your attitude isn't going to be of positive help to Sara. Drudging up and dwelling upon her trauma can only be detrimental to your sister's mental wherewithal. Her recovery will be a process, and I promise you we will…." "Carl should have been fired and charged with sexual assault of a patient at this hospital and should be imprisoned before you try and counterattack that statement, Liz. I understand the ramifications from a stockholder's perspective. Still, there have to be consequences paid and being upfront with you. I haven't filed a lawsuit against NIA as of yet, for the inadequate significant breach of security to allow an employee to be able to rape an inmate; it should be a prisoner's inalienable right not to be victimized or harmed while incarcerated. I believe this to be non-negotiable!"

"Excuse me, Kamryn. I empathize with you. I was there with you. Remember, I witnessed the whole enchilada and saw what Carl was doing. It is an open-and-shut case. No doubt, the board has been called into a special session next week to convene and analyze all these allegations. The Correctional

Officers Union is standing behind Carl. Please don't blow this up and go to the press. Remember, you have plenty of clients and friends invested in NIA. Think what would happen to their investment; you would harm so many innocent people. Let's take this case against Carl to fruition, and if we don't end with the results you deem necessary, then I will give you my blessings. Go to the press." Kamryn squints, rolling her shoulders in disdain "what if Sara was your sister or daughter? Is this the same advice you'd be giving uuhhh...."

"Please hold off. I implore you not to file a lawsuit against NIA right now. Your sister Sara has secured more freedom than nearly all other inmates. I wouldn't want that to change now!" "Is that what it sounds like, Liz?" Kam glares at her over the desk. "You're the one who better freakin tread lightly, Doctor. Are you threatening me? If so, let me warn you that I don't give a rat's ass about your Mickey Mouse threats. I will pull Sara out of here as fast as your broom goes up your...." Liz slams her hand on her desk... "Whoa, uuhhh now. Oh shit, no, I'm so sorry. I could see how you could misinterpret my words, no threat whatsoever, not at all if you wouldn't have jumped down my, umh, throat. Bad choice of words, I suppose, but I was only going to point out that some of the staff here have their entire 401k tied to NIA and might be upset that...." "Upset my ass. My sister matters here, not the employees, don't you get it, Liz?"

Kamryn reaches for the door handle. "I'm very disappointed with you and this Prison. Perhaps there truly is more to the eye... regarding what's happening at this prison or hospital. Something stinks here. My sister better not be retaliated on for anything that I do... that you can put into your pipe and smoke. Now that's a Fkn Threat!"

"Stop, please; it's not my intention to cause you any stress. Will you only wait until the conference next week? You know that your Uncle is the Board Chairman and NIA CEO. He is also Sara's Attorney, Mr. Terrance Hallinan. Think about the family objectives, Kam. Not being too presumptuous, but don't you think you should confer with him before making rash, decisive conclusions? Please, Kamryn, can we part this morning with the same feelings we had at the onset of our get-together?"

Kam twists back around at the door to face her "yes, we can; someone must defend the underdogs. This is my sister. It's personal. You do understand this?" "Of course, I would be the same if the roles were reversed," they shake hands, "have a fun visit with Sara." What Liz didn't know, and Kam thought was none of her business and better to keep to herself as she made her way to the cafeteria to find Sara. That was her ole Uncle Hallinan, and she had a serious falling out about five years back because of his strategy of sending her sister Sara to this facility. Kam had claimed his motives were purely selfish. This was a public relations P.R. move in Kam's mindset since he was the most prominent shareholder, CEO, and Chairman of the Board here at NIA. Sara's admittance here brought more notoriety to this Institution for his part, Terrance agreed. He only shrugged his shoulders; she hadn't spoken to him since!

Kam spies Sara, who pops up from her chair and rushes over to her hugs ensued. "I'm so happy to see you, big sis, and since you will be on the lake with your honey next Thursday, I'm not going to see you again until July 20th, so every second is important to me!" "How are you, Lil sister?" Kam takes her bald head into her hands; scratches on her head have almost disappeared, scabs barely visible, and were happily healing.

Nice that Kam couldn't see a mark elsewhere; all the superficial injuries had healed up… with a closer examination in a few more days, she knew there wouldn't be a mark on her epidermis proving the physical trauma of the sexual assault. Hidden was the ongoing mental abuse. Kam knew the pictures taken after the attack, along with the video, would be essential to winning any litigation against NIA. She'd be there for the inquiry next week. She was adamant that Sara would receive fair and proper treatment and justice for what she'd been through. Kam wished she had her phone at the time, but unfortunately, all electronics were locked into a box before entering the Prisons population for fear that an inmate would gain access to them. Indeed, Liz would produce the pictures. Why wouldn't she, thought Kam? Uhm, am I being too paranoid?

They sat at their regular table as Sara finished off her waffles and some bacon. Kam grabbed some coffee and talked comfortably as her sister chewed eagerly. She seemed enthused and full of life this morning, a welcome change from the doldrums she'd witnessed days before… perhaps Doctor Ame Amaya was to thank for that!

Kam says just what she was thinking, "I was wondering what you would think if I got a second tattoo. I know we have identical 'Cloverleafs' not like that, though" in between bites. Sara grins "not only do we have the same tattoo, but it's in the same place with a syrup smile yep over our left boob so perfect sister I love it!"

"Whatcha think of a tattoo right above my left butt cheek with Edwards Zodiac symbol and mine with an arrow through a heart." "Sweet Kam, I like it. When we get to my Salon, could you draw it for me?" Sara laughs at me… knowing I can't draw, not a chance. "You know I'm a useless artist. It's you that has all the talent. I can draw stick people or smiley faces. That's about it, Sara." They both laugh. For Kamryn, the relief of listening to her sister giggle was healing her heart all by itself. Oh, how she loved her so much. Sure, she had faults, but who didn't? "It's such a wonderful day outside. Dontcha want to spend time in the park or go for a walk, sister?" "Okay, Kam, it's only 9:39 am, but I want to have enough time to give you a complete makeover before your trip to Lake Shasta. Don't you leave tomorrow morning to go up to Redding?"

"Yes, Edward will be there today and set up the houseboat. It's only a 3-to-4-hour drive, and I take off from Marin tomorrow at around noon. I should be up there early afternoon." Hands in palms, they stroll down the shaded path, cool temperatures in the lower 70s, glorious sounds of chirping birds, children on the swings and slides at the playground, happy voices, lots of visitors here seeing their missing family members, Inmates today. "Hey, how are you really doing with the Carl thing? …'thing' uhm, him attacking you and trying to control you. I mean, sorry, it's a tough subject."

Sara squinted and then released a slight giggle, then a sigh escaped her lips, "listen, sis," finding Kam's eyes. "Well, it's not like I'm getting laid or having sex like you are, Kam. If he weren't a fat smelly slob who always had disgusting body odor, it wouldn't have been so bad, right?" "Sara, please no; what are you saying?" "Geez, just kidding, Kam, I suppose that being almost 40 years old, I'm peaking sexually or something like that. But no, it was awful, degrading, humiliating. I'm doing my best to try and compartmentalize all of it, and I want to not talk about it, to forget it. Can we please give it some time before discussing it again?"

Kam stops and hugs her sis. "Of course, we can. I worry about you. One promise that I ask you to make to me is if any other pressures or strains cause you conflicts or emotional or physical pain from now on, I want you to let me know immediately, okay?" "I promise you, Kam, that I will; hey, did you get your favorite safety box number today?" "Nah, 711 wasn't available. I got 571 instead. Why do you ask?"

"Oh, I know that you're a tad bit superstitious, liking odd numbers, and all were sisters and lived together for most of our childhood. Not many secrets did we ever have?" "Wait, Sara, that's not correct. I was shipped away at seven years old mommy, and daddy were going through financially hard times. Heck, I grew up in New York, and our childhood was, you know, actually, aah, we were not together that much as children. Better to change the subject." They both shake affirmative nods, then Kam couldn't let it go. "I'm sorry and always have been that you had to live with Mother's death from breast cancer and daddy dying in that hot tub with the neighbor lady. No, for sure, Sara, you had an awful childhood."

Sara allowed a pitiful grimace to cross her stretched cheeks, listening to what she'd already known but pacified her sister. "While I lived with our wealthy Aunt with vacation homes in the Hampton's, you suffered damn sis I ..." "Enough, Kam, let's do the paddle boats today. Okay, I get the green one!" "I know Kamryn, your favorite colors are red and purple, and mine are green and blue... Lol, they buckle on some life preservers, and off they paddle!"

Later like 33 minutes, Sara grabs her older sister by the forearm "come on, let' s get some drinks to take them to my Salon. I'll grab some extra Ice. When do you plan to leave today?" "The same as always between 3:45 and 4:15. I can stay longer if you want me to?" "No, Kam, that won't be necessary... but thanks." "That gives me almost five hours to do your manicure, pedicure, wash, and style your hair and makeup." Kam grins. "Let's get some sandwiches to take with us for lunch, too, okay?" "Whew, 5 hours of pampering, listening to your soothing music, and chatting, what more could a girl ask for... Yay!"

With Kam's fingers in her grasp and emery board in motion, "you know what, Kam, I was thinking that your quite amazing to recover from that last wedding fiasco, that piece of shit cheating on you; Rocky was a monster, he was a definite hunk a 10+ 'Rocky' had a body that...."

Kam snatches her hand away and leaps up "you promised never ever to bring his name up again, ever say it. You know that man shredded my heart, please, Sara. My stomach goes upside down whenever I think about ugh... stop it, or I'm going to leave. I can't even go to the movies with …" "Yeah, the actor called 'The Rock' "Why are you bringing this up again? Edward is nothing like him?"

"I apologize. I will not use that name again now, please, Kam. Sit back down; I didn't mean to get you upset here. Take a big sip of this yummy, iced tea!" Kam gulps some tea down, and they take a break and eat their lunch. Sara is like playing 99 questions, wanting to change the ambiance in her Salon, picking her sister's brain for all kinds of minute details about her life.

Finally, Kam settles in, and she seems to be the center of attraction and doesn't shut up telling her Lil sister about her life on the outside and all the new technological advances and changes in the outside world. Sara was amazed, sucking it up like a sieve! "What do you think about filing a Lawsuit against NIA and Carl? In actuality, last Thursday, there should have been an outside agency called in and a Police report done. Carl should have been taken to Jail booked, and probably the piece of shit would have been released on bond!"

"I've told you this is a private facility institution, and they have their own guidelines; I don't know, Kam, whatever you think I want to do, I trust your judgment, so it's up to you!" "Well, okay, It depends on what happens next week; Doctor Honcho told me this morning that the NIA board was called in for an emergency meeting to address your sexual assault. Unfortunately, I'd like to be there… but I will be on the houseboat. But if they decide to do nothing, then you and I must seriously decide what our next moves will be. I witnessed the attack, and I haven't been able to get it out of my mind!"

"Well, you punched and kicked the shit out of him, Kam. That was impressive for sure thank you, sista." "Even though I only see you once a week, I must say that it's been a pleasant surprise not watching Carl hover about and around us. I can't imagine the relief it is for you to be here 24/7 and not be bribed for sex constantly." "That's true, and no pressure this last week for sex; I was able to get some rest. It is nice to know he isn't lurking around the next bend or standing outside of my cell like he always used to!"

"But I must admit he did help me a lot, uh, tremendously; in fact, he was the one that decorated this room and brought me…." "Sara, whatever he did was for an ulterior motive, umh, reasons. I wonder how many other inmates were being abused by him in my gut; I believe he had a small harem of enslaved inmates here, doing his bidding!" Sara laughs hardily. "I don't know that there are that many psychos that are good-looking like your sister," they chuckle.

"When are you going to grow back your hair? This hair phobia, Sara, geez, you have such beautiful naturally wavy blonde hair; your eyebrows are gone, you shave shit, you don't have a lick of hair on your body; I don't get it?"

Sara, as per usual, retorts, "okay, Kam, when are you going to stop dying your hair?" "Fair question, I guess. I haven't decided yet." "Sista, I don't want to refer to him by name, but you cut your beautiful blonde locks into a butch cut after Rocky left you alone at the altar, then have dyed your hair dark black ever since!"

"Rocky nearly killed me; you know how Suicidal I was… after 7 ½ years, you'd think I'd be over that bastard he ahh… uh, maybe I should say his name… a thousand times. Face my demons, become angry, and cuss like fk 'Rocky.' Oh crap, I just said his name, lol. I wish he were dead sometimes…." "Kam, it takes two to tango. Crystal, your very best friend, Maid of Honor, and lifelong BFF, shouldn't have been screwing 'Rock,' especially the night before your Wedding. You can't forgive nor forget that, and your other true friend from elementary school, Trudy ole Rock, was hitting on her too at the same time! He was a Fkn Slut not worthy of you, my loving sister. You're in a much happier place now, Kam. Be happy! Smile!"

"Sara, I have to tell you this has been quite the experience with you today; I have never conversated this long with anyone. I was like a motor mouth. We conversed on subjects never broached before, even discussed our… taboo topics. Look at me; I'm not sweating. I'm almost calm, like on downers or valiums. This has been good for me to break past obstacles. Wow, I'm way relaxed. Heck, Lil sister, we took on all kinds of topics that were buried, lost in my closed closet of a mind." Sara hugs her. 'Again, I was enriched by feeling the love from my sister… Gosh, I loved Sara!'

"For some reason, I didn't listen to your constant concerns that Rocky wasn't the man for me. I will never be able to forgive myself for not including you in that Wedding. How horrible and unforgivable was that for you, my poor little sister?" "Yes, that still hurts me, Kam, but you have been here for me through my long-lasting trial and this ongoing hell. Why you wouldn't accept that Rocky had tried several times to get into my panties was beyond me. He won, and you took his side, and Walla, I was left off the Wedding party list. Oh well, that's history, and we live in the now and present for the future. Check it out!"

"No, Sara, let's not continue this conversation any longer. I'm feeling strange, weird." "Here, Kam, drink some more fluids; maybe lunch is upsetting you. Sorry I have distressed you. My fault for bringing up your past trauma regarding 'Rock' drink some more iced tea… and let me start your hair. I love you, Kam." "I love you too, Sara, my little sister, and one day you will get out of this prison!" "Yes, perhaps one day… we can only dream!" laughs Sara Yes.

364

7/7/17 Present Time... Interstate Hwy 5 … Northern California.

Oh… I was filled with exuberance driving North on Hwy I-5, singing to the thumping music, and looking forward to a glorious 11-day and night vacation. Nothing but fun; I'd enjoy water sports, Sea-Doo's, snorkeling, wakeboarding, skiing, tubing… kneeboards, swimming, and lounging on inner tubes on the lake. BBQ's Sun and fun-loving sex relaxation with my Lover. We are soon to be Newlyweds. What wasn't there to like about these thoughts? Wow, exhilarating indeed.

Her gorgeous Corvette was such a rush to drive, hugging the rolling hills into Corning, California, yes… the magnificent sight of Mount Shasta with snow still on its very top peaks. The highway seemed to run right into the mountain, so cool of a façade mirage the sky was a dark blue… not a cloud in sight. A.C. blasting it was 111 degrees outside, she punched the accelerator to whip in and out of behind a Semi truck and trailer trap… grinning. Yeah, boys, not going to pin me in. What fun, as she is once again free of traffic, pulling into the slow lane going fast. The 2-lane Hwy was crazily crowded.

Mindful of her surroundings, constantly checking the rearview mirror, oops, just cut off a woman truck driver with a giant dog sitting in the passenger seat. She changed the music genre to a mellow tune, 'Dave Brubeck's song Take Five' perfect as she thought of the parallel. Lol, she did 'Take Five' Hwy I-5 and smirked.

Then suddenly, the instant gut-wrenching feeling devoured her blissful ride, one that anyone who has driven roads in this world might feel. It's a sickening feeling, bad head rush, ugh, a gut call, albeit flashing lights of an

Ambulance or emergency vehicle or, in this case, a CHP, lights disrupting the serene ambiance, picturesque afternoon her blood pressure shot up as her right foot did the wrong maneuver it pressed down on the brakes. Why? Wrong? Uhm, because it's a predisposed natural instinct showing guilt possibly ill-perceived. The cops see that you hit the brakes because they think you are acting guilty knowing this, you Brake…

Gravel spitting up, she yanks off onto the soft shoulder, now stopped on the side of the road. The CHP cruiser stopped like 15 feet behind her, and she watched as the Officer climbed out of the pulsating-lit car. She was determined to sweet talk and flirt her way out of a ticket.

Well, that was until the bullish domineering woman meandered grindingly slow over to her driver's side window. Hitting the down button, a heat furnace engulfed the Corvette… ice cold air vacated the cockpit, and sauna-dry Death Valley-like air took her breath away. Sweat bubbles were already forming on her forehead. Reading the badge on the left pocket of…"well, surprise, surprise, it's you again, so you didn't learn your lesson, huh?" Holding the ticket book with a toothy smirk. "Gotcha this time, doing 93 mph that was slickly navigating, jutting in and out between those truckers looked to me to be a case of Reckless Driving also, but I will let the Judge decide that!"

Officer Citation opened her book "you know the drill, License Registration, and Insurance, please!" "The officer's radio static blasts into the dry air. She turns away, hearing an excited voice with added static over her radio attached to her breast pocket. Officer Citation's face turned even redder; something got her attention. Her radio was going off. 'Alert Amber Alert Child Abduction dark blue Toyota Tundra 2005 plate 666BSFK spotted by the Rolling Hills Casino!'

'Amber Alert keeps replaying, 5-year-old boy blonde hair blue eyes.' Officer Citation snapped the book closed "fk, it's your lucky day, but I'm sure I will see you again." She rotates around and runs 'wow, she moved faster than I thought she could.' Back at the CHP cruiser, throwing rocks, gravel, and dirt fishtailing across both lanes, leaving tread marks. Burnt grass and ear-piercing squealing tires. Officer Citation spun across the medium, now going in reverse the opposite direction South on I-5.

Whew, that was close. The window shoots back up. She shoves the transmission in gear... the A.C. was trying to regain the advantage. Sighing with relief, a few miles down the road, her blood pressure had nearly dropped to normal... then the phone chimes, Bluetooth activated "hey there, how ya doing, sweetie?" "Oh, fantastic, Edward, but it's God awful hot up here, for Christ's sake, boiling. How do people live up here and not be roasted alive?" He chortles loudly, "many live around the lakes and soak their bodies in the cool water, umh, yuh... Redding Electric is the stock to be in up here, my financial wizard wife... to be everyone lives in Air Conditioning!"

"Where are you at, Kam?" "Just left the Corning signs," "so a good 45 minutes or more away," "uh, I guess, so you want me to stop at a grocery store and pick anything up?" "Nah, got everything handled, babydoll putting the Steaks on the grill in 25 minutes with some stuffed baked potatoes. Aah, I have your favorite Hollandaise sauce with Asparagus sautéed lightly and some special white Wine chilling!" He paused. "Kam, I'm really looking forward to this vacation with you!"

"Oh, yum, me too; I can't wait to see you. My tummy is screaming; now I'm starving." "I love you, Kamryn. Drive carefully, honey. No speeding tickets on this trip, lol!" She decides to set the cruise control at 73 mph, and his voice comes back over her car radio's speakers. "Kam, I will be at the dock. I've reserved a perfect cove for us. The houseboat fits like a glove, with total privacy, with all our toys attached. We are going to have the time of our lives, girl. I love you; goodbye for now." "I love you too, Edward... bye."

She decides to stop in Shasta Lake City, pulls off on Shasta Dam Blvd finds the Sentry Grocery store for a self-serving purpose. She bought a cold six-pack of beer and another case for the houseboat. It was still blistering hot outside, and a refreshing brew would take some of the heat and anxiety away from her meeting with Edward. Checking her dash clock, she'd made great time and couldn't wait. The Bridge Bay exit was less than 5 miles away, and finally, she would see the beautiful Bridge Bay Resort on Shasta Lake. Wow, this was going to be so much fun. She thought, sighing, then a wide-assed smile was stuck on her cheeks.

<u>One day earlier, 7/6/17, Thursday NIA. Later that evening,</u>
<u>after Kamryn's visit!</u>

The head nurse on a call says to Doctor Honcho, "aah again, I must apologize for bothering you once more. Sara is out of control. She is worse now than I have ever seen her; ugh, delusional way off the charts. Doctor Honcho, umh, Liz, you have an alert to contact you if there are any medical issues with Sara. Well, we had to sedate her and place her in a Solitary room. She's in a straitjacket. It's the same ole same thing!" "What do you mean, same ole thing, Renae?... hold on, Renae." Liz rubbed her forehead and moved away from her husband, who was sipping some Sleepy-time tea and watching TV replays of the best plays on ESPN.

"Liz... Sara had passed out during her sister's visit. When she regained consciousness, she went berserk like the other episodes she's had in the last 5 to 7 months. This Episode was the worst of all time. Screaming and howling... got physical, and she lost her mind like always it was after Kamryn, her sister, left her. It's traumatic, and I don't know...." "Renae, it's after 11 pm. Why are you calling me again?" "Umh, it's different this time, Doc, we tried to let her out of the jacket, but unlike previous times when she had calmed down, we allowed her to go back to her cell; this time, she went berserk on us!" "Umh, she went into another Frenzied crazed animal state of being... scratching and clawing, and OmLord, the expletives were from a wild woman, deranged she was fearsome like possessed. I have it all on video scary like I...." "Nurse Renae, I will be in tomorrow morning. Don't contact anyone else about this issue. I will deal with it okay now if that's all, and no one is dead, right... I need to get some rest. Keep her restrained until I get there. Thanks, and Good Night!"

<u>7/7/17 Friday morning.</u>

Doctor Liz Honcho was enjoying a cup of expresso as she reviewed last night's video of Sara. Immediately her thoughts were perplexed. Maybe it would be better to limit Kamryn's visits at least till after the Wedding. Nurse Renae was correct in her observation dead on. Never had Sara gone hog wild and used such foul language. Certainly, she had used obscenities and swear words before, but not like this. She must have reacted badly to the medication change since Carl's assault!

Liz speaks into the recorder, 'The Psychotropic drugs might have caused Ms. Sara Sloan's hallucinations. One of this new therapy's significant drawbacks is its side effects. Sara's mantra was always the same, consistent; her claims never changed. They were a constant Liz sat back to reflect on the violent struggles and skirmishes involving her staff and Sara. The video was difficult to watch. Sara had stood up and kicked a guard in the groin, dropping her where she was standing with a savage kick. An outright assault on an officer.

Liz rubbed her eyes. Whoa, my beautician is getting out of control… ahhhh, strange conundrum. It was only last month that her sister Kamryn had proudly said she had a breakthrough with Sara. They openly discussed the problematic 'Al persona…' well, so much for that reality. Sara was regressing at an alarming rate. If this continued, she'd have no recourse but to drop her classification and limit her movement at NIA!

Liz replays for the 5th time… Sara strapped to a chair in her urine, crying, shaking, and convulsing literal insanity shouting that she was cramping up, hurting, unable to move. The staff had her locked in steel chains in a chair. Sara was suffering badly. The pain matched her dizzy, drugged-out mind. She was in her own 'Dightmare.' Her brain wasn't functioning, and words were slurred. Liz picked up her phone and speed-dialed Terrance Hallinan, Sara's Uncle, who was also the CEO of NIA and Sara's attorney. Maybe if he'd come in to visit her, it might change Sara's disposition. Uh, Liz was grasping at sinking straws. As per usual, the call went to voicemail.

<u>Dazed, Confused in another dimension aligning with Hell.</u>

***

Each time she awakes or seems too… dizzy and hurting, she blinks her eyes open; she releases a prolonged mournful yowl, crying out. 'Where am I? What was happening? Why couldn't she focus? This was the worse hangover in history felt drugged to oblivion. Something was drastically wrong with this entire picture. Why couldn't she maintain one subject? She was so convoluted couldn't concentrate her thoughts buzzed from one to another. I'm going crazy. Am I in a hospital? Was I in a car accident?'

Her mouth was so dry, and her tongue felt like it had developed cracks. Her saliva had stopped secreting… her throat closed, and she was breathing in gasps. Was she dying? The claustrophobia was ripping her mind apart in pieces. I tried to scream, yet no sounds. Was this Hell? Was she dead? How did she get here? Why can't I see anything? Am I blind? She prayed, or did she… was she insane?

Suddenly Doctor Honcho appeared, and the shouting began. She was irate. "What the Hell are you people doing? Are you trying to kill Sara? She's got vomit all over her, sitting naked with feces and urine, chained, and shackled to an iron chair in a fkn strait jacket. Get her out of there now! She cannot breathe. Listen, she is wheezing. Get her the fk out of that chair, or I'll put you all in it! I should fire all of you. I'm writing up all of you… move it now!"

"Doc… Doctor aah Doctor Honcho umh we have been doing our rounds and ma'am we're swamped we.…" "Bullshit," Liz looks up into the camera and microphone. "I want the last five hours of video: Naw, the hell with that. I want the video and audio from the moment Sara was brought into this room on my desk and sent to my email ASAP. 'Damnit,' take off the poor girl's blinders."

Liz stares down at Sara as the guards and nurses scramble to unfasten the strait jacket unchaining her shackled legs and handcuffs, bleeding, raw. "Get the poor girl some water with a straw OmGod. Look at her chapped lips, Nurse Renae. I want to see the charts. When was the last time Sara was given fluids?" Liz stomps out, "your asses are mine…how cruel and sadistic; how would you like to be treated like this obscenely and inhumanely? What have you done to her? All of you should be ashamed of yourselves."

A nurse runs out of the solitary confinement cell. "I'm going to get her a big glass of water, ma'am. Oh God, I'm sorry!" "Sorry, huh ain't no excuses. Look at the poor thing, can't even hold her head up?" With disdain dripping from Liz's lips, Sara moans as she is told to sip on the straw. Sara was so weak that she could move the water up only two-thirds of the way. Liz steps in, takes the straw with her finger over the end… siphons some into the straw, and releases it on Sara's parched tongue "get a gurney in here; I want, and I.V. started for hydration a full checkup. Take her to the medical wing. I want her vitals… get moving, folks!"

The staff was spun out, not conditioned to this verbal abuse. Most were worried about their jobs and bonuses. It was a flurry of activity. "Sara, Sara, Sara, can you see me?" while Liz shines a pen light into her cloudy eyes, nothing.

She could hear her name or someone's, but the words reverberated. Uh, came out of an echo chamber, thinking she was speaking… nothing, the injection of drugs every three hours or so, oh, I'm so messed up with zero comprehension couldn't see what had happened? Why couldn't she remember anything? Was she attacked? Did she have a concussion, an accident, obviously in a hospital, it seemed? Gosh, every joint in her body ached. Her wrists and ankles felt raw; ughhhh, better off to be dead than feel like this. No help me, please God, where are you? What's going on? A permanent fog too thick to see through, a hole with quicksand. Yes, she was sinking into the abyss!

Doctor Honcho's last stop on her rounds was at the infirmary. Still infuriated by Sara's treatment, the staff was written up and put on notice. Each one of them had ten days to appeal upcoming sanctions. She couldn't wait to read their orchestrated versions of events; duh, the video didn't lie!

"Hello, Doctor… hi Doctor Chafe, how is Ms. Sloan?" "Ugh, Liz, do you want the long or short version?" "Short, but please forward your report to my office!" "Okay, she will make it; she overdosed on a multitude of medications. The mixture could have been terminal. She had an adverse reaction, internal glands filled with toxicity. I have her on fluids; her vitals are nearing normal. We've taken several vials of blood for testing. I find it strange that she had a toxic reaction. Her body should have built up a tolerance; this is very unusual...." "She's had a bad week, Doctor Chafe, and..." "Yes, I've heard the rumors. You know this hospital is like Payton Place... the guard Carl had Sara on her knee's sexually abusing her, and then there are other rumors spreading that Carl had her doggy style, or there's this one...." "Doctor Chafe, that's enough. The Warden and I would appreciate that if you hear any of the staff spreading rumors that you put a stop to it at once!" "Uhm, Yes, ma'am."

"The last thing we need here at NIA is negative press, and for other Inmates to get wind of this, then their family members could start a hysteria, a neurosis which could cannibalize your job as well as the rest of the staff. Do you get my drift?" "Umh, yeah, I understand fully now... mum's the word Doctor Honcho. You can count on me, ma'am. I will do you one better. I will call my subordinates in and have a meeting regarding this very hot issue!"

"All right, let me know how that goes. I will be back in on Monday to check on her. If there are any changes to Sara, please call my home number. Now I have to call her sister Kamryn. This catastrophic situation can't continue. We will have to limit her visits here to see Sara... it's for the safety and well-being of our patient. Damn! Oh, Doctor Chafe, when Sara regains consciousness, contact me immediately!"

"I sure will, Doctor Honcho... when Sara was brought here, she was in a catatonic state, moaning, grunting, and groaning. She is bruised all over... her arms, back, breasts all over her upper body, and ankles. Her chins were scraped by the chains and bleeding. The restraints were way too tight, ma'am… cutting off Sara's circulation and blood supply to her toes and fingers. I hope there will be no permanent damage." "Yes, Doctor, I saw the way she was confined. She was being tortured, Doctor, plain and simple. I've written up all employees on the shift that was culpable for her mistreatment! Goodbye!"

Liz hits the down arrow from the 5th floor and ruminates to herself in a bout of self-pity 'gosh, I hope Sara recovers quickly. My 25-year High School reunion was on the 15th of July, a Saturday.' Liz realized she had to be proactive… Sara had to recover enough to do her total makeover. Omg, it's a must; I have never had as many compliments in my life until after her 5-hour makeover. She wily thinks is her responsive show of empathy for Sara selfishly based… ughhhh no, it's not about that!

'No question Sara is a genius, a makeup artist extraordinaire, and what she does to my hair is unreal then helping with matching up outfits to coalesce with my entire ensemble man, oh man, I need Sara back in her Salon.' She drives out of the main gates of NIA. Thinks kinda selfish am I aah so what… it is what it is… or is as it should be she laughs, shrugs her shoulders.

-45-

The engaged couple is in Northern California, on Lake Shasta. It was supposed to be the start of a glorious vacation.

Pullin off at the infamous Bridge Bay Resort exit, with excitement palpable, she veers to her left to the private docks where her honey's parents moored their deluxe houseboat. Indeed the finest she would ever see. She parks in a designated spot... opens the Corvette's door, and the hush of the hot country air takes her lungs by surprise. Hyperventilating with anticipation, she takes her groceries down to the security gate and enters her key. And Walla ambles down the floating dock damp with perspiration. The Lakes water a tease to her body's system. Oh, how she wished she could catapult in right then.

Walking past all kinds of houseboats and pleasure crafts on each side of her, 'hi there,' said a couple sitting on their deck sipping from a bottle of wine. She said, 'well, hello to both of you too, have a wonderful evening!'

At the very end of the dock, she spots the massive 75 ft houseboat that she'd be vacationing on...." She sees another neighbor lounging with a book. The lady looks up from the deck of a magnificent yacht. "Well, look who it is. Hi Kamryn, how are you doing, sweetie? How was the drive?" "Your man is killing all of us down here at the end of the dock. That BBQ smells so delicious." Stopping as her memory evades her, the middle-aged woman in a flowered one-piece bathing suit and large sombrero hat with obviously perfect false teeth, bright and shining white. The woman's too skinny of a husband, bones with sagging skin, looks at her with a tinge of mannish virility long lost as his perusal of her a bit beyond the curves.

"Your right. I can smell that barbeque, and I'm famished, starving. It was a pleasant drive from the Bay Area, and oh, I look forward to relaxing for a while with my honey. You two have a fantastic evening... nice to see you both again!"

Sweeping past the sunbaked couple, the dark green and black houseboat loomed just ahead! Sneaking onboard, she deposits her suitcases and luggage from the pushcart she'd been rollin. Spies him, his back to her, facing forward, concentrating on the BBQ. She slinks in tippy toes, obsequiously making her way to within five feet of him. Music, a sound buffer 'Sinatra' bellows out 'My Way' as she watches his luscious hips flex in and out all around as he is having fun.

In a split second, he impulsively spins around. His chef's hat holds his head. A broad smile creases his countenance, and his arms fling out to the sides as he puts down the spatula. She springs into his waiting arms, the embrace sensual, the kiss far better than either one expected they breathe one another in, the smells… a combination of barbeque and wanton unrestrained licentious lust, the need to ravish and lavish their bodies the yummy barbeque smoke in the mix.

"Oh, Kamryn, I surely love you. I know it's only been a few days since I last kissed you and smelled your skin, but. I've missed you enormously!" "Aah, Edward, I've missed you more than words or even your imagination could ever comprehend, um, no words uh, I could express that would…."He picks her up and whirls her petite frame around in a swirling dance move with mixed emotions, yearning to be inside her, and says. "We should get this houseboat out to the special cove. It's so darn secluded, like private. I located it earlier today. Our Ski boat is saving the spot, but I'd like to devour you instead. Damn, but we'll have to wait." She replied with a sensual circuitous lip and winked her sexiest expression. He clutched her. "We have plenty of time to enjoy our love heck, Kam; for the next ten days, we could go completely au-natural… nude!"

She reaches out and touches the deck. Okay then, I will help you untie this monstrosity. He turns down the barbeque on simmer; a quick peck that lingered pushes himself clear of his fiancé's grip, and he shakes his head. In less than seven minutes, they were floating past the No-Wake Zone.

Luck was on their side. Their Ski boat was still beached on their private island. No one had trespassed or encroached on the little island beach they'd call home. They were just north of the Shasta Dam, a gorgeous, cloistered cove. A family of landlocked deer greeted them as he beached the considerable houseboat. "Hey," he yelled back, "Kam, check it out, a Bald Eagles nest." Pointing at one of the tallest trees up on the ridge, "the trees will give us shade in the morning till noon. What do you think impressive… huh?"

Kam's reply was heard, not verbalized, a splash into the water, followed by a light-hearted whooping squeal, "aah, this is pure Heaven, babe, jump in. Let's go for a swim, Edward?" He turned off the barbeque; dinner would wait. I'm coming grinning large, didn't have to ask him again; seconds later, a cannonball splash… and he was swimming in the water by her side. Such unadulterated fun! Giggling, splashing each other, kissing, horseplay, he'd dive down under the surface and tug on her feet, pulling her down. They hopped up on some inner tubes to let the sun bake down on their bodies for a few moments. They'd found heaven, holding hands and listening to the music that blasted from their houseboat… Bose speakers, hey, this was living life blissfully. Does it get much better than this?

The BBQ was scrumptious, the anticipation of loving, foreplay continuously verbalized, eyes and expressions a build-up of the inevitable bonding, conversationalists two peas in a pod they couldn't wait for their scintillating dessert, her revealing more of her sweet skin. "Hey, you haven't touched your wine, darling?" "My tummy is churning with the expectation of being with you non-stop for the next 11 days. This cold Apple juice works, for now, sweetheart," said she.

"Kamryn, I never ever thought I could fall 'In Love' again, given up on the relationship trip. My feelings didn't happen overnight took several years till I could open up my damaged spirit and heart, and I thought that God's plan for me was only for me to be alone. Lord knows I've suffered from my past relationships, but now I think I'm the happiest ever. I love you and can't wait until we are forever married!"

Their eyes were lost in each other, the setting serene on the upper deck under a large umbrella. A table for two was a perfect size. She pours him some more white wine and smiles. "I love you with all that I am, forever. Our Wedding day will be the best day of my life. Gosh, this dinner is fabulous. Thank you so much!"

He grinned, 'well' as he spread his arms out, waving them around, looking out and around him "privacy, the only way anyone could see us is from the air. I think it's time for some dessert!" with a wink. He was holding her small, manicured hand up. She winked and grinned. "I have a confession or breakthrough that will shock you, uhm. No doubt it was like an epiphany for me!" He rolled his shoulders in anticipation of her words.

"We have been going out together and dating for now, three years, nine months, and five days. Only yesterday, a manifestation materialized clearly, conspicuously initiated by my lovely Lil sister, my Sara." "Let me interrupt you, Kam. I've been at odds with how we should proceed with litigation against NIA. Now I've concluded that what happened to Sara wasn't an isolated act. NIA isn't an island. We need to expose this sexual assault and go for the throat. Even though I've had a convoluted, tortuous, and haunting past with your sister, she is Sick. I can never forgive her, but I can reconcile that she's insane, Kam, so...."

"Edward, it's just like you to steal the moment, please, I have a mind-altering epiphany, a profound change from yesterday, and it's all because of Sara. I realize she's the last person you want to talk about, but she is my sister!" "Sorry, babe, uh, Kam, I just had that on my mind. I will not interrupt you again. Please go on!" He reaches over and takes her hand in his. "Okay, back to where I was on a subject we've never broached before, hidden away deep behind thick walls that surrounded my heart and soul. Sara brought up the horrific time of my last serious

relationship. My wedding from hell… that never happened. Just his name mentioned would have stifled, hampered me, put me into a stupor, and almost put closure to us… Yes us!"

He squeezes her hand, pulls it to his lips kisses softly, "after all, we had so much to overcome from the beginning or at the onset of our relationship. Hate was all that we had, and it's been a miracle that we got past all the obstacles. We are the result of what could only be termed as Destiny, just to be sitting here on Lake Shasta on a wonderous houseboat In Love and about to be Married for life. My sister purposely said the most hurtful and despised name because she wanted to help me overcome my past. My heart was broken, but somehow I endured and survived him… 'Rocky' Yeah, Rocky nearly destroyed my ego and who I was. She not only mentioned his name once but over a dozen times. We'd agreed his name was Taboo. But hey, I overcame it, umh, it was amazing, like therapy. We talked about him like never before." He squeezed her thigh and rubbed her palm lovingly.

"Something clicked in my skull. It's time to leave the 'Rocky' part of my past where it should be buried deep in a vault. I've been so selfish towards you and immature on many occasions. I still recall the toxic and awkward silence that followed when I referred to you as Edward. Your parents had an unusual reaction of confusion upon their faces… not understanding why I called you Edward?"

"Kam, it's all right, I understand, and so did my parent's heck, it's my middle name; refreshingly, you're the only one alive that calls me Edward. I enjoy it, Kamryn. Okay, let's move on, let's…." "Well, that's changing as of now because I've changed more than you can realize since yesterday. I will no longer let my past haunt my future. The problem was always regarding your first name. Not only did it rhyme with his damn name, Rock/Brock, but because of my sister, the memories were so terrible… but now let me say this to you, my lover for the very first time; my Special Agent for the FBI, Mr. Brock Edward Dame, I love you."

Brock stands up with a wide shit-eating grin. He thought his skin would tear, "well, well, first name basis, huh? I like the way my name sounds coming from your succulent lips!" "Brock, brock… Brock," she screams. They laugh as he swirls Kamryn around, giggling together in Virgin bliss with deep-tongued kissing hugs for days. Brock says, "I guess I owe thanks to Sara… wow, I thought I'd never say that!"

Brock pops another cork out "now, are you going to indulge me and celebrate with a few glasses of this fine Cabernet wine?" "Yes, I shall. I think first I have a surprise for you. Be right back, BRB. "He raises his voice over the subtle music. Whoa, I think I've had enough surprises for tonight, lol."

A few moments later, she holds up a Blueberry Cheesecake. "I know how much you enjoy Blueberry Cheesecake, Brock…." Instantly a nasty twinge hit his intestines, thinking back to the last time he had Blueberry Cheesecake delivered to him. *It was with his former 'Fiancé Agent Lucie Link.' It was sent to them at the Restaurant they were having dinner at by the Vipress herself, the sister of his lover Sara.* Still, he rolled with it rather belatedly, "dessert for us, yes, right on, girl, aah, this is going to be the best vacation of my life, Kam!"

A vast evil-tweaked smirk engulfs her cheeks. 'Yep!' "One neither one of us will ever forget, that's for sure. Hey, maybe next week we could take a boat ride over to the Sacramento Arm of the lake and check out where we're getting hitched up, Brock." 'Brock,' she and he laughed "wow, calling me by my first name is going to take a while to get used to!"

Doctor Chafe was beside himself angry as he viewed the bright arterial blood on the sheets around the now chained and once again shackled Sara sedated again. "Doctor, I heard her scream out, then I rushed into her room here, and Ms. Sloan had ripped her I.V. out! Sara was kicking and fighting, saying to let her alone, 'leave me alone, where am I? What the hell kind of place is this?' 'Were some of her words it is all on video. I had no choice but to inject her with the sleeping agent, then one of the guards put restraints on her. That's why I paged you, Doctor Chafe. Did I not follow proper protocol, sir?"

Doctor Chafe sighed and took in his top nurse, who had been by his side for 11 years, flustered, blushingly red, and thoroughly frustrated "you did the right thing," as he lowered his hands on her meaty shoulders, "write out a report, I want copies of your daily logs, I need to attach all files and upload all the videos to Doctor Honcho. She is paying special attention to this Inmate. I will need to send her a text and an email regarding this incident!"

7/10/17 Monday 7:15am NIA.

Liz Honcho is reading the complete reports on the Sunday upheaval at NIA's Hospital ward for the second time. Unfortunately, it was again about Sara.

Liz thinks, gosh, I have to bring her out of this fugue, uh, fantasy world that she has constantly visited for the last seven-plus months. Looking at her patient Sara's charts counting at least 13 times, Sara has had psychological breakdowns and episodes of Schizophrenic delusions. Sara's multiple personalities are taking over her body. Liz was checking and running a cross reference on an interactive chart. Kamryn's visits exacerbated each episode. In fact, the argument justifiably could be made that Kamryn was the provocation uh

cause of many of Sara's latest issues, sadly unbeknownst to her. Her visits incited and instigated well; call the kettle black, thought Liz. Kam induced this mania, Sara's psychosis. Kamryn's visits aligned with each of Sara's delusional episodes… every time in the last seven months that Kamryn had visited, Sara had to be restrained and injected with sedatives. &.

She picks up her cell phone and pushes in Kamryn's number, which instantly goes to voicemail. Then it dawns on her that she was on the Lake on vacation. She notes to herself, 'I need to address this with Kamryn before she plans on coming here to NIA to revisit Sara.' Her desktop phone buzzes 'Yes' 'Ms. Sloan is being moved to conference room # 15. Doctor Honcho, Sara remains restrained and will be on a gurney. She is cognizant or at least consciously delusional, ma'am.' 'Thank you. Make sure she has been given sustenance, food, and liquids. I will be along after I finish some research.' Liz thinks she must do something. Her Anniversary was the following week, and Sara had to come back to life!

Twenty-five minutes later, at NIA, in a 17 X 30 ft room, a refreshment bar with people congregating around it, three separate screens for viewing, a super long table made of solid Oak with matching chairs sitting uncomfortably were two guards, one female, one male. Doctor Chafe, Nurse Renae, Nurse Puffin, and others are in wait mode.

Doctor Liz Honcho enters. She stares across the expansive room, counting the members of her staff. "This is a premeeting for I want us all dialed in, no discrepancies when the Board of Directors are here next week. We must be on the same page regarding an NIA Correctional Officer's alleged sexual attack on Sara. Also on the agenda will be how we explain to Kamryn why her sister is being isolated!" Every person's reaction was similar; all acquiesced and were on alert.

"All right, let's get this meeting going." Liz walks over to the gurney that contains Sara "how are you doing today, Sara?" a slurred, raspy voice. "I'm not Sara, damnit!" Liz turns about, 'I explicitly ordered no more tranquilizers!' "I had to administer a shot of Diazepam. Her blood pressure anxiety was through the roof, hyperventilating the Valium should be wearing off soon," declares Doctor Chafe.

Liz rolls her eyes without a rebuke, "we have a lot to focus on today, and most of you are here because each of you is part of the team who provides Sara with her primary health care here at NIA. This ongoing dilemma of her taking on her sister Kamryn's personality and mind-body is disconcerting. According to our records, this is the 13th consecutive time that this has occurred, and every time it's been associated, ughhhh, it happened after a visit from Kamryn. I want your input now; think all of you, why is this time escapade by Sara worst of all? What happened... I want ideas on how to combat this to bring her out of this fugue. Come on, folks, give me fkn viable answers. We will discuss the Carl situation and the upcoming Board meeting. Still, this inherent problem needs to be resolved, or at least a plan of attack formulated today!"

-46-

The Sara Sloan inquisition.

Liz has Sara rolled in her wheelchair to the front of the room near the podium her team of professionals looks on. Liz steps forward, rolling her shoulders and nodding... "Okay, Sara, before we get started, do you have any questions? Umh, do you understand why we are here?"

"I'm Kamryn Amaya. I work for Schwab Financial. I am the Vice President of the Financial Consultant Division, Liz Doctor Honcho, I was in your office only last week discussing Sara's assault, and you know me; I'm Kamryn. Listen to me, please I can prove it!"

Liz shakes her head for the umpteenth time "listen, Sara, we have gone over this three dozen times if we've gone over it once. Please shut up and stop this delusion. I realize you want to be Kam, but you're not. If we take the cuffs and shackles off and sit you up, will you promise not to harm yourself or try to attack our staff?" asks Liz.

"I am not Sara!" "Is that a yes or no, Sara?" she screams "where is Sara? Why am I in this bed? What the fk is going on? Unchain me now. I will own fkn NIA and fire each of you. Get me out of here!" Liz grimly says, "it appears she is back with us somewhat. Get her some coffee or something to drink!" "Ma'am, are you sure that we should take off her restraints? She's a wild one… yah no!" worries a guard. "I don't want anything from you people. Let me out of this Insane Asylum. I'm going to Sue you for everything your worth. I will leave you all bankrupt. You'll be homeless, you freaks. You will be lucky to collect Unemployment, you assholes!"

"Sara, now calm down or will have to…." She mutters, "I want to talk to my Attorney and my fiancé' Brock Edward Dame. He is the Head of the FBI in Northern California. You're all going to pay for this," as she rubs her wrists where blood droplets were forming.

"Where is my sister? Why am I here? What day is it? What's going on here? Are you all Insane? Where are my clothes? Get me out of here…?" She rubs her eyes, tears not flowing. She'd… been cried out, and then her hands went to her head. She wails, shrieking with rage, "What have you done to my hair? You've fkn shaved my head, no oh no… Wtf? Oh shit!"

"Calm down, Sara or Kamryn. As Liz tilted her head at the group and winked, they acknowledged the subtle winking, nodding, and leaning forward on their chairs. "So, Kamryn or Kam, what is it that you remember from last Thursday, July 6th? BTW today is Monday, July 10th!"

Kam's mouth explodes wide open, agog shocked, "4 days, OmLord, I've lost four days. I was supposed to be with Edward, uuhhh, Lake Shasta houseboat vacation, my Fiancé not possible…" all of this spinning in her head out of control, her mind messed up. The medication's residual effects had to be playing tricks on her conscious state. This is like the worse nightmare of all time. Kamryn sinks down in the chair, closing her eyes. Thinks 'um gotta relax now, breathe slowly, wake me up? This has to be a bad dream. Have I had a stroke?' She stares and focuses on Liz. "I have a severe migraine like a freight train is running from each ear to the other I need a phone… I need to call Edward!"

"Kam, will you please drink some water? You're dehydrated. It will help with your migraine!" "I will only drink water from a bottle that hasn't been tampered with. I don't trust any of you, I…." "I understand you're a bit paranoid," as two bottles of water unopened are handed to her, she twists the lid on one and empties it down her throat, then does the same to the second one and is given a third bottle that she holds on to.

Doctor Chafe whispers to Liz, 'there is a new Psychotropic drug that we could…' Kam can hear and yells, "Oh no, NO, no, I want no more of your fkn drugs. I can't think as it is… I've lost four fricken days. All I want is to leave here. I want to talk to Sara can you get her for me, where is she? Is she in her Salon? I want to talk to my family Attorney Uncle Terrance Hallinan. Now I demand a phone call and to be set free. You're treating me like a Criminal, a Prisoner. This is a nightmare. Wtf is going on here?"

    <u>"Sara-Kam or whomever you think you are at this moment.</u>
I feel it is in our best interest to lay out some ground rules…
or parameters first and foremost. If you have another outbreak
and go berserk, the guards will secure you once again to a
gurney and put a muzzle on you like a dog, or we will be forced
to put you back in a Strait-Jacket! Sara, if you continue to give
us trouble, next will be hypodermic needles, and you will be
incapacitated and immobilized. Listen, you're a patient here
at NIA, a Prisoner, and an Inmate. You will cease with your
demands and obstinate and derisive comments, words, or
threats. I will not tolerate this is that understood I …." "Hold
on here, Liz…." "I'm Doctor Honcho to you." "No, you're not.
We are on a first-name basis. You haven't answered one of my
questions. Have I entered the Twilight Zone? I'm to be
Married in less than two months. I, I'm not Sara!" She stares
out at the faces, some with their eyes lowered 'something is
beyond wrong here; I need help; this is Insane.'

    "What are you doing… to me? I ask you not for anything
except for a simple phone call to my Attorney or my Fiancé
who, as I've told you, is a Federal Agent for the FBI in charge
of the Northern District of California!" Liz ignores her and
says, "all right if you will watch the screen in front of you I, I
believe we can help you to understand our perspectives Sara,
this is a joint effort today. Look around you. We are here to
help you as a group, observe you, and answer a few of your
pertinent inquiries. We are here to help you and discuss several
impending interactions in which you will be involved,
primarily the sexual attack by one of our Correctional Officers.
We want to respect you and treat you accordingly. We demand
this reciprocated. We will assess and formulate a game plan to
bring you back from this personality-shift uhm, paradigm. To
date 'we have logged seven thus far of your multiple
personalities, some with domineering attributes. These
aggressive entities are dominant, and you're scaring the staff,

386

Sara!" Kam shocked, hearing Liz's words, did the only thing she could "ok, I'm listening to you, Liz."

"<u>Sara'</u> is, of all of them, the most dominating. The mental disease you suffer from is Schizophrenia along with a multitude of…." Kamryn sees the date on the video that was uploaded. "Please, enough of this crap. This video is from over five months ago. I want to see my sister Sara now. At least you could bring her here, and we can clear up a lot of…." Liz loses her composure, raising her voice, "Pay attention to the Video and shut up, Sara!" Kam's heart was beating past her chest, light-headed, not entirely cognizant of her predicament, but soon it would all cave in on top of her like tons of bricks. On the 75-inch screen, she sees her sister Sara sitting in a chair in a strait jacket shouting incoherently… blabbering, but some of her words are crystal clear <u>'I'm Kamryn Amaya. I work for Schwab in San Francisco… I'm not Sara, you assholes!'</u>

Kam looks, and yet it doesn't ring true. Liz fumes, "check this out, Sara. Here is another video dated like four months ago. See the calendar on the wall in the background, look at your forehead, and see all the cuts and bruises on your arms. This is when you took off running and dived into the pond after hearing your sister Kamryn was getting married and not visiting you for a couple of weeks. *How can you not see this? It's from four months ago; watch this!"*

Kamryn now starts to sweat profusely because she remembers this incident vividly. Omg… this was four months ago. She was there when Sara harmed herself, jumping into the pond. OmLord, there she was next to her sister Sara, in her cute pants suit, then the video shifted in disbelief. She watches her naked sister in a rubber room, banging her body into the walls, shrieking. <u>'I'm Kamryn Amaya, I'm Kam, Kamryn. I wanna call my Attorney Hallinan and my Fiancé Brock Edward Dame. I demand a phone call now!'</u> *"Here's another video from 3 months ago"* ' They watch, '<u>I want a phone now</u>

you're keeping me against my will. I am not Sara! You're all going to pay for this. I will sue you all. You're going to be homeless; I will own all of you…" Liz shouts, "look at the date Sara on the wall; it's 4/10/17!… over three damn months ago, Sara!" .

In horror, Kamryn sees Sara staring into the camera, her 'Feral eyes,' wild blood dripping from her chin. 'My fiancé is a powerful FBI Agent. I want to call Edward now! why don't you believe me? I'm really Kamryn. I can give you all my stock trades from last week. I can prove without a doubt that I am not Sara… I can easily substantiate everything, damnit, you're all piece of shit freaks!'

By this time, Kamryn's head is hanging, her mouth wide open in shock. She grabs the water bottle and takes a sip. Her tongue was stuck against the roof of her mouth, thinking for the first time, 'oh No!' Liz continues the Chronological timeline with the same theme redundantly exposed 'Sara saying, pleading, acting exactly as Kam had been up to this point; it was like an exact replica of the same act Sara was playing her perfectly months before… eloquently and to the point hitting every narrative thus far… OmLord.'

"This is from two months ago" by this time, Kam's mind could no longer maintain any logic and couldn't focus. She was in a Zombie state of being. 'How could this be happening?' In this video, both Doctor Honcho and Sara were on the screen. Sara was the calmest, yet almost appeared totally calculating and rational. She heard her sister's voice say, 'Doctor Honcho, please help me prove that I am Kamryn Amaya. I'll do anything DNA fingerprints, Iris scans. I can provide you with my losing options. Calls and winning Puts in the stock market, even last week's trades. I'll give you a blood test, whatever!'

Liz, with the rest of the group of NIA staff… were irritated beyond understanding. Many were agitated and didn't want to deal with Sara any longer… get her off their workloads. The professionals who dealt with her by providing medical assistance were at the end of their ropes. They sat bewildered at how Sara couldn't see herself for whom she was. This act was monotonous, consistent with the same-ole same theme. Most thought she should get back to her routine. Several of them had missed scheduled appointments in her Salon.

"Fk Liz, this isn't me. It's Sara. You have been freakin conned, scammed true, very fkn clever my sister Sara is a genius, no questions she's played this out like a Mastermind, and you folks have chewed it up, metabolized it, and shit it out. Let me use the damn Phone now!"

"Stop," Liz pounces up, peering down at Kam, "stop interrupting me. I let you speak, be respectable, listen. I have grown tired of all your expletives and cuss words. Your crass gutter mouth has you close to being gagged. Listen, I've explained this to you dozens of times. I will just one more time. In fact, better than that, you can watch a video of my words verbatim!"

<u>Liz sighed and rolled her eyes okay for the last time. "Sara, please pay attention. Kamryn is your older sister true by 7 minutes, your identical twin's Fingerprints, DNA, even matching tattoos; you are the same in every single way developed from a single fertilized egg ovum…. Damnit again, your Identical twins Sara…." "So what? That's not a new epiphany," Kam yelped out a high-pitched screech. "I'm fkn Kamryn" "Shut up, Sara, you know as well as us your DNA tests and all evaluations will come out the same as your twin sister… Here. Look, this video was only three weeks ago. Watch it. See you once again. You're in a Strait-Jacket." In disbelief, Kamryn drops the water bottle… 'Omg, how could this be happening?'</u>

"See yourself, look… Sara, you're once again in another one of these delusional states only three weeks ago after you recovered from a potent sedative shot. This was when you returned from your subconscious state of being. Pay close attention now. Let me turn the volume up because you're murmuring, droning on, and mumbling, be quiet!" Kam sees Sara speaking. "Please, Liz, why don't you check the security camera's out? Sara shaved my head bald. She made a wig from my hair that she trimmed for months and escaped pretending to be me. I have been set up, Liz. She's probably driving my Corvette right now!"

Kamryn shot up, suddenly blinking, then took her fingers, felt her head, and then eyebrows. 'OmGod, no hair, none Gone... then, not caring, reached down to her vagina where she had a half inch of a hairline landing strip, her cooter was freakin bald... Oh fk, not a hair remained anywhere on her body. No, she bellowed out, 'No, Sara, you didn't, God, no?'

Liz continues, gawking condescendingly, "in your Salon, while you worked your beautification magic recently due to curious nosey onlookers spying on my staff and me from our security rooms... I had blacked out all the cameras in your Salon for privacy's sake. But please watch last Thursday's video to verify and establish authentication that Kamryn left your Salon as she always had. Your sister didn't hesitate to go to box #571 and stick her key in this box. This demonstrates the fact that only Kamryn knew her box number. Here she exits the triple doors and goes directly to her car again. She doesn't hesitate. This in itself substantiates your ongoing delusion contradicting all your faulty arguments. How can you sit there holding onto these idiosyncratic ignorant beliefs? After seeing... should be believing Sara. Pull out of it now!" 'Kam flashes back suddenly at the peculiar questions that Sara had asked her just last Thursday 'did you get your favorite box number, # 711? She nonchalantly said no, # 571. This is too bizarre to comprehend. It's gotta be a hallucination, truly a delusional apparition.'

"The last seven months, you have progressively become increasingly lost in these delusions, symptomatic of a mental loop instigated by your sister's visits, like a mantra of sorts. There're hours of videos of you saying exactly what you have repeated today, all fantasy and prevarications, uhm, make-believe, please think, snap out of it now, Sara!" shouts Liz.

Kamryn vomits and spews bile like in the movie 'The Exorcist,' letting her mind drift back, shaking in pain. She recalls Sara asking innocently, 'hey Kam, what car was I driving? Did I park in the shade over by the fountain? Sara asked me about my plans for the rest of the week. Where was Edward at? Omg, not on the houseboat? Uh, not with my evil sister who hates him. She'll kill him. 'Oh, fk. Looking back at the frozen video screen, I just watched my sister Sara leave NIA looking like me, identically wearing my clothes and getting in my Corvette. She'd shaved me bald, oh damn, that's why she shaved her body of all of her hair... we're identical twins. Oh no, she'd been cutting my hair and making a wig from, ugh... of my hair. She wore my hair out of this fricken prison... No, please, God, this can't be happening!'

Then it hit Kamryn her brain had thawed. 'If I am here, then is Sara with my boyfriend, fiancé Edward OmLord she will murder him!' Kamryn blanks out and blacks out. Nurse Renae is the first one to her side. Doctor Chafe yells, "take her to the infirmary. I want her vitals as Renae wraps on the blood pressure strap 197/121 super high out the door... the gurney rolls. Liz exclaims, "I thought she was on valium. Her BP is skyrocketing. Page me when she has stabilized; thanks!"

<u>Kamryn wakes in the infirmary.</u>

Kam awakes hours later in the exact place she had first found herself after Sara had obviously drugged her with the iced tea she kept urging her to drink. She keeps her eyes closed this time as water seeps out of her eyelids. It was the best she had felt since the drugging started, still thought the drug hangover prevented her from formulating a plan.

Images now found realities, reasons, and strategies, clever manipulations. No, Sara wasn't Insane in the sense of intellectual analysis and analytics. Nope, she was a shrewd, cruel, Masterminding genius... Savant, a Scholar, accentuated by her artistic prowess, drew her own algorithms. She perpetrated the ultimate Mission Impossible Kam's head spun and swum in circles. Whoa, replays floated back and forth across her wet cheeks. Panic then took hold as the machine beside her began sounding an alarm. She hears the doctor come in and order some more of the hypertension medicine. She had another I.V. under her skin... Kamryn tried to fight it but lost as she dropped out of her conscious state of being into a much darker swamp.

Later that same afternoon, Liz headed for the parking lot while on the phone with Doctor Chafe. "If she wakes again in the Kam state of mind, let's try that new miracle Psychotropic drug out for a few days. We need Sara back" doesn't say what she was really thinking out loud, which was, I do need Sara back for my reunion. It's but days away! 'Okay, yes,' he declares and ends the call.

Liz was not feeling a bit guilty for her ulterior reasons and motives that she had to have Sara back in the living 'one way or the other, got to get that bitch back in her Salon, fk that's what I get dealing with insanity laden Freaks!' The night shift staff on Kam's floor at the infirmary had one distinct rule of thumb; if an inmate was unruly or loud, umh obnoxious, sedate them, period, drug them to oblivion, even gag them. 'After all, most of the prisoners were Nuts, uhm, insane, ugh, so what did it matter?'

At the foot of Kam's gurney was a chart with her medical records printed out. She stealthily sits up and reads the printed-out outstanding order that was recently activated 'new prescription drug to be administered when her blood pressure and vitals return to near normal.'

Shit, she was going to be a test rat, remembering one of the doctors saying something about this new Psychotropic drug, damn. She's got to get out of here before they drug her into insanity, uh… make her go insane. 'I am not unstable. I am beginning to see and feel the Evil of my Twin sister, a diabolical monster now unleashed on Brock, whom she had always promised revenge… anger with unrelenting animus and hatred toward him. I must alert him need to get to a phone.'

Kam pretends to wake at 8:05 am, sweating in the cool 69 degrees still in this daymare, and speaks calmly, 'I want to make a phone call, please?' She hears an admonishment, 'no phone calls until your return to the general population, Sara!' The nurse barely seemed to care for her or the other comatose victims who lay about like docile reptiles around her, and she was playing Solitaire on the computer in front of her nose. 'Hope you lose,' shouted Kamryn… 'I'm not Sara, damnit, I'm being treated inhumanely here; just one phone call, let me talk to someone that's in charge!'

"Sara, if you rip out that I.V. again, I will have you chained and shackled down with a fkn gag down your throat. Be quiet. I'm working here!" 'Hey freak, shut up. I'm trying to rest over here,' says another Prisoner lying in a place to Kam's left. Raising her head to peer around, she counts nine other gurneys in her sight. Five of the Inmates were gagged, chained, and shackled down.

Despite that being the case, Kam couldn't resist. She pushes the call button for the intercom, 'what do you want?' 'I need to use the bathroom' 'Oh, for Pete's sake,' the nurse paused her Solitaire game. 'They didn't shove a fkn catheter up your urethra fk these incompetent assholes' walks over and picks up Kam's chart. Saw the outstanding order for the New Age Psychotropics and believes that will shut her up. She walks over, unclips the I.V. and monitors, then takes a wheelchair between gurneys and helps Kam into it. Rolls her to a handicapped bathroom "there you go, hurry up, will yah?" While Kam is in the restroom, the nurse loads a tube of the new drug, ready to be injected into the hanging I.V. line.

Kam is then rolled back to her bed and adamantly barked, "I want to speak with the Warden immediately or whoever is in charge of NIA." "Sara, it's almost 9 pm. The Warden has long left the grounds" "please let me call my boyfriend just one call or even text or my attorney, please!" "Sara, you really have to be quiet." She reattached the I.V. adding the new Psychotropic blend mixed with the saline mixture. In total frustration, Kam shrieks a piercing cry out, "why, God, why is this happening to me? Please help me!" The chatter came from around her... *"oh poor, Poor baby, come to mommy,' 'shut the fk up bitch, I'm warning you,' 'hey nurse, can you shut the bitch up?' shouts another inmate.*

Other inmates start to mimic Kam. The nurse walks over and leans down "last warning, or I will bag your ass up and gag you. Shut up. I have work to do now," she said, hurrying off to her awaiting solitaire game.

Kam feels the drugs affect... her skin crawling instantly, a change inside her body futility wrapped in indignation, feelings like bugs were migrating up and into her veins. A hateful, cold rush shutters and shakes her joints. Kam whips her head around, locates the I.V. line, and decides that she must yank it out of her arm in slow motion. Her right-hand moves in a clawing grasp but never makes it! It would be the last thing she would recall for several days.

<u>Kamryn was lost inside her mind.</u>

'In her younger days, she had experimented with a few hallucinogens, Ecstasy, and Magic Mushrooms; well, she partook truly due to peer pressure during her college days. She was fond of the fun high, and some of the light shows at a few concerts and rave parties which were accentuated by the hallucinogens. She stopped this young adult experiment because of the aftereffects of these drugs. For her, they caused an inevitable comedown worse than an alcoholic hangover. Invariably she'd drop into a deep-down depression, surely enjoying the extreme highs on the drugs, um, euphoria fun laughing hysterically, but then the opposite was three times worse. Wishing for death during the downward spiral of coming off the drugs!' She decided they weren't for her.

Kam was now locked up in prison, switched out by her sister… her brain and body were floating in the air… above the earth. Her view was like five-dimensional, her life on live video from her childhood, her teen days of distress, and the ongoing adulthood trauma. Her mind buzzed. Her presence was unfocused, her life distorted with no future and a factual past of untruths her sister Sara had never loved her. Kam had no control over her destination. She was a locked down passenger on a journey voyaged on without a direction, the drugs that were forced on her, injected in an I.V. Ugh, secreted systemically within her internal glands. She was lost in an abyss without hope and felt total, stifling despair.

It was a wild ride, all in vivid colors fading back five years plus ago. In a Courtroom, Sara is on trial, her uh, our Uncle Attorney Terrance Hallinan grilling Agent Brock Edward Dame on the stand his lover, best friend, and Fiancé Agent Lucie Link lay comatose still from the savage attack and fall from the third floor of the hotel, onto the asphalt.

Kam could still feel the stares of disgust from the many witnesses and family members of Sara's victims. She had an ugly feeling espoused towards her. Some of the crude people that Sara had hurt had thrown eggs at her and cussed her out. The Marshals had to escort her to court and out to her car. Her sister seemed to gloat and revel in the publicity and notoriety of her case, sneering and scowling at the crying family members of her victims. According to the AUSA Prosecution team, Sara was guilty of at least 39 murders that they could prove conclusively.

Once again, like on a time machine, she sat in the courtroom's front row, a spectacle as she watched the Macho man FBI Agent Brock Dame, on the stand; weakness showed this tough man was breaking down. My sister Sara's defense team brutally attacked Brock Dame, rehashing Agent Lucie Links jumped from the hotel balcony at the Sheridan Garden Inn. Kam didn't want to show the slightest bit of empathy for Brock, for, in her eyes, he was a despicable man, albeit handsome... he was the enemy!

The strategic storyline by the Hallinan Law Firm was played out over several weeks that both Lucie and Brock and the FBI had driven Sara... crazy insane. She'd become despondent, melancholy delusional, and she retaliated irrationally for Sara was mentally challenged from her childhood's past and caustic memories, her mother dying from breast cancer, her dad being electrocuted in a hot tub with a neighborhood woman.

There were many charges against her sister, but the most serious of which could be proven was 'Attempted Murder of an FBI Agent Lucie Link.' In total, she had seven felonies lodged and filed against her from that one incident, uh, crime! The 39-plus Serial Killings that she had been suspected of committing became only subjective suppositions and hypothetical meanderings. At best, not a thread of evidence could substantiate the alleged allegations.

Kam had tried her darndest to give Brock the Evil stare, hate him for what he had done to her sister. If not for the FBI's harassment of Sara. Kam believed there wouldn't be a case at all; of course, no doubt my sister wasn't a Serial Killer. How utterly preposterous and absurd, besides detesting Brock Dame, his name was too close to her jilted ex-lover Rocky Blake…'Brock… Rock' add the 'b to Rock,' and the name left… had destroyed her life at her wedding. Every time she heard the name Brock she thought of the detestable freak Rock who'd eviscerated her soul, cheated on her, ugh, destroyed her trust in men. 🐦.

Flash forward… three months at the same courthouse, the downtown San Francisco Federal Building, a miscalculation by Kam put her in a stuffed elevator next to their adversary Agent Brock Dame. Not a word was said. Their eyes met several times. She thought it was the last time she would ever see the man up close anyways, but wrong flash to around three years and nine months ago. A Thursday, she was at NIA visiting her sister… disbelieving her own eyes. He stood across the parking lot with his head in his hands, distraught, apparently. The Macho man was crying. She drove right by him and his white Crown Vic. what the heck was he doing at NIA? 🐦.

Her sister had been locked up in the Asylum for years. If she ever regained her sanity, there would be additional hearings. She made it her business to find out why he was at one of the Out-Patient buildings at NIA. Flash: He was there visiting his Fiancé Lucie, who was under the observation and care of a World Renown Neurologist who was contracted out by NIA.

She was still in recovery and could be forever a vegetable from the awful fall. Lucie Link had broken nearly every bone in her body miraculously… her body was almost totally healed.

It was the brain damage and head trauma that lingered. She was out of the coma but could not speak, not a syllable since the crushing blow to the asphalt. Flash: 5 weeks later, Brock drove up and parked three car spaces away. This time there was no mistaking the awkward silence as he walked past her as she opened the door of her vehicle.

On the 7th floor of NIA was where patients who were not incarcerated and were not inmates would seek medical help. Professionals from all over the Globe congregated in a think tank on this same floor. Top-class innovators, a New Wave of experimental Stem Cell Therapies and Bone Marrow procedures, and the absolute best and most innovative Doctors were hired by NIA. The Federal Government considered medical care for Lucie Link of utmost importance. Brock would visit her at least once a week.

Flash: a couple of weeks later, a Thursday, ironically the same day that she visited Sara, he was there visiting Lucie on the same schedule it appeared. Kam saw him pushing Lucie in a wheelchair from an adjacent building used for rehabilitation. He saw her and looked away, seeming angry or hurt. She entered the NIA Guard gates and visited Sara. She stopped at the outpatient hospital cafeteria to get an iced tea on her way out. Fumbling her phone out of her purse in line at the cash register Brock with a bag in hand, was leaving the counter as her phone tumbled to the tile. They both bend over, not 15 inches apart. He snags it. They stood up, then realized who they were and blushed clumsily, obviously uncomfortable, embarrassingly, no doubt! "Umh aah, thanks" she swiftly takes it from him and turns away.

Flash: Two weeks later… Kam had an awful visit with Sara inside the prison, was in a terrible mood, decided to follow her Thursday routine, and went into the adjacent Outpatient cafeteria to snag another iced tea walking in the automatic doors as Agent Dame was walking out. She couldn't restrain herself and lost her composure and temper. "Can't you find another day to come here? I'm tired of running into you!" Then she looked down OmGod he was pushing, in a wheelchair, um, drooling Lucie, the love of his life. She felt like melting into the ground. Shamefully instant empathy, he, with pain and hurt eyes sorrowful his eyes were filled with tears mutters, "I've been transferred up to Northern California to be able to be with Lucie. My only day off is Thursday. I'm sorry I will see what I can do." He ducks his head and sadly disappears.

That did it. Her conscious ate her up the whole week until the following Thursday, she would apologize, but she didn't see him. Flash: several more weeks passed by, then she spotted him sitting alone in the cafeteria, feelings exuding from him emotional upheaval and anguish, apparently trying and doing his best to keep his composure by rubbing his temples. She stopped. "Excuse me, Agent Dame. I wanted to apologize for being so blatantly rude to you and Lucie a few weeks ago. I'm humbly sorry!"

That did it. His eyes couldn't dam off the flow, and he muttered, 'thanks, please excuse me' and quickly walked towards the men's restroom. I could tell hell, umh; anyone could. Some people were staring in our direction. Brock was lost in love, despairing his Soulmate… in oblivion for some damn reason; I still can't reconcile why fk I sat down at his table where he had only nibbled a few bites out of a grilled cheese sandwich. He finally came out with a startled stare and walked over to his, uhm… our table. "I heard you before 'Kamryn' no worries, in any case. I understand how you must feel about me, so why are you sitting at my table?"

Silence only permeated this awkward confrontation. We oddly showed perplexed expressions "that's just it, Mr. Dame, I don't have a clue how I feel towards you. I read the S.F. Chronicle article about Agent Lucie Link and the distinct possibility or likelihood that she would remain in a vegetative state, umh, ah, where there hasn't been much improvement in her condition. I wanted to express to you how horrible I felt that I hurt you further with my derisive tone and insulting words!"

Then it happened. He sat down next to me and put his hand on mine… "I was lost as tears bubbled. I love Lucie with all that I am. I never thought I could love again. I need her back. She's my only friend, my best friend soulmate! I wish I were dead; with no energy, I'm utterly lost without Lucie. She is the 'Light that was my Life!"

Then he bowed his head into his palms. The proud Macho man shattered, heartbroken, was it maternal or what; before Kam knew it, she was kneading the back of his head, holding him. His hair felt so lush and natural to her. Rubbing him felt oh so good to her… why?

The weight of the situation hit her about the same time it waylaid him. She said, "aah, I'm so sorry for you," as the legs of the chair squeaked underneath her as she got up and took off in a double step, nearly wanting to run! WTHell was she doing? Oh fk!

Ironically, Kamryn, at various times in this haze of the Psychotropic experimental drugs, could envision herself from above the gurney. It came rotated in blinks or flashes like a movie script that bounced back and forth, disjointed… and ubiquitous. She was being shown the replay of her courting of Brock in pure HD, not in control, though, kinda pinned down a 'captive voyeur!'

Flash: Very next Thursday, leaving NIA through the guard gates, who pulled up directly behind her. Ah, yeah! Agent Brock Dame, they were stopped in line with a problem with someone three cars up in the line. She looked at him in her rear-view mirror. It was sunny both wore sunglasses. Then he exited his vehicle and ambled up to her door. She lowered her window "hey there, I'd like to thank you for last week properly.

I sort of lost it. Can I buy you dinner at the Kenwood Winery? No strings attached, please, uhm, to talk… I need someone to talk to. If not, I….” Kamryn giggled, “stop it, Agent Dame, you're going to talk us right out of dinner. The answer is yes, I'm starving.” Omigod, the most handsome dimpled smirkish smile, broke loose, mindbogglingly contagious she couldn't help it and grinned right back. Thankfully, someone honked from behind them. He rushed back to his cruiser, and as they say, the rest umh became history.

Although she felt immense guilt for dating the very man who had arrested and locked up her little sister, how could she live with herself? He had major obstacles to overcome himself to date the sister of the person who forced his wife to be… to jump from the hotel balcony. It took months like a snail's slow courtship. Dating him was rewarding and fulfilling, even taking short vacations together. The chemistry was their attraction, pheromones on blast. He turned left. She was already there. She'd be telling a story, he'd finish her words, they were cohesively bonded, and gosh, they would laugh spontaneously, like hysterically, at a moment's notice. They had fun together with actual coherence, but it was our humor, giggles, and laughter that was so Special! %.

Their relationship seemed more of a BFF, like best friends, sure. We'd pet or massaged one another, with no sex or intimacy for almost 15 months. They even worked out together, spoke for hours on end via phone and FaceTime, and discussed in detail their goals, um, aspirations. Even voiced disagreements resolved some mini arguments, resentments, and ultimately their hurt feelings. Their guilty conscience for dating one another, above the surface and below into our deepest hidden alcoves, we openly bared our souls. The hardest quandary or barrier they faced was broaching the obscene subject matter... <u>Aah, how do either of them have the audacity to allow this relationship to get off the ground? R U</u>

<u>Kidding me?</u> He would say at times, 'What are we doing?' Open wounds and scabs would fester deep in their souls, and their scars itched. This would never vanish after our trials and tribulations. Our relationship was a Work in Progress, yet Laughter overcame all!

They mutually decided it was best for her to use his middle name Edward for the caustic trauma that Rocky had scarred her with… and to keep them a secret from Sara and Lucie. He understood that his first name, 'Brock,' was too close to 'Rock.' So he was happy to be called Edward. It would also help him with how Lucie Link would refer to him. Once he said that Brock was dead, yes, I'm Edward. I like that it helps me mentally. Great idea, Kamryn. I'm now someone else, not Lucie's Brock; I'm your Edward, lol. He just made it clear that he didn't want to be called ED!

(In less than two months, she was to become Kamryn Linda Dame against all odds. They did overcome all obstacles, love healed all, and 'Yes, they were In Love!')

Kam wakes from the fugue caused by the Psychotropic medications three days later in a cell. Looking around, I thought it must have been Sara's old cell. Gut-wrenching reality took her conscious mind into overdrive; Sara, the conniving manipulator, was pretending to be me. Is she with Edward? Certainly, he would be able to tell the difference. Yes, we were identical twins, but we had unique differences, such as our mannerisms and expressions. I regret not getting the matching tattoos Brock suggested on my left forearm.

It wasn't her imagination. After she distanced the look and altered and changed her hair color from her natural blonde to a Raven black, the Press and Newsies started leaving her alone no more pictures on the front pages of Newspapers across the Globe. Social Media even slowed its maniacal, hyped attack on her.

However, she will never forget an article <u>"This is Sara's identical Twin Kamryn Amaya the same enzymes blood, and DNA flows through her internal glands her skin matches, who's to say she doesn't have the same mental makeup as Sara? One day Kamryn may Snap!"</u>

Dying her hair was one way of distancing herself from her twin and the negatives of being identical twins. After several months, Kam fell in love with the hair color and look and even contemplated dying her blonde pubic hair and did so a few times with a beard dye from 'Just for Men,' but Edward liked the Blonde trail. Flash: Kam drifts off again now in her teenage days.

<u>-48-</u>

<u>Shasta Lake Houseboat, Edward, and Brock… Kam and Sara?</u>

So I'll bite Kam. What makes the female gender the best kind of 'hitman' or lol 'hitwoman?' I mean, for sure, you couldn't physically battle a male. You're not as powerful nor as resilient after a bruising fight with a person that outweighs you by what? Hell, look at us. I, uh, weighed 221 pounds yesterday at the gym and had my fat ratio tested at 6.9%. My weight is primarily lean muscle mass. You, my dear, are about 135 pounds of tight tendons and taut muscles. How could you ever overpower me, my darling?" She winked and tapped her forehead. It's right here in one of the largest and most complex organs in the human body…Brains."

Brock cackles into a riotous yowl, 'whoa' slapping his forearm, "these mosquitos are out for blood; got to get some spray." She took the lead. "Yeah, us Females' were frenzied in a greedy, ravenous piggish way, sucking blood voraciously." "Hey," as he took the last bite of the scrumptious Blueberry cheesecake, "the mosquitos are after dessert also"… they laughed. "Hey babydoll, can you grab the Skin so Soft spray? You know it's only the 'Female' mosquitos that bite and sucks your blood, Kam." "Yup, Brock, like mosquitos… it's been synonymous throughout time that the females of the human race, uh, of our civilization, can be the most dangerous gender, not the males."

Brock looked over at his sweetheart. They were having another one of their philosophical debates, elongated renderings, um musings, and each taking turns to build up their arguments debating any and all topics brought forth. This was their kind of competition and fun. After one of them would develop a hypothetical belief, they'd verbally and analytically reinforce the analogy or tear down the subject matter. Tonight Brock thought ole Kamryn was on a roll regarding the dominating and subtle 'Femme fatale.

She stands up and starts pacing in front of him. "A seductress with the enticement of tempting sexual interaction can disarm the male's instinctive state of awareness, survival, and preservation of the male's perpetuation of safeguarding oneself. Males are vulnerable to an alluring sexy, tantalizing female. Their natural suspicions are subtracted from a testosterone buildup that puts blinders towards their counterparts, making them susceptible that's why throughout history, the female assassins were and are the most prolific!"

"Wow, Kamryn, I never knew you were a history buff. Please go on; I'm enjoying this lecture and learning as you go. Give me some examples, Professor Kamryn. Yeah, uhm babe, how is it you formulate this assumption" Brock snickers. "I love you, Kam!" "My dear man, not an assumption but a mere fact." Gazing right back at him with a matching smirk, "let me further elaborate, my lover!" She pinches his arm.

"Ramses 3rd in 1155 B.C. the King of Egypt was assassinated by members of his own Harem of women who conspired to kill the Pharaoh during sexual acts they murdered him, or how about from the 'Apocryphal' the Old Testament Book of Judith she liberated the city of Bethulia. After Judith used her charms and sexuality to become intimate and seduce him, then she severed his head 'he lost his head to a pretty girl.' Decapitation… his name was 'Holofernes' in 1621 A.D., yep, a sexy 'Siren' got his head! Not the little one, I remind you … uuhhh yuh following me, Brock?" He merely rolled his hand like go on…

"Or how about the Kenite woman, 'Jael,' in the 12th century when 'General Sisera' was murdered with a Peg of wood driven through his scalp while he slept? His assassination occurred in the General's tent after a scintillating night of sex and drinking." "Wow, I'm flabbergasted. Your unreal girl, uhm, Kam, do you have any more examples? He chuckles, "I might need to write down all of this and take notes." She continues, "Actually, Brock, this subject could last till tomorrow, and I wouldn't come close to how many female assassins had successfully exterminated famous men throughout the annals of time." "Men who were after sexual conquests here's another how about the 'death of Marat' a famous painting depicts the scene of the French Revolutionist Jean-Paul Marat dead in his bathtub following his slaying by the woman Charlotte Corday 1793. Or, more recently, another female killer took the life of Selena, the Queen of Tejano music, a superstar killed by Yolanda Saldivar, who befriended her. Or how about the two women that conspired to murder the brother of the North Korean dictator… Kim. You see, women are so unassuming, Brock the weaker sex really; females have the ability to fly under the radar stealth mode, men let their guard down they disregard a woman's abilities to kill." Brock had sat up, feeling pains in his stomach and an eerie feeling of trepidation.

"Take the Black Widow who devours the male Black Widow, her mate, after sex. The lists go on and on!" 'Brock, with imperfect timing, felt suddenly light-headed. Was it from the Wine, too much wine?' He had this fuzzy feeling. His legs felt heavy and lethargic. He was placing his palms on the table.

"Kam, that was remarkably interesting and scary. I could easily see how a man could underestimate a woman, especially if they were heterosexual in lust for sexual pleasures. A lover could disarm you through the falsehoods encompassing intimacy!" For you to memorize, all those historical events is simply mindboggling. You're fantastic. I had no idea!"... 'Ugh!'

'An odd twinge, weird electric current floated by his Amygdala, instantly anxious... uh. The neurons processed eerie emotions of anxiety that filled his nervous system, an un-copacetic head rush he was struck peculiarly with apprehension, a warning sign from his brain that something was inherently wrong, an ephemeral narrative.' Thought patterns drift by obscure, undefined nebulous transformation. 'Something happened in a flashback. Ugh, foggy, the kiss was unlike any he'd ever received from Kam, like strange their tongues were not dancing in unison, kind of out of sync. Something was wrong, but what... his skin was tingling.'

Never did Kamryn go off on a tangent like that, the conversation, and her mannerisms queerly unusual, the eyes the same. It's not... there's a difference, ughhhh, as he tried to lift his head to look into her smiling eyes; was it a stare of malice, animus, or enmity? The feeling he interpreted was hostility, even outright hatred. The way she said I love you felt and sounded flat like lip service, emotionless an act, superficial whoa, what am I thinking? She only zoomed into him as he dropped his wine goblet. She hops up to clean up the mess "oh, Brockbaby, how clumsy of you. I got it, and I'll get you another glass. Oh wait, I haven't even taken a sip of mine. You can have it, babe, 'BRB' be right back gotta get the dust-pan!"

Evil, the smell of sin, noxious corruption… his dislocation from being on point in complete control of his faculties, his mind whirls. Was this for real happening? Not possible, his hair tingled the second that word left her mouth; Brockbaby, no one had ever called him that but the Serial Vipress herself, Sara Amaya, whose alias was Sara Sloan. He was thinking, moving his lips in utter shock without noise uuhhh Naw. He had been poisoned, thinking out loud in a hoarse, scratchy voice as Kamryn returned with a mug of 'beer' the dustpan in her other hand with a whisk broom.

'Beer… Kam' as he slurs, "you don't drink beer. Your allergic to Hops? Never once have you drank a beer." Then that word Omg echoed and reverberated and slashed his throat 'Brockbaby' then she repeated the word! "Incorrect 'Brockbaby' I'm actually allergic to Wine." Lmao!

His next word, a proper noun, "SARA' your freakin Sara!" Brock moves deliberately. She watches with glee, intentionally allowing his feeble purposeful attempt to grasp his cell phone. "Umh aah, I feel compelled to tell you that when I consolidated all my stuff from the San Diego storage unit to my San Francisco storage building which is on Auto-Payment and still is all mine. I left some of my custom-made poisons and many other toys but did bring my blocking tech device. So no cell calls now until I turn it off, silly boy. Now leave your cell phone alone!" He grasped his throat, having a difficult time breathing.

"Brockster, I want to remind you while your memory/mind still works, lol, that I had predicted, even promised you, that I would get you one day. You would be mine, all mine, Brock. I never break a promise, 'Never' now I couldn't be happier feeling like singing and dancing a jig! Finally, we can consummate our love for one another. This is truly a dream Cum true for us both. Oh, I'm so fkn tight Brockster like 'Virginesque' Yep!"

Sara slugged down her cold beer "oh, looks like I will need another beer. Luckily, I stopped along the way to pick up a case of beer. I promise you, Brockbaby, it will be a long, fun, rewarding vacation, honey. You wait and see, and I can't believe you chewed up all that poison I sprinkled on your large slice of cheesecake. Ah, delish! Oh yeah, you also drank my special potion in your Red Wine. The 'Vipress Serial Killer' is back. Yep! kinda like that moniker, I bid you adieu or Aloha, a Hawaiian salutation if you will!... Oh, Brocky, I wonder if you're going to beg me to stop torturing your body... yummy."

<u>Kamryn awakens again...</u>   <u>... 7/11/17 NIA Tuesday</u> <u>Evening...</u>

It seemed each time that she came partially out of the medically induced fugue, awakening confused in a stupor, they would verbally berate her like she was a captive, and then another dose of drugs was injected into her bloodstream. This happened again just now. Kam was drifting on dark clouds. She went in and out of hopelessness. She now prayed for death. No longer did she fight for life. Nope, begging and wanting to die, the desire to live in this cruel world was stifled, snuffed out.

She decided that there was not a higher being 'In Heaven.' How could her faith in the All-mighty God allow this torture of her soul and spirit, her life being internally disemboweled? She was helpless; 'God, please take my life!'

Her eyes flickered open; yes, she was still here... there, damnit "hello there, Sara, are you feelin' any better? Would you like something to drink and eat?" asks Liz. "We've been feeding you intravenously. Please try and drink some water!"

Kam should have known this woman's name. She looked familiar but had no recollection whatsoever. Her surroundings seemed ambiguous. A vague and conflicting emotion simultaneously took precedence. She was in a life-or-death spiral, tumbling in a chamber of un-rectifiable condemnation with ultimate doom imminent and no power to censure or rebuke the powers to be... she barely nodded.

Liz snaps her fingers 'get her something to drink water, Apple juice, Cranberry juice, and some cottage cheese with peaches. Sara, are you with us?' 'Sara' Kam's defensive mechanisms involuntarily kick in reflexively, laying on a bunk in one of the prison cells allocated for medical lock downed inmates. Kamryn debated... argued internally, and screamed and shouted, 'yelled all in Silence!' This was like being a POW, a Prisoner of War locked away from society at NIA.

She was at the Mercy of her captives, being brainwashed, manipulated, and abused with chemicals that displaced her motivation to survive this ordeal. A resolve oriented with apathy took the gut-wrenching hold of her inner Spirit, yet a sliver a ray of sunlight, shown through the wired glass in the cell where windows should have been. A quandary mixed and jumbled a hodge-podge of reckoning. A question posed to self should she go along with being Sara? Would they stop chaining and shackling, drugging her unmercilessly, unrelentingly? Was this the correct answer, or was the decision made only for self-preservation?... Doctor Honcho again asked, "Sara don't you want to go back to your cell?" Kam then nodded in the affirmative, which to her immediate expectation, changed the expression of the Doctor whose name tag reflected Liz Honcho.

The doctor grinned horribly at her. A toothful ghastly ghoulish countenance prevailed. Kam surmises… oops, I need to adjust my approach, but what am I thinking, confused in a dizzy plague of surrealism, was this 'fantasy or fiction?' Wait, isn't or aren't those words synonymous?' Liz has a giddy look of excitement and pats her shoulder "seeya in the morning, Sara! I'm glad you are on the way back to us… I must consider if I will allow your sister Kamryn to visit again until we make some adjustments. We can't have this reaction after she visits with you, Sara!" I just nodded.

"Dontcha want to get out of that bed?" she yelled at the orderly "get the restraints off her now. Let's get you back to what you love to do, Sara. Your Salon is waiting. You have missed so many appointments since last Thursday. I'm counting on you being able to perform your magic for me… my Anniversary and Reunion is in two days. It's vitally important to me to look the best I can… so what can I do to help you, Sara?" I only blinked and frowned.

"How is the new medication working?" Kam had yet to utter a word, but one thing was for sure she didn't want any more forced drugs shoved and shuttled through the I.V. no more could she sustain. "Give me a reason to get you the heck out of here, Sara, back to your cozy sanctuary, your room, and all of your belongings back in the Population. It's beautiful outside!" I opened my mouth; at least, I believed I did, but no words fell out. "Don't you want the freedom you worked so hard to gain? You have your TV in your cell, and Sara, what about the joy of drawing… your artistic abilities are second to none. Don't you miss that? And what about phone calls?" Asks Liz. *Kam's ears perked up. Phone calls umh Phone calls Yes, precisely what she needs, but even if she held a phone in her hand, she was lost, a blur, couldn't remember the phone numbers must have a phone book in Sara's cell gosh, no more medications! Felt like she had amnesia...* 🗯.

Kam was afraid that her memory was no longer obtainable. Did the drugs eat away who she was and had been? Is she lost and forever discombobulated? A twinge of hopelessness hovers like a film over her pupils. Then she says her first words trying to play the Sara card now, "No more drugs, please!" Kam's only words done, Liz leans over her bunk "okay, no more drugs. I will be here first thing in the morning to sign you out of the infirmary. Keep it together, Sara, goodbye!"

<u>Lake Shasta... Houseboat Sara and Brock.</u>

Enjoying her 5th beer on a warm evening kicking back on Lake Shasta, legs up, music blasting, aah, the taste of freedom living life once again the way it's supposed to be NIA was Trauma based gone now forever. Lol... wonder how sissy Kam was doing Lmao. Sara wanders from room to room. This houseboat had everything; it was a spacious home on the water. Brock had tethered off the Sea Doo's, and on the deck of the houseboat, he'd secured a rowboat, rafts, and even a couple of Kayaks. The family Ski boat was beached on the other side of where the houseboat was anchored at. She had never navigated a houseboat, but fortunately, that wasn't part of her plans. She could pilot the 25 ft Ski boat, no prob!

<u>Sara's schizophrenic entities are starting to get restless, Al...</u>

<u>the Ventriloquist, yelped.</u>

Sara's frontal lobe tingled, then, from the base of her skull, a vibration felt all the way out her inner ears. Static was heard like a CB radio, then laughter hilarious incongruent with her mindset rattling from within her head static '<u>Alert Amber Alert</u>

<u>**Child Abduction dark blue Toyota Tundra 2005.'**</u> **then more laughter contagiously released.**

Sara can't help it. She joins in they both giggle, laughing so hard good ole 'Al' he undoubtedly came in handy with his Ventriloquist skills throwing voices and noises. They laugh so hard she chokes over her own saliva, water drips into her beer, and rubs her eyes, wiping the tears away! 'Okay, fk Al, I'll give you the Props you deserve. You fkn played the hulking Officer Citation CHP. She bought the Amber alert hook, line, and sinker; your static sound was off the charts!

'Stop it, Al,' he slowly contains himself... 'yah gotta admit that was a good one, Sara' 'umh yes, Al, your skills surely saved my or our bacon, Bacon yah get it CHP cop pig... duh. Now, Al, enough you broke our or your Oath to live in the background. I'm the boss, Al, and I didn't invite you into existence. Get back now.' Sara intimates to Al, 'get back in our mind to where you belong, Al.' 'It's boring in here. I saw an opportunity to help us. That's all, sorry... shit.' 'Al, I don't want to rehash this again. You murdered our Papa against my objections; Papa loved us... me!' 'Sara, I've told all of us how sorry I am. Please forgive me, damnit. I'm here with you. Don't hesitate to access my many attributes and talents.' 'Enough, Al. I have to think now. Please don't re-surface, come forth or materialize again. Stay put till I need you. I love you, Al!' 'I Love you two, Sara.' Sara wondered if her other diverse personalities would stay put, hoping not to hear the logic of Ame reverberate in her skull.

Darnit, Brock was dead weight; Sara struggled to drag him down the hallway on the indoor-outdoor carpet; shit, your one heavy dude. She was sweating in the warm night air. It was just after 11 pm... her 5' 3" frame and 135 pounds were worn out, still 87 degrees, a heat wave on the way, almost always en vogue in Shasta County!

On 7/13/17, Thursday, Kam leaves her medical cell... inside NIA's prison.

Luckily, Kam hadn't had any more episodes from the drug's lingering effects. She would never, of her volution, ever ingest um or take any of the medications that were forced into her. Gratefully, the residual effects of the injected pharmaceuticals lessened over time. The question she constantly posed to herself was, did she have permanent damage? Only time would answer that question. Doctor Chafe, she hears say to a guard escort, 'take Sara to her housing unit. All her privileges are to be reinstated!' Kam is pushed in a wheelchair to the elevator down to the first floor, where she is told to get up. Nurse Renae quickly checked her vitals, slowly helped her walk, and worked with her to ensure her equilibrium had returned. After 25 minutes, Kam's mobility had regained enough for her to traverse the prison hallways, although her stomach was empty and very queasy.

She walked directly to the cafeteria for breakfast and some much-needed coffee, thinking only of phone numbers and calls. She didn't verbalize a single syllable to anyone, still in a daze of disbelief, but if she were going to survive this macabre existence, not only endure but emancipate herself from this slavery, she'd have to be slick. 'Ugh, to be free again, exonerate herself and prove this injustice and take revenge out on her evil twin, she had to maintain and focus, analyze, and play the game to Win!'

She was still partially disoriented, but as every second passed by without the inducement of additional drugs in her system, her faculties were dethawing, which yielded a rational mind with a high aptitude for equations, a mathematician, stock market wizard; she had always been quick-witted.

'To escape this Insane Asylum, she not only had to be clever and cunning but must mold herself systemically and systematically into the role of her treacherous evil Twin sister Sara who diabolically planned this strategy right down to gluing her hair into a wig using her cut hair for eyebrows.' Then sickeningly shaving my entire body of all hair, the gall of Sara to take her time to undress and shave every centimeter of me… so sick I had to be completely fricken nude in her salon. I don't have a single hair on my body, right down to my toes! Oh, how Kam despised her sister. I'd been utterly violated… what a chance she'd taken. What if, by accident, a guard would have walked into her makeshift salon? Every breath, each inhale was now Hate-filled. She would plunge a dagger through Sara's throat in a split second, and soon enough, vengeance would be Mine!

Kamryn couldn't… nor wouldn't dwell on where Sara was. She needed to be proactive, make a plan, and be flexible yet staunch. Her brain thrust had never let her down before. She must be cognizant, determined, and relentless in using all her resources, which were conundrums in prison. She was limited but would persevere downing her third cup of coffee, which enhances and lubricates her constipated bowels. Her internal system was clogged up from her forced, sedentary drug-based existence.

Sitting on the toilet, the relief after seven days and nights of constipation was Heavenly better than an Orgasm. Her description nearly induced her to let loose a subtle, arcane, elusive dimple. Still, it retracted before it broke the surface.

Kamryn was still dressed in hospital attire, a gown, and slippers. She made her way back to the nurse's station. Renae took notice. "Hi Sara, are you feeling like yourself again?" "Yes, better already, thank you. My mind is still kinda scrambled; I seem to have forgotten some very important phone numbers!" Kam, a numbers-oriented gal, had put most of her critical phone numbers on speed dial. No need to use her memory… sad but true.

"No worries, Sara," as Renae switches screens on the desktop computer. "I will print out all your approved phone numbers… for you, honey." "Well, thanks a lot," as she receives an 8 X 11 piece of paper over the counter from Renae, she adds, "looks like you still have 77 minutes left on this month's minutes."

Kam nodded even though she didn't understand the monthly limits making her way to a bank of hard-wired phones like old phone booths. Several other inmates were congregating about the phones with lists of numbers in their hands. After the 5th time trying to call her Fiancé, 'Edward' ughhhh Brock Dame, and being unable to get an outside line, frustration mounting asks a fellow inmate what she was doing wrong. "You must include your inmate number in the sequence of numbers to start with," said a kind, wickedly distorted face that belonged to an elderly lady who seemed to her to be docile and harmless, then thinks, yeah, sure, probably an AXE Murderer… .

After three connections to Edward's cell and the voice mail enacted, his VM was full, with no more room for her message. She decides to call Uncle Attorney Hallinan's office and is pleasantly surprised that her call is picked up on the 3rd ring "this is Ms. Jewel… Sara. What can I do for you?" "Oh, I'm so happy to hear a familiar voice, Ms. Jewel. This is Kamryn here. There has been a terrible mistake; my sister Sara has escaped as you know, we are identical twins. I…" Kam felt like the mouthpiece of the phone was covered… there was a long pause.

"Sara, please, you continue to have these delusions, and honey, they are not healthy. You have been calling this office with these same claims dozens of times or more Mr. Hallinan is very busy unless you have something pertinent to discuss with him. I…?" "Let me speak with him, please?" "He is in court and will be till later this afternoon as long as they can settle on a jury panel. Let me pass you through to his VM, Sara; thank you for calling." Beep… 'umh Mr. Hallinan, aah Uncle, we need to speak in person. It's vitally essential, crucial for you. It's regarding the litigation going forward and an upcoming press release. Your aware that I was sexually assaulted here at NIA.' Terrance, with you being the CEO and Chairman of the Board here, I believe I could help put this, as you might say, under the carpet; please make a trip here to Napa. It will be worth your time and your stockholders. I'm looking forward…" beep… the recording ends.

Kam hung up with her first glimpse of a smile. I need a face-to-face to be able to convince Terrance that I am Kamryn we have a history. We've spent a lot of alone time and shared bunches of experiences and secrets that only he and I are aware of, especially when Sara was being prosecuted. If only I could get him here! She then pushes her phone number on the keypad knowing her sister, the Vipress, had her phone in her possession. It goes directly to VM, is turned off, and Kam shakes her head. But refuses to let this sink her newly founded optimism regarding her message to her Uncle. Her devious sister thinks she's laid the perfect trap, but who laughs first, maybe will be crying at the end? Her goal was to be hysterically laughing at the conclusion of this saga! Swinging Sara's head by her hair! Growling intensely!'

Kam must think like her devilish sister. The Devil is in the details, of course. She knew I'd be calling Terrance first thing. She feels and thinks that she has covered every base. Not so quick, sissy. I will find a loophole and have you recaptured. Never will I ever visit or communicate with her demon ass again. It wasn't a maybe; now Kam had to consider it a fact she'd been wrong all along, being a stalwart and steadfast advocate for Sara's innocence. Now feeling the vixen's wrath, she had to admit Sara was the Serial Killer, the Vipress, after all. Sara was Guilty of the sins that she committed.

There had been several copycat killings but none with the same poison chemical solutions or ingredients. For the entire time of Sara's incarceration, not one murder had the same M.O. No newspaper clippings or letters were sent to the FBI. It was then from behind Kam that she heard a distinct sound "well, Sara, I'm so happy to see you out and about; how are you feeling? You want to get back to work in your Salon?" "Not yet, Doctor Honcho. I'm still not myself!" Kam tries to exaggerate her hands and fingers shaking, "the drugs have had lingering effects taken their toll. I can't even maintain a semblance of normalcy. I'm sorry!"

Liz's face contorted, visibly angry, seething even, her whacked-out eyebrows and nose hair twitched. "Sara, as you have known, been aware of for now over a month, I have a Highschool Reunion, my 25th year anniversary. This is super important to me. I have to look my best by tomorrow at 6:15 pm. I understand that you have had a setback and realize that you might have a drug hangover, but with that being said, why don't you go to your cell and get some rest? I will come on my day off tomorrow morning for my complete makeover, and Sara, don't disappoint me!" What could I do but nod?

"This afternoon, I have that conference to handle regarding Carl and the alleged sexual assault!" "Alleged attack what you were there, oh, isn't this par for the course? The victim always has the burden of proof, so tell me, Liz, why wouldn't I be at this so-called conference? I want to testify!" Kam waits for a response, then shuffles away as someone else draws Liz's attention. Kam says to herself, 'guess it's time to see where the wicked, nasty Sara lived. Checking her sheet of phone numbers, she sees a cell number on a door as she walks down another hallway looking for Sara's cell #555. Muses, it should have been #666. Now she was on a mission to find where the hell her temporary home would be... Sara's cell living quarters.

Following the signs to the 500 block, she passes a guard station and cameras in all the corners of the ceilings. She was standing in front of the steel door with the number 555. With a loud clacking noise, her door cracked open, and she saw a total of five diagonal windows, maybe 5 inches wide by 25 inches vertical she could hear noise from other cells, music and TVs, someone screaming, another crying and praying for something maybe, this was a freakin nut ward!

Kam's first step into the room-cell felt eerie frightening, stuffy, and musty odor clogged her nasal passage. The door closed behind her. She was now locked up. Oh, shit, locked in, couldn't leave. I looked up to the cameras, three of them I'm under constant surveillance, nowhere to hide. It seemed this was the start of Hell. Suddenly Kam, with her back to the wall hiding her face, unable to take another step, breaks down. She slides to the concrete floor, her head weighing heavy. In her life, never had she been in jail or guilty of any crime besides parking tickets, speeding, and moving violations. She recalls the first visit to NIA. She was petrified, scared to death of the guard towers, razor wire, and concrete and steel walls. As she raised her head and looked around, she was in a Maximum-Security Prison for the Criminally Insane with no way out set up by someone she truly loved and cared about. She starts sobbing uncontrollably and rolls over on the cold concrete floor in a fetal position.

'Hey Sloan, you, all right? Do you need medical attention in there,' says a guard who was obviously watching the cameras. Oh no, as she juts up, 'No, I'm all right, thanks' 'then if you're fine, why don't you take yourself to your bunk and get off the floor?' Forcing herself to try and regain her composure.

For hell's sake, she didn't need any more medications. Stands up and took her first honest look at her new cell. It was much larger than cells in jails that she'd seen on TV, and Movies had to be like 11X14 feet with a ceiling height of about 10ft.

The Sloan reference had always bothered Kam even when it was said referring to her sister, the press and the FBI took the name Sloan and made it infamous that the Serial Killer always signed all letters with Ms. Sloan, and it stuck, but her last name was Amaya. Sara Amaya! The Amaya sisters in school not fondly did this memory crawl through her memory.

Looking up, there were three inset halides in the ceiling, controlled elsewhere, one chair, and a desk table contraption built in and attached to the wall. Easels with canvases, paint brushes soaking with paint of all colors, a TV that looked like a 35-inch flat-screen, and stereo with speakers on a built-in shelf. A large bookshelf lined with books of all genre's shelves in front of the desk filled with nick-knacks and a twin bunk bed (Twin ugh).

A small sink with a few Tupperware plates, bowls, cups, and plastic utensils, and an open closet that held Sara's clothes, shoes, and sweat workout outfits. A dresser was attached to the wall with five drawers bolted down lamps with dimmer switches for reading or writing at the table or desk. She saw humongous stacks of 11X14 drawings on thick Art Paper.

Kam looks at a doorless opening that the camera no doubt could peer inside, at least part way, she thinks, steps into the area, and then moves into the white-painted concrete room. Sadly, like on television shows, a stainless-steel toilet sink, an all-in-one unit, a spout for drinking water to her left was a curtain, and a small shower built in made of rigid fiberglass. Looking around, this was the only place that didn't have a video camera, so there was a smidgen of humanity umh, privacy left to the Inmates as long as they were classified at the highest rank, a number five.

Walking out of the bathroom, she takes in the white walls made of concrete with some shelves with books and, pictures, personal stuff. Then Kam sees stacks of books. Wow, the witch was a reader, for sure! The cell was immaculate with a bit of dust but other than that super clean. She spots a fan on each side of the room and flips the switch. Aah, air movement. In the ceiling were vents for air circulation, a closed system, with heater vents at the base of the floor. She flipped on a lamp to brighten the dreary room. The three lights inset in the ceiling were on dim that probably... the guards monitored. Surely each Cell was aligned to a control panel. Her eyes lit up OmLord, no way up to 7 feet high on the back wall were drawings in color pastels, chalk crayons markers, painted on 11X14 inch thick paper all taped to the wall, almost like a panoramic mural.

She turns and peers into an alcove, her breath taken away. Oh shit, she hops up and walks closer. Geez, the little Monster was a busy bee. There were 3-foot stacks of these drawings in the alcove, which had to be tens of thousands of drawings. Kam wanders back to the bunk, sits down at the edge of the bed, and then closes her eyes. *No, not possible, please, this can't be... umh no way, an instant headache Migraine she was vanquished she laid her body down-shook, trembles passed out-shock this was her reality, now her life!* .

Awakens sometime later; heck, it could have been moments still not feeling like her ordinary self-sniveling. Sadly, she tried to hide her shaken, wet face. She didn't want to be a highlight show for the voyeuristic guards, nor couldn't afford to be forced to take more medications. She was a long way from thinking like herself, confused and in shock. She cried silently and finally succumbed to sleep!

Abruptly she is awakened. A horn is sounding. 'Chow time, chow time, Chow time' she sits up and takes a moment to get her bearings. Ugh, not a 'Daymare' she was really in prison… picks up a cheap Timex watch on the headboard. 5:45 pm hunger pangs. Yes, she must eat, stands at the door, and waves at the camera. Nothing happens, then waves with both hands at the cameras, umh, nothing, sees the red button, and pushes it. 'Yes' 'I'm hungry!' the door is buzzed, and out goes Kam to the chow hall, her first dinner in Prison. Omg wonder what all the freaks look like. She'd never been inside NIA for dinner, thinking she had always left Sara before 5 pm.

Where will I sit? Freaked out and nervous, she follows the crowd down the hallway, all going in the same direction as rats in a maze would. Ugh!

-50-

Shasta Lake, on Brock's parent's Houseboat… Sara is in Charge, and Brock is sick to his stomach.

It's so damn dark, and my eyes are open; fk, my jaw feels like it's locked in place, saliva overruns my lips… drool, feeling bloated and cramped, and my legs are prickling and stinging a sensation like numbness in my limbs. Not a trace of a feeling in my toes. My arms are splayed wide open in an awkward way, throbbing. Maybe the pain is good. At least I can feel all my extremities other than my toes.

I'm lying on my back; I can feel myself breathe and feel my heart beating. It's so dark that I can't see… nor could I hear anything whatsoever. Am I entombed? My mind is opaque, bleary, and distorted. The memory then flashes back a Hot flash, the Wine and Cheesecake, the woman across the table that in every way resembled, um, appeared to be my Lover Fiancé, Best friend, and forever Soulmate Kamryn. Wasn't!

How could I have failed to recognize and read her demonizing glare, unmistakable feeling in the air, same eyes looked back into mine... except instead of Love, they displayed transparent contempt ughhhh. It was hatred that peered into my dilated pupils. I'm a fool and didn't roll with my inherent intuition. Why didn't I catch the subtle nuances of the provocatively stimulating embrace of the taste of her mouth, tongue movement Alien? Aggressive and bold, kind of lewd, almost a nasty filthy unloving act kissing like a prostitute doing her trade, ugh, job, a necessary fake attraction.

Not Kamryn's lips or mouth. Should I have made a move and disabled Sara then... Wtf? What was wrong with me? It should have been as plain as the nose on my face. She wasn't my lady but the Vixen murderer Vipress Sara. Why didn't it register where the fk was I, uh, my guard down, but in my defense which matters not, 'how could this be Sara?'

I needed to stop beating myself up. A life lesson 'hindsight was always 20/20.' This was contrary to the positive person I am. A quick buzz went through my mind as Sara was going off on the female assassin's soliloquy in a 'weird voice, not hers. Sadly, I recalled thinking that Kam was exhibiting a subtle, uhm, slight form of craziness. Weirdly always in the back of my mind... knowing Schizophrenia was hereditary like I'd researched before getting too attached to Kam. Then discarded the notion saying internally, am I nuts? In retrospect, I don't think I could have attacked her once I figured out that she'd poisoned me... I was dizzy at that time. I was glued to my seat. The poison or sedatives were taking their toll, fed to me in my wine and cheesecake.

Now I must find the dexterity and courage to overcome all obstacles in my life. Where was my wife-to-be, Kamryn? What did the Vipress do to her? Our lives depended on my skillset. How did the Sick, Insane Sara escape the maximum-security Prison NIA? Brock thinks, 'I must add up and analyze this situation. What do I know? The last memory was seeing her satisfaction with the malice and glory of Sara gloatingly reveling in her triumph, drinking a beer with the expressions and amused stares of Gotcha. With a sickening feeling of despair, I was like paralyzed, facing an executioner, weakened, dizzy and confused. Sara was lusting with arousal enjoying herself fulfilling her earlier conversation about Female assassins. Not all became crystal clear and relevant, until now 'the clever slithering Snake… fk her!' I still feel sick. My stomach cramped and ached, and I felt like I was going to have some severe diarrhea…

I must have been served a form of tranquilizer; my body stopped reacting to my brain's signals. It demanded a disconnect, my nervous system, not my own, like a statue in decomposition. My eyes grew heavy, the lids closed, and that was it. My ears heard the last noises. Wicked laughter rang loud. I can still remember Sara's raging howls of hysteria and her words garbled raucously.

So with that being reviewed and assimilated no need to overanalyze. I'm not dead yet. Unless dead feels like this, I can't see, hear, or smell anything. First, I will try to move my fingers on my left hand, yes, counting my fingers. All good on both, but my hands feel stiff. I confidently try to raise my arms, but oops, no way restrained. Next, I find my toes, although numb, all move, so I kick up my legs. Nope, unable to do so, gathering all my power, I jerk up my upper torso with all my might yet could only move mere inches.

Hot sweat bubbles on my skin. The simple deduction, I was securely restrained, lifting my head up as far as I could, a soft landing once I laid it back down on a pillow. The softness under my body, a mattress this, bodes well enough for me to conclude that she could have me splayed out on the floor. I thought she had a molecule of kindness towards me, and this was a good sign! 'But I was deadly wrong, umh, essentially… my life was on a downward spiral… pain was all that was left until I felt nothing at all!'

NIA, Kam, in the cafeteria with Lunatics.

Buffet-style dining, a line in front of her of around 35 inmates and perhaps another 105 already eating seated all females. Kam surmised these had to be the best of the best levels of Fives. Knowing the prison was separated by custody levels, feeling fortunate that Sara was a level five, the least restrictive inmate classification, she'd not dealt with security issues like others that were deemed more dangerous and hostile to the staff and other inmates. At the first table she passed, she'd witnessed an elderly woman with her teeth out by her plate, in a clear plastic cup, her fingers inside the spaghetti. A youngish girl sat next to her aah messy face talking with her mouth full of noodles.

Guards were posted by the entrances, and exits music was playing like Carnival type. Kam saw some inmates that were so medicated that it was three minutes between bites… Zombies. Some were seriously twitching, others seemed deformed, some scratching themselves raw, gesticulating arms and legs. A loud chatter was even more audible when there was a pause in the circus music. Many of the women were speaking animated at invisible things and people. She was inside a Looney bin, and there was Insanity surrounding her; she really was in an Insane Asylum!' .

Appetite squelched and quickly diminishing passes a woman asleep with her face planted downward in her plastic plate of spaghetti. Then a woman in the far corner was waving at her. At least, it seemed that way. However, she could have been waving at an Alien Monster for all she knew. The woman

stood up and yelled, "I've saved your seat like always, Sara. Why are you standing over there?" Kam apprehensively tried to appraise this Nut. What's the worst thing that could happen, ugh, get stabbed by a plastic fork or knife and hit over the head with a plastic tray?

Prisoners were refilling their trays at the food bins at the buffet beside the hot racks inmate women were working behind the food bins… with hairnets and white hats. She made her way over to the woman who yelled her name oops, my sister's name, Sara. 'Hi, Sara,' smiled a toothless grin except for three rotten yellowish nubs for teeth… standing next to another inmate. I looked at the food with trepidation. She started to add food to her tray; the garlic bread looked all right.

I get on the heels of this inmate, making our way past the crowd to the table she'd saved for us, following the toothless woman, happy that only one other woman was sitting at the table for four, watched her pull a chair out and lay a napkin on her lap. "You fkn bitch… you stood me up yesterday!" In a whisper, Kam exclaims, "excuse me, what are you talking about?" "No excuse for you. I had my visit today and wanted to look pretty. I had an appointment with you!" "Look, I was sick. I'm sorry okay?" "That ain't going to get it with me. Sorry is for suckers; I ain't no sucker. You fkn disrespected me. My mom only comes here every three months!"

"Hey, relax. I will make it up to you." Kam turned her attention to her food, took her first bite of the spaghetti, and followed it up with crunchy garlic bread 'from the corner of her eye' she saw the tray being hurled at her head. The madwoman was upon her. The tray slammed against her left cheek with a glancing blow, and the fork that she was wielding scrapped over her Bald scalp and knocked her to the floor. The maniac was trying to chew on her face, kicking. Fingernails were ripping into her skin like an enraged Cannibal.

Kam, with her fork, stabbed the crazed lunatic in her open mouth, skewering her tongue like a sausage, blood and spit spraying, realizing her advantage grabbed the deranged fool by her hair, taking clumps out... being bald was a definite plus. Kam let all her pent-up frustrations blow up, and she attacked the woman to 'Kill, tear her to fricken pieces!'

Suddenly they were pounded flat... guards had them sprawled down on their stomachs, blood all over the orange jumpsuits. Handcuffs were put on oh so tight, their wrists yanked behind their backs, and both lifted up by the steel cuffs. Kam felt her shoulder almost snapping out of the socket. The Chow Hall had erupted in screams and chaos... fights started all over. Food was tossed at each other, and inmates were throwing trays. It was a food war. Insanity reigned for sure this craziness seemed to last a long time, but that wasn't the case for... in a matter of moments. A special force entered wearing full-on protective gear, Masks on all of them. In their hands were Stun guns, batons, clubs, and whistles blowing like a Swat team of guards drove up with flat trailers behind Golf carts. Fixed on the trailers were cages, three in total. Kam was lifted and tossed headlong into one of them.

The steel bars slammed shut behind her. The other two cages were filled, and off they went. She fell forward, losing her equilibrium as she saw another set of Golf carts driving in, thinking, either I fight here or die. Survival was now her mantra... like animals in cages. They were taken into a narrow corridor with Iron doors and no windows. The driver stopped, and the doors popped open on the cages. Two prominent healthy, manly female correctional officers snatched her up and dragged her into an open cell.

They took the cuffs off aggressively, physically held her down as they stripped off all her clothes, then ordered her to pull her vagina lips apart and cough. Then she bent over with her butt in the air, stretched her ass apart, and coughed again.

They were checking my body cavities for weapons. Disgusting and humiliating, I was dazed and confused. But I knew these female guards would beat me to a pulp with their batons if I put up a fight. They acted like all they needed was a little excuse. They were mean, yet they seemed to enjoy themselves as I caught them staring and smirking and rubbing their genitalia!

After this humiliation and loss of dignity, the iron door rammed close. The cell was dank and stunk, super small, with no bed, just the stainless-steel combo toilet sink, nothing else concrete, one light dimly on, grateful that she was left her clothes for it was cold, then she noticed that she had no shoes they were confiscated. Over the speaker system, I hear…'Inmate Sloan do you have any injuries that need to be attended to?' "I don't know, can't see my head… no mirror, but I'm still bleeding. I have lumps and bruises, blood dripping down my forehead, red marks, and scratches all over, and my shoulders hurt badly. They might be out of their socket there killing me… my back hurt ah spine was burning like it was on fire…." "Sloan, I don't give a flying Fk about all that shit. It's either a yes or no, and that would be a yes you will be placed in the order of worse injured, and you're not as bad as most of them!"

At about that time, my adrenalin started to wear off, felt a stinging from my hands… I spotted my right-hand fingers leaking blood, nails ripped at the cuticles, index finger twisted, swollen wrist with welts from the handcuffs… trying to open and close her hands. Only pain resulted in the attempt. She couldn't clench or move her fingers. Great!

Hunger pangs back. She definitely lost a bunch of weight since being held captive against her will, nowhere to lie down on cold concrete, thankful she had socks on her feet. Funny, it seemed now she longed for Sara's cell. This was a pit she was in. I guess it could get worse, always can get worse now inhabited inside solitary confinement. Oh yes, that would be the answer life here could get worse, way worse, no doubt, 'Life as I knew it was over!'

<u>**7/15/17 NIA Saturday. 10:05am.**</u>

Over the last night, Kam had been brought to the Infirmary bandaged up her right hand in a soft cast, the other arm in a sling. I thought I was lucky for actually avoiding a 'Shot' or a write up a 100 Series violation which would have resulted in her losing Sara's spacious cell, reducing her freedom, and moving to another floor with the classification raised. This is what happened to the misguided hair client who had attacked her. She was now reduced to level 4, locked down on another floor.

The Captain and Lieutenant LT. had viewed the security footage from the chow hall… showing that all Kam was guilty of was self-defense. What a miserable night she had frozen during the night well. Uhm, actually, that would only be a guess. There was no way to tell day from nite.

Being fortunate to be able to leave the cell via God-given dreamland, her imagination had them lying on a beach. Kam was with her Fiancé Brock Dame… on a make-believe Honeymoon. Sweet dream, walking hand in hand naked on the black sandy beach in Costa Rico, pure bliss. A tear hung, formed larger, then dropped, then a banging sound her door opened.

Hands-on hips, a 'sneering scowl' displayed in the dull light, a bent over angry face, lips turned up. It was Doctor Liz Honcho. "Sara, I leave you for just one day, and you get yourself beat up. Let me see you stand up." Kam edges up weakly, sore as hell, and props herself up against the wall hurting in places she didn't know existed on and in her body, 'Oh, she moans, ouch' aching and stiff, hurting in obvious pain.

Liz stomps into the room and takes a closer look at her "how the hell are you going to do my makeover with your hand in a cast and the other in a sling?" Liz grabs her left hand up, and Kam gasps. It was bruised purple and red, missing three fingernails, and bent. "Fk, just my pathetic dumb luck to have to count on an Inmate. Now, what am I going to do?" Liz is saying this more to herself than to Kam. "Tonight is the night of my reunion."

A sad display of expressions like a wounded dog mashes into Kam's eyes. "I should leave you in this solitary confinement cell and let you Rot; that's what you deserve. You have let me down for the last time!" Kam speaks for the first time through scabbed lips, "I was attacked, assaulted, only defended myself. Some of my injuries were caused by the guards. I didn't plan this, Liz. What should I have done? Let the Madwomen kill me and play dead, for God's sake, Liz. How is any of this my fault? Please tell me?"

Creepy silence paused, a stare off Kam's perception collided with commiseration 'could have been a stroke of luck this fight and injuries. How would she ever handle applying makeup or a makeover, uhm, styling hair, or even doing Liz's nails? In a million years, she'd still be lost, with zero talent in those departments. Ugh. She could barely manage her own makeup, and Sara or someone else always did her nails.'

As far as drawing pictures or painting, Kam was lucky to be able to draw 'stick people.' No artistic talent whatsoever wouldn't know where to start on the Homely Liz Honcho. Sara and I were Identical Twins on the outside but complete opposites in the way their brains worked and with the way their talents and natural attributes were dispersed. Sara was gifted in the ways she wasn't. Kam had zero talent as an artist and not a sliver of knowledge of how to start a 'Makeover.' She'd instead go all-natural, no makeup, hair in a ponytail, a plain Jane look, more a Tomboy all her life.

Kam adhered to society's stereotypes and dressed and looked the part of a Female Professional certainly. Schwab and her clients were put at ease with the perceived Financial consultant look-style and grace. Her plain, unassuming look was the envy of many of her male counterparts. She wasn't into the glamorous stereotypical career woman. No, she was the down-to-earth female who was happy to be in her skin. She recalled many ugly stares of extreme resentment, especially when going to the gym to 'work out' and sweat her ass off. Other females fixed themselves up like they were in a Beauty Pageant. They did more checking each other out than the guys did!

Wthell was wrong with these women? Sick... men mostly went to the gym to actually work out, unlike most gals, not fake, and sure there were the G.Q. types fake as shit, worried about the 'Look.' Her man, Brock, wanted her to skip makeup and loved her for her natural skin and beauty. Yep! If she had her druthers, she'd kick it in sweats or shorts with slippers or sandals, lol, and then she realized just where she was. Humor exited from her mindset-depression sucked her downward!

Breaking the soundlessness with a strategy for pacification, "hey doc, why don't you take the pictures of yourself that are on your desk to a Professional stylist and tell the beautician here is the look I'm after. Can you please replicate this?" Liz stared back at her. 'Well, finally, a smile popped out of her grizzled countenance.' "Sara, I must have over 25 pictures of the three makeovers you did for me. That's a fantastic idea. I better get going!"

"Liz, why don't you use the latest one, the 8X10 on the left side of your desk, you know, the one with the Turquoise eyeliner and matching blouse!" Liz stops cold, nearly stumbles, and flips around, frowning into a grimace. "Sara, how the hell do you know about that picture that was only printed last week?" With sarcasm, I said, "umh, that would be further proof I am Kamryn, and I was in your office for the meeting over the Sara sexual assault. Would you like to go word verbatim over some of that conversation, Liz?"

She twists her body uncomfortably as if perplexed, then, like diarrhea flowing, flushed the idea, "come on out of there, follow me… you're going to be locked down in your cell for the next 72 hours. You can thank me for that unless you want to stay in here?" Lol. Kam was already in gear, albeit in slow-mo, at the rears of Liz. "Which outfit should I wear? Uuhhh, I want to know, um, what you think better flatters my figure the best?" "How about the picture on your wall just to the right of the picture of Niagara Falls, the pink and purple if you add…." "Sara, you have never been in my office on the 5th floor… what is going on? Did your sister tell you about those pictures, or what?"

"No, Doctor, we need to talk. I can prove…." "Stop this nonsense at once. Which outfit should I wear? I don't have time for this. We can talk about all of this after this weekend!" I thought about how to answer this absurd question. "Doctor…" "umh, call me Liz. Haven't we been on a first-name basis since you have been doing my makeovers, Sara?" "Okay, Liz, why wouldn't you stick to the same outfit that we dressed you in after the last makeover." "Yes, perfect. Why didn't I think of that? It's what I shall do. Thank you, Sara."

"I had only one small tray for breakfast slid into the door slot. Do you think I could be allowed to go to the cafeteria, Liz? I'm starving!" "But of course, but afterward, you go lock down, do you hear me?" "Yes, ma'am, I will."

'Shasta Lake Houseboat Brock Dame restrained!'

A yank-tug pulling pain as his pubic hairs are removed by their roots, a clump was torn from his sensitive skin. "Wake up, you asshole!" Brock was indeed alive. He stopped pretending to be asleep. It was futile, and he wiggled his head. She rips the duct tape from his eyes, taking a fraction of his eyebrows and lashes off. She was almost nose to nose. He couldn't focus "listen, you bastard, it's gotta be 119 degrees out there; this is a Hell Hole that I've been in all afternoon while you slept your ass off. I've had to sit in the lake on an innertube with a useless umbrella. The fkn generator shut down. It's boiling in here!"

'Instantly like psychosomatic, he felt his body's sweat perk up, a stream of perspiration dripped from his face, it was like a bath without humidity, the heat was sauna-like.' "Listen, you piece of shit, I took the generator manual out and checked everything trying to troubleshoot this problem... but to no avail can't live like this. Do you have a clue or any ideas on how to get the A.C. on?" Brock's eyes only rolled "aah, I guess this would help," as she tore the duct tape from his lips, taking hair from his mustache with it.

She raises up the manual and starts reading it to him "listen to this, it's the part of the troubleshooting section where supposedly the fixes for problems exist, yet nothing works" he says nothing. "Well, are you going to help me or not?" He jerks his body with all his strength, and his arms and legs barely move three inches. "Naw, Brockbaby, your all mine ain't no escape. I'm going to do what I want to, yay, some of which you should enjoy, other stuff you will not be able to tolerate unless you are restrained, but lucky for me, that's the way you will remain. I can assure you that I will thoroughly enjoy myself.

I'm in full bloom. Entirely blissful dreams do come true through perseverance. There is a God, Brock!" She slaps him swiftly across his right-side cheek. "But Brock, I can't start to work on you till I can stop sweating. I'm fkn melting, dude," as she wipes the sweat dripping from her forehead. "I have to get this A.C. fixed." Brock clenched his teeth and stared at her disdainfully, slowly wobbling his head in the... no-mime stance.

Sara's facial expression becomes distorted as she holds up a large pair of steel chrome Pliers. "I'm going to bust out your front teeth and pluck out your tongue... yah dare me, Brockster, counting to three, one, two, three...." 🦋.

Kam at NIA.

On her way back from grazing at the salad bar, a fill-up of minestrone soup on her direct line back to her cell for the 72-hour lockdown, she takes an alternative route, path and stops in front of the phone banks... all were being used, so she waited. Finally, one was abandoned. The inmate had a tissue in her hand.

Disgustingly in order to use the phone, she had to verbalize her sister's evil moniker into the mouthpiece 'Sara Amaya' for the voice activation system to work, which would then allow her to make calls out of NIA. Next, she'd enter her passcode. She was repeatedly frustrated and continually denied access, and the phone would go dead. That's right, 72-hour sanction, uh, her phone privileges were cut off... no hope of her calling Edward, aah Brock, squashed, head down. She is bumped into by a super thin female officer who takes her by the arm. 'Sloan, you're supposed to be locked down!'

Kam was escorted back to her chambers with only despair accompanying each foul footstep, the physical pain muted by the emotional distress again for the umpteenth time, dwelling on Suicide with no way out. The Iron door slammed loudly closed and bolted in again!

She drops to her bruised knees to cry, then thinks better of this and struggles back up on her feet. The camera's rollin all was needed was forced sedatives and more narcotics. She spies an escape from the invasive prying eyes like perverts probably watching her now, walks past 3-foot-high stacks of Artwork, and sees a word on a piece of yellow tape in black marker… <u>Start Here!</u>.

By-passes this demand from her warped sister and, in the closet, selects some shorts, a long comfy shirt, and underclothing. In a wastebasket, she takes out the plastic bag, yes (perfect to place over her head and 'breathe no more'… did she have the guts?). Maybe later, she thinks and ties the plastic bag off on her right hand to protect the cast, and in relative privacy, she undresses in the shower out of the jerk-off's scrutinization. I had to admit the hot waters spray felt so fabulous, now invisible to the prying eyes. Her peace and Salvation from meddling vulturistic eyeballs!

Even with the dimensions of a small shower cubicle, she was able to sit down and let the warm water bounce off her Bald, scraped, and bruised scalp while water fell from her tear ducts. Now was the time to let go, as congruently, the liquid fell. Ambivalently with mixed feelings, she weighed her life as an Innocent Prisoner versus the chances of her being able to escape this torture chamber realizing only one thing, despair-filled knowing… Suicide was her only way out!

How could she sustain herself here at NIA? What could lift and rebound, um, rebuild her resolve? All energy waned, despondency siphoned her determination, fortitude melted hope was amorphously opaque, choking, sobbing obscurely. The dull clouds in her mind disguised any form of optimism. After around 45 minutes, a noise next to her naked prone body "hey, what are you doing in there?" the curtains are suddenly torn back. The mere shadow… the size of this physically brutish creature was intimidating, 6'5" tall and 277 pounds at a minimum. Her nickname was Mini, as in a refrigerator, Kamryn scared shitless at the guard's size, mumbled, "just in the shower, ma'am!"

"Alrighty then, if we don't see any movement in your cell… then we need to check it out. Enough water wasting, Sloan. Get out of the shower now!" Kam was left alone, still sitting on her wrinkled water-logged butt. Her cast was damp, even wet in areas after peeling off the plastic bag she had taken out of the garbage can, the same one she mused about tying over her head. Ugh, wouldn't you know it? There were tiny pinholes perforated throughout the plastic, safeguarding the inmates from attempting suicide.

Shaking her noggin, she got out of the shower, dried off, dressed, sits with her feet crossed on the edge of the bed. Wow, this is a luxury Suite compared to the 'hole' 'SHU,' or solitary confinement hops up, take's the remote, and turns on the TV. Her favorite channel, CNBC financial news, the stock market was closed because it was a Saturday, but she would get caught up on the last week's market action.

It was gravity, no, or inertia. Nope, a strong desire compelled her like a magnet to walk over to where the words <u>'Start Here'</u> was displayed. Like a diabolical infectious disease standing non-moving this sign, a note from her evil twin, no doubt was curiosity goin to get the better of her, Okay? Uneasy, even fearful, filled with dread, 'well hell, what else do I have to do or to lose? I'm locked in a Nut ward, for God's sake!' 'Perhaps there will be a clue or strategy I can glean from her drawings.'

Kamryn reached down and picked up a 7-inch stack of thick sheets of paper… drawings 11X14 inches, not wanting to accept what the caricatures in color meant, the exaggerated characteristics like cartoon figures. Sara was always drawing, even at the youngest of ages. She had to sit down feeling flush with her temples pounding, her body aching, and still. Pain resonated from the attack at the chow hall.

At the desk with the stack of drawings, she saw that each sheet was numbered in chronological order #1 flipped over; father and mother leaning over a crib Twin 'baby girls' written at the bottom of the picture were Daddy, Mommy, Kamryn, and Ame! She was shell-shocked, staring at the name 'Ame,' a name from their past. It had been almost 25 years since she'd seen that spelling of many Amy's Aimee's different variations of the name but never any Ame's.

She paused, contemplating what she had already known; Ame was the artist who drew all of these pictures. It didn't matter... she could draw masterpieces on cardboard. Ame was a once-in-a-lifetime talent. She could make oil paintings and portraits on canvas come alive. Her graphic detail was mind-blowing. Kam used to watch Ame sketch in awe, a natural talent. Everyone would be mesmerized by what she could do to a piece of paper or canvas. Omg, the oil paintings, portraits, and pastel landscapes are all in graphic detail, which is beyond amazing.

Each drawing progressed in time, events Disney World, Yosemite family adventures, vacations, and trips # 13 had their Grandfather in caricature. 'Papa' who took to Ame like a fish to water his favorite. Kam sat back in the uncomfortable stationary chair, still feeling the pain... resentment, yes, jealousy still biting and gnawing at her. Papa would take Ame for weekends to Las Vegas while I was left home many times, heck, too many to count! Although sometimes I was invited as # 15 is turned over. Yep! in the drawing, the three of them were in Vegas at a circus, smiles around. She remembered they were only four years old, and mommy was pregnant in the hospital with daddy by her side.

Papa had the both of us for over a week. It was so much fun. Instinctively Kam grinned. Papa made his living putting on shows. He was a headliner on the Las Vegas Strip, a renowned Ventriloquist performing on stage in massive arenas and Vegas's largest and most engaging casinos. Heck, Papa traveled all over the planet. He was World Famous. Ame was his favorite because she could mimic and copy like Sesame Street's characters hell, Ame could copy anyone's voice, even commercials, after hearing them only once! She could click off doorbells, sirens, dogs barking, meows, and loud growls that would have your hair stiff like right behind your ear, throwing her voice. This she could do at the age of like five years old… it would leave me stupefied. She caused a lot of trouble in Kindergarten… with our friends Ame… she had a cruel, mean streak. She liked to pretend that she was a boy and even had a name for him, Al. Let me tell you. <u>Al was a Monster</u>! Papa would refer to her as Al when he practiced and taught her the nuances and enhanced her skills as a precocious Ventriloquist. Sara's psychotic mind and brain were occupied by four main characters counting her… Sara, Ame, Al, and Donny. 🐦. But suddenly Sara was like normal… like me!

Then just as fast as this genetically inherited flaw of Al's evil arose, it vanished. The exceptional talent disappeared forever by the time we were seven years old. Ame had lost all her mental aptitude for throwing her voice or imitating. She would no longer be an impersonator at our parties. It was quite sad because all our friends would egg her on. It was fun if we closed our eyes. Al could be our parents, or even our teachers, anyone of us. It was a blast. We giggled for hours! Al was a supreme ventriloquist being trained by Papa!

Kamryn had always felt it was convenient and suspicious that suddenly Al disappeared, leaving Sara with only her other invisible friend partner Ame. We had a smattering of Schizophrenia in our bloodlines. Oh well, so it is what it is! Since Sara had been locked up here at NIA, I'd read that Al had separated from Ame. There were multiple personalities in Sara's cranium!

Yes, as Kam closes her eyes in remembrance and shakes her head, 'Ame or Al' was the best form of entertainment back then. Sara didn't exist. My Lil sister Ame was awesome, overshadowing all of us. With her stunning intellect, she was a walking brain.

Then she spied something on # 19 incongruous with the pictorial scene and started flipping back to previous pages, yet she held it up and brightened the area with the lamp that hung over the desk. There it was. A chill went racing up her spine. Ame Amaya was hidden in each caricature, a signature hidden like Waldo. This was significant for Kamryn Amaya. 'Because after her Lil sister Sara was vanquished, they got along like '2 peas in a pod' with logical, analytical reasoning, loving, empathetic, and compassionate they were inseparable. A few adoring gifts that Ame brought to the table, her Art and super intelligence, and Ame was a chameleon.'

Oh, how she missed the interaction for over 25 years. Ame was lost… gone forever, nope… the proof is right here as Kam looked at all the pictures. This was impossibly untrue because Ame was the artist damn. Sara couldn't draw any better than I could. As I said, stick figures were my best… <u>please pardon my language, I'm so upset… put yourself in my position K.</u>' Then I flipped over # 21, the picture of our parents and all three children… my Lil brother Ken sat in a highchair at the table jelly all over his face. I was leaning over him, cleaning his face. She smiled and thought, how did she know it was her wiping Ken's face? Ahh, because her twin was busy making funny faces at their little brother in the drawing? That's what Ame was known for… she was so darn detailed with her drawings.

Kam got up to get a drink of water and noticed some instant Lipton tea heck, why not? Not as refreshing as iced tea, no ice, lol, enjoying her visit down memory lane like an animation film play or silent movie. First days in school, mom and dad were in our backyard at a BBQ birthday party, our swimming pool, and dad and mom's hot tub lol that we were only allowed in when one of them was in it with us. However horrible her situation was, she felt somehow more optimistic. Hope was there, letting out a slow rumble and a chuckle to think she was frightened to death at what Sara had set up for her to see. These drawings lifted her spirit so high. Building confidence like a skyscraper, she knew that, ultimately, she would prevail. This is and was her life, with so much more to live!

If Kam could have a Heart to Heart with Ame, she was optimistic that 'Good would prevail over Evil.' The problem was that Sara took charge and overpowered Ame. I really thought Ame was eliminated decades ago. Evidently, I was wrong. Aah, picture # 29, Papa with the three of us in a waiting room. We, twins, were five years old, and Ken was two years old. At the hospital, the night that our little sister Valerie was born, oh, how pretty she was, like a Lil Barbie Doll 'baby Valerie.' Kam leans back and reminisces with her lungs deeply engorging oxygen. Oh, if it had only stayed like this, her family would be in total blissful happiness. ☯.

Unfortunately, Havoc was just over the horizon like a Nuclear bomb exploding shrapnel and tearing flesh. Their family was destroyed, totally eradicated, and obliterated… Toast! Sad. Number 35 depicted a 360-degree spin. Kam grasped her heart, clenching with bleeding fingertips, stupefied by the sequences of # 35, 36, and 37, which were a juggernaut of unfathomable consequences and an overwhelmingly squalid nauseating loathsome indignation. No, Beyond Criminally Evil, Kam was hyper-ventilating as she slammed down the three sheets 'livid, vivid' memories surfaced and stayed with her. She couldn't let it go. Her baby Twin sister was indeed a murderess!

Kamryn was drawn back to # 35. Their mom was lying out on our pool deck, and little brother Ken was in the floater in the pool. Sister Sara was swimming under the water. Kamryn would never forget that day as if it lived in negative infamy just below the surface of her partitioned mind. She was spending the day at her best friend's house # 36, a drawing of her mother rushing into the house. The bottom description reads, 'baby Valerie crying screaming 'Al's doing Lol'… meaning Sara 'Al' had thrown her voice, making the sound of baby Val crying from inside the sliding screen door in our living room. OmLord # 37 'Al-Sara' flips three yr. old Ken upside down… bubbles displayed floating up a smiling tooth full gleam with Vampire teeth glistening red, bottom depiction reads 'Al drowned Ken no more BRAT!'

Oh God, the police investigation clearly came to the wrong conclusion calling Ken's death an accidental drowning… No sister Sara was a killer at the age of 5 yrs. This devastated the family… in tatters # 41 the funeral 43 an argument at our dining room table mom looked ravished, torn back listless dad had thrown a plate of food across the room. I was crying with baby Val. Sara was stoically unmoved, perhaps amused. Kam felt frozen in time as if playing a game of Freeze tag. She was transfixed solemnly. Could she tear the drawings all up and rip them into shreds?

NO, Sara was unbeatable controlling her mind from far away elsewhere, perhaps in the Starter stack of drawings of maybe another 55 sheets, the outside chance compelling her to continue praying there would be a clue? A mistake on Sara's behalf, a Key to her Freedom! Should she? Did she have the strength and conviction to follow through, umh, could she continue walking to the closet, counting three more piles of Ame's drawings? Did she have the courage and fortitude to face all the adversity that might spill out from the paintings? 'In the End,' she knew she would turn over every sheet. Maybe there would be a trace of evidence, a note written by Sara, a confession that would exonerate her and free her from this exile. She wanted out of this Prison, uh, Insane Asylum… NIA.

Kam understood that she had to explore and examine every single centimeter of Sara's cell, every possible hiding place, each 'nook and cranny' not a 'pebble or paper unturned.' So, with a new profound enthusiasm, her inner strength and resolve prevailed with a firm, steadfast conviction that she could do this Hell, she had to! She flipped up # 47. Papa was holding Ame's hand. She's crying, sobbing hysterically. Daddy was holding my hand, I was balling my eyes out, and mommy was in between baby Val in a stroller.

Al and Ame… (Sara) was sent to live with Papa at five years old after Ken's death. I remembered this OmLord so scary for Ame and me, but it wasn't long before we were reunited again. My parents were never the same after my brother, ugh, their only son, had drowned. But no, Ken was killed by 'Al-Sara, Ame,' of the trifecta. Ame was far and away my steadfast favorite. It had been literally over two decades since I broached any of these identities with Sara. I was forced out of the house and sent to my Aunt's place in New York a few years later.

I closed my eyes and drifted back to some childhood distress, wondering why a kid's trauma always was more memorable than a child's happiness. Donny was Sara's pervert. I wish I could forget a scene that encroached and was emblazoned into my mind like a freakin Tattoo. I was visiting during spring break. Sara and I had just turned 13 years old. I woke up early in my bedroom, which was next to my sister Sara's bedroom. I could hear what seemed to be an aggressive tone, uh, argument in her room, so I bolted over to her door and listened to a guy's voice and Sara screaming bloody murder. I opened the door, and Sara was straddling a chair, her legs up and spread wide open, and this massive dildo was in her left hand, jamming it home. Donny's voice was yelping.

'Yeah baby,' oh Hellyeah....' In Sara's delusional mind, Donny was screwing her. Uh gross! Sara didn't need imaginary lovers, for she had Donny, who would go down on her in a flat-jack second. Supposedly the guy was a stud. At least, that's what my sicko sister told me once when she was inebriated. Donny was Sara's invisible sexual partner.

I honestly thought the different entities inside her head were obsolete, gone, and buried in her pre-adolescent mind. I felt like many psychologists stated she'd grow out of them. I stopped and had to laugh out loud. I moved from New York City and Wallstreet back to San Francisco after Sara was arrested and indicted on the attempted murder of Agent Lucie Link. I wanted to help our Attorney Uncle in his defense of my sister. I'd spoken to Sara, and she described this guy that worked for her at her psychiatric practice. His name was Don. He had worked as a secretary for her... Naw, another figment of my demented sister's imagination. Don, she told me all about him, that they were in love and how he was gobs of fun... Omg, actually, Don was Donny, her make-believe boyfriend, and lover.

Thinking back a few decades, I can still hear Al's voice for Donny. Wow, I'm glad I didn't get the schizophrenic bug from my family tree. Uuhhh, some sick shit, for sure. When Ame would draw Donny, he was the 'duh' spitting image of us... Sara and I, but with short hair and a boyish countenance wearing his pants down below his ass with boxers. She drew him sexy, like kissing and fondling her. It was kinda funny back then, but not now!

The subsequent 17 sheets, dated back over 20 years ago, represented many of Al's practical jokes, pranks, and depictive paintings at school at Papa's house, much that Kam wasn't privy to part of her twin's life unshared, Sara's multiple personalities caused her extended stays in and out of Psychiatric Hospitals. Outpatient hospital treatments, tests, and experiments included ongoing brain scans and MRIs. At a young age, Omigod Sara had already been diagnosed with Schizophrenia. With seven diverse personalities, different people all residing in one body. This disorder involved hordes of pharmaceuticals, poor sister Sara! 'I thought the Doctors got it wrong I only counted three identities besides Donny, so yeah, four!'

Kam recalls this era in time when stress cannibalized her family. She had started to bite and chew her fingernails, wet the bed, not controlling her bladder, couldn't sleep, always upset insecurity set in deep in my bones. Mother and Father were play-acting walking zombies daddy would drink alcohol from morning to nighttime, and fights between them increased horrible, awful fights the police called out several times.

The blame game was always where the disputes ended. It was momma's fault that Ken had drowned… blame was also leveraged on Sara's head. Even though she was only five years old, she should have been paying attention to her little brother. What was she doing? Daddy would ask. When mommy got to baby Val's crib that fateful day, Valerie was sleeping soundly and wasn't crying or making a sound. We were all in counseling daddy had lost his job and was now on his 3rd job. Mom was hanging on; she had been suspended several times her boss empathized with the family's plight.

Turning over sheet 67, oh shit… fright took hold of me. Ugh, numbers 67-71, causing minestrone soup to crawl up my throat, uh, an acid taste. The following drawings were colored in pastels, pictures of a creek… children jumping from rocks, playing in the water, and others digging out a makeshift cave. 'Stunned out of this negative reverie, the sound of jangling rattle of keys at the steel door, my tiny tray slot slaps down with a thud 'get over here, Sloan, or I'm just goin to push your food through to the floor!'

Kam rushes over, almost tripping on air, and takes the tray 'thank you,' she says to an invisible person, 'yuh, have 15 minutes, and were picking that tray back up. You're on lockdown for three days!"

"Despite the unsettling drawings, hunger took precedence, devouring the chicken fried rice steamed Broccoli, whole wheat bread, and cranberry juice. Not bad, as she wipes her chin with some toilet paper and lays down for a short nap. Her bladder wakes her up three hours later. The time is 9:35 pm, 7/15/17, Saturday night. Wanders back to the pile of drawings on # 70 showed a pool and a water hose and 'Al Sara' with a butch cut. Kam knew Sara never allowed her blonde locks to be buzzed off. The image was of Al, one of her alter egos.

A gruesome picture unfurls, looking at # 71. Al was holding a hose. The cave had collapsed in Al's eyes, a smiling caption <u>'3 bullies buried alive ahh too bad.'</u> Kam rubbed her eyes. Having known the three children pretty well, she had gone to birthday parties and the skating rink with them. They were classmates… Counselors were brought to the school for weeks.

The funerals were awful. A gut-wrenching time… an emotional time indeed. I cried so hard, really lost, not understanding, or reconciling how I had just seen my friends at school the same day, and then they were gone dead forever!

I now can recall that day at the funeral. Sara sat right next to me. All of us were crying along with the deceased kids' parents; Sara just sat there without an expression the counselors had brought her in several times because she seemed apathetic towards their deaths. Not seeming to care, and iota, I supposed she should have been crying like the rest of us now. The truth is she was more likely celebrating gloating with her lips sealed. My Twin was a murderer. She tried once to smother our little sister Valerie in her crib for crying… screaming at the top of her lungs. I stopped her and warned her never to touch Valerie or Else I would tell her doctors, mom and dad, and Papa! She took me seriously and never touched our baby sister again. Well, I now knew with proof what happened to my brother Ken and my friends at school! 'Sara-Al' drowned Ken in our pool, now killed three classmates, already a Serial Killer for real before she was nine years old!

I got up and left the desktop to take a look at the three remaining stacks of drawings nearly three feet high, then took another gander across at the wall with taped drawings. Gosh, 'Sara/Ame' was busy. 'I wondered what other surprises lay in wait for me in the thousands of drawings left and which ones I'd bring to Doctor Liz Honcho and my dear ole Uncle Terrance Hallinan, the CEO of NIA… Optimism rang out loudly. I would be exonerated soon enough.'

-52-

<u>Shasta Lake Houseboat. Hot as Hell, Sara was counting down. Pliers in her hand!</u>

Before Sara finished her countdown to one, Brock yelled at her, "Go to the mechanical room, where the generator is. Look on the bottom left side. There is a toggle switch. Flip it to the right. This will allow the generator to access the main fuel tank. I think it only shut down cuz it ran out of gas. Now, after flipping the switch, wait for it to prime itself for maybe five minutes, then push the green start button!" Sara hops up from hovering over him on his chest "okay, that's what I shall do, thanks!"

Brock waits for her to pounce onto the floor and leave the houseboat's master bedroom, then again rips at his leather and chain restraints 'why can't this be like the movies like a Hercules or Superhero show?' Why can't I summon enough power or access my adrenaline glands to poof up and break free? After trying again and again, the attempts were futile. He was going to have to outsmart the witch Sara and be clever. He would strangle the snake if he could only get one hand on her. She would never break from his vise-grip of hatred!

The vents suddenly pushed out waves of cool air over his body, and the sweat that had beaded up all over his body transformed into a cold sweat. It felt good. He blinked and shook his head. Nah, it couldn't be a cold chill. A sensation hit him, whoa. No, his testicles were in a direct position for the air vent's directional blow. Which meant he was naked the bitch had stripped all of his clothes off. How demoralizing as his penis shrunk from the cold blast, he didn't feel a stitch of clothes. Oh, how he despised the reality of vulnerability, a sense he'd never known didn't ever play bondage games. Sure, it was all right if he was in control of the S&M, he guessed, but he never engaged in that form of sexual gratification. Nope, he wasn't into the submissive subservient slave games, yet he didn't mind portraying the Master! Yep! He rebuked himself for thinking like that, 'get real, Brock, this is a life-or-death situation that deserves a worthy adjustment.' I will Kill Sara after I find out about her sister Kamryn, my fiancé!'

He was a trained veteran engaged in wars in Iraq and Afghanistan, Special military Forces, a platoon leader in Delta Force, FBI, and commander and Director for the Northern California District. Leader of the Swat A-1 Team. He is a Man's Man, a protagonist, and a damn good guy. This is what he believed. Now he had to strategize. There had to be a way out of this predicament. He would find a weakness, just a slight mistake, and he'd kill her!

Bang like a spark lit and hit him. Oh shit Wait, no way; suddenly, his head was on fire, lost in the leftover drug abyss. 'If Sara was here, where the Hell is his Kamryn? Where was Kam? Did the Vipress murder her?' he had to stop this train of

446

thought. It led nowhere but to futility must keep his composure. He took a shuttering breath gotta stay focused. I'm no good unless I can escape this trap!

He would play it cool and be calm. Don't antagonize the witch. Stay objective. Sara was fricken dangerous how many people had she already murdered? Sara was a cold-blooded snake. His head fell back to the pillow. It's about the here and now, nothing subjective, don't dwell on negatives thinks musing all right… 'After all, if Sara wanted me dead, I'd be history already, not tied up. This was a major plus must think of the positives… or was she planning on torturing him slowly to a bloody death? Rationale hit him sideways with a solid conclusion it dawned on him. Uh, finally, his mind cleared. Ah, if Sara was here on the houseboat, then his lady had to be locked up at NIA. How the hell did she escape? His mind reverts to the table where they were enjoying the barbeque….' Suddenly he felt her appear in the room but couldn't lift his head enough to see her.

"Hey there, Brockbaby, whew, it's cooler in here already." "I need to use the bathroom, Sara. You're going to have to let me up!" She disappears out of view, returns, and holds up an empty milk carton. "Oh, Brock, your weeny is turning teeny; you must not like the cold." She grabs it and puts it in the open carton's spout, "okay, ready, set go. This is kinda fun never felt one of these as piss runs out of the main vein cool cum on Brock. Let me feel it pee now. Yeah, getting shy with me, huh? What's it called piss fright?"

"I don't have to take a leak; I need to take a dump, poop-bowel movement shit, all right!" "Oh, crap, I hadn't thought of that. Guess I could get a pan and put it under your ass damn. This isn't cool, dude! Not fkn cool at all!" "I'm not into shit, aah, wiping your ass, oh fk. I'm not Nurse material; Dude, not a good nurse type. Cleaning shit might make me barf fkn vomit here, umh, while I figure this shit out. Open your mouth." "For what? I'm not thirsty."

Holding a short funnel in her hand and a bottle with a label he couldn't read, "listen, Brock, if I have to, as I warned you before, I'll bust out your front teeth and put this fkn funnel down your throat so let's do this the easy way make this as simple as possible okay?" Brock shakes his head, thinking that she wanted to pour poison down his throat, but then Nah... that doesn't make sense. She could have poisoned me dead before.

"All right, I guess it does no harm in telling you what this fluid is. The stuff in this bottle is a cleansing agent made to pass drug tests. Barbiturates that I grinded up in your cake and wine will not show up during your postmortem examination!" She winks. "Now cum on, Brockbaby, let's do this!" "My autopsy. What, you're planning to kill me, Sara? why?" He swallowed hard, yet no saliva was to be found 'so that's why he was alive. She had to cover her tracks and needed his body's metabolization, his system functioning to process this drug cleaner, or I'd be dead now. "Umh, I see that funny look on your face, babe?" "Oh, no worries, dude, you're not going to die that easy we have all kinds of plans and things to do besides our answer and question forum. We have so much to cover; heck, I'm sure you wanna make love to me as I do you. It will be our Dream Cum true, Brockbaby. I will be all yours and you mine... Yum!"

Sara giggles, then adds, "we, uh, if you allow yourself, may have lots of fun. I know, despite what you may think, I will have the time of my life with you! I have dreamed flicked my Clit-masturbated too many times, fantasizing about this time with you. Yummy!" She squeezed his thigh, "yeah, no, you lost a day sleeping away. Today is 7/9/17, a Sunday heck... we're not due off the lake till the 16th... no one will find us out here, so we have days to explore each other, Brock!" He grimaces and barks, "Sara, do you actually think I can get it up for you? Your insane!"

"Oh, Brockster, your so funny…you know how a penis works. A little rub a dub, and it's an involuntary action. I'll get it going for you. My velvet tongue is magical! I'm in charge here, buddy." Smiling, "well, you're all tied up. I guess I will be the explorer for a while, but I will surely become bored with you, which will happen, babe. That's just how my life works. When I've, or we've had our fun… You will then become a delicatessen for all the fish at the bottom of this lake. Now open up!" He gulps down most of the liquid, nearly choked, but he manages. She slaps him viciously across his face, and his nose starts to bleed. Then she dabs his chin. "You drooled some out, Brock. You're going to cum to realize I'm in charge here. You obey me… my every command, or you will suffer greatly and feel my wrath as she clenches her fist and leverages a wicked punch hitting his spread-Eagled body squarely in the testicles he jerks about. He bites his tongue but wouldn't give her the satisfaction of hearing his sound of agony "you're wrapped to the four-poster bed that you and my sister oh so enjoyed." His stomach was heaving, churning the pain, the agony, of the surprising solid whack to his groin had him not paying attention to his captor!

He opens his eyes, and she is standing above him, checking his ligatures "important for you to listen to me; I will not have you bruising your wrists on the leather. There must be no signs of torture if, by a miracle, your body is somehow discovered years from now!" "Gosh, whatever happened to Mr. Brock Edward Dame, umh, he simply got too drunk and drowned in Lake Shasta. Aah, poor, poor fool!" Sara laughed heartily, displaying a scowl for the ages, then flicked her tongue out, wiping her lips.

Sara starts in a low hum-warming up to a decent howl and laughing uproariously, "oh, this is so much fun!..." "Your Insane,

Sara. If I were you, I'd kill me. Now get it over with!" "Okay, but see, you're not me, lol, nanny-nanny goat lol No! And we have so much to do; you'll see." "Still, Sara, it changes nothing. I have to go to the bathroom!" "Oh, yeah-shit, that's right. I will be back. Hold it in, no mess, gotta figure this out, damnit, why didn't I think of this?" She mutters to herself, like Duh; biological functions are necessary. Geez, gotta figure this out… Sara.

'Maybe I should ask my brilliant companion Ame? Gosh, laughing within, I don't want to let her big mouth out. She'd never shut up better to leave her with Al and my currently docile lover Donny Yep!'

Kamryn plots to get an interview with Doctor Liz Honcho and have Uncle Terrance visit her at NIA.

A sigh of surrender exhaled as her lungs discarded carbon dioxide. In a ball curled up on the bunk bed, one pillow between her legs, the other under her head in a fetal position, how to reconcile her dilemma with the hopelessness of the given circumstances? Is there a malleable, flexible strategy that she could employ? The simple truth was that she was Kamryn Amaya. Her predicament was unyielding so many quandaries to calculate.

Kam felt the opposite of stress and anxiety that she'd surmise ordinary people would feel. Instead of being restless, her skin and mind were wired to her eyelids and felt laden with weights… using a mantra that has been useful throughout her life. She posed questions repetitively, with constant reiterations. She first spoke aloud, then in whispers, only silently connecting with her mind, her conscious inner self melding with her subconscious state of being. She welcomed sleep and the possibilities that her analytical mind would solve this dilemma, the collusion of all that was she… bring about all possibilities, hoping to find peace and tranquility oneness with self-trusting her inner being Spirit and Soul! While she rested, Kam begged and implored her subconscious to be vigilant and come up with a plan. Amen!

Alas, instead of drifting away in a graphical blissful world of semantic illustrations, her inner self led her down a path. A five-syllable word meant everything to her… 'Com-part-ment-ta-lize… compartmentalize divided into segments to analyze her situation from outside the box. She had some powers of her own and must use all of her assets. Think like an observer, uuhhh third-party person who is rendering or interpreting all information with proficiency and unemotional disattachment, knowing her sister's smug demeanor and arrogant, egotistical disposition 'mien.' Despite the lack of compunction on Sara's behalf-mistakes-miscalculations, wrought with narcissistic compulsion, these flaws would be Sara's undoing and galvanize my escape from purgatory. Visiting a black hole that Kamryn spastically ignored shamefully, so she now had to embrace her heritage. I could not deny who I was… using her inner resources. This was survival; Sara had won the battle… I'd win this War!

What am I? Stop the denial. All the mental characteristics genetically flowed freely through my endocrine system, mind, blood, soul, and Spirit. The constitution of genetics, a disease she most feared prevalent in her bloodline passed down from generation to generation inherited handed down, is no longer a subtext or subjective. No, admit it embrace it, be objective, uh, a concrete-based manifestation was externally exhibiting what she internally analyzed with unbiased truths. Face reality, Kamryn. Now it's not too late, do it. Your paranoia is warranted. Be strong, do it, ah concentrate, she muttered one word over and over, 'Now.' <u>'Compartmentalize!'</u>

As sinister as Sara was, they were formulated from the same egg. Sure, she has won round One with a couple of knockdowns. I need to get off the canvas and attack. I had to stay focused and be dogmatic. I had to be objective… no more hiding behind the veils of Nun's headdresses. My family tree, uh, ancestors dating back as far as the 1700s, had a touch of Insanity. Stop, not just a hint of craziness. Let's look at it from a case-by-case history of Psychopathic Delusional behaviors, mentally deranged disorders conflicting multiple personalities, chronic Psychosis of a violent abnormal convolution to harm and destroy others, Sociopaths with a desire to maim and digest metabolize humans... of all varieties.

Great-great-great Grandma was burned at the stake and deemed deranged a Witch back from the Salem Era madwoman. She wasn't an ordinary witch. If there was such a thing, nope, she was a Sorcerer with many Warlocks and Witches that catered to her. The most used term from generations back was Schizophrenia, usually offering itself at the onset of pubescence, unless you were Special then much earlier, like sister Sara!

Kam was rolling over, clenching her pillow snugly, willing herself not to delve into the many relatives... ancestors that were beheaded. Hung from a rope till dead... put to death for odious, wicked, and heinous crimes, her 'Family Tree' was arousingly repulsive. A chainsaw should have cut it down. A backhoe shoulda pulled it out by the roots... then cremation!

Instead, her dreams fast-forwarded to Papa. Through years of counseling, he had discarded his demons, the multitude of Ventriloquists, magicians, sorcerers, enchantresses, and even a wizard or three. It was mindboggling her family tree the questions posed for decades, why would we have offspring, children with these genetic flaws? Why risk another tyrant or mass murderer? One of our ancestors owned a medical institution in England. He'd impregnated his sister, and their daughter was born. The three of them, for decades, experimented on prisoners. They were only discovered ughhhh caught when an unruly gang of vigilantes torched the prison. It was then that the dozens of corpses were found, and also located were dozens of torture chambers that were being occupied at the time of the burning! Not Good, No! ☾.

Sara had shown signs well before puberty when my kitty cat was found bloody, trying to claw its way out of the dryer. The look on Tabby, her eyes on the glass looking out of the dryer, was horrific. I instantly became hysterical, crying uncontrollably. 'Sara-Ame-Al-Don' laughed hysterically, saying, "Tabby must have been cold. That's why she jumped into the dryer!" Sara giggled. 'Then Al made meow mews and started to Purr!'

Sara started therapy at five years old. Luckily, I hadn't had any symptoms. Blessed, yes, now as an adult, I have continually rethought my parent's reasoning, rationale, well, my mom's for having any of us and propagating Insanity. Still oddly naïve, I believed that Sara had outgrown it all and wasn't the Serial Killer Vipress that the media and Police had professed. Wrong!

A dubious first, my Great Aunt was like the inaugural prisoner at the infamous 'Belleview Mental Hospital Asylum for the criminally Insane in upstate New York. Sadly, the Females were by far the most deadly vile and ruthless, way worse than the males in our family line. Scientists did much speculation and research. It always seemed the experts concluded the same assumptions: Inbreeding cousins, even mothers procreating with sons.'

Who cares? Switch gears oddly, her bloodline's IQ was beyond superior geniuses with exceptional gifts and creative powers. Generations of intellectuals, Scientists, Physicians, Savants, scholars, masterminds, and even several chess champions World Class intellects, some of which all along were honing, umh, sharpening their collective evil skills! Turning personality disorders into positive manifestations, manipulating the public as politicians are known to do self-serving uhoh, we have stories to tell… Yup!

Kam knows the buck stops with her. Fortunately, the offspring had slowed many in the family abstained from having children, for we were a cursed family and should have our own abortion clinic. I will never have a child after having my uterus removed long ago! Yet Brock and I would conceive with a surrogate proxy, Brock's sperm would impregnate another woman, and we would have a blessed family. We had discussed the likelihood of having two children! The world could breathe collective sighs as she inhaled a large breath. Neither Sara nor I can have babies. Thankfully, the end of our Bloodline… Yes, a substantial worthwhile sigh left Kamryn's lips. Enough reminiscence 'I will find my way out of this Asylum, for Sara has to be stopped. No doubt I will find proof to enable my release and her subsequent recapture returned to this same Prison only, not this cozy, pleasant cell, but the basement of Hell. Nope, this time they will lock her ass up in the Dungeon across the way, where the worst 'Inhumans are kept!'

Kam finally drifts off, finding R.E.M. asleep. Her conscious state of being was worn out. Now time to recharge the batteries, for I had an uphill battle, unswerving tasks, and burdens that I must overcome. She'd catapult all barriers with final resolve, accuracy, and dogmatic perseverance. The buzzer-like alarm chirps annoyingly at 5:55 am, abruptly awakening her… breakfast is served through the slot 'hey Sloan. I have an extra tray…you want it?' 'yes, thank you!' yay… she pulls both from the door slot. And makes some instant Folgers coffee a potent double scoop with a brand-new outlook and perspective. The artificial light was bright. Adding some cheese out of a jar from Sara's shelves to her powdered scrambled eggs, she munched the turkey bacon, determined to get through the drawings without any resoundingly negative stumbling blocks. Remembering her operative word from her meditational sleep, 'compartmentalize' all. Be unemotional and objective. See the pictures from a third-person vantage point, from the outside, with a nonchalantness!

After a poop run, she grabs a small stack of numbers 73 through 81, perusing the drawings of a relatively benign family outing to start... Papa was performing in Las Vegas. Little Val, baby Valerie swinging merrily at a circus, all three sisters were riding a Merry-go-Round. Papa, dad, and mom are in focus. Ame was quite the Artist. The pictures came alive like an animation show, only taking her seconds to put to canvas any thought Ame had... could be drawn. Kam often sat and watched her in Awe or stood amazed at her Lil sisters' talent, younger by 7 minutes.

I had other talents and skills, an affinity for numbers, Math-eidetic with an unmatchable compassionate heart, forgiveness, sensitivity, and sympathy, almost empathetic to a fault, and a staunch believer in the '10 Commandments.' By drawing #83, she was convinced that therapy was improving Ame's disposition, not a sign of violence or devilry... malice departed. Sara was drawing roses, even depictions of happy smiling faces, hearts, Sunshine flowing, and flowers like she wasn't Insane!

The following pages showed her parents, who seemed to be on the road to recovery from her brother's death two years in the past. Baby Valerie was now three years old. Daddy was once again fully employed, as was mother. The scars were there, but life's evolution rolled on we were nine years old. I was visiting from upstate New York with my Aunt, and 'Sara, Ame, and Al' were allowed back from Papa's house. We were a family once again. A family of five, not counting the hidden entities that were ensconced in the mind of sister Sara.' Kam knew what was coming as her fingers were wet with perspiration. She gripped the pages in front of her on the desk... cataloged. Remember, do this, Kam. Move on, do it!

The end started on pg.93. How could my family absorb so much adversity? Turmoil and trauma, the results were on the paper drawn by Ame... answers for me to visualize. A family can't survive all these atrocities; sadly, it's a mere villainous and iniquitous truth! Sheet #95 family all together except baby Valerie in dad's station wagon. We were going to dinner at our fav McDonald's. Dad stops to pick up our little sister Valerie at the daycare center adjacent to her Kindergarten school... Police are all over the place, lines are spread out in Yellow tape, parents are sobbing, and teachers, daycare nurses, and employees'... heads are in their hands.

Alarmed, my mom was the first out her door, the car still rollin, followed by dad. They were accosted before they made the gated playground. Sara and I sat rigidly up on the edge of our seats. Not a word was spoken then mommy hit the ground and imploded with a scream. I will never be able to forget this trauma. I awake during sleep, sweating, hearing loud bells ringing and horrific screaming. This was my childhood. I lived alive in my subconscious. My life had become to be my worst nightmare.

<u>Daddy barges through the police officers knocking them aside. His hands held out above his head. He was shouting and yelling for his daughter, his baby girl, Valerie falling to his knees, and several women came to his aid. Mommy was already extremely Ill with breast cancer. She fell, withering, twisting all over the asphalt. She shrieked for her daughter, baby Val! Our sister, baby Valerie, had been abducted from the daycare center... Omigod, no!</u>

Sara and I could hear most of what was said. 'Not 35 minutes prior, a white van had pulled up, and a man had jumped out and jumped over the 3-foot chain-link fence and stolen the little child. The Strawberry Blonde girl was abducted and gone. Valerie's

Kamryn's tears were wetting picture #97, turning it upside down, wiping her face, and blowing her nose. She took a time-out; coffee induced a bowel movement again. Off she went to shower again! The hot water fell, and the steam was continuous. Wishing she could stay sitting in the shower forever, but she had to be proactive. If she did nothing, she'd rot and die in prison. Her motivation hadn't lost any momentum thinking back to the day the family was quickly demolished and pulverized. Baby Val would never be seen again!

We never received any ransom notes, not any demands whatsoever, zero calls, and never was a body found. Valerie could still be alive, abducted, or kidnapped at five years old, but who would ever know? Our lives would never be the same because of notoriety, public outcry, and overbearing scrutiny. There were news people at our front door continuously. There was no escape. The publicity sucked what was left of our lifeline, which withered and died. Stigmatized Papa came in and took Sara and me for months to try and give our parents some relief. There was none to be had, a son drowned at not three years old and a daughter at five years old kidnapped, most likely sexually abused, dismembered after being tortured to death!

Papa was a Saint... all that was left of us on my mother's family side; Grandma had died well before we were born in a tragic plane crash on her way to Las Vegas to be with him. Papa had shunned and tried to abstain, not to procreate or to proliferate the mental disease, and didn't want any responsibilities tied to his tainted bloodline.

Papa had only one child, my mother. He was wealthy beyond comprehension, worked for fun on the Vegas Strip for decades, invested in the stock market, and initiated 'Trust Funds' for Sara and me. He was always there for our family financially, especially when daddy sank to the lower depths of the bottle and lost his job again.

Dad's broken mental state was precariously on a slippery slope. His intrinsic value and existence were determined by how drunk he could get before noontime. He was still inebriated when his eyes opened. Mother was also fired after Valerie's kidnapping… cancer was cannibalizing her, and she was taking prescription pills for mood elevation and sedatives for pain. She was tranquilized to a zombie state, her words slurring heavily from her parched lips a continuum.

I was shipped back East, and Sara remained within this quagmire, lost and constantly in and out of counseling programs. Papa paid the bills and helped them, uh, my parents, as best as he could, provided therapy counseling and paid for everything for them, but they wouldn't attend. They were beyond saving, it seemed. He made sure that Sara went to school and had tutors. Sara saw a boatload of Professionals before Social Services stepped in and tried to take control, but Papa wouldn't have it. He stepped up proudly to meet each and every challenge. Thank God for Papa. Oh, how I loved Papa always, even till this day, I'd say, 'I love you, Papa, sweet dreams!'

<u>Kamryn is in Sara's cell studying Ame's Drawings.</u>

One of the oldest sayings that I could remember was 'when it rains, it pours, or when you think things couldn't get worse, well, then you're wrong, a 'Murphy' like Law or rule. I'm here to tell you you're lucky that you weren't part of my family. No, you want proof; well, there I was, staring at picture #127, which was of mama lying in the hospital. I was brought back from my Aunt's house in New York. My dad, Papa, Sara, and I were by her side for a double mastectomy, and mom was drowsing in and out of consciousness.

Our mother had been diagnosed late. Sadly, she had done everything she could to be proactive way before she was an adult, constantly getting tests. Since we had a predilection, um, another weakness, Cancer, another negative trait in our flawed bloodline, she had been proactive since her late 20s, demanding mammograms. But even with the precautionary screenings that she'd insisted on, even though many of the physicians told her she was too young to be so worried, one such doctor had labeled her mother, calling her a hypochondriac. Because of faulty technicians, radiologists, and an irresponsible doctor, by the time they caught the tumor, she was already at stage 4. A death sentence for my mom, who had defeated the insanity valiantly that was genetic. She then was going to succumb to cancer; what a screwed-up life!

By drawing #131, 'Al' was back in the picture literally, giving our mother the final dose of medication and alcohol, including half a bottle of sleeping pills, killing our mother and her pain no more misery for mom. I knew mom was being monitored by Hospice and didn't have long to live, and Al committed a mercy killing. Although I could not fly back out of New York again to say goodbye to mom in person, I talked with her twice or thrice a day when she was cogent. She knew I loved her. I hugged and held her the last time I was with her. We hugged and talked of Love and of God and where she was going to Heaven. We would be together again! I wasn't ready to say goodbye, but when is a person really prepared?

The caption under #131, <u>'Al is mother's little helper!'</u> Kam puts both hands out and holds the end of the desk as she peers down at pictures of her mother's funeral # 135. No one came; I flew out. Dad was passed out drunk and wasted on the kitchen floor. Papa again does his best in the following picture, taking us out for pizza and bowling number 137 glimpses of smiles as all the pins were knocked down a Strike! Sara's feet were off the ground with celebration. Yes, it was written at the bottom of the paper. <u>'Sara with a Strike!'</u>.

Drawings numbered between 141-145 almost stopped Kamryn's heart, the accident that wasn't an accident, after all, OMLord. Daddy was Murdered, a double slaying that changed their living arrangements and household dynamics forever. Our mother had died, and now our father was dead, along with a neighbor lady. Only Papa was left. The murders were ruled an accident after being investigated thoroughly, although Ame's drawing of # 145 proved otherwise. With Boombox Radio in her hands, Sara thrust it into the Hot Tub with daddy and the woman inside having sex. My mother's former best friend fking in the same hot tub we spent hours in as children both electrocuted. Sparks were flying about in the pic. 'Sara's ghoulish eyes sparked with intensity! 'Well, these pictures are worth thousands of words. I gotcha Sara, your Guilty!'

Number 146 was a close-up of Sara's face contorted and grinning with a hateful smirk # 147 153 was of the police. Papa's social worker's… psychiatrist's faces were drawn, then dad's funeral # 155, but no one showed up. From the night of the double slaying, Sara ceased to be the same person forever, for all intents and purposes. She flexed in and out of personalities at a whim uhm, scary. Sara refused any acknowledgments of doing so, none whatsoever!

I couldn't wait to finish all of Ame's drawings now, feeling like I had proof of an honest admission of Sara killing our father and neighborhood lady. Felt quite energized seeing a stack of colorful Oil Paintings on canvas. I regrettably had to pick them up and then made a Beeline to the Toilet on my bruised and now bleeding knees, dizzy with anxiety and gripped with the harrowing grossness and evil!... I wretched and vomited all the food in my stomach with bile and contemptible acid coming up my esophagus volcanic-like. In a daze, I kneeled in front of the Stainless-Steel toilet.

I took a break and sucked down some potable water from the sink. Knowing I had to finish with the drawings, heck, what else did I have to do? I was going to be locked down for another two days. After an hour or so of contemplation doing crossword problems in one of Sara's puzzle books, I moseyed on over and took a stack of drawings labeled 'PG-19... XXX.'

They were Pornography-based drawn pictures of the freaks Donny, and Sara, with Ame being the voyeur. Ame had drawn portrayals ughhhh, and they were disgustingly sick and vivid of Donny screwing her with a Horse or Donkey dick, her body contorted, her Ass up in the air, full-on fellatio, and cunnilingus. The depictions were lively, and Graphic based beyond details. Ame had to have spent hours with these Oil paintings. I could make out the sweat pores spilling from Don's Glutes as he Rocked Ame. Captions of the song's names and music were written at the bottom of the pages of her Make-believe sexual exploitations. Donny, Ame, the Psychiatrist, and the Secretary were in the Jacuzzi. I gasped and realized what bothered me the most in the pictures. Sara was staring right through me. At the bottom of the last painting, she had penned, ' by the time you're enjoying these lovely paintings, I will be enjoying your Fiancé I'll have your Brock

Out of the shower 25 minutes later, I got back at it. I couldn't have my focus supplanted… Pit-bull determination with unyielding and unwavering perseverance. I remembered that time period… 'Sara demanded after she'd killed daddy and the neighbor woman that from that point forward, she wanted to be referred to as Sara Sloan. No longer would have dad's last name 'Amaya.' She became Ame Amaya, the Psychologist, Al the Ventriloquist, and even another personality, Donny, the head secretary. I suppose she'd spent so much time with Psychiatrists that she had that act covered. Besides that, Sara had extensive education, uhm, the best that money could buy. She, like me, had numerous earned degrees.

Sara was our mother's name, Sloan was her maiden name, and Papa's last name. Sara couldn't stand to hear our last name, Amaya! Sara decided that the name Amaya was for the trash, like cheaters. Enraged that daddy didn't wait for mom to be buried, barely a week had passed, and he was screwing our neighbor. I remained Kamryn Amaya, and Sara Amaya played with her alias for nearly 25 years. She was a Sloan; I had called my sister by her legal name Sara Amaya.

Lunchtime at the steel door… it was an excellent time to take a break. After a tiny nap… Kam returned to work and was in the middle of the second stack. Ame aah… Sara's alter ego, Al, was back in the foreground. He showed up for 161 to 169 explicitly the killings of the teachers at the hotel. The caption 'Cheating teachers taught lessons.' Al was again on canvas with short blonde hair, butch cut-tight jeans, and a black T-shirt. He was feeding a large juicy steak to a Saint Bernard in a backyard. The painting was named 'yummy the last meal poison,' then the knife throwing Al… 'the wife beater and Crispy mother of three children… dead as doornails.

Kamryn was numb by now. Nothing raised her blood pressure. There wasn't a question that Sara was the Serial Vipress Killer her sister was the 'Dark Angel.' Taking a toll on the philanderer's infidelity and playing like a Saint, eliminating some of the debaucheries amongst humans. She went after the incessant cheaters with precise and irrevocable determination and felt vindication after she'd eradicated another cheater.

The turning point was catching daddy... Sara had levied Hate and contempt against their father. She's flipped an insanity switch. Kam wasn't making an excuse for her dad. He was most likely five sheets to the wind. The neighbor whore had always flirted with daddy when mom wasn't around, especially in the pool! This was enough for Sara's Insanity to fulfill its destiny, her Psychopathic underpinnings to fall from this dimension into her own world. She sought to cleanse the world of cheaters, salacious philanderers, and adulterers. That's my conclusion, plain and not so simple now... I, Kamryn, needed to prove all of this and get out of this Prison. I will do this!

Shasta Lake Houseboat. Sara is in Control. Brock's demise is not a foregone conclusion, but close!

Sara re-enters the master suite in the deluxe houseboat. In her right hand was a 38-caliber revolver. Placing it down on the end of the table by the bed, she takes an additional pillow and puts it under Brock's head. He can now see on a level with her as she sits in a covered chair. Sara asks, somewhat perturbed, "Why, in movies, books, and TV shows, there never are references of a kidnapped person having to use the bathroom to take a shit, a natural human function. These biological functions can change the plot line drastically, yuh see!"

Brock purposely lets out a toxic fume with an added flapping of his butt cheeks, reverberating fart flatulence 'stink then smiles!' She jumps up and says, "fkn gross disgusting, your dead inside, dude." She is already holding her nose closed, then grabs the decorative pillow. "I can't help it. What can I do? let me up, or I'm going to let it blow!" Sara was nearly sick to her stomach, knowing after that stench, ugh, the odor filled the room. He wasn't kidding. Sara, this is your fault that sedative or poison has my stomach doing somersaults. I have to go to the bathroom, or it's going to juice out, girl! She wanted nothing to do with playing nurse, cleaning his ass, or a shitty mess. If so, vomiting, retching, and throwing up would be the ultimate outcome. This brought her back to when mom forced her to clean baby Valerie's diaper. She could do the peed ones but couldn't make it through the poopy diapers. Uh, good thing I never had or will have children... yep!

Sara could barely handle her own feces; it was a phobia, uh, was the best way to describe it. Even though she wanted to deny it, she'd been diagnosed with a rare Phobia. When she was a child, she'd get deathly sick being around Ken or Valerie's poopy diapers. She'd have to wear nose plugs in public restrooms and couldn't even glimpse a floating log of shit. Brock's incessant stench had her stomach in knots and cramping, realizing she was allergic to other's feces and her own. Sara, couldn't even visualize the toilet paper after a bowel movement. Throughout Sara's childhood, she'd experienced panic attacks, it started way before kindergarten and had never left her mind. Sara would feel anxious when she had the urge to poop... for to her, it was always a horrible experience. Sara couldn't get around it.

At seven years old, walking with one of her friends to the playground Sara, got violently sick after accidentally stepping into a pile of runny dog poop... and dropping to the ground in a seizure-like... twisting mess. Mom had discussed this event with one of my psychiatrists, and after another sphere or stint of testing, it was determined that I was a 'Coprophiliac.' Sufferers of this fear experience anxiety even though they realize their fear is irrational. They can become convulsive if they come into contact with feces or sometimes even… seeing feces. <u>Fear of feces is termed 'Coprophobia,' a word that was derived from the Greek… 'kopros'… dung. No, I couldn't even look at my own shit in the toilet. This was a terrible affliction. I truly believed I'd planned everything out like the mastermind I am… how did I forget that Brock might have to poop?</u>

<u>Sara's had two options… kill Brock or let him use the restroom.</u>

Sara couldn't very well shoot him dead or strangle him, for if his body were found, the FBI would obviously label it a homicide, besides his body still had her toxic sedatives. An autopsy would discover that. "Brock, this is how we will do this. I will loosen your right wrist enough so you can work yourself free, starting with your left hand and then your feet. This gun will be pointed at you from seven feet if you flinch. Ugh, Make a fast movement of any kind. I will empty the gun into your body; I will not hesitate. Yea, get my drift, pal?" Brock's expression remained squeamish, as if he'd blow at any second.

"After your bathroom run, you will get back on the bed and put the straps back on your feet one at a time… of course. I will stand over you and secure each one, then, in reverse mode, put your left hand into the leather cuff again. If you give me a reason, I will shoot you dead." Brock had another plan that included not being restrained. He kept quiet and only acquiesced to her orders "please, Sara, hurry, I'm going to explode. I'm cramping up the…." He watches her facial expressions and puts it on heavier, pushing more gas to escape his anus cavity. I feel 'asparagus bubbling out, whew' an agitated Sara gun leveled on his heart loosens his wrist, then steps back calmly in charge, 'damn, why didn't I think about this? My mistake!'

Brock was beyond stupefied… thinking, what the hell is wrong with this killing freak? She was going to let him go use the bathroom R.U. Freakin kidding me… He sat up, shaking his hands, bringing blood back to his extremities. His toes were nearly numb, checking her out now… with both hands grasping the 38 caliber gun. With a nonwavering killer stare, he started waddling, uhm, strolling to the bathroom, her now stepping behind him but way too far for him to spin around. He's got to figure something out, not returning to that deathbed. All was working according to his plan thus far, 'pushing his advantage' with her being feces allergic, utters 'yeah know' as he sat on the toilet "it would help this process if you didn't stare/scare me down with a gun… I'm getting Poop shy!"

She let loose a chortle that morphed into a cackle, "you asshole, after you arrested me, I was placed into a rubber room naked. Not a stitch of clothes in the middle of the floor was a stinking hole to use the fkn bathroom. If this situation weren't so fkn pathetic, it would be funny. I should have just put on nose plugs and gloves and dealt with you. Ugh, my stupidity, but there will be no more concessions… shit, and move it Now!" "Calm down, Sara. I need to relax my abdomen."

"Oh, that's right, how utterly humiliating, and inhumane me being inside that rubber room at the prison you helped put me in, you bastard. I had no toilet paper, uuhhh, like I was going to commit Suicide by stuffing it down my throat or something, so the piss-ant guards pushed some through a slot in the door. The guards gave me a few squares of toilet paper. They were grinning. Surely they got their jollies. They watched and recorded my every move, including some banter and wisecracks. I was left with no dignity or humanity. I was on display, all 5' 3-inch, 125 pounds blonde and drop-dead gorgeous they were probably stroking their cocks off up in the control room or flicking clits. It wouldn't surprise me if one of them hadn't put my videos on the Internet, so I don't have a slight bit of empathy for your situation. Hurry the fk up!"

While sitting on the commode, he changes his tact, "how did you do it, Sara, escape? Let's chat it up. It will help me not concentrate on the gun you have leveled at my head and your eager invasive eyes." A greedy smirl 'smirk-growl' instantly popped out, then a raucous giggle, her expressions of delight. "Oh, my escape, it was a Classic. It should be part of a movie script or a novel. None better, uhm, you can forget that movie… <u>'One flew over the Coo Coo's nest.' I'm a mastermind the newspapers, ughhhh, Social Media… 'Sara, the Genius.'</u> For sure, my plan was always evolving. That's how you have to do it adlib at times, countermeasures to roll with the punches, creative contingencies uh, alternatives with dogmatic and relentless objectives, Brock, I am a God!"

Brock let go of a squeaky squirting pile of diarrhea, aah, perfect timing, then flushed, continuing to act like it was squeeze and go. Sara shook her head and muttered, 'fkn disgusting anyways,' after Sara paused to dry heave and spit up some phlegm into a cloth rag…scowling at him the whole time with utter disdain… "Okay, my plan. I concocted it over time, analyzing it like <u>I was a four-person think tank.</u> I guess it was about three years after sister Kam moved from New York. First, I had to play on Kam's natural weakness of empathy and compassion, throw in some Love You's, and kiss up easy-peasy. Sell my dear big sister Kamryn into visiting me regularly, like every single week. Her soft trusting weak-ass good-hearted soul was super easy-peasy to manipulate. Yup!" Brock explodes again…

"Remember, Brockbaby Kamryn and I are absolutely Identical right down to matching tattoos that we'd got when together after turning 18 years old. 'I was able to pin her down to visit me on a schedule… every Thursday, well, ahh, a simple deduction that would be the day I'd perform my Magic. The only difference between her and me throughout our lives was our attire and clothing or if we cut our hair and had different hairstyles. But then the Bitch changed her hair color at my Sentencing in Federal Court. She went from blonde like me to Raven black or 'Midnight gloss.' That was the name of her hair dye. The reason for the hair color change told me all that I needed to know, and bang… gave me my original brain thrust. It was her way to lessen the harassment of looking identical to me. However, she said she loved me the same… Sure!" 🌀.

"So, when she visited, she never had blonde hair, always a brunette. This turned out to be a Godsend, or as I'd like to call it, a Devil-send. Uh, it helped the staff and guards to relax and ease up because of our similarities. To separate us further, where no one would give Kam or me a double-take look anymore, I then strategized brilliantly to evolve into becoming a 'hair-a-phobic,' lol ingenious shaved every hair off my body. Not even a pubic or butt hair remained. Believe me, 'Brockbaby,' it wasn't easy with those plastic razors." She paused and blew her nose. "Okay, I had been in the selection department trying to propagate an accomplice, for, without an outside source and unknowing partner, my plans would implode or barely get off the ground. I did have a few guards to choose from. Working my sexual innuendo's ah verbiage, it was easy to snatch up um ascertain the weak link." Sara coughed, wiping her nose suddenly clogged, ugh, "come on, Brock, shit or get off the pot!" "I'm constipated from your drugs Sara, cramping up!"

"Damnit, anyways, back to my academy award mission impossible. Remember, I needed a guard in upper management, Walla, then I found him. I nurtured this weak-minded man who was the Shift Manager of all the guard's correction officers, yah no, his slob-ass name was Carl. A major cog and key to my strategy. Yeah, no, the type of guy who had been married forever. Sex had dried up, all used up. No lust nor passion… it happens. Duh 'ole had' boring he resorted in porn to stroke off. Frustrated sexually, 'perfect a vulnerable sucker' 'ahh, the wrong word that became me, ugh!' I provided him relief with sensual Blow Jobs; I might brag and add the best he'd ever have. No one else has my talented throat! If you're lucky, you may just get a mouthed massage." Brock tried to grin and then smirked "okay, why not! you don't bite, do yah?" She flipped her eyebrows up and winked. ⚜.

He sat stoically on the toilet seat, waiting and hoping for a chance to lunge and take her down. "Who knows, Brockster, you play your cards right. You might even get a taste, ahh, or I might get a taste. Lol. 'Okay, umh anyways, where was I?' That's right, my sister pulled strings with NIA management and the staff. It wasn't too difficult or tricky. It didn't hurt to have our Uncle as CEO of NIA, lol. Right to the top of the food chain, the Hierarchy starts with one of Papa's best friends for life. A family friend Uncle Terrance Hallinan the infamous Attorney. He is my Attorney and NIA Chairman of the Board, a Trifecta! Shit, I ascended the levels quickly from naked and humiliated in the basement of the dungeon to the Penthouse of the Prison!" She clapped her palms together, giggling.

"This was when I started working Carl hard, lol pun. He was doing my bidding, keeping track of my sister via Private Investigators. I paid for all with cash out of one of my secret accounts, 'then you shocked the Shit out of me, man Brock really… Kamryn, my sister, you started courting and screwing, sis.' What the hell is wrong with you… huh, you were supposedly In Love with poor biddy Agent Lucie Link… Wedding plans Fiancés. Wtf were you two thinking you guys started dating R U Fkn Kidding me, the weirdest twosome ever? Sick!" She shook her head in utter disbelief. "How could you date the sister of the woman that made your fiancé a vegetable?" "Whoa, now, nelly, stop right there, Sara. It was a mutual attraction. I never stopped loving Lucie."

"Brock, you became part of the equation, which I don't mind telling you was an ultimate shocking surprise because I was going to kill you either way." 'Flush, flush, flush.' "My inherent natural knack and talent in cosmetology soon took my next bullet points forward, and three of my phases were accomplished. First, shave my body, separating the resemblance with Kam. 2nd, find a guard for my accomplice, and thirdly, find seclusion, a private place to unfold my ultimate plan. My 'Salon'… it didn't hurt that I could take an ugly frog, enhance, and beautify superficially, improving a woman from the doldrums like ratings of 3 or 5's into like 7 to 9's. Shit, Brock, you saw most of my disguises. I am a genius when it comes to morphing into other looks! Could work in Hollywood, Yep!" Brock unrolled some toilet paper.

"I can change anyone's appearance tremendously. There's nothing I can't do with makeup and the proper props…

Nothing I can't do. I started by being a hairstylist. My objective was to do Kam's hair only, but what no one could ever guess was my ingenious master plan. I'm so smart, so I would brush my sister's hair every time she'd visit, trim it at times, and always save all her hair in my brush. This went on for months and months, then a couple of years later, finally, I had enough to sew together. I made a splendid, superb replica of Kam's head of hair. I'd style her real hair, then match it to the wig of Kam's hair." She gulped her bottled water and smooched up her nose, looking at her, ah, Kam's Apple watch.

"After like 31 months with this pressure, one of the attorney's visiting rooms was made into a Salon. Yes, my own room. It was slow initially, but I had more clients than I could handle in no time. One was the most important regular, Dr. Liz Honcho. I was constantly in her ear as I turned her ugly mug into something extraordinary, way more respectable I would let her catch me staring up at the cameras whenever I could. After weeks of her regular appointments, she finally caught on."

"I whispered in her ear,' Liz, you know I overheard some of the guards talking about your makeover the other day. Too bad you couldn't switch off the security system while I did your makeover. It's no one's business but ours. It feels weird, like them watching us peeping Tom's, wondering what the staff is saying or even if they're snapping pictures of your face and make-up. Liz, no biggie, aah, if you can handle the voyeurs, umh, it's fine with me! Liz sneered up at the cameras, and I knew I was under her skin." "Sara got to admit it. That was clever." She paid him no attention and was on a roll...

"But unfortunately, or fortunate, depending on your perspective, I became a novelty at NIA and even did a makeover for the Warden. This is where Carl helped me. Also, he was definitely instrumental in my escaping NIA. Just for him to obtain the room, my 'Salon' umh, lucky it wasn't in use an Attorney visiting room OmLord awesome. I put pressure on Doctor Honcho and the staff. My Sister got involved. The more I did 'make-overs' of the upper echelon of NIA, the more privacy I was allowed. Given that none of the women wanted the nosey guards watching them get make-overs via camera, then Liz herself, aah Doctor Honcho, became paranoid as I was beautifying her. 'I'd continue to work her... a stubborn woman indeed, 'but in the end! I played her to the tee' pretending coyly to glimpse at the camera up on the wall. All I wanted, Brock, was for the cameras to be disabled for phase 4 to be thoroughly completed. I needed total privacy to strip Kamryn and quickly shave her body, then get redressed in her clothes... Lol!" Brock snarled and pushed some more juice from his body.

"Within a few weeks, the Salon was offline, and Carl also played a huge part in this; he was essential. Picking his small brains was simple as pie. I learned all the nuances of in's and out's procedures, what to expect when I would make my way out of NIA, knowing the processing of visitors… how it worked until I was outside the gates of NIA. The big dummy hadn't a clue, lol."

-54-

Brock couldn't believe that Sara had untied him because she couldn't handle a bowel movement. Wow… Straight up bizarre! .

Brock flushed again, wiped, and still sat on the warm toilet seat, not ready to get up, for he had yet to calculate how he would overpower her. No chance to jump from the commode and hit the Psycho! She'd unload a cartridge into his body before he reached her. He kept nodding, egging her on with his startled, amused expressions like he was in Awe. She ate it up and motormouthed on! One thing he'd learned in a short time, Sara liked to gloat and talk about herself, a no-question narcissist of the highest degree.

Then Brockbaby, I moved slickly into phase 5… for the last like nine months, I'd freak out, I mean go fricken crazy, after Kam would visit me, pretending to be Kamryn, like I'd been switched out… you know the strategy of the boy crying Wolf, lol. .But I was the girl playing Wolf slyly. Yep… I was Kamryn… and Sara had escaped. OMG! Oh Yeah, it was freakin fun! Well, until they grabbed me and dragged my body over the cold concrete, I was sedated and strapped into strait jackets several times. Having a lot of practice, I went insanely

472

delusional the 'Whole 9 yards' and called my Uncles Attorney's office like dozens of times. I told them I was Kam, and Sara had just left NIA and escaped. Lmao Yep! I was crazy, and unrelenting my claims of being Kamryn was one of the main components of my master plan. It was essential because if somehow Kam could convince them that I'd actually escaped, then I wouldn't be here holding this gun on you, Brock." She howled, then bounced back to her narrative. "I pretended to be Kam even with my bald look, which was nothing like the Raven-haired beauty that my sister was." Glowingly, she waved the pistol around as if contemplating and gloating over her dastardly nasty deeds.

"I had to analyze all that my sister would do every time she'd visit me, what her routine was when she left the prison. For when she woke up from being drugged in my Salon, her head and body would be shaved bald, and she'd be dressed like me. I knew Brock that your Fiancé would fight back and argue and be combative, claiming that she was who she really was. Lmao." "Your something else, Sara. I have to hand it to you. I wouldn't believe it if I weren't living it!"

"Yeah, Brock, you thought you'd got me… anyways, not wanting to be redundant like I said to you earlier about the Wolf   . I'm a genius, you know, have an IQ of like 153 uhm, my analogies fell on the old folklore or saying, the story well kinda like The little boy and the Wolf Fairy Tale, he kept crying that there was a Wolf about to chew him up, the villagers believed him in the beginning, but he kept Crying Wolf 'In the End' well you get my gist anyhow I kept crying that I was Kam from the rooftops I burned up the phone lines. Yup!" She cackled.

"When the day came, it was oh so perfect. Kam was so fkn excited to be with you on this houseboat, lol. It made me sick; that woman, uh sister dear, was head of heels captured by you, huh? She surely sank her teeth into the jugular vein of love for you. What a fkn fool, a sicko! I easily picked her brain about you and your plans and this houseboat she was spewing like that diarrhea from your ass.

Kam told me of all the pre-wedding plans. I saved up my pills, medications, uhm, and the sedatives and mouthed them when the nurses gave them to me. They'd say, 'open your mouth Sara' to check to see that I swallowed the pills, but with my tongue, I'd slip them to one of my cheeks. You no Brock, many inmates would save their pills and try to take them all at once to commit suicide at NIA, or the resourceful inmate would try and sell their mouthed pills." Brock forced out another flatulence. She disregarded the stench and wouldn't be stopped, on a definite roll……

"Next phase, umh, step was to get rid of Carl. He could be a liability. He knew my mannerisms, and we had a history. I had hired Private Investigators through him. He did a lot of fundamental groundwork for me anyways… One of the intricacies of my complex scheme was the aftermath of the switching of Kam for me. So for months after Kamryn's visits, I'd go berserk, uh, Insane. This was to beguile the staff, especially Liz. I claimed to have manifested into my older sister Kam. I would freak out and pretend with the semantics of an Academy 'A' winner Actress. I claimed vehemently and violently that I was your fiancé. I even placated her with helping with her plans regarding your wedding. I helped pick out the gross wedding dress and putrid Bridesmaids' outfits." Sara pantomimed and played like sticking the gun barrel deep down her throat, gagging like.

"This vacation that I'm enjoying with you, Brockbaby, was all she could talk about. I became excited cuz she described how sweet this houseboat was and all the fun I would have… not her gosh, I was hot and bothered wet with excitement yum like foreplay."

'The longer the Megalomaniac spoke, the angrier I became. She started lowering the pistol in her lap. I sat, muscles clenching. Little was she aware I would not be going back to that bed or was going to allow her to restrain me again. This is when 'push will become Shove,' and I would gladly die to get my hands around her carotid artery, ugh, ugly throat. I'm going to strangle the wench… my Lover and best friend was locked in the Insane Asylum. I had to save Kamryn.'

Sara started to Crow, quacking, wiggling her chin back and forth, raising her eyebrows into a sniggering cackle laughing uncontrollably while waving the gun in front of her. "Hell, you'd had to have been their Brocky, your Ex-Kam in the Captain's chair in my Salon. We chatted it up. I fed her iced tea laced with some super-duper potent, strong tranquilizers. She drank them up and down. I spent the day earlier picking her brain on which box she had placed her personal property in, even where she had parked her Corvette. Simple once she went unconscious, I moved like a Cheetah shaved her head bald eyebrows, and that cute Pussy trail, I'm sure you sniffed it and adored it from time to time!"

"I placed Kam's head back in a resting position and dressed her in my old prison clothes; then I took to the already made wig I'd spent months making and hiding from the guards. It was Kam's hair. How much better could it have been? I permed it into a new hairstyle, placed it on top of my cute baldness, and became Kamryn. I put her clothes on, stripping in less than a minute. It was a hot day. She wasn't wearing much but a short blouse, undies, and capris. My only unknown variable or fear was that if a guard or staff member had walked in, I would have been busted with amazing speed. I did it. Remember, I left nothing to chance!" "Wow, that's some story, Sara!" She tossed up a stop signal palm, like, shut up!

"My timing for this part of the complex and ingenious 'Mission Impossible' plot was timed, um, planned for the shift change of the staff and guards while they left their posts anxious to get on with their Thursday evening. Their replacements were on the way. I became Kam!" Then Sara smirked, sticking her tongue out said, "I'll fill you in on the rest after I have you back in place! Now let's get your dirty ass back to the bed, Brockbaby. I'm horny, honey. I have dreamed of making love to you for years, which will never happen again. We only have a short time to giddy up and make love Brockster." I tried to switch her focus back to her titillating escape. "So what, you just left Kamryn in the Salon chair and strolled right out the doors? Like Walla, bam out the concertina wires passed the guard towers, stole your sister's Corvette, and drove up here. How'd that work and feel, Sara?" Sara again busts up laughing "oh yeah, I've wished I were a bug on the wall watching Sister Kam in my cell, wondering what the hell happened. She must have totally lost it for real and gone insane. Way too funny, uh hysterical… so perfect. Gosh, I should write a scintillating horror thriller. Naw, write a book about me, the 'Femme Fatale' mastermind. That's It"

<u>Kamryn at NIA, ready to prove that Sara had escaped, that she wasn't Sara!</u>

Bolt action creaking hinges her cell door flung open 'Sloan, let's go your wanted upstairs!' Kam gets up, hurries over, and picks up a stack of Ame's drawings to take with her. "Who wants me? Is it Doctor Honcho or my Uncle Terrance Hallinan?" Come on; you're wasting my time, Sloan…." "For what, no more medications? I'm not taking anything else, nothing!" "Move it, Sloan, now, not yesterday. And leave those papers here. I'm to escort you, and your still under restrictions, no phone calls, no library." Kam drops the drawings on the table and is led into an elevator. She watched the elevator open and smiled inside. She'd been on this floor several times before. But this wasn't the office she'd last visited Liz in. It was at the end of the hall. The guard stopped and knocked at the office door with the name Doctor Liz Honcho attached to a gold and black placard. "Please have a seat, Sara," Liz says. Kam looks up at Liz aah, the makeover, or what was left of it, made her look like a sad clown.

Raising her palms to her chin, noticing her stare, "as you can see not happy with the results of my makeover, but I had a blast at the reunion. How are your hands and body recovering?" "The same heck, Liz, it was just a few days ago; thanks for asking, though...." "Sara, I've given much time and thought analyzing your therapy medications and all the counseling, and we still haven't made a lick of progress from second base!"

"This is one of my offices that I bring patients to for video displays of their counseling sessions, but I had you brought up here for a dual purpose!" For the first time, I looked around and saw a humongous monitor on the wall and two Lazy boy chairs and a platter of cheeses, meats, veggies, and chips in between on a standing table, a pitcher of melting iced tea! Liz pushes her chair back. "Sara, join me in these comfy chairs and enjoy some tasty treats. I'm sure it's been years since you have had anything like this!" "I'm Kamryn, and no, I regularly snacked on hors d oeuvres and appetizers like on that platter, but yes, I will enjoy some, thanks!" Liz scowls briefly, then regains her superiority okay and pours them some tea.

They sit with paper plates loaded up and cups of tea. "I have put together... aah well, actually some of my staff have a combined composition of various videos, sort of a montage of you, they separated some of your Schizophrenic personalities. Maybe this will help your mind to accept who you are and perhaps be helpful in your rehabilitation. It has been a lifesaver for others with similar disorders as yours, Sara!" Liz flicked a remote, and the curtains closed over the window that showed the beautiful pond and fountain she'd walked along so many times with her Demonic sister. The lights dimmed, and then on the screen was Sara sitting in a chair in a still picture. "I'm going to warn you that this may be a bit unsettling, and if you want me to pause or just shut it down, I will, and we can try this at a different time, but this is and will be part of your programming from this day forward, I want to warn you, Sara, this can be terrifying for some patients."

"Really, Liz, do it. I'm going to be watching Sara's antics, not anything to do with me! By the way, I have confirmation in Sara's cell that I am not Sara and beyond that, evidence that Sara has killed many people, umh, my dad and little brother ughhhh, but the guards wouldn't let me bring the drawings. I can prove beyond a shadow of a doubt...." "Shush now," declared Liz.

I frowned and scowled at Liz... and turned to the video screen, watching Sara get up, pointing her finger at an empty chair across a small table. She spoke but not in her normal voice, *'listen, Sara, I feel you're making giant strides in your treatment program and in our counseling sessions, but we need to move on chronologically. Sara, I drive here from San Rafael weekly to visit you and Al. We need to accomplish more in our counseling sessions, Sara. We've covered your caustic childhood. It's time..."* "Doctor Ame Amaya, I want to tell you another story about this Patti Dame character. She was married to Agent Brock Dame, whom the awful scandalous Agent Lucie Link was courting!' I didn't kill the slut, Patti Dame... Darn, life is so unfair, uh. It has been like a witch hunt. Doctor Ame, next you know, I was charged with attempting to kill Lucie, Doctor Ame, I did nothing to Lucie. I didn't push her from the hotel. She jumped. This doesn't seem right. I want out of here; I'm innocent!"

Liz pauses the film. "So, what do you think of what you just saw?" Kam shook her head "well, it's obvious. Sara is playacting. She is acting like Ame. She's insane. You hear two voices, yet she is the only person in the room, and she's walking around, pointing her finger at an invisible person in an empty chair. For the record, I have heard Ame's voice thousands of times. It was one of Sara's favorite personalities!" I take a drink of the iced tea, "this is an interview between Sara and Ame. It's all pretty simple. Right… Doctor Honcho!"

Liz fast forwards now to a familiar setting. 'Sara is in her cell. The same cell that Kam was now told was her home.' Sara was pacing back and forth in a rage, totally animated. 'Donny,' I don't know what we're going to do about Ms. Slimson. She has a severe case of Anorexia with Bulimic undertones; Don, cancel the rest of my appointments today. Let's go to our favorite restaurant. Why don't you get us reservations at San Rafael Joe's, umh, get over here first. I'm in need of a stress release cum to Ame… Donny!'

Kam sits, fidgeting, covering her eyes. Oh, gross, stop it as … Suddenly Sara disrobes, laying her nude body on the bed, and starts fingering herself, moaning and gyrating, 'oh, OH, oh Donny!' "Stop it. I've seen enough, Liz geez, really?" Liz laughs subtly "yeah, kinda visual, huh? Do you remember doing this? Sara, your Donny's voice is so macho and sexy. What do you think of what you just saw, or shall I continue the show?" "Jeez, my sister is demented. She is sick. I've heard Don's voice before. It's another of my sister's imaginative characters, her invisible boyfriend lover and sex slave, ole hot to trot Donny! I will show you many paintings with Donny and Ame in them. Most are quite XXX-rated. And, yes, Liz, I'm aware of Ame!" Liz says, "well, I'd like to see these drawings one day and hear your explanations for each because surely you're the artist, young lady; we're not done here, Sara." Since I needed to use strategy, uh, patronize Liz, I tossed some applicable verbiage out.

"Ame was an academic. She is a Forensic Psychologist and Psychiatrist with the degrees to match and actually had an office in San Rafael… Ame has been around since Sara was young. I think she was developed from all the counseling and invasive medical procedures she underwent as a child! I have seen enough, Liz. Can we get to the point?" "Sara, that is where you're wrong. I'm in charge here, and yuh better get that through your demented delusional screwed-up head. You've seen enough when I say you have; now pay attention and watch this." Liz paused and shook her head, bending over and taking up her tea. "Whoa damn, I'm sorry, Sara, geez, that's not like me. I'm trying to help you now. Pay attention! Please humor me, Sara, and watch this quick excerpt; <u>This is YOU… Sara playing 'Al' pretending to be your sister Kam; I have spoken with Doctor Honcho, and you know I'm paying for your counseling sessions with Doctor Ame Amaya, in fact, I have never met her and will be driving to San Rafael later today… Kam, I'm serious. What you see here at NIA isn't real this is like a military base for mercenaries. I…." Liz flips the video off "what the hell are you saying about NIA, Sara? You better be careful, I have yet to show this to your Uncle Hallinan, but this could end your existence… immediately!</u>

Then Liz portrayed a ghoulish grimace and didn't expound any further on the mercenary stuff and fast-forwarded the video of me… saying This is fricken freaky watch this like Stephen Kingish… Ughhhh, I sat stone-faced, shocked out of my 'normal mind' on the video screen was a bald head painted black with what looked like different colored magic markers. Her head turned away, and then slowly, the morbid face looked directly into the cameras with painted eyebrows and red teardrops down the cheeks. A Monster, Sara had painted Al's face onto the back of her bald skull. So she could swivel her head around in the mirror and either be Sara or Al. Omg, it was the killer freak! Sara's face showed the second scariest of her Schitzo personalities when she whipped her bald head around, and it was Al who stared right at you! Oh, damn, Sara and Al were standing yelling at Papa, a master Ventriloquist. Al had far more skill at throwing and mimicking other voices… He could have retired on the Vegas Strip. In the video, Sara stood with her version of Al, hands on hips screaming at Papa, "If you were not so fkn nosey Papa, I wouldn't have to poison you with the peanuts. Now your dead asshole, don't fk with Al!"

I quickly jumped to my feet, spilling the plate and the tea "oh no, stop it, please stop it." Tears formed and flowed immediately. 'This was torture. How Evil could someone be that had the same blood in their veins as me? Liz was up, grasping me.' "I know Sara, how hard this must be, you poor child; come here," as she reached to hug Kam. Who jolted backward with disdain and a form of hatred "that's not me; I can prove it! I can't watch anymore no more!"

I was instantly crying, sniveling, and mumbling, "What you just showed me, Liz, is that Al is guilty of murdering my Papa, umh, my grandfather. His death was never solved. The case went Cold; Al was suspected because he lived with Papa at the time of his peanut poisoning. My Papa was deathly allergic to peanuts!"

"Relax, come on, sit back down here. This is good for you, only a few more minutes. I will save the other three hours and 51 minutes on the next disks for our next meeting. You have done outstanding, Sara, but let me get your take on the last clip on this disk?" I was allowed to use her bathroom to blow my nose and wash up. I stared into the mirror at a face that frightened me. Who was I? Dazed and confused, residual effects of the barbiturates I surmised, back out I went to see Liz waiting and patting my chair with her hand "sit, sweetie!"

We watched the video as Sara was walking with her hairbrush, miming it as a microphone talking, then both Kam and Liz zoomed into each other's eyes. "It was impossible the voice was an exact replica of Liz's. If you closed your eyes, you'd swear that Doctor Ame Amaya and Doctor Liz Honcho were having a heated argument. Liz was yelling at Ame. They both seemed they would come to blows. The brush bobbed with her head as she spoke into it! It was Al's talented Ventriloquist skills talking into a hairbrush, imitating Liz to a tee! It became apparent that the hairbrush was a phone in Sara's demented minds. She'd made dozens of calls to Liz… I flashed with an epiphany. Whoa, that's what Sara had said. Umh, Carl was useful. Yes, he'd brought in phones for Sara to use to pretend and mimic being me, uhm, to be me calling Liz and others. Yeah, super slick. Damnit, and I didn't see it coming like a blind 'S' turn with a thousand-foot cliff on both sides.

"Sara, your talent is miraculous. Listen, we have the Board of Directors meeting next month, and I wanted to put on a talent show for them using our inmates. What do you think?..." "No, fk No, I'm tired of saying the same thing to you, Liz. I'm not Sara. When will you listen to what I have to say?" Liz stops and sighs, then relents, 'Umh, didn't you say you had a couple of things to go over with me? I'm done with the videos for today. We can finish this form of your therapy next week!"

Liz straightens up, pulling out her cell phone "here is a text from Kamryn. She sent it while on vacation." What a kind sister you have. She was checking in on you and the Carl debacle. Liz reads the text, 'I want vindication for Sara. I have yet to file charges and a lawsuit against NIA. This will not be washed down the drain or under the carpet. As always, I will be visiting next Thursday; I need answers then! ⚔… ⚜.

I lost my temper… Too much stress! ☾.

After hearing Liz tell me that my sister Sara was going to keep my Thursday visits on schedule, I lost it… I flinched and sprung up… erect and rigid, standing at full attention, and yelled loudly and belched out as if spewing Lava. My scalp tingled, "that Bitch is coming here…" seething inside. "I'll rip that wig of my hair from her bald head and shove it down her fricken throat… I'm going to take her down!" Instantly I recognized my mistake, rather than be spontaneous, I needed to analyze before spouting off. I shut-up, watching Liz wave her hands in disarray.

"Sara, I had reservations about bringing you to my viewing room. It's proved to be a tremulous and caustic experiment. Maybe I should inform your sister that I think we should put any more visits by her on hold until we can address…." "Oh, no, Doctor, you can't do that, Liz… please, I would die, um, I have to see her next week, Liz. I'm sorry; I just lost it temporarily. I will promise to be on my best behavior."

A frown, then Liz said, "will you follow me into the adjoining room? I have made up my mind to engage you with another homeopathic… perspective. The treatment plan is unorthodox. It can either have major positive results or could set you back into another fugue. It's another therapy I've never used before. I…" "Doctor, please, no more medications, please, or restraints" "no, that's not where I was going with my thought process and discussion. Can you please not interrupt me, Sara?" I shook my head in aggreance.

"So your first video showing was the initial shock method to show you… your personality deficit and Schizophrenic disorders. This is in the same realm theme but with a smoother transition. I know you said you didn't want to continue watching yourself interacting with your alter egos, but if you want me to allow your sister to visit next week, you will oblige me." I was angry, but what could I do but acquiesce? Stepping past the threshold into the nearly vacant room with two couches and a loveseat? There was a small 'Twin' bed, a wet bar, and a refrigerator with a much smaller monitor attached to the wall.

"Please sit on the couch and make yourself comfy here are a few pillows, this time, you're going to be in charge of what you see or don't view. It's up to you. The monitor in front of you will be powered up," Liz takes a laptop out of a desk. She starts it up, slipping in a memory disk, then places it in front of Kam with a thick folder of forms and paperwork. "I have personally spent hours researching your history like a prized pupil as far back as High School and have isolated and selected approximately 75 minutes of recorded video for you to check out. I'll be alongside you if, at any time, you want to discontinue this experiment; we can and will!"

Kam mulls over another disastrous video display of schizophrenia with her sister's insanity, but if she wants to have the demon visit next week, she must pass this test! "Now I want to pre-empt you… This video has some statements and questions that I'd enjoy or like your input on at any time. We are currently being taped with three cameras in use, both audio, and video, so that we can review our interactions again. This is a learning experience, innovative and risky!" I was sketchy, to say the least, and had to admit there had to be residual drugs in my system, perhaps melting at this very moment, and I felt queasy.

"Let me say that I am highly impressed with your Resume from what I've gleaned… you graduated with honors at the top of your class at U.C. Berkeley with degrees in Psychology and Forensic Psychiatry, three years at Kaiser Permanente, residency work, and a Ph.D. Sara, you had follow-up courses and then received a bachelor's degree at the renowned Stanford University in Business Administration very impressive, and on top of all that… you mastered the Real Estate profession. You were an entrepreneur having a successful business with offices in San Rafael, San Diego, and L.A. I'm highly impressed, young lady. When they arrested you, your main office in Marin County had 21 employees! You are educated or, shall I say, overeducated. I haven't a position here at NIA that you couldn't excel at, Sara!"

Kamryn had a matching pedigree in Economics etc. I wondered where Liz was going with this narrative. I didn't have to wait long! "Before you started your Real-estate business Sara, amazingly, at your peak, you had three offices in Marin County employing… what 17 Psychiatrists. From what I can learn, all three practices were phenomenally successful with high-end clients. This went on for years. Why did you abruptly close down two of the 3 Psychiatric Offices, reducing your patient load? Why?" "Why is this relevant, doc?" "Liz, call me Liz, just curious, not trying to pry, let's just do some girl chat-like friendly interaction, Sara. Please, I am eager to learn and understand you. I'm here only to help you, so please play along!"

'Kam was bored, silly Wtf?' Get to the point, man, she thought but kept her mouth closed, just listening. "A few minutes back, you watched yourself play act… out your imaginative office manager Donny, but Sara, he wasn't your imagination, was he? He was as real as you and me, not fictitious, but reality-based. You're in such a quandary of mixed dimensions that you don't know the real world from the fractional or fantasy. Let's face the truth with Integrity. Now that you have had some elixir in the iced tea, this should relax you and allow you to drop your natural defenses to break through your force fields and open your mind for this therapeutic form of release and to elicit an epiphany of whom you are and can be… so humor me okay Sara?"

At that point, if I had a dagger, I'd jam it down her throat; she'd drugged me with the iced tea. Geez, talk about 'Déjà Vu.' That's how my sister got me. I had to keep my cool what was the word, oh yeah, um, Compartmentalize? That's why I felt like I didn't give a shit about anything, just blasé whatever, no prob. I thought, let's do this boring reenactment if this brings my deadly Twin here to NIA to visit. I will do nearly anything. This is like fkn Deja-Vu; just like my sister drugged me using Iced Tea, this piece of shit Doctor does the same thing. I can't trust anyone. No wonder I feel so confused, paranoid, and dazed! I was thinking like in a loop. Didn't I just think that ughhhh! Drugs…

Liz patiently waited until I stopped fidgeting around and looked into her eyes… "So why did you close the Psychiatric offices?" "I grew bored. I didn't just close my other offices; I sold them for a combined 235% profit to another Doctor's group. I kept a small base of patients. Liz, my sister, and I are 'Trust Fund' babies. It wasn't about monies or the sales!" "Thanks for clearing that up. It's a start, so your secretary, his name was Don Feline or Donny he." "Liz, why did you bring him up?" "Please try not to be so defensive. There is a method to my madness!"

Kam decided to play along in this charade of her being Sara. For sure, she had made Don's acquaintance via phone. As far as she was concerned, it was Al using his vocal skills. Kamryn spoke almost daily with Sara when she lived in New York City. "Sure, okay, Don was my everything office manager, secretary, gopher, even lover, so what? He was the glue that held the doors open at the 4th street San Rafael office. He was irreplaceable and invaluable, so where's this going?" "Sara, listen, I'm only trying to understand your motives for…." "Liz, this feels more like an interrogation, fk. Are you writing a book or something shit!" "Shall we continue if you want your sister's visit to be approved? Let's get past this, okay?" *'There it was, the outright blatant threat, or was it bribery? Yeah! Ms. Liz Honcho of Integrity, my ass… not!'*

"I will not broach a single topic that isn't relevant or doesn't relate with the 75 minutes of your video interviews with Police and investigators, newspapers, etcetera… please humor me!" "Liz, there's nothing humorous about this subject matter to me." "Please remain calm. I'm here only to help you. Let me fast-forward a bit. For I remember your negative press, all your interviews, and front-page news, they railroaded you out of town. What were your exact words that became the most played phrase by the morning disc jockeys? It was all over the Radio? It even made it to Saturday Night Live celebrity status, Sara! Heck, it became a craze even here at NIA shirts were made putting your words into print <u>'If I were you, I'd jump. Jump, do it!'</u> 'Then the War Veteran Hero jumped off the Golden Gate Bridge all on real-time videotape broadcasted around the globe' Liz clicked on the Laptop. 'Here it is, your patient, aah, Mr. Fred Flight jumping to his death suicide, umh, then the world went down the drain for you, didn't it?" Liz paused to see if there was a reaction from Sara, but she remained unmoved.

"Lawsuits galore, Fred's family went after you… you were tied up in litigation for years, the Medical Board pulled your licenses, you were suspended, your liability Insurance wasn't enough, and you were subpoenaed and ended up in Civil Court, correct?"

Kam remembered this tragic situation and was there for her sister. It was an awful time. That's when Sara started drinking and, for a short time, got involved primarily in other heavier drugs, including Cocaine. Whatever drug Liz had slipped into my tea, I decided they weren't a bad thing; they actually had me feeling mellow, but ole Liz wouldn't get another drink by her 'fool me once on you, fool me twice my fault!'

In fact, it was Kam's idea for a career change for Sara, and she'd flown out to San Rafael to visit her distraught sister, put her into a rehabilitation center to get her off the Cocaine and alcohol, again being the loyal sibling, uh what a freakin sucker I was uhm am... "So, Sara, you bounced right back up. I admire your tenacity and resilience. You fell back on your business degree and parlayed that with a Real Estate license. You had a wildly resounding successful chain of offices in less than three years. Your agents were selling upper-scale homes, mansions, beachfront, and commercial properties, then went into property management and development. Geez, there you were in Magazines, became a Jet-setter, you were a star among the stars!"

"I'm sorry, Liz, but why is any of this relevant? Uh, what does this have to do with being locked up in this Insane Asylum, ugh, factory?" "Quite the contrary, it has everything to do with your mental state of mind. You were able to blend in Society with lucrative prominent business endeavors. You headlined Real Estate Seminars and were on the front lines, Sara. Your business acumen in the real estate industry was on the cutting edge, innovative strategies you were always at the Vanguard of any breakthroughs." She took up her tea and sipped. <u>Indeed, when Liz looks back at this video recording of our interview, she'll see when I switched out my drugged tea for hers, lol.</u> "Without further Ado, I will play the first clip or segment. It's only a 5-minute skit with no interruptions. Let's watch, okay." She hits play on her remote, and the scene unfolds. Kam sees her sister standing in her cell, waving her arms, slowly walking, and then she sits down. <u>*'Doctor Ame, I was being picked on; what would you do? So I threw my voice and imitated the bully, Ralph. He was in the front row of the classroom. The teacher asked us students what the capital of Florida was. I*</u>

*made Ralph say, "whom the fk cares?" he was called to the office."
"Then a different voice with authority says, Al, how did that make
you feel?"*

"Liz, what is this? Huh, we've established that Ame, Donny, and Al are prime inhabitants of Sara's schizophrenic mind. This is getting old and boring I mean, please already get to the point..." "Kamryn, you're not paying attention; please, enough with the argumentative attitude. Can't you hear the octaves, intonations, and the voice patterns are precise, even your voice? You couldn't tell the difference, so what? Yes, this is a certainty!" "Sorry, Liz, but haven't we already concluded that Sara, or call it Al, is a master ventriloquist? He imitated my voice and yours expertly, so what...." "Shush, Shut up!' Look at this video. It was before we stopped the security cameras from filming in the Salon. This was only you, Sara, who was speaking to Ame and arguing with Al and then Don. The argument was escalating, then your sister Kam's voice could be heard with Liz trying to calm them all down. Must I back up the video recording? I find it amusing to listen to my unique voice being spoken by Al. Not only that, but my sentiment was dead-on with the words I would have said in the playacting situation I've said... <u>'Shut up, Or I will Lock you all up in solitary confinement!'</u> uhm, too many times to count!"

Liz punches play again, and we see... Sara was fuming and berating her with the words, <u>'Doctor Honcho, I have a contract with NIA, and I will be dammed if you're going to stop me from seeing my clients Sara and Al. Ain't no fkn way I will go to the board, Honcho' 'Doctor Amaya, please control yourself. Be professional. Let's talk this out?' 'Honcho, you need to butt out said, Sara. My Doctor is Ame Amaya... 'Al, please contain yourself,' Don interjects. Kam says," Sister, please calm down, Sista. Mine your own business!'</u>

Liz finally clicked pause, laughing and slapping her knees... Kam was beyond flabbergasted. She had just witnessed her sister carry on a six-person show. Each one of them had utterly diverse and unique voices with expressions to match their conversations that flowed rationally. Every one of the characters was copacetic, aligned, animated, and entrenched on the same page. Sara could do a One-person theatric performance, but once again, this was a redundant and useless waste of time! .

After Liz stops the bizarre macabre performance, she exclaims, "I've watched this numerous times, and so has your Uncle Terrance Hallinan and our entire Hierarchy. You're invaluable. It's astounding how if I closed my eyes, I'd swear it was me talking, you're an amazing imitator, but your other talent is equally impressive. You're an artist, a woman that can change anyone's appearance. Take your Ventriloquism and makeover skills. You could be another piece of our progressive machine here at NIA. We need your skill base here, Sara; your skills are second to none. I want you to consider joining your Uncle and our team!" I'm trying not to act weird, but Liz was freaking me out.

"I, or let's say… We need your special skills, uhm, and attributes. You have so much to offer our NIA militia, umh, team. I will leave it to that for now. Still, Sara, you will be attending a high-level conference soon. Our military advisors could use your talents on some of the upcoming missions to our utmost advantage! Ah, and you, little lady, your benefits for joining our team and cohesively working to meet our steadfast goals can be rewarding, Sara. Uhm, what we could do by adding your expertise to our team of mercenaries?" Liz suddenly glared at her cup of tea, then looked at me and smirked largely, showing her teeth. Realizing that Sara had switched up the tainted tea… Liz was getting loose-lipped knowing she better be quiet until Terrance approves this line of discussion.

"I will have you escorted back to your cell now!" "Wait, WTHeck do you want of me here? What is this place, NIA?" Then I shut up, for I remembered Sara telling me it was a training facility for the Russian Mafia or something bizarre like an American militia group, uuhhh, the SOJ... State of Jefferson. Like a terrorist group on American soil infiltrating facets throughout the United States. God, I had thought what a conspiracy freak, but now whatcha think? I was drugged, so all of this might be my imagination next thing you know, I was back in Sara's cell.

I almost found some odd comfort in being locked down in this prison cell. I was exhausted by the visit of five hours with Liz, but in the end, she promised to listen to what proof I had, and she'd be open-minded. I again told her that she wasn't speaking to Sara and that I was Kamryn. I passed right out for the following few hours, and then bang didn't sleep a wink from that point. The next thing I knew, a breakfast tray was passed through the door. I tried to rest my stinging eyes and couldn't break from the thought that Sara was with my fiancé on his parent's houseboat. Sara had quizzed me repeatedly about my relationship. Still, oddly I didn't catch any foreboding vibes at the time... Sara wanted to know where the houseboat was moored on Lake Shasta. Not so odd now... that I understood her plan and how she'd bring it to fruition, huh? Sara needed to know where Brock was, for there were many resorts to choose from on Shasta Lake.

If there were one individual Sara hated more than any human alive, it would be Brock, my fiancé's real first name. After what I've learned from her drawings and the meeting yesterday with Liz, vengeance is all that fuels her. Sleepless, Zombie material, the guard at 11 am was again going to be escorting me to Liz's office. This time I would lay out the proof and see if I could speak with my Uncle and have the authorities check out the houseboat that Sara, I believed, was now on with my husband-to-be.

<u>The following day I awoke early in the morning with optimism!</u>

I sat across from Liz, "Sara, how are you today?" "Liz, I want to get right to it. Please listen and analyze what I have to say to you. After this morning's meeting, I believe you will come to the same conclusion as any rational person." "Sara, there isn't any reason to be condescending, but as I promised you yesterday, I will listen to your story!" "Okay, here's an example; do you remember a couple of visits back you were at your desk speaking to me and knocked over your coffee?" Liz had a startled expression, but I soldiered on. "While you were talking to your husband, you swore and hung up on him and almost fell when you rolled your chair back and stood up! Liz, you were wearing pink slacks with a white shirt, right?" Liz stopped breathing. Her face flushed "how the hell would you know that?" Rollin her shoulders. She looked into Kam's face "what else can you tell me?"

A knock on the door "Doctor Honcho, the Warden, needs you upstairs immediately. It's urgent." "Oh, all right, could you have someone take Sara back to her cell, please!" She turns to Kam and says, "we will continue this subject matter tomorrow sleep, well tonight!" "Tonight, why can't we get together after you meet with the Warden? This is important!" "Sara, I have meetings the rest of the afternoon. Now I must go!"

Kam had a mini bounce in her step. 'I saw Liz question herself, umh, how the hell did I know about the spilled coffee? She's now uncertain. I have even more ammo to enhance more doubt. Just a speck of doubt now lingers in Liz's head. She'll realize that I was telling her the truth, uh, that Sara had switched us out and escaped NIA. I feel good and believe she will soon know what I'm saying is true. The seed is planted now; I must fertilize and water it. I must scrutinize how I will attack her conscious state with substance and memories that only she and I would know.'

Kam followed a red line on the concrete to her cell, thinking, how about this; 'last year when I bought seven cases of Girl Scout cookies from her Granddaughter, umh, what was her name? Damn, it… wait, umh, 'Dawn,' she was a cutie pie with bright red hair. My purchase had enabled Dawn to be the grand Champion seller of her entire troop!'

There's a glimmer of hope, and where there is hope comes optimism; confidence will build with momentum and guide me through a promising turn of events. The steel door slammed shut behind her closed for the first time when she didn't mind. She ran and jumped up and plopped on the bed with a well-deserved sighing smile! Wondering how my fiancé is doing, my lover and best friend?

-56-

On Shasta Lake, Brock is still on the toilet in the Houseboat.

"Hey, how about a quick shower, Sara? What's the harm? I'm a sweaty mess. I don't have the convenience to jump into the lake, right, so why not… you can contain me here in the bathroom, ah, if yah want to get a thrill and watch me shower. Let me hop in for a few minutes. Hell, you can stand at the doorway and point that gun at me. I'm going nowhere!"

"Brock, this isn't a game here. You seem extremely calm, like relaxed, reserved, and even accepting your eminent demise. It's cool, though… go ahead, shower, and wash your ass. It will be your last. I'd rather have your body clean for what I have planned, for

it is much more convenient than me giving you a fkn sponge bath!" she chuckles.

Brock is sure of a few things, one being that the maniac will kill him, has a gun, and will use it. Two, he will not allow her to tie or chain him down again. This ends today or tonight. He's going out fighting, not groveling on his knees never would beg fk it. She'd have to kill me. Strange how his brain was assimilating all of this life-or-death situation rolling back in time. He supposes being in Law enforcement and the military most of his adult life. That is why Death didn't scare him; heck, all living things die.

Hell… I have seen and been around so much death in my lifetime. He'd absorbed three bullets in self-defense, taken five lives of criminals, and was credited for 17 kills in the Middle East that could be traced to his weapons. I watched the love of my world, Agent Lucie Link, leap from the balcony. I moved on. Lucie sadly is confined to a wheelchair and is Paraplegic.

Amazingly I found another 'Angel' Kamryn, who is now incarcerated in NIA because of the devil that stood before me.

If I have to take another bullet or three, uh, it'll be worth it… this will be determined when Sara is within five feet of me. I will leap at high-speed, swiftly attack and disable her, turning my body, so most of my vital organs are not exposed when she shoots me! I had made a firm decision to fight, live or die. I wasn't going to be restrained again. Being vulnerable before, unable to move with her in control of me, was the worst physical feeling I'd ever had, and mentally it was frustratingly exhausting.

"Sara, the Authorities will never rest after you murder an FBI Agent, uh me! Are you aware that all my fellow Agents and the Director of the FBI know that I'm out here on Lake Shasta, and next Thursday, a boatload of my friends, including many Law Enforcement Officers with spouses and children, umh, their significant others were going to join Kam and me out here so…!"

"I don't really give a rat's ass or care. You're the only loose 'link' uh, get that one, Lucie Link," cackling. "I'm free to live my life as I see fit. Kam has taken my place. You're the only person alive who could expose me. Unfortunately, there's no deal, no way, really, Brock, what can I do? I'm forced to kill you. Try and put yourself in my shoes. What choice do I have? With you out of the way and Kam locked up? I own my destiny!" Sara clapped her hands together, smirking. "Think about that, and Brock give me an alternative?" as she grins with resolve. He tries some of his logic, "perhaps you haven't examined this dilemma as methodically or in detail as you might think. Typically there are other options and interpretations. Remember, you are a sole survivor and thinker. I have other opinions and feel you're missing the ultimate repercussions of Kamryn's disappearance. She oversees an entire division of a financial team for Schwab, has dozens of associates and colleagues, and travels with many of them to New York on business. She has literally dozens of close friends who will be here for our Wedding, and next week, about 15 of them are showing up for a pre-party at a campground right on this Lake on the Shasta Arm where this houseboat is supposed to be. How will you replace her, Sara? You're never going to be able to fool her friends. You have a 'Zero' personality and are a Sociopath. It's like talking to a fkn Robot communicating with you!"

He thinks he has her reeling, so he adds to his advantage; "you might resemble her physically, but your no match for her vivacious personality, her quirkiest behaviors her closest friends have shared so many experiences, memories no way for you to take her place she has one-of-a-kind relationships and clicks… Deals are pending, associates. You're a fish outta water Sara! It would be like a fkn duck floating on molten lava… impossible, Sara!" He scrunched up his nose and continued, "Kamryn, inside and out, is all good, a wonderful human being she is…." "Shut the fk up! Hurry up in the shower. Yeah, you're absolutely correct about sticking out like a sore thumb and replacing goodie two shoes at her place of employment, but as I see it, that will never happen. See, Brocky, accidental drowning will be the Medical Examiners' ruling once you end up missing. This will be assumed because your body will never be found. I being sweet Kamryn, I'll play oh so fkn distraught I will go into a self-imposed exile… I will cease to exist. Yep!"

Sara hits the wall with the gun, "after your body has been missing for a while, Kam's world will be flipped over. She will be in a quagmire of depression. I will never return to her place of employment. Nope, I'll ask for a temporary leave of absence from work. I will stop my weekly visits to NIA. The 'tragic loss of you, my love' will be the impetus or the propulsion, if you will, thrusting me into the limelight and out of my comfort zone. After this quick burst of notoriety, I will literally disappear, which would seem normal in the realm of things you know to mourn and languish in the grief-laden darkness play the world's belief of how the bereavement process works and how humans are supposed to be and are accepted. Lol! Brock, with all your research about me. I'm surprised that you don't understand how I think. You are aware of my College degrees in Psychology…." "Yes, Sara, I know you were privileged to have the coffers of your Papa, who put together a trust fund with your Uncle Terrance Hallinan, the piece of shit attorney that I battled against in your case. Sure you have been blessed with the proverbial Silver Spoon…." "Screw you, Brock, I was born into a cursed existence with… ahh enough!" "Why'd you get all worked up? Sara, I was only stating." A foreign sound of a boat motor getting closer stopped all dialogue. After a few minutes, the rumbling, revving engine disappeared.

"Cum on, Brocky, let me play this out for you. Your dreary doomsday prologue can be my epilogue turned inside out too. Think, feel this! The grieving bride… to be sympathy garnered after your body hasn't been found for a month or so. I will tell everyone I can't go on. I need to get the hell away. I'll pack up and move to Europe gone… money has never been a concern. Buy a flat in London or Paris, and then I can get back on track with my life's work! Lol, Sara Sloan is back from the dead!" She Snickers into a laughing howl. Yup!

"Except Brockbaby, umh, my name, and M.O. will change. I have learned from my mistakes. I was too brazen and allowed my immaturity and vengeance for retaliation to take me down. If I hadn't gone after your Agent Lucie Link, I would have walked; you Fed's hadn't any clues or evidence all circumstantial. It was my stupidity; I'll admit that now but I will not make any more errors in this life. I promise you that, and FYI, remember I promised you that I'd get you, and here we are. I don't break promises, Yea!"

"Oh, you mean re-start the Vipress Serial Killer Act?" "Why not, everywhere you turn, any civilizations involving human beings have and will always include lewd and lascivious, cheating, unfaithful lustful, salacious, and lecherously immoral men and women, hearts broken emulsified drained shredded of all hope, lives snuffed out!" "Wow, what an overwhelming crusade, a campaign of twisted retribution in your convoluted warped, twisted minds, as in plural… bizarrely, you can call this a justifiable murder. *How do you categorize the killing of me? I've never strayed or cheated on any woman in my life. I am like you would say, Integrity based oh, and do I need to remind you, Sara, you wrote me letters about my moral fortitude and behaviors? Of how you desired me wanted me as your man because I quote, 'Brock, you're my soulmate, a moral and*

I'm watching her, knowing those insanity-laden eyes from the night before when she was going off about the female assassins now a softer, more maternal female-ish gleam. She lowers the gun to her lap sitting near the entrance of the bathroom. I was toweling off!

After the longest silence, a super pause between us, she nodded, then morphed and seemed to regain her balance, re-fortified with hate! "Brock, I certainly desired you. I still get wet thinking of us, but in a bizarre twist, my sister caught you so weird, like we were always meant to be my look and our body types. You have a pheromone affinity towards Lucie, my twin, and me. Even your Ex Patti looks a lot like us. You're attracted to the petite female body style, especially blonde!... Dude speaking for me, I'm enthralled by your body type and macho persona. We could have been so grand together, Brock fk, but I gotta kill you. Sad Huh!" "Sara, you don't have to do anything, girl. We can work this out!" She disregarded his words.

"Way weird wrong still blows me away how you and Kam hooked up unreal, and your death will not be appetizing, not in the least it's true I haven't a bone of contention to pick with you. Brock, you are also correct that I have zero remorse and regrets. I never lamented any of the necessary killings. No, or for that matter, albeit, uhm, the accidental deaths I was responsible for were my bad… I guess, but they were merely collateral damage. I never felt the need to repent. With that being said, I will not, as I usually do enjoy my handiwork. Your demise will be sad, but 'in the end,' your only like the other Agents, just collateral damage, my dear boy; bad luck if you will!" .

Brock realizes that even with the gun held loosely in her lap, she was too far away to lunge and grab her without a frontal bullet or three, so suddenly, he kicks the bathroom door shut in her face and ducks to the side of the threshold no shots fired, instead no noise except his heavy breathing of anticipation…

Next, he hears her sarcastic overtones mixed with laughter… through the thin door. "Now, Brockbaby, what do you think you accomplish by locking yourself in that bathroom? Honey, you can't climb out that cubby hole of a port hole window. I sit here comfortably with nine bullets in the chamber. In the bag by my leg, I have a Police Edition Stun gun, my special squirt gun with my magic potion of poison, and all sorts of toys for our Sexual fantasies cum on out, Brocky!" Brock said nothing, 'knowing he was royally screwed, only delaying the inevitable, he'd have to lunge at her and take the chance; oh well!'

"Hey stud, you know I haven't been laid in way over five years, so I was planning on some 'Cowgirl Action' with yah, kind of kinky you restrained spread Eagle me taking a ride on your hard pogo stick even brought along a cow-girl hat and bandana!" "Not going to happen, Sara!" "Don't rain on our parade of fun. Guess what I found on Kamryn's iPad. Yep, you and my older sister doing it 'wet and wild,' umh, the whip-cream, and the kitchen table, bouncing into the hot tub. <u>Oh yeah, a 'flick your clit promotion' indeed. Hell, you should open your own Porno production, Brockster! Whew, so very sexy, yum, delish, yummy!" "Shut up, Sara, you bitch!" "aah, did I get under your skin, Brockster? Now cum on out of there, and you can get under my skin too,"… she giggles Evilly.</u> .

"Now, you need to hurry up and open that door. We don't want to destroy your parent's houseboat, do we?" I opened the door and showed my luscious dimples, grinning confidently, the opposite of how I'd felt…. "This is how I see it, Sara; logically, I have to die accidentally for your plan to work, right?

Bullet wounds would lead the FBI directly to you and this houseboat, and then you're finished before you start your European escapade! I've investigated too many drownings. There is an inherent problem with me drowning here in Lake Shasta. First, no question that my body will float to the top of the lake, for with the natural gases bodies release, I will become bloated and buoyant and float to the surface. If you try to anchor me down, the forensic scientists will ascertain the undeniable trademarks of being weighted down fact foul-play murder." Sara glowered at me confidently. "Oh, I'll humor you if you must go ahead and keep running at the mouth and waste more oxygen."

"My body will float back to the water's surface. It's a fact, Sara, that all bodies in this lake that had drowned have arisen. This is a manmade lake ain't nowhere for my body to become lodged. Nope, your history, girl. Suppose I have a bullet hole. Then you're busted. If I have ligature marks, busted, poison in my system, uh, you're guilty of murder, the Medical Examiner will use the proverbial fine-tooth comb. I'm FBI Sara. The investigation will be relentless, and my death will lead directly back to you. Please don't be so futile not to believe that Kamryn isn't using all of her substantial resources to get the staff and your Uncle to believe what you've done. Ughhhh, no doubt Kam is making a viable case at NIA that you impersonated her and escaped. Not even an inept 'Mayberry Sheriff' couldn't umh wouldn't come to the conclusion that you Sara…!"

She screams out of control, "Enough, Brock, quite enough. I'm growing bored with all your bullshit!" "Woman, I am unlike many others. I haven't a fear of death. I don't fear death, as funny as it may seem. The only thing I fear is 'Betrayal aligned with Deception' by someone whom I have released my Spirit, Soul, and Heart to a person whom I Love. I'll admit it I have a fear of commitment. I'd rather die than have another woman hurt me with lies, deceit, and chicanery. I'm in your car there, Sara. As unlikely as that sounds, women I have loved and given my all to have always terrorized me, frauds, double-dealing hypocrites. A woman's treachery knows no bounds. My heart cannot handle any more pain! You took from me Lucie, the love of my life forever. Now I've found another soul-mate, my Loving fiancé and wife-to-be Kamryn. You murdered my ex-Patti-Dame wow, shit. I feel like I'm decomposing, rotting. If not for Kam's plight, I'd gladly give myself up to you. Kill me. I don't give a fk no...." Sara rubbed her forehead forlornly. His last words had apparently touched home in her psycho-fractured minds. Brock hopes he can get within 7 feet of her.

"Enough elucidation on your behalf preaching to the choir what are we going to do? I truly can't find anything about you that I dislike. I kinda admire you, and you know, Luv u a tiny bit, Brock. I know it's like so weird. You're the first man that I have felt this way about. You're as good as it gets for me within your gender; I can't let you go free. We will not be married and live forever in Bliss!" "Why not Sara... why the hell not? Why couldn't we get hitched?" <u>Silence pervades and permeates... his words echo off of her inner chambers within her diverse mindset... thoughts provoked, umh, possibilities stoked. Sara mulls over her response with giddiness.</u>

<u>-57-</u>

<u>Kam at NIA... Optimism Reigns.</u>

Dinner banged through the cell door. Not hungry, flipping back over #189 took her appetite away. Al killed our beloved Papa, poisoning him years after her parents died... he was the only close family Kam had left. Papa truly loved her, but unfortunately, after his daughter, uhm, my mother and father died. Papa couldn't take care of both my sister Sara and me. Since one of Sara's entities was Papa's favorite, Al... who was a budding ventriloquist with a bunch of talent, Papa decided to raise Sara. I was sent once again to my Aunt Tammy and Uncle Jason in New York.

Fortunately, my Aunt could take me in, and she nurtured me for the first few years. It wasn't fun! I studied hard and got lost in my schoolwork, and read a ton of books, living in a fantasy land of fiction. Kam had been shipped off several times, going back and forth from New York to California during her childhood. Ugh, it wasn't a stable childhood, but she can't complain. Unfortunately, my Aunt re-married and abandoned her and her mother's maiden name <u>Sloan.</u> Kamryn was staring at corroboration of what Liz had shown her on video that Al indeed killed their adorable Grand-Papa.

Aunt Tammy wasn't immune to our genetic flaws and was arrested a couple of years ago for attacking her new Mother-in-law. This raised suspicions that she'd poisoned her previous mother-in-law and thus that Cold Case was back on the burner. Then the authorities exhumed my Uncle, and toxicology testing proved that he'd been murdered, ughhhh, poisoned with antifreeze, making his sweet tea even Sweeter. 🌿. It turned out that Uncle Jason had a hefty life insurance policy... Auntie Tammy would be locked up for the rest of herlife, and so goes the 'Sloan Curse!'

Papa left all his monies, his entire fortune, to a Trust Fund. He would never be there for them physically, but he left them a great start in this life. He was a compassionate man. Sure he had his demons, yet he had overcome so much adversity, a more muscular-willed man she'd never know. How could 'Al-Sara' kill Papa Sloan? Heartless, evil. Is there really any justification for the God-fearing people to believe in a higher power of righteousness watching us?

Brushing the stream of tears from her cheeks, break time, another long shower, and to get away from the peeping Tom's and be able to think. Time alone with hot water spraying on my body. Re-wrapping her soft cast, the injuries were healing, and feeling better. She twisted the faucets and waited for the water to heat up. Sits down in the tiny cubicle, the only escape from prying eyes. The steam surrounds her, then the worry comes back into her head, missing her Fiancé… her resolve was slowly melting at times. It was a task to breathe involuntarily, this being the case at that very instant.

I felt wired out from thinking with worry and stress for like 15 hours consecutively. My brain and mind only wanted to rest. The exertion of constantly being on point was exhausting continual strain struggling to strive relentlessly nonstop. This situation was urgent; even dire exigencies personified Sara could be in the houseboat right now! Being all alone led her to purposely change her inclination to dwell upon the loathsome reality that she had failed to reconcile with the nonacceptance of her theme. The meeting with Liz empowered her that a plan was in force. But that energy was sapped by the fact that she was locked in Prison without a recourse. Could she die here at NIA?

It was a conflict of attrition, pessimism vs. optimism… umh, can I convince her that I'm not Sara a remembrance secured her mindset. Approximately nineteen months ago, during an Impromptu meeting on New Year's Eve, Brock and she were at a fantastic Ball downtown San Francisco, the magnificent Opus One Theater at this gallant extravaganza. She had bumped into Liz knocking her champagne out of her hand then. They recognized one another and started laughing; Liz and her husband joined Edward and her at their club seats after some small talk.

We all had drinks and appetizers, hit it off, and had a grand time cheering as the clock struck midnight. We jumped up and down, hugged and even kissed each other, and continued celebrating until about 1 am. How could Liz forget that… this would undoubtedly prove that I am Kamryn? I even tripped her husband, George, with him falling over me onto the dance floor. I gave them my old business card with the words, 'sorry, George, for tripping you. Happy New Year's, Kamryn and Edward.' After I replay this to Liz, I'm outta here. She can't deny that Sara would not know of that night 19 months plus ago… done deal!

Then with grandiosity peaking as a backup strategy, if I could have a face-to-face with Uncle Terrance Hallinan, our family attorney, I could easily convince him of my true identity. We have too much history. We became inseparable during Sara's trial. Papa was his childhood friend from elementary school. Crazy 'ole Sara' with a tempered smile flicks across her dimples. She has underestimated me and my relationships with relevant and distinguished individuals; I will be free soon!

If all goes well, I should be out of here in the next few days with the incriminating drawings. A case or cases could be made against dear Lil sister circumstantially, albeit hell, the one picture of the blonde girl tossing the boom box radio into the hot tub is proof enough, correct? Ruled accidental no, yeah, better re-open that puppy… Daddy was murdered by his seven-year-old daughter Sara along with the slutty neighbor. Kam stood up invigorated and soaped up and nearly felt like singing a tune… Not. Rinsed and stepped out feeling 101% better than when she entered the enclosed shower after drying off and slipping on a robe, feeling revitalized and raring and ready to do a mental battle with Liz and her Uncle.

Now she wished that she had eaten something for dinner. Lol, no room service here, yet the cafeteria stayed open until 9 pm. It was only 7:55 pm; aah, what the hell? She reached out and pushed the Emergency call button by the steel doors opening. 'Sloan, what's up?' 'I'm hungry, wishing for a sandwich or whatever?' 'hold on, Sloan, it says here on your chart you didn't eat anything on your dinner tray!' 'I know my stomach was upset.' There was silence, no reply for an inordinate amount of time.

'Sloan, Doctor Honcho left orders for us to comply with any requests for food, so a sandwich and some cottage cheese with vegetable soup is on its way!' 'Well, thank you very much...' 'Don't thank me. I wouldn't care if you starved to death chewing and cannibalizing your own body parts. It would be a fitting end for a non-human such as yourself! It's my job bitch... True-that!' The sounds of a cackling rooster came over the speakers.

I walked away. Wow, what an admonishment one thing for sure, that dude didn't like me, and he was delivering my food may be better just to let him vent and be nonchalant, flipping on the television, 'geez, I wonder if I should even eat the food such hate deservedly... uhm well if I were Sara?'

Letting her mind drift into one of the 'fake reality shows,' a farce totally scripted by amateurs, what the populace buys... believes. They should really be named 'unreality shows,' but whatever sells to the brain-dead masses!

Shasta Lake Houseboat, Sara's dilemma.

Brock had ducked once more into the houseboat bathroom to towel off... "Tell you what I'm going to do, Sara. I will open this door in a towel and walk out your options are plain and clear. Shoot me dead with the 38 caliber. Or fire the projectile prongs of the Stun gun you say you have... or shoot me with the poison. That's up to you, but here is a fact you can chew on. I won't allow you to cuff me back down on that bed if you're planning to kill me, then let's get it done... K whatcha think, Sara?"

"Brock, despite my feelings for you, don't dare to misjudge my instinctual drive to survive if it's you or me. Your history, Dude. Have you forgotten I'm a 'PsychoSociopath?' Sure, killing you will cause a bout of indigestion like a Fart... puff gone. I will shoot you square between your eyes. That's my only option. You could easily overpower me. You're a lot stronger and have special training in hand-to-hand combat, so if you walk out and approach me, you leave me no other options. You're a dead man!"

"Remember, if you put a bullet in me, your original plan goes down the toilet. It won't work. My body will have...." "That wasn't my entire plan, I..." "umh, I have an idea Sara where you can still keep full control of me and this situation. How about you give me some space and backup? Take out the 50,000-volt Stun gun that will definitely disable me temporarily, at least until I rip the prongs out of my skin, that is." "I'm listening. Go ahead, but don't be upset if your only wasting your breath, boy!"

"I will then make my way back to the bed, and we can discuss alternatives that may be a win-win for us?" Sara thinks to herself that he believes I'm weak-hearted towards him, but the fool hasn't a clue he isn't leaving this boat alive. She decides to play along "okay, I'm ready. Come on out, Brocky!"

The door swings open, and he walks casually out, but... casual was a façade. All he wanted to do was get close enough to pounce, destroy, ah rip Sara's head off her shoulders. But he forced a smile, "you see," as he slowly stepped past her, she was out of reach. He climbs up on the bed, his back against the headboard. Sara had both guns pointed at him, not buying any of his crap, standing with her back against the furthest wall about nine feet off.

"A moment ago, you said something about your entire plan. Please fill me in; I've drank the drug cleaner, so let's pretend that I am back in restraints. How were you going to get me to cooperate? Get me in a boat. I weigh 221 pounds.” “Yup, your one heavy solid man. It was tough as all get out… to drag you down the stairs and get you into the bed. Dragging you back up the stairs will be much more difficult, but I can do it.” “As we have discussed earlier, the M.E. will scrutinize my body. You couldn’t sedate me again. That defeats your purpose of….” “So here is my plan. I was going to stick a funnel down your throat and pour a bottle of Crown Royal in it, wait 15 minutes, and add a bottle of Scotch. You pass out and are fricken completely inebriated… drunk, and blackout.

Then I was going to get the cart that I used to load my stuff from the dock onto the houseboat, load your drunk ass into it, roll you down the beach to where the Ski boat is, and lug your heavy ass into it. Start up the ski boat and pull a sea doo behind the boat, take you to another cove, throw you overboard, being blacked out drunk, you would drown. Then I’d pull the Sea-Doo in, start it up let it go in circles while all that’s left of you is alcoholic bubbles from the bottom of the Lake. Lol!” Brock sat mouth wide open, matching his eyes. “Whew, you are a crazy witch….” “The Sea-Doo would eventually run out of gas when or if your body were found, the cause of death would be alcohol-related. Of course, I would tell the investigators how I begged you to wear a life vest, but you were too macho and drunk!” lol Yep!” �֍.

‘I sat back a lot less relaxed after taking all of her words in’ fk, that plan was mind-blowing, very calculated, flawless even. “I have to admit, Sara, that was brilliant. All sounded plausible. One hitch could have been if you were pulled over at night by a Sheriff boat?” “Wait, Brock, why couldn’t I verbalize a cogent and credible explanation like, umm, my Fiancé drank too much, and I’m taking him back to our houseboat? For you wouldn’t have any marks or injuries. Brock, you would be too inebriated to communicate, just plain ass drunk!” “Sara, that might have been feasible, uh, could have possibly worked, but not any longer, girl!"

Sara smirked and winked, blowing him a kiss… thinking yeah, no, I'm not a paranoid individual. Don't sweat the small things. A Veteran of in-the-moment spontaneity, she relishes a challenge, thinking okay… "So I'll bite; why would I get pulled over by the Police driving the boat? I'd have the running lights on at night and not speeding?" "Sara, if you want to kiss me, get your ass over here…." He chortles, "anyways, you're right; all of that is fine and dandy where it gets sticky. The part IMO that becomes caustic is where you start the Sea-Doo up. It's illegal to ride a Sea Doo at night, with no lights, no excuses, a Red flag, and sure ticket trouble." Rubbing his tongue against his front teeth, an acidic film, 'gotta brush my teeth again.' Brock scowled toward her underneath his skin but kept a nonchalant expression upon his countenance… 'Sara made him nauseous, her kitschy black wig sewed together with the hair of my Kamryn… lover and fiancé straight up sickening ugh. How I hate this Psychotic Bitch. I need to get the upper hand!'

Sara was pissed off muses over this fkn dilemma, even with the best-framed plan's one adaption, an adlib. Here I sit, had everything under my control in place if only I had the stomach to clean up his Ass after he shit-pooped. My phobia has sidetracked my ultimate plan, albeit temporarily. 'How simply stupid, a mistake. Now I have to keep it from being a fatal mortal miscalculation, a misjudgment that could cost me my life and freedom. Oh, how fkn stupid to let this man out of the restraints!' Maybe I am nuts!'

"I don't know what was in that disgusting liquid you forced down my throat, but I have to get to the bathroom again. Should sell that stuff as a laxative /constipation aid loosens the bowels," he gets up slowly. She follows him, guns drawn, and they return to the bathroom, the sounds of flowing streams of diarrhea the same smell. "Flush it, for hell's sake Brock. Oh, how nauseating!" "Sorry!' he says rather disingenuously, 'it's you that is to be blamed for my raw butt!" "So much for your shower, dude fk. This is brutal."

Washing his hands and brushing his teeth, Sara nods and looks on. This dude is so relaxed, even confident, and here I stand with his life in my hands. I guess the epitome of 'No Fear' I have to admire the guy 'there he was, gargling mouthwash, uuhhh asshole.' "Whew, I feel better now," as he steps back to his comfy position on the bed. "Okay, where were we at? Oh, that's right, your scheming intentions to murder me!" 'She catches a quaint scowl,' a flash perhaps antiquated or maybe not. Was it a smile? She had a hazardous precarious situation of which she had to resolve and control. How? "Brock, I am not a person that enters a fray threadbare, not 'half-cocked.' I've had years to develop the manifestations of my master plan... there are many moving parts calculated integrally with mathematics and denoted integers...." "What the hell, Sara, stop with your mumbo-jumbo will yah you do not impress me with your words, cuz you make zero sense. What are you trying to do? Please don't try and show me how you have mastered the English vocabulary. Don't think so, girl, so my analytical, scholarly, profound, and highly efficient murderess spit it out in plain-ass street dialogue. You sit there like a giant kitty cat that has trapped a fat juicy rat!"

Laughter emits from her cruel unsavory lips. He listens and thinks to himself, 'she's like a Cirrhosis, a disease that thinks she holds an Ace that finishes this 'card game' a full-on Royal Flush.' "Brockster, I'm not all that alone here. I have a partner, dude" smirking, he guffaws, "sure, girl," and decides to continue egging her on sarcastically, raising his arms palms outward to his sides. _"Aah, woman, unless I missed it, umh, it's only us out here on the lake. Is your partner or conspirator invisible? Oh, wait, I know; geez, why didn't I think of it, Sara?_

Her temper erupts, red-faced anger rising. She cocks the 38-caliber "funny, huh, really funny you are having a blessed time over there?" "Sara, don't let your lack of control over all your multiple whacked-out personalities get the best of you thus far; you've maintained well; I am impressed. Tell me, am I still speaking to Sara, or are you, Wilma? I'm Fred Flintstone…" he starts hacking hard, laughing hysterically, slapping his thighs "oh crap, maybe I went into the wrong profession. Could have been a comedian!" .

"Brocky, you got some balls… gall, but don't you see I control your fate, Boy, and your woman's fate. Just as I took care of your Ex-wife Patti Dame, dead and cremated, and don't forget how I diminished your lovely bride to be… poor-poor Poor Lucie Link, she's now a paraplegic who thought she could fly… now broken wings brain dead yay. Yuh, see, I have beaten you at every turn. I win, you lose. Now I am on a straightaway coasting downhill. I will place my foot on the pedal, and you will be fumes gas from my ass!" Yeah.

'Well, ouch, she's got me there. If I allowed those words into my mind and heart, they would eat me like a toxic acid. No, I must keep on rolling forward in this debate to break her resolve!' "Sara, you truly missed your calling. It would help if you wrote Horror Flicks… Novels that, ultimately, the predator makes one final mistake like dominoes, her world caves in, and she mutates into a polliwog!" lol. 'Humorlessly, they locked into tunnel vision stare down… pause' "But you have piqued my interest. Didn't you say that you control my woman's fate? How so she's in NIA, your replacement. She is far away from your tentacles, and BTW, why don't you take her hair off your head? It's disgusting, don't you think?" .

510

"On the contrary, pal, your assumption is false although in miles you're correct… but I can still reach out and extinguish Kam's life. Kamryn isn't so far away in reality. I'm confident that you will be fishbait before the night ends. Brockbaby… nevertheless, I am emphatically in the driver's seat. I remain in charge of your pathetic ass… I see your eyes and expressions. You don't like me… dude. No worries, and you can't believe I'm a killer without remorse, just a slaughterer… butcher, a person who indiscriminately murders a brutal and cruel woman who wantonly takes pleasure in eradicating human trash. Yes, that would be correct. I'm a garbage collector extractor compressor. I'm... uh, you're like one of those fricken useless do-gooders ah counselors thinking you'll get in my head for morality's sake, huh? Brockster, I could eat a ham and cheese omelet off your dead ass forehead. I don't have an inkling of empathy for you or anyone. But like the neighbor psychopath, sociopath, I can pretend to care… LMAO. .She was verbally countering him effectively, and the tension in the master bedroom was rising.

"Whew, you're lost, shut-up… girl. What the hell are you insane, stupid, or what? Oh yeah, that's right. Sorry forgot I'd lost count of your many disorders and diagnoses. I can't follow your gibberish. Can't you speak fkn plainly? Your words don't align with mine. Spit it out, will you? Not into word-solving puzzles!" She tossed up her palm. "I'm far from stupid or ignorant there is a plan 'B' and 'C' in my mixed bag of tricks. Hopefully, neither you nor my sister will have to experience either of the alternatives." "I'm terrified; hey, how about something to eat, woman? I'm starving to death, uhm, dying from boredom. I may perish at any second!" grinning. "Humor, huh is that your best way to deal with stress? You make jokes to lessen your fears, Boy?" "Psycho, I'm hungry, okay, so get to your point already. I'd rather die with a full stomach, all right… no, not joking, Sara!"

"Where does a person like you come from? You're a piece of work, Brock. I do like your Cocky to the end attitude but believe me. This will End!" "Hey, why don't you give the Wig a rest? You will never be Kamryn!" "Brocky, I am super-duper comfortable in my skin. *Let's get back on point," she says; they gaze over at the clock radio. "Aah, we're about 17 minutes from your epiphany, and you will clearly see your discombobulated situation. Our parameters and rules will change. I expect your total loyalty and a touching kneel at my dainty toes. You will 'Kowtow' bastard."* 🎵.

-58-

Sara surprises Brock with leverage to control him.

He spies an Evil smug smirk and feels a nervous twinge rush through his veins. She takes out a basic flip phone from a bag and looks across at him, stating, "a burner phone, untraceable throwaway phone, my friend who will be calling uses the same… 'pay attention now Brock,' be quiet. I am going to put the call on speaker unbeknownst to the caller!"

The phone jingles on time "sshhh Brock," "hello," "Hey Sara, how's it going out there?" "Umh, it could be better, but first. Where are you calling from?" "I'm at an 'In and Out' burger in the parking lot, no problems!" "I'm dying for updates. It would help if you filled me in on Kamryn. Don't leave a single thing out; I'm fkn excited now, come on!" raged Sara. "No, that would take hours. Let me give you a quick synopsis. I will summarize points of interest. If you want further details on any of them, stop me, okay?"

512

"Your sister went absolutely fricking berserk beyond what we expected, got out of control hostile, man, she was an aggressive hussy, and actually attacked one of my nurses. She had to be restrained, placed into a Straitjacket, and then sedated. She was injected with a new Psychotropic medication and dropped to the floor instantly like jelly ah, incoherent, ranting and raving like a lunatic. Just like we assumed she would, repeating like a broken record, 'My Name is Kamryn' Not Sara!" "Fk Yay!" Shouted Sara, along with loud crispy cackles smiling and clapping while Brock sat at the end of the bed. He was nauseous and absorbed sickeningly what he was listening to on Sara's phone speaker. He clenched fists and teeth and was highly agitated, disturbed that these deviates were discussing his girl. His heart sunk to new lows, and a queasy feeling ripped his intestines into knots.

"They had to move her to the infirmary where once again she became hysterical. We had her chained to a gurney and shackled. She was delusional on a delirium road trip to hell. It gets even better ohhh after she was injected again with a strong experimental drug. She started hallucinating and shit she…." Abruptly Sara barks, "I have a situation where I might need your assistance. It's not good, and we might have to use our number one pragmatic contingency." "What, Sara, you're scaring me…." "Do you have that lethal dose prepared?"

"Yes, Sara, but as I've told you, it's not a lethal dose. I don't want to do that at NIA. Remember, your sister isn't just anyone. Ole Terrance Hallinan is part of your family. We need not bring on alarms. The dose is waiting on Kam. It will scramble her mind permanently from the injection forward. She will shit piss herself and drool, brain-dead catatonic. She will cease to think on her own or even recognize herself or her life. Ain't that what we want, Sara?"

"All right, so she will essentially be a Zombie, a vegetable isn't that what you're saying?" "The proper medical term is

'Catatonia Schizophrenia with intervals of Catalepsy,' often becoming or morphing into a stupor of violence towards herself or others!" "Renae,' please, I don't give a rat's ass about medical terms. Listen, you have Kam under control, right?" "Yes, Kamryn is in your old cell like we wanted, Sara. Going to move her out soon after I set her up with the contraband. As we discussed, her security level will be dropped, and she'll be locked up next door at the dungeon. Why, what's up, Sara? You are freaking me out. Uh, isn't everything going to plan?" "Renae, have you already been drinking? I told you we have a situation. I need your help with a change of plans!" "I'm all ears, Sara, and no, not buzzed at all. Hope it's not a serious issue!" "Nah, it can be rectified, but it will take your utmost vigilance. You need to stay on your toes!" "No problema!"

Sara takes a huge breath and stares over at Brock measuring his reactions so far, hoping now to see a weakness 'one thing for sure, he's a calculating man who doesn't wear his emotions on his sleeve.' "Renae, if you gave the word or called NIA, how long would it take to put the final injection into Kamryn's vein?" "I would do it myself, Sara. Remember, I'm the head Nurse here, and Kam is mine... she's on my patient load. There would be no reason to call or to have anyone else involved. Keep it all in-house. I could inject her once I started my shift in the morning. It would take perhaps seven minutes for it to start to take effect, then bye-bye, Kam!"

"So, the mixture is already in a syringe with her name on it?" "Yes, as we discussed before you left NIA." Brock stands up. Sara motions with the gun and then pushes mute on the phone. "Brock, do I have your attention now?" He nods reluctantly... affirmative she unmutes, "you, still there, Sara?" "Yep, sure am, Renae. I broke a Cardinal rule by deviating from the original plan. This divergence will cost us some added due diligence on my behalf; it's only time... I or we are still in the prominent position of control!"

"Okay, I have to meet with the husband in 45 minutes to make dinner. What the hell happened? We had this down to a science like $1 + 1 = 2$!" "Look, short story Brock isn't restrained at this time, and we're discussing the upcoming wedding plans that he and Kamryn had put together!" "No, Fkn way. OmLord, no, he's an FBI Agent, no Sara, this isn't going to work. I will be locked up in the dungeon along with you for the rest of our lives. This wasn't part of anything we planned, nor did I want a part of it. Now you got me on Front Street out on an Island or plank they would hang me. I will not see the light of day, girl. You're going down too. He must be eliminated, Sara. I will not ask the obvious question?"

"Oh, let me guess what the obvious question is, Renae, were you going to ask me 'are you fkn insane' cuz yes, I'm certifiably Insane. I understand your anger, but I have paid you handsomely!" "Umm, you can have the Santa Monica Beach House back, Sara, fk this, but let me tell you, I'm no fool either, girl. I've covered my Ass as well. You think I'm wearing blinders, girl, if it comes out that I ended up with your 9-million-dollar bungalow. What are the authorities going to think, Sara?" "Bungalow, my butt, it's a 3,900 square foot Beach house, Renae." "Damnit, you freak, I can't go down for this, fk I should ahhhh…."

"Relax, Renae!…" "My fkn ass Sara you fricken Relax. I'm not part of this fiasco, neither a co-defendant nor a conspirator. This is bullshit. You have nothing on me. I may very well lose my license for conning a patient out of a property, but nothing criminal where is the fkn Agent at? Does he know about me? Geez, Wtf is wrong with me uuhhh? Greed shit? I'll rot in Prison. How, ugh, why did I get involved with a lunatic? Fk, have I lost my mind?"

Sara uproariously laughs loudly, howling, "aah like duh-9 million reasons I'd think it's not time to fold up the tent or run home with your tail between your legs to mommy you're fine because of my error gaffe. I'm going to double down with cash for you to retire in splendid luxury!" A softer tone prevails "you have this under control, Sara. Please tell me there is nothing to worry about?" "Absolutely under control, and you're the optimal key, trust me. Hasn't everything unfolded exactly like I said? The only loose stone or variable is Brock. With him on ice were home free. No worries, Renae; please calm down. You will blow a fuse!" "Sara, you're sure that Carl hasn't a clue of any of this, right?" "No question, he only provided me with outside help with private investigators and stuff. I wouldn't have known that Kam was out there dating Brock without him. He has been suspended for his sexual molestation of me in the closet and will not be at NIA again, I bet. Carl is a docile Lamb without any knowledge, just a pawn, but he will be eliminated anyways!"

With a slight tone… change of acquiescence, "Okay, what do you want from me? Also, you didn't answer my question. Where is Brock, and is he aware of my involvement? How are you going to contain an FBI Agent who already has suffered the loss of one Fiancé, and now his next wife-to-be is locked

down!…" "Geez, Renae, stop with the dramatic, heart-wrenching bullshit. Brock is getting exactly what he deserves."

Brock weighed his options 'should he blare out something and alert this nurse named Renae that he was privy to all and put additional fear in her brain? She seemed nervous enough and apprehensive it was worth Sara's wrath, so he yelled out!' "Renae, I'm sitting here with Sara. Your…" Sara pushed mute with her gun-shaking mouth open like she'd been slapped. "Brock, if you utter one more fkn word, I will have Renae inject Kamryn immediately!"

Unmutes, all they could hear was Renae screaming hysterically and shouting… yelping at the top of her lungs…. Sara grimaced and scowled at Brock… shaking the gun at him, her head wobbling to and fro…. After what seemed an eternity,

"Renae, are you...." "What? You've had me on speaker phone Bitch!" not a question but a statement; Renae's voice morphed into utter tranquility... she was calm and reserved, the opposite of what Sara expected. "Yes, I am holding a gun on him and wanted to use the leverage of you injecting Kam to bring him to heel." "Sara, I'd appreciate you letting me know if you're allowing anyone to eavesdrop on my conversation." "He will not say another word, so Renae, let's get back on track. The key to keeping Brock in line is Kamryn. He will be held in check with the real threat of ending her cognitive reality. He will comprehend that with only one call. It will be the end of Kam for all intents and purposes, correct!"

"This is crazy. How long do you think you can maintain this threat if he gets next to a phone calls his office or...." "Renae, that's the key NIA is fully secure. Even if the Fed's raided the place, how could they? It's a fortress. Kam would be a Zombie before they got past the first gate. That's a promise!" She again gauges his expressions and mannerisms. What alternative do I have? 'The Monster sits on the bed, glaring at me. This is insane. No logic. The second that bastard gets a chance, he will take me out and waste my ass!'

"Renae, I can shoot him dead," squinting her eyelids at him under furrowed brows, "but I'm going to need your help up here to bury his body. The FBI will put out a missing person alert for Agent Brock Dame. Being his Fiancé, I would be the number 1 suspect. They would put me on a rotisserie barbecuing my succulent meat! This has to seem feasible and believable...." "Sara, the original plan for him, drunk out of his mind on the Sea-Doo, that's a foolproof plan, girl. I don't know. This is way fked up!" "That's not going to work now we, uh, I need to be creative. I'll handle it, Renae!"

"Sara, you're the one who has screwed up. This is 1,000 percent your fault. He was supposed to die, umh, meet his demise in an accident. Remember, fish food at the bottom of the lake." "Not going to happen, unfortunately, so keep this phone on you for now. If I don't text you every 15 minutes with our code, inject the hypodermic needle into Kam. Can you do this, Renae?" "Yes, it will cause a hassle, umh. I will cancel dinner and tell hubby I was called into work, no problem. What do I tell my husband if he sees the other phone? Because I'm going to have it handy, um, to monitor your texts, shit. Damnit, I hate this sneaking around as if I'm an adulterous vixen. This is just great, Sara. Geez, you screwed up a wet dream all right, I will work it all out for now, but I'm warning you, the only link to me is you, and this is your fault!"

"Enough, Renae. You must never threaten me or degrade me in one of your patronizing tones... I will be in contact at 15-minute intervals. I'm in charge. Nurse Renae, remember that you never want to piss me off. Goodbye!" They sat in silence. Both are lost in their diverse minds 'contrarian thinking on opposite spectrums. One recapture and kill Brock; the other fight for freedom, kill Sara, and save his fiancé.'

Brock tries to act as calm as a cucumber... "Clever, very succinct. I have to ask you the obvious question why even involve Renae in this sick plot, and what did you get with Carl?" "Sshhh, simple, I went from being stripped nude in the Prison Dungeons basement, locked inside a rubber room drugged out. Nurse Renae is the supervisor in charge of all the Nurses just underneath... Liz umh, Doctor Liz Honcho... Renae and Liz are best friends, and she co-signs anything Renae wants. Liz does basically whatever Renae asks and signs forms without even looking at them anymore. Over the years, Renae has garnered her complete trust. This is just the way it is. Yeah, yay think it was an accident for me to move up to level 5 in less than five years. Impossible. I should never have seen the light of day. I was the alleged mass murderer, and the next thing you know, I had my Salon... think about it. It was all part of my master plan. Carl was also a huge pawn in my strategy." "Sara, there are other options. I'm sure we can work this out in favor of you and Renae."

"Shush… to answer your question and show you my brilliance, um, Renae and I knew where all the cameras were. She played her part to 'Oscar caliber' quite the plump dynamite actress worked Kam and Liz like stepchildren and helped manipulate Liz to have the cameras turned off in the Salon, no easy task. NIA is a maximum Prison. I had to have her as an accomplice. No, she is a liability. After your drowning incident, I was going to kill Renae dead… Dead women tell no tales-no lies, no witnesses!"

"I get it, no doubt. What of Carl now?" "Aah, Carl presents no problem. He can barely tie his shoes. His mind is in a loop-he deserves a cell at NIA, dumb as the box of pebbles, but I will untie his shoes and fill them with bricks. Carl is the walking dead." Lol. 🦋.

She glances at the clock "in 9 minutes. I need to text my code to Renae. Come on, let's get some dinner. How about you start up the barbeque? I'll marinade some baby back ribs, oh, by the way. All your electronics took the plunge! So sorry cum on honey…." Brock stalls and then gets up off the foot of the bed. Sara declares, "I thought you were starving… umh, I'm Famished," giggling "let's do this!" she chortles like a schoolgirl. He frowns convoluted, and steps past Sara 'her guns lowered, now what?'

-59-

<u>Kamryn locked down at NIA… plotting out her next moves.</u>

The evening sinks behind Ame's mundane drawings. All blended the same beyond redundant, fought with her willpower to not succumb to the addictive graphics of past lives. Wondering if she should pick out selective sequences. Yes was the answer, she muttered to herself, 'put together a stack of the drawings to take with her in the morning for her much-anticipated get-together with Liz.' Each time she dwelled upon her relationship with Brock Dame, her tummy erupted with a combination of gastric pains and cramps. She'd be getting sick to her stomach, as has been the case lately. It wasn't easy keeping food down.

Having another notion, uhm premonition, a suspicion that haunted her, could Sara really fool her fiancé? Was this even remotely possible? The body was the same; the mind and personality were as opposite as an apple and orange, not a chance that he wouldn't discover the anomaly. The stark comparisons weren't too much, yet she still worried. Such was human nature 'parts of us, despite our egos, are insecure, especially when our Hearts and Spirits are tied or leveraged to another person!'

Ouuhh, another cramp spreads up from her nervous digestive system. She rushes towards the bathroom. What was going on? Premenstrual syndrome prior to menstruation, or was I pregnant? She added to the constriction with a chuckle. Aah, not likely what an absurd thought I'd had; a hysterectomy which took all of that out of play. But that's precisely how her guts felt like they were dissolving and liquifying. I have never conceived nor been with child heck... 40 years old is barely around the corner. I still can't deny the odd feeling that something felt different a seed had been germinated, planted, and was growing down inside of me. No way the plumbing was gone, wasn't it? Please, no praying; Sara was the only person to accompany me to the operation...uh, hysterectomy. Ahh, paranoia, no periods since then. Am I going crazy? With her family disease of toxic genetics and her heredity filled with Psychopaths, the last thing this World needed was another miscreant like Sara.

She sat back with a coarse tissue, relaxed, then tremulously pain shuddered past her midsection. Kam almost laughed at her twisted thoughts, wiping away the possible ramifications of her convoluted, mixed-up brain. Flush down the drain out of her mind. She had to admit it; her optimism was running on fumes. Her loose bowels and bile that came up from her upset stomach were never-ending. But 'In the End' denial refusal of the truth seems to always show itself as would be predicated in this living example. She laid down and closed her eyes, trying to find the subject matter that was meant to propagate a positive, even a Fairy Tale of falseness… would defend against the doldrums that were upon her, which only relented in her unconscious world. Sleep was necessary.

Kam didn't want to dream. Nothing would ease the pain, no vacuum to suck away the black hole of her situation, nada, her stomach still vacated of food, refused the tray from the vehemently angry guard. Kam allowed sleep to encapsulate her restless mind.

<u>Kamryn's latest Nightmare.</u>

Oh yes, there she was, floating out in a celebration, an occasion sprung from the depths of the quicksand that engulfed her on stage, a divine, religious, and sacred experience. Her flowing silk wedding dress finally sanctified a marvelous wedding. The gathering with Mount Shasta's vantage point over the horizon, she was floating on Lake Shasta with ethereal bliss glowing in the distance. The world's most handsome groom, the scene was ephemeral as he slipped his Grandmother's unique wedding ring on her finger. A lopsided wink preceded the embrace and the kiss. Omg <u>(no, Not I, it wasn't me, Kam, but Sara, who was marrying Brock, she smiling, smirking winking at me Gottcha!)</u> waking in a huffy sweat. Oh No! Sleep wouldn't revisit her the rest of the night, tossing and turning at 9:45 am and three cups of instant coffee. She'd had pushed the red button on the wall five times.

"Sloan, as I informed you, Doctor Honcho is in meetings this morning. I left her a message, and she sent the guard station a message back not to bother her or interrupt her again… earlier. I also forwarded a message to her Inbox, so lay off the button, will you?" Pacing to and fro like a caged animal already had a bout of flu-like sickness, a hot shower helped a little didn't want to watch TV or peer at paintings and drawings, so she decided to practice some Yoga. Ah, stretching exercises, put some motivating Jazz on the radio, and did her best to clear her convoluted and twisted mind. Kam was confident she had an ally in Liz and seemed to believe she was pliable, having undaunting proof that she couldn't possibly be Sara. All she needed was her ear and attention for 25 minutes. Enough doubt would surface that the first steps into freedom were within her grasp. She could feel it, uhm, taste it!

Then a girly song came on, turned it up, and slow danced across the floor, a song that her man and her would make love on repeat too. Oh, how her juices flowed. Her eyes flinched open and closed. Oh God… I miss him; I love him with all that I will ever be! He bought the CD and dedicated the song <u>'can you feel it'</u>… Artist 'Kem.' Yes! All 6 minutes and 07 seconds again and again! I wanna feel it forever! Sitting down later after another shower, hell mused hadn't showered this much since forever with a pen and paper pad, writing out details of her argument that she would pose to Liz. Bullet points precise articulations of enough circumstantial evidence to win a judgment in a Federal Trial!

A rude clanging interruption as the lunch tray came banging through the slot in the door…crap. It was 11:59 am, her patience wearing thin, leery, weary, and teary. Approaching the Red button, should she fear the wrath of the guard? Aah, shit, as she tossed caution into the Tornado! 'Sloan, do you have an emergency? That's the only reason for you to be ringing my freaking control room… last warning. I can make sure you'd have a reason to push that button. There are a few raging Heifers who'd love to share that cell with you for a short period of time. Shall I send one in to visit with Yah? I'm sure they can satisfy their every whim. You can play their Ragdoll? The only reason your sort of whole is your because of your Uncle, CEO [redacted].'

Kamryn takes a step back from the iron door… 'No, sir, I was just concerned. I had an important interview with Doctor Honcho. I will not bother you again, sorry!' <u>'That has been duly noted. Leave us alone!'</u> Depression and hopelessness reared their ugly heads again. Nothing she could do. She doesn't dare get close to that button anymore. I'm going to make sure that sister dear suffers. Then she took another step back, burying her head in her hand's frustration… of the unknown was eviscerating her entire will to fight back. Knowing if she gave up, she'd die inside of NIA. Hate wasn't part of her makeup, but she'd suppose she could make one exception, an internal alteration. Kam had lost every single physical fight with Sara when they were children… her sister was plain-ass mean and fought with blind passion. With furry, her anger unleashed more adrenalin, she guessed.

Kamryn's temper was prickling the surface of her epidermis. Consistently lost, unable to reconcile her mental whereabouts, suicidal, and nearly didn't care if Sara had won. Then her memories bounced back to her Papa, and angrily she snarled you stop feeling sorry for yourself. Her Papa would say, 'do something, Kamryn, fight back uhm; my babydoll, I'm always with you!'

Well, no time like the present back at the desk, the stack of color drawings sitting within reach continuing the pictorial of Sara's demented life confirmation of the 'Vipress' was now depicted in color on every page. No names, no legitimate permissible or 'Bona-fide,' proof, only horrific scenes of death, the contorted countenances caused by Sara's poison. Bedroom scenes like #221 labeled 'filth removed' a dash then number '23', obvious the circled number denoted her 23rd murder. Strange as it seemed to Kam, all the killings by 'Al' were not added to the total. Also absent was the double slaying of daddy and the Slutty neighbor by Sara. So, how could anyone trust the numbers on these 11X14 sheets growing numb with disdain and incomprehensible violence? The intricate details in Ame's art were stupendous... choking on her own saliva. Kam slammed down a page on the table, petrified.

The caption at the bottom of the entire portrait told it all 'Brockbaby' #235, yes her man enters the fray. Sara's pictures now took on a tense awareness... the following sheets had a couple in FBI jackets leaning over a woman's body at a luxurious Hotel, 'Agent Brock Dame and Agent Lucie Link' written across the page. This upset Kam. The two of them were close, her arm around his waist obviously together although working the murder scene, 'Ame had somehow put some magic in their relationship. Staring again at the picture, it was perhaps Lucie's eyes or maybe the way she leaned or hovered by Brock!'

#241 was the clencher. Kam's gut vibrated, doubling up like she'd done 505 consecutive sit-ups on an incline board. Her hands held onto her tummy 'felt the sickness' caption read 'The Loving Couple in Oceanside.' The picture showed her fiancé with his hands covering Lucie's hands. Their eyes communicated undeniable attraction, the lust. She knew those stares. She'd been in Lucie's seat thinking, oh no, those sexy looks were only for her... wrong. He Loved Lucie, and tears fell despite her attempt to reign them in, trying to be stoic and composure laden. Nope!

The next series, 242 through 247, was of the Oceanside café and other patrons. The disguised murderess at a table waiting to kill Brock and Lucie watched the guy drop the date drug in an unsuspecting victim's drink. The would-be rapist changed

Sara's agenda. She went into attack mode, another double murder. Somehow Kam felt dehumanized. There wasn't a way for her to reconcile what she was viewing really as she rubbed her head. <u>The next sequence of drawings sank Kam into a fugue. She laid down with doubled-up pain on her thin wafer called a mattress… Ohno, there, Brock with on Fisherman's Wharf on his knees proposing to Lucie Link… oh, how fricken romantic… I'm definitely in second place in Brocks warped and melted Heart.</u> 🐍.

Kamryn, exhausted, blanked out and awoke later… and got the picture, clearly, she had the evidence to sink Sara into a lifelong prison sentence for premeditated murder. The artwork by Ame was undeniable proof. Who else would know this but the Vipress Serial Killer herself? Wasn't this enough circumstantial evidence to lock her sister up… for the rest of her hateful life, for if she could bring these drawings to a prosecutor, Sara would be history. If there still were a Death Penalty, she'd own it, but certainly, she'd never see the light of day with all of her drawn evidence. Sara was given practically no time for the 'Attempted Murder' of FBI Agent Lucie Link the Judge handed down the maximum sentence of 10 years. This was because… without a doubt, Lucie had jumped of her own convolution from the 3rd-floor balcony at the hotel and, of course, her million-dollar legal team that included Uncle dearest. Sara could be Paroled after her sentence, umh, if she regained her faculties and sanity heck, Sara was well on her way. Then the video that Liz displayed to her came back to memory Sara with four of her personalities, no sis had a ways to go.

Then a huge, suppressed sigh, nope, a realization hit Kamryn square in the jaw. Oh no, it wasn't Sara who had to be concerned with all these chronological pictures, no, Oh, no, it was me, uhm, my problem. I'd be the one held culpable for every killing proof lay in the stacks of drawings, all in a perfect sequence, 'Sara's Supreme

Setup,' an ambush by sister dear… Kam was being framed for murder. Who else knew about this? &.

Omg… Sara left these drawings in her cell to punish me and destroy my willpower to ensure I'd never get out of NIA! If the staff finds and studies these drawings, I'd be indicted for multiple murders… Sara was ruthless. No doubt there were tons of hours in drawings all on the camera's film ohmy… when will the other shoe drop? Should she destroy every last one of these, logic asks what would someone else do in this desperate, forlorn situation? The guard's eyes were watching her every move, recording her on a 24/7 loop. What would happen if she did start to tear them to pieces? No garbage disposal: they certainly wouldn't fit down the toilet. The guards collect the trash. The only thing she could do was start the shower and quickly take the thousands of pictures in there with her. No way… Busted!

The next question was why her sister left them here. What was her purpose and intention? Because the calculating freak didn't do anything without a planned and concise reason. Sara must have known it would be like an addiction that she would have to pick up each one and look at her handy work of Evil. So I played my part with determination and fortitude because the only conclusion for these pictures to be here… is they were meant to be found and used against me in a court of law, aah. <u>Yes…when would the other shoe drop… soon?</u> Most likely, real soon, Sara knew Kam was no quitter, but… interrupting her chain of thought, a dinner tray was banged through the slot in the door.

By the 11 o'clock news, she had her fill of Sara's Art, knowing that Ame was the true artist in the family, the best alter ego that lived within Sara. My honey Brock Dame was sketched across many pages. Also on display was the stalking of his ex-wife Patti Dame and subsequent murder in the parking lot at that bar. Sara disguised as a decrepit old lady

526

with a cane in her hand. Ahh, too much, umh, enough to digest. I'm surprised that Brock isn't mentally deranged with all he has gone through at my sister's hands. Really, it's amazing how we humans can overcome uh persevere such tumultuous trauma scars on our souls, yet our Spirits remain to stay intact throughout our suffering.

Sometimes our human constitution, power within… inner strength ah, and heart supersedes all adversities. The history of humankind proves this to be valid, with pinging in her midsection as she lays down for the night. Tomorrow she will put an end to this or at least set the 'wheels in motion, freedom retribution all she needs is Liz's ear!'

At 5:35 am, she is awakened by Doctor Chafe and Nurse Renae by his side. Kam rolls up with boogers in her sleepless eye crevices "please, Ms. Sloan, can you sit in this chair for us? We need to check out your right hand, remove your soft cast, and give you a once over," begrudgingly, she slowly moved, smelling her lousy morning breath and tasting the vile name and reference to Sloan… flushed past her tonsils, done with this debate her last name is Amaya, damnit.

In under 15 minutes, she had a new soft cast on and returned to bed to resume her attempt to sleep. At least she could rest her body. Sleep never took hold, 'tossed turned,' fretting with anxiety, distress, and fear of the unknown heart beating loudly. Agonizing over her predicament with a gnawing uncertainty out of her control, the torment grasped her by the throat, vexed and provoked the dreadful, revolting reality that she was locked inside of an Insane Asylum. Under others' control, the loss of dignity, freedom, and being a non-entity. Spoken to with such disrespect and scornful hatred and demeaning words, the noses of the staff pointed upward, peering at her… sneeringly insulting, portraying utter contempt and dislike, aligned with disdain filled their countenances matching derisive stares. Their treatment felt like I was part of an exhibit at a zoo, uhm… animal. Hyperventilating, she ran to the toilet to Vomit!

She was later sitting in the shower with the hard spray of hot water splashing about, laying the groundwork for the preceding day and how to preface the facts to Liz. Knowing the meeting with Liz was where all her hope resided, dwelling upon this, she dried off, made some instant coffee, and ate the fruit and oatmeal from the breakfast tray, all along scribbling and condensing her notes steadfast with the ultimate objective at hand.

Thinking of Sara now and what life she'd lived here, this predicament could worsen before it got better. Sara had only two visitors on her visiting list since she was locked up, she and their Uncle. What contacts did she have? Answer none! Without some external connections, she could rot inside NIA! Suddenly she just had to do it, whatever the consequences were. With a ton of reluctance and built-up apprehension, she pressed the Red button 'what's up, Sloan?' 'Please excuse me, but I have an appointment with Doctor Honcho today. She was busy in meetings all yesterday.' 'Sloan, first get this through your screwed-up head. There isn't any excuse for you… But I will put in your request; leave me alone!'

Kam was thrilled, for at least it wasn't the same voice as the angry guard the day before, with no faces to align with their malignant voices, which were ambiguously broadcasted over the speaker system. However, the theme stayed true a different correctional Officer uh guard with the same stereotypical standard polluted attitude, but how could I blame them if I were in their shoes? How would I approach or speak to a Mass Murderer?

She was working diligently putting forth a timeline, a non-debatable argument strictly facts, ma'am. Kam, who affectionately called him Uncle Terrance, their family attorney and Papa's very best friend of his life. This was the only other ally that she had. The executor of Papa's Will... in charge of their Trust Fund. Even as a young teenager, she had watched him in the courtroom. He was magnanimous and lit up the space he inhabited with overpowering charisma. He inspired in her an enthusiasm for details and unrelenting facts she wrote furiously in the notebook. Kam thought, uh, wait, she was putting the carriage in front of the Horse. First, she had to sway Liz. Then she'd parlay that success with a meeting with her Uncle.

<u>Finally, Kamryn was called out of her cell to visit with Doctor Liz Honcho.</u>

This was her life. The facts had to be irrefutable; the case she would characterize not only chronicle would be a historical record of Liz's interactions, including with her husband and the words they'd spoken to each other over the five-plus years that they had known one another! 'Once I'm done with that narrative, Liz will have doubts in her mind proof that I am Kamryn! It's all going to happen with impeccable timing as the thought whirled lingering, visualizing her moment as she finished the last of her practiced dissertation in the aluminum mirror, and the steel door grinded open 'let's go, Sloan' she leaped up with a spring in her toes 'Yes!'

With reserved happiness, she was led to a different office, Liz's private domain personal retreat inside of NIA. I was clutching my notebook like a parachute rope, 'life or death.' I was confident in the familiar way I had trained and disciplined myself in all of life's challenges. The guard ordered me to sit down in a hallway outside her door.

Moments later, Liz cracked the door "come on in, inmate Sloan, have a seat. Would you like some espresso or anything to drink this time? I promise I will not add any additives," she smirked! "No thanks," I sat on the other side of a magnificent desk table formation. The lacquer finish was impressive. What a comfy room, I thought. Liz's back turned towards her bay window, and she seemed preoccupied staring out upon the acres and acres of trellised grapes that, with a fermentation process, would ultimately produce yummy wine in the near future. Spinning around, she excused the guard and then said!

"How have you been, Ms. Sloan?" Kam looks around quizzically, perplexed at why Liz was using a formal approach. What could have changed from only the other day? "Umh, Liz, it is as good as to be expected. Thank you for asking." "Please refer to me by my proper name Doctor Honcho… Ms. Sloan!" "Uuhhh, didn't you tell me to refer to you as Liz only two days ago? Ugh, aah sure, well okay, is something wrong hum?" Kam looks up at the camera 'it must be some form of a protocol as strange as the about-face was. She paused, then moved on.'

"All right, Doctor Honcho, I've spent hours detailing a concise record of our interactions away from NIA, I believe after I …" "Ms. Sloan, are you still in denial, delusional Psychotically claiming to be Kamryn Amaya?" "Please, I have five different occasions that will stimulate your memory. These examples will leave no doubts, no questions about who I am. Let me start with New Year's Eve at the Orpheum Theater in downtown San Francisco. I can describe what you wore with your husband, George, and check this out. I can …."

Liz throws up a hand in a stop sign position, her countenance unfriendly, bordering on wicked. Liz acted as if she was an imposter from the other day. Who was she less than 45 hours before hum? Was she willing to listen and communicate on level ground? Liz showed due respect before… shit. She was the Schizophrenic. I had studied in some manuals that some Psychiatrists go nuts or insane since there constantly dealing with lunatics. As Professions go, Psychiatrists commit Suicide at the highest rate. Was Liz a fricken Psychotic doctor? She'd gone from being loquacious and open-minded to now a cold tyrant, an alien. Help! ✍.

Kam started to feel sick-instantly a headache and sweat beaded up despite the A.C. vents blowing icicles. Gosh, she felt like dropping to her knees and praying, begging. 'OmLord, help me!' "Ms. Sara Sloan, I need to set the record straight here. Pay attention, for I will say this, but one time… first, stop harassing my staff at NIA. If I wanted to see you, I'd have you fetched up!" "But wait, Liz, aah Honcho or whatever, you're the one who told me that we would get together and talk the next day. What has happened since? What's going on? Please, I implore you to help me. I can make it worth all your while. Listen to me; I have facts!"

"Make it worth my while. What are you trying to do? Bribe me, Sloan? That will be your last interruption. The next will result in a muzzle being placed tightly over your mouth. Just nod if you understand this?" Kam nods, blushing in shock, totally disillusioned, and beginning to shake, kowtowed, and admonished. The assault continued, "if I have to, I'll have you sedated and placed in a fricken rubber room ugh, back to my…." Liz pauses and mutters, 'damnit, I lost my train of thought!'

"Umh Sloan, get this, listen, your walking on thin Ice here at NIA. Mind your own business and leave the staff alone. Try to be an exemplary model inmate, for I can assure you that the only way you're leaving this institution is in a body bag or coffin in the back of our Coroner's van. Get used to it no hope for you ever to escape this prison. When your Parole hearings come up, other staff members and I will stand up and tell it like it is, then play the video you saw the other day and show the Parole board that you're still a danger to society!

<u>"You think your slick, huh, Sloan"</u> *<u>as she shakes a stapled packet of paper. "I got the report from Nurse Renae about how you're scamming me and talking behind my back, spewing hatred, thinking your this mastermind con who is going to be my special Pet and that you purposely spent hours picking Kamryn's brain for</u>*

<u>memories of times with me. I'm no fool, Sara. It's you that's</u> *<u>Insane!</u>"* **Despite her courage and resolve, hopelessness like lightning bolts shattered her Spirit; Kam's face morphed into terror, tears developed and fell in torrents, blindsided, lost in an Abyss, and sank into a Fugue as Liz went on with her rant.**

"If you continue to parade around here as if your Kamryn spewing the fiction BullShit that the real Sara escaped, you were swapped out, or whatever demented mind games you come up with. I will induce you with some highly potent Psychotropic meds, and I'll have you believing that you're a fkn Orangutang!" Liz slammed her coffee cup on her table, shattering it in a temper tantrum. "These Pharmaceuticals I'm going to shove into your veins are mixtures of high-potency hallucinogens. They should do the trick. She cackled, morphing into a howl. I will prescribe you this treatment regimen starting today. It will be a real hoot, cuz by the time you're done with this treatment. I guarantee you will not care who the hell you are or who you were. You might start to think that you're a Poodle and bark and crawl about licking your own asshole. That's your next step here at your Forever home. NIA!" She sneered repulsively.

"This is where you will be till you die, Sloan NIA. It's up to you to change your attitude, or I will take away your Salon. And if you cause any trouble from here on out, you will lose your luxury cell and Level # 5 classification!" 'What could I say, nada? My chin fell with all hope, diminished,… staring at the stapled packet of papers, uh, reports from Nurse Renae, with my name on the top of the large file. Wondering how many of the staff were in on Sara's conspiracy, or was I paranoid genetics were coming back to haunt me?... Am I the person who was… and is Insane? 🖋.

Hope evaporated in Doctor Liz Honcho's office for Kamryn.

Liz leans over, stretches her arm out, and pushes the Red button. A guard instantly appears "get her out of my sight!" 'Then Kam spots a new 5X7 color photo of Liz, her husband, and Nurse Renae. The three of them were standing on a beach in Santa Monica by a Beach House that Kam had visited several times back when she was managing Sara's property holdings. 'Liz was in on the 'SARA' conspiracy, uh, in cahoots. She had to be working with Sara, fk no, Omg no, please, how? Why would Renae & Liz be at Sara's property other than ughhhh? The shock dropped her to her knees as she tried to get up from the chair but was cognizant not to let on that she'd spotted the Beach House that Sara had tried to sell her seven years ago! .

"Get up, Sloan, get your slime off my carpet," shouted Liz in a Rage. The guard rudely jerked her up by her armpit "for this impish act, I'm adding three more days to your lockdown. Get outta here, Inmate!" The journey back to the cell was far from uneventful the guard shoved me from behind into the elevator. I stumbled and hit my forehead on the side wall. As the doors shut, he kicked me in the ribs "yuh, wanna suck my cock also bitch?" Slaps me violently across my face "that's for Carl, you fkn bitch!"

I couldn't breathe, gasping for oxygen, but I realized I better get up before he kicked me again, wondering who was operating the cameras. He looked down upon me with evil intentions. The doors opened. "let's go, Sloan," I tried to get past him without touching him, but again, he shoved me aggressively with his foot out, tripping me as I rolled on the concrete, sprawling sideways into a garbage can. "What, Sloan, you forgot how to walk or something?" Laughing, standing to the side with him, was a large female guard who yelped mockingly, "get the fk up, Sloan! No more protection from Doctor Liz Honcho. She said for us to do as we want, with you… you're in for a change of venue. We got ur ass now. Lmao Yep!" Kam had no reply. Her face bled from her nose and lips. Kam never thought she'd be so happy to see her Prison cell. He leaned into her against the door, ground into her back, then the door banged open with one final kick in the lower back, tumbling down onto the ground "get in there, you slut. I might cum visit you before my shift is out!" Bruised and battered, she fell across her bed, suddenly feeling bad vibes 'what was it? What was wrong or different? Umh, was someone hiding in the bathroom?'

Why was the hair on the nape of her neck prickling, an alarm beaming in from her subconscious? She wobbled into the shower area. On the stainless-steel mirror, drawn in Ruby Red Lipstick, were the words 'Your Ass is mine now, Sloan. I'll be Cuming for you soon, Greek style!' Kam staggered out and fell face forward on the hard mattress. A coarse tissue wiping the dripping blood from her chin, ah oh, she noticed the notebook she'd carried with her to Liz's office was no longer around. She'd lost it when getting beaten. There wasn't any reason to panic. What good did it do me anyways, her Spirit broken, shredded, shattered, locked in an Insane Asylum for the rest of my life! Could it be worse… huh, sure, it could be. Tears this time flowed like a river without any sign of ever relenting!

I crawled to the bathroom, my sanctuary, turned the shower on, undressed and climbed in, sat again under the water, and prayed to God to take her life 'please just let me die, please end my life, please. I started praying, 'our dear heavenly Father, kill me now, give me a heart attack, staring at the shower curtain! Maybe she could hang herself. Yes, the decision firm… Kamryn would hang herself by the shower curtain. Bye Bye now! ✿.

Brock stood in front of the BBQ, peering at the baby-back ribs... he just watched Sara text off the third time to Nurse Renae on the dime at 15-minute intervals. She again set her alarm. It was indeed a strange conundrum standing in front of the grill like Déjà vu wishing it was his loving bride to be... his Kamryn, with him. 'Naw, the fiendish anti-Christ lurked about setting the table for dinner on the deck. The night air was hazy and smokey, not from the BBQ but from a nearby fire raging over in the Whiskey Town area. Hopefully, my parent's home and property were safe!'

He checked the time. It was 7:07 pm. It was still 87 degrees out. The sultriness had returned to Redding, California summer time's first real heat wave. Sara walked past him with a provocative swaying of her hips, wearing her short wrap-around slip and bikini top. Sara had Kam's body... a drop-dead gorgeous knockout he'd enjoyed too many times to count. His familiarity with Kam's contours, curves, and smells had him thirsting, um, blinking his eyes. All he wanted to do was 'taste her. Gosh, he lusted and yearned for his girl! What an Evil twist of fate!'

"How are the ribs coming, Brocky?" "umh, give me another seven minutes. I just lathered them down again." "All right, I cut up some Watermelon, made a salad for us, and a pot of barbecued flavored beans with some corn on the cob heck, we're going to have a feast, man!" "Sara, do you really think I'm going to sit down with you and eat dinner? How silly and ignorant would that be? Did you already open a bottle of poisoned wine for me? Really isn't this like 'Take two?' Your goal to sedate me I...." "I promise you I am not up to any backhanded tricks, no drugs; let's have a relaxed meal with good music and conversation. Is that a possibility?" Her words ease and nonchalance flow dumbfounded him, harboring not an inkling of trepidation. No Fear whatsoever, he could reach over, pick up the girl by her throat and break her neck in seconds. She hasn't a prayer in physical combat, yet she struts about… flirts as if this is some Romantic dinner arrangement. She's definitely Psycho crazier than a bed bug. Brock would rather engage with a 17-foot Crocodile than touch the Vipress, but he'd play along with her sex talk… Talk was cheap, knowing there was a method to this woman's madness. Sara couldn't afford for him to live. This was an end game, no other way to look at it, he had one option to save Kamryn and himself, and that was to get the phone after Sara tapped in her passcode, then call 911… "Hey, Brockster, I will play the 'taster' like in 'Medieval Times' before the King would eat his meal… chosen slaves or whoever would taste his food. That is what I will do that way; you will have no worries, all right?"

He took the ribs from the flame and turned to her. "I'm starving for sure let's give it a go. I will open my own bottle of wine, which you are allergic to or dislike intensely." "No worries, I have a cold beer in the refrigerator, come on, join me here!" "He knew the ribs were clean of contaminates not tainted, a salad bowl and all the rest of the food was like in a shared container. He observed her. She had no sleeves, only a Bikini top, so not an option to defile his food with a powder residue!

He nearly smiled to himself. What the hell was he doing sitting at a table with a notorious Serial Killer and going to enjoy dinner? Yep, he was starving, but also, he was still alive, yup. This is the Vipress herself who murdered his Ex-wife Patti and forced Lucie to jump from the balcony to the asphalt to get away from her. Now his Fiancé inside the Asylum in place of her; his appetite was diminishing, dwindling, an Acid secretion hit the back of his mouth, felt oddly disengaged from himself like a neutral party sitting from afar!

She took bites out of his bean salad, chewed, and swallowed even the corn on the cobb. They ate in relative silence with some of his favorite Blues playing over the houseboat's deluxe sound system. He recognized the artist and CD. It was Kamryn's 'Joe Bonamassa' on the album 'Dust Bowl.' The song was one of his most liked and so… suitable for the setting he found himself within! The next song was oh so apropos 'Prisoner,' he sang along. The barbeque ribs were delicious… jeesh Brock sighed. At first, he had to force the food into his mouth, all the while watching Sara… he licked his lips. The meal turned out scrumptious… he placed his fork on the table. Brock was satiated, umh, full. He was in motion. His natural predisposition, um, habit, took hold, and he opened another bottle of wine after he saw her start her second bottle of beer.

"Oh, I forgot to tell you I canceled all our visitors for tomorrow so your friends will not be interrupting us… took your phone and Kam's and sent texts, then had to speak with a few of the persistent nuisances they had planned to be here on 7/13 Thursday… through the fricken weekend to be with us. I mean you and my Goody Two Shoe sister Kam. What the heck were you and my sister thinking like, really? Why would you want all that company, geez? Not so romantic, huh? Lucky with my ventriloquist skills, they didn't doubt they were speaking with your honey. Lol." Sara's show of entitlement angered Brock… "No, don't you mean Sara ahh, not your ventriloquist skills but one of the other psychopaths in your distorted and delusional mind, isn't it Al's voice, uh, isn't he the ventriloquist? You freak…." "Shut up, Brock!" Downing her beer and quickly grabbing another one.

"Well, unfortunately, Brock, some of your pre-wedding party group wouldn't take my advice and stay home… nope. One stupid bitch told me that a bunch of them had rented cabins and would be on the lake anyways. I hope and worry…

that they are not going to bother us and our privacy, but that didn't stop them from driving up here. Besides those obstinate fools, some of Kam's stubborn friends are staying at Bridge Bay the Hotel bringing their watercrafts… and going to party hardy. I'm betting that they will be looking for us and find us out here at our lovely cove. Can't hide a Houseboat this freakin big… kind of pisses me off, Brock!"

Brock grinned, this time an absolutely genuine smirk. 'He and Kam had some loyal friends that were fun and devoted, and this party had been planned for over three months. Ain't no way they were not going to be up here on the lake they'd find them even with 365 miles of shoreland, and curiosity got the best of him. Asking, "So, during your texting and conversing, did any of them want to speak with me?"

It was her turn to smile, "yep! Crazy, every fkn one of them asked, even my sister's best friends from Schwab. One statement stands out 'Beverly,' said Quote Verbatim, 'Kam, you have already had him for almost a week. This party will go on. We're all going to be there. Let me speak with Edward. Stop being so damn selfish; you got the rest of your life with him, GF!" Then this Bev laughed loudly; "we're going to find you, and the party will start. Yuh got that, BFF." .

This brings a huge, dimpled teeth-exposed smile. He rolls his shoulders and stretches macho-like with a laughing cadence, declares, "that's good ole Bev, she is a character, vibrant as all get out, tells it like it is aah… with that being said Sara, what's your plan? I'm having a difficult time reconciling your train of thought, umh, logic. Really, how is it all going to work out? What, how fricken absurd hum, uh, are you going to text Renae every 15 minutes for the next week? Sara, do you think our wedding party won't find us here on my parent's giant houseboat?"

He wipes the napkin across his messy face. She sits back, taking a guzzle of beer "yes, a quandary we do face together, an undaunting dilemma indeed, for self-preservation is the strongest human instinct. How I analyze it, the only reason you haven't tried to choke me out is that you know that it would be futile, for Renae would inject your honey. You need to access a phone and would invariably try to stop Renae's injection of Kam. Also, I do concur with your train of thought. There isn't a logical way for me to send a text off every 15 minutes. So something has to change here!" She reached across the table to click her beer on his wine glass, and he obliged.

"The misconception, belief that we'd both be awake, I mean Renae and I, uhm, 24/7 even to do so, it's an end game, Brock. Zero alternatives unless you have another idea heck, we will be inundated with like 11 partygoers tomorrow!" Sara rethinks her decisions and says, "I suppose I should have shot you dead and taken my chances, but the FBI would be all over my ass, I'd be in an interrogation room being sweated. My freedom has only two obstacles Nurse Renae and you. Unfortunately, you both must be eliminated unless you want to make love to me, be my husband, never to leave or part um, never to deceive or betray me to love me till the end of your days?"

A clangorous rip-roaring cackle explodes with dripping watermelon juice down his chin "make love to you, Sara, omg, I'd rather chew glass." He pours another full glass of Cabernet. "Brock, I don't get it all my life. I've heard a hard prick had no conscious look at this body. It's the same one that you have been hitting regularly. Um, yum, we're identical twins, Brockster... uh, each and every curve is the same, except you will find me a tighter fit... inside my vaginal cavity, ah, tunnel of love. Yum, um, you'll be a will snug fit, for sure... since it's been forever since I've had company down there. Not begging, but will you please indulge me? It's been years! I believe you will enjoy my craziness. I am Wet & Wild, and insatiable, Brockbaby!" He displayed a lopsided smirk, said zilch.

"I will even take the reins and ride you 'cowgirl' style whatcha say, boy?" He seemed elsewhere, not listening to her pleading, chewing away, and looking at the grey sky smoke blotting out the clouds, his mind… ears in shock. She was hitting on him, wanting to have sex with him. This was like the making of a Horror Movie. "Well, Brockbaby, I'm waiting. What do you say?" oops, the alarm goes off-she says aloud. "Oh gosh, I better text the code to Renae, or poor Kam will become a blabbing drooling vegetable. Think about my proposal. I'm losing my patience; excuse me, dear Brockster!"

Reflecting backward pensively, he was well aware that this make-believe farce had a distinct and inevitable expiration date, and that was before the full-on entourage showed up tomorrow afternoon, so in less than 17 hours or so, an attempt on his life was all but guaranteed. His options were not conducive to parlaying a cheerful ending to the upcoming confrontation. Constantly butting heads with this vixen wouldn't be instrumental in keeping his girl from harm. Sara was using both passcode-protected phones, so they were useless unless he could get her passcode. He'd need her codes. If he waited till she put her code in to attack her and beat her to a pulp, he could then call the Director of the FBI, his boss in minutes, have the Warden of NIA in communication, stop the perilous danger that Kam unwittingly faced.

The timing was essential; everything would happen 'snake quick,' with one crunching punch to Sara's evil face, and she'd collapse like a falling stack of dominoes. Sara re-appears, "well, I bought sister dear another 15 minutes. Shall we get busy in the bedroom or out here under the hazing stars, Brocky?"

"Sara, earlier you said something about an 'age-old wives tale.' A hard pecker indeed has no conscience, especially through adolescence. It's a 'hard thing to manage,' pun intended. But as we males mature, speaking for myself, my cock is attached to my heart, feelings, mind, and conscious state controlled by the impulses of my brain. Despite many men having separate names for their love muscle or their penis, obviously, mine is affectionately referred to as 'Brock Junior or BJ,' this organ is part of me, and I am in control of...." "Duh, shut up. Get to the point. Enough gibber jabber, dude!"

Brock decided to let her feel his wrath... "I can say this without reservations I could never find enough blood to fill an erection for you. It would be a useless frustrating endeavor for us. I have nothing for you, Sara all I have for you is...." "Sshhh, stop, don't say it, Brock. You're ruining our night. My mouth can do wonders. Let me give it a shot. What do you have to lose? I mean, um, I'm so fricken horny for you, wet and glistening. Let me try my handi-work. Whatcha say?"

Draining the rest of the bottle into his glass, he takes in her wicked glare. How could he play this out in his favor? If he had her nude on the bed when the 15-minute alarm went off, waited till she punched in the code, then assaulted her. Then I could take control and chain her down to the bed, then use her phone to handle business; sure, that will work. Timing is everything, then maybe call ole Nurse Renae with a deal that she can't refuse. Yes, doable done!

Sara was feeling the pressure of indecision. Part of her wanted to have him inside her, loving, sensual, and lustful another part wanted to end this in any way possible by shooting him dead. 'Between a Brock and a hard place,' her control flinched. 'I'm Sara in charge, but I was wavering. Al had tried once again to come out of hiding and rear his big, opinionated mouth, and waiting in the wings, the exiled Ame, damnit to hell, Ame was giving her fits. Having multiple personalities had its ups and downs. The only reason Brock didn't launch an assault on her is because of her leverage holding sister dear's life in her paws. I was still in control;

this was always the case. Sara was getting anxious but held her water for the time would come. There wasn't a doubt that… she would overcome and end up on top.

<u>'Don't do this, Sara… shouts Ame in her skull.' Ame was logically trying to espouse other options. In our Inner Ear 'Brocks, a good man, you said so yourself.</u> Stop enough' Sara squeezed her nose to gain some pain and control of her conspirators that were compartmentalized near the surface of her minds. Her inner selves are in conflict their censorship fails. She pops the top off another beer and sits back down at the table. He reaches for the bottle opener, a cool bottle of Red Zinfandel in his left hand. She downs half the beer in gulps; he says, "need some more alcohol for a primer, Sara? I thought you were anxious to be with me in bed." She reaches up and snatches off Kam's hair Wig. He could see blonde nubs were already growing out. Suddenly an alarm sounds as he watches her move quickly. She is less than three feet from him. The sequence was as follows on her Apple phone; the alarm sounded. Sara then taps a code in that phone and resets the alarm. Then she picks up the basic no-frills throwaway phone, taps a password in, then the code is done. She was texting Renae and waiting for her response, which came directly back.

He warms up an inner Smile 'the next time will be her last time. He thinks with a determination that once she inputs the code to Renae, he will hit her in the jaw, take the phone, redial the texted number, and take the proactive, aggressive approach, chain Lil missy Sara to the bed, as he was once hours ago.' She takes a swig and wipes the foam from her lips "this is like Russian Roulette… we know this ends tonight; one of us has to make the first move. I'm no match for you, Brock… physically. Hey, the sex talk was fun, but let's face it, a waste of time. Our focus wouldn't be true!" "Wrong, sweet Sara, I'm up for your Cowgirl rides, and then I will flip your ass up… and into my personal erotic rotisserie. Let's get busy

down in the Master bed, hell. I can play your Master," he chokes, laughing raucously!

"Brock, you're not serious. You're working angles and not sexual ones. You want my burner phone and code. You think me bare ass naked will make it much easier for you to overpower me, uuhhh, correct?" He slowly sips the Red wine "that be a fact. By tomorrow the cat will be out of the bag… why don't you give yourself up, Sara? Why not? You still have a reasonable chance at Parole!" Sara cackled into a snicker and almost choked into a full-blown howl. "Oh sure, after I have escaped with my ingenious and elaborate plan, the authorities are just going to slap my hand and say, 'bad girl' Nah, if I turned myself in, I'd be locked up for the rest of my life!"

Brock couldn't argue with her. She was no doubt correct, he felt slightly buzzed better slow down on the Vino. <u>"Sara, you said it, not me, but I fully agree with you. There isn't any way forward for you… you're going to be locked up until you are Grey and moldy. You're squelched like a bout of impotence, but for you, my Serial Killer, there isn't any Vagina like dysfunctional drugs, Nah."</u> He howled hysterically… "man, I'm good, should be on stage!" Sara sat back with an amusing smirk, and he soldiered on. "Whoa, I can't imagine your frustration. What because you couldn't wipe my cute ass? How's the mighty brain-thrust and wishful master planner feel now? As I see it, your ingenious plan misses some transitional objectives. It leaves too many loose ends, such as Kamryn in your place at NIA, me free here sipping wine, Nurse Ratchet or Renae, who sounds like she isn't going away, and I think you underestimate guard Carl. Sure, I could be wrong on all points but don't think so… 'Give yourself up, Sara, okay." Nope! ◖.

Kamryn was waterlogged, worrying about the Lipstick threat on the stainless-steel Mirror.

After over an hour, Kam heard a familiar sound, a guard checking on her, "what are you doing in here, Sloan?" As the curtain was ripped open, the same gargantuan female officer stood staring down at her sitting under the water. "Taking a shower is all I'm about to get out in a few minutes." "See that you do; stop wasting our water!"

Left alone again, she closed the curtain. The steam and hot water had cleared her mind somewhat. She wouldn't let Sara and her sinister accomplices win. No, Suicide was the weak-ass way out, nope. 'I have to think for two, for I am with child Brock's baby; all indications prove so. I feel morning sickness, cramps, and bloated, which I've read about, right down to super sensitive nipples. I'm going to be a mother; suicide kills both of us, and I am not willing to kill our innocent baby. *'Wait, that's not possible. Am I going nuts, uh crazy, is the pressure and depressive stress devouring my mindset… of who I am? Are my genetic predispositions finally dethawing? Am I insane? Didn't I have a hysterectomy? Sara drove me home from that horrible medical procedure; right weirdness bounced past her pupils. Is she mentally losing it? Are genetics coming to fruition? Oh, no, her family's Insane genes ….'*

We had made a pact that we would both get hysterectomies at the young age of 21 years. Most doctors refused the operation because of our age. But after we brought in our Family Tree umh chart showing our tainted bloodline, we convinced a doctor to perform the operations. Even at that young age, I had Endometriosis. Besides, I'd stopped having my menstrual cycle at about 19 years old. My gynecologist had first suspected it was from stress and my propensity to work out like a professional athlete. Still, after some tests, I was diagnosed with 'Poly ovary syndrome,' and I stopped having a period.

Pregnant, what a trip; wow, I mumbled aloud, 'get a grip' I'm no more pregnant than the Queen of England is. However, I drifted back to a debate with Sara, who tried to convince me not to have the hysterectomy after she'd had it done. Her argument was, hey, our bloodline dies with you. Who knows, maybe your child will be blessed. I recall yelling at her and asking then, why'd you get the operation?

With the virulent strain of Insanity in our hereditary line, did the Psychotropic injections, all the forced medications, bring out another me? No, please, no, as she sucks in a massive inhalation of Oxygen. I am fine now just lost it for a sec. Geez, that was kinda scary. 'Get a clue, Kam!' So, Sara had major allies in Nurse Renae and Liz. They were at the beach house; either one of them could end her life at any time. I still have one last resource that I haven't tapped into! That is Attorney Uncle Terrance Hallinan. I must get a face-to-face with him, need to be clever, play the part of Sara, and seek an attorney visit. We cannot be taped on camera in a private attorney visit. I can do this. My phone calls are being scrutinized and listened to by Liz, or at least I must assume all phone calls from inmates are recorded. I need to play it cool and adapt, ugh, to become in sync… synonymous with my environment, which is being an inmate inside NIA at this time!

I need not create any ripples. Bide my time and get him down here so I can convince him that I am Kamryn. How could Terrance ever forget the strip club he took me to? Lol, I will prove without a doubt that 'I am not Psycho Sara.' Standing up and toweling off, I will be a model Prisoner Inmate from here on out. Walking over to the block wall on the other side of the bed and carefully searched the drawings taped up all over the walls of the cell. Pictures of Sara's Salon and her makeover clients plastered the wall, and many illustrations of the park, ponds, and wildlife; even Carl was in a few. She stopped when she saw the drawing of Sara diving into the pond on a recent visit.

Kam was also in the scene & something else was in the picture, but she couldn't place it. She tore it off the wall and brought it to the desk. Flicks on the bright halide, there in the window was a person looking out, shivers down her spine, oh hell no... looking out was Nurse Renae. The planned dive into the water and trauma was all a game of theater and Drama. It was orchestrated and part of the show!

In the middle of the last stack, she turns the page. I was in the drawings, vibrant and full of life in my garden at home in Marin County #313. There I was, downtown San Francisco in a dark blue pants suit entering the office at Schwab someone had been following me. Sara had surveillance on me, an investigator, ugh, or maybe it was Carl or someone he'd hired... for my evil twin. No question that someone was providing Sara with photos of her life. The timeline and subsequent pictures were of a time period of approximately 17 months ago #339 sat her back in a flush of shivers and spasms. It was of Brock and me at Pier 19 in San Francisco. How could I be so damn naïve trusting Sara? She is a Monster, like a fungus that kept growing and spreading. 'Then, as if she had any fricken Tears left, a Cloud Burst a drawing of Brock on his knees proposing, me spilling the Carmel Popcorn oh please... ughhhh!' It was like the second coming after Kamryn had seen the pictures of Brock proposing to Lucie at about the same area in Fisherman's Wharf... Kam surely was just another Lucie Link, like a replay. She wondered if Brock truly loved her like he most certainly did with his so-called Soulmate Lucie. Kam raised her chin and took in a long breath... and muttered, 'leave it alone, Kam. This isn't helping the situation. At least,

I have proof enough that the witch had a private investigator or someone following me, uh us.'

Kam took a break, then, after a while, she was back at the table... like possessed, kept flipping the pages, then stopped shell shocked. It was the drawing of the Houseboat on Lake Shasta. These paintings were obviously most recent, like in the last month, after Sara had known of the vacation planned with Brock, a disturbing rendition of 'her fiancé fastened to a bed naked took the last of her breath away.'

In the last drawing, #357, the scene is ubiquitous and vague yet drew her in... the meaning of the depiction was albeit disconcerting. A pit in her throat, choking her stomach like a leech, clawed at the inner linings of her soul. In the background is the greenish houseboat, and in the foreground is an empty lake beside an untethered Sea-Doo. The caption was but one word 'Seeya!'

My palms were sweating, my head was throbbing, stomach cramped. How could Sara have had the forethought ... and then closed my eyes. Then it dawned on me, of course. I fed her all the details unbeknownst that I was the guilty party, uhm, in collusion with my unknown Arch Enemy, my own freakin sister! 'Tell me, wasn't this enough proof that she was not only a fool to leave all her drawings and painting of her traitorous acts of horror, but a full-blown narcissistic heathen, wanting to hurt me further! Wait, not really, because it's all unsubstantiated, given that many of these drawings had... dates from last month. Like Sara was a Seer, uh fortune teller of the future, a Nostradamus... ugh. Obviously, this was from her delusional fantasy world!'

Suddenly I had sharp white flashes like when I would sneeze violently, shoved past my vision. I flipped up the next drawing. Omg... A painting of a man floating with his body nearly submerged in a mud puddle. The pain resonated systematically... eviscerating and cannibalizing my entire spirit. I suppose I'm not strong enough mentally ... or emotionally to remain in this conscious dimension. I shut down feebly and faded out. Later! .

<u>**Chaos on Shasta Lake... Life or Death or Both?**</u> .

    Brock wonders, instead of drinking glass after glass of wine, shouldn't he be consuming coffee in lieu of the alcohol... numbing his senses? His preferred caffeine high consistently invigorated his senses with clarity and decisive action. Why was he slacking and self-medicating? All alcohol could do was impair his reactionary times. Directly across from him, she slowly finished another brew. Shit, she could pound them for her size; then he saw the label of the last beer, 'non-alcohol,' mused, so she was the responsible one. He was now on the same page; he would make some strong coffee. He gauged her eyes, her focus, uh, for all her malicious intent, yes, Sara the Vipress was ready to counterattack his inevitable assault to disable her.

    Strangely... not coincidently, another CD of a different genre started to be heard over the sound system, the artist <u>'Papa Roach'</u> ironically, the name of the song was <u>'Last Resort,'</u> and then the alarm sounded at about the same time as Sara's song ended. She watches his body tense in his Stars and Stripes bathing suit with a matching T-back-tank top. His muscles were defined, moving like an athlete's handsome hunk body... to <u>'die'</u> for! What a damn waste... Lol, Sara flicks her tongue out like a snake, rotates it around her curvaceous rounded pink lips, and holds up the radio's remote. "Brockbaby, this is the song I have played repeatedly for years, even while locked away in that awful prison NIA... that you stuck me in. The name of one of my all-time favorite songs is <u>'Desire'</u> by the incredible singer-artist <u>'Meg Myers.'</u> Ssshh, let's listen to it and feel every luscious word... that's meant for

you." She checked her phone. "Yup, we have just enough time. The song is about five minutes long! 🎵"

Sara taps pause on the stereo remote as the last of the drums echo across the deck of the houseboat. Sara picks up the throw-away phone. Brock pounces across the table to intercept the text and take the phone and disable Sara. His focus was on the phone, his first mistake, and she Plunged a hypodermic needle to the hilt deep into his shoulder. He shakes it off, gripping the phone in his left hand. A step behind her as she takes off running, she knows if he catches her, she's history. A dead woman, he lunges towards her for a final last grasp. She leaps off the deck of the houseboat into the lake and disappears into the dark water. He swears, takes the phone, and sees that the text had been sent to stop the injection into Kamryn. He then punches in the emergency number 911 then. Collapses to the deck in a dismantled heap!

About ten minutes later, after hearing nothing from Brock... Sara warily grabbed the rails, water dripping from her body, started the ascent up the ladder, and roared, 'nice try, Brockbaby nice!' She wiped lake water from her forehead and eyes. 'Babe, are you still with us, Brocky? Hey, you there? I knew it would take several minutes to knock you down couldn't inject you until I was sure I could get away. The water feels great cum on in Brock.'

She tentatively reaches the top rung peers cautiously over the deck and hesitates to step onto the deck until seeing his crumpled form over by the railing. It was time to go to work, with so much to accomplish in so little time. She rushes over and sees the phone 911 on the screen, but 'Enter' wasn't pushed. Whew, she turns it off and goes to her bag of goodies. Guesswork was how long the sedative sleeping tranquilizer would be effective, taking his body weight into the equation.

Sara props him into a sitting position, prying his mouth open, carefully inserting a feeding tube she'd lubricated earlier down his throat, and snakes it into his stomach. Not wanting to drown him, she poured the remaining cleaning agent cleanser fluid to negate the sedative into the tube, hoping there was enough to clear the narcotic shot she'd given him. She then went over to the bar and selected some Maker's Mark Whiskey, shouting 'Brockster, only the best for my Boy,' and that went down his throat with ease… Yum!

After another select bottle of Dewar's Scotch, grinning, 'you're a fkn Stud Brocky didn't even choke or even show any signs or reactions.' With the precision of a surgeon, she had lubed the tube to ensure that the Medical Examiner wouldn't see any visual marks on his esophagus. Now, she had to be gentle in getting him into the boat. But, before doing so, she phoned Renae, "relax, all is fine; the original plan will be exercised; no worries." "Aah, thank God, what a fkn relief once we are together; you have to fill me in on the details. I'm hiding in our bathroom. Ole hubby is getting suspicious and told me I was acting weird. Man, Sara, I was sweating the proverbial bullets. Damn, now I can rest, putting this phone away. Thanks, Sara!"…'dial tone.'

It took every ounce of her strength, the burden of his weight and the inertia, a struggle unlike any she'd ever attempted. The gravity was overwhelming… finally trying her best not to bruise him, using a sling for a rope down the ladder into the wheelbarrow she'd borrowed from the dock that she used to load her beer and belongings into the houseboat exhausted lugging around a 221-pound man Smiles… 'dead weight! 'Oh Yeah!'

She was finally getting him into the Ski boat, starting it up, pulling the Sea-Doo on a rope behind, tailing her as she went out to the deep black water watching the Garmin depth finder at about 517 feet deep. She stopped the boat leaving the running lights on just in case of a Sheriff boat, remembering what Brock had intimated. A quick cursory look at his docile body with satisfaction, what a waste of a man. Not a suspicious bruise or welt or cut on him. The injection spot was A-Okay. She reached over and grabbed her briefcase for the last part of her vicious, savage, and sinful act.

Before flipping the switch, she had taken one of her rubber waterproof Teva shoes off and placed it in his mouth not to cause his teeth to shatter and break. Her shoe would act like a mouthguard of sorts. She'd flipped the lever twice the third time, resulting in what she wanted foam exploding from Brock's nose and mouth, the smell of shit and urine the Portable Defibrillator had fried ole Brockie's brain. No doubt this added cruelty was cryptic. She had intended the portable unit to be used as a torture machine on his testicles... butt. 'In the End,' she didn't let the defibrillator go to waste. Yep! she Howled. Her laughter ricocheted over the small white caps of the smokey pitch-darkness of Lake Shasta.

Finished, um done, speculates now only left were the final eliminations of Nurse Renae and Carl. She could and would relax thoroughly afterward and then be able to in peace execute her future plans. Umh, perhaps she could also use this portable unit on Renae's body. Wouldn't that be fun? She eases Brock over the side of the boat. With the boat's anchor around his throat, he floats for a few seconds, then slithers down, sinking, watching the bubbles disappear, blowing him kisses, pulling the Sea-Doo, starting it up, untying it, and watching the water bike run in circles. One thought lingered negatively; would the authorities wonder why there wasn't an anchor in the ski boat? Ahh… no worries.

Sara feeling satisfied, even euphoric, starts to laugh. This is way fun, grinning largely as she eases the boat's shifter forward, heading back to the houseboat for some real beer, maybe a Martini… Yay! Fk Yes! 🐍

-62-

91 Days Later.

Sara sat, stewing in anger, transfixed, enraptured, watching for the 5th time the video clip given to her by her paid accomplice Renae. The gall and utter nerve of her threats unveiled in the video were… life-changing. The fact that the snake Renae involved someone else had Sara livid, and worse yet, an entire Law practice in Napa. How can the winch guarantee that the attorney didn't peel open the packets given to him by Renae and watch it out of curiosity, worst-case scenario? In the video, Renae laid out all the facts, trying futilely to absolve herself of any guilt. Her robotic monologue was played out like 'matter-of-factly' droning on about her role in our conspiracy. This memory disk had Sara ready to barf… leaving absolutely nothing out, including their verbal pact and the paperwork for the nine-million-dollar beach house that was the crux of our deal.

To Sara's surprise, the betrayer Renae used some hidden video cameras and taped a few of their previous meetings inside her office at NIA. This proves undauntingly… Renae's premeditation of evil, the backstabbing wench. Renae showed her true colors. Omg, Sara had misjudged this snake's true

552

objective to extort and Blackmail her… damn! Sara was not thinking about security measures or protecting herself ughhhh in her defense. She was still incarcerated at NIA and didn't have her electronic blocking device available. 'The leech' 'Renae' had been skeptical and doubtful of the plan I had contrived. We walked the grounds at NIA for hours, her my Nurse and I her patient, both agreeing and organizing and coordinating the planned project. I dangled the Santa Monica Beach House like a treasured fruit from a vine. The audacity of Renae's traitorousness left bile that causticity stuck to her tongue. She'd put together over three hours of our conversations implicating her and me in this conspiracy all freakin recorded; what an idiot I am to have trusted this traitor! She'd die slow, a horrible demise… Yup. ◖.

<u>Nurse Renae could only smile, she'd done it.</u>

Renae had what she thought was leverage, uh, Life Insurance and protection to ensure that Sara wouldn't and couldn't eliminate her. She had retained a Lawyer and a family friend. Renae was clever; at least, this was her belief. She'd delivered two packages to an attorney whom she'd met at one of her husband's fundraisers. He was running for a local office… hoping to be Mayor of Marin County soon thereafter. The attorney was flirtatious, and Renae liked the married man… she'd visited with him and had a written agreement that he'd open the packages she'd left with him if something disastrous happened to her… in case of her demise or untimely death. If she went missing for six months without checking in, action would be taken. Sort of like a 'LivingWill' only to be opened and revealed upon her death. Renae wasn't a fool and smirked into her compact mirror, knowing that ole Sara was steaming mad by now… having sent her the evidence that would protect her life. The vixen has met her fricken match. If Sara stepped out of line, she was going down; ah, I'd have to work out a plea bargain with the Feds, uhm, with an AUSA… sure I'd do some cushy prison time. Most likely at a cozy, quaint camp… so what a girl gotta do, what a girl must.

Sara had to give it to her… Way clever, for she was my loose link, having me leveraged and under her thumb! In Sara's mind, that was beyond unforgivable Renae's words, 'you better pray that I don't have an accident or even a heart attack because if I do, the evidence at the attorney's office will bury your ass!' Lol, Lethal injection, Sara dear! At this very moment in time, Sara sat on a stool in her San Francisco storage unit, closing the laptop and exiting. Sara said aloud, 'ok, you wanna play a death match of Chess with me? No worries, you put me in Check! That's your first mistake!'

Back at NIA. Kamryn in her own Fugue.

Kam hadn't seen an Obstetrician or anyone regarding the round hard pouch that grew from her abdomen. Her stomach protruded like a balloon from her petite figure. Lucky Sara had left some baggy clothes with the Prison garb, but she knew she couldn't hide the pregnancy much longer and needed to seek medical care. She still spotted blood and cramps daily and had no childbearing experience. She was blind to what was expected.

One unknown fact that I constantly mulled over was how many months or days have I been pregnant. Kam guessed maybe four months. Shouldn't she be ingesting prenatal vitamins? For sure, this Prison food wasn't adequate! For certain, if Doctor Honcho discovered her pregnancy or Nurse Renae or hell, if anyone found out, she'd be forced into an abortion like the rest of the impregnated inmates. It wasn't an anomaly that inmates here at this mental institution ended up pregnant. Kam had learned from Sara that it didn't matter if the inmate were five months or seven months pregnant, an abortion would be ordered, and the baby would be murdered. Some of the scandalously corrupt correction officers defiled, raped, and had consensual sex with prisoners. It wasn't brainy for the predator guards to typically avoid inmates with outside connections and visits. But if your poor soul was forgotten and you hadn't any correspondence with the outside world, the guards were undoubtedly privy to this. You were open territory because no one cared about you. They'd lock you up in solitary confinement after the abortion for a while. Also, rumors were spread that some guards had ongoing sex videos filmed in some isolated confinement cells.

Kamryn had worked some magic of her own in the last three months with the survival of her baby and herself… major priorities. Kam was sitting on her bed, reflecting on a few positives and what would become of them. Being cognizant that all her correspondences were being monitored and most likely never did a letter that she'd written leave NIA. There was no way to communicate with the outside world if they didn't let you. Our phones and mail were all regulated by NIA, and if you were not allowed visitors, uhm, you were at the mercy of the prison. Kam took the unprecedented action of befriending another inmate, knowing that it was a Major risk she could be sold out or betrayed, but desperation seeks strange bed partners. This inmate had a connection that she needed to use. Kam's new friend had retained the same Law practice that her Uncle Terrance owned in San Francisco. Terrance had never replied nor come to visit, so she sent a letter using the inmate's name and registration number. The letter was short, curt, and concise.

Hopefully, the letter wouldn't be tracked back ("My dear Uncle Terrance, I would like to donate 1/3rd of my Trust Fund to one of your chosen charities. I need a face-to-face with you in complete privacy for reasons I will explain to you in person. Please don't make an appointment to visit me better to show

<u>up for an impromptu visit. All will become transparent when
we are in each other's company sincerely 'Sara.'</u>) Oh, how
Kamryn despises not leaving her real name on the letter
thought it was wise in case it was intercepted.

After three more weeks had passed by, she started to
formulate another letter… then. 'Out of the blue,' she was
summoned to the office on her main floor. She had been
relaxing, feeding the Ducks at a table by the pond some crusty
breadcrumbs, when she heard her name over the
loudspeakers. 'Sloan, you have an attorney visit in #5' she tried
not to run, feeling nervous, nausea ripening, she swallowed
hard with emotions OmGod finally, some hope. She almost
started skipping in excitement; her heart was whirling, but she
calmed herself. With difficult restrain hurriedly as she could,
entering the doors, an unfriendly guard was standing with a
clipboard 'here, Sloan, sign this.'

The female guard scowled at me, the same one who would
always bust me in the shower, and led me down the hall, a
familiar hallway for Sara used to have the Salon around the
corner. Attorney visit in # 5 'my throat nearly collapsed; heart
skipped several beats' pulling my composure intact, I entered
the room. My Uncle was dressed in a 3-piece suit with
sunglasses on. He gave me his customary grin. "Glad to see
you, Sara," he reached out, and I fell into his strong arms,
holding me. It was nice to feel the warmth and a hug. Then he
held me out at arm's length to assess… stared at me with a
great big smile… "Look at you letting your Blonde hair grow
back… wow, look at your complexion, and you are putting
some color on your face, a Suntan… you look terrific!"

I waited until the door closed behind us, rubbed my belly,
and said, "look, Uncle, I'm over four months pregnant." He
slapped his forehead and opened his mouth. "Oh Sara, you're
such the card. I have missed your humor," and he couldn't
stop laughing. I felt freaked out. What could be so funny?

"Sara, actually, you are thinner, almost anorexic. It would be good for you to put on some weight, but you still look fabulous! I'll see to it that I speak to Ursula Anders, the Warden here, and get you on a special diet. We'll fatten you up some; okay, now let's get down to business!" I shook inside, and a twinge spun a vibration in my cranium.

'I'm not all here; I must have had a nervous breakdown. My Uncle was probably right; I wasn't pregnant. I had to regain my composure and build momentum, not dwell on this mania umh manic lunacy, move on, and stay focused. He had a large briefcase and folders laid out on the table before me. I looked around cautiously, paranoid "do you remember when I was 13 years old, and you caught me in your Limo with your Son Manny, who was 15 years old at the time?" He laughed "yes, how could I forget that it was your Papa's 69th birthday." Then he stopped and became serious, "but that wasn't you. It was Kamryn!"

"Manny had my bra off, and his hand cupped my left boob." He shook his head "yeah, the kid was grounded for a month!" "Uncle, do you remember the most embarrassing time in my adolescent life? I'll never forget you picked me up from school. I was so excited that you took me out for ice cream I was 12 years old. We were celebrating because I was presented with an award for my 4.3 GPA. I was in 6th grade, and all of a sudden, there I was in your plush BMW, blood pouring out of me my first ever period in white shorts… staining your beige seat!" Terrance quickly stands, shoving the chair aside, angered "that wasn't you Sara it was Kamryn." "Do you remember what you said to me, Uncle Terrance? Do you recall what you did to help me?"

"Yes, but why don't you tell me!" "I was crying, scared, embarrassed. You soothed me by telling me that you loved me and everything was going to be all right. You pulled over to the side of the road, stopped and took off your brown suit coat, and helped me unbuckle the seat belt and wrapped it around my pants and body. Then, Uncle, you kissed me on my forehead, wiping my sobbing tears away, then drove to Walgreens drug store and bought like three different kinds of Tampons, Kotex's pads. You had no idea what I needed, but you bought everything!"

He exploded and burst out laughing. "Well, I didn't have any experience raising a daughter, hate to admit it. I was petrified, scared out of my element. I could face down an angry Jury and Judge, but you and your sister...." "Since I was staying with Papa cuz mom and dad were dead, and Papa wasn't home, it was you and I for the day to be together. Oh, by the way, no one but you and I could ever know what you did next, Uncle. 'God, I Love You, Uncle' you then took me to a fancy Hotel, got a great big room, and told me to take a shower. When I got out, you had one of your secretaries there. Her name was Maddie. She came into the bathroom with me and helped me choose what to use and how to do it!" Terrance's eyes never left her face; shock and bewilderment glazed over his countenance.

"When I got out of the bathroom, I nearly feinted you had bought me like five outfits from a fancy clothing store in the hotel. I played model with Maddie helping me try on the outfits OmGod I felt so special I'd forgotten all the pain and embarrassment. Then you said come on, we went down the elevator, and I saw the man just finishing putting on the new seat covers. You grabbed my right hand, and we skipped to my Lou all the way to the car, then off to 31 flavors for ice cream!... Yes!"

Terrance's complexion had changed, his brows furrowed 'no-not possible, nope' shaking his head vigorously, he asked me, "what was the name of the hotel?" I told him it was the Sheridan, and I chose the pink overalls that were his favorite! Oh yeah, and I dropped my Rocky Road ice cream cone onto my lap!" lol. Mesmerized, silence prevailed and lingered. His whole demeanor had been altered since we started reminiscing. Strangely, he seemed more kicked back, not as shocked as I had envisioned that he'd be. He shook his head up and down with a quirky smirk. "All right, okay, I will play along with you after the trial of Sara. Where did we go after the plea agreement was signed, and what secret did I divulge to you and only you that day?… Ugh, till this day, no one else knows my secret!"

'Uncle,' I bent my head downward and sighed "you told me that you had been diagnosed with prostate cancer and were undergoing treatments, but you would be fine. We were at the Restaurant 'Fridays,' and you were drinking Scotch. I was having a glass of Red wine. We had Crab cakes as an appetizer! Then you took me to my first-ever Strip Joint, which genuinely unnerved me. I was lost as we sat right up by the stripper's pole. You made me throw dollars, then fought with me furiously for me to let the cute redhead give me a lap dance lol I hate to admit it, but I actually had fun. You asked me which girl you think you should have lap dance on you, and I picked out the sultry Strawberry Blonde with a set of enormous boobs!"

Tears welled up in his hard, stoic face & eyes. 'Kamryn?' He leaped up out of his chair, arms wide open 'yes, Uncle, it is me' we both shed tears. We were hugging and holding one another. He said, "I thoroughly believe you. I have the entire rest of the day. Tell me, please… what has happened. I'm all ears, my favorite niece!" 'I explained what had happened. He listened intently at first; it was difficult for him to believe the complicity of Nurse Renae until I brought up the Beach house. He then nodded and admitted he had been invited down to Santa Monica years back by Sara after she'd bought it with some of her Trust Fund monies. He openly wondered how Renae and her husband Ron could afford the Beach house!'

Nine days later, Kam was still at NIA.

Kam laid back on a pillow. If she were a kitty cat, she'd been purring… and continued the replay of the extraordinary and super special visit. Uncle Attorney Hallinan still was standing, leaning his hands on the table. His face was flush-countenance was perplexed with a form of compassion I'd not recognized before, never ever over the dozens of times watching him in court had I seen him sweat. Well, he did perspire on the tennis court for sure, my Uncle played semi-pro tennis on the local circuit, but he had a reason for sweating.

He then called me by my real name, 'Kamryn, I love you, girl. This isn't going to be a quick process, so don't get your hopes up to high. I will have to be extremely cautious on how to move forward, uh, around this precarious conundrum. It will indeed need to be a delicate and calculated formula akin to walking on eggshells while trying to sneak up on a Cobra. With Sara escaping NIA, this could bring down all that I've worked for, and can you imagine all our investors? Please, Kam, stop being outspoken here about you being

swapped out by Sara. Remember, I'm the CEO of this conglomerate, and we're in the process of expanding into Europe. I will have to take some time and evaluate how we move forward. No worries, I will be calling you out of NIA Kam, but not today. We will stay in touch stealth-like.' **Omg, it felt so good, like it had been forever since I'd heard anyone mention my name… in referencing me. It was like the whole world was lifted from my shoulders. 'Kam, will you please remain here? I need to retrieve my phone from the personal property box and make some calls. I will alert the guards that I will be back. Oh, don't worry; coincidentally, Renae and Liz are off today, no worries!'**

I'd told him, 'I'll be right here, Uncle, thanks…' Thirty-five minutes later, he re-entered. 'Kamryn, I have some super news

for you. I am going to have a team of Special Forces locate your sister Sara, and they will kidnap her. Then we will drive her into this Prison facility in a coroner's Van, and she will replace you here at NIA. I can empathize with you, Kam, for you deserve to walk out of here with me. Still, unfortunately, we live in a complex society uhm world, and on a whim, if any of this information was released, such as the Serial Killer Vipress had escaped NIA, not only would our Public Company lose Billions of dollars, all the Pension funds ETF'S and all… 'Hell, Kamryn, as I informed you moments ago, we're also considering expanding NIA's footprints into Europe. We have a lot to lose if the catastrophic news were released that your sister had escaped NIA.' I stared up into Terrance's anguished face and asked him have you forgotten…'Uncle, please, I am a Stockbroker running a Financial Consultants division for Charles Schwab. Uncle, you don't have to extrapolate or expound on how this event would go VIRAL, and yes, NIA's Bonds and Warrants… our Stock would drop like a proverbial Rock in the toilet. I get it, Uncle, but dammit, I want out of here like Now!

He reached out and pulled me into his chest 'you're as good as free; unfortunately, with the way your sister cleverly set you up, putting on the melodramatic show by using Carl in the sexual assault, her luridness has bounced across the social media world, already putting NIA on the defensive, placing herself on front street. Sara was ingenious then leaving you here posing for her. The switch was unremarkable, performed with amazing discipline, and skillfully orchestrated such a complex scheme. We have to worry about the control that Nurse Renae wields. We need to move slowly, Kam; we don't know if there are other accomplices. Truly I don't believe Liz is involved, but please remain vigilant and be patient!'

'But are you not the Chairman of the board here at NIA? You're the CEO, Uncle. Why can't you have me released and arrest Sara today?' 'Kamryn, your too far intelligent to even ask that question. I know emotions play a big part, but....' 'Uncle, I've been threatened multiple times. I'm one hypodermic needle ordered by Renae or now Liz from being a vegetable Zombie, and this would kill who I am and will ever be! I've thus far been lucky, for after a meeting with Liz, she'd let the guards have free reign on me, but that only lasted a few days. I was slapped around and physically beaten. I was able to stop the inevitable assaults, rape, and beatings because of using my influence of having you as my ally... my Uncle. I'd threatened Liz that if anything happens to me, I will be telling you.' I couldn't help it, um, couldn't turn off the faucet staring at him that day in the visiting room. Tears had streamed down my cheeks, dripping at an alarming rate onto the tabletop. He'd pulled her in for an entrenching hug lasting a long wonderous interval, then whispered the following words 'Kamryn, as baffling and burdensome as this may seem, listen to me. I will let no one touch you. We must move you from here to another holding area; I'm thinking of Napa County Jail. I will get you a new DNA Test for Science has made leaps and bounds. I believe we can now separate the DNA of identical twins. I will file all the necessary paperwork. This must be done in stealth mode, unbeknownst to Renae and Liz. We don't know if others are involved in this conspiracy?'

I remember my body shaking while he rubbed my head soothingly. He continued to pacify me, 'So please lay low. Yes, it would be awesome if I could use my prestige, political power, and leverage to contact Wash. DC. Use my influence with the Attorney General and powers to be and walk you out of here this very day with you in my grasp, but your sister's cunning plot... her swapping you out has to be proven. Please understand that Sara's Killing spree was Hyped for months. Her case was a whopper because of all the publicity. It was a Worldwide phenomenon, ah, an event like the O.J. case. It went on Viral mode, uh, auto drive. It didn't help that a similar killing spree was occurring in Europe at the same time as the Sara case was being adjudicated. Don't worry, my favorite Niece, I will get you out of here, and you can testify against your sister Sara... now babygirl, you stay... on the 'lowdown.'.

'If I wasn't so upset,' aah, I almost laughed. I said, 'Uncle, it's not the 'lowdown,' it's called keep it on the 'down low.' 'Uncle Terrance, I'm well versed in the pressures your under being a financial guru in charge of a division of Schwab's financial core in San Francisco. If any of this information were to hit the mainstream or be leaked out that the serial killer, Sara, had escaped NIA the Stock as we discussed! It'd be like an asteroid from space crashing, plummeting to make a crater in the Earth. NIA might never recover. This Prison would go on Lockdown and be infiltrated by all Federal entities. The public would be marching with signs outside these razor-wired towers, no doubt that Billions of dollars would be lost. Stock and Bondholders would suffer devastating losses. Yes, Uncle, I understand why you must keep this on the Downlow! But can't you do what you initially said, kidnap Sara? She replaces me here, and we're done!'

Terrance didn't say a word, merely acknowledging my statements with his chin and eyes. 'I will also monitor you from afar via closed circuit security. I will put someone on the cameras 24/7. No one will touch you. I can link into the system here and see everything. You will be protected. This may take 2 or 3 weeks, but it's happening. As I said, you must be tolerant, umh, patient and stay in stealth mode. I will be here to accompany you out of here. Believe me, Kam, I promise you, girl!... I love you Kamryn Amaya.' .

They embrace, 'please, Uncle, hurry. I am not safe here, and you will not be able to protect me from your office in San Francisco. I told him about the words written in lipstick and how the guards were abusing me. I could be raped, sodomized, or murdered in a split second!' I told Uncle Terrance about the time only days after the traumatic situation in Liz's office when a couple of the female guards had torn me out of the shower nude, yelling to stop wasting the water. They forced me onto my knees, telling me they would be back after count time for some real fun. I was lucky they never returned.

'I promise, Kam, I'm sorry, don't stress. I will take care of this for you and us. No one will hurt you. I am stopping in to discuss just this with the Warden before I leave here and will have a lengthy conversation with Liz. I will have my Limo drive to her house if I have to. Please believe me. I love you; you'll be safe till I get you out of here!' Hugs again ensued then he waved and nodded stoically with certainty trying to instill strength in me. Then he was gone, and with his departure went my security blanket, and with repressed optimism, I was led back to my cell.

SARA, tying up loose ends acclimating to freedom.

Grinning as only she could, Sara 'Kamryn' had played every card to its hilt after the love of her life Soulmate Fiancé, had perished and drowned. This tragedy unfolded like molasses. She played it with solid, stoic silence breaking down in tremulous crying and shaking fits. The Academy Awards would have all been Sara's. No doubts remained!

After what happened to Brock, her fiancé, she didn't have to employ or deploy much pressure. All the sympathies that could be mustered were on free-fall from her mandated leave of absence from Schwab, which she then followed up with her resignation, formally quitting and walking away 'her boss told her the door was always open after she had finished grieving, mourning or when she wanted her job back, it would always be there for her.' Nope!

A broken human needs to grieve in their own way and might need rehabilitation and counseling with rest to overcome losing the man she would have spent the remaining of her life with. Kamryn's friends would look away, hurting for her, lol… uhm, at Sara and never holding her eyes. Sara didn't allow a conversation to get out of her control when speaking with Kam's friends, she acted awkward at times, but that was easily sold because of the trauma and torture she was enduring. 🐾 Sadness was the prevailing theme, empathy laden! She avoided all of Kam's friends as best as possible, kept her mouth zipped, stopped answering texts and phone calls, shut down Kamryn's Instagram, Twitter, and Facebook accounts, eliminated all social media, and stopped all emails.

Sara had accomplished a dream come true. Another of her plans culminated with the expertise of a sculptor. She turned the key in the door of her new Salon, which had its Grand opening on 10/31/17, a Tuesday Halloween, appropriately already had sub-contracted out seven stations to aspiring beauticians. Sara had the finest, most innovative equipment money could buy installed. Her Salon was second to none! Her aspirations, convoluted and jumbled, wanted to continue the Sara Vipress Fun in Europe but were waylaid by her obsession with beautifying the female gender. She now evolved into and rotated her dreams following a newfound desire she'd developed in NIA to start a chain of her Salons luring and aligning her ambition for remaining legal till the dust had cleared… perfect Yes! Envisioning with a smidgen of grandiosity, a Salon on Rodeo Drive in Beverly Hills, maybe she'd one day own a preeminent studio in Hollywood. Why not give it a whirl, Right?

Sara decided to lay low and handle the extracurricular issues or loose strings left at the wayside until she had squelched all opposition to her well-being. Time was on her side. Soon she'd not have to glance over her shoulders, and that's the way Sara wanted to live, so the decision was easy-peasy. Renae, Carl, and big sister Kamryn were soon to only exist in the netherworld… then, and only then, would she expand her horizons!

Well, how not Ironic? Guess who her first customer was. Yeah, Renae enters her Salon's doors, eyes meet acknowledgment "hi Renae, your right on time as per usual for your makeover. You are such a punctual individual, one of your better attributes. Now let me see what I can do about your fkn mug!" There weren't any embraces or warm words. Both were in monotone mode, suspicious and weary of one another. Still, if they were going to live copacetically as estranged partners, this was a tasteless necessity "thanks, Sara, I'll take the full-on treatment service head to toe. Wow, this blows away that little room at the Prison," subtly grimaced with a fake smile… Yup! ⚶.

-64-

<u>Kamryn… 15 days since Uncle Terrance's visit at NIA.</u>

'Sloan, you gotta visit!' this belched over the loudspeakers. Kam was getting something to drink in the cafeteria. Her heart jumped along with her anticipation of walking out of this Hell hole. Maybe it was Terrance. It had been 15 days and counting. She walked to the visiting room area. 'Sloan, check in at the front desk!' she ambled over now, almost in a waddle, trying hard to disguise her excitement. Kamryn stood in a line waiting… then she was next walked up to the counter and was given a message from Doctor Liz Honcho, Co-signed by Nurse Renae. It read, '<u>Sara, your sister Kamryn is here to visit you today due to your aggressive nature towards her and this being her first visit since the catastrophe involving her Fiancé… We have to make different arrangements. We cannot permit you to go off half-cocked and</u>

Kam thought about what arrangements and what catastrophe regarding her Fiancé Brock Dame. Geez, she'd heard nothing about him… Wtf was going on? She'd heard not a word about Brock. Uncle Terrance said nothing. She'd tried dozens of times to call Brock's cell phone to no avail. It went to voicemail, and the FBI refused to accept her phone calls from NIA. People outside of Prison didn't nor couldn't understand how easy it was for the staff and powers to control all communications. They could limit her from any outside contact… no mail was received or sent. It all stopped at the mail room. I wasn't allowed any phone calls to unauthenticated numbers. All numbers on my calling list had to be approved. Then if so, the answering party had to accept the call by pushing a designated number… seclusion was a reality. I was totally Isolated, not even allowed the local newspapers.

Liz obviously mandated that no mail I sent went anywhere but sat on her desk. Likewise, any mail sent to me with my name and registration numbers ended there. Also, I was unable to communicate even with my friends. No, my phone account was limited to just three numbers; preposterously, I was only allowed to contact the… phone that Sara had that was originally mine. The sister bitch had stolen it along with my life! The other two phone numbers I was permitted to try and call were of my Uncle, Attorney Terrance Hallinan's office and his personal cell phone.

I had heard nothing Zilch from or about Brock for months, sadly. I had to assume my fked up sister Sara had pulled it all off pretending to be me and was now married to my Man. What else would you think, huh I was lost in despair with the knowledge base that soon enough, all would be reconciled. It was not going to be long before I'd be free. Brock and I would resume our Loving relationship! I almost fell to my knees, dizzy with stress. *I reread the orders from Doctor Honcho for the third time, 'I have ordered you to be secured to a wheelchair, feet and arms restrained, so hopefully, this will be only a temporary inconvenience, and future visits can occur like normally as has been the case in the past let's get past this first hurdle Sara' signed Doctor Honcho!*

I had stopped dead in my tracks fk no, no way, why would I first and foremost visit with that Psychopath? I hated her with every fiber of my being. I could refuse the visit, and that was what I would do. The last thing I would do was allow myself to be chained to a freakin wheelchair while the worst human alive pushed me around. Nope, not going to happen, ain't no way! A guard rolls a chair over with straps, 'here, Sloan, have a seat!' Kam's anxiety goes beyond the roof. She started grinding her teeth, blood pressure stroking out, breathing hard. She said to herself, remember you have Uncle Terrance on your side. This is but temporary, but still trying to relax, which was impossible.

Should she really refuse the visit, could she? Yes, this wasn't a forced visit, like a prosecutor with a subpoena. How was this even close to being legal or legit? I'm a prisoner restrained in a wheelchair against my will; how could I stop this from happening? Hell, refuse, right? Can you imagine the claustrophobia of being locked down in a wheelchair and rolling down a dock with water deep on both sides? I tossed caution into the breeze, knowing Terrance was, of course, working on my release. Oh no, what to do? still apprehensive <u>(Kam would look back on this decision for eternity; this would be a life changer!)… Don't!</u> ✦.

How could this be a good idea? She pulls down, adjusts her baggy shirt, and thinks of her twin, ugh, evil sister Sara. The tide, uuhhh, the riptide is turning. Soon Sara will be back Caged at NIA for the rest of her screwed-up and demented life. With the knowledge that Uncle Terrance was working hard and promised he would set her free soon, she fixated on this for strength and conviction gritted, grinding her teeth so she could face Sara the Monster with resolve and commitment to do just what Sara had done to her 'turn-about-was-fair play' deception, fraud trickery… Yup!

What was the ole saying? Oh yeah, 'what was good for the goose was good for the gander' yeah, bet you the Worm had turned, and two could play this game to hell with this killing murderous Bitch. What she's done to me is unforgivable. <u>Since I have had zero news about my Fiancé or what Sara was up to… pretending and impersonating me, my decision was a foregone conclusion. I sat in the Wheelchair strapped down.</u> How naïve was I? I Used to be the bleeding-heart anti-death penalty person. I had donated thousands of dollars to the American Civil Liberties Union, believing that inherently the Death Penalty Violates the Constitutional ban against Cruel and Unusual punishment and the guarantee of due process of law… Fk That… I was Dead Wrong! If anyone deserves the Needle, it is Sara. I'd make her pay for all of this if it were the last thing I'll ever do! 'ahhohh!'

Kam's heart was shredded. What kept her strong enough to persevere from losing complete control was the fact that her Uncle acknowledged and knew without question that she was Kamryn and that Sara had pulled off a spectacular escape. Terrance was solid integrity based. He would save me, and Sara would be put to death eventually! Yay!

Then a familiar voice from directly behind me says, "Hey there, sista dear?" I said nothing, nada, no reply, for hell's sake. I'd heard that same voice for my entire life, ugh, in my peripheral vision. I saw cold black hair growing and flowing thick from her scalp. "So, let's go for a 'roll umh stroll' like the rhyme, sis?" I calmly said, "What fkn rhyme? Why did you come here to visit me, hum, let me guess, to rub it in my face, you despicable Bitch? Leave me alone, Sara, you freaking freak!"

Sara howled derisively, then leaned over to my left ear and whispered, "ohhh, poor baby Kamryn now, I suppose you have a reason for this hostility, reasons to be a bit angry. I get it. I'd be like, well, the same as you, but I'm just not as fkn Stupid as you are, big sista," laughing heartily. "Be careful many of your words, Sista, or statements will be disregarded or not valid, and you should understand right out of the gate I will not discuss subjects, or topics that are not conducive to the furtherance of my agenda umh, understand I'm in control here! Everything is offline unless I initiate it and decide that we can discuss it. I don't have to remind you that eyes and ears are everywhere. I will not be playing your game, loser, Sara!"

"Kamryn is my name, and you fkn know that... you Psychotic Neanderthal. I have nothing else to say to you. Get away from me, or I will scream!" *Sometimes I'm an idiot. I should never have let myself be tethered in this chair.* "Scream damn, that wouldn't be a good idea that would bring attention to us, the guards with nurses would cum running shit you would be jeopardizing yourself, Kam, needles injections heck, haven't you witnessed this before like Deja Vu you don't want that now do yah?" Lol!

I sat docile and let my arch-enemy take charge. Sara pushed the wheelchair to the end of the Pier overlooking a serene setting with Ducks, Geese, and waterfowl with a beautiful Flamingo off on another shore a glorious day indeed. I felt like throwing up. A flock of birds flew by, and two Swans nibbled each other, almost cuddling in a premating foray on the flowing ripples of the giant pond.

Kam looks out over the vast water, wondering if the better term would be a lake, not a pond, rolled out about 75 feet on the wooden pier. Kam's personality had been altered due to the suffering she'd experienced. Kamryn knew she had a nervous breakdown and was doing her best to keep it together. She had to be strong. Kam was no longer a shy, docile naïve soul. Peering out, squinting her eyes, and seeing her future… flashing red lights before her. What a perfect murder her monstrosity of a sister might have planned. Heck, how perfect was this her being chained to a wheelchair… bam Sara slips and falls, pushing her off the Pier accidentally? Oops, she lets me slide chained and shackled inside of a wheelchair into the lake, drowned. Kam speaks up and doesn't scream, shout or yell, "what are you doing, Sara? Are you going to drown me cuz I gotcha on the sly… you're like the 'Walking dead!' little troll that you are. You'll be sitting here again. Sara, tell me about Brock now!"

"Oh, sista, please cum on, dear. So dramatic are you?" Kam noticed a few nurses sitting on a bench along with several patients at the end of the pier, feeding Ducks and some Pigeons. There were NIA patients out on the dock, and everywhere she looked… Sara shoved me between the other victims who used wheelchairs. I saw a rowboat glide by and three paddleboats with visiting children. The sun was brilliant, a gorgeous Napa day.

A woman in one of the rollin chairs looked upon her then, in a garbled, slurred voice, said, 'Hello!' Kam instantly choked on her saliva in Shock. She stared directly into Lucie Link's eyes! It was Agent Lucie Link… Sara jumped and was also surprised, then quickly recovered "how is she doing?' asks Sara of the caregiver pushing Lucie.

The Nurse said, "for someone who had nearly every bone broken in her body, brain trauma, she is doing amazingly. She's now swimming all on her own, healing nicely. She has just begun to speak again. Actually, umh, last night, Lucie said a complete sentence. I'm her day nurse," said the lady Ms. Kare. As nosey as hell, Sara asked, "what did she say last night?" <u>"I didn't hear it, but the night nurse reported that she said, 'I Love you, Brock, and that's forever!"</u> Suddenly Lucie's eye's glowed and refocused. She looked around and tried to stand, her hands clenched, shaking, and showing her fist. Nurse Kare held her down with a snarl, and then <u>Lucie said, "Yes, I love Brock Dame, and I will Kill You! Sara… 'Damn right!"</u>

Nurse Kare said, "OmLord, what Lucie, what did you say?" I shouted loud enough to be heard 25 yards away, "Lucie OmGod, your memory is coming back! 'Right on, Girl!" Another nurse nearby stood up "well, uh, I'll be darned; it's a damn miracle I told you getting the patients outside by the lake in the parks out of their restricted confinements was going to be beneficial for them and could bring them back to life I mean we never really know what our patients are thinking unless they can speak… this is awesome wait till Lucie's parents hear about this Nurse Kare!" .

The other nurse continued entering our space, now entirely leaning over Lucie 'didn't I tell you this is community land shared by the prison and by our medical staff? We should all utilize this outdoor paradise. This makes me so happy to hear Lucie articulate without slurring her words!' I watched Sara's face morph into what… She was a demon; she exclaimed and interjected, or shall I say rudely interrupted, the two nurses debating over why this was the reason the patients were improving. "Aah, I heard that Agent Lucie Link was always going to be a vegetable, Omg, and look at her; she is as pretty as the day I…." "God works in mysterious ways." I wished Nurse Kare would have let Sara complete her words!

I felt nausea creeping up my throat, feeling sick hearing Brock's name and Lucie's love for him. A horrible spine, itching, tingling, and burning pain shot up my back and hovered at the nape of my neck. In another wheelchair was a young girl, maybe seven years old, who was in an automobile accident. Both of her parents had died in the accident. She had severe head trauma her eyes were glossy like dead fisheyes, but if I had a guess, I was pretty sure she was enthralled watching the gorgeous Swans dancing on the water! Abruptly Sara declares, 'Let's go!' she takes the wheelchair and spins it around back the way we had come. Over my shoulders, I hear my devious sister mutter, "It's insane having trauma patients comingling with murderous inmates. I don't get it?" then she added, "even though only level #5 prisoners are allowed out here!" I said nothing… was caught up in the memory of Brock and Lucie, 'my Brock Dame; undoubtedly, we live in such a Cruel world!'

I was well aware of the toxic risks of verbally attacking Sara. She was Insane and unpredictable. I could accept the consequences. What was killing me was the non-talk about Brock and the supposed catastrophe, what happened with the Wedding that I was to become Ms. Kamryn Dame. I knew now why I had agreed to this visit. I had to hear about my man… dealing with Sara's personality deficit was another matter in itself, yet I tossed caution to the wind two-thirds of the way back down the Pier.

"Karma is a Bitch;' Karma will be my revenge for all your vile acts against me and humanity! Where's my man at Sara huh? Where is Brock?" Suddenly, she halted the chair, nearly tipping me forward and over 'lucky I was strapped in,' spun around to face me, then leaned in over my head between my breasts with a raspy voice… And I heard this threat; "Kamryn, your one poke of a needle, then your clinically brain dead be careful. Don't push my buttons because I barely give a shit about you. In fact, I detest your goody-two-shoes demeanor. Your pathetic!" .

Then she shoved the wheelchair into fast gear. "I knew it wasn't a good idea to visit you today?" I was quiet, only wanting to get out of this chair and away from the Evil twin behind me! She stopped abruptly again and said, "Oh, Sista dear, I have to let you in on a special secret. I opened my first Salon in Marin County, and it's already been a wild success. I mean, I have seven stations all rented out and am booked out for a month already. I spoke with Uncle Terrance yesterday. He's in London in high-level meetings regarding the expansion of NIA… hell isn't that grand? Think about it, my noxious sister, uh, suppose he's able to pull off the business venture. In that case, you may be able to transfer to London, that is, if I don't decide to make you a vegetable before then… and sista, the odds are about 15% that you make it another month here, sane. Your destiny is vegetable-like. Oh, the reason I spoke with our Uncle was to ask him for help in expanding my business and opening a Salon in San Francisco! So life couldn't be better for me, aren't you happy for me?" she starts ripping out throaty howls!

I sat frozen in place, instantly discombobulated. My mind evaporated sweat poured from me. I was lost, hopeless, and couldn't comprehend Sara's words about my Uncle, who promised me Sara would be re-captured, and I'd be free. But here she was, ahh. The Vipress was standing inside the Razor wire, an easy capture and exchange for me. This proves that Terrance lied to me. Perhaps he was involved and colluded with Sara all along. My life was over. I no longer cared if I lived or died. 'I was well done, Toast! later!'

65

My Gawd, I couldn't fathom what my vision displayed...

OmLord Bang; suddenly and disturbingly, metaphorically, a thunderbolt struck Kamryn, fatally penetrating her inner-self melted uhm,... an <u>OBE 'out of body experience of nonfiction'</u> entering the long Pier heading directly at them was an older couple. Kam knew them well. Brock Edward Dame's Mother and Father were walking toward her and Sara. Kamryn wondered what they must think of her. How to signal them? Was there anything she could do to inform them that the monster pushing her in the wheelchair was her murderous alien sister?

In front of the parents I'd met at least a half dozen times... rolling towards Sara and me, was a wheelchair. Her Fiancé, umh, my honey's head was shaven, bald, and leaning downward. Like me, Brock was strapped into the chair, ahh, at that exact instant... Sara saw them and gasped, stopping dead in her tracks. Stunned, but as quick as a Mongoose, Sara recovered, 'Oh fk,' she muttered, yanked back on the wheelchair and stopped the forward momentum, and leaned over me again "you say one word, and you're a dead girl Kam, one word, I promise you that!" Her sinister laden, raspy whispers were pure unadulterated evil, 'I was entranced and stupefied OmLord my Brock was in a fricken wheelchair...I don't remember saying a word of acknowledgment toward Sara; ugh, perhaps I nodded?'

The Pier was approximately nine feet wide, and Sara stopped alongside Brock. I was about three feet from being able to touch and hold him. He was to my left. If we could outstretch our arms and hands, we could feel each other again! Sara blurted out, 'Omg!' and rushed into Brock's mother's arms with false love dripping sewer laden, the empathy misplaced by genuine apathy. His Father hovered over both of them, sandwich hugging; he said, "Kamryn, oh God, Kamryn!"

With disdain, Brock's dad looked down dispassionately, staring hatefully at me in my chair. "I know you said you'd be visiting your sister today. Never thought we'd run into you I…." Sara leaped towards Brock, tugging his head up into her bosom and kissing the top of his head. "Oh, I love you, Edward, oh I love you with all that I am. I will visit you after I deposit my sister!" Sara holds Brock tight, looking up at the adoring parents "why did they release him from the Stanford Neurology Hospital? I was just there yesterday. No one said anything to me about transferring him here?"

Brock's mother acknowledged my evil sister, "Kam, it's God-given direction. We are Blessed indeed with the help of a professor working on astounding and wondrous breakthroughs in Neurology. He Lectures at Stanford University. He is the Director of NIA's Neurological Institution. He believes Brock can be revitalized and fully recover and has taken a personal interest in his treatments." "Kamryn, it surprised my wife and I that Mr. Terrance Hallinan here at NIA has contracted with some of the finest clinical Physicians on our planet. Blessedly, there now employed here. It's amazing to see the documented improvements by patients that you would automatically assume would never recover!"

'I kept my mouth closed. My only show of emotions was puffy eyes' I fell into despair, my stomach cramped… waves of agony spun through my body, trembling as wetness streamed toward my chin… gravity fallen. What did Sara do to my honey? My man looked half dead, and my heart sank to new depths. I could barely breathe looking at him. I wanted to Scream but bit my tongue, for my sister would definitely kill me or disable me permanently. Her threats were not veiled. The hate spewed in her voice. 'I had to be strong and hold on to the fact that Brock was alive and sitting in a wheelchair, not three feet away. There is hope!'

Mr. Dame points to the 5-story building outside the concertina razor wire, adjacent to a guard tower. "There are all kinds of changes in Stem Cell Therapies. Brock has already made stupendous gains in just under three months. He's able to walk with a walker and able to recognize some images. We pray that we will have our son and your Fiancé back soon. Brock will fully recover; we believe this... where there is a will, there is a way, God willing."

I whispered under my breath towards his bent overhead, chin wanting to touch his luscious chest, which was heaving up and down slowly. My Lover was alive. What did she do to him? 'I Love you. It's a miracle we're going to have a life together; I will always be here for you. I'm always yours forever!' 'I was in a fugue of euphoria, cloud nine-like tingling high as my endorphins kicked in. Life suddenly was worth living again!'

Sara was fuming, having difficulty keeping her sneering expressions intact. Sadly, the parents couldn't read body language, for Sara was wringing her hands, folding her arms over her breasts. Her nonverbal cues revealed far more than her words could convey. She shook her head and glared down at me, whispering under her breath. 'How could the bastard have lived? Fk, there isn't a chance in Hell' scornfully smirking with Vipress venomousness, her loathsome hatred-based emotions hard to restrain. Sara tried to repulse her arousing impulses to put her fingers around the bastard's throat, strangle the prick, close his throat off, and spit in his dilated eyes. <u>'How could this piece of shit have survived? I watched the bubbles dissipate. He was drowned dead I watched the dark lake with floodlights for about seven minutes the dude sank to the bottom... this is damn impossible, fk. I have no luck in this screwed-up life!' Dang, I'd wrapped the boat's</u>

<u>anchor around the despicable prick's neck... There's no Devil... No!'</u> .

Sara couldn't let it go as I watched her grab my man's wrist squeezing it as hard as she could, lifting his head in a façade of Love. Brock's parents smiled, looking at Sara, not seeing what I did. She dug her fingernails in deep, wanting to splay his skin, then stopped. 'Whoa, didn't want any marks on him.' Sara kneeled again, trying to catch his eyes to see if he recognized where he was or who she really was, then grinned from within. His eyes were cloudy and blank. 'Nada!' Sara rolled her shoulders, looking up at Brock in disbelief, the shock still blazing up from her bowels, 'are you fkn kidding me? How did he float up onto a shore some 75 yards from where I slung him over the side of the boat? The depth finder showed that the bottom of the lake was over 517 feet down... Ughhhh, what bullshit, where's the Devil when I need him, where's my helper, idol at... man oh man, life isn't fair!'

Sara sighed internally. At least she wasn't busted, arrested... super-duper; fortunate for her, the drug-cleansing solutions she'd poured down his throat worked like a charm. It could have been worse. After a boater had found Brock face down on a narrow beach and called 911... The Paramedics had airlifted him to Mercy Hospital in Redding, then the FBI was alerted, and he was flown to a secret FBI Lab that tested all his bodily fluids and gave him a thorough physical. Next, Brock was transferred to Stanford Universities Neurological Trauma center.

The FBI's CSI teams cordoned off the small island that Brock was found face down on and then backtracked to where we'd spent days on Brock's parent's houseboat... which was almost a quarter mile away from where Brock had washed up on the shore. Not a stone was unturned; every facet and component they'd gathered in his recovery on the Shasta Lake beach was also tested and analyzed. They reenacted the entire accident scene and reviewed Brock's condition with a fine-tooth comb. Sara had spent over seventeen hours inside interrogation rooms, scrutinized down to a Gnats ass. So she was damn lucky, and Sara acknowledged this but now wanted him and this situation to go the way of the Dinosaurs. She kissed his bald forehead and reached down in his lap, clenching his 49er ball cap, saying aloud, "it's sunny out here. I don't want you to get a sunburn, my honeybunny…."

Fortunately, an enormous amount of Alcohol was found in his system, a 3.7 B.A.C. blood alcohol count, no other drugs, not a clue of her use of the defibrillator on his head. Maybe because his hair had covered the impact points not going to overthink it. The diagnosis thus far is that the lack of oxygen caused brain damage. Still, Sara knew she had scrambled his brains with the electric shocks. $%!

Sadly, what was for sure was that now she had another loose end and added mission that must be completed for Devil's sake. The last thing Sara needed was another miracle fkn recovery. Are you kidding me? Was Lucie enough? She had to finish the job and kill the bastard before some 'Einstein Doctor' brought Brock back to reality from his catatonic brain-dead state! She grimaces, hiding a scowl. Geez, will her work ever end? Brock's mom peers over at me, believing I'm the dastardly Sara… glaringly, "wow, you were not kidding me. Besides your hair color, she's a spitting image or identical to you. Sara seems to be a little more skinny than you. Does she talk?"

Sara's hateful glaring eyes measured me "no, she doesn't speak much, heavily sedated medicated, for she can be violent, that's why I have her restrained. But she's my sister, and I love her despite all she has done; I'm all she has left!" Brock's mother's expression displayed utter contempt, for whom I wasn't sure, but I thought it was oddly directed towards sister dear, but then remembered the person she'd glared at was me. I was the person who ended their son's romance with Lucie

Link. I didn't think they cared for the pretender of me, Sara. I had a displaced feeling that they still wanted their son to marry and be with Agent Lucie Link. Could I be wrong? After a long pause, Sara unleashes more hogwash. "Well, it seems now I will have two reasons to visit NIA … for the most important person in my life, uuhhh, the love of my life, Brock Edward Dame. Mr., and Ms. Dame, we will still be married."… *"Never!..." I blurted out. 'Oh, shit!…'* Instantly, three elements of this impromptu gathering became relevant. First, Brock moved. Second, Sara leaped toward me viciously, clenching my chin and mouth. Thirdly Cindy… Brock's mother shouted, "Kamryn, what did Sara say?"

Sara leaned over me, blocking the parent's view, pulled my encumbered head down, and hoarsely declared, 'one more word, and I will kill you and him.' Next, she wiggled her head up to answer Cindy. "It's the medication. She is delusional at times. I visit her hoping for moments of lucidity; unfortunately, lately, she is like a potato head just sitting in her feces." Cindy's face upturned grossly uh "how do you do it, Kam? That's disgusting!" Sister took advantage of shock value and changed up the subject matter.

"So, how difficult was it to enter this Prison? I mean, didn't the guards and staff scrutinize you? Wasn't it a hassle? I don't get…." Brock's father interrupted, " No, actually not. The Professor of Neurology suggested we take Brock on strolls through the park, like grounds here, specifically around the ponds aah water, to see if he reacted in any way. Look over there; Agent Lucie Link's parents bring her here all the time. It's therapeutic and far better to get the patients outdoors anyways. To answer your question, we were given three passes at the outpatient center and told that they'd allocate more visitor passes if we applied. Kamryn…" He waved his arms wide, "look at all the children visiting these privileged inmates, remember like my wife and I were told, this part of the prison is a camp-like environment or for campers, uhm, low custody trustee-like inmates. It was no trouble getting in here. They opened the triple gates checked our Identifications, and here we are... by the way. Brock is on the fifth floor, room # 517." "Thanks; I will visit him later this afternoon!"... Not!

During the interaction between Mother and Father and Sara, all my tear-fallen eyes could do was flutter as I shook nervously in despair, my lover and best friend brain dead. My man sat in a vegetable state. All I wanted to do was touch his skin, smell him again, love him, and let him know that he would be all mine forever. I'd never give up on him!

Kamryn's eyes never left the sight of Brock. *She watched the muscles in his neck contract and pulse outwards. His head arose, his cloudy eyes found hers, and chills popped over Kam like unreal he looked right into her soul, his flexed eyes focusing pin-pointed, then his mouth crookedly gaped open slightly and mimed... his lips parted no sound emitted only one word unmistakable. <u>(KAM!)</u> a flicker as just one tear dropped from his right eyelid. Kam then Mimed three words, <u>'I Love You,' ... Brock's left eye winked three times.</u> He lowered his head slowly, his muscles relaxed, and he returned to his former self vegetable-like,* but he wasn't! Yay!

Luckily, none of our interactions were witnessed or seen by the three standing adults. Kamryn's heartbeat was as one with her husband-to-be. She was energized, umh, thrilled that hope abounded and optimism had found a foothold. Fate, there is a God, and Karma, Yes! I had questions for days. I can't express how difficult it was for me to keep my mouth closed, but soon enough, Sara would feel my wrath. I would demand the answers to how Brock was injured. What happened to him? What did she do to him? I was beyond angry but was steadfast, knowing I was in a vulnerable position. Duh!

66

A woman visits San Francisco from London, England.

****

Forty-nine miles away, far up in San Francisco's Skyline, stood a magnificent specimen of the female persuasion, supple soft full lips, rosy, red, big bright greenish eyes, eyelashes movie stars paid thousands for, and cheeks that flashed adorable dimples. Her teeth were as straight as a Laser, and her hair was a vibrant orange-reddish, blonde streaked um auburn natural, the beauty of voluptuousness, a Venus both genders couldn't resist gawking at… her pheromones and endorphins were popping... Yum! .

She saw dainty ears with diamond studs on her succulent lobes in the reflection of the mirrors. She knew she was an instant 'hardon' uhm, 'slick wetness.' Her body left no doubts that she was an avid 'workaholic.' Her stature and strut were of confidence. Still petite, standing 5'5" and weighing a brawny 135 pounds, the three-piece suit accentuated her figure cut up at the hips, tailor-made only for her. The provocative neckline set with a silver-lined necklace with glistening diamonds, ample breasts… full and pointed in the cum and get them position… nipples trying to escape, all 'Au Naturel.'

Her taut-pierced belly button and hips swayed as she strolled down any path. Her ass was plump full-on lustful. To see her bend over was a treat. Blood flowed in some flaccid organs. This had caused several accidents in London, England, a beauty undeniably! From a distance a month prior, she'd been at a groundbreaking ceremony in Westminster, England, only nine minutes from the Buckingham Palace gates in London. NIA had purchased a large plot of land to build a state-of-the-art Neurological Hospital. Terrance

Hallinan cut the ribbons. The Backhoes and Bobcats started rumbling to work. She was enamored with the man!

Now she was in California at 711 Montgomery street, just across from the 853-foot-tall Transamerica Pyramid building. She was on the 37th floor at the top of a Skyscraper owned by the distinguished World Renown Attorney Mr. Terrance Hallinan in the superbly decorated penthouse… she was enthralled, staring around at the paintings and artifacts. It was like a museum… a cultural experience. Indeed!

Swinging her feet in a pair of gladiator-strap stilettos, she knew she was a dream for any person to ravish. Her skin exuded sexuality and yum with intense delight as she grinned in the floor-to-ceiling mirrors. If not for her feet and toes, she thought herself perfect, hating her feet, ahh, Men's feet. She despised her hairy toes and was damn flat-footed. She had always hidden them, no sandals, flip-flops, ugh, toe-bearing shoes. Nope, I never would make it as a Cinderella type… uuhhh, forget the golden slipper.

'Oh, how she wanted a transplant of her feet' although she had talented toes, she could wave hello and goodbye with them and pick up things like pencils, papers, and even clothes like fricken monkey's feet. Oh, how she abhorred her clawed feet. She'd missed an appointment in London to have electrolysis, uh, to kill the roots of the hair that grew up off her toes, umh, well call it like it was, she'd escaped Europe! Although she enjoyed pedicures, her toenails matched her manicured fingers polished with an Opal black tint. She finally mused, well, hell, enough about me and my ugly Duckling feet. Her London accent was Sexy and alluring, even seductive, but she was not a woman to be held nor to acquiesce. Nope, she was a total control freak. She'd cultivated herself at the best educational institutions in the World for the affluent and wealthy and had degrees from Cambridge and Oxford Universities.

Baby Valerie had grown up. Yep! Sara's and Kamryn's baby sister in person, 'Valerie Amaya' reached over and signed the purchase agreement that Terrance had slid across his spacious desktop… A 9.5 Million-dollar 3-story home overlooking Mount Tam in Marin County. With the Pacific Ocean at her doorstep, the Trust Fund baby came back to Roost and finally returned from Europe with total confidentiality. No one knew of her arrival other than her Uncle. This was his and her secret pact. Valerie was in her mid-30s, barely five years younger than her Twin sisters. Little did Uncle Terrance know Val was under a massive investigation from Germany, France, and Italy, aligned scrutiny from too many countries to name. It seemed a Serial Killer was and had been on the prowl and loose all over Europe. The hunt was ongoing for the Ventriloquist… Makeup artist Extraordinaire mass killer. Valerie was a cocky woman with master's degrees umh Baccalaureate prestige… Valerie was the cream of all the crops!

Doctor Valerie Amaya, Forensic Psychologist: "So, Uncle, you really think I have the possibility of being the Director of the entire NIA complex?" He only grinned, which morphed into a widely dimpled smile, then finally, after a slight pause, "Valerie, of course, you do!" Valerie had kept track of her sisters after her escape and murder of her captors, who had abducted her from the Kindergarten School Yard at only five years old. Valerie lived her childhood in bondage entirely in trauma. Her abductors were sexual deviates, a husband and wife. Val became their bloody captive, a toy to violate… their molestations met no borders. They did what they wanted to her body, and she was forced to engage the insidious couple or was beaten mercilessly. She became their sex slave. This started from when Valerie was only five years old… It continued for years Until!

Sister Sara, the 'Vipress,' had notched many killings on her belt. A mere amateur, Val was the ultimate competitor ravaging Europe and carried much more weight having to wear 3 Championship belts, which tripled Sara's exploits and expertise… in killing deemed useless and harmful deviates. A true Veteran and Professional, Baby Val was finally back home once again… oh. How she had missed the States, nearly drooling, teeth bared, scowling into the mirror!

Home Sweet Home, geez, now if I could only do something about these feet, Nope!

-67-

Sara scolded and taunted me… I, Kamryn… felt blessed to have silently communicated with my fiancé Brock Dame…

***

Sara finally shoved my wheelchair away from Brock and his parents back down the dock, muttering to herself angrily. Once we were out of earshot, she said to me, "you're going to pay for opening your trap." I retorted vehemently, "I want to know what happened to Brock. I wanna hear what the hell you did to him, and I want no bullshit. Also, you freakin bitch, I'm going to make sure you rot in hell… I want…"

Laughing derisively, she said, "don't you interrupt me, or I will gag your ass right here on this path. I'm taking you back to your home, the Prison lobby, lol, but listen to me, Kamryn, despite what you may think or believe. I did nothing to Brock… oh hell, I had a wonderful time with him. Sex was out of this world. He kept asking me excitedly, 'wow, girl, you're on fire. Where did you get all of this energy, your insatiable where did all these new moves cum from? Your animalistic, so fkn passionate sex is off the charts with you, the best I've ever had. Oh, Brockbaby couldn't get enough of your Sister! Delish."

Sara paused speaking while she pushed me by a few correction officers… "I think you will appreciate what I told him; 'Brock, I'm so comfortable and confident in us being together for the rest of our lives. I just let my lust and passion take control. I am so in love with you, wildly turned on by you. My Passion shall never die, babe. We will have intimacy with experimentations that will blow your imagination. I will be all you will ever desire. You're so straight-up yummy, Brock! Then we made love again, sista. He is such a freakin stud. Kamryn, I get it now. Brock is a beast. His aggressive style and zero inhibitions, oh Yeah!

"You're a Liar, Sara. Go ahead, gag me. I don't give a shit. Brock would know the difference between us. He's not so shallow. It's all bullshit, I …" "Ssshh, I'm warning you, Kam, shut up now." We were close now… to the entrance of the lobby "what happened to him, Sara? What did you do to him? You didn't marry him pretending to be me, you skank!".

Sara pulled her scarf from around her neck and shoved it in my mouth. I tried biting her. The guards looked on and only smiled. I wanted to push it out with my tongue, yanking my arms on the straps and kicking my tethered feet. No one came to my assistance for 'I was the Serial Killer in their minds.' "Kam, you don't deserve answers. Besides, you're not going to be cognizant long enough to analyze shit. You're going to be brain-dead real soon. I admit to nothing. I am totally innocent of hurting Brockbaby. The Brockster got fkn drunk and wouldn't listen to reason and jumped on one of the Sea Doo's, and that was the last that I saw of him; bye Bye now!" *I whirled my head around, facing the dock where I almost lost my breakfast, hugging… were the foursome of Lucie and Brock's parents, and … side by side sat Lucie and Brock facing one another.* .

"Kamryn, I own the staff here at NIA. If I finalize my decision, you will not make it a week and will be foaming and drooling over yourself. Answer me this question, why did Uncle Terrance visit you the other day? Huh, what's up? What was that about? I was informed that you had a private meeting with him in my old Salon room. Tell me now!" I couldn't speak, gagged, then she brought her face close to me and winked with a snarl, "I have a meeting with Uncle in an hour, so no worries, I'll straighten out whatever you started!"

Sara pointed her finger downward and wildly smirked. "Oh, I almost forgot you're going to be Indicted by the Grand Jury. Yep, back to Court; you go soon. I'm sure the AUSA Prosecutors would have sought the death penalty if it were still in vogue, but no worries, sista, you know your 10-year sentence for the attempted murder of Lucie Link is almost up. But guess what? I betcha you will achieve the status of being called a Lifer. A life sentence is your next accomplishment. Gotta give it to good ole Ame's drawings and paintings that will substantiate your killings of Papa and Daddy and the slut. The proof is overwhelming Doctor Liz Honcho even has the video of you drawing the 11 X14 paintings. Your busted babydoll oh 'Sista wouldn't want to be you 'Seeya Adios Yep!"

<u>'Epilogue and Afterlife.'</u>

Where do I start? Such a diverse and complicated set of characters, I suppose we can delve in with the sisters Kamryn and Sara. To begin with, how will Kam obtain her freedom? Will Sara be incarcerated again? Does Nurse Renae inject Kamryn, and is she now brain-dead? Don't forget that 'baby Val.' Yep! sister Valerie has just arrived from Europe from her rampage… killing spree. Will she hook up with Sara and form a dynamic duo? How will Sara deal with Nurse Renae and Carl? Remember, she is highly driven and motivated to tie up loose ends. She also now must worry about Agent Brock Dame coming back to cognizance and implicating her, so he is at the top of her list.

What are the actual dynamics between Sara and her Attorney, Uncle Terrance Hallinan? Is he complicit or in cahoots? Does Sara refrain from her Vipress killings? Happy to work at her new dream of expanding her beautification business, her Salon's… Nope! So many loose ends need to be tethered, and most of the lingering questions will be resolved in the subsequent novels in the NIA series. The follow-up of 'Sara' has been written and already published. The book's appropriate name is <u>Kam,</u> the next one up and could put closure to many inquiries.

Questions and musings that need reparation include Agent Lucie Link and Agent Brock Dame. Will they somehow miraculously recover with the new innovations in Stem Cell Therapies and become viably energized? What is really happening at NIA with CEO and Attorney Terrance Hallinan? Nurse Renae and Doctor Liz Honcho?

From the 'Feral Eyes First book,' we know that Wendi Feral and Jax Foul also reside at NIA. They are intricate pieces of the stealth militia we know live at Napa's inpatient hospital and prison. The many forthcoming pages describe the various missions

588

the elite NIA team engages in. They will be hair-raising and suspense-laden, no doubt. Rico Captor and Rascal Savage will be back at the forefront, along with many interrelating characters from 'Feral Eyes.' Sara's journey is just getting heated up. She has to maneuver through the Covid Pandemic and into the future.

<u>'Feral Eyes' and 'Feral Eyes 2' are meant to be read first, then 'Sara' and 'Kam'; some of the characters are interrelated, and most reappear again in the finished novel 'Covid-57.'</u>

Stay tuned, for I also anticipate that many twists and hairpin turns will come to fruition aligned with the engineering of Lombard Street in San Francisco.

<u>**Not the Last Words...**</u>

<u>**The natural sequence of books to be read or listened to is as follows… 'Feral Eyes' > 'Feral Eyes 2.' Or if you want to jump right into the volcano… start with 'Sara' and then read or listen to 'Kam.' Most of the novels in the NIA series share original characters, but they are exclusively independent for the most part.**</u>

This is the Third book in a series of 13 that have all been written. Unfortunately, I am the sole Author without a team of Editors. Nope, I don't have a Literary Agent; I will be Self-Publishing… it's just poor ole me. Therefore, the numerous errors in my novels are all mine; I'm sort of old school. I use a notebook and different colored pens for plot changes; I'm aware my punctuation sometimes stinks, although rarely, it's purposeful.

When I started putting pen to paper, I didn't know what an undertaking I was getting into. Whoa, this is Work! with a Capital W! I wish I could hire someone to do the hard part of bringing my writings to fruition because I honestly enjoy putting pen to paper.

I'd much rather write than do almost anything else, but this work formulating a Book is mind-blowing, and yet I step into Libraries and Walla; there are books forever; I am in Awe of them all.

I recently finished a Novel I've named 'Covid-57' for a simple reason… I envisioned the Pandemic we are trying to survive 'Covid-19', which will, in the end, be three times worse. Thus 3 X 19 = 57. I must say this 1,100-plus-page Novel reads like Non-Fiction, simultaneously exhilarating and ominous to write. It is the last book finished in the NIA series. Although 'Covid-57' is a stand-alone effort. I will publish Covid-57 with four other completed books at nearly the same time. The

Novels in the NIA Series are 'Feral Eyes, Feral Eyes 2… Sara, Kam, and Sonja, Church, Ted, and Ted 2.

I'm also excited about a book titled 'The Clinic.' I will soon add a preview of this novel based in San Diego and Mexico. Within the words and pages of 'The Clinic,' there is much truth about covert prison camps throughout Mexico; these establishments are supported mainly by relatives that pay the guards to keep their relatives alive and unharmed; I've spent time interviewing family members with inside information about this ongoing travesty.

Non-Fiction accomplishments 'Charity, Take a Chance, Take a Chance 2, Take a Chance 3… S.C.J Sacramento County Jail, Savant Style Trading' an informative book about trading the Stock Market, nuances, and how to profit, using basic algorithms…

Since this is a Lone endeavor or enterprise, I haven't many people to thank, Lol…but I have a single person I want to praise. His name is Gerald Ward, and he was employed by the Sacramento Public Library and was the leading publisher at 'I-Street Press.' He just retired last December 2021. Gerry has been instrumental in this process of preparing my novels for print. Unfortunately, he's not an editor, but he is a fantastic photographer and knows his way around the Art of publishing… His extensive library of Photos has been used on the covers of the Feral Eyes books.

<u>Last but Never Least, I would be remiss if I didn't Dedicate all my writing to my Dear Mother! 'Barbara Jean Hayes Meyers.'</u>

As a small child, I watched her write page after page in notebooks; she wrote thousands of pages. Her Genre was Romance. She loved to write, always dreaming of one day publishing a book. Sadly never did. These books are for you,

Mom… sorry, I am not talented in the Romance arena; perhaps one day, I will give it a College try.

Thank You for reading what I enjoyed writing, Glen 'Rocky' Meyers. Oh, BTW, I include in many of my novels this phrase 'From the Corner of his eye' or my eye reason in praise of one of my favorite books by 'Dean Koontz!'

Please visit Gembooksrock.com for the author's biography.

I'm responsible for every error and mistake in my novels. I printed the first edition called an… 'ARC' book… or (Advanced Readers Copies) for some beta readers to let me know what they thought. Ugh, my first test books needed a lot of work… I had literally thousands of mistakes in my writing…The second edition will be cleansed, but it will not be perfect! Thanks for your time. Please visit my website, 'Gembooksrock.com,' soon; I hope to have a business venture uhm offer for you, not costing you a penny, only time… enough! >Glen Rocky Meyers @ Facebook, Instagram. Please visit my website Gembooksrock.com.

Thank you very much for your precious time…

Glen Rocky Meyers@GlenAuthor' Twitter. Soon to be on YouTube.